The Luminaries

ALSO BY ELEANOR CATTON

The Rehearsal

'A remarkable achievement . . . [Catton] has surpassed the daring and assurance of her previous effort with a massive, intricate, painstakingly detailed and deliciously readable historical yarn set amid the scrabbling greed of a mid-1860s gold rush in Hokitika on New Zealand's South Island . . . *The Luminaries* is a novel that can be enjoyed for its engrossing entirety, as well as for the literary gems bestowed on virtually every page' *Quill & Quire*

'Eleanor Catton is nothing if not ambitious . . . With astonishing intricacy and patient finesse, Catton brings to life the anomalous nature of 19th-century New Zealand' David Grylls, *Sunday Times*

'A brilliant exercise in 19th-century language. The account of gold-prospecting in New Zealand is wonderfully intricate' Philip Hensher, *Spectator*

'This fiendishly clever and extraordinary piece of fiction will confirm Catton as one of the brightest stars in the international writing firmament' *Bookseller*

'For the scale of her ambition and the beauty of its execution, somebody should give that girl a medal' Lucy Daniel, *Daily Telegraph*

'It's awesomely – even bewilderingly – intricate . . . There's an immaculate finish to Catton's prose, which is no mean feat in a novel that lives or dies by its handling of period dialogue. It's more than 800 pages long but the reward for your stamina is a double-dealing world of skulduggery traced in rare complexity' Anthony Cummins, *Evening Standard*

'Irresistible and gripping . . . the things that most impress are the cunning withholding of information, the elegant foreshadowing, the skilful looping back on the narrative' *Irish Independent*

'In *The Luminaries*, the Victorian novel meets the Wild West (or South). Wilkie Collins's *The Woman in White* is an obvious antecedent but I most thought of the Bob Dylan song "Lily, Rosemary and the Jack of Hearts". If that's your pipe of opium you may well find this addictive – it's very clever' Paul Dunn, *The Times*

'A tour de force of narrative control . . . Catton does an incredible job of bringing to life the time and place and the utter ruthlessness that greed engenders in human beings . . . The voice works beautifully because of its exquisite control of language . . . The novel is like a huge Rubik's Cube, with panels of plot sliding and reforming, to create new patterns and perspectives' *Vancouver Sun*

'A remarkable tour de force, breathtaking in the layer upon layer of astrological lore it reveals throughout its great length. Decoding such an allegory can be absorbing – like tackling cryptic crossword puzzles. I think, however, that *The Luminaries* has much more to offer' Andrew Riemer, *Brisbane Times*

The Luminaries

Φ

ELEANOR CATTON

Victoria University Press

VICTORIA UNIVERSITY PRESS
Victoria University of Wellington
PO Box 600 Wellington
vup.victoria.ac.nz

National Library of New Zealand Cataloguing-in-Publication Data

Catton, Eleanor, 1985-
The luminaries / Eleanor Catton.
ISBN 978-0-86473-988-9
I. Title.
NZ823.3—dc 23

Printed in Australia by Griffin Press

*for Pop, who sees the stars
and Jude, who hears their music*

NOTE TO THE READER

The stellar and planetary positions in this book have been determined astronomically. This is to say that we acknowledge the celestial phenomenon known as *precession*, by which motion the vernal equinox, the astrological equivalent of the Greenwich meridian, has come to shift. The vernal equinox (autumnal in southern latitudes) formerly occurred while the Sun was in the constellation of Aries, the first sign. It now occurs while the Sun is in Pisces, the twelfth. Consequently, and as readers of this book will note, each zodiacal sign 'occurs' approximately one month later than popular information would have it. We mean no disrespect to popular information by this correction; we do observe, however, that the above error is held in defiance of the material fact of our nineteenth-century firmament; and we dare to conjecture, further, that such a conviction might be called Piscean in its quality—emblematic, indeed, of persons born during the *Age of Pisces*, an age of mirrors, tenacity, instinct, twinship, and hidden things. We are contented by this notion. It further affirms our faith in the vast and knowing influence of

the infinite sky.

CHARACTER CHART

STELLAR:
Te Rau Tauwhare, *a greenstone hunter*
Charlie Frost, *a banker*
Benjamin Löwenthal, *a newspaperman*
Edgar Clinch, *an hotelier*
Dick Mannering, *a goldfields magnate*
Quee Long, *a goldsmith*
Harald Nilssen, *a commission merchant*
Joseph Pritchard, *a chemist*
Thomas Balfour, *a shipping agent*

Aubert Gascoigne, *a justice's clerk*

Sook Yongsheng, *a hatter*

Cowell Devlin, *a chaplain*

PLANETARY:
Walter Moody
Lydia (Wells) Carver, *née* Greenway
Francis Carver
Alistair Lauderback
George Shepard
Anna Wetherell
Emery Staines

TERRA FIRMA:
Crosbie Wells

RELATED HOUSE:
The Wells Cottage (Arahura Valley)
The Reserve Bank (Revell-street)
The *West Coast Times* Office (Weld-street)
The Gridiron Hotel (Revell-street)
The Aurora Goldmine (Kaniere)
'Chinatown Forge' (Kaniere)
Nilssen & Co. (Gibson Quay)
The Opium Den (Kaniere)
Godspeed (a barque, reg. Port Chalmers)
Hokitika Courthouse (Magistrate's Court)
The Wayfarer's Fortune (Revell-street)
Hokitika Gaol (Seaview)

RELATED INFLUENCE:
Reason
Desire
Force
Command
Restriction
Outermost (formerly Innermost)
Innermost (formerly Outermost)

(deceased)

TABLE OF CONTENTS

PART ONE

A Sphere within a Sphere

27 January 1866

42° 43' 0" S ∫ 170° 58' 0" E

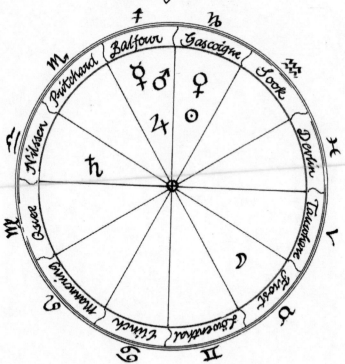

MERCURY IN SAGITTARIUS

*In which a stranger arrives in Hokitika; a secret council is
disturbed; Walter Moody conceals his most recent memory;
and Thomas Balfour begins to tell a story.*

The twelve men congregated in the smoking room of the Crown
Hotel gave the impression of a party accidentally met. From the variety of their comportment and dress—frock coats, tailcoats, Norfolk
jackets with buttons of horn, yellow moleskin, cambric, and twill—
they might have been twelve strangers on a railway car, each bound
for a separate quarter of a city that possessed fog and tides enough
to divide them; indeed, the studied isolation of each man as he pored
over his paper, or leaned forward to tap his ashes into the grate, or
placed the splay of his hand upon the baize to take his shot at billiards, conspired to form the very type of bodily silence that occurs,
late in the evening, on a public railway—deadened here not by the
slur and clunk of the coaches, but by the fat clatter of the rain.

Such was the perception of Mr. Walter Moody, from where he
stood in the doorway with his hand upon the frame. He was innocent
of having disturbed any kind of private conference, for the speakers
had ceased when they heard his tread in the passage; by the time he
opened the door, each of the twelve men had resumed his occupation (rather haphazardly, on the part of the billiard players, for they
had forgotten their places) with such a careful show of absorption
that no one even glanced up when he stepped into the room.

The strictness and uniformity with which the men ignored him might have aroused Mr. Moody's interest, had he been himself in body and temperament. As it was, he was queasy and disturbed. He had known the voyage to West Canterbury would be fatal at worst, an endless rolling trough of white water and spume that ended on the shattered graveyard of the Hokitika bar, but he had not been prepared for the particular horrors of the journey, of which he was still incapable of speaking, even to himself. Moody was by nature impatient of any deficiencies in his own person—fear and illness both turned him inward—and it was for this reason that he very uncharacteristically failed to assess the tenor of the room he had just entered.

Moody's natural expression was one of readiness and attention. His grey eyes were large and unblinking, and his supple, boyish mouth was usually poised in an expression of polite concern. His hair inclined to a tight curl; it had fallen in ringlets to his shoulders in his youth, but now he wore it close against his skull, parted on the side and combed flat with a sweet-smelling pomade that darkened its golden hue to an oily brown. His brow and cheeks were square, his nose straight, and his complexion smooth. He was not quite eight-and-twenty, still swift and exact in his motions, and possessed of the kind of roguish, unsullied vigour that conveys neither gullibility nor guile. He presented himself in the manner of a discreet and quick-minded butler, and as a consequence was often drawn into the confidence of the least voluble of men, or invited to broker relations between people he had only lately met. He had, in short, an appearance that betrayed very little about his own character, and an appearance that others were immediately inclined to trust.

Moody was not unaware of the advantage his inscrutable grace afforded him. Like most excessively beautiful persons, he had studied his own reflection minutely and, in a way, knew himself from the outside best; he was always in some chamber of his mind perceiving himself from the exterior. He had passed a great many hours in the alcove of his private dressing room, where the mirror tripled his image into profile, half-profile, and square: Van Dyck's Charles, though a good deal more striking. It was a private practice, and one he would likely have denied—for how roundly self-examination is condemned, by the moral prophets of our age! As if the self had no relation to the self, and one only looked in mirrors to have one's arrogance confirmed; as if the act of self-regarding was not as subtle, fraught and ever-changing as any bond between twin souls. In his fascination Moody sought less to praise his own beauty than to master it. Certainly whenever he caught his own reflection, in a window box, or in a pane of glass after nightfall, he felt a thrill of satisfaction— but as an engineer might feel, chancing upon a mechanism of his own devising and finding it splendid, flashing, properly oiled and performing exactly as he had predicted it should.

He could see his own self now, poised in the doorway of the smoking room, and he knew that the figure he cut was one of perfect composure. He was near trembling with fatigue; he was carrying a leaden weight of terror in his gut; he felt shadowed, even dogged; he was filled with dread. He surveyed the room with an air of polite detachment and respect. It had the appearance of a place rebuilt from memory after a great passage of time, when much has been forgotten (andirons, drapes, a proper mantel to surround the hearth) but small details persist: a picture of the late Prince Consort, for example, cut from a magazine and affixed with shoe tacks to the wall that faced the yard; the seam down the middle of the billiard table, which had been sawn in two on the Sydney docks to better survive the crossing; the stack of old broadsheets upon the secretary, the pages thinned and blurry from the touch of many hands. The view through the two small windows that flanked the hearth was over the hotel's rear yard, a marshy allotment littered with crates and rusting drums, separated from the neighbouring plots only by patches of scrub and low fern, and, to the north, by a row of laying hutches, the doors of which were chained against thieves. Beyond this vague periphery, one could see sagging laundry lines running back and forth behind the houses one block to the east, latticed stacks of raw timber, pigpens, piles of scrap and sheet iron, broken cradles and flumes—everything abandoned, or in some relative state of disrepair. The clock had struck that late hour of twilight when all colours seem suddenly to lose their richness, and it was raining hard; through the cockled glass the yard was bleached and fading. Inside, the spirit lamps had not yet succeeded the sea-coloured light of the dying day, and seemed by virtue of their paleness to accent the general cheerlessness of the room's decor.

For a man accustomed to his club in Edinburgh, where all was lit in hues of red and gold, and the studded couches gleamed with a fatness that reflected the girth of the gentlemen upon them; where, upon entering, one was given a soft jacket that smelled pleasantly of anise, or of peppermint, and thereafter the merest twitch of one's finger towards the bell-rope was enough to summon a bottle of claret on a silver tray, the prospect was a crude one. But Moody was not a man for whom offending standards were cause enough to sulk: the rough simplicity of the place only made him draw back internally, as a rich man will step swiftly to the side, and turn glassy, when confronted with a beggar in the street. The mild look upon his face did not waver as he cast his gaze about, but inwardly, each new detail—the mound of dirty wax beneath this candle, the rime of dust around that glass—caused him to retreat still further into himself, and steel his body all the more rigidly against the scene.

This recoil, though unconsciously performed, owed less to the common prejudices of high fortune—in fact Moody was only modestly rich, and often gave coins to paupers, though (it must be owned) never without a small rush of pleasure for his own largesse—than to the personal disequilibrium over which the man was currently, and invisibly, struggling to prevail. This was a gold town, after all, newbuilt between jungle and surf at the southernmost edge of the civilised world, and he had not expected luxury.

The truth was that not six hours ago, aboard the barque that had conveyed him from Port Chalmers to the wild shard of the Coast, Moody had witnessed an event so extraordinary and affecting that it called all other realities into doubt. The scene was still with him—as if a door had chinked open, in the corner of his mind, to show a band of greying light, and he could not now wish the darkness back again. It was costing him a great deal of effort to keep that door from opening further. In this fragile condition, any unorthodoxy or inconvenience was personally affronting. He felt as if the whole dismal scene before him was an aggregate echo of the trials he had so lately sustained, and he recoiled from it in order to prevent his own mind from following this connexion, and returning to the past. Disdain was useful. It gave him a fixed sense of proportion, a rightfulness to which he could appeal, and feel secure.

He called the room luckless, and meagre, and dreary—and with his inner mind thus fortified against the furnishings, he turned to the twelve inhabitants. An inverted pantheon, he thought, and again felt a little steadier, for having indulged the conceit.

The men were bronzed and weathered in the manner of all frontiersmen, their lips chapped white, their carriage expressive of privation and loss. Two of their number were Chinese, dressed identically in cloth shoes and grey cotton shifts; behind them stood a Maori native, his face tattooed in whorls of greenish-blue. Of the others, Moody could not guess the origin. He did not yet understand how the diggings could age a man in a matter of months; casting his gaze around the room, he reckoned himself the youngest man in attendance, when in fact several were his juniors and his peers. The glow of youth was quite washed from them. They would be crabbed forever, restless, snatching, grey in body, coughing dust into the brown lines of their palms. Moody thought them coarse, even quaint; he thought them men of little influence; he did not wonder why they were so silent. He wanted a brandy, and a place to sit and close his eyes.

He stood in the doorway a moment after entering, waiting to be received, but when nobody made any gesture of welcome or dismissal he took another step forward and pulled the door softly closed behind him. He made a vague bow in the direction of the window, and another in the direction of the hearth, to suffice as a wholesale introduction of himself, then moved to the side table and engaged himself in mixing a drink from the decanters set out for that purpose. He chose a cigar and cut it; placing it between his teeth, he turned back to the room, and scanned the faces once again. Nobody seemed remotely affected by his presence. This suited him. He seated himself in the only available armchair, lit his cigar, and settled back with the private sigh of a man who feels his daily comforts are, for once, very much deserved.

His contentment was short-lived. No sooner had he stretched out his legs and crossed his ankles (the salt on his trousers had dried, most provokingly, in tides of white) than the man on his immediate right leaned forward in his chair, prodded the air with the stump of his own cigar, and said, 'Look here—you've business, here at the Crown?'

This was rather abruptly phrased, but Moody's expression did not register as much. He bowed his head politely and explained that he had indeed secured a room upstairs, having arrived in town that very evening.

'Just off the boat, you mean?'

Moody bowed again and affirmed that this was precisely his meaning. So that the man would not think him short, he added that he was come from Port Chalmers, with the intention of trying his hand at digging for gold.

'That's good,' the man said. 'That's good. New finds up the beach—she's ripe with it. Black sands: that's the cry you'll be hearing; black sands up Charleston way; that's north of here, of course—Charleston. Though you'll still make pay in the gorge. You got a mate, or come over solo?'

'Just me alone,' Moody said.

'No affiliations!' the man said.

'Well,' Moody said, surprised again at his phrasing, 'I intend to make my own fortune, that's all.'

'No affiliations,' the man repeated. 'And no business; you've no business, here at the Crown?'

This was impertinent—to demand the same information twice—but the man seemed genial, even distracted, and he was strumming with his fingers at the lapel of his vest. Perhaps, Moody thought, he had simply not been clear enough. He said, 'My business at this hotel is only to rest. In the next few days I will make inquiries around the diggings—which rivers are yielding, which valleys are dry—and acquaint myself with the digger's life, as it were.

I intend to stay here at the Crown for one week, and after that, to make my passage inland.'

'You've not dug before, then.'

'No, sir.'

'Never seen the colour?'

'Only at the jeweller's—on a watch, or on a buckle; never pure.'

'But you've dreamed it, pure! You've dreamed it—kneeling in the water, sifting the metal from the grit!'

'I suppose ... well no, I haven't, exactly,' Moody said. The expansive style of this man's speech was rather peculiar to him: for all the man's apparent distraction, he spoke eagerly, and with an energy that was almost importunate. Moody looked around, hoping to exchange a sympathetic glance with one of the others, but he failed to catch anybody's eye. He coughed, adding, 'I suppose I've dreamed of what comes afterwards—that is, what the gold might lead to, what it might become.'

The man seemed pleased by this answer. 'Reverse alchemy, is what I like to call it,' he said, 'the whole business, I mean—prospecting. Reverse alchemy. Do you see—the transformation—not *into* gold, but *out* of it—'

'It is a fine conceit, sir,'—reflecting only much later that this notion chimed very nearly with his own recent fancy of a pantheon reversed.

'And your inquiries,' the man said, nodding vigorously, 'your inquiries—you'll be asking around, I suppose—what shovels, what cradles—and maps and things.'

'Yes, precisely. I mean to do it right.'

The man threw himself back into his armchair, evidently very amused. 'One week's board at the Crown Hotel—just to ask your questions!' He gave a little shout of laughter. 'And then you'll spend two weeks in the mud, to earn it back!'

Moody recrossed his ankles. He was not in the right disposition to return the other man's energy, but he was too rigidly bred to consider being impolite. He might have simply apologised for his discomfiture, and admitted some kind of general malaise—the man seemed sympathetic enough, with his strumming fingers, and his rising gurgle of a laugh—but Moody was not in the habit of speaking candidly to strangers, and still less of confessing illness to another man. He shook himself internally and said, in a brighter tone of voice,

'And you, sir? You are well established here, I think?'

'Oh, yes,' replied the other. 'Balfour Shipping, you'll have seen us, right past the stockyards, prime location—Wharf-street, you know. Balfour, that's me. Thomas is my Christian name. You'll need one of those on the diggings: no man goes by Mister in the gorge.'

'Then I must practise using mine,' Moody said. 'It is Walter. Walter Moody.'

'Yes, and they'll call you anything but Walter too,' Balfour said, striking his knee. '"Scottish Walt", maybe. "Two-Hand Walt", maybe. "Wally Nugget". Ha!'

'That name I shall have to earn.'

Balfour laughed. 'No earning about it,' he said. 'Big as a lady's pistol, some of the ones I've seen. Big as a lady's—but, I'm telling you, not half as hard to put your hands on.'

Thomas Balfour was around fifty in age, compact and robust in body. His hair was quite grey, combed backward from his forehead, and long about the ears. He wore a spade-beard, and was given to stroking it downward with the cup of his hand when he was amused—he did this now, in pleasure at his own joke. His prosperity sat easily with him, Moody thought, recognising in the man that relaxed sense of entitlement that comes when a lifelong optimism has been ratified by success. He was in shirtsleeves; his cravat, though of silk, and finely wrought, was spotted with gravy and coming loose at the neck. Moody placed him as a libertarian—harmless, renegade in spirit, and cheerful in his effusions.

'I am in your debt, sir,' he said. 'This is the first of many customs of which I will be entirely ignorant, I am sure. I would have certainly made the error of using a surname in the gorge.'

It was true that his mental conception of the New Zealand diggings was extremely imprecise, informed chiefly by sketches of the California goldfields—log cabins, flat-bottomed valleys, wagons in the dust—and a dim sense (he did not know from where) that the colony was somehow the shadow of the British Isles, the unformed, savage obverse of the Empire's seat and heart. He had been surprised, upon rounding the heads of the Otago peninsula some two weeks prior, to see mansions on the hill, quays, streets, and plotted gardens—and he was surprised, now, to observe a well-dressed gentleman passing his lucifers to a Chinaman, and then leaning across him to retrieve his glass.

Moody was a Cambridge fellow, born in Edinburgh to a modest fortune and a household staff of three. The social circles in which he had tended to move, at Trinity, and then at Inner Temple in his more recent years, had not at all the rigid aspect of the peerage, where one's history and context differed from the next man only in degree; nevertheless, his education had made him insular, for it had taught him that the proper way to understand any social system was to view it from above. With his college chums (dressed in capes, and drunk on Rhenish wine) he would defend the merging of the classes with all the agony and vitality of the young, but he was always startled whenever he encountered it in practice. He did not yet know that a goldfield was a place of muck and hazard, where every fellow was foreign to the next man, and foreign to the soil; where a grocer's cradle might be thick with colour, and a lawyer's cradle might run dry; where there were no divisions. Moody was some twenty years Balfour's junior, and so he spoke with deference, but he was conscious that Balfour was a man of lower standing than himself, and he was conscious also of the strange miscellany of persons around him, whose estates and origins he had not the means to guess. His politeness therefore had a slightly wooden quality, as a man who does not often speak with children lacks any measure for what is appropriate, and so holds himself apart, and is rigid, however much he wishes to be kind.

Thomas Balfour felt this condescension, and was delighted. He had a playful distaste for men who spoke, as he phrased it, 'much too well', and he loved to provoke them—not to anger, which bored him, but to vulgarity. He regarded Moody's stiffness as if it were a fashionable collar, made in some aristocratic style, that was unbearably confining to the wearer—he saw all conventions of polite society in this way, as useless ornamentations—and it amused him, that the man's refinement caused him to be so ill at ease.

Balfour was indeed a man of humble standing, as Moody had guessed. His father had worked in a saddlery in Kent, and he might have taken up that mantle, if a fire had not claimed both father and stable in his eleventh year—but he was a restless boy, with frayed cuffs and an impatience that belied the dreamy, half-focused expression he habitually wore, and the dogged work would not have suited him. In any case, a horse could not keep pace with a railway car, as he was fond of saying, and the trade had not weathered the rush of changing times. Balfour liked very much to feel that he was at the vanguard of an era. When he spoke of the past, it was as if each decade prior to the present year was an ill-made candle that had been burned and spent. He felt no nostalgia for the stuff of his boyhood life—the dark liquor of the tanning vats, the rack of hides, the calfskin pouch where his father stored his needles and his awl—and rarely recalled it, except to draw a comparison with newer industries. Ore: that was where the money lay. Coalmines, steelworks, and gold.

He began in glass. After several years as an apprentice he founded a glassworks of his own, a modest factory he later sold for a share in a coalmine, which in due course was expanded to a network of shaft mines, and sold to investors in London for a grand sum. He did not marry. On his thirtieth birthday he bought a one-way ticket on a clipper ship bound for Veracruz, the first leg of a nine-month journey that would take him overland to the Californian goldfields. The lustre of the digger's life soon paled for him, but the ceaseless rush and hope of the fields did not; with his first dust he bought shares in a bank, built three hotels in four years, and prospered. When California dried he sold up and sailed for Victoria—a new strike, a new uncharted land—and thence, hearing once again the call that carried across the ocean like a faery pipe on a rare breeze, to New Zealand.

During his sixteen years on the raw fields Thomas Balfour had met a great many men like Walter Moody, and it was a credit to his temperament that he had retained, over these years, a deep affection and regard for the virgin state of men yet untested by experience, yet untried. Balfour was sympathetic to ambition, and unorthodox, as a self-made man, in his generosity of spirit. Enterprise pleased him; desire pleased him. He was disposed to like Moody simply for the reason that the other man had undertaken a pursuit about which he evidently knew very little, and from which he must expect a great return.

On this particular night, however, Balfour was not without agenda. Moody's entrance had been something of a surprise to the twelve assembled men, who had taken considerable precautions to ensure that they would not be disturbed. The front parlour of the Crown Hotel was closed that night for a private function, and a boy had been posted under the awning to watch the street, lest any man had set his mind on drinking there—which was unlikely, for the Crown smoking room was not generally celebrated for its society or its charm, and indeed was very often empty, even on the week-end nights when the diggers flooded back from the hills in droves to spend their dust on liquor at the shanties in the town. The boy on duty was Mannering's, and had in his possession a stout bundle of gallery tickets to give away for free. The performance—*Sensations from the Orient!*—was a new act, and guaranteed to please, and there were cases of champagne ready in the opera-house foyer, courtesy of Mannering himself, in honour of opening night. With these diversions in place, and believing that no boat would risk a landing in the murky evening of such an inclement day (the projected arrivals in the shipping pages of the *West Coast Times* were, by that hour, all accounted for), the assembled party had not thought to make provision for an accidental stranger who might have already checked in to the hotel some half-hour before nightfall, and so was already inside the building when Mannering's boy took up his post under the dripping porch facing the street.

Walter Moody, despite his reassuring countenance, and despite the courteous detachment with which he held himself, was nevertheless still an intruder. The men were at a loss to know how to persuade him to leave, without making it clear that he *had* intruded, and thus exposing the subversive nature of their assembly. Thomas

Balfour had assumed the task of vetting him only by the accident of their proximity, next to the fire—a happy conjunction, this, for Balfour was tenacious, for all his bluster and rhapsody, and well accustomed to turning a scene to his own gain.

'Yes, well,' he said now, 'one learns the customs soon enough, and everyone has to start where you are standing—as an apprentice, I mean; knowing nothing at all. What sowed the seed, then, if you don't object to my asking? That's a private interest of mine—what brings a fellow down here, you know, to the ends of the earth—what sparks a man.'

Moody took a pull on his cigar before answering. 'My object was a complicated one,' he said. 'A matter of family disputation, painful to relate, which accounts for my having made the crossing solo.'

'Oh, but in that you are *not* alone,' Balfour said cheerfully. 'Every boy here is on the run from something—you can be sure of it!'

'Indeed,' said Moody, thinking this a rather alarming prospect.

'Everyone's from somewhere else,' Balfour went on. 'Yes: that's the very heart of it. We're all from somewhere else. And as for family: you'll find brothers and fathers enough, in the gorge.'

'You are kind to offer comfort.'

Balfour was grinning broadly now. '*There's* a phrase,' he said, waving his cigar with such emphasis that he scattered feathers of ash all over his vest. '*Comfort*—! If this counts as comfort, then you're a very Puritan, my boy.'

Moody could not produce an appropriate response to this remark, so he bowed again—and then, as if to repudiate all puritanical implication, he drank deeply from his glass. Outside, a gust of wind interrupted the steady lash of the rain, throwing a sheet of water against the western windows. Balfour examined the end of his cigar, still chuckling; Moody placed his own between his lips, turned his face away, and drew lightly upon it.

Just then one of the eleven silent men got to his feet, folding his newspaper into quarters as he did so, and crossed to the secretary in order to exchange the paper for another. He was wearing a collarless black coat and a white necktie—a clergyman's dress, Moody realised, with some surprise. That was strange. Why should a cleric elect to get his news in the smoking room of a common hotel, late on a Saturday night? And why should he keep such silent company, in doing so? Moody watched as the reverend man shuffled through the pile of broadsheets, rejecting several editions of the *Colonist* in favour of a *Grey River Argus*, which he plucked out with a murmur of pleasure, holding it away from his body and tilting it, with appreciation, towards the light. Then again, Moody thought, reasoning with himself, perhaps it was not so strange: the night was very wet, and the halls and taverns of the town were likely very crowded. Perhaps the clergyman had been obliged, for some reason, to seek temporary refuge from the rain.

'So you had a quarrel,' Balfour said presently, as if Moody had promised him a rousing tale, and had then forgotten to begin it.

'I was party to a quarrel,' Moody corrected him. 'That is, the dispute was not of my own making.'

'With your father, I suppose.'

'It is painful to relate, sir.' Moody glanced at the other man, meaning to silence him with a stern look, but Balfour responded by leaning further forward, encouraged by the gravity of Moody's expression to believe the story all the more worth his hearing.

'Oh, come!' he said. 'Ease your burden.'

'It is not a burden to be eased, Mr. Balfour.'

'My friend, I have never heard of such a thing.'

'Pardon me to change the subject—'

'But you have roused me! You have roused my attention!' Balfour was grinning at him.

'I beg to refuse you,' Moody said. He was trying to speak quietly, to protect their conversation from the rest of the room. 'I beg to reserve my privacy. My motive is purely that I do not wish to make a poor impression upon you.'

'But you're the wronged man, you said—the dispute, not of your making.'

'That is correct.'

'Well, now! One needn't be private about *that!*' Balfour cried. 'Do I not speak truly? One needn't be private about another fellow's

wrong! One needn't feel ashamed of another fellow's—deeds, you
know!' He was being very loud.

'You describe personal shame,' Moody said in a low voice. 'I
refer to the shame that is brought upon a family. I do not wish to
sully my father's name; it is my name also.'

'Your father! But what have I told you already? You'll find fathers
enough, I said, down in the gorge! That's no turn of phrase—it's
custom, and necessity—it's the way that things are done! Let me
tell you what counts for shame on the diggings. Cry a false field—
that's worthy. Dispute the pegging on a claim—*that's* worthy. Rob a
man, cheat a man, kill a man—*that's* worthy. But family shame! Tell
that to the bellmen, to cry up and down the Hokitika-road—they'll
think it news! What's family shame, without a family?'

Balfour concluded this exhortation with a smart rap of his empty
glass upon the arm of his chair. He beamed at Moody, and lifted
his open palm, as if to say that his point had been so persuasively
phrased as to need no further amendment, but he would like some
kind of approbation all the same. Moody gave another automatic
jerk of his head and replied, in a tone that betrayed the exhaustion
of his nerves for the first time, 'You speak persuasively, sir.'

Balfour, still beaming, waved the compliment aside. 'Persuasion's
tricks and cleverness. I'm speaking plain.'

'I thank you for it.'

'Yes, yes,' Balfour said agreeably. He seemed to be enjoying himself very much. 'But now you must tell me about your family
quarrel, Mr. Moody, so that I may judge if your name is sullied, in
the end.'

'Forgive me,' Moody murmured. He glanced about, perceiving
that the clergyman had returned to his seat, and was now absorbed
in his paper. The man next to him—a florid type, with an imperial
moustache and gingery hair—appeared to have fallen asleep.

Thomas Balfour was not to be deterred. 'Liberty and security!'
he cried, waving his arm again. 'Is that not what it comes down to?
You see, I know the argument already! I know the form of it!
Liberty over security, security over liberty ... provision from the
father, freedom for the son. Of course the father might be too

controlling—that can happen—and the son might be wasteful . . . prodigal . . . but it's the same quarrel, every time. Lovers too,' he added, when Moody did not interject. 'It's the same for lovers, too: at bottom, always, the same dispute.'

But Moody was not listening. He had forgotten, for a moment, the creeping ash of his cigar, and the warm brandy pooling in the bottom of his glass. He had forgotten that he was here, in a hotel smoking room, in a town not five years built, at the end of the world. His mind had slipped, and returned to it: the bloody cravat, the clutching silver hand, the name, gasped out of the darkness, again and again, *Magdalena, Magdalena, Magdalena*. The scene came back to him all in a snatch, unbidden, like a shadow passing coldly over the face of the sun.

Moody had sailed from Port Chalmers aboard the barque *Godspeed*, a stout little craft with a smartly raked bow and a figurehead of painted oak—an eagle, after St. John. On a map the journey took the shape of a hairpin: the barque set off northward, traversed the narrow strait between two seas, and then turned south again, to the diggings. Moody's ticket afforded him a narrow space below decks, but the hold was so foul-smelling and close that he was compelled to spend most of the voyage topside, hunched below the gunwales with his leather case clasped wetly to his chest and his collar turned up against the spray. Crouched as he was with his back to the view, he saw very little of the coastline—the yellow plains of the East, which gave way by subtle incline to greener heights, and then the mountains, blue with distance, above them; further north, the verdant fjords, hushed by still water; in the West, the braided streams that tarnished when they met the beaches, and carved fissures in the sand.

When the *Godspeed* rounded the northern spit and began her passage southward, the weatherglass began to fall. Had Moody not been so ill and wretched he might have felt afraid, and made his vows: drowning, the boys on the docks had told him, was the West Coast disease, and whether he could call himself a lucky man was a question that would be settled long before he reached the goldfields, and long before he first knelt down to touch the edge of his dish to the stones. There were as many lost as landed. The master

of his vessel—Captain Carver was his name—had seen so many
lubbers washed to their deaths from his station on the quarterdeck
that the whole ship might properly be called a graveside—this last
spoken with a hushed solemnity, and wide eyes.

The storm was borne on greenish winds. It began as a coppery
taste in the back of one's mouth, a metallic ache that amplified as
the clouds darkened and advanced, and when it struck, it was with
the flat hand of a senseless fury. The seething deck, the strange
whip of light and shadows cast by the sails that snapped and
strained above it, the palpable fear of the sailors as they fought to
hold the barque on her course—it was the stuff of nightmare, and
Moody had the nightmarish sense, as the vessel drew closer and
closer to the goldfields, that she had somehow willed the infernal
storm upon her self.

Walter Moody was not superstitious, though he derived great
enjoyment from the superstitions of others, and he was not easily
deceived by impression, though he took great care in designing his
own. This owed less to his intelligence, however, than to his experience—which, prior to his departure for New Zealand, could be
termed neither broad nor varied in its character. In his life so far
he had known only the kind of doubt that is calculated and secure.
He had known only suspicion, cynicism, probability—never the
fearful unravelling that comes when one ceases to trust in one's own
trusting power; never the dread panic that follows this unravelling;
never the dull void that follows last of all. Of these latter classes of
uncertainty he had remained, until recently at least, happily unconscious. His imagination did not naturally stray to the fanciful, and
he rarely theorised except with a practical purpose in mind. His
own mortality held only an intellectual fascination for him, a dry
lustre; and, having no religion, he did not believe in ghosts.

The full account of what transpired during this last leg of the
voyage is Moody's own, and must be left to him. We think it sufficient to say, at this juncture, that there were eight passengers aboard
the *Godspeed* when she pulled out of the harbour at Dunedin, and
by the time the barque landed on the Coast, there were nine. The
ninth was not a baby, born in transit; nor was he a stowaway; nor

did the ship's lookout spot him adrift in the water, clinging to some scrap of wreckage, and give the shout to draw him in. But to say this is to rob Walter Moody of his own tale—and unfairly, for he was still unable to recall the apparition wholly to his own mind, much less to form a narrative for the pleasures of a third.

In Hokitika it had been raining for two weeks without reprieve. Moody's first glimpse of the township was of a shifting smear that advanced and retreated as the mist blew back and forth. There was only a narrow corridor of flat land between the coastline and the sudden alps, battered by the endless surf that turned to smoke on the sand; it seemed still flatter and more contained by virtue of the cloud that sheared the mountains low on their flanks and formed a grey ceiling over the huddled roofs of the town. The port was located to the south, tucked into the crooked mouth of a river, rich in gold, which became a lather where it met the salt edge of the sea. Here at the coast it was brown and barren, but upriver the water was cool and white, and said to gleam. The river mouth itself was calm, a lakelet thick with masts and the fat stacks of steamers waiting for a clearer day; they knew better than to risk the bar that lay concealed beneath the water and shifted with each tide. The enormous number of vessels that had foundered on the bar were scattered as unhappy testament to the hazard below. There were thirty-some wrecks in total, and several were very new. Their splintered hulks wrought a strange barricade that seemed, dismally, to fortify the township against the open sea.

The barque's captain dared not bring the ship to port until the weather improved, and instead signalled for a lighter to convey the passengers over the rolling breakers to the sand. The lighter was crewed by six—grim Charons to a man, who stared and did not speak as the passengers were lowered by chair down the heaving flank of the *Godspeed*. It was awful to crouch in the tiny boat and look up through the impossible rigging of the ship above—she cast a dark shadow as she rolled, and when at last the line was struck and they pulled away into open water, Moody felt the lightness on his skin. The other passengers were merry. They exclaimed about the weather, and how splendid it had been to come through a storm. They wondered about each shipwreck that they passed, sounding out the names; they spoke of the fields, and the fortunes they would find there. Their cheer was hateful. A woman pressed a phial of sal volatile into the bone of Moody's hip—'Take it quiet, so the others don't come wanting'—but he pushed her hand away. She had not seen what he had seen.

The downpour seemed to intensify as the lighter neared the shore. The spray from the breakers brought such a great quantity of seawater over the gunwales that Moody was obliged to assist the crew in bailing the boat, using a leather pail thrust wordlessly upon him by a man who was missing every tooth except his rearmost molars. Moody did not even have the spirit to flinch. They were carried over the bar and into the calm of the river mouth on a white-capped wave. He did not shut his eyes. When the lighter reached her mooring he was the first out of the boat, drenched to the skin and so giddy he stumbled on the ladder, causing the boat to lurch wildly away from him. Like a man pursued he staggered, half-limping, down the wharf to solid ground.

When he turned back, he could only just distinguish the fragile lighter bucking against her mooring at the end of the wharf. The barque herself had long since vanished into the mist, which hung in plates of clouded glass, obscuring the wrecked ships, the steamers in the roadstead, and the open sea beyond. Moody reeled on his feet. He was dimly aware of the crew handing bags and valises out of the boat, the other passengers running about, the porters and stevedores shouting their instructions through the rain. The scene was veiled to him, the figures gauzed—as if the journey, and everything pertaining to it, had been claimed already by the grey fog of his uncertain mind; as if his memory, recoiling upon itself, had met its obverse, the power of forgetting, and had conjured the mist and driving rain as a kind of cloth, spectral, to screen him from the shapes of his own recent past.

Moody did not linger. He turned and hurried up the beach, past the slaughterhouses, the latrines, the breakwind huts along the sandy lip of the shore, the tents that sagged under the greying weight of two weeks' rain. His head was down, his case clutched tightly against him, and he saw none of it: not the stockyards, not the high gables of the warehouses, not the mullioned windows of the offices along Wharf-street, behind which shapeless bodies moved through lighted rooms. Moody struggled on, shin-deep in slurry, and when the sham front of the Crown Hotel rose up before him he dashed towards it and threw down his case to wrench with both hands at the door.

The Crown was an establishment of the serviceable, unadorned sort, recommended only by its proximity to the quay. If this feature was an expedience, however, it could hardly be called a virtue: here, so close to the stockyards, the bloody smell of slaughter intermingled with the sour, briny smell of the sea, putting one in mind, perpetually, of an untended icebox in which an uncured joint has spoiled. For this reason Moody might have disdained the place offhand, resolving instead to venture northward up Revell-street to where the fronts of the hotels broadened, brightened in colour, acquired porticoes, and communicated, with their high windows and their delicate fretwork, all those reassurances of wealth and comfort to which he was accustomed, as a man of means ... but Moody had left all discerning faculties in the pitching belly of the barque *Godspeed*. He wanted only shelter, and solitude.

The calm of the empty foyer, once he had closed the door behind him, muting the sound of the rain, had an immediate and physical effect upon him. We have noted that Moody derived considerable personal benefit from his appearance, and that this was a fact of which he was wholly sensible: he was not about to make his first acquaintance in an unfamiliar town looking like a haunted man. He struck the water from his hat, ran a hand through his hair, stamped his feet to stop his knees from shaking, and worked his mouth in a vigorous way, as if testing its elasticity. He performed these motions swiftly and without embarrassment. By the time the maid appeared, he had arranged his face into its habitual expression of benign indifference, and was examining the dovetailed join at the corner of the front desk.

The maid was a dull-seeming girl with colourless hair and teeth as yellow as her skin. She recited the terms of board and lodging, relieved Moody of ten shillings (these she dropped with a sullen clatter into a locked drawer beneath the desk), and wearily led him upstairs. He was conscious of the trail of rainwater he left behind him, and the sizeable puddle he had created on the foyer floor, and pressed a sixpence upon her; she took it pityingly and made to leave, but then at once seemed to wish she had been kinder. She flushed, and after a moment's pause, suggested that he might like a supper tray brought up from the kitchens—'To dry out your insides,' she said, and pulled back her lips in a yellow smile.

The Crown Hotel was lately built, and still retained the dusty, honeyed trace of fresh-planed lumber, the walls still beading gems of sap along each groove, the hearths still clean of ash and staining. Moody's room was furnished very approximately, as in a pantomime where a large and lavish household is conjured by a single chair. The bolster was thin upon the mattress, and padded with what felt like twists of muslin; the blankets were slightly too large, so that their edges pooled on the floor, giving the bed a rather shrunken aspect, huddled as it was beneath the rough slope of the eave. The bareness lent the place a spectral, unfinished quality that might have been disquieting, had the prospect through the buckled glass been of a different street and a different age, but to Moody the emptiness was like a balm. He stowed his sodden case on the whatnot beside his bed, wrung and dried his clothes as best he could, drank off a pot of tea, ate four slices of dark-grained bread with ham, and, after peering through the window to the impenetrable wash of the street, resolved to defer his business in town until the morning.

The maid had left yesterday's newspaper beneath the teapot—how thin it was, for a sixpenny broadsheet! Moody smiled as he took it up. He had a fondness for cheap news, and was amused to see that the town's *Most Alluring Dancer* also advertised her services as the town's *Most Discreet Accoucheuse*. A whole column of the paper was devoted to missing prospectors (*If this should reach the eyes of EMERY STAINES, or any who know of his whereabouts* ...) and an entire page to Barmaids Wanted. Moody read the document twice over, including the shipping notices, the advertisements for lodging and small fare, and several very dull campaign speeches, printed in full.

He found that he was disappointed: the *West Coast Times* read like a parish gazette. But what had he expected? That a goldfield would be an exotic phantasm, made of glitter and promise? That the diggers would be notorious and sly—every man a murderer, every man a thief?

Moody folded the paper slowly. His line of thinking had returned him to the *Godspeed*, and to the bloody casket in her hold, and his heart began to pound again. 'That's enough,' he said aloud, and immediately felt foolish. He stood and tossed the folded paper aside. In any case, he thought, the daylight was fading, and he disliked reading in the dusk.

Quitting his room, he returned downstairs. He found the maid sequestered in the alcove beneath the stairs, scrubbing at a pair of riding boots with blacking, and inquired of her if there was a parlour in which he might spend the evening. His voyage had wrought considerable strain in him, and he was in sore need of a glass of brandy and a quiet place to rest his eyes.

The maid was more obliging now—her sixpences must be few and far between, Moody thought, which could be useful later, if he needed her. She explained that the parlour of the Crown had been reserved that night for a private party—'The Catholic Friendlies,' she clarified, grinning again—but she might conduct him instead, if he wished it, to the smoking room.

Moody returned to the present with a jolt, and saw that Thomas Balfour was still looking at him, with an expression of intrigued expectation upon his face.

'I beg your pardon,' Moody said, in confusion. 'I believe I must have drifted off into my own thoughts—for a moment—'

'What were you thinking of?' said Balfour.

What had he been thinking of? Only the cravat, the silver hand, that name, gasped out of the darkness. The scene was like a small world, Moody thought, possessed of its own dimensions. Any amount of ordinary time could pass, when his mind was straying there. There was this large world of rolling time and shifting spaces, and that small, stilled world of horror and unease; they fit inside each other, a sphere within a sphere. How strange, that Balfour had been watching him; that real time had been passing—revolving around him, all the while—

'I wasn't thinking of anything in particular,' he said. 'I have endured a difficult journey, that is all, and I am very tired.'

Behind him one of the billiard players made a shot: a doubled crack, a velvet plop, a ripple of appreciation from the other players. The clergyman shook out his paper noisily; another man coughed; another struck the dust from his shirtsleeve, and shifted in his chair.

'I was asking about your quarrel,' Balfour said.

'The quarrel—' Moody began, and then stopped. He suddenly felt too exhausted even to speak.

'The dispute,' prompted Balfour. 'Between you and your father.'

'I am sorry,' Moody said. 'The particulars are delicate.'

'A matter of money! Do I hit upon it?'

'Forgive me: you do not.' Moody ran his hand over his face.

'Not of money! Then—a matter of love! You are in love . . . but your father will not approve the girl of your choosing . . .'

'No, sir,' Moody said. 'I am not in love.'

'A great shame,' Balfour said. 'Well! I conclude: you are already married!'

'I am unmarried.'

'You are a young widower, perhaps!'

'I have never been married, sir.'

Balfour burst out laughing and threw up both his hands, to signal that he considered Moody's reticence cheerfully exasperating, and quite absurd.

While he was laughing Moody raised himself up on his wrists and swivelled to look over the high back of his armchair at the room behind him. He had the intention of drawing others into their conversation somehow, and perhaps thus diverting the other man from his purpose. But nobody looked up to meet his gaze; they seemed, Moody thought, to be actively avoiding him. This was odd. But his posture was awkward and he was being rude, and so he reluctantly resumed his former position and crossed his legs again.

'I do not mean to disappoint you,' he said, when Balfour's laughter subsided.

'Disappoint—no!' Balfour cried. 'No, no. You will have your secrets!'

'You mistake me,' Moody said. 'My aim is not concealment. The subject is personally distressing to me, that is all.'

'Oh,' Balfour said, 'but it is always so, Mr. Moody, when one is young—to be distressed by one's own history, you know—wishing to keep it back—and never to share it—I mean, with other men.'

'That is a wise observation.'

'Wise! And nothing else?'

'I do not understand you, Mr. Balfour.'

'You are determined to thwart my curiosity!'

'I confess I am a little startled by it.'

'This is a gold town, sir!' Balfour said. 'One must be sure of his fellows—one must trust in his fellows—indeed!'

This was still more odd. For the first time—perhaps because of his growing frustration, which served to focus his attention more squarely upon the scene at hand—Moody felt his interest begin to stir. The strange silence of the room was hardly testament to the kind of fraternity where all was shared and made easy . . . and moreover, Balfour had offered very little with respect to his own character and reputation in the town, by which intelligence Moody might be made to feel more assured of *him*! His gaze slid sideways, to the fat man closest to the hearth, whose closed eyelids were trembling with the effort of pretended sleep, and then to the blond-haired man behind him, who was passing his billiard cue from one hand to the other, but seemed to have lost all interest in the game.

Something was afoot: of this he was suddenly certain. Balfour was performing a role, on behalf of the others: taking his measure, Moody thought. But for what purpose? There was a system behind this battery of questions, a design that was neatly obscured by the excess of Balfour's manner, his prodigious sympathy and charm. The other men were listening, however casually they turned the pages of their papers, or pretended to doze. With this realisation the room seemed suddenly to clarify, as when a chance scatter of stars resolves into a constellation before the eye. Balfour no longer seemed cheery and effusive, as Moody had first believed him to be; instead he seemed overwrought, strained; even desperate. Moody wondered now whether indulging the man might serve better purpose than denying him.

Walter Moody was much experienced in the art of confidences. He knew that by confessing, one earned the subtle right to become confessor to the other, in his turn. A secret deserves a secret, and a tale deserves a tale; the gentle expectation of a response in kind was a pressure he knew how to apply. He would learn more by appearing to confide in Balfour than by openly suspecting him, simply because if he placed his trust in the other man, freely and without reservation, then Balfour would be obliged to confer his own trust in exchange. There was no reason why he could not relate his family story—however vexing it might be to recall it—in order to purchase the other man's trust. What had happened aboard the *Godspeed*, he had no intention of divulging, of course; but in this he did not need to dissimulate, for that was not the story that Thomas Balfour had requested to hear.

Having reflected upon this, Moody changed his tack.

'I see that I must win your confidence yet,' he said. 'I have nothing to hide, sir. I will relate my tale.'

Balfour flung himself back into his armchair with great satisfaction. 'You call it a tale!' he said, beaming again. 'Then I am surprised, Mr. Moody, that it concerns neither love nor money!'

'Only their absence, I am afraid,' Moody said.

'Absence—yes,' Balfour said, still smiling. He gestured for Moody to continue.

'I must first acquaint you with the particulars of my family history,' Moody said, and then lapsed into silence for a moment, his eyes narrowed, his mouth pursed.

The armchair in which he was sitting faced the hearth, and so nearly half of the men in the room were behind him, sitting or standing at their various sham pursuits. In the several seconds' grace he had secured for himself by appearing to collect his thoughts, Moody let his gaze wander to his left and right, to make note of the listeners sitting closest to them, around the fire.

Nearest the hearth sat the fat man who was feigning sleep. He was by far the most ostentatiously dressed in the room: a massive watch chain, thick as his own fat finger, was slung across his chest, between the pocket of his velvet vest and the breast of his cambric shirt, and affixed to the chain at intervals were knuckle-sized lumps of gold. The man next to him, on Balfour's other side, was partly obscured by the wing of his armchair, so that all Moody could see of him was the glint of his forehead and the shiny tip of his nose. His coat was made of herringbone, a thick woollen weave that was much too hot for his proximity to the fire, and his perspiration betrayed the posture of apparent ease with which he had arranged himself in the chair. He had no cigar; he was turning a silver cigarette case over and over in his hands. On Moody's left was another wingback armchair, pulled so close to his own that he could hear the nasal whistle of his neighbour's breath. This man was dark-haired, slim in build, and so tall that he appeared folded in two, sitting with his knees together and the soles of his shoes planted flat upon the floor. He was reading a newspaper, and in general, he was doing a much better job of pretended indifference than the others, but even so his eyes were somewhat glassy, as if they were not quite focused upon the type, and he had not turned a page in some time.

'I am the younger son of two,' Moody began at last. 'My brother, Frederick, is five years my senior. Our mother died near the end of my school years—I returned home only for a short time, to bury her—and shortly thereafter my father married again. His second wife was unknown to me then. She was—she is—a quiet, delicate woman, one who frighted easily, and was often ill. In her delicacy she is very unlike my father, who is coarse in his manner and much inclined to drink.

'The match was poor; I believe both parties regretted the marriage as a mistake, and I am sorry to report my father treated his new wife very badly. Three years ago he disappeared, leaving her, in Edinburgh, without provision to live. She might have become a pauper, or worse, such was the sudden destitution in which she found herself. She appealed to me—by letter, I mean; I was abroad—and I returned home at once. I became her protector, in a modest sense. I made arrangements on her behalf, which she accepted, though somewhat bitterly, for the shape of her fortunes was much changed.' Moody gave an awkward dry cough. 'I secured for her a small living—employment, you understand. I then travelled to London, with the purpose of finding my father. There I exhausted all possible methods of locating him, and spent a great deal of money in the process. Finally I began to see about turning my education into an income of a kind, for I knew that I could no longer rely on my inheritance as surety, and my credit in the city had become very poor.

'My elder brother knew nothing of our stepmother's abandonment: he had left to seek his fortune on the Otago goldfields, some few weeks before my father disappeared. He was inclined to fits of whimsy of this kind—an adventurous spirit, I suppose you might call him, though we were never close with one another after childhood, and I confess I do not know him well. Months passed, and even years; he did not return, and nor did he send any news at all. My letters to him went unanswered. Indeed I still do not know if they ever reached his hands. At length I too booked my passage on a ship bound for New Zealand, my intention being to inform my brother of the changes in our family's position, and— if he was alive, of course—perhaps to join him on the diggings for a time. My own fortune was gone, the interest on my perpetuity was long since exhausted, and I was in a great deal of debt. While in London I had studied at the Inner Temple. I suppose I might have stayed on, and waited to be called to the Bar . . . but I have no real love for the law. I could not stomach it. I sailed for New Zealand instead.

'When I landed at Dunedin, not two weeks ago, I learned that Otago's gold had been all but eclipsed by new findings here on the Coast. I hesitated, not knowing where to venture first, and was rewarded for my hesitation in the most unexpected way: I met my father.'

Balfour made a murmur, but did not interrupt. He was staring into the fire, his mouth pursed judiciously around his cigar and his hand loose around the base of his glass. The eleven others were equally still. The billiard game must have been abandoned, for Moody could no longer hear the click of the balls behind him. There was a sprung quality to the silence, as if the listeners were waiting for him to reveal something very particular ... or fearing that he might.

'Our reunion was not a happy one,' Moody continued. He was speaking loudly, above the drumming of the rain; loudly enough for every man in the room to hear him, but not so loudly as to make it seem as if he was aware of their attention. 'He was drunk, and extremely angry that I had discovered him. I learned that he had become extraordinarily rich, and that he was married again, to a woman who doubtless was innocent of his history, or indeed of the fact that he was legally bound to another wife. I was, I am sorry to admit, unsurprised. My relations with my father have never been warm, and this was not the first time I had caught him in questionable circumstances ... though never in a situation of this criminal magnitude, I should hasten to say.

'My real amazement came when I inquired after my brother, and learned that he had been my father's agent from the outset: they had orchestrated the abandonment together, and had journeyed south as partners. I did not wait to encounter Frederick too—I could not bear it, to see them both together—and made to leave. My father became aggressive, and attempted to detain me. I escaped, and made the immediate plan to journey here. I had money enough to return to London directly, if I wished, but my grief was of a kind that—' Moody paused, and made a helpless gesture with his fingers. 'I don't know,' he said at last. 'I believed the hard labour of the diggings might do me well, for a time. And I do not want to be a lawyer.'

There was a silence. Moody shook his head and sat forward in his chair. 'It is an unhappy story,' he said, more briskly. 'I am ashamed of my blood, Mr. Balfour, but I mean not to dwell upon it. I mean to make new.'

'Unhappy, indeed!' Balfour cried, plucking his cigar from his mouth at last, and waving it about. 'I am sorry for you, Mr. Moody, and commend you, both. But yours is the way of the goldfields, is it not? Reinvention! Dare I say—revolution! That a man might make new—might make *himself* anew—truly, now!'

'These are words of encouragement,' Moody said.

'Your father—his name is also Moody, I presume.'

'It is,' Moody said. 'His Christian name is Adrian; perhaps you have heard of him?'

'I have not,' Balfour said, and then, perceiving that the other was disappointed, he added, '—which means very little, of course. I'm in the shipping line of business, as I told you; these days I don't rub shoulders with the men on the field. I was in Dunedin. I was in Dunedin for three years, near about. But if your pa made his luck on the diggings, he'd have been inland. Up in the high country. He might have been anywhere—Tuapeka, Clyde—anywhere at all. But—listen—as to the here and now, Mr. Moody. You're not afraid that he will follow you?'

'No,' Moody said, simply. 'I took pains to create the impression that I departed immediately for England, the day I left him. Upon the docks I found a man seeking passage to Liverpool. I explained my circumstances to him, and after a short negotiation we swapped papers with one another. He gave my name to the ticket master, and I his. Should my father inquire at the customhouse, the officers there will be able to show him proof that I have left these islands already, and am returning home.'

'But perhaps your father—and your brother—will come to the Coast of their own accord. For the diggings.'

'That I cannot predict,' Moody agreed. 'But from what I understood of their current situation, they had made gold enough in Otago.'

'Gold *enough*!' Balfour seemed about to laugh again.

Moody shrugged. 'Well,' he said coldly, 'I shall prepare myself for the possibility of their arrival, of course. But I do not expect it.'

'No—of course, of course,' Balfour said, patting Moody's sleeve with his big hand. 'Let us now talk of more hopeful things. Tell me, what do you intend to do with your pile, once you have amassed a decent sum? Back to Scotland, is it, to spend your fortune there?'

'So I hope,' Moody said. 'I have heard that a man might make a competence in four months or less, which would take me away from here before the worst months of winter. Is that a probable expectation, in your mind?'

'Quite probable,' Balfour said, smiling at the coals, 'quite probable, indeed—yes, one might expect it. No mates in town, then? Folk to meet you on the quay, join up—lads from home?'

'None, sir,' Moody told him, for the third time that evening. 'I travelled here alone, and, as I have said to you already, I intend to make my own fortune, without the help of other men.'

'Oh, yes,' said Balfour, 'making your own—well, going *after* it, in the modern way. But a digger's mate is like his shadow—that's another thing to know—his shadow, or his wife—'

At this remark there was a ripple of amusement around the room: not open laughter, merely a quiet expulsion of breath, issued from several quarters at once. Moody glanced around him. He had sensed a slackening in the air, a collective relief, at the conclusion of his narrative. The men had been afraid of something, he thought, and his story had given them reason to put their fear aside. He wondered for the first time whether their trepidation was connected in some way to the horror he had witnessed aboard the *Godspeed*. The thought was strangely unpleasant. He did not want to believe that his private memory might be explicable to another man, and still less, that another man might share it. (Suffering, he thought later, could rob a man of his empathy, could turn him selfish, could make him depreciate all other sufferers. This realisation, when it came, surprised him.)

Balfour was grinning. 'Ay—his shadow, or his wife,' he repeated, nodding appreciatively at Moody, as though the jest had been Moody's, rather than his own. He stroked his beard several times with the cup of his hand, and laughed a little.

For he was indeed relieved. Lost inheritance, falseness in marriage, a highborn woman *put to work*—these betrayals belonged to a different world entirely, Balfour thought; a world of drawing rooms, and calling cards, and gowns. It was charming to him, that such changes in fortune might be counted as tragedies—that the young man might *confess* them, with the stern, controlled embarrassment of a man who had been taught to believe, from the moment of his birth, that his estate would never change. To speak of that here—at the vanguard of the civilised world! Hokitika was growing faster than San Francisco, the papers said, and out of nothing ... out of the ancient rotting life of the jungle ... out of the tidal marshes and the shifting gullies and the fog ... out of sly waters, rich in ore. Here the men were not self-made; they were self-*making*, as they squatted in the dirt to wash it clean. Balfour touched his lapel. Moody's story was pathetic, and had aroused in him an indulgent, fatherly feeling—for Balfour liked very much to be reminded that he himself was modern (entrepreneurial, unencumbered by connexion) while other men still foundered in the trappings of an outworn age.

This, of course, was a verdict that said less about the prisoner than about the judge. Balfour's will was too strong to admit philosophy, unless it was of the soundest empirical sort; his liberality could make no sense of despair, which was to him as a fathomless shaft, possessed of depth but not of breadth, stifled in its isolation, navigable only by touch, and starved of any kind of curiosity. He had no real fascination with the soul, and saw it only as a pretext for the greater, livelier mysteries of humour and adventure; of the soul's dark nights, he had no opinion. He often said that the only inner void to which he paid any kind of notice was appetite, and although he laughed when he said it, and seemed very well pleased, it was true that his sympathy rarely extended to situations where sympathy was expected to extend. He was indulgent towards the open spaces of other men's futures, but he was impatient with the shuttered quarters of their pasts.

'In any case,' he went on, 'mark this as your second piece of advice, Mr. Moody: find yourself a friend. Plenty of parties about that'd be glad for an extra pair of hands. That's the way, you know—find a mate, then form a party. Never known a man to make it solo. You kitted with a costume, and a swag?'

'I'm afraid I am at the mercy of the weather on that count,' Moody said. 'My trunk is still aboard ship; the weather was too inclement to risk crossing the bar tonight, and I was told to expect my belongings at the customhouse to-morrow afternoon. I myself was conveyed by lighter—a small crew rowed out, very bravely, to fetch the passengers in.'

'Oh, yes,' Balfour said, more soberly. 'We've seen three wrecks in the past month alone, coming over the bar. It's a frightful business. There's a penny to be made in it, mind. When the ships are coming in people don't pay too much attention. But when they're going out—when they're going out, there's gold aboard.'

'I am told that the landing here at Hokitika is notoriously treacherous.'

'Notoriously—oh yes. And there's nothing to be done about it, if a vessel's on the long side of a hundred feet. She might blow off a full head of steam and it's not enough to force her over. Capital firework show, with the flares shooting up all around. But then— it's not just the steamers. Not just the big ones. It's any man's game on the Hokitika Bar, Walter. That sand will ground a schooner on the wrong tide.'

'I well believe it,' Moody said. 'Our vessel was a barque—none too large, agile, hardy enough to weather the most dreadful of storms—and yet the captain wouldn't risk her. He elected to drop anchor in the roadstead, and wait for the morning.'

'The *Waterloo*, that her name? She's a regular, in and out from Chalmers.'

'A private charter, as a matter of fact,' Moody said. 'Name of *Godspeed*.'

He might have pulled a pistol from his pocket, such was the shock that name produced. Moody looked around (his expression was still mild) and saw that the attention of the room was now openly fixed upon him. Several of the men put down their papers; those who had been dozing opened their eyes; and one of the billiard players advanced a step towards him, into the light of the lamp.

Balfour, too, had flinched at the mention of the barque's name, but his grey eyes held Moody's gaze coolly. 'Indeed,' he said, seeming in an instant to shed all the effusion and bluster that had characterised his manner up until that point. 'I confess to you the name of that craft is not unknown to me, Mr. Moody—not unknown—but I should like to confirm the captain's name also, if you have no objection.'

Moody was searching his face for a very particular quality—one that, if he had been pressed, he would have been embarrassed to name aloud. He was trying to see if Balfour seemed haunted. He was sure that if the other man's mind leaped to imagine, or to remember, the kind of preternatural horror that Moody himself had encountered aboard the *Godspeed*, then its effect would be only too visible. But Balfour merely looked wary, as when a man hears of the return of one of his creditors, and begins in his mind to tally his excuses, and methods of escape—he did not look tormented, or afraid. Moody was certain that anyone who had witnessed what he had would bear the mark of it. And yet Balfour was changed— there was a new shrewdness to the other man's aspect, a new sharpness to his gaze. Moody felt energised by the alteration. He realised, with a surge of excitement, that he had underestimated him.

'I believe the captain's name was Carver,' he said slowly, 'Francis Carver, if I remember rightly; a man of considerable strength, with a brooding look, and a white scar upon his cheek—does that description match your man?'

'It does.' Balfour was scanning Moody's face, in turn. 'I am very curious to know how you and Mr. Carver came to be acquainted,' he said after a moment. 'If you would indulge the intrusion, of course.'

'Forgive me: we are not acquainted,' Moody said. 'That is, I am sure he would not recognise me if he saw me again.'

He was resolved, in accordance with his strategy, to field Balfour's questions politely and without reservation: it would give him licence later to demand some answers of his own. Moody had no small genius for the art of diplomacy. As a child he had known instinctively that it was always better to tell a partial truth with a willing aspect than to tell a perfect truth in a defensive way. The appearance of co-operation was worth a great deal, if only because it forced a reciprocity, fair met with fair. He did not look about him again, but instead kept his eyes wide and his face open, and directed his speech wholly to Balfour, as if the eleven staring men on his periphery did not trouble him in the least.

'In that case,' Balfour was saying, 'I shall hazard to guess that you purchased your ticket from the ship's mate.'

'Paid him into his own pocket, sir.'

'You had a private arrangement with the man?'

'The scheme had been devised by the crew, with the master's consent,' Moody replied. 'An easy enough way to turn an extra shilling, I suppose. There were no berths of any kind—one was allotted a place below decks, and instructed to stay sharp and keep out of the way. The situation was not at all ideal, of course, but my circumstances compelled my immediate departure from Dunedin, as you know, and *Godspeed* was the only scheduled departure on the day I wished to leave. I did not know the mate prior to our transaction, nor any of the other passengers, nor any of the crew.'

'How many passengers came in under this arrangement?'

Moody met Balfour's gaze levelly. 'Eight,' he said, and put his mouth on his cigar.

Balfour was quick to pounce upon this. 'That's you and seven others? Eight in sum?'

Moody declined to answer the question directly. 'The passenger list will be published in Monday's paper; of course you may examine it yourself,' he said, with a slightly incredulous expression, as though to imply that Balfour's need for clarification was not only unnecessary, but unbecoming. He added, 'My real name, of course, will not appear there. I travelled under the name Philip de Lacy, this being the name of the man whose papers I purchased in Dunedin. Walter Moody, as the authorities have it, is currently somewhere in the South Pacific—bearing eastward, I expect, towards the Horn.'

Balfour's expression was still cool. 'Please allow me to inquire one thing further,' he said. 'I should like to know—merely—whether you have cause to think well or ill of him. Mr. Carver, I mean.'

'I am not sure that I can answer you fairly,' Moody said. 'I have on my authority only suspicion and report. I believe that the man was under some duress to leave Dunedin, for he was anxious to weigh anchor despite predictions of a coming storm, but I am entirely ignorant of the business that compelled his haste. I did not formally meet him, and saw him only from a distance during the voyage, and then only rarely, for he kept to his cabin much of the time. So you see my opinion is not worth very much. And yet—'

'And yet . . .' Balfour prompted, when Moody did not go on. He waited.

'To be frank with you, sir,' Moody said, turning squarely to face the other man, 'I discovered certain particulars concerning the ship's cargo, while aboard, that made me doubt her errand was an honest one. If I am certain of one thing, it is this: I wish never to make an enemy of Mr. Carver, if that event is in my power to avoid.'

The dark-haired man on Moody's left had stiffened. 'Found something in cargo, you said?' he interposed, leaning forward.

Aha! Moody thought, and then: *now is the time to press my advantage.* He turned to address the new speaker. 'Please forgive me if I neglect to elaborate,' he said. 'I mean no disrespect to you, sir, but we are strangers to one another; or rather, *you* are a stranger to *me*, for my conversation with Mr. Balfour tonight has reached more ears than his alone. In this I am disadvantaged, not unto myself, as I have represented myself truthfully, but unto you, for you have made my acquaintance without introduction, and heard my piece without invitation or reply. I have nothing to conceal, concerning this or any journey I have made, but I confess,' (he turned back to Balfour) 'it rankles to be questioned so relentlessly by an interrogator who divulges nothing of his own design.'

This was rather more aggressively worded than was Moody's habit in speech, but he had spoken calmly and with dignity, and he knew that he was in the right. He did not blink; he stared at Balfour and waited, his mild eyes wide, for the other man's response. Balfour's gaze flickered sideways to the dark-haired man who had made the interruption, and then back to meet Moody's own. He exhaled. He rose from his chair, tossed the stump of his cigar into the fire, and held out his hand. 'Your glass needs refilling, Mr. Moody,' he said quietly. 'Please be so kind as to allow me.'

He went to the sideboard in silence, followed by the dark-haired man, who, when he had unfurled himself to his full height, almost grazed the low ceiling of the room. He leaned close to Balfour and began to mutter something urgently in his ear. Balfour nodded and muttered something back. It must have been an instruction, for the tall man then moved to the billiard table, beckoned the blond-haired man to approach him, and conveyed a whispered message to him. The blond-haired man began nodding, vigorously and at once. Watching them, Moody felt his habitual quickness return. The brandy had roused him; he was warmed and dried; and nothing caused his spirits to lift more surely than the promise of a tale.

It often happens that when a soul under duress is required to attend to a separate difficulty, one that does not concern him in the least, then this second problem works upon the first as a kind of salve. Moody felt this now. For the first time since he had disembarked from the lighter he found that he was able to think upon his recent misadventure clearly. In the context of this new secret, his private memory was somehow freed. He could recall the scene that haunted him—the dead man rising, his bloody throat, his cry—and find it fabular, sensational; still horrific, but somehow much more explicably so. The story had gained a kind of value: he could turn it into profit, by exchange.

He watched the whispered message pass from man to man. He could not distinguish any proper nouns—the jumble of unfamiliar accents made that impossible—but it was evident that the matter under discussion was one that concerned every man in the room. He forced his mind to evaluate the situation carefully and rationally. Inattention had led him to err in judgment once already that evening; he would not err again. Some kind of heist was in the offing, he guessed, or maybe they were forming an alliance against another man. Mr. Carver, perhaps. They numbered twelve, which put Moody in mind of a jury ... but the presence of the Chinese men and the Maori native made that impossible. Had he interrupted a secret council of a kind? But what kind of council could possibly comprise such a diverse range of race, income, and estate?

Needless to say that Walter Moody's countenance did not betray the subject of his thoughts. He had calibrated his expression precisely between grave bafflement and apology, as if to communicate that he was very sensible of the trouble he was causing, but he had no idea what that trouble might be, and as to how he should proceed, he was willing to take anyone's direction but his own.

Outside, the wind changed direction, sending a damp gust down the chimney, so that the embers swelled scarlet and for a brief moment Moody could smell the salt of the sea. The movement in the hearth seemed to rouse the fat man nearest the fire. He levered himself from his armchair with a grunt of effort and shuffled off to join the others at the sideboard. When he had gone, Moody found himself alone before the fire with the man in the herringbone suit; the latter now leaned forward and spoke.

'I should like to introduce myself, if you have no objection,' he said, snapping open his silver cigarette case for the first time, and selecting a cigarette. He spoke with an accent identifiably French, and a manner that was clipped and courteous. 'My name is Aubert Gascoigne. I hope that you will forgive that I know your name already.'

'Well, as it happens,' Moody said, with a little jolt of surprise, 'I believe I also know yours.'

'Then we are well met,' said Aubert Gascoigne. He had been fishing for his matches; he paused now with his hand in his breast pocket, like a rakish colonel posing for a sketch. 'But I am intrigued. How is it that you know me, Mr. Moody?'

'I read your address this evening, in Friday's edition of the *West Coast Times*—am I right? If I remember correctly, you penned an opinion on behalf of the Magistrate's Court.'

Gascoigne smiled, and pulled out his matches. 'Now I understand. I am yesterday's news.' He shook out a match, placed the side of his boot against his knee, and struck his light upon the sole.

'Forgive me,' Moody began, fearing that he had offended, but Gascoigne shook his head.

'I am not insulted,' he said when his cigarette was lit. 'So. You arrive as a stranger in an unfamiliar town, and what is your first move? You find a day-old paper and read the courthouse bulletin. You learn the names of the lawbreakers, on the one hand, and the law enforcers, on the other. This is quite a strategy.'

'There was no method in it,' Moody said modestly.

Gascoigne's name had appeared on the third page of the paper, beneath a short sermon, perhaps the length of a paragraph, on the iniquity of crime. The address was preceded by a list of all the arrests that had been made that month. (He could not recall any of those names, and in truth had only remembered Gascoigne's because his former Latin master had been Gascoyen—the familiarity had drawn his eye.)

'Perhaps not,' Gascoigne returned, 'but it has brought you to the very heart of our disquiet nonetheless: a subject that has been on every man's lips for a fortnight.'

Moody frowned. 'Petty criminals?'

'One in particular.'

'Shall I guess?' Moody asked lightly, when the other did not go on.

Gascoigne shrugged. 'It doesn't matter. I am referring to the whore.'

Moody raised his eyebrows. He tried to recall the catalogue of arrests to his mind—yes, perhaps one of the listed names had been a woman's. He wondered what every man in Hokitika had to say about a whore's arrest. It took him a moment to find the words to form an appropriate answer, and to his surprise, Gascoigne laughed. 'I am teasing you,' he said. 'You must not let me tease you. Her crime was not listed, of course, but if you read with a little imagination you will see it. Anna Wetherell is the name she gives.'

'I am not sure I know how to read with imagination.'

Gascoigne laughed again, expelling a sharp breath of smoke. 'But you are a barrister, are you not?'

'By training only,' Moody said stiffly. 'I have not yet been called to the Bar.'

'Well, here: there is always an overtone in the magistrate's address,' Gascoigne explained. '*Gentlemen of Westland*—there is your first clue. *Crimes of shame and degradation*—there is your second.'

'I see,' Moody said, though he did not. His gaze flickered over Gascoigne's shoulder: the fat man had moved to the pair of Chinese men, and was scribbling something on the flyleaf of his pocketbook for them to read. 'Perhaps the woman was wrongly indicted? Perhaps that is what captured everyone's attention?'

'Oh, she wasn't gaoled for whoring,' Gascoigne said. 'The sergeants don't care a straw about *that*! As long as a man is discreet enough, they are quite content to look the other way.'

Moody waited. There was an unsettling quality to the way that Gascoigne spoke: it was both guarded and confiding at once. Moody felt that he could not trust him. The clerk was perhaps in his middle thirties. His pale hair had begun to silver above his ears, and he wore a pale moustache, brushed sideways from a central part. His herringbone suit was tailored closely to his body.

'Why,' Gascoigne added after a moment, 'the sergeant himself made a proposition of her, directly after the committal!'

'The committal?' Moody echoed, feeling foolish. He wished that the other man would speak a little less cryptically, and at greater length. He had a cultivated air (he made Thomas Balfour seem as blunt as a doorstop) but it was a cultivation somehow mourned. He spoke as a disappointed man, for whom perfection existed only as something remembered—and then regretted, because it was lost.

'She was tried for trying to take her own life,' Gascoigne said. 'There's a symmetry in that, do you not think? Tried for trying.'

Moody thought it inappropriate to agree, and in any case he did not care to pursue that line of thinking. He said, to change the subject, 'And the master of my vessel—Mr. Carver? He is connected to this woman somehow, I presume?'

'Oh yes, Carver's *connected*,' Gascoigne said. He looked at the cigarette in his hand, seemed suddenly disgusted with it, and threw it into the fire. 'He killed his own child.'

Moody drew back in horror. 'I beg your pardon?'

'They can't prove it, of course,' Gascoigne said darkly. 'But the man's a brute. You are quite right to want to avoid him.'

Moody stared at him, again at a loss for how to reply.

'Every man has his currency,' Gascoigne added after a moment.

'Perhaps it's gold; perhaps it's women. Anna Wetherell, you see, was both.'

At this point the fat man returned, with his glass refreshed; he sat down, looked first to Gascoigne and then to Moody, and seemed to recognise, obscurely, a social obligation to introduce himself. He leaned forward and thrust out his hand. 'Name's Dick Mannering.'

'It's a pleasure,' Moody said, in a rather automatic tone. He felt disoriented. He wished Gascoigne had not been interrupted quite at that moment, so he could have pressed him further on the subject of the whore. It was indelicate to attempt to revive the subject now; in any case Gascoigne had retreated back into his armchair, and his face had closed. He began turning his cigarette case over again in his hands.

'Prince of Wales Opera House, that's me,' Mannering added, as he sat back.

'Capital,' said Moody.

'Only show in town.' Mannering rapped the arm of his chair with his knuckles, casting about for a way to proceed. Moody glanced at Gascoigne, but the clerk was staring sourly into his lap. It was clear that the fat man's reappearance had severely displeased him; it was also clear that he saw no reason to conceal his displeasure from its object—whose face, Moody saw with embarrassment, had turned a very dark shade of red.

'I could not help but admire your watch chain, earlier,' Moody said at last, addressing Mannering. 'Is it Hokitika gold?'

'Nice piece, isn't it?' Mannering said, without looking down at his chest, or lifting his fingers to touch the admired item. He rapped the arms of his chair a second time. 'Clutha nuggets, in actual fact. I was at Kawarau, Dunstan, then Clutha.'

'I confess I'm not familiar with the names,' Moody said. 'I assume they're Otago fields?'

Mannering assented that they were, and began to expound on the subject of company mining and the value of the dredge.

'You're all diggers here?' Moody said when he was done, moving his fingertips in a little circle in the air, to indicate that he meant the room at large.

'Not one—excepting the Chinamen, of course,' Mannering said. 'Camp followers is the term, though most of us started off in the gorge. Most gold on a goldfield's found where? At the hotels. At the shanties. Mates spend the stuff as soon as they find it. Tell you what: you might do better to open a business than to head to the hills. Get yourself a licence, start selling grog.'

'That must be wise advice, if you have acted upon it yourself,' Moody said.

Mannering settled back into his chair, seeming very contented with the compliment. Yes, he had quit the fields, and now paid other men to work his claims for a percentage of the yield; he was from Sussex; Hokitika was a fine place, but there were fewer girls than was proper in a town of such a size; he loved all kinds of harmony; he had modelled his opera house upon the Adelphi at the West End; he felt that the old song-and-supper could not be beat; he could not abide public houses, and small beer made him ill; the floods at Dunstan had been dreadful—dreadful; the Hokitika rain was hard to bear; he would say again that there was nothing nicer than a four-part harmony—the voices like threads in a piece of silk.

'Splendid,' Moody murmured. Gascoigne had made no movement at all during this soliloquy, save for the compulsive rhythm of his long, pale hands, as he turned the silver object over in his lap; Mannering, for his part, had not registered the clerk's presence at all, and in fact had directed his speech at a spot some three feet above Moody's head, as if Moody's presence did not really concern him either.

At length the whispered drama that was taking place on their periphery began to approach a kind of resolution, and the fat man's patter subsided. The dark-haired man returned, sitting down in his former position on Moody's left; Balfour came after him, carrying two sizeable measures of brandy. He passed one of the glasses to Moody, waved his hand at the latter's thanks, and sat down.

'I owe an explanation,' he said, 'for the rudeness with which I was questioning you just now, Mr. Moody—you needn't demur, it's quite true. The truth is—the truth is—well, the truth, sir, deserves a tale, and that's as short as I can make it.'

'If you would be so kind as to enter our confidence,' Gascoigne added, from Balfour's other side, in a rather nasty show of false politeness.

The dark-haired man sat forward in his chair suddenly and added, 'Does any man present wish to voice his reservations?'

Moody looked around him, blinking, but nobody spoke.

Balfour nodded; he waited a moment more, as if to append his own courtesy to that of the other, and then resumed.

'Let me tell you at once,' he said to Moody, 'that a man has been murdered. That blackguard of yours—Carver, I mean; I shan't call him Captain—he is the murderer, though I'll be d—ned if I could tell you how or why. I just know it, as sure as I see that glass in your hand. Now: if you'd do me the honour of hearing a piece of that villain's history, then you might ... well, you might be willing to help us, placed as you are.'

'Excuse me, sir,' Moody said. At the mention of murder his heart had begun to beat very fast: perhaps this had something to do with the phantom aboard the *Godspeed*, after all. 'How am I placed?'

'With your trunk still aboard the barque, is what he means,' the dark-haired man said. 'And your appointment at the customhouse to-morrow afternoon.'

Balfour looked faintly annoyed; he waved his hand. 'Let us talk of that in a moment,' he said. 'I entreat you, first, to hear the story out.'

'Certainly I will listen,' Moody returned, with the slightest emphasis on the last word, as though to caution the other man against expecting, or demanding, anything more. He thought he saw a smirk pass over Gascoigne's pale face, but in the next moment the man's features had soured again.

'Of course—of course,' Balfour said, taking the point. He put down his brandy glass, laced his knuckles together, and cracked them smartly. 'Well, then. I shall endeavour to acquaint you, Mr. Moody, with the cause of our assembly.'

JUPITER IN SAGITTARIUS

In which the merits of asylum are discussed; a family name comes into question; Alistair Lauderback is discomfited; and the shipping agent tells a lie.

Balfour's narrative, made somewhat circuitous by interruption, and generally encumbered by the lyrical style of that man's speech, became severely muddled in the telling, and several hours passed before Moody finally understood with clarity the order of events that had precipitated the secret council in the hotel smoking room.

The interruptions were too tiresome, and Balfour's approach too digressive, to deserve a full and faithful record in the men's own words. We shall here excise their imperfections, and impose a regimental order upon the impatient chronicle of the shipping agent's roving mind; we shall apply our own mortar to the cracks and chinks of earthly recollection, and resurrect as new the edifice that, in solitary memory, exists only as a ruin.

We begin, as Balfour himself began, with an encounter that had taken place in Hokitika that very morning.

Φ

Prior to the dawn of the West Coast rush—when Hokitika was no more than a brown mouth open to the ocean, and the gold on her beaches shone quiet and unseen—Thomas Balfour lived in the province of Otago, and conducted his business from a small shingle-roofed building on the Dunedin harbour front, under a calico

banner that bore the legend Balfour & Harnett, Shipping Agents.
(Mr. Harnett had since abandoned the joint venture, of which he
had owned only a one-third share: he was now enjoying a colonial
retirement in Auckland, far from the Otago frost, and the fog that
pooled white in the valleys in the chilly hours before the dawn.) The
firm's advantageous location—they were squared with the central
wharf, and enjoyed a view towards the distant heads of the harbour—brought distinguished custom, and among their many
clients was the erstwhile Superintendent of Canterbury, a spade-
handed giant of a man whose reputation was one of conviction,
expansion, and zeal.

Alistair Lauderback—this was the statesman's name—had
enjoyed a sense of constant acceleration over the course of his
career. He was born in London, and had trained as a lawyer before
making the voyage to New Zealand in the year of 1851—setting
sail with two goals: firstly, to make his fortune, and secondly, to
double it. His ambition was well suited to a political life, and especially to the political life of a young country. Lauderback rose, and
rose quickly. In legal circles he was much admired as a man who
could set his mind to a task, and not rest until he had seen the project through; on the strength of this fine character, he was rewarded
with a place on the Canterbury Provincial Council, and invited to
run for the Superintendency, to which post he was elected by a
landslide majority vote. Five years after his first landing in New
Zealand, the network of his connexion reached as far as the
Stafford ministry, and the Premier himself; by the time he first
knocked upon Thomas Balfour's door, wearing a fresh kowhai
flower in his buttonhole and a standing collar whose flared points
(Balfour noticed) had been starched by a woman's hand, he could
no longer be called a pioneer. He smacked of permanence: of the
kind of influence that lasts.

In his countenance and bearing Lauderback was less handsome
than imposing. His beard, large and blunt like Balfour's own, protruded almost horizontally from his jaw, giving his face a regal
aspect; beneath his brow, his dark eyes glittered. He was very tall,
and his body tapered, which made him seem even taller still. He

spoke loudly, declaring his ambitions and opinions with a frankness that might be called hubristic (if one was sceptical) or dauntless (if one was not). His hearing was slightly defective, and for this reason he tended to bow his head, and stoop slightly, when he was listening—creating the impression, so useful in politics, that his attentions were always gravely and providentially bestowed.

In their first meeting Lauderback impressed Balfour with the energy and confidence with which he spoke. His enthusiasms, as he announced to Balfour, did not pertain wholly to the political sphere. He was also a ship owner, having cherished, since boyhood, a passionate love for the sea. He possessed four ships in total: two clipper ships, a schooner, and a barque. Two of the crafts required masters. Hitherto he had leased them on charter, but the personal risk of such a venture was high, and he desired to lease the ships instead to an established shipping firm that could afford a reasonable rate of insurance. He listed the names of the ships in rote order, as a man lists his children: the clippers *Virtue* and *Corona Australis*; the schooner *Lady of the Ballroom*; and the barque *Godspeed*.

As it happened, Balfour & Harnett was sorely in need of a clipper ship at that time, of the very dimensions and capabilities that Lauderback described. Balfour had no use for the other ship on offer, the barque *Godspeed*, as that craft was too small for his purposes—but the *Virtue*, pending inspection and trial, would make the monthly passage between Port Chalmers and Port Phillip very comfortably. Yes, he told Lauderback, he would find a master for the *Virtue*. He would purchase insurance at a fair premium, and lease the ship on a yearly term.

Lauderback was Balfour's contemporary in age, and yet from that first meeting the latter deferred to him almost as a son to a father— showing a touch of vanity, perhaps, for the aspects of Lauderback's person Balfour most admired were the same aspects he cultivated in his own. Something of a friendship formed between the two (a friendship that was rather too admiring on Balfour's part ever to develop into intimacy) and for the next two years the *Virtue* ran unimpeded between Dunedin and Melbourne. The insurance clause, for all it had been painstakingly crafted, was never consulted again.

In January 1865 Robert Harnett declared his intention to retire, sold his shares to his partner, and moved north to milder climes. Balfour, with a typical absence of sentiment, relinquished the harbour-front lot immediately. Otago's boom was past its prime, he knew. The valleys were rutted; the rivers would soon be dry. He sailed to the Coast, purchased a bare patch of land near the mouth of the Hokitika River, strung up his tent, and began to build a warehouse. Balfour & Harnett became Balfour Shipping, Balfour bought an embroidered vest and a derby hat, and around him the town of Hokitika began to rise.

When the barque *Godspeed* pulled into the Hokitika roadstead some months later, Balfour recalled the name, and identified the ship as belonging to Alistair Lauderback. As a gesture of politeness he introduced himself to the ship's master, Francis Carver, and thereafter enjoyed a cordial relationship with the man, formed on the nominal bond of their mutual connexion—though privately Balfour thought Mr. Carver rather thuggish, and had pegged him for a crook. He held this opinion without bitterness. Balfour was not awed by force of will—unless it was of the sort that Lauderback displayed: charismatic, even charmed—and he could not love a villain. The rumours that dogged Mr. Carver at his heels did not intimidate him, and nor did they strike a chord of boyish admiration in his heart. Carver simply did not interest him, and he wasted no energy in his dismissal.

In late 1865 Balfour read in the paper that Alistair Lauderback was set to run for the Westland seat in Parliament, and some weeks after that Balfour received a letter from the man himself, requesting the shipping agent's collaboration once again. In his campaign to win the Westland province, Lauderback wrote, he wished to appear as a Westland man. He entreated Balfour to secure lodgings for him in central Hokitika, to furnish the rooms appropriately, and to facilitate the shipment of a trunk of personal effects—law-books and papers and so forth—that would be of crucial importance to him over the course of his campaign. Each item of business was described in the expansive, flourishing script that Balfour associated, in his mind, with a man who could afford to waste his ink on curlicues. (The thought made him smile: he liked to forgive Lauderback his many extravagances.) Lauderback himself would not arrive by ship. Instead he would make his passage overland, crossing the mountains on horseback to arrive triumphal at the heel of the Arahura Valley. He would make his entrance not as a pampered statesman travelling in comfort in a first-class berth, but as a man of the people, saddle-sore, muddied, and stained with the sweat of his own brow.

Balfour made these arrangements as he was instructed. He secured for Lauderback a suite of rooms overlooking the Hokitika beachfront, and registered his name at all the clubs that advertised craps and American bowls. He put in an order at the general store for pears, washed-rind cheese, and candied Jamaica ginger; he solicited a barber; he rented a private box at the opera house for the months of February and March. He informed the editor of the *West Coast Times* that Lauderback would be making the journey from Canterbury via the alpine pass, and suggested that a sympathetic mention of this brave endeavour would recommend the newspaper most favourably to Lauderback's future administration, should he win the Westland seat, as he was likely to do. Balfour then dispatched a message to Port Chalmers, instructing the master of the *Virtue* to collect Lauderback's trunk, once it had been sent down from Lyttelton, and convey it to Hokitika on the clipper ship's next circuit to the Coast. Once all this was done, he bought a demijohn of stout from the Gridiron Hotel, put up his heels, and quaffed it, reflecting as he did so that he might have liked politics— the speeches, the campaigning; yes, he might have liked it very well indeed.

But as it happened Alistair Lauderback's arrival in Hokitika was not accompanied by the burst of fanfare that the politician had envisaged, when he first set down his plans in his letter to Balfour. His expedition across the Alps indeed captured the attention of the diggers on the Coast, and his name indeed featured very prominently in every gazette and newspaper in town—but not at all for the reasons that he had intended.

The story recorded by the duty sergeant, and published the next morning in the *West Coast Times*, was this. Some two hours' ride from their final destination, Lauderback and his company of aides had happened to pass the dwelling of a hermit. It had been hours since their last refreshment, and night was falling; they stopped, intending to request a flask of water and (if the dwelling's owner would oblige them) a hot meal. They knocked on the door of the hut and received no answer, but by the lamplight and the smoke issuing from the chimney it was evident that someone was inside. The door was not latched; Lauderback entered. He found the dwelling's owner slumped dead at his kitchen table—so freshly dead, he later told the sergeant, that the kettle was still boiling on the range, and had not yet run dry. The hermit appeared to have died of drink. One hand was still curled around the base of a bottle of spirits, near empty on the table before him, and the room smelled very strongly of liquor. Lauderback admitted that the three men did then refresh themselves with tea and damper on the hermit's stove before journeying on. They did not stop for longer than a half hour, on account of the dead man's presence in the room—though his head was resting on his arms, which was a mercy, and his eyes were closed.

On the outskirts of Hokitika their company was further delayed. As they advanced upon the township they came upon a woman, utterly insensate and soaking wet, lying in the middle of the thoroughfare. She was alive, but only barely. Lauderback guessed that she had been drugged, but he could not elicit any kind of intelligence from her beyond a moan. He dispatched his aides to find a duty sergeant, lifted her body out of the mud, and, while he waited for his aides to return, reflected that his electoral campaign was off to a rather morbid start. The first three introductions he would make, in town, would be with the magistrate, the coroner, and the editor of the *West Coast Times*.

In the two weeks following this ill-starred arrival, Hokitika did not pay the impending elections much mind: it seemed that the death of a hermit and the fate of a whore (this, as Lauderback soon discovered, was the profession of the woman in the road) were subjects with which an electoral candidacy could not be expected to compete. Lauderback's passage over the mountains was only very briefly mentioned in the *West Coast Times*, though two columns were devoted to his description of the dead man, Crosbie Wells. Lauderback was unperturbed by this. He was anticipating the parliamentary elections with the same relaxed self-possession with which he awaited all acts of providence, and all rewards. He had determined that he would win; therefore, he would win.

On the morning of Walter Moody's arrival in Hokitika—the morning we take up Balfour's tale—the shipping agent was sitting with his old acquaintance in the dining room of the Palace Hotel in Revell-street, talking about rigs. Lauderback was wearing a woollen suit of the lightest fawn, a hue that took moisture badly. The rain on his shoulders had not yet dried, so that it appeared as if he was wearing epaulettes; his lapels had turned dark and furry. But Lauderback was not the kind of man for whom a sartorial imperfection could lessen the impact of his bearing—in fact, the very opposite was true: the damp suit only made the man look finer. His hands had been scrubbed that morning with real soap; his hair was oiled; his leather gaiters shone like polished brass; in his buttonhole he had placed a native sprig of some sort, a pale, bunched flower whose name Balfour did not know. His recent journey across the Southern Alps had left a ruddy bloom of health in his cheeks. In sum, he looked very well indeed.

Balfour gazed at his friend across the table, only half-listening as the statesman, talking animatedly, made his case in defence of the ship-of-the-line—holding up his two palms as main and mizzen, and making use of the salt cellar as the fore. It was an argument that Balfour would ordinarily find engrossing, but the expression on the shipping agent's face was anxious and detached. He was tapping the base of his glass against the table, and shifting in his seat, and, every few minutes, reaching up to pull hard on his nose. For he knew that with all this talk of ships, their conversation would turn, before long, to the subject of the *Virtue*, and to the cargo that she had been charged to carry to the Coast.

The crate containing Alistair Lauderback's trunk had arrived in Hokitika on the morning of the 12th of January, two days before

Lauderback himself. Balfour saw that the shipment was cleared, and gave instructions for the crate to be transferred from the quay into his warehouse. To the best of his knowledge, these instructions were obeyed. But by an unhappy twist of fate (so much unhappier, that Lauderback stood so high in Balfour's esteem), the shipping crate then vanished altogether.

Balfour, upon discovering the crate was missing, was horrified. He applied himself to the project of its recovery—walking up and down the quay, inquiring at every door, and registering queries with every stevedore, porter, mariner, and customs officer—but his effort was to no avail. The crate was gone.

Lauderback had not yet spent two nights together in the suite of rooms on the upper floor of the Palace Hotel. He had spent the past fortnight making his introductions at camps and settlements up and down the Coast, a preliminary tour of duty from which he had only been released that very morning. Thus preoccupied, and believing the *Virtue* to be still in transit from Dunedin, he had not yet asked after his shipment—but Balfour knew that the question was coming, and once it did, he would have to tell the other man the truth. He swallowed a mouthful of wine.

On the table between them lay the remains of their 'elevenses', a term Lauderback used to refer to any meal or dish taken at an irregular hour, whether morning or night. He had eaten his fill, and had pressed Balfour to do likewise, but the shipping agent had repeatedly declined the invitation—he was not hungry, most especially for pickled onions and lamb's fry, two dishes whose smell never failed to curl his tongue. As a compromise to his host, out of whose pocket he was dining, he had drunk an entire pitcher of wine, and a mug of beer besides—Dutch courage, he might have called it, but the spirits had done little to conquer his trepidation, and now he was feeling very sick.

'Just one more piece of liver,' said Lauderback.

'Excellent stuff,' Balfour mumbled. 'Excellent— but I'm quite satisfied— my constitution—quite satisfied, thank you.'

'It's Canterbury lamb,' said Lauderback.

'Canterbury—yes—very fine.'

'Caviar of the highlands, Tom.'

'Quite satisfied, thank you.'

Lauderback looked down at the liver a moment. 'I might have driven a flock myself,' he said, changing the subject. 'Up and over the pass. Five pounds a head, ten pounds a head—why, I'd have made a fortune, selling up. You might have told me that every piece of meat in this town is salt or smoked: I'd have brought a month of dinners with me. With a pair of dogs I might have done it very easily.'

'Nothing easy about it,' said Balfour.

'Made myself a killing,' said Lauderback.

'Saving every sheep that breaks its neck in the rapids,' said Balfour, 'and every one that's lost, and every one that won't be driven. And all the miserable hours you'd spend counting them—rounding them up—chasing them down. I wouldn't fancy it.'

'No profit without risk,' returned the politician, 'and the journey was miserable enough; I might at least have made some money at the end of it. Heaven knows it might have improved my welcome.'

'Cows, perhaps,' said Balfour. 'A herd of cows behaves itself.'

'Still going begging,' said Lauderback, pushing the plate of liver towards Balfour.

'Couldn't do it,' said Balfour. 'Couldn't possibly.'

'You take the rest of it then, Jock, old man,' said Lauderback, turning to his aide. (He addressed his two attendants by their Christian names, for the reason that they shared the surname Smith. There was an amusing asymmetry to their Christian names: one was Jock, the other, Augustus.) 'Stop your mouth with an onion, and we shall not have to hear any more tripe about your blessed brigantines—eh, Tom? Stop his mouth?'

And, smiling, he bent his head back towards Balfour.

Balfour pulled again at his nose. This was very like Lauderback, he thought; he encouraged agreement on the most trivial of points; he angled for consensus when a consensus was not due—and before one knew it, one was on his side, and campaigning.

'Yes—an onion,' he said, and then, to get the conversation away from ships, 'Mention in the *Times* yesterday about your girl in the road.'

'Hardly *my* girl!' Lauderback said. 'And it was hardly a mention, for that matter.'

'The author had a fair bit of nerve,' Balfour went on. 'Making out as if all the town deserved a reprimand on the girl's account—as if every fellow was at fault.'

'Who's to credit his opinion?' Lauderback waved his hand dismissively. 'A two-bit clerk from the petty courts, airing his peeves!'

(The clerk to whom Lauderback so ungenerously alluded was of course Aubert Gascoigne, whose short sermon in the *West Coast Times* would also capture Walter Moody's attention, some ten hours later.)

Balfour shook his head. 'Making out as if it was *our* error—collectively. As if we *all* should have known better.'

'A two-bit clerk,' Lauderback said again. 'Spends his days writing cheques in another man's name. Full of opinions that no one wants to hear.'

'All the same—'

'All the same, nothing. It was a trifling mention, and a poor argument; there's no need to dwell on it.' Lauderback rapped his knuckles on the table, as a judge raps his gavel to show that his patience has been spent; Balfour, desperate to prevent a revival of their previous topic of conversation, spoke again before the politician had a chance. He said, 'But have you seen her?'

Lauderback frowned. 'Who—the girl in the road? The whore? No: not since that evening. Though I did hear that she revived. You think I ought to have paid a call upon her. That's why you asked.'

'No, no,' said Balfour.

'A man of my station cannot afford—'

'Oh, no; you can't afford—of course—'

'Which brings us back to the sermon, I suppose,' Lauderback said, in a newly reflective tone. 'That was the clerk's precise point. Until certain measures are in place—almshouses and so forth, convents—then who's accountable in a situation like that? Who's responsible for a girl like her—someone who has no one—in a place like this?'

This was intended as a rhetorical question, but Balfour, to keep the conversation moving, answered it. 'No one's accountable,' he said.

'No one!' Lauderback looked surprised. 'Where's the Christian spirit in you?'

'Anna tried to take her life—to end her life, you know! No one's accountable for that except herself.'

'You call her Anna!' Lauderback said reprovingly. 'You are on first-name terms with the girl; I'd say you have a share of responsibility in caring for her!'

'First-name terms didn't light her pipe.'

'You would shut your door to her— because she is an inebriate?'

'I'm not shutting any doors. If I'd found her in the thoroughfare I'd have done just as you did. Exactly as you did.'

'Saved her life?'

'Turned her in!'

Lauderback waved this correction aside. 'But then what?' he said. 'A night in the gaol-house—and then what? Who's there to protect her, when she lights her pipe all over again?'

'No one can protect a soul against themselves—against their own hand, you know!' Balfour was vexed. He did not enjoy discussions of this kind; really, he thought, it was only marginally better than the relative merits of ship-rigged and square. (But then Lauderback had been a poor conversationalist this fortnight past: despotic in tone, by turns evasive and demanding. Balfour had chalked it up to nerves.)

'Spiritual comfort, that's what he means—spiritual protection,' put in Jock Smith, meaning to be helpful, but Lauderback silenced him with the flat of his hand.

'Forget suicide—that's a separate argument, and a morbid one,' he said. 'Who's there to give her a chance, Thomas? That's my question. Who's there to give that sorry girl one clean shot at a different kind of a life?'

Balfour shrugged. 'Some folk are dealt a bad hand. But you can't rely on another person's conscience to live the life you want to live. You make do with what you're given; you struggle on.'

In which remark the shipping agent showed his uncharitable

bias, the obstinacy that hung as a weighted counterpoint beneath the lively indulgence of his outward air—for, like most enterprising souls, he held his freedoms very chary, and desired that all others would do the same.

Lauderback sat back and appraised Balfour down the length of his nose. 'She's a whore,' he said. 'That's what you're saying, isn't it? She's just a whore.'

'Don't mistake me: I've got nothing against whores,' Balfour said. 'But I don't like almshouses, and I don't like convents. They're dreary places.'

'You are provoking me, surely!' Lauderback said. 'Welfare is the very proof of civilisation—it is its finest proof, indeed! If we are to civilise this place—if we are to build roads and bridges—if we are to lay a foundation for the future in this country—'

'Then we may as well give our road builders something to warm their beds at night,' Balfour finished for him. 'It's hard work, shovelling stones.'

Jock and Augustus laughed at this, but Lauderback did not smile.

'A whore is a moral affliction, Thomas; you must call a thing by its name,' he said. 'You must insist upon a standard, if you stand at a frontier!' (This last was a direct quote from his most recent electoral address.) 'A whore is a moral affliction. That's the end of it. A bad drain for good wealth.'

'And your remedy,' Balfour returned, 'is a good drain for good wealth, but it's a drain all the same, and money's money. Leave off the almshouses, and let's not go turning any of our girls into nuns. That would be a d—ned shame, when they are so outnumbered as it is.'

Lauderback snorted. 'Outnumbered and outfoxed, I see,' he said.

'Responsibility for whores!' said Balfour. He shook his head. 'They'll have a seat in Parliament next.'

Augustus Smith made a rude joke in response to this, and they all laughed.

When their laughter had subsided Lauderback said, 'Let's not talk in this vein any longer. We have discussed that day from all corners and all sides—it makes me tired.' He indicated with a circular sweep of his hand that he wished to return to their previous conversation. 'With respect to the ship rig. My argument is simply that how one conceives of the advantages depends entirely on where one stands. Jock holds his perspective as a former able seaman; I hold mine as a ship owner and a gentleman. In my mind, I see the sail-plan; in his, he sees tar and oakum, and the breeze.'

Jock Smith responded to this jibe conventionally, but with good cheer, and the argument was revived.

Thomas Balfour's irritation was revived just as quickly. He felt that he had spoken wittily on the subject of asylum—Lauderback had praised his rejoinder!—and he wished to persist with that topic of conversation, in order that he might seize the opportunity to do so again. He did not have anything witty to say about the ship rig, and its advantages—and neither, he thought sulkily, did Jock, nor Augustus, nor Lauderback himself. But it was Lauderback's custom to begin and end conversations at whim, changing the subject simply because he had tired of a certain issue, or because his authority had been trumped by another man's. Thrice already that morning the politician had protested the introduction of a new theme, returning always to his imperious patter about ships. Every time Balfour began to speak of local news, the politician declared himself sick to death of useless brooding about the hermit and the whore—when in fact, Balfour thought with annoyance, they *hadn't* discussed either event in any real detail, and certainly not from all corners and all sides.

This internal expression of feeling followed a pattern, though an unacknowledged one. Balfour's admiration of Lauderback was so vaulting that he preferred to deprecate himself than to criticise Lauderback, even privately, when the two men disagreed—but deprecation always waits to be disputed, and, if the disputation does not come, becomes petulance. Over the past fortnight Balfour had kept his silence on the subject of Lauderback's encounter with the dead man, Crosbie Wells, though the circumstances of the hermit's death held a considerable amount of curiosity for him; he had not discussed Anna Wetherell, the whore in the road, at all. He had acted according to Lauderback's wishes, and had waited for his own to be acknowledged in turn—an event that required a degree more solicitude than Lauderback possessed, and so had yet to come to pass. But Balfour could not see this deficiency in the man he so admired; instead he waited, became quietly impatient, and began to sulk.

(We shall add, in conciliatory tones, that his sulking was of a very superficial sort: at a single kind word from Lauderback, his good humour would be restored.)

Balfour pushed his chair a little further away from the table, wishing in a childish way to make his boredom obvious to his host, and cast his gaze over the room.

The dining room was nearly empty, owing to the uncommon hour of their meal, and through the serving-hatch Balfour could see that the cook had taken off his apron and was sitting with both elbows on the table, playing at solitaire. Before the hearth sat a large-eared boy who was sucking on a stick of jerky. He had evidently been posted there to keep an eye upon the clothes-irons, which were warming in a rack above the coals, for every half-minute or so he wet his finger and held it close to the trestle to test the heat. At the table nearest theirs sat a clergyman—a freckled fellow, none too handsome, with a snub nose and a droop to his lower lip, like a simple child's. He had taken his breakfast alone; he was now drinking coffee and reading a pamphlet—no doubt rehearsing the sermon he would deliver the following day, Balfour thought, for he nodded slowly as he read, as a man keeping tempo with a silent address.

The large-eared boy wet his finger again, and held it close; the clergyman turned a page; the cook squared a playing card with the edge of the chopping block. Balfour fiddled with his fork. Finally Lauderback paused in his diatribe to take a draught of wine, and Balfour seized his chance to interject.

'Speaking of barques,' he said (they had been speaking of brigantines), 'I've seen your *Godspeed* over the bar a fair few times, this past year. She's yours, isn't she—*Godspeed*?'

But to his surprise, this remark was met with silence. Lauderback only bowed his head, as if Balfour had put to him an issue of the gravest philosophical import, and he desired to meditate alone upon the question.

'Hell of an outfit, she is,' Balfour added. 'Marvellous.'

The aides exchanged a glance.

'Surely that brings home our point, Mr. L,' said Augustus Smith finally, breaking the spell. 'Even a barque handles better than a brigantine; she does it with half the crew and half the fuss. He can't deny that.'

'Yes,' Lauderback said, rousing himself. He turned to Jock. 'You can't deny that.'

Jock was chewing; he grinned through his mouthful. 'I will deny it. Give me half the weight in rigging over half the crew—there's your fuss. I'd take speed over handling any day.'

'How about a compromise?' said Augustus. 'Barquentine.'

Jock shook his head. 'I'll say it again: three masts is one too many.'

'More speed than a barque, though.' Augustus touched Lauderback's elbow. 'What about your *Flight of Fancy*? She was fore-and-aft rigged on the mainmast, was she not?'

Balfour had not intuited the aides' objective—to divert the conversation away from the subject he had introduced—and he thought that perhaps the politician had not heard him correctly. He raised his voice and tried again. 'Your *Godspeed*—as I say. She's a regular, these parts. Hell of an outfit. I've seen her over the bar a fair few times. Seems to me she's got both speed *and* handling. My word, she's a marvellous craft.'

Alistair Lauderback sighed. He threw his head back and squinted up at the rafters, and a foolish smile trembled on his lips—the smile of a man who is unused to embarrassment, Balfour realised later. (He had never, before that morning, heard Lauderback confess a weakness of any kind.)

At last Lauderback said, still squinting upward, 'That barque is no longer in my possession.' His voice was strained, as though his smile had made it thinner.

'That so!' Balfour said, surprised. 'Made a swap, did you—something bigger?'

'No: I sold her, outright.'

'For gold?'

Lauderback paused, and then said, 'Yes.'

'That so!' Balfour said again. 'Just like that—you sold her. Who's buying?'

'Her master.'

'Hoo,' said Balfour, exhaling cheerfully. 'Can't envy you there. We have heard some stories about that man around here.'

Lauderback did not reply. Still smiling, he studied the exposed beams of the ceiling, the cracks between the floorboards of the rooms above.

'Yes,' Balfour repeated, sitting back, and tucking his thumbs beneath his lapels. 'We have heard some stories around here. Francis Carver! Not a man I'd care to cross, all right.'

Lauderback looked down in surprise. 'Carver?' he said, frowning. 'You mean Wells.'

'Master of the *Godspeed*?'

'Yes—unless he sold it on.'

'Burly fellow—dark brows, dark hair, broken nose?'

'That's right,' said Lauderback. 'Francis Wells.'

'Well, I don't mean to contradict you flat,' Balfour said, blinking, 'but that man's name is Carver. Perhaps you're confusing him with the old fellow who—'

'No,' Lauderback said.

'The hermit—'

'No.'

'Who died—the man you came across, two weeks ago,' Balfour said, persisting. 'The dead man. His name was Wells, you know. Crosbie Wells.'

'*No*,' Lauderback said, for the third time. He raised his voice slightly. 'I am not mistaking the name. Wells was the name on the papers, when I signed the barque across. It was always Wells.'

They looked at each other.

'Can't understand it,' Balfour said at last. 'Only I do hope you didn't get stiffed. Strange coincidence, isn't it—Frank Wells, Crosbie Wells.'

Lauderback hesitated. 'Not quite a coincidence,' he said carefully. 'They were brothers, I thought.'

Balfour gave a shout of laughter. 'Crosbie Wells and Frank Carver, brothers? Can't imagine anything more unlikely. Only by marriage, surely!'

Lauderback's foolish smile returned. He began stabbing with his finger at a crumb.

'But who told you that?' Balfour added, when the other did not speak.

'I don't know,' said Lauderback.

'Carver mentioned something—when he signed the papers?'

'Maybe that was it.'

'Well! If you say so ... but to look at them, I'd never have believed it,' Balfour said. 'One so tall and striking, the other such a wastrel—such a runt—!'

Lauderback quivered; his hand made a compulsive movement on the table, as if to reach and grasp. 'Crosbie Wells was a wastrel?'

Balfour waved his hand. 'You saw him dead.'

'But only dead—never living,' said Lauderback. 'Strange thing: you can't tell what a fellow really looks like, you know, without animation. Without his soul.'

'Oh,' Balfour said. He contemplated that idea.

'A dead man looks created,' Lauderback continued. 'As a sculpture looks created. It makes you marvel at the work of the design; makes you think of the designer. The skin is smooth. Fine. Like wax, like marble—but not like either: it doesn't hold the light, as a wax figure does, and it doesn't reflect it, like stone. Has a matte finish, as a painter would say. No shine.' Suddenly Lauderback seemed very embarrassed. He rounded off by demanding, rather rudely, 'Have *you* ever seen a man fresh dead?'

Balfour tried to make light of it ('Dangerous question to ask— on a goldfield—') but the politician was waiting for an answer, and at length he had to concede that he had not.

'Shouldn't have said "seen",' Lauderback added, to himself. 'Should have said "bore witness".'

Augustus Smith said, 'Jock put his hand on the fellow's neck—didn't you, Jock?'

'Ay,' said Jock.

'When we first came in,' said Augustus.

'Meant to rouse him,' said Jock. 'Didn't know that he had already passed. He might have been sleeping. But here's the thing: his collar was damp. With sweat, you see—it hadn't yet dried on him. We figured he couldn't have been more than half an hour dead.'

He would have said more, but Lauderback made a sharp movement with his chin, to silence him.

'Can't figure it out,' Balfour said. 'Signed his name Wells!'

'We must be thinking of different men,' said Lauderback.

'Carver has a scar on his cheek, right here. White in colour. Shaped like—like a sickle.'

Lauderback pursed his lips, then shook his head. 'I don't recall a scar.'

'But he was dark-haired? Thick-set? Brutish, you might say?'

'Yes.'

'Can't figure it out,' Balfour said again. 'Why would a man change his name? And *brothers*! Frank Carver—and Crosbie Wells!'

Lauderback's mouth was working beneath his moustache, as if he was chewing on his lip. In quite a different voice he said, 'You knew him?'

'Crosbie Wells? Not a bit,' said Balfour. He settled back in his chair, pleased to be asked a direct question. 'He was building a sawmill, way out in the Arahura—well, you saw the cottage; you've been there. He'd done his shipping through me—equipment and so forth—so I knew him to look at him. Rest his soul. Had a Maori fellow for a mate. They were in on the mill together.'

'Did he strike you—as a kind of a man?'

'As what kind of a man?'

'Any kind.' Lauderback's hand twitched again. Flushing, he amended his question: 'I mean to say: how did he strike you?'

'No complaints,' Balfour said. 'Kept his business to his business, you know. From his talk I'd call him London-born.' He paused, and then leaned forward conspiratorially. 'Course, they're saying all sorts about him, now that he's gone.'

Again Lauderback did not respond. He was being very strange, Balfour thought; the man was tongue-tied, even red-faced. It was as if he wanted Balfour both to answer some very specific question and to cease talking altogether. The two aides seemed to have lost interest—Jock was pushing a piece of liver around his plate, and Augustus's head was turned away; he was watching the rain beat at the window.

Out of the corner of his eye, Balfour considered them. The two men were as satellites to Lauderback. They slept on bolsters in his room, accompanied him everywhere, and seemed at all times to speak and act in plural, as if they shared a single identity between them, as well as a name. Until that morning Balfour had thought them pleasant chaps, convivial and quick-witted; he had thought their devotion to Lauderback a fine thing, though their constant presence had occasionally worn his nerves rather thin. But now? He looked from one to the other, and realised that he wasn't sure.

Lauderback had hardly spoken a word to Balfour about the final chapter of his journey over the Alps, two weeks prior. Most of what Balfour knew about the night of his arrival had come from the *West Coast Times*, which had published an abridged version of the account Lauderback had given, in writing, to the law. Lauderback was not suspected of having played any part in the deaths, one attempted, the other actual: the coroner's report removed any doubt that Crosbie Wells had died of purely natural causes, and the physician was able to prove that the opium by which Anna Wetherell had nearly perished was her own. But Balfour wondered, now, whether the paper's account had been the truth.

He watched Jock Smith push his piece of liver back and forth. It was very strange that Lauderback seemed, all of a sudden, so intensely curious about the living character of Crosbie Wells; it was even stranger to think that Crosbie Wells, who had been mild, and common, and lacking in any kind of influence, should enjoy a familial connexion—or *any* kind of connexion!—to the notorious Francis Carver. Balfour could not believe it. And then there was the matter of the whore in the road. Was that event just a coincidence, or did it connect somehow to Crosbie Wells's untimely passing? Why had Lauderback been so reluctant to speak of either encounter—reluctant, that is, until now?

He said, partly to rekindle the conversation, and partly to keep his imagination from drifting to make unfounded accusations of his friend, 'So you sold the barque to Carver—only you thought his name was Wells—and he told you, by the bye, that he had a brother Crosbie, squirrelled away.'

'I can't remember now,' Lauderback said. 'It was nearly a year ago. Long gone.'

'But then you come across the same man's brother—fresh dead—a year later!' Balfour said. 'On the other side of the Alps, no less . . . in a place you've never set foot before! There's queer odds on that, wouldn't you say?'

Lauderback said, rather loftily, 'Only a weak mind puts faith in coincidence'—for it was his habit, when under pressure, to assume a condescending air.

Balfour ignored this maxim. 'Alias Carver?' he mused. 'Or alias Wells?' But he was watching the politician as he spoke.

'Shall I fill us another pitcher, Mr. L?' said Augustus Smith.

Lauderback rapped the table. 'Yes: fill us another. Good.'

'*Godspeed* weighed anchor around two weeks back,' said Balfour. 'She goes back and forth from Canton, does she not—tea-trading? So I expect we won't be seeing Carver around these parts for a while.'

'Let's drop the subject,' Lauderback said. 'I made a mistake with the names. I must have made a mistake with the names. It doesn't signify.'

'Hang tight,' said Balfour. A new thought had struck him.

'What?' said Lauderback.

'It *might* signify. Given that the sale of his estate has been appealed. It might signify to the widow, if Crosbie Wells had a brother tucked away.'

Lauderback was smiling again, tremulously. 'The widow?'

'Ay,' Balfour said darkly, and was about to go on, but Lauderback said, all in a rush, 'There was no sign of a wife at the cottage—no sign at all. To all appearances he—the fellow—lived alone.'

'Indeed,' Balfour said. Again he was about to elaborate, but Lauderback interrupted:

'You said that it might signify—news about a brother. But a man's money always goes to his wife, unless his will says otherwise. That's the law! I don't see how a brother could signify. I don't see it.'

He bent his head towards his guest.

'There *is* no will,' Balfour said. 'That's the problem. Crosbie Wells never made one. No one knew if he had any family at all. They didn't even know where to send a letter, when he passed— they only had his name, you see, not a home address, not even a birth certificate, nothing. So his land and cottage are returned to the Crown . . . and the Crown has the right to sell it on, of course, so it goes on the market and it sells the very next day. Nothing stays long on the market around here, I can tell you. But *then*, with the ink still drying on *that* sale, a wife turns up! No one knew a scrap about a wife before that day—only she's got the marriage papers— and she signs herself Lydia Wells.'

Lauderback's eyes bulged. Now, at last, Thomas Balfour had his complete attention. '*Lydia Wells?*' he said, almost in a whisper.

Augustus Smith looked at Jock, and then away.

'This was on Thursday,' Balfour said, nodding. 'The Court can't fault her papers—they've sent away to Dunedin, of course, just to verify. But something's off. The way she pops up so quickly, wanting to get her hands on the estate—when Crosbie never spoke of her. And another thing is fishy: this lady is a d—n class act. How Crosbie Wells managed to get himself married to a lady like that— hoo!—is a mystery that I for one would pay to know the answer to.'

'You've seen her—Lydia—here? She's here?'

The name was familiar in his mouth: so he knew her, Balfour thought; and he must have known the dead man, too. 'Ay,' he said aloud, careful not to let any trace of his suspicion show. 'Coming off the packet steamer, Thursday. Dressed up to the nines, she was; swarming down the ladder like a regular salt. Dress in a knot over her shoulder, drawers gathered up in her hand. All the hoops and buckles on display. I'm blowed if I know how Crosbie Wells landed a piece like her—I'm blowed.'

Lauderback was still looking shocked. 'Lydia Wells, wife of *Crosbie* Wells.'

'Ay—so her story goes.' Balfour studied his acquaintance, and then suddenly put down his glass and leaned forward. 'Look here, Mr. Lauderback,' he said, placing his palm upon the table between them. 'Seems you're holding on to something that's preventing you from talking plain. Why don't you share it?'

This request, so simply made, unlocked a dam in Alistair Lauderback's heart. As is the case for so many governing men, who are accustomed to constant service of the highest quality, and who rarely find themselves alone, Lauderback tended to think of his attendants in utilitarian terms. Certainly Balfour was a nice enough chap—shrewd in his business, cheerfully intemperate, and ready with a laugh—but his value as a man was equal to the value of the role he filled: in Lauderback's mind, he was replaceable. What lay beyond his most immediately visible qualities, the politician had never troubled himself to learn.

It is always a starkly private moment when a governor first apprehends his subject as a man—perhaps not as an equal, but at least as a being, irreducible, possessed of frailties, enthusiasms, a real past, and an uncertain future. Alistair Lauderback felt that starkness now, and was ashamed. He saw that Balfour had offered friendship, and he had taken only assistance; that Balfour had offered kindness, and he had taken only the benefit of use. He turned to his aides.

'Fellows,' he said, 'I want to talk to Balfour man to man. Go on and leave us for a spell.'

Augustus and Jock rose from the table (Balfour observed with a flash of competitive triumph, unusual for him, that they both looked very put out) and left the dining room without a word. When they had gone, Lauderback exhaled deeply. He poured himself another measure of wine, but instead of taking a draught he held the glass between the heels of his hands, and stared at it.

'Do you miss England, Tom?' he said.

'England?' Balfour raised his eyebrows. 'Haven't set foot in sunny England since—well. Since before my hair was grey!'

'Of course,' Lauderback said apologetically. 'You were in California. I had forgotten.' He fell silent, chastising himself.

'Round here, everybody's always talking about home,' said Balfour. 'Can't help but think that the pleasure's in the missing.'

'Yes,' said Lauderback, very quietly. 'Just so.'

'Why,' Balfour went on, encouraged by the other man's assent, 'most boys keep one foot on the boat, you know. Head back as soon as they've made their dust. What do they do? Buy a life, find a sweetheart, settle down—and then what do they dream about? What do they wish for? They dream about the diggings! Back when they could hold the colour in their hands! When all they did here was talk about home. Their mothers. Yorkshire puddings. Proper bacon. All of that.' He tapped the base of his glass upon the table. 'England—that's the old country. You miss the old country. Of course you do. But you don't go back.'

While he was waiting for the politician to begin speaking, he looked around him. It was well after ten o'clock in the morning, and the dinner crowd had not yet begun to trickle in—which they would presently, for it was Saturday, and a Saturday following a week of rain. The boy at the hearth had gone, taking the rack of hot irons with him; the cook had put away his playing cards, and was hacking at a bone; the scrubbing boys had surfaced from their quarters and were stacking plates and making noise. The clergyman at the table next to theirs was still sitting at his coffee, which had long since cooled. His gaze was focused on the print of the pamphlet he held in his hand and his mouth was pursed in concentration. It was clear that he was not paying his neighbours the slightest attention—but even so, Balfour brought his chair a little closer to Lauderback's, so that the politician would not have to speak so loud.

'Lydia Wells,' Lauderback began, 'is the mistress of an establishment in Dunedin whose name I should like only to say once, if you don't mind. The place is called the House of Many Wishes. Stupid name, really. I suppose you've heard of it.'

Balfour nodded, but only slightly, so as to imply neither total familiarity nor total ignorance. The establishment to which Lauderback referred was a gambling house of the most decadent order, famous for its high stakes and its dancing girls.

'Lydia was—a fond acquaintance of mine at that establishment,' Lauderback continued. 'There was no money involved. No money changed hands at all—you must understand that. Understand it because it's the truth.' He tried to glare at Balfour, but the shipping agent's eyes were lowered. 'Anyway,' he said after a moment. 'Whenever I was in Dunedin I would pay a call on her.'

He waited, challenging the other man to speak, but Balfour remained silent. After a moment he continued.

'Now, when I first came to your offices, Tom, you'll recall that *Godspeed* was in need of a master. You didn't want her, and in the months after that I had a fair bit of trouble finding a man I could count on to take up the contract. She was anchored in Dunedin then. *Lady* needed caulking, and I was out of pocket for repairs on *Virtue*, as you might remember. All sorts of bills to pay. In the end I made a snap decision, and leased *Godspeed* privately to a chap named Raxworthy who wanted to set up a run between Australia and the Otago fields. He was a Navy man. Retired, of course. He'd commanded a corvette in the Crimean War—up in the Baltic— and he had a Victoria Cross to show for it. He'd been everywhere. Used to say that if he'd been trailing a rope behind him, he could have tied a knot right around the world. He'd been discharged from the navy on account of gout—bad enough to get his long-term leave, which was due to him anyhow, but not quite bad enough to make him want to swallow the anchor altogether. *Godspeed* suited him—he's an old-fashioned type, you know, and she's an old-fashioned girl.

'I went back to Akaroa after that, and didn't hear from Raxworthy for a spell. But I was back and forth down the island fairly frequently, and the next time I called in at Dunedin, I found myself in a bit of trouble. There was a husband. Lydia had a hus-band. He'd come home while I was gone.'

Balfour narrowed his eyes. 'Crosbie Wells?'

Lauderback shook his head. 'Not him. This man was the brute you know as Carver. To me he was Wells. Francis Wells.'

Balfour nodded slowly. 'But now the very same woman's saying she's the wife of *Crosbie* Wells,' he said. 'Somebody's lying somewhere.'

'In any case—'

'Either lying about a marriage,' Balfour said, 'or lying about a name.'

'In any case,' Lauderback said with annoyance, 'that doesn't matter—not just yet. You have to hear it in the proper order. Back then, I didn't even know Lydia was married. When she was at the gambling house she used her maiden name, you see—Lydia Greenway, she was; I never knew her as Lydia Wells. Of course, once the husband showed up I saw that I was in the wrong. I tried to back right off. Tried to settle things the proper way. But the chap had me in a bit of a corner. I'd just taken up the Superintendency; I was a Councilman. I was recently married myself. I had my reputation to think about.'

Balfour nodded. 'He played the cuckold. Tried to make a few pounds extra on the side.'

Lauderback's mouth twisted. 'It wasn't that simple.'

'Oh—the trick's an old standard,' Balfour said, trying to commiserate. 'Plays right into the heart of every man's fear, of course—and then the blackmail is almost a relief, when it comes. Pay up, and you'll never hear from me again, all of that. Most often the girl's involved. I suppose he told you that she was expecting.'

Lauderback shook his head. 'No.' He resumed staring at the vessel in his hand. 'He was much cleverer than that. He didn't ask for any money—or for anything at all. At least not right away. He told me that he was a murderer.'

The carriage clock on the mantel struck a quarter till the hour. The clergyman at the table next to theirs looked up, patted his thigh, and retrieved his pocket watch from his trouser pocket, in order to synchronise the hands. He wound the key, twitched the dial, wiped the face of the watch with his napkin, and replaced it in his pocket. He then turned back to his pamphlet, cupped his hands around his eyes to narrow his field of focus, and resumed reading.

'He was very controlled when he said it,' said Lauderback. 'Polite, even. Told me there was a fellow on his tail, a mate of the man he'd killed. He didn't tell me whom he'd murdered, or why—just that it was on account of a murder that he was being pursued.'

'Didn't give you any names?'

'No,' said Lauderback. 'None at all.'

Balfour frowned. 'Where do you figure in all that? I hear that as another man's quarrel. Or another man's boast. But in either case, nothing to do with you.'

Lauderback drew closer. 'Here's the heart of it,' he said. 'He told me I'd been marked as his mate. As his associate. When this avenger caught up with him, and came to take *his* life . . . well, after that, the man would come for me.'

'You'd been marked?' Balfour said. 'Marked how?'

Lauderback shrugged and sat back. 'I don't know exactly. Of course I'd been at the gambling house a fair bit—and I'd been out and about with Lydia, here and there. I might have been spied upon.'

'Spying's one thing,' said Balfour. 'But how could a man be marked without his knowing? Marked—like a tattoo—without his knowing! Come—this is only half a tale, Mr. Lauderback! Where's the meat of it?'

Lauderback looked embarrassed. 'Well,' he said. 'Have you heard of a twinkle?'

'A what?'

'A twinkle. It's a piece of glass, or a jewel, or a scrap of a mirror, that's inserted into the end of a cigar. One can still smoke quite easily around it, and when the cigar's in the mouth, like so, you can't see it at all. Gamblers use them. The gambler's smoking while he plays; he takes the cigar from his mouth, like this, and holds the thing in his hand in such a way that the twinkle shows him a reflection of another player's cards. Or he uses it to show his partner his own hand, if he's playing doubles. It's a type of cheat.'

Balfour held an imaginary cigar in his hand, splaying his first two knuckles, and extended his arm across the table.

'Now,' he said, 'that seems like a d—ned inefficient way to cheat. So many ways it could fail! What if you were holding your cards close, now? What if you kept them flat on the table? Look: if I reached my arm across the table, like so . . . you'd pull your cards back, wouldn't you? Go on—you'd shrink away!'

'Never mind the details,' said Lauderback. 'The point is—'

'And a fool of a risk,' said Balfour. 'How's a man to make an excuse for a tiny mirror stuck into the end of his cigar?'

'The point is,' said Lauderback. 'Never mind the details. The point is that Wells—Carver, I mean—said that he had a twinkle on me.'

Balfour was still flexing his wrist and cocking his elbow, squinting at the invisible cigar in his hand. He stopped now, and closed his fist. 'Meaning,' he said, 'some way to read your cards.'

'But I don't know what it was,' said Lauderback. 'I still don't. It's driven me mad.' He reached for the pitcher of wine.

Balfour was wearing a sceptical expression. What kind of leverage was this? A vague mention of revenge, no proper names, no context, and some rubbish about a gambler's cheat? This was not enough to merit blackmail. Plainly, Lauderback was still concealing something. He nodded to indicate that Lauderback should fill his glass.

Lauderback set the pitcher back on the table and resumed. 'Before he left,' he said, 'he asked for one thing, and one thing only. Raxworthy was short a hand on the *Godspeed*—it had been advertised in the papers, and Wells had heard about it.'

'Carver.'

'Yes: Carver had heard about it. He asked me if I'd put in a word for him. He was going down to the quay in the morning to apply. Asked me the favour man to man.'

'You did as he asked?'

'I did,' Lauderback said heavily.

'There's another twinkle on you, maybe,' said Balfour.

'What do you mean?'

'Another connexion, now—the ship—between you both.'

Lauderback thought about that for a moment, seeming very

dejected. 'Yes,' he said. 'But what could I have done? He had me tied up.'

Balfour felt a sudden rush of sympathy for the other man, and regretted his previous ill humour. 'Ay,' he said, more gently. 'He had you tied.'

'After that,' Lauderback went on, 'nothing happened. Absolutely nothing. I went back to Canterbury. I waited. I thought about that d—ned twinkle until my heart near gave out. I confess I rather hoped that Carver would be killed—that the thug would catch him, so I would know the fellow's name before he came for me. I read the *Otago Witness* every day, hoping to see the blackguard's name among the dead, may God forgive me. But nothing happened.

'Nearly a year later—this is almost a year ago, maybe February, March last year—I get a letter in the mail. It's an annual receipt from Danforth Shipping, and it's filled out in my name.'

'Danforth? Jem Danforth?'

'The same,' said Lauderback. 'I've never shipped with Danforth— not for personals—but I know him, of course; he rents part of *Godspeed*'s hold for cargo.'

'And *Virtue* too, on occasion.'

'Yes—on occasion, *Virtue* too. All right: so I examine the receipt. I see that there's a recurring shipment on *Godspeed*'s trans-Tasman route under the name of Lauderback. My name. Again and again, on the westbound voyage across the Tasman—each voyage, there it is, shipper Danforth, carrier *Godspeed*, master James Raxworthy, one shipment of personals, standard size, paid in full by Alistair Lauderback. Me. I tell you, my blood went cold. My name, written so neatly; that column of figures, going down.

'The amount due was zero pounds. Nothing outstanding. Each month the account had been paid in cash, as the record showed. Someone had engineered this whole business in my name, and paid good money for it, to boot. I had a quick look over my own finances: I wasn't missing any money, and certainly nothing to the tune of eighty, ninety pounds in shipping fees. I'd have noticed a slow leak of that kind, wherever it was coming from. No. Something was cooking.

'As soon as I could, I left for Dunedin, to see about the affair myself. This was—April, I suppose. May, maybe. Some time in the early autumn. When I reached Dunedin I hardly even stepped ashore. I made straight for *Godspeed*. She was at anchor, and rafted up to the wharf, with the gangway down; I boarded, seeing no one at all. I was intending to speak to Raxworthy, of course—but he was nowhere about. In the fo'c'sle, I found Wells.'

'Carver.'

'Carver, I mean. Yes. He was alone. Holding a policeman's whistle in one hand, a pistol in the other. Tells me he can blow the whistle any time. The harbour master's office is fifty yards from where we're standing and the hatch is open wide. I keep quiet. He tells me there's a shipping crate in *Godspeed*'s hold with my name on it, and a paper trail that connects my name to that shipment every month for the last year. Everything legal, everything logged. In the eyes of the law, I've been paying for this shipment for a year, back and forth from Melbourne, back and forth, back and forth, and nothing I can say will disprove that fact. All right, so what's inside it, I ask. Women's fashions, he says. Dresses. A pile of gowns.

'Why dresses, I ask. He gives me a smile— horrible—and says, why Mr. Lauderback, you've been sending for the latest fashions in Melbourne every month for a year! You've been keeping your lovely mistress Lydia Wells in good nick, you have, and it's all on the books, to boot. Every time that trunk arrives in Melbourne, it's shipped in to a dressmaker's on Bourke-street—the very best, you understand—and every time it leaves, it's packed full of the finest threads that can be had for money, this face of the globe. You, Mr. Lauderback, are a very generous man.'

Lauderback's voice had become sour.

'But how is it that this shipping case came to be registered in my name, I ask him, and he has a good laugh at that. He tells me that every rat in Dunedin knows Lydia Wells, and what she does to make her bread. All she had to do is tell old Jem Danforth I was keeping her in bells and ribbons, but please could he keep *her* name out of it, out of respect for my poor old wife! The fellow believed her. Logged the shipment in my name. She paid in cash, saying the

cash was mine—and nobody mentioned a word to me. Thinking
they were being discreet, you realise: thinking they were doing me
a d—ned good turn, by not letting their Christian judgment show.

'But this isn't the half of it. Women's fashions are not the bloody
half of it. *This* time, he says, there's something else in the trunk
besides gowns. I ask him what. A fortune, he says, stolen, and all of
it pure. Stolen from whom, I ask. Stolen from yours truly, he
answers, and by my own wife, Lydia Wells—and then he laughs,
because of course that's part of the lie: they're in on it together, the
two of them. Well, what's *he* doing with a fair fortune in pure, I ask
him, and he tells me that he has a claim up Dunstan way. Was it
declared, I say, and he says no. Undeclared means untaxed, which
means this shipment is in breach of duty—or at least, it will be, if
Godspeed sails on schedule with the next day's tide.

'Now, there in the fo'c'sle Carver lets me think about all that for
a moment. I'm thinking about what it looks like from above. It
looks like I've been going behind the husband's back for a good
long while, to court his wife as my mistress. There's proof of that.
It looks like I've stolen a fair fortune from the man, and I mean now
to ship the gold offshore. It looks like I've engineered the whole
business to bankrupt and ruin him, both. That's adultery and theft
and even conspiracy right off. But the real clincher is that the gold's
undeclared. I'm facing charges for breach of customs, evading duty,
illegal trafficking, all of that. I'm looking at a lifetime in gaol—and
I don't have a lifetime left, Thomas. I don't have a lifetime left. So
I ask him what he wants, and finally he shows his cards. He wants
the ship.'

'Is he an able seaman at this point?'

'Yes. He works under Raxworthy and he wants Raxworthy gone.
He's figured it all out: how I'm going to sack Raxworthy that very
night, how I'm going to cancel the contract on the crew, and sign
the ship over to him free and clear. This is an insult, you understand. I laugh. I say no. But he's got that God-d—ned whistle, and
he pretends to make a move to call the harbour master in.'

'Did you ask to see the gold in the case?' said Balfour. 'How did
you know he wasn't bluffing?'

'Of course I asked to see it,' said Lauderback. 'We did all that. Oh, he had laid his foundations with care—I have to credit him for that! There were five dresses in the trunk. Each of them last season's fashions, in keeping with his story; ready for the dress-maker's in Melbourne, you see. But hear this! The gold wasn't just lying free in the case, beneath the gowns. It had been sewn into the very seams of the dresses. By Lydia herself, no doubt: she was a dab hand with a needle and thread. You wouldn't have guessed at all, until you lifted them out, and felt the weight of them. But a customs officer might not have troubled himself to do that, you see—unless he was tipped off, and knew where to look. When you opened the case, even when you rummaged around, it was just woman's fashions, nothing else. Yes: it was a very clever plan.'

'Let me get my head around this,' Balfour said. 'If the ship had sailed on schedule . . .'

'Then Carver would have come across the trunk in the hold, acting as though he'd never seen it before. He would have brought it up to Raxworthy, feigning outrage and distress and what have you. They were his wife's dresses, after all—and my name was on the papers. He would have demanded to bring the law to my door, on account of the theft, the adultery, the breach of customs, all of it. *Godspeed* would never have left the harbour; she'd have been turned around before she reached the heads. Then the law would have come for me—and clapped me in arms.'

'But surely . . . if that happened, and the law was called in . . . you might have just blamed it all on Lydia Wells,' Balfour said. 'Surely *she* would have been gaoled—'

'Oh yes, she certainly would have been,' Lauderback replied, cutting him off. 'But I was not going to risk my own freedom merely to have the satisfaction that *she* would get her comeuppance too! The two of them would certainly have sided against me, if the whole confounded business came to trial, and *that* would have bought her a great deal of sympathy—for seeing the light, you see; for repenting; for standing by her lawful husband, and all that rot.'

'If he really *was* her lawful husband,' Balfour pointed out. 'Now it seems that *Crosbie* Wells—'

'Yes, yes,' Lauderback snapped. 'But I didn't know that then, did I? Don't tell me what I ought to have done, and how I ought to have done it. I can't bear that. A game plays how a game plays.'

'Well,' said Balfour, sitting back, 'I'm blowed.'

'He wore me down,' said Lauderback. He spread his hands in a gesture of defeat. 'I signed her over.'

Balfour thought for a moment. 'Where was Raxworthy that night?'

'At the d—ned gambling house,' Lauderback said. 'Having an evening of his life, no doubt, with Lydia Wells at his elbow, blowing on his dice!'

'Was he in on the secret?'

'I don't think so,' Lauderback said, shaking his head. 'He had shore leave that night—there was a naval occasion, an official event of some kind. Nothing untoward. And I never got a funny feeling, afterwards.'

'What's he doing now?'

'Raxworthy? Helming the bloody *Spirit of the Thames*, and bored as a tiger in a carriage car. The man can't stand steam. He's furious with me.'

'Does he know?'

Lauderback looked angry. 'I'm a public figure,' he said. 'If anybody knew about this, you'd know. I'd be sunk. Does he know? Of course he doesn't know!'

He had become suddenly impatient with his own story, Balfour saw. The narration of the events had only rekindled his shame at having been made a fool.

'But the sale of the ship,' Balfour said after a moment. 'That's public knowledge—printed in the papers.'

Lauderback swore. 'Oh yes,' he said. 'According to the paper, I sold that d—ned ship for a very reasonable price indeed, and all in pure. Of course I never saw a penny of it. The gold stayed in that d—ned trunk, and when *Godspeed* made her voyage to Melbourne the next day, the trunk was collected on the other side—as it had been every month for the past year. And then it disappeared, of course. I couldn't do a thing about it, without bringing down all hell around my ears. God only knows where that gold is now. And he's got the ship, to boot.'

Lauderback toyed angrily with the cruet stand.

'What was the true value of the gold in the trunk—to your eye?'

'I'm no prospector,' Lauderback said, 'but by the weight of the gowns I'd estimate it was a couple of thousand, at least.'

'And you never saw that gold again.'

'No.'

'Or heard tell of it.'

'No.'

'Did you ever see the girl again—Lydia Wells?'

Lauderback laughed harshly. 'Lydia Wells is no *girl*,' he said. 'I don't know what she is—but she's not a *girl*, Thomas. She's not a *girl*.'

But he had not answered Balfour's question.

'You know she's here—in Hokitika,' Balfour reminded him.

'So you mentioned,' said Lauderback grimly, and would not say more.

What a strange, unbroken beast is adulation! How unpredictably it rears its head, and tears against the bridle of its own making! Balfour's worship of the other man—that which had so easily become petulance—now became, in rising flood, disdain. To have lost so much—and over a *mistress*! Over another man's wife!

Disdain, for all its censorious pretension, is an emotion that can afford a certain clarity. Thomas Balfour watched his friend drain his glass and snap his fingers for another round, and was scornful— and then his scorn gave way to mistrust, and his mistrust to perspicacity. There were elements of Lauderback's story that still did not fit together. What of the timely death of Crosbie Wells? Lauderback had yet to address *that* coincidence—just as he had yet to explain why he believed that Carver and Wells had been, of all things, brothers! What of Lydia Wells, who had swept into Hokitika to claim her rightful inheritance, arriving so promptly after his death that the harbour master asked, half in jest, if the Hokitika Post Office had installed a telegraph? Balfour knew without a doubt that he had not been told the whole truth; what he did not know, however, was the reason for this concealment. Whom was Lauderback protecting? Himself merely? Or someone else?

Lauderback's eyes had sharpened. He leaned forward and stabbed the table with his index finger. 'You know,' he said, 'I've just had a thought. About Carver. If his name really *is* Carver, then the sale of the ship is void. You can't sign a deed in another man's name.'

Balfour made no reply. He was distracted by his new appraisal of the other man, and the critical distance that had opened as a sudden gulf of doubt between them.

'And even if his name is really Wells,' Lauderback added, brightening further, 'even if *that's* true, Lydia can't be married to two men at once, can she? It's as you said: either lying about a marriage, or lying about a name!'

A boy brought a fresh pitcher of wine. Balfour picked it up to refill their glasses. 'Unless,' he said as he poured, 'it *wasn't* both at once. She might have divorced the one, and married his brother.'

He used the word 'brother' carefully, but Lauderback, who had become excited by this new possibility, did not notice. 'Even in that case,' he said, 'if Carver's name is really Carver, then his signature is a false one, and the sale of the ship is void. I tell you, Thomas: either way we've got him. Either way. We've caught Carver in his own lie.'

His relief had made him reckless. Balfour said, 'So—you're out to catch him, now?'

Lauderback's eyes were shining. 'I shall expose him,' he said. 'I shall expose Francis Carver, and take *Godspeed* back again.'

'What about the avenger?' Balfour said.

'Who?'

'The fellow who was after Carver. The one who has a twinkle on you.'

'Never heard a peep,' said Lauderback. 'I expect he made all of that up.'

'You mean he didn't kill a man?' said Balfour, lightly. 'You mean he's not a murderer?'

'He's a blackguard, is what he is,' Lauderback said. He pounded the table. 'A blackguard and a liar! *And* a thief! But I shall catch him on it. I shall make him pay.'

'What about the elections?' Balfour said. 'What about Caroline?' (This was the name of Lauderback's wife.)

'I don't need to risk all *that*,' Lauderback said scornfully. 'I can do it privately. Catch him on the contract. Blackmail him—as he did me. Give him a taste of his own medicine.'

Balfour stroked his beard, watching him. 'Well, now.'

'Carver will have destroyed his own copy of the bill of sale, most likely, if it's proof of a lie ... I suppose I'll have to get my copy notarised, to be safe.'

'Well, now,' Balfour said again. 'Perhaps we ought to steady up.'

But Lauderback had sat forward in excitement. 'There's no need—I can begin right away!' he exclaimed. 'I know exactly where the contract is. It's packed in my trunk, in that shipping crate you're taking care of for me.'

Balfour felt his guts clench. His face flooded red. He opened his mouth to reply—and then, in cowardice, closed it.

'Has the *Virtue* been and gone already?' Lauderback said. 'You were expecting her last week, I think.'

There was a roaring in Balfour's ears. He ought to have come clean about the disappearance as soon as the two men were left alone. *Stupid*, he shouted internally, *stupid!* But could he not simply tell Lauderback the truth? It had been no man's fault that the shipping crate had disappeared—it had been an accident, a blunder of paperwork most likely—and it would show up, sooner or later, in some unlikely situation ... a little battered externally perhaps, but none the worse for wear. Surely Lauderback would understand that! If he was calm and honest in making his confession—if he admitted fault—

But then Balfour's heart gave a judder. There must be a correlation between the trunk in Lauderback's story—the one packed with women's dresses, that had made the trans-Tasman crossing every month for a year—and the trunk containing Lauderback's effects, the fraudulent contract among them, that had so recently vanished from the Hokitika quay. There *must* be, when Balfour had never before mislaid a shipping crate, nor had one stolen, not in all his years in the business! His heart began to pound. Francis Carver had blackmailed the politician once before; perhaps he had done so for a second time! Perhaps *Carver* had stolen the shipping crate! The man was familiar on the Hokitika docks, after all …

Lauderback was casting his eye over the table, looking for a cold morsel; he had not noticed the change in Balfour's demeanour, as the latter turned over this new possibility in his mind. 'Has she been through—the *Virtue*?' he repeated, without impatience.

'No,' said Balfour.

The room seemed to constrict around the lie.

'Not here yet?' said Lauderback. He found a waxy onion on the plate Jock Smith had left behind and popped it into his mouth. 'So I beat my own clipper ship—and on horseback! I wasn't expecting that! Nothing went belly-up at sea, I hope?'

His good humour was quite restored; he was even giddy. Such a tonic for the spirit is the promise of revenge!

'No,' Balfour said again.

'She's still in transit, you said?'

Balfour paused a fraction of a second, then he said, 'Ay—still in transit. That's right.'

'Coming West from Dunedin, is she? Or up and through the Strait?'

Balfour was sweating. He watched the movement of Lauderback's jaw as the other man chewed. In the end he chose the more protracted route. 'Up and through.'

'Oh well,' Lauderback said, swallowing. 'These things can't be helped, I suppose. Not in the shipping business. But you'll let me know the moment it gets here—won't you?'

'Ay—of course. Yes. I will.'

'I shall look forward to it,' said Lauderback. He hesitated. 'I say—Tom—there's another thing. You must understand that what I've told you this morning—'

'Strictest confidence,' Balfour blurted out. 'Won't tell a soul.'

'With my campaign at the point of—'

'No need for that.' Balfour shook his head. 'No need to say it. Mum's the word.'

'Good man.' Lauderback pushed his chair back and slapped his knees with both hands. 'Now,' he said. 'Poor Jock, and poor Augustus. I have been unutterably rude.'

'Yes—poor Jock, poor Augustus, yes,' said Balfour, motioning with his hand that Lauderback was free to leave—but Lauderback, humming now through his teeth, was already reaching for his coat.

Thomas Balfour's heart was beating very fast. He was unused to the awful compression that comes after a lie, when it dawns upon the liar that the lie he has uttered is one to which he is now bound; that he must now keep lying, and compound smaller lies upon the first, and be shuttered in lonely contemplation of his own mistake. Balfour would wear his falsehood as a fetter, until the shipping crate was found. He needed to do it quickly—and without Lauderback's knowledge, let alone his help.

'Mr. Lauderback,' he said, 'I think you ought to go and play the politician for a while. Go shake some hands, you know. Throw the dice. Play some bowls. Spend a night at the theatre. Leave all this aside.'

'What about you?'

'I'll go down the wharf and ask a round of questions. What Carver's up to, where he's gone.'

A shadow of alarm passed over Lauderback's face. 'Thought you said he'd gone to Canton. Isn't that what you said? Tea-trading?'

'But we ought to make sure,' Balfour said. 'We ought to be ready.' He was thinking about the missing shipping crate, and the new possibility that Francis Carver might have stolen it. (But what need had Carver of avenging himself *twice* upon Alistair Lauderback—when the first blackmail had come off without a hitch?)

'Discreetly,' said Lauderback. 'Discreetly—when you ask your questions.'

'Nothing to it,' said Balfour. 'The fellows know me down on Gibson Quay, and you remember I've done a fair patch of shipping with *Godspeed*. Anyway: better me than you.'

'Yes—better,' said Lauderback. 'Yes. All right. You do that, then.' He nodded.

In fact this was the very kind of delegation to which Alistair

Lauderback was accustomed, as a man of means. It was not strange to him that Balfour should devote his Saturday to straightening out another man's affairs. He did not pause to wonder whether Balfour could be risking his own reputation, by associating himself with a story of cuckoldry, blackmail, murder, and revenge, and nor did he spare a thought for how Balfour might be recompensed. He felt only relief. An invisible order had been restored: the same kind of order that ensured his boiled egg was ready every morning, and the dishes cleared away. He plumped the knot of his necktie with his fingers, and rose from the table as a man refreshed.

Lightly Balfour said, 'And you ought to steer clear of Lydia Wells, I think. Just because—'

'Of course, of course, of course,' said Lauderback. He picked up his gloves with his left hand, and reached to shake Balfour's hand with his right. 'We'll get the bastard, won't we?'

Suddenly Balfour realised that Lauderback knew exactly the nature of the twinkle by which Frank Carver had him tied. He could not have explained how he arrived at this sudden realisation—but all at once, he knew.

'Yes,' he said, shaking Lauderback's hand very firmly. 'We'll get the bastard, by and bye.'

MARS IN SAGITTARIUS

In which Cowell Devlin makes a poor first impression; Te Rau Tauwhare offers information at a price; Charlie Frost is suspicious; and we learn the crime of which Francis Carver was convicted, years ago.

When a restless spirit is commissioned, under influence, to solve a riddle for another man, his energies are, at first, readily and faith-fully applied. But Thomas Balfour's energies tended to span a very short duration, if the project to which he was assigned was not a project of his own devising. His imagination gave way to impa-tience, and his optimism to an extravagant breed of neglect. He seized an idea only to discard it immediately, if only for the reason that it was no longer novel to him; he started in all directions at once. This was not at all the mark of a fickle temper, but rather, of a temper that is accustomed to enthusiasm of the most genuine and curious sort, and so will accept no form of counterfeit—but it was, nevertheless, something of an impediment to progress.

Balfour was ready to rise from the table and quit the Palace Hotel when suddenly it struck him that it would be a great shame to leave a pitcher of perfectly good wine half-filled. He poured the last of it into his glass and was raising it to his lips—and then he saw, over the rim of the glass, that the clergyman at the nearby table had put aside his tract and folded his hands. He was looking at Balfour intently.

Like a child caught thieving, Balfour put down the glass.

'Reverend,' he said. (It was, on reflection, rather early in the day to be drunk.)

'Good morning,' returned the reverend man, and from his accent Balfour knew at once that he was Irish; he relaxed, and allowed himself to be rude. He picked up his glass again, and drank deeply.

The clergyman said, 'Your friend is a lucky man, I think.'

What an unfortunate face he had—caught in a perennial boyhood, with that bunched mouth, that pouting bottom lip, those teeth like nubbins. One envisaged him in shorts and gaiters, munching on a slab of bread-and-dripping, carrying a parcel of books that had been buckled together with an old belt of his father's, slapping it against his leg as he ate. But he was thirty, perhaps forty in age.

Balfour narrowed his eyes. 'Don't recall we were speaking for your benefit.'

The man inclined his head, as if conceding a point. 'No, indeed,' he said. 'And to the benefit of no other man either, I should hope.'

'Meaning what, precisely?'

'Merely that no man ought to profit from overhearing bad news. Least of all a member of the clergy.'

'Bad news, you call it? Thought you just said he was lucky.'

'Lucky to have you,' the clergyman said, and Balfour blushed.

'You know,' he said angrily, 'it doesn't count as a confession, just because it sounds like a secret, and you heard it on the sly.'

'You are quite right to make that distinction,' the clergyman said, still in pleasant tones. 'But I did not overhear you by design.'

'As to your design—as to what's intentioned and what's not. Who's to know it?'

'You were talking very loud.'

'Who's to know your design, I meant?'

'With respect to my intentions, I'm afraid you'll have to trust in my word—or in my cassock, if my word is not enough.'

'Trust what in your word and your cassock? Trust what enough?'

'Trust that I did not mean to eavesdrop,' said the clergyman patiently. 'Trust that I can keep a secret, when I'm asked.'

'Well,' Balfour said, 'you've been asked. I'm asking. And you ought to leave off mentioning luck and bad news. That's your opinion—that's not what you heard.'

'You're right. I do apologise.'

'Unsolicited, you know. And not appreciated.'

'I do apologise. I shall be silent.'

Balfour waved his finger. 'But you should leave off because I've asked you—not because of the confessing rule. Because it wasn't a confession.'

'No indeed: we agree on that.' He added, in a different voice, 'In any case, confession is a Catholic practice.'

'But you're Catholic.' All of a sudden Balfour was feeling very drunk.

'Free Methodist,' the reverend man corrected, without offence; but he added, as a gentle reprimand, 'You can't tell a great deal about a man from his accent, you know.'

'It's Irish,' said Balfour, stupidly.

'My father hails from the county Tyrone. Before I came here, I was in Dunedin; before that, I was in New York.'

'New York—now there's a place!'

The reverend shook his head. 'Everywhere is a place,' he said.

Balfour faltered. After this admonishment, he felt that he could not pursue the subject of New York—but he could not think of anything else to speak about, beyond the subject he had already forbidden the reverend man to pursue. He sat a moment, scowling; then he said, 'You're stopping here?'

'At this hotel?'

'Ay.'

'No: in fact my tent is flooded, and I'm taking my breakfast out of the rain,' the clergyman said. He spread his hand to indicate the detritus of the meal before him, long since cold. 'You see I have taken rather a long time of it, to make the shelter last.'

'You don't have a church to go to?'

This was a rather rude question, and one to which Balfour already knew the answer, for there were only three churches in Hokitika at that time. But he was feeling somehow thwarted by the man, in a way that he could not quite identify, and he wished to regain the upper hand—not by shaming him, exactly; but by cutting him down to size.

The clergyman only smiled, showing his tiny teeth. 'Not yet,' he said.

'Never heard of a Free Methodist. I suppose it's one of the new ones.'

'A new practice, a new polity,' said the man. He smiled again. 'But an old doctrine, of course.'

Balfour thought him rather smug.

'I suppose you've come on a mission,' he said. 'To turn the heathens.'

'I notice that you make a great many suppositions,' said the clergyman. 'You have not yet asked a question without presuming to answer it as well.'

But Thomas Balfour did not take kindly to this kind of observation: he would not be instructed on the formation of his thought. He pushed his chair back from the table, indicating that he intended to take his leave.

'To answer you,' the clergyman went on, as Balfour reached for his coat, 'I am to be the chaplain of the new gaol-house at Seaview. But until it is built'—he picked up his pamphlet, and slapped it in an explanatory fashion against the palm of his other hand—'I'm a student of theology, that's all.'

'Theology!' said Balfour. He pushed his arms into the sleeves of his coat. 'You ought to be reading stiffer stuff than that, you know. Hell of a parish you're walking into.'

'God's people, even so.'

Balfour nodded vaguely and made to leave. Suddenly a new thought struck him.

'If you called it bad news,' he said. 'I'm going to wager that you were listening for a good long while.'

'Yes,' said the chaplain humbly. 'I was. It was a name that caught my attention.'

'Carver?'

'No: Wells. Crosbie Wells.'

Balfour narrowed his eyes. 'What's Crosbie Wells to you?'

The chaplain hesitated. The truthful answer was that he did not know Crosbie Wells at all—and yet in the fortnight since that man's death, he had done little else but think of him, and ponder the circumstances of his death. He conceded after a pause that he had had the solemn honour of digging Wells's grave, and performing the last rites over his coffin, as it was lowered into the ground—an explanation that did not satisfy Thomas Balfour. The shipping agent was still regarding his new acquaintance with an expression of patent mistrust; his eyes narrowed still further when the chaplain (who ordinarily bore up very well under doubtful scrutiny) suddenly winced, and dropped his gaze.

The chaplain's name—as Walter Moody would discover some nine hours later—was Cowell Devlin. He had arrived in Hokitika upon the clipper ship *Virtue*, which was leased and operated by Balfour Shipping, and which had conveyed, along with sundry passengers, timber, iron, fasteners, many tins of paint, assorted dry goods, several crates of livestock, and a great quantity of calico, the now-vanished shipping crate containing Alistair Lauderback's trunk, and inside that, the copy of the contract under which the barque *Godspeed* had been sold. The *Virtue* had reached Hokitika two days before Alistair Lauderback himself; the Reverend Cowell Devlin had first arrived in Hokitika, therefore, two days before the death of Crosbie Wells.

Immediately upon landing, he had reported to the Police Camp, where the gaol's governor, George Shepard, wasted little time in putting him to work. Devlin's official duties would not begin until the completion of the new Hokitika gaol-house, high on the terrace of Seaview; in the meantime, however, Devlin might make himself useful around the Police Camp, and help with the daily management of the temporary gaol, which was, at that time, the residence of two women and nineteen men. Devlin was to teach each one of them to fear their Maker, and to instil in their wayward hearts a proper respect for the iron cladding of the law—or so the gaoler phrased it. (Devlin would soon discover that he and Shepard differed very radically in their pedagogic sensibilities.) Having taken a brief tour of the Police Camp and praised the style of its man-agement, Devlin inquired whether he might take his lodging in the gaol-house each night, so as to sleep among the felons, and share their bread. The gaoler received this proposition with distaste. He did not exactly reject Devlin's inquiry, but he paused, licked his lip with a pale, dry tongue, and then suggested that Devlin might do better to take up residence in one of Hokitika's many hotels. Shepard went on to warn the chaplain that his Irish accent might invite demonstrations of partisanship from Englishmen, and the expectation of a Catholic sensibility from his fellow Irish; he advised him, finally, to be discerning when choosing his company, and still more discerning when choosing his words—and with this pronouncement, he welcomed Devlin to Hokitika, and promptly bid him good morning.

But Cowell Devlin did not have funds enough to support several months' lodging in a hotel, and it was not his habit, furthermore, to indulge another man's pessimism about partisan displays. He did not take Shepard's advice, and he did not heed his warning. He purchased a standard-issue miner's tent, strung it up some fifty yards from the Hokitika beachfront, and weighted the calico pock-ets with stones. Then he made his way back to Revell-street, bought a mug of small beer at the most crowded hotel he could find, and began to introduce himself, to Englishmen and Irishmen alike.

Cowell Devlin was, to all intents and purposes, a self-made man—but because this epithet is rarely used to describe members of the holy orders, we ought to clarify its usage here. The cleric spent the present moment in a state of constant visualisation, con-juring in his mind the untroubled future self he had determined that he would one day become. His theology, too, followed this pat-tern: he was a hopeful believer, and to his many disciples he spoke of a utopian future, a world without want. When he spoke, he freely interchanged the language of auspice with the language of dreams: there was no conflict, in Cowell Devlin's mind, between reality as he wished to perceive it, and reality as it was otherwise perceived. Such an inclination might, in the context of another man's temperament, be called ambition, but Devlin's self-image was impregnable, even mythic, and he had long ago determined that he was not an ambitious man. As might be expected, he was given to bouts of very purposeful ignorance, and tended to pass over the harsher truths of human nature in favour of those that could be romanticised by whimsy and imagination. With respect to these latter articles, Devlin was an adept. He was an excellent storyteller, and therefore, an effective clergyman. His faith, like his self-image, was complete, equable, and almost clairvoyant in its expression—attributes that, as Balfour had already observed, occasionally made him seem rather smug.

At eleven o'clock on the night of the 14th of January—the night that Alistair Lauderback arrived in Hokitika—Cowell Devlin was sitting cross-legged on the floor of the Hokitika gaol-house, speaking with the inmates about Paul. Sometime around sundown it had begun to rain, and the chaplain had decided to stay late, in the hope that the downpour was only a temporary one—for he was new to Hokitika, and did not yet understand the dogged persistence of the weather on the Coast. The governor was at work in his private study, and his wife abed. The prisoners were mostly awake. They had listened to Devlin's sermon at first politely and then with real interest; they were now, at the chaplain's encouragement, offering testimonies and philosophies of their own.

Devlin was wondering whether he ought to retire for the night and venture out into the rain when there came a shout from the courtyard, and a thump against the door. This roused the gaoler, who emerged from his study with a linen cap upon his head and a rifle in his hand, a combination that ought to have been amusing, but was not. Devlin rose also, and followed Shepard to the door. They peered into the rain—and saw, just past the circle of light that was thrown by the gaoler's lantern, the duty sergeant Ellis Drake. He had a woman in his arms.

Shepard opened the door wider and invited the sergeant to step inside. Drake was a greasy, nasal fellow of limited intelligence; hearing his name, one was put in mind not of the naval hero but of the common duck, a species he closely resembled. He conveyed his captive into the gaol-house by the vulgar method of the fireman's hold, and deposited her with little ceremony upon the floor. He then reported, nasally, that the whore had either committed a crime against society or a crime against God; she had been found in a posture of such abject insentience that a distinction between gross intoxication and wilful harm could not be made, but he hoped (tipping his hat) that some hours in the gaol-house might serve to clarify the matter. He nudged her senseless body with the tip of his boot, as if to reiterate his point, and added that the instrument of her crime was likely opium. The whore was enslaved to the drug, and had often been seen in public while under its effects.

Governor Shepard gazed down at Anna Wetherell, and watched her hands curl and clasp at nothing. Devlin, not wanting to act out of turn, awaited the gaoler's decision, though he wanted very much to kneel and touch the woman, and check her body for signs of harm: he was greatly saddened by the notion of suicide, and considered it the most dreadful assault upon the soul that any body could possibly make. The three men looked down at the whore, and for a moment no one spoke. Then Drake confided that if he had to make a definitive indictment, he was of the belief that she had attempted the more atrocious crime; the gaoler had better wait for her to come around, however, so as to ask the girl himself.

Shepard collected Miss Wetherell's body as he was bid, propped her up against the wall, and shackled her. He ensured that she could breathe and was performing that function tolerably; he then looked at his pocket watch, and commented upon the lateness of the hour. Devlin took his cue, and donned his hat and coat— though as he left the gaol he cast a yearning look over his shoulder. He wished that the girl had been arranged more comfortably. But the gaoler was bidding him good night, and in the next moment the door had been shut and locked behind him.

When Devlin returned to the Police Camp early the next morning Anna Wetherell was still unconscious; her head had lolled sideways, and her mouth was slightly agape. There was a bluish-purple bruise upon her temple, and her cheekbone was painfully swollen: had she fallen, or had she been struck? Devlin had no time to investigate, however, or to press the gaoler for more information on the circumstances of the girl's arrest: it transpired that a man had died during the night, and Devlin was requested to accompany the physician to the Arahura Valley to assist in the collection of the dead man's remains—and perhaps also to say a prayer or two over his body. The dead man's name, Shepard informed him, was Crosbie Wells. On Shepard's information he had died peacefully, of age, infirmity, and drink; there was no reason, at this stage, to suspect homicide. In life, Shepard went on, Wells had been a hermit. He would be remembered neither as a good nor as a wicked man, for his acquaintances had been few, and no family had survived him.

The chaplain and the physician drove northward up the beach, and turned inland once they reached the mouth of the Arahura River. Crosbie Wells's cottage, situated some three or four miles upriver, was of simple construction—a timber box beneath a sloping roof of sheet iron—though Crosbie Wells had afforded himself the handsome luxury of a glass window, set into the north side of the house. The cottage was plainly visible from the Christchurch road, for it was elevated some twenty feet above the riverbank, and was surrounded by a cleared plot of land.

All in all, the dwelling made for a very lonely picture—and all the more so, after the man's corpse had been wrapped in blankets and carried from the room. Every surface was tacky and furred with dust. The bolster was stained yellow, the pillow sprayed with mould. A side of bacon, hanging from a rafter, was cracked and greasy-dry. Empty demijohns of liquor were ranged around the room's perimeter. The bottle on the dead man's table was likewise empty, signifying that the hermit's last action had been to drain his vessel, rest his head on his hands, and sleep. The place had an animal smell—the smell of loneliness, Devlin thought, with sympathy. He knelt before the range and pulled out the ash drawer—intending to build a fire in the stove, in order to burn off the dead-seeming odour of the room—and saw a piece of paper, trapped between the grating and the bottom of the drawer.

It appeared as if someone (Wells, presumably) had attempted to burn the document, but had closed the door of the range before the paper caught; the document had only caught fire along one edge before it dropped between the slats of the firebox to the drawer below, and was only very slightly charred. Devlin plucked it out and brushed it clean of ash. It was still legible.

On this 11th day of October 1865 a sum of two thousand pounds is to be given to MISS ANNA WETHERELL, formerly of New South Wales, by MR. EMERY STAINES, formerly of New South Wales, as witnessed by MR. CROSBIE WELLS, presiding.

Next to Wells's name there was a shaky signature, but next to the other man's name, only a space. Devlin raised his eyebrows. The deed was therefore invalid, for the witness had signed before the principal, and the principal had not signed at all.

Devlin recalled the name Anna Wetherell: this was the whore who had been admitted to the gaol-house late the previous night, drugged with opium. He halted a moment, frowning, and then suddenly folded the deed in half and thrust it between the buttons of his shirt, against his skin. He continued building the fire. Presently the physician came back inside (he had been feeding the horses) and the two men sat and shared a cup of tea, looking out the plate-glass window over the river, and to the clouded mountains beyond. Outside, the horses champed at their nosebags, and stamped their feet; on the tray of the cart, the blanket covering Wells's body gained a film of beaded silver, from the rain.

Cowell Devlin could not quite justify his impulse to conceal the deed of gift from the physician, Dr. Gillies. Perhaps, he thought, he had been impelled by the atmosphere of quiet in the dead man's house. Perhaps he had meant the act of suppression as a gesture of respect. Perhaps his curiosity had been aroused by the name Anna Wetherell—the attempted suicide, found unconscious in the Christchurch-road—and he had concealed the paper out of an obscure wish to protect her. The chaplain mused over these various possibilities as he drank his tea. He did not speak to the physician, who was likewise silent. When they were done they washed their cups, covered the fire, closed the door, and clambered back upon the cart, to convey their sorry freight back to the Police Camp in Hokitika, where a post-mortem was to be conducted upon the dead man's remains.

It was characteristic of Cowell Devlin that he would not attach a precise motivation to an action of questionable integrity, and that he chose, instead, to indulge a kind of dreamy confusion about his motivations as a whole. It was characteristic, too, that he saw no real obligation to confess this action—either then, or in the fort-night that followed, for it was not until the night of the 27th of January, two weeks later, that he showed this purloined deed of gift to anyone. Devlin believed himself to be a virtuous man, and his self-conception remained, in the face of all contradiction, impreg-nable. Whenever he behaved badly, or questionably, he simply jettisoned the memory, and turned his mind to something else. On the way back to Hokitika he held the deed flat against his chest with the palm of his hand. He spoke only to remark upon the power of the breakers, as the surf furled white against the shore beside them. The physician did not speak at all. After they returned to the Police Camp, and had carried Crosbie Wells's body inside, Devlin did half-heartedly consider sharing the deed with Governor Shepard, but he was distracted by a new commotion, and the opportunity expired. Anna Wetherell, it turned out, was beginning to revive.

Her eyes fluttered behind their lids, and her tongue shifted in her mouth; she made a murmuring noise. Her fever appeared to have broken, for there was a spray of beaded perspiration on her brow and nose, and the orange silk of her dress had turned brownish at her collar and beneath her arms. Devlin dropped to his knees before her. He clasped her hands in his—they were soft, and chill to the touch—and called to Shepard's wife for water.

When at last the girl woke, it was as if from a death. Her head reared back, and her eye rolled forward; she made a rasping noise. She seemed to register where she was, but the after-effects of opium had left her ravaged; evidently, she did not possess the energy even to express surprise. She drew her hands weakly away from Devlin's grasp, and he retreated. He noticed that her hands moved at once to encircle her corset—as though her belly had been punctured, he thought, and she was trying to staunch the wound. He spoke, but she did not respond, and presently she closed her eyes again, and drifted back to sleep. An altercation broke out in another quarter of the gaol-house, and Devlin was called over to officiate; this duty, and others pertaining to his station, claimed his attention for the remainder of the afternoon.

At the end of the day the justice's clerk arrived from the court-house to collect bail from any miscreant who could raise the necessary sum. At the sound of this newcomer's voice, Miss Wetherell lifted her dark head, made damp by fever, and beckoned. (The clerk was another new face in town, slim and very dapper; Gascoigne was his name.) The whore extracted several coins from between the sorry bones of her corset, and pressed them one by one into the clerk's open palm. She was shivering a great deal, and wore a look of great humiliation. The bail was recorded as met, and Governor Shepard was then obligated to release her, which he did promptly. Devlin did not attend her hearing at the Magistrate's Court the next day, for he had been charged with the task of digging a grave for the hermit, Crosbie Wells. He heard later that she had declined to plead, and had paid the fine that was levied against her without argument.

The day after the burial, a four-thousand-pound fortune was discovered in Crosbie Wells's cottage—exactly twice the sum named in the partially burned deed of gift, which Devlin had since stowed between the pages of his Bible, between the end of the Old Testament and the beginning of the New. Still Devlin did not confess; still he did not show the deed to anyone. He told himself that once Anna Wetherell was stronger—once the episode of her near-suicide was safely behind her—he would show the piece of paper to her; for the moment, however, he judged it prudent to keep the information to himself.

Now, in the dining room of the Palace Hotel, Devlin reached out and placed his hand over the battered cover of his Bible, which was unmarked except for a small Canterbury cross, stamped into the leather in gold. The movement was protective: although he did not yet know that the enclosed deed, pressed, apocryphal, between

Malachi and Matthew, was to be of great importance to Thomas Balfour, as it would be to sundry other men, still he felt the need to keep it close to him. He knew that the deed—receipt of a gift that was never given, codicil to a will that was never made—was valuable somehow, and he was loath to part with it until he knew what its exact value truly was.

'Grave-digging,' said Balfour, taking his derby hat from its hook and running his fingers around the brim. '*That's* something you'll need to read up on.'

'I do not know of any tracts on the subject,' Devlin said.

'For your new parish,' said Balfour, ignoring him. 'There's a gallows going in.' He put his hat on, pushed it back off his forehead with his thumb, and turned to leave. At the door he lingered. 'I don't know your name, Reverend,' he said.

'And I don't know yours,' Devlin returned. There was a silence—and then Balfour burst out laughing, tipped his hat to show his pleasure, and strode from the room.

Φ

Saturday in Hokitika was a day of bustle and appointment. The diggers flooded back to the township in droves, swelling the total population to some four thousand, and filling the dosshouses and hotels along Revell-street to riotous capacity. The clerks at the Magistrate's Court were overrun with petty claims and mining rights, the brokers with pledges, the merchants with orders from the rich men, and petitions for extended credit from the poor. Gibson Quay was a hive of industry; it seemed that with every hour that passed, a new timber frame was hammered into place, a new door was hung, and a new store unfurled its banner to billow and crack in the Tasman wind. Every spoke on the great wheel of luck was visible on a Saturday—there were men rising, risen, just falling, fallen, and at rest—and that night every digger would either drink his sorrow, or his joy.

Today, however, the heavy rain had discouraged all but the most urgent traffic in the streets, and Hokitika did not throng with its usual crowd. The few bedraggled men Balfour passed were hunched under the awnings of hotels, cupping their hands to keep their cigarettes alight. Even the horses had an air of grim surrender. They stood muzzled by the wet cones of their nosebags, unmoving in the torn muck of the road, and as he strode by they showed not even a flicker in the half-lidded slack of their eyes.

As Balfour turned into Revell-street he met with such a lash of wind and rain that he was obliged to clamp his hat to his head with his hand. According to Saxby's Weather Warnings, that dubious oracle published daily in the *West Coast Times*, the deluge would let up within a day or three—for Saxby was expansive in his predictions, and allowed himself a generous margin of error on either side of his guess. In truth the specifics of his column changed but rarely: downpour was as much a part of the Hokitika constitution as frost and sunburn had been in Otago, and red dust in the Victorian hills. Balfour quickened his pace, pulling his coat tighter around his body with his free hand.

There were a dozen-odd men upon the covered veranda of the Reserve Bank, pocketed in groups of three and four. The windows behind them were fogged pearl-grey. Balfour scanned the faces, squinting through the rain, but saw nobody he recognised. A ragged plume of smoke directed his gaze downward, to a figure sitting alone: a Maori man was squatting under the eave with his back against a piling. He was smoking a cigar.

His face was tattooed in a way that reminded Balfour of the wind patterns on a map. Two large swirls gave fullness to his cheeks, and spokes radiated upward from his brows to join his hairline. A pair of deep whorls on either side of his nostrils lent an almost prideful definition to his nose. His lips had been coloured blue. He was wearing serge trousers and an open-necked twill shirt, unbuttoned to the sternum; flat against the brown skin of his chest hung an enormous green pendant, shaped like an adze. He had almost finished his cigar, and as Balfour approached, he threw the butt into the thoroughfare, where it rolled down the camber of the road and then came to rest, still reeking, against the wet edge of the grass.

'You're that Maori fellow,' said Balfour. 'Crosbie Wells's mate.'

The man moved his eyes to Balfour's, but did not speak.

'Give us your name again? Your name.'

'*Ko Te Rau Tauwhare toku ingoa.*'

'Crikey,' Balfour said. 'Give us just the name part.' He held his palms close together, to signify a small amount. 'Just the name.'

'Te Rau Tauwhare.'

'Can't say that either,' Balfour said. He shook his head. 'Well—what do your friends call you, then—your white-man friends? What did Crosbie call you?'

'Te Rau.'

'Not much better, is it?' Balfour said. 'I'd be a fool to try, wouldn't I? How about I call you Ted? That's a good British name for you. Short for Theodore or Edward—you can choose. Edward's a nice name.'

Tauwhare did not respond.

'I'm Thomas,' Balfour said, placing his hand on his heart. 'And you're Ted.' He leaned over and patted Tauwhare on the crown of his head. The man flinched, and Balfour, in surprise, quickly snatched back his hand and took a step backwards. Feeling foolish, he stuck out his leg and shoved both hands into the pockets of his vest.

'Tamati,' said Tauwhare.

'Come again?'

'In my tongue, your name is Tamati.'

'Oh,' Balfour said, very relieved. He took his hands out of his pockets, clapped them together, and then folded his arms. 'You've got a bit of English—good!'

'I have a great many English words,' said Tauwhare. 'I am told I speak your language very well.'

'Crosbie teach you a bit of English, Ted?'

'I taught *him*,' said Tauwhare. 'I taught *him* korero Maori! You say Thomas—I say Tamati. You say Crosbie—I say *korero mai*!'

He grinned, showing teeth that were very white and very square. Evidently he had made a joke of some kind, and so Balfour smiled back.

'Never had a head for languages,' he said, pulling his coat tighter across his body. 'If it's not English, it's Spanish—that's what my old dad always said. Listen, though, Ted: I'm sorry about your mate. I'm sorry about Crosbie Wells.'

Tauwhare's expression became sober at once. '*Hei mauma-haratanga*,' he said.

'Yes, well,' Balfour said, wishing that the other man would stop talking in his own tongue, 'it was a d—n shame, is what it was. And now all this kerfuffle—all this bother, about the fortune and so forth—and his wife.'

He peered expectantly at Tauwhare, through the rain.

'*He pounamu kakano rua*,' said Te Rau Tauwhare. With his first two fingers he touched the pendant that hung around his neck. Perhaps it was a talisman of some kind, Balfour thought: they all had them, the Maori fellows. Tauwhare's was almost the size of his hand, and polished to a shine; it was made of a dark green stone, clouded with bands of a lighter green, and was fitted to a braid that ran around Tauwhare's neck, so that the narrow end of the adze sat high in the notch of his collarbone.

'Say,' Balfour said, opting for a shot in the dark, 'Say, where were you when it happened, Ted? Where were you when Crosbie died?'

(Perhaps the Maori fellow could start him on his way; perhaps he knew something. It wouldn't do to ask too many questions about the town, of course, for fear of attracting suspicion, but a Maori man was a much safer bet than most: his acquaintance was, most likely, very limited.)

Te Rau Tauwhare turned his dark eyes on Balfour, and considered him.

'Do you understand the question?' Balfour said.

'I understand the question,' Tauwhare said.

He understood that Balfour was asking about the death of Crosbie Wells, and yet had not been present at his funeral—that shameful excuse for a funeral, Tauwhare thought, with a flash of anger and disgust. He understood that Balfour had made only the most superficial show of sympathy, and had not even removed his hat. He understood that Balfour was looking to make a profit in some way, for he had a greedy look, in the way that men often did when they saw a chance to receive something and give nothing in return. Yes, Tauwhare thought: he understood the question.

Te Rau Tauwhare was not quite thirty years of age. He was handsomely muscular, and carried himself with assurance and the tightly wound energy of youth; though not openly prideful, he never showed that he was impressed or intimidated by any other man. He possessed a deeply private arrogance, a bedrock of self-certainty that needed neither proof nor explication—for although he had a warrior's reputation, and an honourable standing within his tribe, his self-conception had not been shaped by his achievements. He simply knew that his beauty and his strength were without compare; he simply knew that he was better than most other men.

This estimation did make Tauwhare anxious, however: he felt that it pointed to a spiritual dearth. He knew that any self-reflexive certainty was the hallmark of shallowness, and that valuation was no index of true worth—and yet he could not shake his certainty about himself. This worried him. He worried that he was only an ornament, a shell without meat, a hollow clam; he worried that his own self-estimation was a vain one. He therefore apprenticed himself to the spiritual life. He quested after the wisdom of his ancestors, so as to teach himself to doubt himself. As a monk seeks to transcend the lesser functions of his body, so did Te Rau Tauwhare seek to transcend this lesser function of his will—but a man cannot master his will without the expression of it. Tauwhare could never strike a balance between surrendering to his impulses, and fighting them.

The *iwi* to which Tauwhare belonged was Poutini Ngai Tahu, a people who had once commanded the entire western coast of the South Island, from the steep-sided fjords in the south to the palms and stony beaches in the far north. Six years ago the Crown had purchased this extensive tract of land for a sum of three hundred pounds—reserving for Poutini Ngai Tahu only the Arahura River, sections of its banks, and a small parcel of land at Mawhera, the mouth of the river Grey. The negotiations had at the time struck Poutini Ngai Tahu as unfair; now, six years later, they knew the

purchase to be patent theft. The thousands and thousands of diggers who had since flocked to the Coast in pursuit of gold had each
purchased a prospector's licence at a pound apiece, and land at a
price of ten shillings per acre. That profit alone was considerable—
but that was to say nothing of the value of the gold itself, hidden
in the rivers and mingled in the sands, whose aggregate value was
so colossal it had not yet been given a figure. Every time he thought
about the wealth his people ought to have commanded, Tauwhare
felt a swell of anger in his chest—an anger so bitter and tormented
that it manifested as pain.

Thus it was to the Crown, and not to Poutini Ngai Tahu, that
Crosbie Wells had paid his fifty pounds, when he purchased a hundred rolling acres at the eastern end of the Arahura Valley—an
acreage that was thick with totara, a finely grained wood that
answered well to a knife, and did not weather under salt or storm.
Wells was pleased with his purchase. His two great loves were hard
work and hard work's reward—whisky, when he could get it, and
gin when he could not. He built himself a one-roomed cottage
overlooking the river, cleared a space for a garden, and began to
build a timber mill.

Te Rau Tauwhare travelled up the Arahura Valley relatively frequently, for the reason that he was a hunter of *pounamu*, and the
Arahura River was filled with that treasure: smooth, milky-grey
stones that, when split, showed a glassy green interior, harder than
steel. He was a competent carver, even, some said, an excellent one,
but it was in sourcing the stone from the riverbed that he was truly
and uniquely skilled. *Pounamu* was as dull and ordinary on the exterior as it was bright and iridescent within; Tauwhare, with his
practised eye, did not need to scratch or split the stones at the riverbank, but carried them back to Mawhera untouched, so that they
could be blessed and broken in the ceremonial way.

The acreage purchased by Crosbie Wells banked on to Poutini
Ngai Tahu land—or, as we should properly say, banked onto the
portion of land to which Poutini Ngai Tahu had been so recently
confined. In any event, it was not long before Te Rau Tauwhare
encountered Crosbie Wells—having been attracted by the sound of

Wells's axe, ringing through the valley as he split kindling for his fire. Their acquaintance began cordially, and became frequent; over time Tauwhare began to call in at Crosbie Wells's cottage each time he was near. Wells, it turned out, was an enthusiastic pupil of Maori life and lore—and so Tauwhare's visits became a tradition.

Te Rau Tauwhare loved any chance to enlighten other men upon those qualities that best defined him, and never more than when his audience flattered those aspects of his person about which he cherished a deeply private doubt: namely, his *mauri*, his spirit, his religion, and his depth. Crosbie Wells, over the coming months, questioned Tauwhare relentlessly about his beliefs, as a man, and as a Maori man, and as a Maori man of Ngai Tahu allegiance. He confessed that Tauwhare was the first non-European with whom he had ever spoken; his curiosity, so expressed, had all the qualities of thirst. Tauwhare, it must be said, did not learn a great deal about Crosbie Wells during this time; the latter seldom spoke about his own past, and it was not Tauwhare's habit to ask a great many questions. He considered Crosbie Wells a kindred spirit, however, and often told him so—for, like all fundamentally confident persons, Tauwhare was very happy to compare himself to others, intending all such comparisons as compliments of the most heartfelt kind.

On the morning after Crosbie Wells's death Tauwhare arrived at his cottage with a gift of food, as was their custom—he supplied the meat, and Wells the spirits, an arrangement that satisfied both men. In the clear space before Wells's cottage he met a cart, departing. Holding the reins was the Hokitika physician, Dr. Gillies; beside him sat the gaol-house chaplain, Cowell Devlin. Tauwhare did not know either of these men, but when his gaze moved to the cart, he saw a familiar pair of boots, and, beneath a folded blanket, a familiar form. Tauwhare gave a cry, and dropped his gift upon the ground in shock; the chaplain, taking pity on him, suggested that he might accompany his friend's body back to Hokitika, where it was to be prepared for burial, and thereafter, interred. There was no room for Tauwhare on the driver's seat, but if he wished it, he could sit on the rear tongue of the cart, so long as he remembered to keep his feet out of the way.

The hoteliers and shopkeepers stood in the doorways along Revell-street as the cart rattled into Hokitika and turned down the main road. Some trotted forward for a better view, peering up at Te Rau Tauwhare—who stared back, blank-faced, limp. One of his hands was loosely gripping Wells's ankle. The man's body rolled and juddered with each lurch of the cart. When they reached the Police Camp Tauwhare did not move. He sat waiting, still holding Wells's ankle, while the other men conferred.

The Hokitika cooper had agreed to knock together a pine coffin, ready for the funeral, and to fashion a rounded wooden headstone on which he would paint Crosbie Wells's name and the two dates that bounded his life. (Nobody was sure of the actual year of his birth, but the year 1809 had been inked upon the flyleaf of his Bible: this was a plausible birth date, for it would place Crosbie Wells at fifty-seven years of age, and it was this date that the cooper would inscribe on the dead man's wooden headstone.) Until these two orders were completed, however, and until the grave was dug, the gaol's governor had directed Crosbie Wells to be laid out on the floor of his private study at the Police Camp, with a muslin bed sheet between his body and the ground.

When the body was arranged with his hands folded across his chest, the gaoler ushered everyone from the room and pulled the door closed, causing the hallway to shiver. The interior walls of the gaoler's house were made of patterned calico that had been stretched tight and tacked to the building's frame, and when the timber creaked in the wind, or was disturbed by a heavy footfall or the sudden slam of a door, the walls all quivered and rippled, like the surface of a pool—so that, watching them tremble, one could not help but call to mind that two-inch space between the doubled cloth, that dead space around the framing, full of dust, and patterned by the moving shadows of the bodies in the room beyond.

Someone has to stay with him, Tauwhare insisted. Wells could not be left alone, lying on the floor, without even a flame burning in the room, with no one to watch over him, touch him, pray over him, pray for him, or sing. Tauwhare tried to explain the principles of the *tangi*— but they weren't principles, they were rites, too sacred for explanation, too sacred even to defend: they were simply the way things ought to be done, must be done. A spirit has not fully departed until the body is interred, he said. There are songs, and prayers . . . The gaoler reprimanded him, calling him a heathen. Tauwhare became angry. Somebody has to stay with him until the burial, he said. I will stay with him until the burial. Crosbie Wells was my friend and my brother. Crosbie Wells, the gaoler returned, was a white man, and unless a passing shadow has deceived me, certainly no brother of yours. The funeral will be on Tuesday morning; if you want to make yourself useful, you can lend a hand to the digging of his grave.

But Tauwhare stayed. He kept vigil on the porch, and then in the garden, and then in the alley between the gaoler's cottage and the Camp—and from each station he was chased away. At last the gaoler emerged from the gaol-house with a long-handled pistol in his hand. He would shoot Tauwhare if he saw him within fifty yards of the Camp at any hour before the moment Crosbie Wells's body was lowered into the ground, so help him God, he said. So Tauwhare backed up fifty paces, counting the steps, and sat down against the wooden façade of the Grey and Buller Bank. From this distance he watched over his old friend's body, and spoke beloved words for him, on the final night before his spirit sailed away.

'When Crosbie died,' said Tauwhare, 'I was in the Arahura.'

'You were in the valley?' said Balfour. 'You were there when he died?'

'I was setting a trap for kereru,' said Tauwhare. 'Do you know kereru?'

'Some kind of bird, is it?'

'Yes—very tasty. Good for stewing.'

'All right.'

Balfour's derby hat had begun to drip. He took it off and banged it against his leg. Already his suit had darkened from grey to a sodden charcoal. His shirt had become translucent, showing through it the pink of his skin.

'I set the trap before nightfall, to catch the birds in the morning,' Tauwhare said. 'From the ridge you can see Crosbie's house—from above. That night four men went in.'

'Four?' said Balfour, replacing his hat. 'You don't mean three— one man on a black stallion, very tall; two other men with him, shorter, both on bay mares? That's Alistair Lauderback—and Jock, and Augustus. The men who found his body, you know—who alerted the police.'

'I saw three men on horseback, yes,' said Tauwhare, nodding slowly. 'But before they arrived, I saw one man on foot.'

'One man alone—well! You're all right, aren't you, Ted?' said Balfour, suddenly very excited. 'Yes—by golly, you're all right!'

'I was not alarmed,' Tauwhare continued, 'because I did not know that Crosbie Wells died that night. I did not know he was dead until the morning.'

'One man—entering the cottage, alone!' said Balfour. He began to pace. 'And *before* Lauderback! *Before* Lauderback arrives!'

'Do you wish to know his name?'

Balfour wheeled on his foot. 'You know who it was?' He was almost shouting. 'Yes, good Lord! Tell me!'

'We will trade,' said Tauwhare immediately. 'I will set my price; you will counter. One pound.'

'Trade?' said Balfour.

'One pound,' said Tauwhare.

'Hang tight,' said Balfour. 'You saw a man go into Wells's cottage on the day of his death—the very day of his death, two weeks ago? You really saw somebody do that? And you know—without a shadow of a doubt—who that man was?'

'I know the name,' said Tauwhare. 'I know the man. No cheating.'

'No cheating,' agreed Balfour. 'But before I pay—I want to make sure that you do really know him, you see. I want to make sure you're not taking me for a ride. Big man, was it? Very dark hair?'

Tauwhare folded his arms. 'Fair play,' he said. 'No cheating.'

'Of course it's fair play,' said Balfour. 'Of course it is.'

'We will trade. I have set my price at one pound. Now you counter.'

'Heavy—was he heavy? Thick-set? I'm just making sure, you see. I'm making sure you're on the level. Then I'll start trading. *You* might be cheating *me*.'

'One pound,' said Tauwhare stubbornly.

'It was Francis Carver, wasn't it, Ted? Isn't that right? It was Francis Carver—the sea captain? Captain Carver?'

Balfour was guessing—but it was a good guess. A wounded look passed over Tauwhare's face, and he exhaled audibly.

'I said no cheating,' he said, in a tone of reproof.

'I wasn't cheating, Ted,' said Balfour. 'I just knew it already, you see. I'd only forgotten. Of course Carver made a trip up to Crosbie Wells's cottage that day. That was him, wasn't it—Captain Carver, the man you saw? You can tell me—it's not a secret, because I already know.'

He searched the man's face, making sure.

Tauwhare's jaw was rigidly set. Under his breath he muttered, '*Ki te tuohu koe, me maunga teitei.*'

'Well, Ted, you've done me a d—ned good turn here, and I won't forget it,' said Balfour. By now he was thoroughly saturated. 'And you know—if I ever need something done, I'll come to you, won't I? And you'll get your coin some other way.'

Tauwhare lifted his chin. 'You need Maori,' he said. He did not phrase it as a question. 'You need Maori, you come to me. I do not do odd jobs. But you need language, and I will teach you many things.'

He did not mention that his skill was as a carver. He had never sold *pounamu*. He would not sell *pounamu*. For one could not put a price upon a treasure, just as one could not purchase *mana*, and one could not make a bargain with a god. Gold was not a treasure—this Tauwhare knew. Gold was like all capital in that it had no memory: its drift was always onward, away from the past.

'All right—but you'll shake, won't you?' Balfour seized Tauwhare's dry hand in his wet one, and shook it vigorously. 'There's a good man, Ted—there's a good man.'

But Tauwhare was still looking severely displeased, and he withdrew his hand from Balfour's grip as soon as he was able. Balfour felt a twinge of regret. It would not do to make an enemy of the fellow—not with so much of this business yet unsolved, he thought. There was a chance that Tauwhare's testimony might have to be called upon at a later time; there was a chance that he knew something about the relations, whatever they were, between Crosbie Wells and Francis Carver—or between those two men and Lauderback, come to think of it. Yes: it would be useful, to keep the man appeased. Balfour reached into his pocket. Surely he had something small, some token. They were fond of tokens. His fingers found a shilling and a sixpence. He pulled the sixpence out.

'Here,' he said. 'You can have this, if you tell me some Maori. Just like you taught Crosbie Wells. Eh, Ted? Then we'll have done business, just as you wanted to. All right? Then we'll be friends. Then you won't be able to complain.'

He pressed the silver piece into the other man's palm. Tauwhare looked at it.

'Now, tell me,' said Balfour, rubbing his hands together. 'What does . . . what does Hokitika mean? Hokitika. Just the one word, that's all I'm after. And I'd call that a tidy price, by the bye—a six-pence, for a single word! I'd call that a song!'

Te Rau Tauwhare sighed. Hokitika. He knew the sense of it, but could not translate. This happened so often between the languages, English and Maori: the words of one tongue never found their exact equivalent in the other, just as there was no white man's herb that one might perfectly exchange for *puha*, and no white man's bread that exactly called to mind *rewena pararoa*: however close the flavour, there was always something approximated, something imagined, or something lost. Crosbie Wells had understood this. Te Rau Tauwhare taught him korero Maori without using any English at all: they used their fingers to point, and their faces to mimic, and when Te Rau said things that Crosbie Wells did not understand, he let the sounds wash over him, like prayers, until their meanings clarified, and he could see inside the word.

'Hokitika,' said Balfour. He wiped the rain from his face. 'Come on, mate.'

At last Tauwhare lifted his finger and described a circle in the air. When his fingertip returned to the place from which he had begun, he jabbed his finger, sharply, to mark the place of return. But one cannot mark a place upon a circle, he thought: to mark a place upon a circle is to break it, so that it is not a circle any longer.

'Understand it like this,' he said, regretting that he had to speak the words in English, and approximate the noun. 'Around. And then back again, beginning.'

Φ

The Reserve Bank was always very crowded on a Saturday at noon. Diggers stood about with their hands full of gold; the Libra-scales rattled up and down as the ore was measured and recorded; the junior bankers ran back and forth from the archives, checking claim papers, marking tax payments, and receiving fees. Along the wall that faced the street were four barred cubicles where the bankers sat; above them hung a gilt-framed chalkboard, upon which was written that week's yield in ore, with subtotals for each district, and a grand total for the Hokitika region as a whole. Whenever a sum of raw gold was banked or bought, the chalked numbers were erased and then totalled anew—typically to a murmur of appreciation from the men in the room, and occa-sionally, if the total was a remarkable one, to a round of applause.

When Balfour entered the bank the attention of the crowd was focused not upon this chalkboard but upon the long table opposite, where the gold buyers, identifiable by the bright copper satchels that they wore upon their belts, inspected the raw ore for purchase. The buyer's work was slow. He weighed each nugget in his hand, scratched and tested the metal for impurities, and examined it through a jeweller's loupe. If the ore had been sifted, he filtered it through sieves of matting to check the flakes had not been cut with grit or gravel, and sometimes shook glistering handfuls over plates of mercury, to ensure that the metals bonded as they should. Once he declared the stuff pure and fit to be valued, the digger in ques-tion shuffled forward, and was asked to state his name. The Libra-scales were then calibrated until the arm hung parallel with the desk—and then the buyer poured the digger's pile of gold into the left-hand tray. To the right-hand tray the buyer added cylinder weights, one by one, until finally the scales lurched, and the tray bearing the man's fortune shuddered, and swung free.

That morning there was only one buyer present: a slick-haired magnate, wearing a pale green hunting jacket and a yellow tie—a gaudy combination, and one that might have served to mark him rather too obviously as a moneyed man, had he been doing business alone and unprotected. But the Hokitika gold escort was on hand. This small army, a uniformed infantry of ten men, presided over every sale and purchase of the colour. Later they would oversee the bullion's transfer into an armoured van, and ensure that it was safely conveyed offshore. They stood behind the buyer, and flanked the desk at which he sat—each man armed with a .577 Snider-Enfield rifle, a massive, gleaming piece of the most modern design. It took a cartridge as long as a man's index finger, and could blow a fellow's head to bloody dust. Balfour had admired the Snider-Enfield when the model was first shipped in, but seeing ten armed men in this enclosed space gave him an anxious premonition. The room was so crowded he doubted any one guard could find the room to raise his weapon to his shoulder, let alone discharge a round.

He shouldered his way through the diggers to the bankers' cubicles. Most of the men in the room were present as spectators only, and so parted to admit him; it was in very little time at all, therefore, that Balfour found himself at a barred cubicle, facing a young man in a striped vest and a neatly pinned cravat.

'Good morning.'

'I'm wanting to know if a man named Francis Carver has ever taken out a miner's right in New Zealand,' Balfour said. He removed his hat and slicked back his wet hair, an action without a perceptible benefit, for the palm of his hand was very wet also.

'Francis Carver—Captain Carver?'

'That's the man,' said Balfour.

'I am obliged to ask who you are, and why you are requesting this information.'

The banker spoke without affect, and in a mild tone of voice.

'The man owns a ship, and I'm in the shipping trade,' Balfour said smoothly, replacing his hat. 'Tom Balfour's my name. I'm looking to set up a side venture of a kind—tea-trading, back and forth from Canton. Just canvassing the idea at this point. I want to find out a bit more about Carver before I make any offers of business. Where his money's spread. Whether he's ever been bankrupted. That kind of thing.'

'Surely you could just ask Mr. Carver yourself,' replied the banker, speaking in the same inoffensive tone, so that the remark did not come off as rude, but, merely, as pleasantly offhand. He might have been passing a broken wagon in the street, and observing, quite affably, that there was a very simple way to mend the axle.

Balfour explained that Carver was at sea, and could not be contacted.

The banker seemed unsatisfied with this explanation. He considered Balfour, and put his finger against his lower lip. Evidently, however, he could not conjure a further objection that might give him reason to decline to pursue Balfour's request. He nodded, pulled his ledger towards him, and wrote a note in a thin, precise script. He then blotted his page (a little unnecessarily, Balfour thought, for the ledger remained open) and dried the nib of his pen with a square of soft leather. 'Wait here, please,' he said. He disappeared through a low doorway, beyond which lay an antechamber of some kind, and soon returned carrying a large folder, bound in leather and marked on its spine with the letter *C*.

Balfour drummed his fingers as the banker untied the clasp upon the folder and opened it. He scrutinised the young man through the bars of the grille.

What a contrast this young man posed to the Maori in the street! They were rough contemporaries in age, but where Tauwhare had been muscled, tense, and proud, this fellow was languid, even cat-like: he moved with a kind of casual luxury, as though he saw no need to spend his strength on swiftness, and nor did he see any reason to conserve it. He was lean in body. His hair was brown in hue, long, and curly at the tips; he wore it tied in a ribbon at the nape of his neck, in the fashion of a whaler. His face was broad and his eyes spaced widely; his lips were full, his teeth very crooked, and his nose rather large. These features conspired to form an expression that was both honest and nonchalant—and nonchalance is a form of elegance, when it demands much, and declines to reveal its source. Balfour considered him a very elegant young man.

'Here,' the banker said at last, pointing. 'You see—Carswell, here, and then Cassidy. Your man's not here.'

'So Francis Carver doesn't own a miner's right.'

'Not in Canterbury, no.' He shut the folder with a soft thud.

'What about an Otago certificate?'

'I'm afraid you will have to go to Dunedin for that.'

This was a dead end. In Lauderback's story the gold in the crate had hailed (allegedly, of course) from Dunstan, which was an Otago field.

'You don't keep records of Otago men?' Balfour asked, disappointed.

'No.'

'What if he came in on Otago papers? Would there be a record at the customhouse—from when he first arrived?'

'Not at the customhouse,' said the banker, 'but if he made any dust, he'd have to have it counted and weighed before he left. He's not allowed to transfer it to another province, or out of the country, without declaring it first. So he'd come here. We'd ask to take a look at the miner's right. Then we'd make a record in this book that he was working under Otago papers, but on a Hokitika claim. There's nothing in this book; therefore, as I said just now, we can safely assume he hasn't prospected anywhere hereabouts. As for whether he's prospected in Otago, I've no idea.'

The banker spoke with the controlled alarm of a bureaucrat who is requested to explain some mundane feature of the bureaucracy of which he is a functioning part: controlled, because an official is always comforted by proof of his own expertise, and alarmed, because the necessity for explanation seemed, in some obscure way, to undermine the system which had afforded him that expertise in the first place.

'All right,' said Balfour. 'Now, there's one more thing. I need to know whether Carver has owned shares in any mining company, or if he took out shares on a private claim.'

A flicker of doubt disturbed the banker's mild expression. For the briefest moment, he said nothing, and again it seemed as if he were trying to think of a reason to decline Balfour's request, to declare it unorthodox, or to press to know the reason why. He looked at Balfour with a gaze that was no less piercing for its mildness—and Balfour, who was always made uncomfortable by scrutiny, scowled very darkly. But, as before, the banker applied himself to the task demanded of his office. He wrote another note upon his ledger, blotted it, and then politely excused himself to pursue this new request.

When he returned with the shares records, however, he looked openly uneasy.

'Francis Carver *has* speculated in this area,' he said. 'You wouldn't call it a portfolio: it's only one claim. Looks like a private agreement. Carver takes home a return to the tune of fifty percent of the mine's net profit every quarter.'

'Fifty percent!' Balfour said. 'And only one claim—that's confidence for you! When did he buy?'

'Our records show the date as July 1865.'

'That far back!' Balfour said. (Six months ago! But that was after the sale of the *Godspeed*—was it not?) 'Which claim is it? Who's owning?'

'The mine is called the Aurora,' said the banker, enunciating very carefully. 'It is owned and operated by—'

'Emery Staines,' Balfour finished for him, nodding his head. 'Yes, I know the place—up Kaniere way. Why, that's capital news. Staines is a great friend of mine. I'll go and talk to the man myself. Thank you very much, Mr.—?'

'Frost.'

'Thank you very much, Mr. Frost. You've been extraordinarily helpful.'

But the banker was looking at Balfour with a strange expression on his face.

'Mr. Balfour,' he said. 'Perhaps you haven't heard.'

'Something about Staines?'

'Yes.'

Balfour stiffened. 'He's dead?'

'No,' said Frost. 'He vanished.'

'What? When?'

'Two weeks ago.'

Balfour's eyes went wide.

'I am sorry to be the one to break the news—*if* you are his great friend.'

Balfour did not notice the barb of emphasis in the banker's remark. 'Vanished—two weeks back!' he said. 'And no one's talking? Why haven't I heard about it?'

'I assure you that many men have been talking,' said Frost. 'A notice has been published in the Missing Persons column every day this week.'

'I never read the personals,' said Balfour.

(But of course: he had been with Lauderback, this fortnight past, facilitating introductions up and down the Coast; he had not been frequenting the Corinthian, as he habitually did in the evenings, to share a mug of beer with the other camp followers while they exchanged the local news.)

'Perhaps he found a strike,' he said now. 'That could be it. Perhaps Staines found a paying seam, up in the bush somewhere, and he's keeping it quiet—until he's staked the ground.'

'Perhaps,' the banker said courteously, and would not say more.

Balfour chewed his lip. 'Vanished!' he said. 'I can't understand it!'

'I rather wonder whether this news will be of import to your partner,' said Frost, smoothing the open page of his ledger with his palm.

'Who's my partner?' Balfour said, with some alarm—thinking that the banker was referring to Alistair Lauderback, whose name he had been careful not to use.

'Why—Mr. Carver,' Frost said, blinking. 'Your prospective partner in business—as you have just informed me, sir. Mr. Carver has a joint investment with Mr. Staines. So if Mr. Staines is dead . . .'

He trailed off with a shrug.

Balfour narrowed his eyes. The banker seemed to be implying, however vaguely, that Carver was in some way responsible for

Emery Staines's disappearance ... an implication for which he surely did not have any proof. His attitude was very clear, and yet he had not really expressed an opinion of any kind, upon which he might be faulted. The tone of his voice implied that he did not like Carver, even though his words expressed sympathy for the man's possible loss. Balfour, feeling the cowardice of this equivocation, almost became angry—but then he remembered that he was shamming. He was not going into business with Carver, and need not take his part in an argument against him.

But then young Frost smothered a smile, and Balfour saw, with a sudden rush of indignation, that, in fact, the younger man was mocking him. Frost had not believed his false story for a moment! He knew that Balfour was not going into business with Carver; he knew that this falsehood had been fabricated to mask some other purpose—and then he added the insult of diminishment to the injury of exposure, by finding Balfour amusing! It rankled Balfour to be second-guessed, but it rankled him still more to be ridiculed, especially by a man whose days were spent in a three-foot-square cubicle, signing cheques in another man's name. (This last was Lauderback's phrase, half-remembered from earlier that morning; it came to Balfour's mind as his own.) Suddenly angry, he leaned forward and curled his hands around the bars of the grille.

'All right,' he said quietly. 'You listen. I'm no more going into business with Carver than you are. I think the man's a thug and a crook and all the rest of it. I'm up against him, d—n it. I've got to get a twinkle on him: something I can use.'

'What is a twinkle?' the banker asked.

'It's stupid—never mind it,' Balfour snapped. 'The point is that I'm looking to round him up. Give him over to the law. I think he skimmed a fair fortune out of some other fellow's claim. Thousands. But it's only a hunch, and I need hard evidence. I need a place to start. All right? That investment story I gave you just now was a bunch of guff. Cock and bull.' He glared at the banker through the bars of the grille. 'What?' he said after a moment. 'What, then?'

'Nothing at all,' said Frost. He squared the papers on his desk, and gave a cryptic, tight-lipped smile. 'Your business is your own. I wish you only luck, Mr. Balfour.'

Φ

The news about Emery Staines had rattled Balfour severely. Shipping crates and blackmail was one thing, he thought, but a person disappearing was quite another. That was a sombre business. Emery Staines was a good digger, and much too young to die.

Outside the courthouse Balfour stood and breathed heavily for a moment. The small crowd outside the bank had dispersed to their luncheon, and the Maori man was gone. The rain had thinned to a persistent drizzle. Balfour cast his eye up and down the street, somewhat at a loss for where next to go. He felt excessively dejected. *Vanished*, he thought. But one did not simply vanish! The boy could only have been murdered. There was no other explanation for it—if he had not been seen for two weeks.

Emery Staines was easily the richest man south of the black sands. He owned more than a dozen claims, several of which had shafts that descended to depths of thirty feet, at least. Balfour, who admired Staines exceedingly, would have guessed his age at three- or four-and-twenty—not so young as to be unworthy of his luck, and not so old as to suggest that he might have acquired it by some less than honest means. In fact such a suggestion had never crossed Balfour's mind. Staines had been gifted with a thoroughly good-natured beauty, the kind that is earnest and hopeful without ever declaring itself to be so; in temper he was affable, optimistic, and delightfully quick. Even to think him dead was hateful. To think him murdered was worse.

Just then the Wesleyan chapel bell struck half past twelve, releasing a flurry of birds: they burst out of the makeshift belfry and scattered, dark against the sky. Balfour turned his face to the sound, feeling as he did so a sudden ache in his temple. His senses were turning from dull to sharp—the effect of the spirits he had consumed that morning—and the responsibilities of his situation had begun to weigh heavy upon him. He no longer felt inclined to ask questions on Lauderback's behalf.

He wrapped his coat around his body, turned on his heel, and began walking towards the Hokitika spit—a place that was, for him, a habitual refuge. It was his pleasure to stand on the sand in foul weather, clutch his coat across his body, and look out past the clustered masts of the ships at anchor, swaying en masse, impelled variously by the river's rushing current, the surf, and the wind—the howling Tasman wind, that stripped the bark from the trees at the beachfront, and bent the scrub to crippled forms. Balfour enjoyed the fierce indifference of a storm. He liked lonely places, because he never really felt alone.

As he slithered down the muddy bank to the quay, the wind suddenly dropped. Smiling, Balfour peered into the mist. The rain had stolen all chance of a reflection from the wide mouth of the river, and the water was as grey and opaque as a pewter plate. The bucking masts had slowed their motion when the wind died away; Balfour watched them, calmed by their weighty roll, back and forth, back and forth. He waited until they were almost still before moving on.

The quay curved around the mouth of the river to meet the spit, a narrow finger of sand that was battered on one side by the white surf of the open ocean, and lapped on the other by the confused wash of the river, its waters mingled now with salt, and stripped of gold. Here, on the calm side of the spit, a short wharf projected from the quay. Balfour stepped down onto it, landing with a flat sole, and the structure shuddered beneath his weight. Two stevedores, quite as sodden as he was, were sitting on the wharf some twenty feet away; they started at the jolt, and turned.

'All right, chaps,' said Balfour.

'All right, Tom.'

One was carrying a brass-capped boathook; he had been using it to swipe at the gulls, which were diving for their supper on the rocks below, and now he resumed this idle purpose. The other was keeping score.

Balfour strolled up behind them, and for a time nobody spoke. They watched the moored vessels pitch back and forth, and squinted out, through the rain.

'You know what the trouble is?' Balfour said presently. 'Down here, any man can make himself over. Make himself new. What's an alias, anyway? What's in a name? Pick it up as you pick up a nugget. Call this one Wells—this one *Carver*—'

One of the stevedores glanced around. 'You got a quarrel with Francis Carver?'

'No, no.' Balfour shook his head.

'Quarrel with a man called Wells?'

Balfour sighed. 'No—there hasn't been a quarrel,' he said. 'I'm wanting to find out a thing or two, that's all. But quiet—on the sly.'

The gull returned; the stevedore swiped again, and missed.

'Foul-hooked through his wing, nearly,' said the second man. 'That's five.'

Balfour saw that they had dropped a square of biscuit on the gravel below.

The stevedore who had spoken first nodded his head at Balfour and said, 'Are you wanting to chase up Carver, or chase up the other one?'

'Neither,' Balfour said. 'Never mind. Never mind. I've got no quarrel with Francis Carver—you remember that.'

'I'll remember,' said the stevedore, and then, 'I say, though: if you're wanting dirt—and on the sly—you ought to ask the gaoler.'

Balfour was watching the gull circle closer. 'The gaoler? Shepard? Why?'

'Why? Because Carver did time under Shepard,' said the stevedore. 'On Cockatoo Island, for all of ten years. Carver dug the dry dock there—convict labour—with Shepard looking on. If you're wanting dirt on Carver, I'd make a bet that Gov. Shepard is the man to dig it up.'

'At Cockatoo?' Balfour said with interest. 'I didn't know Shepard was a sergeant at Cockatoo.'

'He was. And then the very year after Carver gets his leave, Shepard gets a transfer to New Zealand—and follows him! How's that for bad luck?'

'The worst,' agreed his fellow.

'How do you know this?' Balfour said.

The stevedore was addressing his mate. 'That's a face *I'd* never want to see again—my gaoler, day in and day out, for ten years—and then, as soon as I'm free—'

'How do you know this?' Balfour persisted.

'I apprenticed on the dockyards there,' the stevedore said. 'Hey, now—*that's* a corker!'

For he had struck the gull across the back with his stick.

'You don't happen to know what Carver was booked for—do you, lad?'

'Trafficking,' the stevedore said immediately.

'Trafficking what?'

'Opium.'

'What—into China? Or out?'

'Couldn't tell you.'

'Who booked him, though? Not the Crown.'

The stevedore thought about this, and then shrugged. 'I don't really know,' he said. 'I thought it was something to do with opium. But maybe that was just something I heard.'

Presently Balfour bid them both goodbye, and moved on along the spit. As soon as he was well alone, he planted his feet apart, thrust his hands into his pockets, and looked out over the white roar of the ocean—past the screw jacks and greased rollers, past the wooden lighthouse at the spit's far end, past the dark hulks of the ships that had foundered on the bar.

'See, now!' he muttered to himself. 'That's something—that's something, all right! Carver *must* be the man's real name! He can't be using an alias—not in Hokitika, under the gaoler's own nose—when he served time beneath the man, in a penitentiary!' Balfour slicked his moustache with his finger and thumb. 'Here's the rub, though. What in heaven's name provoked him to make the claim—with proof in writing, to boot—that his name was Francis Wells?'

In which Joseph Pritchard outlines his theory of conspiracy; George Shepard makes a calculated offer; and Harald Nilssen agrees, in a tone of remonstration, to pay a call upon Ah Quee.

It was at this point that Balfour's role as narrator was usurped—a transferral that was marked, on the shipping agent's part, by the lighting of a new cigar, the filling of a fresh glass, and an enthusiastic 'Now, correct me if I'm wrong, boys!'

This exhortation was apparently directed at two persons: Joseph Pritchard, the dark-haired man on Moody's left, whose stifled intensity of silence was matched, as Moody soon discovered, by the stifled intensity of his unhurried speech, and another man whose physical presence we have not yet had cause to remark. This second man had been playing at billiards when Moody first made his entrance; Balfour now introduced him, with an admiring thrust of his cigar, as Harald Nilssen, born in Oslo, late of Bath, undefeated master of the three-card brag, and a d—ned fine shot—to which Nilssen added, springing forward to augment his own commendation, that he carried a muzzle-loading Enfield musket, the British Empire's finest, and the only firearm he had ever deigned to touch. These two men were more than willing to take Balfour's exhortation at face value—Nilssen for reasons of vanity, for he could not bear to be the leading role in a sensational tale, and not the leading actor, too; and Pritchard for reasons of precision.

We shall therefore leave Thomas Balfour standing on the wharf with his hands in his pockets, squinting into the rain. We shall turn our gaze some two hundred yards to the north, and alight at the Auction Yards on Gibson Quay—where, behind the rostrum, an unpainted door leading to a private office bears the legend *Nilssen & Co., Commission Merchants*.

In deference to the harmony of the turning spheres of time we shall resume our tale exactly at the moment Balfour left off—in Hokitika, on Saturday, the 27th of January, at five minutes before one in the afternoon.

Φ

At midday on a Saturday Harald Nilssen could usually be found in his office, sitting before a stack of contracts, wills, and bills of lading, patting his breast every ten minutes or so to check again the silver pocket watch that would release him to his luncheon—which he took with medical regularity each day at the Nonpareil. Nilssen recommended this routine to any who would listen, believing very stoutly in the curative properties of dark gravy, pastry, and ale; he did much recommendation, in fact, and often made an example of his own customs for the profit of other, less visionary men. He derived an especial pleasure from argument, so long as it was of the preposterous, hypothetical variety, and so loved to fashion absurd theories of abstraction from the small but dedicated circle of his own tastes. This attitude was affectionately reinforced by his friends, who thought him vivacious and amusing, and scorned by his detractors, who thought him affected and self-absorbed—but these latter voices were subdued in Nilssen's ears, and he spent no effort to better make them out.

Harald Nilssen was famous in Hokitika for the high style of his dress. That afternoon he was wearing a knee-length frock coat with silk-faced lapels of a charcoal hue, a dark red vest, a grey bow tie, and cashmere striped morning trousers. His silk hat, which was hanging on a hatstand behind his desk, was of the same charcoal hue as his coat; beneath it was propped a silver-tipped stick with a curved handle. To complete this costume (for so he perceived of his daily dress: as a costume that could be completed, to effect) he smoked a pipe, a fat calabash with a bitten-down stem—though his affection for the instrument had less to do with the pleasures of the habit than for the opportunity for emphasis it provided. He often held it in his teeth unlit, and spoke out of the corner of his mouth like a comic player delivering an aside—a comparison which suited him, for if Nilssen was vain of the impressions he created, it was because he knew that he created them very well. Today, however, the mahogany bowl was warm, and he was pulling on the stem with considerable agitation. The hour of his luncheon was past, but he was not thinking of his stomach, and nor of the ruddy-cheeked barmaid at the Nonpareil, who called him Harry and always saved the choicest edges of the piecrust for his plate. He was frowning down at a yellow bill upon his desktop, and he was not alone.

At length he pulled his pipe from his teeth and lifted his eyes to meet the gaze of the man sitting opposite him. He said, in a low voice, 'I've done no wrong. I've done nothing below the law.'

He spoke with only a very slight Norwegian accent: thirty years in Bath had made him all but British in his inflexions.

'It's who stands to profit,' said Joseph Pritchard. 'That's what a justice will be looking for. Seems you made a very tidy profit by this man's death.'

'By the legal sale of his estate! Which I took on *after* he was already in the ground!'

'In the ground—but warm, I think.'

'Crosbie Wells drank himself to death,' said Nilssen. 'There was no cause for an inquest, nothing untoward. He was a drunk and a hermit, and when I received these papers I believed his estate would be small. I had no idea about the 'bounder.'

'You're saying this was just a lucky piece of business.'

'I'm saying I've done nothing below the law.'

'But *someone* has,' Pritchard said. '*Someone* is behind this. Who knew about the 'bounder? Who waited till Crosbie Wells was six feet deep, then sold off his land so quiet and so quick, without ever going to auction—who put the papers in? And who planted my laudanum under his cot?'

'You say *planted*—'

'It was planted,' Pritchard said. 'I'll take my oath on that. I never sold that man a dram. I know my faces, Harald. I never sold a single dram to Crosbie Wells.'

'Well then, there you are! You can prove that! Show your records, and receipts—'

'We have to look beyond our own part in this design!' Pritchard said. When he spoke vehemently he did not raise his voice, but lowered it. 'We're *associated*. Trace it back far enough, and you'll find an author. It's all of a piece.'

'Do you suggest this was planned—in advance?'

Pritchard shrugged. 'Looks like murder to me,' he said.

'Conspiracy to murder,' Nilssen corrected him.

'What's the difference?'

'The difference is in the charge. It would be conspiracy to murder—we'd be convicted for the intention, not for the act itself. Crosbie wasn't killed by another man's hand, you know.'

'So we've been told,' Pritchard said. 'Do you trust the coroner, Mr. Nilssen? Or will you take a spade in your own hands, and bring the hermit's body up?'

'Don't be ghastly.'

'I'll tell you this: you'd find more than one corpse in the hole.'

'Don't, I said!'

'Emery Staines,' Pritchard said, relentlessly. 'What the devil happened to him, if he wasn't killed? You think he turned to vapour?'

'Of course not.'

'Wells died, Staines vanished. All in a matter of hours. Wells is buried two days later . . . and what better place to hide a body, than in another man's grave?'

Joseph Pritchard always sought the hidden motive, the underlying truth; conspiracy enthralled him. He formed convictions as other men formed dependencies—a belief for him was as a thirst—and he fed his own convictions with all the erotic fervour of the willingly confirmed. This rapture extended to his self-regard. Whenever the subterranean waters of his mind were disturbed, he plunged inward, and struggled downward—kicking strongly, purposefully, as if he wished to touch the mineral depths of his own dark fantasies; as if he wished to drown.

Nilssen said, 'That's useless speculation.'

'Buried together,' said Pritchard. He sat back. 'I'd bet my life.'

'What does it matter what you guess—what you wager?' Nilssen burst out. '*You* didn't kill him. *You* didn't murder anybody. It's on another man's head.'

'But somebody certainly wants to make it seem as if I did. And somebody's certainly made *you* look like a d—ned fool, for chasing a herring that turned out to be red!'

'You're talking appearances.'

'Juries care about appearances.'

'Come,' said Nilssen, somewhat weakly. 'You can't really think that a *jury*—'

'—Will be necessary? Don't be an ass. Emery Staines is Hokitika royalty. Strange as that sounds. Folk who couldn't pick the Commissioner from a line-up of drunks know Staines's name. There's no doubt there'll be an inquest. If he fell down the stairs and broke his neck with a dozen men to witness, there would be an inquest. All it's going to take is one shred of evidence to connect him to the Crosbie Wells affair—his body, probably, whenever they find it—and bang, you're implicated. You're a co-conspirator. You're on trial. And *then* what are you going to say to defend yourself?'

'That I'm not—that we didn't—*conspire*—'

But uselessness overcame him, and he did not go on.

Pritchard did not interrupt the silence. He stared intently at his host and waited. At length Nilssen resumed, struggling to keep his voice calm and practical:

'We mustn't keep anything back. We must go to the justice ourselves—'

'And risk the charge?' Pritchard's voice became lower still. 'We don't know half the players, man! If Staines was murdered—look, even if you don't believe the rest of what I'm saying, you must admit that it's a d—ned coincidence he disappeared when he did. If he was murdered—and let's say he was—well, somebody in town has got to know about it.'

Nilssen tried to be haughty. 'I for one am not going to stand about and wait with a noose around my neck—'

'I am not proposing that we stand about and wait.'

The commission merchant sagged a little. 'What then?'

Pritchard grinned. 'You say there's a noose—well, all right. Follow the rope.'

'Back to the banker, you mean?'

'Charlie Frost? Maybe.'

Nilssen looked sceptical. 'Charlie's no double-crosser. He was as surprised as anyone when the 'bounder turned up.'

'Surprised, that's easy to fake. And what about the fellow who purchased the land? Clinch—of the Gridiron Hotel. He must have been tipped off somehow.'

Nilssen shook his head. 'I can't believe it.'

'Perhaps you ought to try.'

'Anyway,' Nilssen said, frowning, 'Clinch doesn't stand to gain a penny, now that the widow's made her claim. *She's* the one you should be worried about.'

But Pritchard did not have an opinion about the widow. 'Clinch doesn't stand to gain a penny—from Crosbie Wells, maybe,' he said. 'But think on this. Staines leases the Gridiron to Clinch, doesn't he?'

'What are you driving at?'

'Only that a fellow's never sorry when his creditor is dead.'

Nilssen turned red. 'Clinch wouldn't take another man's life. None of them would. Charlie Frost? Come off it, Jo! The man's a mouse.'

'You can't tell from looking at a man what he's capable of doing. And you certainly can't tell what he's done.'

'This kind of speculation—' Nilssen began, but he did not know what form his protestation was to take, and he again fell silent.

Nilssen did not know the vanished prospector, Emery Staines, at all well—though if asked, he would have declared the opposite, for Nilssen tended to profess intimacy whenever it flattered him to do so, and Staines was very much the kind of man with whom Nilssen would have liked to forge an intimate acquaintance. Nilssen loved to be dazzled, and never was he more dazzled than by the selfhood of a man he very much admired. Emery Staines, being possessed of both youth and conviction, was naturally an enviable type. Calling him to mind now, Nilssen had to agree with Pritchard that it was exceedingly unlikely that Staines had departed Hokitika in secret, of his own volition, in the middle of the night. His claims required constant maintenance and supervision, and there were more than fifty men in his employment—why, his absence would be costing more than pennies, Nilssen thought, and the debt would be mounting every day. No: Pritchard was right. Staines had either been kidnapped, or—far more likely—he had been killed, and his body had been very effectively concealed.

The current information held that Emery Staines had last been seen around sundown on the 14th of January, walking south down Revell-street in the direction of his house. What happened after that, nobody knew. His barber came calling at eight the next morning, and found his door unlocked; he reported that the bed was rumpled, as if recently slept in, but the fire was cold. All valuables were present and untouched.

Emery Staines had no enemies, as far as Nilssen was aware. His disposition was bright and very open, and he had the rare gift of managing to act both generously and humbly at once. He was very rich, but there were many rich men in Hokitika, and most of them were a good deal more unpleasant than he. It was unusual that he was young, of course, and that might be a cause for envy in an older, more disappointed man—but envy was rather a weak motive for murder, Nilssen thought, if indeed the young man had been killed.

'What would drive any man to quarrel with Staines?' Nilssen said aloud. 'That boy radiates luck—the Midas touch, he has.'

'Luck is not a virtue.'

'Killed for his money, then—?'

'Let's put Staines aside for the moment.' Pritchard leaned forward. 'You took home a fair cut of Crosbie Wells's fortune.'

'Yes—I told you, ten per cent,' Nilssen said, turning back to the yellow bill of sale on the desk before him. 'Commission on the sale of his effects, you know; but now that the will's been disputed, the payment's void. I shall have to pay it all back again. The property ought not to have been sold.'

He touched the edge of the bill with his finger. He had signed the document, and its copy, at this very desk two weeks prior—and how his heart had sunk as he had penned his name. In Hokitika the sale of effects on a deceased estate was never a profitable venture, but his business was not prospering, and he was desperate. How shameful it was (he had thought), to have travelled half the girth of the globe only to see his fortunes fall so far—only to scrabble for scraps beneath the tables of richer, luckier men. The name on the bill—Crosbie Wells—had meant nothing to him. From what he knew Wells was just a loner, a wretched twist of a man who drank himself into a stupor every night and dreamed of nothing. Nilssen signed his name in bitterness, in exhaustion. He was going to have to rent a horse, sacrifice a day of work, ride out—where?—to the forsaken Arahura, and pick over this dead man's effects as a vagrant trawls through a gutter, looking for food.

And then, wedged into the flour canister, the powder box, the meat safe, the bellows, the cracked basin of an old commode—and all of it glistering, heavy, and soft. His commission had come in at just over four hundred pounds; for the first time in his life, he was flush. He might have packed up and sailed to Sydney; he might have returned home; he might have begun anew; he might have married. But he had no time to enjoy it. The day his commission was finally cleared was the very day of Mrs. Wells's arrival; within hours, the sale of the estate had been appealed, the inheritance disputed, and the fortune seized by the bank. If the appeal was granted—as it certainly would be—Nilssen would be obliged to pay his commission back again, in full. Four hundred pounds! It was more money than he earned in a year. He ran his finger down the edge of the bill, and felt a lonely stab of outrage. He wished, as he had wished many times in the last week, that he could be given someone to blame.

But Pritchard was shaking his head: he wasn't interested in the dead man's will, nor in the legal implications of its contest. 'Never mind all that, for the moment,' he said. 'Think back to the cottage. You saw the pile with your own eyes?'

'I was the one to discover it.' Nilssen spoke with a touch of pride. He relaxed a little at the memory. 'Oh—if you'd seen it—I might have turned it into leaf and covered a whole billiard table, legs and all. Heavy as anything. And how it *shone*.'

Pritchard didn't smile. 'You said that it wasn't dust and it wasn't nugget. Do I have that right?'

Nilssen sighed. 'Yes, that's right: it had all been pressed into squares.'

'Retorted,' Pritchard said, nodding, '—which takes equipment, and skill. So who was the smith? Not Wells himself.'

Nilssen paused. This was a point that had not crossed his mind. The way that Pritchard was setting forth his argument—confidently, arrogantly—was unpleasant to him, but he had to concede that the chemist had made several connexions already that he himself had missed. He sucked on his pipe.

Nilssen had no great knowledge of the workings of a goldfield. He had only attempted to prospect for the colour once, and found it miserable work—lugging pails of water to and from the river to sluice the stones, slapping at the sandflies that crept up his jacket until he was mad enough to dance. Afterwards his back ached and his fingers stung and his feet stayed spongy and swollen for days. The pinch of grit he had taken home, knotted into the corner of his kerchief, was taxed and taxed and then weighed to the smallest fraction of an ounce—yielding, at last, five dirty shillings, an impossible disappointment, barely enough to cover the rental of his horse to and from the gorge. Nilssen did not try his luck again. He was by natural faculty and self-styling a Renaissance man, accustomed to showing immediate promise in whatever field to which he applied himself; if he did not master a trick on his first attempt, he gave up the trade. (He was not without humour about this practice: he often recounted his abortive episode in the Hokitika gorge, exaggerating the discomforts he had sustained in light-hearted deprecation of his own constitutional delicacy—but this was an interpretation that was reserved for him alone, and he became embarrassed if another man took on this same perspective, so to speak, or agreed with him.)

The theory that Joseph Pritchard had put to him was logical enough, up to a point. Somebody—more than one person, perhaps—must have known about the fortune hidden on Crosbie Wells's estate. The fortune was too large, and the sale of his property too furtive and too swift, to deny that probability altogether. Furthermore, the phial of laudanum that had been discovered in close proximity to the man's dead body suggested that somebody— perhaps the same somebody—had been present in the cottage either just prior to or just after the hermit's death, presumably with some intention of harm. The phial was Pritchard's, purchased from his emporium and bearing a label signed in his hand: its bearer must therefore have been a Hokitika man, travelling northward, not a stranger, travelling south. This ruled out the dignitaries who had first discovered Crosbie's body, and had brought the news of his death to the town.

Privately Nilssen did believe that Pritchard was right to hold the purchaser of the estate, Edgar Clinch, in suspicion—and the banker, Frost, as well. He did not suspect them of having a part in Emery Staines's murder, as Pritchard evidently did, but it seemed to him that Clinch must have acted on a tip of some kind, to buy Crosbie Wells's cottage and land so hastily—and whatever that tip might have been, Charlie Frost must know about it. Nilssen could also accept that his own involvement, however innocently undertaken, must look decidedly fishy to an impartial outsider: he had been the one to discover the fortune, after all; he had recorded the glass phial of laudanum in his ledger along with everything else (he had been compiling a list of effects to be sold); and he stood to gain four hundred pounds out of the transaction.

Beyond these admissions, however (which, after all, were only admissions of doubt and probable impression), Nilssen was uncertain. Pritchard had reasoned that the disappearance of Emery Staines could not be coincidental, which was supposition; he had argued that the man had been murdered, which was guesswork; he had suggested that his body had been buried in Wells's own grave, which was presumption; and he had proposed that the legal debacle over Wells's estate had been planned in advance as a kind of eclipse, a decoy—this last, Nilssen thought, was downright fantasy. Pritchard could not account for the phial of laudanum; he could not produce a motivation, or a plausible suspect … and yet the commission merchant could not discount the man's convictions altogether, however much he disliked the manner in which they were expressed.

Nilssen did not share the chemist's rapt intoxication with the plumbing of the deep: the quest for truth did not possess him as it did his guest. Pritchard became very strange when speaking of his passions, the elixirs that he brewed and tasted under the low ceiling of his laboratory, the resins and powders that he bought and sold in clouded jars. There was something cold and hard about the man, Nilssen thought—diverting his own ill feeling, as he often did, into a principle of aesthetic distaste.

At last, and with the air of vexation that always passed over him whenever another man's argument showed a deficiency in his own, Nilssen took his pipe from his mouth and said, 'Well—perhaps Wells had a contact down at the Reserve. Killarney—or a Company man—'

'No.' Pritchard struck the desk with splayed fingers; he had been waiting for Nilssen to guess wrongly, and he had his counter-argument prepared. 'This is a Chinaman's work. I'd bet any money. The joss at Kawarau was always full of fellows without a permit—they shared the miner's rights between them. No man can tell two of them apart, you see, and one name's as good as another, when it comes from a foreign tongue. It's all outside jobs in Chinatown. If this was a Company affair it would look—'

'Cleaner?' Nilssen sounded hopeful.

'The opposite. When a fellow has to cover his prints—when he has to use the tradesman's entrance, instead of coming in through the foyer as he's known to do—that's when he has to start making provisions, sacrifices. Do you see? A man on the inside has to contend with the pawns—with all the pieces of the system. But a man on the outside can deal with the Devil direct.'

It was expressions of this kind that Nilssen particularly disliked. He dropped his gaze again to the bill of sale.

'Chinatown Forge,' Pritchard said. 'You mark my guess. One fellow does all the furnace work. His name is Quee.'

'You'll speak to him?' said Nilssen, looking up.

'Actually,' said the chemist, 'I was hoping that you would. I'm in a spot of bother with the Orientals at the moment.'

'Dare I ask why?'

'Oh—bad business is all. Trade secrets. Opium,' Pritchard said. He turned his hand over and then let it fall into his lap.

Nilssen frowned. 'You ship your opium from *China*?'

'Good Lord, no,' Pritchard said. 'From Bengal.' He hesitated a moment. 'It's more of a personal dispute. On account of the whore who nearly died.'

'Anna,' Nilssen said. 'Anna Wetherell.'

Pritchard scowled: he had not wanted to use her name. He turned his head away and watched the raindrops swell and gather under the lip of the sash window.

In the brief pause before he resumed speaking, Nilssen was startled by the thought that perhaps the chemist loved her: Anna Wetherell, the whore. He tested the possibility in his mind, enjoying it. The girl was uncommonly striking—she moved with a weary, murderous languor, like a disaffected swan—but she was rather more volatile in her tempers than Nilssen liked in a girl, and her beauty (in fact Nilssen would not call her beautiful; he reserved that word for virgins and angelic forms) was too knowing for his taste. She was also an opium eater, a habit that showed in her features as a constant blur, and in her manner as a fathomless exhaustion—this compulsion was unbecoming enough, and now she was a would-be suicide, besides. Yes, Nilssen thought: she was just the kind of girl for whom Pritchard would fall. They would meet in darkness; their encounters would be feverish and doomed.

Here the commission merchant missed his mark. Nilssen's guesses were always of the self-confirming sort: he tended to favour whichever proofs best pleased his sense of principle, and equally, to hold fast to whichever principles best lent themselves to proof. He talked often of virtue, and so gave the impression of a most encouraging and optimistic temper, but his faith in virtue was indentured to a less adaptable master than optimism. The benefit of the doubt, to take the common phrase, was a haphazard gift, and Nilssen was too proud of his intellect to surrender the power of hypothesis. In his mind a protective glaze had been applied to the crystal forms of high abstraction: he loved to regard them, and to wonder at their shine, but he had never thought to take them down from their carved and oaken mantel, so to speak, and feel them, supple in his hands. He had concluded that Pritchard was in love simply because it was pleasant to deliberate the point, examine the specimen, and then return to the beliefs he had possessed all along: that Pritchard was a queer fish; that Anna was a lost cause; and that one ought never undertake to love a whore.

'Yes, well,' Pritchard was saying, 'they're furious about it, you know. The yellow chap who operates the den at Kaniere—Ah Sook is his name—he went to Tom Balfour, after the whore took ill—very upset, you understand. He told Tom he wanted to look over my shipping records, check the last case that had come in on my account.'

'Why not just come to you direct?' Nilssen asked.

Pritchard shrugged. 'Thought I was up to something, I suppose,' he said.

'He thought you poisoned her—on purpose?'

'Yes.' Pritchard looked away again.

'Well, and what did Tom say?' Nilssen said, to prompt him.

'He showed Ah Sook my records. Proved I'm clean.'

'Your record's clean?'

'Yes,' Pritchard said shortly.

Nilssen saw that he had caused his guest offence, and felt an ugly flash of pleasure. He was beginning to resent the implication that they would be equally implicated as conspirators, if (or when) the possible murder of Emery Staines came to light: it seemed to him that Pritchard was considerably more embroiled in this mess than he was. Nilssen had nothing to do with opium, and wanted nothing to do with it. The drug was a poison, a scourge, and it made a fool of men.

'Listen,' Pritchard said, placing his finger on the desktop, 'you need to get this Quee chap to talk with you. I'd do it myself if I could—I've tried the den, but Sook won't have a bar of me. Quee's all right. He's decent. Ask him about the pile—whether it's his gold, and if it is, why it turned up on Wells's estate. You can go this afternoon.'

It rankled Nilssen to be ordered about in this way. 'I don't see why you can't talk to Quee yourself, if your beef is with the other fellow.'

'I'm under the hammer. Call it laying low.'

Nilssen called it something rather different in his mind. Aloud he said, 'What on earth would induce a johnny chink to speak to me?'—taking refuge, finally, in petulance. He pushed the yellow bill away from him.

'At least you're neutral,' Pritchard said. 'You've given none of them cause to judge you one way or another—have you?'

'The celestials?' Nilssen sucked on his pipe; the leaf was almost ash. 'No.'

'You say it with an *Ah* in front—Ah Quee. It's their way of saying Mister.' Pritchard paused a moment, regarding the other man, and then he added, 'Think of it this way. If *we* are being framed, then perhaps *he* is, too.'

As he was speaking, there came a knock at the door: it was the clerk, bearing the message that George Shepard was in the outer office and waiting to be received.

'George Shepard—the gaoler?' Nilssen said, with some trepidation, and a swift glance at Pritchard. 'Did he say why?'

'Matter of profit, he said, mutual gains,' the clerk replied. 'Shall I fetch him in?'

'I'll take my leave,' Pritchard said, standing immediately. 'So you'll find him—the fellow Quee? Say you will.'

'All the way to Kaniere?' Nilssen said, remembering his luncheon, and the barmaid at the Nonpareil.

'It's only an hour's walk,' Pritchard said. 'But make sure you get the right fellow: the one you're after is a shortish chap, very thin, clean-shaven; you'll know his cottage by the chimney that issues from the forge. I'll wait your message,'—and he was gone.

Φ

Nilssen's office seemed much too small to accommodate the massive, rigid bow that George Shepard made upon his entrance. The commission merchant felt himself shrink back a little in his chair, and to compensate for this he leaped up, thrust out his hand, and cried,

'Mr. Shepard—yes, yes, please. I haven't yet had the pleasure of receiving your business, sir—but I do hope that I can be of service—in the nearest future—if I may. Do sit down.'

'I know you, of course,' Shepard replied, taking the chair that was offered him. Seeing that Nilssen's pipe was lit, he reached in his pocket for his own. Nilssen passed his tobacco pouch and lucifers across the desk, and there was a short pause as Shepard filled and tamped his bowl and struck a match. His pipe was shallow, made of briar, with a smart collar of amber set between the bit and the stem. He puffed several times until he was satisfied the leaf was lit, and then sat back in his chair with a calculated glance first to his left and then to his right, as if he wished to square himself with the planes of the room.

'By reputation,' he added, being the kind of man who always finished an utterance once he had set his thought in motion. He breathed out a mouthful. 'That fellow just leaving,' he said. 'His name again?'

'Jo Pritchard is his name, sir—Joseph. Runs the drug hall on Collingwood-street.'

'Of course.'

Shepard paused, forming his business in his mind. The pale light of the day, falling slantwise across Nilssen's desk, froze the eddies of pipe-smoke that hung about his head—fixing each coiling thread upon the air, as mineral quartz preserves a twisting vein of gold, and proffers it. Nilssen waited. He was thinking: *if I am convicted, then this man will be my gaoler.*

George Shepard's appointment as governor of the Hokitika Gaol had been met with little opposition from the men who lived and dug within the bounds of his jurisdiction. Shepard was a cold, formidable character, slow moving in a way that seemed constantly to emphasise the breadth of his shoulders and the weight of his arms; when he walked, it was with long, deliberate strides, and when he spoke (which was seldom) he intoned in a rich and august bass. His manner was humourless and not at all likeable, but severity counted as a virtue for a man of his profession, and it was to his credit, the voters agreed, that no charge of bias or prejudice had ever been laid at his door.

If Shepard was the subject of idle rumour, it was of the conjectural sort, and nearly always concerned his private relations with his wife. Their marriage was to all appearances conducted in absolute silence, with a grim determination on his part, and a fearful inhibition on hers. The woman referred to her own self as Mrs. George, and this only in a whisper; she wore the bewildered, panicked aspect of a tortured animal, who sees a cage where there is none, and cowers at every sudden thing. Mrs. George rarely ventured beyond the gaol-house door except, on rare occasions of civic display, to trip red-faced down Revell-street in Governor Shepard's wake. They had been at Hokitika four months before anyone discovered that she did in fact possess a Christian name—Margaret—though to speak it in her presence was an assault so dreadful that her only recourse was to flee.

'I come to you on business, Mr. Nilssen,' Shepard began. He held the bowl of his pipe in his fist against his breast as he spoke. 'Our present gaol-house is little better than a corral—a holding pen. There is scant light, and insufficient air. To ventilate, we prop open the door upon a chain, and I sit beyond the doorway with my rifle on my knees. It is untenable. We haven't the resources to cope with—more experienced criminals. More sophisticated crimes. A murder, say.'

'No—yes, yes,' Nilssen said. 'Of course.'

There was a pause, and then Shepard continued. 'If you will forgive my pessimism,' he said, 'I believe that Hokitika is about to meet a darker time. This town is at a threshold. Digger law is still the creed of the hills, and here—why, we are but a backwater of Canterbury still, but soon we will be the jewel in her crown. Westland will split, and Hokitika will prosper; but as she rises, she will have to reconcile herself.'

'Reconcile—?'

'The savage and the civil,' Shepard said.

'You allude to the natives—the Maori tribes?'

Nilssen spoke with a touch of eagerness; he cherished a romantic passion for what he called 'the tribal life'. When the Maori canoes came strong and flashing through the Buller Gorge—he had seen them from a distance—he was quelled in awe. The warriors seemed terrible to him, their women unknowable, their customs fearsome and primitive. His transfixion was closer to dread than to reverence, but it was a dread to which he sought to return. In fact Nilssen had been first spurred to make his voyage to New Zealand by a chance encounter with an able seaman at a roadside inn near Southampton, who was boasting (rather improbably, as it turned out) of his own encounters with the primitive peoples of the South Seas. The sailor was a Dutchman, and wore his jacket cut short above his hips. He had traded iron nails for cocoa-nuts; he had permitted island women to place their hands upon the white skin of his chest; he had once made a present of a knot to an island boy. ('What kind of knot?' Nilssen begged, coming forward; it was a Turk's Head; Nilssen did not know it, and the seaman sketched the looping floral shape upon the air.)

But Shepard shook his head at Nilssen's interjection. 'I do not use "savage" in the native sense,' he said. 'I allude to the land itself. Prospecting is an ugly business: it makes a man start thinking like a thief. And here the conditions are foul enough to make the diggers still more desperate.'

'But the diggings can be made civil.'

'Perhaps—after the rivers are spent. After the prospectors give way to dams and dredges and company mines—when the forests are felled—perhaps then.'

'You do not have faith in the power of the law?' Nilssen said, frowning. 'Westland is soon to have a seat in Parliament, you know.'

'I see that I am not making myself clear,' Shepard said. 'Will you allow me to begin again?'

'By all means.'

The gaoler began immediately, without altering his posture or his tone. 'When two codes of justice are available at once,' he said, 'a man will always use the one to inveigh against the other. Consider a man who thinks it just and right to bring a complaint to the Magistrate's Court against his own whore—expecting both the exercise of the law, and his exemption from it. He is refused, and perhaps he is even charged for consorting with the girl; now he blames the law and the girl both. The law cannot answer for his digger's sense of what is due, and so he takes the law upon himself, and throttles her. In former days he would have solved his quarrel with his fists, at once—that was digger's law. Perhaps the whore would perish, or survive, but either way his action was his own. But now—now he feels his very right to demand justice has been threatened, and *that* is what he acts upon. He is doubly angry, and his rage is doubly spent. I am seeing examples of this kind every day.'

Shepard sat back, and replaced his pipe in his mouth. His manner was composed, but his pale eyes were fixed very intently upon his host.

Nilssen never refused an opportunity to provoke a hypothetical. 'Yes, but—to follow your argument,' he said, 'surely you are not suggesting a preference for digger's law?'

'Digger's law is philistine and base,' Governor Shepard said calmly. 'We are not savages; we are civilised men. I do not consider the law to be deficient; I mean to point out, merely, what happens when the savage meets the civil. Four months ago the men and women in my gaol-house were drunks and petty thieves. Now I see drunks and petty thieves who feel indignant, and entitled, and speak righteously, as if they have been unjustly tried. And they are angry.'

'But—again—to conclude,' Nilssen said. 'After the whore is throttled, after the digger's rage is spent. Surely the civil law then returns to condemn this man? Surely he's punished justly—in the end?'

'Not if his fellows rally round him, to preserve his digger's rights,' Shepard replied. 'No man holds to any code as strong as he does when his code's affronted, Mr. Nilssen, and there's nothing more brutal than a gang of angry men. I've been a gaoler sixteen years.'

Nilssen sat back in his chair. 'Yes,' he said. 'I take your point; it's this twilight that's the danger, between the old world and the new.'

'We must do away with the old,' Shepard said. 'I will not suffer whores, and I will not suffer those who frequent them.'

Shepard's autobiography (a document which, if ever penned, would be rigid, admonishing, and frugal) did not possess that necessary chapter wherein the young hero sows his oats and strays; since his marriage, his imagination had conjured nothing beyond the squarish figure of Mrs. George, whose measures were so familiar, and so regular, that he might have set his pocket watch by the rhythm of her days. He had always been irreproachable in his conduct, and as a consequence, his capacity for empathy was small. Anna Wetherell's profession did not fascinate him in the least, and he had no boyhood memories of tenderness or embarrassment to soften him towards the subtleties of her trade; when he looked at her, he saw only a catalogue of indiscretions, a volatile intelligence, and a severe want of promise. That a whore might attempt to take her own life did not strike him as a remarkable thing, nor a very sad one; in this particular case, he might even call a termination merciful. Miss Wetherell lived by the will of the dragon, after all, a drug that played steward to an imbecile king, and she would guard that throne with jealous eyes forever.

It is fair to say that, of the seven virtues, Governor Shepard inclined towards the cardinal four. He was well apprised of the Christian doctrine of forgiveness, but only as a creed to be studied, and obeyed. We do not mean to diminish his religion by remarking that forgiveness is a thing that one must first be obliged to ask for in order to know how to give, and Governor Shepard had never in his life met any imperative to ask. He had prayed for Miss Wetherell's soul, as he did for all the men and women in his keeping, but his prayers were expressions of duty rather than of hope. He believed the soul to inhabit the body, and consequently, that the body's desecration was an assault upon the soul: a common whore, when judged by this substantive theology, fared ill indeed, and Anna Wetherell was malnourished, mistreated, and as wretched a picture as any he had seen. He did not wish her damned, but he believed, privately, that her salvation was impossible.

Miss Wetherell's spiritual fate, and the method by which she had sought to determine it forever, did not interest him; her corporeal merits did not interest him either. In this Shepard was set apart from the majority of men in Hokitika, who (as Gascoigne was to remark to Moody some seven hours later) had been talking of little else for a fortnight. When they exhausted the former subject, they fell back upon the latter, an arrangement that kept them in conversation for a great while.

Nilssen's pipe had gone out. He rapped the bowl against his desktop to empty the ash and then began to refill it. 'I believe Alistair Lauderback means to make a change,' he said, unlacing the strings of his tobacco pouch with his free hand. 'If he is elected, of course.'

Shepard did not answer at once. 'You've been following the campaigns?'

Nilssen, busy with his pouch, did not notice the other man's hesitation. When the gaoler had first entered Nilssen had been fearful of himself, even guarded, but he rarely dwelled long in a state of embarrassment. Shepard's theory of law had roused his intelligence, and gratified it, and he again felt master of his faculties. The absorbing rituals that attended the filling of his pipe—the worn thinness of the leather strings, the dry spice of the tobacco—had restored a kind of order to his senses. He replied, without looking up, 'Yes indeed. Reading the speeches every day, and with keen attention. Lauderback is here now—in Hokitika—is he not?'

'He is,' Shepard said.

'He will take the seat, I think,' said Nilssen, rubbing a pinch of tobacco between his fingers. 'The *Lyttelton Times* is backing his play.'

'You value him?'

'Tunnels and railways,' Nilssen said, 'that's his game, isn't it? Progress, civilisation, all of that. Strikes me that your thinking squares quite nicely with Lauderback's campaign.' He struck a match.

Shepard made to reply, then hesitated. 'I don't make a habit of speaking my politics in another man's office unless I'm invited to do so, Mr. Nilssen.'

'Oh—please,' said Nilssen politely, shaking out the match.

'But with your leave,' nodding his great pale head, 'I will say this. I too think that Lauderback will take the seat—Parliament and the Super both. He has a great force of personality on his side, and of course his connexion to the Bar and to the Provincial Council speak highly of his character and skill.'

'And this is a re-election for him, of course,' interrupted Nilssen, who very often made a habit of speaking politics in other men's offices, and forgot for a moment that he had granted the other man licence to speak his own mind. 'He's familiar.'

'He is familiar—to his own circle,' Shepard said. 'His loyalty is to Canterbury, and his tunnels and railways—to take your phrase—are the Lyttelton tunnel and the projected railway between Christchurch and Dunedin. As Superintendent he will reapportion whatever funds are not already tied into this tunnel and this railway—as he must, of course, to make good the promises of his campaign.'

'You may be right about the Super,' Nilssen said, 'but as an M.P.? He will *represent* Westland—'

'Lauderback is a Westland man in electorate only,' Shepard said. 'I do not fault him on it—he has my vote, Mr. Nilssen—but he does not know the digger's life.'

Nilssen looked as if he meant to interrupt again, so Shepard pressed on, raising his voice a little. 'I arrive now at the business that compelled this interview. I have the Commissioner's endorsement to begin work upon a new gaol-house, away from the Police Camp, on the terrace north of town. You recall it was a company of convicts who first cleared the Hokitika-road? I intend to do the same thing here: I shall use my own convict labour to build the prison at Seaview.'

This notion appealed to Nilssen's sense of retribution, and he smiled.

'However, as you have already remarked,' Shepard continued, 'Alistair Lauderback's focus is on transport: in his address to the Council he has argued in favour of using convict labour to build and maintain the Christchurch road. The route over the Alps is still treacherous—unfit for a horseman, much less for a coach.'

'The Superintendent has the final word on the matter?' Nilssen asked. 'Are your convicts not yours to employ?'

'Alas,' Shepard said. 'They are only mine to keep.'

The clerk entered, bearing coffee on a wooden tray. He was in a state of considerable excitement, for it was not often that Nilssen had visitors, and never visitors of such enigmatic repute as Pritchard (who was famous for his opium) and Shepard (who was famous for his wife). The clerk had arranged the coffee pot and saucers on the tray with particular attention, and he carried it high with his elbows cocked and his back held very straight. Nilssen nodded approvingly: it was not their custom for the clerk to wait on his employer, but Nilssen was pleased at the effect it must be creating in the mind of his guest. The clerk set the tray upon the sideboard and began to pour. He was hoping that the men would resume their conversation while he was still in the room, and so tried to pour slowly, feeling a pang of regret at the floating grains of chicory that he had added to the coffee grounds for reasons of economy, and now, with their ugly film of grit, seemed to admonish his pretensions.

Behind him Shepard said, 'By the bye, Mr. Nilssen: what do you know about Emery Staines?'

There was a pause. 'I know that he is missing,' Nilssen responded.

'Missing, yes,' said Shepard. 'He hasn't been seen for almost a fortnight. Very strange.'

'I do not know him well,' Nilssen said.

'Don't you?' said Shepard.

'He is an acquaintance—but not a friend.'

'Ah.'

Nilssen seemed about to cough; then he burst out, 'Are you *quite* finished, Albert?'

The clerk set down the coffee pot.

'Shall I leave the tray, sir?'

'Yes, yes—then go, for God's sake,' Nilssen said. He lurched for the cup as it was handed him, causing a small tide of coffee to slop into the saucer, and set it down before him with a clatter. The clerk brought a second cup to Shepard, who made no move to touch it, and pointed to the desk before him without a word.

'I shall say it plain,' Shepard said, when the disappointed clerk had shut the door behind him. 'I mean to begin work on the gaol-house at once, before the elections, so that when Lauderback takes office the work is already well underway. I am aware that this may seem to others as if I seek to actively thwart the success of his campaign. I come to you to solicit both your business and your discretion.'

'What do you need?' Nilssen said cautiously.

'Materials to build, and perhaps ten or twenty able bodies to begin digging the foundation,' Shepard said, reaching into his breast for the plans. 'I can offer you commission at your standard rate. The site has been purchased already, and approved. Here is the architect's design.'

'This is the original? Or a copy?' Nilssen took the papers from Shepard's massive hand and unfolded them.

'The original. There is no copy,' Shepard said. 'I keep these documents on my person always, of course.'

'Of course,' Nilssen agreed, reaching for his spectacles.

'The reason I have come to you,' Shepard continued, 'and not to Cochran, or Morrison, or another competitor whose business—forgive me—is faring rather better than yours at present, owes only in part to your reputation as an efficient man.'

Nilssen looked up.

'Permit me to speak frankly,' Shepard said. 'The matter is indelicate, I know; I will try and be as delicate as I can. It has come to my attention that you took home a commission to the value of many hundreds of pounds, upon closing the estate of Mr. Crosbie Wells.'

Nilssen started, but Shepard held up his hand to silence him.

'Do not implicate yourself by speaking before you have heard what I have to say,' he said. 'I will tell you exactly what I know. The man's body came through the Police Camp before his burial; given that he had no family or friends to speak of, we conducted the wake at the Camp itself. I had the solemn honour of viewing his body, and of being present while the physician checked his vital organs for signs of harm. Dr. Gillies concluded the cause of death was drink; I, with my slender knowledge of the subject, could only agree with his ruling. Dr. Gillies was careful in his examination of the contents of the dead man's stomach and intestines, however, which contained not only food and spirits, but traces of laudanum—though not enough, I should add, to warrant undue suspicion. I do not believe that Crosbie Wells was poisoned, except by drink.

'Now: even before the wake was over, Wells's land and mill were sold. The land, as you know, was reclaimed by the bank, and was then purchased almost immediately by a Mr. Edgar Clinch; while the transaction was perfectly legal, it is nevertheless curious how swiftly the property changed hands. I understand that you were then called upon to clear the cottage and sell on the dead man's effects, for a fee that would be set against their total value; you accepted this employment, and promptly discovered a great deal of hoarded gold (where was it hidden, in the flour canister?) to the aggregate value of four thousand pounds. A "homeward bounder", to use the local phrase. Now, Mr. Nilssen, you ought have then been able to walk away with your percentage, which was by now a very handsome cut; the whole enterprise was thwarted, however, when Mr. Wells's widow landed on the beach, and declared herself. She was one week too late to attend his burial, but not at all too late to contest the sale of his estate, and any transactions that had taken place as a consequence of that sale.

'As I have said, I do not believe that Crosbie Wells was poisoned,' Shepard said. 'But I also do not believe that the hoarded gold belonged to him, much less to his widow. The apparition of the widow Wells is a curiosity in a tale already rather too curious for my taste.' He paused. 'Have I said anything so far that you know or guess to be untrue? You can decline to answer that if you wish.'

'You mean to blackmail me?' Nilssen managed.

'Not at all,' Shepard said. 'But you must agree this smacks of plotting.'

'Yes. I do.'

'I am not a detective,' Shepard said, 'and profess no inclination towards that field. I care very little about how much you know. But I must have my new gaol-house, and I see an opportunity for both of us to gain.'

'Speak it, sir.'

'The widow Wells has made her appeal, to contest the sale of her late husband's effects,' Shepard said. 'The appeal will take months to action, of course, as legal matters do, and in the meantime the money will be held in escrow by the bank. In the end, I expect that the sale will be revoked, and if no greater plot is exposed, the widow will claim the 'bounder as her own. Incidentally, I have enjoyed several conversations with Crosbie Wells these past few months, and he certainly never spoke of being married—not to me, nor to any other man I've spoken to.'

Nilssen had a vision of a cat tapping a small rodent back and forth with the flat of its paw, its claws in sheath. He was not guilty—he had done no wrong—and yet he *felt* guilty; he felt implicated, as though he had performed a terrible misdeed while sleeping, and had woken to find his bolster smeared with blood. He felt certain that any moment now the gaoler would expose him—but for what crime, he did not yet know. What was the word Pritchard had used? *Associated*. Yes—he felt that acutely.

When he was a small boy Nilssen had stolen a precious button from his cousin's treasure chest. It was a cuff button from a military jacket, brass in colour, and engraved with the lithe body of a fox, running forward with its jaws parted and its ears cocked back. The button was domed, and greyer on one side than on the other, as if the wearer had tended to caress its edge with his finger, and over time had worn the shine away. Cousin Magnus had rickets and a bandy-legged gait: he would die soon, so he did not have to share his toys. But Nilssen's longing for the button became so great that one night when Magnus was sleeping he crept in, unlatched the chest, and stole it; he walked about the darkened nursery for a while, fingering the thing, testing its weight, running his finger over the body of the fox, feeling the brass take on the warmth of his hand—until something overcame him, not remorse exactly, but a dawning fatigue, an emptiness, and he returned the button to the place where he had found it. Cousin Magnus never knew. Nobody knew. But for months and years and even decades afterwards, long after Cousin Magnus was dead, that theft was as a splinter in his heart. He saw the moonlit nursery every time he spoke his cousin's name; he blushed at nothing; he sometimes pinched himself, or uttered an oath, at the memory. For although a man is judged by his actions, by what he has said and done, a man judges himself by what he is willing to do, by what he might have said, or might have done—a judgment that is necessarily hampered, not only by the scope and limits of his imagination, but by the ever-changing measure of his doubt and self-esteem.

'I estimate that it will be at least April before the sale is successfully repealed,' Shepard was saying, with the same perfect gravity. 'In the meantime—immediately, in fact—I propose that you invest the entire sum of your commission into the building of my gaol-house.'

Nilssen raised his eyebrows in surprise. 'But the money is not mine,' he said, for the second time that afternoon. 'It has already been revoked de jure, if not de facto. Once the widow's appeal has been granted, and the sale of the estate declared void, I shall have to pay my commission back in full.'

'The Council can sponsor your loan, with interest,' Shepard said. 'The gaol is publicly funded, after all; by the time your commission is recalled, I will be able to draw down funds from the Reserve, and repay you. We shall have a contract drawn up; you may name your terms. Your investment will be secure.'

'If you have public funding,' Nilssen said, 'then why propose this to me at all? What need do you have of these four hundred pounds?'

'Yours is ready money, and will be privately invested,' Shepard said. 'My Council funding has been approved, but not paid out; if I wait for the sum to be apportioned, and deposited into the gaol's account, I will be waiting for thirty bankers to push my contract across thirty desks, and back again. It will be March, or April, and the elections will be past.'

'And Lauderback will have his convicts,' Nilssen said.

'Yes, and he will have siphoned off a great deal more of the district's budget, besides.'

'Very well,' Nilssen said. 'Let us suppose that I agree to this, and you get your gaol-house. You said that *both* of us would stand to gain.'

'Well, yes,' Shepard said, blinking. 'You will have employment, Mr. Nilssen. You will get your standard commission on the labour, and the iron, and the timber, and the nails, and every small thing. Legal profit—that is how you stand to gain.'

Nilssen could not fault this (certainly, it had been many weeks since he had contracted work that promised this degree of yield), but Shepard's method of proposition was making him very uncomfortable. The gaoler had used the word *murder*, and called that crime 'sophisticated'; he had waited until Albert was present as a witness to ask about Emery Staines; and when he narrated the story of the Wells affair, he had made a great show of preventing Nilssen's interruption, lest the commission merchant implicate himself by speaking too much or too soon—thereby assuming that he *could* implicate himself in some way. Shepard was treating his host as a guilty man.

Nilssen said, 'And what if I refuse your offer—what then?'

Shepard pulled his lips back in a rare smile, the effect of which was rather gruesome. 'You are determined to see this offer as a blackmail,' he said. 'I cannot imagine why that might be so.'

Nilssen could not hold the gaoler's gaze for long. 'I will grant you the loan, and offer my services on commission,' he said at last. His voice was low. He pulled the architect's plans towards him. 'Please be so good as to wait a moment,' he added, 'while I make a record of the materials you require.'

Shepard inclined his head, and at last picked up the cup of coffee that was cooling on the desktop before him. He took up the saucer with great care; in his great hand the china seemed impossibly fragile, as if he might close his fist and with a single motion crush the vessel to a dust. He drained the cup and returned it to the exact position it had formerly occupied upon Nilssen's desk. He then replaced his pipe in his mouth, folded his hands, and waited. The irregular scratch of Nilssen's pen was the only sound between them.

'I shall draw you down a cheque on Monday morning,' Nilssen said at last, as he penned the final sum. 'We can advertise for tender in Monday's paper—I'll send a note to Löwenthal direct. I shall recommend that the labourers meet here, in the Auction Yards, at ten sharp, to be signed—that will give the men a chance to read the paper and spread the word. By Monday noon, weather permitting, we can begin work on the land.'

Shepard's eyes had narrowed. 'You said Löwenthal? Ben Löwenthal—the Jew?'

'Yes,' Nilssen said, blinking. 'We can't advertise without the paper. You could do it by flyer and gazette if you wanted—but everybody reads the *Times*.'

'I hope that we are understood that the investment of your commission is strictly a private matter.'

'We are understood, sir.' There was a pause. 'On my oath,' Nilssen added, and then immediately regretted the phrase.

'Perhaps we ought to insert a clause into our contract to that tune,' Shepard said lightly. 'For peace of mind.'

'You can trust my discretion,' Nilssen said, blushing again.

'I truly hope I can,' said Shepard. He stood, and extended his hand.

Nilssen rose also, and they shook hands.

'Mr. Shepard,' Nilssen said suddenly, as Shepard made to depart. 'The way you were speaking before—about the savage and the civil, the old world and the new.'

Shepard regarded him impassively. 'Yes.'

'I'm curious to hear how that line of thinking applies to all of this—the estate, the 'bounder, the widow Wells.'

Shepard took a long time to answer. 'A homeward bounder is a chance for total reinvention, Mr. Nilssen,' he said at last. 'Find a nugget, and a man can buy his own life. That kind of promise isn't offered in the civil world.'

Φ

Nilssen sat alone in his office for a long time after Shepard left, turning the gaoler's proposition over and over in his mind. A feeling of doubt was seeding in his breast. He felt that he had missed a connexion somewhere—as if he had come across a knotted handkerchief, balled in the watch-pocket of an old vest, and could not for the life of him recall what the knot was supposed to prompt him to remember—what errand, what responsibility; where he'd been, even, when he tied the corners, and tucked the thing away against his heart. He drummed his fingers; he toyed with his lapel. The rain beat against the window. The grey shadows in the room changed places, as the sun sank behind the cloud.

Suddenly he got up, went to the door, and opened it a fraction. 'Albert!' he called, through the chink.

'Yes, sir,' Albert called back, from the outer office.

'Crosbie Wells—the man who died.'

'Sir.'

'Who found his body? Remind me.'

'A company of men, sir,' Albert replied.

'You recall the story?'

'It was in the papers—I can find it for you, if you like.'

'Just tell me what you remember.'

'The party stopped in to refresh themselves, and found Mr. Wells fresh dead—that's my understanding. Sitting at his kitchen table, the papers had it.'

'Give us the name?'—But he already knew. He rested his head against the doorframe, and felt sick.

'That fellow in contest for the Westland seat,' said Albert. 'The Canterbury man. You met him last week at the Star. Alistair Lauderback's his name.'

Φ

Some ten minutes later Nilssen appeared in the doorway of the outer office, snapping out his top hat with such a tremendous crack that the clerk leaped out of his chair. He was holding his stick in a rather brutish fashion, gripping it halfway down its shaft, as if he meant to wield it as a cudgel. His face was very pale.

'Shall I direct any callers to the Nonpareil?' Albert called after him, as the commission merchant made for the door.

'No—leave me be. Tell them to wait. Tell them to come back Monday,' Nilssen snapped, without turning. He quitted the gate-house and strode off down the quay, but when he reached his accustomed pie-house on the corner he did not stop. He drew his coat tighter across his body and turned inland, towards Kaniere, and the goldfields.

MIDNIGHT DAWNS IN SCORPIO

In which the chemist goes in search of opium; we meet Anna Wetherell at last; Pritchard becomes impatient; and two shots are fired.

Joseph Pritchard, upon quitting Nilssen's offices, had not returned immediately to his laboratory on Collingwood-street. He had made his way instead to the Gridiron, one of the sixty or seventy hotels that lined Revell-street along its most crowded and lively stretch. This establishment (which, with its canary trim and false shutters, showed a gay frontage even in the rain) was the habitual residence of Miss Anna Wetherell, and although it was not the latter's custom to entertain callers at this hour of the day, it was not Pritchard's custom to conduct his business according to any schedule but his own. He stamped up the steps and hauled open the door without so much as a nod to the diggers on the veranda, who were sitting in a row with their boots upon the rail, alternately whittling, cleaning their nails, and spitting tobacco into the mud. They looked at him with some amusement as he passed darkly into the foyer, remarking, once the door had thudded shut behind him, that *there* was a man very much determined to get to the bottom of something.

Pritchard had not encountered Anna in many weeks. He had heard about her attempted suicide only third-hand, via Dick Mannering, who in turn had relayed the intelligence of Ah Sook, the Chinese man who managed the opium den at Kaniere. Anna frequently plied her trade at Kaniere Chinatown, and for that reason was known colloquially as Chinaman's Ann—a designation that harmed her popularity in some circles, and greatly accented it in others. Pritchard belonged to neither camp—he held little interest in the private lives of other men—so he was neither titillated nor repulsed to learn that the whore was a particular favourite of Ah Sook's, and that her near-death, as Mannering reported to Pritchard later, had driven the man almost to hysteria. (Mannering did not speak Cantonese, but he knew a handful of written characters, including *metal*, *want*, and *die*—enough to conduct a pictographic colloquy with the aid of his pocketbook, an object that was by now so heavily marked and foxed with use that he was able to perform very sophisticated rhetorical allusions simply by leafing back through the pages and pointing with his fingers to an old quarrel, an old settlement, an old sale.)

It irritated Pritchard that Anna had not contacted him herself. He was a chemist, after all, and, south of the Grey River at least, the sole supplier of opium to the West Coast dens: concerning a matter of overdose, he was an expert. She ought to have called on him, to solicit his advice. Pritchard did not believe that Anna had tried to end her life: he could not believe it. He was sure that she had been forced to take the drug against her will; either that, or the stuff had been altered with the intention of causing her harm. He had tried to recall the remainder of the lump from the Chinese den, in order to examine it for traces of poison, but Ah Sook was much too furious to indulge this request, having articulated (again via Mannering) his vehement resolve never to conduct business with the chemist again. Pritchard was indifferent to the threat—he had plenty of custom in Hokitika, and the sale of opium made up only a very small percentage of his revenue—but his professional curiosity about the event had not yet been satisfied. He needed, now, to question the girl himself.

The hotel's proprietor was not present when Pritchard entered the foyer of the Gridiron Hotel, and the space had an empty, rattling feel. Once Pritchard's eyes became accustomed to the gloom he saw Clinch's valet, who was leaning against the desk reading an old copy of the *Leader*, simultaneously mouthing the words and tracing them with his fingertip as he followed each line of print. There was a greasy patch on the countertop where the motion of his finger had polished the wood to a shine. He looked up and gave the chemist a nod as he passed. Pritchard flicked a shilling at him, which the other caught neatly and slapped onto the back of his hand—'Came up tails,' the boy called out, as Pritchard began to ascend the stairs, and Pritchard gave a snort of laughter. He could be brutal, when his spirits were aggrieved, and he was feeling brutal now. The hallway was quiet, but he put his ear against Anna Wetherell's door and listened for a moment before he knocked.

Harald Nilssen had guessed rightly that Pritchard's relations with Anna Wetherell were rather more tormented than his own, but he was mistaken to conclude that the chemist was in love with her. In fact Pritchard's taste in women was thoroughly orthodox, even juvenile. He would sooner be inclined to fall for a dairymaid than for a whore—however dull the maid, and however striking the whore. He valued purity and simplicity, plain dress, a soft voice, a tractable will, and a small ambition—which is to say, contrast. His ideal woman would perfectly contrast him: she would be knowable where he was unknowable, composed where he was not. She would be a kind of anchor from above and without; she would be a shaft of light, a comfort, a benediction. Anna Wetherell, with all her excess and intoxication, was too like him. He did not hate her for that, exactly—but he pitied her.

In general Pritchard was close-mouthed on the subject of the fairer sex. He did not enjoy speaking about women with other men, a practice which, in his estimation, was always clownish and braying. He kept his silence, and as a consequence his fellows believed him very well accomplished, and women, when they regarded him, believed him enigmatic and profound. He was not unhandsome, and his trade was a good one: he might have been considered a very eligible bachelor, had he worked a little less, and ventured into society a little more. But Pritchard loathed large groups of mixed company, where every man is required to act as a kind of envoy for his sex, and presents his own advantages playfully, under the scrutiny of the room. Large crowds made him stifled and irritable. He preferred close company, and kept few friends—to whom he was fiercely loyal, as he was loyal to Anna, in his own way. The intimacy that he felt when he was with her owed chiefly to the fact that a man is never obliged to discuss his whores with other men: a whore is a private matter, a meal to be eaten alone. It was this aloneness that he sought in Anna. She was a solitude for him; and when he was with her, he kept her at a distance.

Pritchard had truly loved only once in his life—but it had been sixteen years since Mary Menzies became Mary Firkin, and moved to Georgia to pursue a life of cotton and red earth and (so Pritchard had imagined) an expansive slowness, made of wealth and cloudless skies. Whether she had perished—whether Mr. Firkin, too, was living still—whether she had children, born or lost—whether she had aged well, or aged badly—he did not know. She was Mary Menzies in his mind. When he had last seen her she had been twenty-five, dressed simply in sprigged muslin with her hair gathered in ringlets at her temples, her wrists and fingers unadorned; they were sitting in the window box, saying goodbye.

'Joseph,' she had said (he inscribed it in his pocketbook later, to remember it for all of time), 'Joseph, I don't believe you have ever been at peace with good. It is well you never made love to me. You will remember me fondly now. It would not have been so, otherwise.'

He heard quick steps on the other side of the door.

'Oh, it's you,' was Anna's only greeting. She was disappointed: she must have been expecting someone else. Pritchard stepped inside without speaking, and closed the door behind him. Anna moved into the quartered patch of light beneath the window.

She was dressed in mourning, but by the old-fashioned style of the gown (the bell-shaped skirt, the pointed waist) and the faded hue of the cloth, Pritchard guessed it had not been tailored for her new: it must have been a gift, or, more likely, something salvaged. He saw that the hem had been let out: two inches of darker black showed as a stripe against the floor. It was a strange thing to behold a whore in mourning—rather like seeing a dandified cleric, or a child with a moustache; it gave one a sense of confusion, Pritchard thought.

It struck him that he had rarely seen Anna except by lamplight, or by the moon. Her complexion was translucent, even blue, and tended to a deep purple beneath her eyes—as if she had been painted in watercolour, on a paper that was not stiff enough to hold the moisture, so the colours ran. Her countenance was, as Pritchard's mother might have said, made up of angles. Her brow was very straight and her chin was pointed. Her nose was narrow, even geometric: a sculptor might render it in four strokes, with one slice on either side, one down the bridge, and one tuck beneath. She was thin-lipped, and though her eyes were naturally large, she tended to peer upon the world suspiciously, and so rarely employed them to seductive effect. Her cheeks were hollow, and her jawbone was visible, as the rim of a drum is visible, tight beneath the stretched membrane of the skin.

The previous year she had been with child, a state that had warmed the wax of her cheeks, and made plump the wretched bones of her arms—and Prichard had liked her: the round belly, the swollen breasts, hidden beneath yards of lawn and tulle, fabrics which softened her, made her buoyant. But sometime after the spring equinox, when the evenings were becoming longer, and the days brighter, and the sun hung low and scarlet over the Tasman Sea for hours before slipping, finally, into the red wash of the sea, the baby perished. Its body had since been wrapped in calico and buried in a shallow grave upon the terrace at Seaview. Pritchard had not spoken to Anna about the baby's death. He did not frequent her rooms with any kind of regularity, and he did not ask her questions when he was there. But he had wept, privately, when he heard the news. There were so few children in Hokitika—perhaps three or four. One looked forward to seeing them as to hearing a familiar accent of speech, or a beloved ship on the horizon, that put one in mind of home.

He waited for her to speak first.

'You can't stay,' she said. 'I've an appointment.'

'I won't keep you. I wanted to ask after your health.'

'Oh,' she burst out, 'I am sick of the question—sick of it!'

He was surprised by the violence of her answer. 'I haven't visited you in a while.'

'No.'

'But I saw you in the thoroughfare—just after the New Year.'

'It's a small town.'

He moved closer. 'You smell like the sea.'

'I don't. I haven't been sea-bathing in weeks.'

'Something stormy, then. As when a body comes in from the snow, and carries in the cold.'

'What are you doing?'

'What am I doing?'

'By speaking in that way—poetical.'

'Poetical?'

(Pritchard had the bad habit, when conversing with women, of answering a question with another question. Mary Menzies had complained of it once, long ago.)

'Sentimental. Fanciful. I don't know. It doesn't matter.' Anna plucked at her cuff. 'I have recovered my health,' she added. 'And you can save your next question for yourself. I didn't mean any kind of unnatural harm. I meant to take a pipe same as always, and then I fell asleep, and then the next thing I remember, I was in gaol.'

Pritchard placed his hat upon the armoire. 'And since then, you've been hounded.'

'To death.'

'Poor you.'

'Sympathy is worse.'

'Well, then,' Pritchard said, 'I shan't give you any. I'll be cruel to you instead.'

'I don't care.'

It seemed to him that she spoke with pity and blankness, which angered him; he considered showing it, but then he reminded himself that he was on an errand. 'Who's the client?' he said instead, to taunt her.

She had gone to the window, and half-turned in surprise. 'What?'

'You said you've an appointment. Who is it?'

'There's no client. I'm going with a lady to look at hats.'

He snorted. 'I've heard of a whore's honour, you know. You don't have to lie.'

She studied him from what seemed like a great distance—as if he were only a mark on the horizon for her, a distant speck, receding. And then she said, slowly, as if speaking to a child, 'Of course—you didn't know. I'm done with whoring for a time.'

He raised his eyebrows, and then, to cover his surprise, laughed at her. 'Honest woman, are you now? Hats and window boxes, is it? Gloves in the street?'

'Just while I mourn.'

He felt that this answer—stated simply and quietly—made him look foolish for having laughed, and a knot of frustration began to gather in his chest.

'What's Dick got to say about that?' he said, referring to Anna's employer, Mr. Mannering.

Anna turned away. 'He's not happy,' she said.

'I should imagine not!'

'I don't want to talk about that with you, Jo.'

He bristled. 'What's your meaning?'

'I don't have a meaning. Not a special one. I'm just tired of thinking about him.'

'Has he been a beast to you?'

'No,' Anna said. 'Not really.'

Pritchard knew about whores. The mincing types who pretended shock and spoke in high-pitched voices full of air; the buxom, helpful types who wore draped-elbow sleeves in any season, and called one 'lad'; the drunkards, greedy and whining, with chipped red knuckles and watery eyes—and then there was the category to which Anna belonged, the unknowable types, by turns limpid and flashing, whose carriage bespoke an exquisite misery, a wretchedness so perfect and so absolute that it manifested as dignity, as calm. Anna Wetherell was more than a dark horse; she was darkness itself, the cloak of it. She was a silent oracle, Pritchard thought, knowing not wisdom, but wickedness—for whatever vicious things one might have done, or said, or witnessed, she was sure to have witnessed worse.

'Why didn't you come to me?' he said at last, wanting to accuse her of something.

'When?'

'When you took ill.'

'I was in gaol.'

'But after that.'

'What good would that have done?'

'It might have saved you a good deal of trouble,' he said curtly. 'I could have proven that opium was poisoned, if you'd let me testify.'

'You knew it was poisoned?'

'I'm guessing. How else, Ann? Unless—'

Anna moved away from him again, to the bedhead this time, and wrapped her fingers around the iron knob. As she moved he smelled her again—the sea. The intensity of the sensation startled him. He had to check the urge to step towards her, to follow her, and breathe her in. He smelled salt, and iron, and the heavy, metallic taste of foul weather ... low cloud, he thought, and rain. And not just the sea: a *ship*. That tarred ropy smell, the dusty damp of bleached teak, oiled sailcloth, candle wax. His mouth began to water.

'Poisoned,' Anna said, peering at him. 'By whom?'

(Perhaps it was a sensory memory—merely a chance echo, the kind that suddenly flooded one's body, and then vanished just as swiftly. He put it from his mind.)

'The possibility must have occurred to you,' he said, frowning.

'I suppose. I don't remember anything.'

'Anything at all?'

'Only sitting down with the pipe. Heating the pin. After that, nothing.'

'I believed you weren't a suicide—that you didn't mean harm. I believed that.'

'Oh well,' Anna said, 'but it does occur to one, now and again.'

'Of course—now and again,' Pritchard said, too quickly. He felt bested, and took a half step backward.

'I don't know a thing about poison,' she said.

'If I could examine the rest of the lump I could tell you whether or not the stuff had been cut with something else,' Pritchard said. 'That's why I came. I want to know if I can buy some of it back from you to take a look at. Ah Sook won't give me the time of day.'

She narrowed her eyes. 'You want to examine it—or swap it out?'

'What's that supposed to mean?'

'You might be covering your tracks.'

Pritchard flushed with indignation. 'What tracks?' She said nothing, so he said again, 'What tracks?'

'Ah Sook thinks *you* poisoned it,' Anna said at last, peering at him.

'Does he? Bloody roundabout way of doing it, if I wanted to see you dead.'

'What if you wanted to see *him* dead?'

'And lose his business?' Pritchard's voice became low. 'Look here: I don't claim a brotherly feeling or anything of that sort, but I've got no quarrel with Oriental folk. Do you hear? I've got no reason to wish any one of them harm. None at all.'

'His claim tent was slashed again. Last month. All his medicines got spoiled.'

'What—you think that was me?'

'No, I don't.'

'Then what's the story?' Pritchard said. 'Give it up, Ann. What?'

'He thinks you're running a racket.'

'Poisoning chinks?' Pritchard snorted.

'Yes,' Anna said. 'And it's not as stupid as all that, you know.'

'Is that right! Come around to his perspective, have you?'

'I didn't say that,' she said. 'It's not *me* who thinks—'

'*You* think me a cross old man,' Pritchard said. 'I know it. I am a cross old man, Anna. But I'm not a murderer.'

The whore's conviction disappeared as swiftly as it had come to animate her. She shrank back again, stepping sideways towards the window, and her hand moved to the tatted lace of her collar. She began to pluck at it. Prichard felt soothed. He recognised the gesture: not as her own, but as a motion that belonged to a girl, any girl.

'Well, anyway,' he said, trying to make amends. 'Anyway.'

'You're not so very old,' she said.

He wanted to touch her. 'And then this laudanum business—the Crosbie Wells debacle,' he said. 'My mind's been full of that.'

'What laudanum business?'

'Phial of laudanum, found underneath the hermit's bed. It's mine.'

'Corked or uncorked?'

'Corked. But only half full.'

She looked interested. 'Yours—does that mean belonging to you personal, or just bought from your place?'

'Bought,' said Pritchard. 'And not by Crosbie. I never sold that man a dram.'

Anna placed her hand against her cheek, thinking. 'That's strange.'

'Old Crosbie Wells,' said Pritchard, trying to be jolly. 'Nobody ever paid the man a scrap of thought when he was living—and now this.'

'Crosbie—' Anna began, but then all at once, she was crying.

Pritchard made no move to advance towards her, to open his arms, to offer comfort. He watched her fish in her sleeve for a handkerchief and waited, his hands locked behind his back. She was not crying for Crosbie Wells. She hadn't even known the man. She was crying for herself.

Of course, Pritchard thought, it must have been unpleasant, to have been tried for attempted suicide at the petty courts, and hounded by all manner of men, and discussed in the *Times* as a curiosity, and spoken about over breakfasts, and between rounds at billiards, as if one's soul were a common property, a cause. He watched as she blew her nose, fumbling with her thin fingers to tuck the handkerchief away. This was not exhaustion merely: this was a grief of a different kind. She seemed not so much harassed as halved.

'Never mind,' Anna said at last, when she had regained control. 'Never mind me.'

'If I could just take a look at a piece of it,' Pritchard said.

'What?'

'The resin. I'll buy it back from you. I'm not going to swap it out—you can give me just a piece, you know; you don't have to give up the whole lump.'

She shook her head, and in the sharpness of the movement Pritchard caught what was different about her. He strode forward, covering the space between them in three quick strides, and grabbed her sleeve.

'Where is it?' he said. 'Where's the tar?'

She pulled free of him. 'I ate it,' she said. 'I ate the last of it last night, if you must know.'

'You didn't—you couldn't have!'

Pritchard followed her, and turned her by the shoulders so she faced him. He placed the pad of his thumb on her chin and tilted her head back, to better see her eyes.

'You're lying,' he said. 'You're dry.'

'I ate it,' Anna repeated. She shook herself free.

'Did you give it back to Sook? Did he take it back?'

'I ate it. Same as ever.'

'Come off it, Ann. Don't be a liar.'

'I'm not a liar.'

'You ate a lump of poisoned tar and your eyes are clear as dawn?'

She narrowed her eyes. 'Who's to say it was poisoned?'

'Even if it wasn't—'

'You *know* that it was poisoned? You're *sure*?'

'I don't know a d—ned thing about this d—ned business, and I don't like your tone,' Pritchard snapped. 'I just want a piece of it back so I can look at it, for heaven's sake!'

She was roused again. 'And who poisoned it, Jo? Who tried to kill me? What's your guess?'

Pritchard waved his arm. 'Ah Sook, maybe.'

'Accuse the man who's accusing you?' She laughed. 'That's a guilty man's game!'

'I'm trying to help you!' Pritchard said furiously. 'I'm trying to *help*!'

'There's nothing to help!' Anna cried. 'No one to help! For the last time: there was no suicide, Joseph, and no—bloody—*poison!*'

'Then explain to me why you ended up half-dead in the middle of the Christchurch-road!'

'*I can't explain it!*'

For the first time that day Pritchard saw real emotion on her face: fear, fury.

'You took a pipe that night—same as usual?'

'And every day since I made bail.'

'Today?'

'No. I ate the last of it last night. I told you.'

'What time last night?'

'Late. Midnight, maybe.'

Pritchard wanted to spit. 'Don't call me a fool. I've seen you when you're under, and I've seen you coming up. Right now you're sober as a nun.'

Her face crumpled. 'If you don't believe me, go away.'

'I won't. I won't go.'

'D—n you, Jo Pritchard!'

'D—n *you.*'

She burst into tears again. Pritchard turned away. Where would she keep it? He strode to the armoire, opened it, and began rifling through the contents. Her empty dresses, hanging from the rail. Her petticoats. Her bloomers, most of them tattered and stained. Handkerchiefs, shawls, stays, stockings; her button boots. There was nothing. He moved to the dresser, where a spirit lamp sat upon a cracked china plate—this would be her opium lamp—and beside it, a wadded pair of gloves, a comb, a pincushion, an opened package of soap, sundry jars of cream and powder. These items he picked up and then replaced, roughly; he meant to turn the whole room over.

'What are you doing?' Anna said.

'You're hiding it—only you won't tell me why!'

'Those are my things.'

He laughed. 'Keepsakes, are they? Precious mementos? Antiques?'

He wrenched the drawer from her dresser, and upended it over the floor. A cascade of trinkets rattled out. Coins, wooden spools of thread, ribbons, covered buttons, a pair of dressmaker's shears. Three rolling champagne corks. A man's shaving brush—she must have stolen that from somewhere. Matches, stays. The ticket from her passage to New Zealand. Wads of cloth. A silver-backed looking glass. Pritchard raked the pile. There was Anna's pipe—and there ought to be a little box to match it, or perhaps a little pouch, inside of which her resin would be folded in a square of waxed paper, like toffee purchased from a store. He cursed.

'You're a beast,' Anna said. 'You're detestable.'

He ignored her, and picked up the pipe.

It was of Chinese making, fashioned from bamboo, and about as long as Pritchard's forearm. The bowl of the pipe sat some three inches away from its end; it protruded like a doorknob, and was fixed to the wood by means of a metal saddle. Pritchard weighed the thing in his hands, holding it as a flautist holds a flute. He sniffed it. There was a dark residue around the rim of the bowl— so someone had partaken of the pipe, and recently.

'Happy?' she said.

'Watch your lip. Where's the needle?'

'There.' She pointed at a square of cloth among the sorry detritus on the floor, through which was pushed a long hatpin, stained black at the tip. Pritchard sniffed this also. He then inserted the hatpin into the aperture of the bowl and rolled the tip about.

'You're going to break it.'

'Be doing you a favour, then.'

(Pritchard deplored Anna's craving for the drug—but why? He himself had taken opium many times. He had taken it in Kaniere, in fact, with Ah Sook, in the tiny hut that Sook had hung with Oriental fabrics, to still the air so that his precious lamps would not flicker in a draught.)

At last Pritchard tossed the pipe aside—but carelessly, so that the bowl struck the floorboards, and rang out.

'Beast,' Anna said again.

'I'm a beast, am I?'

He lunged for her, not really intending to hurt her, but merely to grab her by the shoulders and shake her, until she told him the truth. But he was clumsy, and she wrenched away, and for the third time that afternoon, Pritchard's nostrils were filled with the rich, briny smell of the ocean—and, impossibly, the metallic taste of *cold*—as if a wind had slapped him in the face, as if a sail had snapped above him, as if a storm was in the air. He faltered.

'Get back,' she said. She was holding her hands before her face, her fingers half-curled into fists. 'I mean it, Joseph. I won't be called a liar. Get back and get out.'

'I'll call you a liar if you d—ned well lie.'

'Get back.'

'Tell me where you've hidden it.'

'Get *back*!'

'Not until you tell me where it is!' he shouted. '*Tell* me, you use-less bloody whore!'

He lunged for her again, in desperation; he saw her eyes flash, and in the next moment she had reached into her breast and with-drawn a muff pistol, the single-loading kind. It was a slip of a piece, hardly longer than Pritchard's finger, but from a distance of two paces it could shatter his chest. Instinctively he put up his hands. The piece was facing backward, with the muzzle pointing up towards her chin, and Anna had to spin the piece to fit it into her hand—but she was frantic, and in that moment three things hap-pened at once. Pritchard stepped backwards, and stumbled on the edge of the rattan rug; behind him, the door burst open, and some-one gave a cry; and Anna half-turned at the noise, started forwards, and shot herself in the breast.

The report from the small gun was hollow, even unremarkable—like the cracking of a topsail far above a deck. It seemed an echo of itself, as if the real shot had fired somewhere much further away, and this noise was just a copy. Stupidly Pritchard wheeled about, turning his back on Anna, to confront the figure at the door. His mind felt full of fog; he registered, in some distant way, that the man who had just entered was Aubert Gascoigne, the new clerk at the Magistrate's Court. Pritchard did not know Gascoigne at all well. Some three weeks ago the clerk had come to his laboratory, seeking to fill a prescription for a bowel complaint—absurdly, Pritchard thought of that now. He wondered whether his tincture had helped the other man as he had promised it would.

For the briefest second, nobody moved ... or perhaps no time passed at all. Then Gascoigne roared an oath, started forward, and fell upon the body of the whore. He wrenched her head back and the pistol clattered to the side—but the white of her neck was unscarred—there was no blood—and she was breathing. Her hands flew to her throat.

'You fool—you fool!' Gascoigne shouted. There was a sob in his voice. He grabbed her tatted collar with both hands and ripped it open. 'Blank cartridge, was it? Wax pellet, was it? Thought you'd give us all another scare? What the devil do you think you're play-ing at?'

Anna's hand was moving over her breast, her fingers touching and tapping in confusion. Her eyes were wide.

Pritchard said, 'A blank?' He leaned down and picked up the pistol.

The barrel was hot, and the smell of gunpowder was in the air. But he could see no spent casing, and no hole anywhere. The wall behind Anna was plastered and smooth, just as it had been a second ago. The two men looked about—at the walls, at the floor, at Anna. The whore looked down at her breast. Pritchard held the pistol out, letting it dangle foolishly from his index finger, and Gascoigne took it up. Deftly he snapped open the barrel and peered into the breech. Then he turned on Anna.

'Who loaded this piece?' he demanded.

'I did it myself,' Anna said, bewildered. 'I can show you the spares.'

'Show me. Show me the spares.'

She clambered up, and went to the whatnot beside the bed; after a moment she returned with a tin box in which seven cartridges were rolling on a scrap of brown paper. Gascoigne touched them with his finger. Then he passed the pistol to the whore. 'Do it just as you did. The very same.' Anna nodded dumbly. She pivoted the barrel sideways and fitted a cartridge into the breech. She then snapped the barrel back correctly, cocked the piece, and handed the loaded pistol back to him. She looked terrified, Pritchard thought—dumbfounded, mechanical. Gascoigne took the pistol from her, stepped back several paces, levelled the piece, and fired at the headboard of her bed. The report sounded just as it had before—this time Pritchard heard a murmur of alarm from the floor below, and rapid footsteps—and they all looked to the spot where he had fired. A perfect hole, darkened slightly at its edges by the heat, pierced the centre of her pillow; a puff of feathered dust had risen up from the stuffing, and as they watched, floated down in a film of gauze. Gascoigne moved forward, and tossed the pillow aside. With his fingers he felt around the headboard of the bed, just as Anna had felt around her neck for injury, and after a moment he gave a grunt of satisfaction.

'It's there?' Pritchard said.

'Hardly made a scratch,' Gascoigne said, testing the depth of the hole with the end of his finger. 'Those muff pistols, they're not worth much.'

'But where—' Pritchard was at a loss. His tongue felt thick in his mouth.

'What happened to the first?' said Gascoigne, echoing him. They all stared at the second cartridge, the visible cartridge, misshapen in his hand. Then Gascoigne looked at Anna, and Anna at Gascoigne— and it seemed to Pritchard that a look of understanding passed between them.

What a wretched thing it was, to behold one's whore exchanging glances with another man! Pritchard wanted to despise her, but he could not: he felt dulled, even bewildered. There was a ringing in his ears.

Anna turned to him. 'Will you go downstairs?' she said. 'Tell Edgar I was playing with the gun, or cleaning it, and it went off by accident.'

'He isn't at the desk,' Pritchard said.

'Tell the valet, then. Just make it known. I don't want anybody coming up; I don't want any fuss. Please do it.'

'All right. I will,' Pritchard said. 'And then—'

'And then you should go.' Anna was firm.

'I want what I came for.' He spoke quietly, glancing sideways at Gascoigne—but the other man's eyes were discreetly lowered.

'I can't help you, Joseph. I don't have what you want. Please go.'

He looked into her eyes again. They were green, with a thick rind of darkness around the edge of the iris, and flecks of pebbled grey clustered around the pupil in rays. It had been months since he had seen the colour in her eyes, since he had seen her pupil as a point, a grain, and not as a blurred disc of blackness, dulled with sleep. She was sober—of this he had no doubt at all. So she was a liar, and maybe even a thief; so she was deceiving him. And her appointment, the man Gascoigne. There was another secret. Another lie. Going with a lady, to look at hats—!

But Pritchard found that he could not renew his anger. He felt ashamed. He felt as though it had been *he* who had intruded, as though it had been *he* who had disturbed an intimate scene in the whore's own chambers, between Anna and Gascoigne. The shame Pritchard felt was of a very crude and childish sort: it came upon him as a rush of bitter feeling, swelling in his throat.

At last he turned on his heel and made to leave. In the doorway he reached back for the handle, to pull the door shut behind him—but he did it slowly, and watched them through the narrowing crack.

Gascoigne began moving just before the door was quite closed. He spun towards Anna and opened his arms for an embrace, and Anna fell into him, her pale cheek rising to fit into the curve of his neck. Gascoigne wrapped his arms strongly about her waist, and Anna's body went limp; he lifted her, so that her toes trailed on the floor; she was clasped against him; he lowered his head and pressed his cheek against her hair. His jaw was clenched; his eyes were open; he breathed fiercely through his nose. Pritchard, with his eye at the door, was overcome with loneliness. He felt that he had never loved, and that no soul had ever loved him. He shut the door as softly as he could, and padded down the stairs.

Φ

'May I interject to ask a question?'

'Yes, of course.'

'Can you show me exactly how Miss Wetherell was holding the pistol?'

'Certainly. Like this—with the heel of her hand right here. I was standing at an angle to her, about where Mr. Mannering is sitting now, in relation to me, and her body was half-turned, like this.'

'And if the gun had fired as expected, what kind of injury would Miss Wetherell likely have sustained?'

'If she was lucky, a flesh wound in the shoulder. If she was unlucky—well, perhaps a little lower. Her heart, maybe. The left side ... The truly curious thing, of course, is even if the cartridge *was* a blank, she still should have been impacted by the empty casing, or burnt by the powder, or seared at the very least. We couldn't make heads or tails of it.'

'Thank you. I'm sorry to interrupt.'

'Is there something you can share with us, Mr. Moody?'

'Presently I will—when I have heard the rest of the story.'

'I must say, sir—you're looking awfully queer.'

'I'm quite well. Please continue.'

Φ

It was still early in the afternoon when Pritchard returned to his drug hall on Collingwood-street, but he felt that it ought to be much later—that night ought to be falling, to make sense of the exhaustion that he felt. He entered by way of the shop, and spent a foolish moment straightening the razor-strops with the corners of the shelves, and tidying the bottles so that they stood shoulder-to-shoulder against the lip of the display cabinet—but suddenly he could not bear himself. He set a card in the shop window informing callers to return on Monday, locked the door, and retired to his laboratory.

There were several orders set out upon his desk, to be made up, but he gazed down at the forms almost without seeing them. He took off his jacket and hung it on the hook beside the range. He tied his apron about his waist by habit. Then he stood and gazed at nothing.

Mary Menzies's words had fixed him—they were his prophecy, his curse. 'You have never been at peace with good'—he remembered them; he wrote them down; and by doing so he made sure her words came true. He became the man whom she rejected *because* she rejected him, *because* she left. And now he was thirty-eight, and he had never been in love, and other men had mistresses, and other men had wives. With his long finger Pritchard touched the shaft of a prescription bottle on the desk before him. She was nineteen. She was Mary Menzies in his mind.

A phrase of his father's returned to him: you give a dog a bad name, and that dog is bad for life. ('Remember that, Joseph,'—with one hand on Pritchard's shoulder, and the other clasping a new-born puppy against his chest; the next day, Pritchard dubbed the young thing Cromwell, and his father nodded once.) Recalling the words, Pritchard thought: *is that what I have done, to my own self, to my own fate? Am I the dog in my father's maxim, badly named?* But it was not a question.

He sat down and placed his hands, palm downward, on the laboratory bench. His thoughts drifted back to Anna. By her own account, she had not intended to commit suicide at all—a claim that Pritchard believed was an honest one. Anna's life was miserable, but she had her pleasures, and she was not a violent type. Pritchard felt that he knew her. He could not imagine that she would try to take her life. And yet—what had she said? It does occur to one, now and again. *Yes*, Pritchard thought heavily. *Now and again, it does.*

Anna was a seasoned opium eater. She took the drug nearly every day, and was well accustomed to its effects upon her body and her mind. Pritchard had never known her to lose consciousness so completely that she could not be revived for over twelve hours. He doubted that such a circumstance could have come about by accident. Well, if she truly had *not* intended to end her life—as she attested—then that left only two options: either she had been drugged by somebody else, used for some nefarious purpose, and then abandoned in the Christchurch-road, or (Pritchard gave a slow nod) she was bluffing. Yes. She had lied about the resin; she could easily be lying about the overdose, too. But for what purpose? Whom was she protecting? And to what end?

The Hokitika physician had confirmed that Anna had indeed partaken of a great deal of opium on the night of the 14th of January: his testament to this effect had been published in the *West Coast Times* on the day after Anna's trial. Could Anna have managed to fool the physician, or to persuade him somehow to give a false diagnosis? Pritchard considered this. She had been in the gaol-house for over twelve hours, over which time she would have been prodded and poked by all manner of men, and witnessed by dozens of others, besides. She could hardly have fooled them all. True unconsciousness cannot be faked, Pritchard thought. Even a whore was not as good an actress as that.

All right: perhaps the drug had been poisoned after all. Pritchard turned his hands over, and studied the whorls on the pads of his fingers, each hand the mirror image of the other. When he pressed his fingertips together, they made a perfect doubled reflection, as when a man touches his forehead to a glass. He leaned forward to look at the whorls. He himself had certainly not altered the drug in any way, and he did not really suspect the Chinese man, Sook, of having done so either. Sook was fond of Anna. No, it was impossible that Sook might have sought to cause Anna harm. Well, that meant the drug must have been poisoned either *before* Pritchard bought it wholesale, or *after* Anna purchased her smaller portion from Ah Sook, to imbibe at home.

Pritchard's source for opiates of all kinds was a man named Francis Carver. He considered Carver now. The man was a former convict, and had a poor reputation as a consequence; to Pritchard, however, he had always been courteous and fair, and Pritchard had no reason to think that Carver might wish him—or his business— any kind of active harm. As to whether Carver bore ill-will towards the Chinese, Pritchard had no idea—but he did not sell direct to the Chinese. He sold to Pritchard, and Pritchard alone.

Pritchard had first met Carver at a gambling house on Revell-street, some seven months ago. Pritchard was a keen gambler, and had been refreshing himself between games of craps, tallying his losses in his mind, when a scar-faced man sat down beside him. Pritchard inquired, as a pleasantry, whether the man was fond of cards, and what had brought him to Hokitika; soon they fell to talking. When in due course Pritchard named his own profession, Carver's expression sharpened. Putting down his drink, he explained that he had a long-standing connexion with a former East Indiaman who controlled an opium poppy plantation in Bengal. If Pritchard was in need of opium, Carver could guarantee a product of unrivalled quality and limitless supply. At that time Pritchard had no stock of opium at all, save for some weak tinctures of laudanum he had purchased from a quack; without hesitation, therefore, he thanked Carver, shook his hand, and agreed to return the following morning to draw up the terms of their trade.

Since then Carver had supplied him with a total of three pounds of opium. He would not supply Pritchard with more than one pound at a time, for the reason (as he very frankly explained) that he liked to keep a very tight hold on his own supply, in order to prevent Pritchard from selling the drug wholesale to other sellers, and making an intermediary profit that way. (In selling opium to Ah Sook, Pritchard was of course doing exactly this—but Carver remained unaware of this auxiliary arrangement, for he was seldom in Hokitika, and Pritchard had not troubled himself to confess it.) The resin came wrapped in paper, pressed into a tin box not unlike a caddy for storing tea.

Pritchard picked up a clout from the laboratory bench and began to clean the dirt from beneath his fingernails—noticing, as he did so, that they were getting rather long.

Would Carver really have dared to poison the drug before he sold it wholesale to a drug emporium? Pritchard might have powdered the resin and turned it into laudanum; he might have sold it piecemeal to any number of clients; he might have used the drug himself. It was true that Carver had an unpleasant history with Anna; he had harmed her badly once before. But even if he wished to kill her by overdose, there was no guarantee that a portion of the poisoned opium would end up in Anna's hands. Pritchard rolled a ball of dirt between his fingers. No: it was absurd to think that any man would devise a plot that comprised so many uncertainties. Carver might be a brute, but he was not a fool.

Having rejected that theory, the chemist now considered the second option: that the drug had been poisoned *after* Anna Wetherell was given a piece of it by Ah Sook to take at home. Perhaps someone had stolen into her rooms at the Gridiron, and poisoned it there. But again—why? Why bother to poison the opium at all? Why not kill the whore by more conventional means—by strangulation, or smothering, or battery?

Defeated, Pritchard turned his mind instead to the things he knew by instinct to be true. He *knew* that Anna Wetherell had not told the whole truth about the events of the 14th of January. He *knew* that someone had partaken of the drug recently from the pipe she had hidden in her room. He *knew* that she had ceased to take opium herself; by her eyes and her motions, he could not doubt that she was as dry as a bone. These certainties, in Pritchard's eyes, could only point to one conclusion.

'Hang it all,' he whispered. 'She's lying—and on another man's behalf.'

So the afternoon wore on.

In time Pritchard picked up his unfinished orders, and, for want of a more diverting occupation, began to work. He was not aware of the passing of the hours until a gentle knock at the laboratory door returned him to the present. He turned—noting, with a dim surprise, that the light had become very thin, and dusk was approaching—and saw Albert, Nilssen's junior clerk, hovering in the doorway with his breath caught in his chest and an abashed look upon his face. He was carrying a note.

'Oh—something from Nilssen,' Pritchard said, coming forward. He had quite forgotten his conversation with Nilssen earlier that afternoon, and the request he had made of him—to find the goldsmith Quee, and to question him regarding the retorted gold that had been discovered on Crosbie Wells's estate. He had forgotten about Crosbie Wells entirely—and his fortune, and his widow, and the vanished Mr. Staines. How silently the world revolved, when one was brooding, and alone.

Pritchard was fishing in his apron for a sixpence—but Albert, blushing furiously, stammered, 'No, sir—' and held up his palms, to show that the honour of having made the delivery was quite sufficient to sustain him.

In fact Albert was sure he had never had so exciting an afternoon in all his life. His employer, upon returning from Kaniere Chinatown some half hour previous, had been in such a state of agitation that he had almost torn the door from its hinges. He had penned the note that Albert was carrying now with all the passion of a symphonic composer in collusion with his muse. He had sealed it badly, dropped wax upon himself, cursed, and then thrust the folded, lumpy sheet at Albert, saying hoarsely, 'Pritchard—to Pritchard—quick as you can.' In the privacy of the chemist's receiving room, just before he entered the laboratory, Albert had pinched the edges of the letter together to make the folded paper form a kind of tube, and by squinting down its length he had made out several words that seemed to him to smack of the gravest piracy. It thrilled him that his employer was up to no good.

'Very well, then—thanks,' Pritchard said, taking the letter. 'Did he say a reply was needed?'

The boy said, 'There's not to be a reply, sir. But he said to stay and watch you burn it, after you'd read it through.'

Pritchard gave a snort of laughter. This was so like Nilssen: first he sulked, and then he complained of the messiness of it all, and then he dallied, and then he tried to remove all the burden of responsibility from himself—but as soon as he became a participant, as soon as he felt crucial, and impressive, then everything became a pantomime, a cloak-and-dagger show; he gloried in it.

Pritchard walked away a few paces (the boy looked disappointed), tore the seal with his fingers, and flattened the paper upon his laboratory desk. The letter read:

Jo—

> *Called on Quee, as per your request. You were right about the gold— his work—though he swears he has no notion how the stuff ended up with Wells. The whore's mixed up in it all—perhaps you knew that*

already—though we can't quite get to the bottom of it—the author, to use your phrase. Seems every man is implicated as we are—peripherally. Too much to set down here. I proposed a council. Orientals too. We meet in the back room of the CROWN, at SUNSET. Will ensure our council not disturbed. Tell no one—not even if you trust them & they are connected & may one day stand beside us as Accused. Be so good as to destroy this—

    H. N.

MOON IN TAURUS, WAXING

In which Charlie Frost forms a hunch; Dick Mannering buckles on his holsters; and we venture upriver to the Kaniere claims.

Thomas Balfour's inquiry at the Reserve Bank of New Zealand that morning had piqued the banker's curiosity on several fronts, and as soon as the former had left the building, Mr. Frost immediately resolved to do some inquiring of his own. He was still holding in his hand the shares profile of the Aurora goldmine, owned and operated by the vanished prospector, Emery Staines. *Aurora*, Frost thought, tapping the document with his lean finger. *Aurora*. He knew that he had seen that name recently—but where? After a moment he laid the document aside, clambered down from his stool, and padded to the cabinet opposite his cubicle, where a row of leather spines were marked with the words 'Returns by Quarter'. He selected the third and fourth quarters of the previous year, and returned to his desk to examine the goldmine's records.

Charlie Frost was a man of scant reputation, for such a thing is only ever claimed, and Frost was a quiet soul, modest in his dress, mild in his features, and disinclined, whatever the provocation, to disturb the peace. When he spoke, it was slowly and with care. He rarely laughed openly, and although his posture was languid and easy, he always seemed alert, as if perpetually mindful of some rule of etiquette that other men no longer observed. He did not like to declare his preferences or to hold forth in speech; in fact he was reluctant, when in conversation, to assert an agenda of any kind. This was not at all to say that Frost lacked agenda, or that his preferences were few; in fact, the many rituals of his private life were regulated in the extreme, and his ambitions were tremendously particular. Rather, Frost had learned the value of appearing to be unassuming. He knew the latent power of obscurity (powerful, because it aroused curiosity in others) and he was capable of great strategy in wielding it—but he took extreme care to keep this talent hidden. The impression that strangers invariably formed, upon first meeting him, was that he was a man of reaction rather than of action, who was managed in business, seduced in love, and steadfastly docile in all his pleasures.

Frost was but four-and-twenty years of age, and New Zealand-born. His father had been a high-level official in the now defunct New Zealand Company, who, upon disembarking at the mouth of the Hutt River and finding a wealth of flat land to be divided and sold, had promptly sent home for a wife. Frost was not proud of the fact of his birth, for it was a rare citizenship for a white man to hold, and he felt that it was shaming. He told no stories about his childhood, spent in the marshy flat of the Hutt Valley, reading and re-reading his father's thumbed copy of *Paradise Lost*, the only book besides the Bible that the family possessed. (By the age of eight, Frost could recite every speech of God's, the Son's, and Adam's—but never Satan's, whom he found pugnacious, and never Eve's, whom he thought feeble, and a bore.) It was not an unhappy childhood, but Frost was unhappy when he recalled it. When he spoke about England, it was as though he missed that place very dearly, and could not wait to return.

With the dissolution of the New Zealand Company, Mr. Frost senior was all but bankrupted, and cast into disrepute. He turned to his only son for aid. Charlie Frost secured scribal work in Wellington, and soon was offered a place at a bank in the Lambton quarter, a position that earned him enough to keep his parents in health and relative comfort. When gold was discovered in Otago, Frost transferred to a bank at Lawrence, promising to send the larger portion of his wages home, each month, by private mail—

a promise he had never broken. He had not once returned home to the Hutt Valley, however, and did not plan to. Charlie Frost tended to conceive of all his relationships in terms of profit and return, and he did not spare a thought for others once he considered that his duty had been served. Now, in Hokitika (for he had followed the rush from Lawrence to the Coast), he did not think at all about his parents, except when he was writing to them each month. This was a difficult task, for his father's letters were abrupt and mortified, and his mother's, full of a dismayed silence—sentiments that grieved Charlie Frost, but only briefly. After his replies had been written and dispatched, he shredded their letters into spills for lighting his cigars, cutting the pages lengthwise so as to occlude their import absolutely; the spills he burned, with great indifference.

Frost thumbed through the returns folder until he found the section that pertained to Kaniere and the Hokitika gorge. The records were listed alphabetically, with the Aurora as the second, beneath a claim that had been named, rather optimistically for the West Coast, the All Seasons. Frost leaned in close to the page to read the figures, and in the next moment, he gave a murmur of surprise.

In the month following its initial purchase, the Aurora claim had performed splendidly, pulling in almost a hundred pounds; come August, however, the claim's profits had dropped off radically, until—Frost raised his eyebrows—virtually coming to a halt. The sum total of the Aurora's profits over the last quarter was only twelve pounds. One pound weekly! That was very odd, for a mine of Aurora's depth and promise. One pound weekly—why, that would be barely enough to cover the overheads, Frost thought. He bent closer over the book. The record showed that the Aurora was worked by one man only. The name was a Chinese one, so the labour would be cheap ... but even so, Frost thought, the digger would still have to be paid a daily wage.

Charlie Frost was frowning. According to the shares profile, Emery Staines had first taken over the Aurora goldmine in the late autumn of the previous year. It appeared that, some weeks after this purchase, Staines had sold fifty-percent shares to the notorious

Francis Carver; however, immediately following *that* transaction—
as this record showed—the claim had run suddenly dry. Either
Aurora had become, all of a sudden, a duffer claim—worth virtually nothing—or someone was doing a very good job of making it
seem that way. Frost shut the folder and stood for a moment, thinking. His gaze wandered over the crowd: the diggers in their slouch
hats, the investors, the escort in their braided epaulettes. Suddenly
he remembered where he had seen that name before.

He put up a card in his cubicle to indicate that the window was
closed.

'You off for the day?' a colleague asked.

'I suppose I could be,' said Frost, blinking. 'I hadn't thought that
I might; I had intended to return after my lunch hour.'

'We'll be closed by two, and there's no more buying today, once
this lot is done,' the other banker said. He stretched his back, and
slapped his belly with both hands. 'May as well see you Monday,
Charlie.'

'Well!' Frost murmured, gazing into the crown of his hat, as
though suddenly perplexed to see it in his hand. 'That's very kind
of you. Thank you very much.'

Φ

Dick Mannering was alone in his office when Frost knocked upon
the door. At his knock, Mannering's collie-dog burst from beneath
the desk in an explosion of joyful energy; she leaped upon Frost,
her tail thumping the floor, her red mouth open.

'Charlie Frost! *You're* a man I didn't expect to see,' Mannering
exclaimed, pushing his chair back from the desk. 'Come in, come
in—and close the door. I have the feeling that whatever it is you're
about to tell me, it's not for everyone to hear.'

'Down, girl,' said Frost to the dog, gripping her muzzle, looking
into her eyes, mussing her ears—and, satisfied, she dropped back
onto all fours, and trotted back to her master, where she turned,
sank down, put her nose upon her paws, and watched Frost from
beneath her brows, sorrowfully.

He closed the door as he was bid. 'How are you, Dick?'

'How am I?' Mannering spread his hands. 'I'm curious, Charlie. Do you know that? I'm a very curious man, these days. About a whole raft of things. You know Staines hasn't shown up—not any-where. We even tried Holly in the gorge, though she's not much of a bloodhound. Gave her a handkerchief to sniff at, and off she went—but then back again, with nothing. Yes, I'm a very curious man. I do hope you've brought a bit of news—or a bit of scandal, if news cannot be had. My word—what a fortnight it's been! Take off your coat—yes—oh, don't worry about the rain. It's only water—and heaven knows we ought to be used to the stuff by now.'

Despite this encouragement Frost was careful to hang up his coat so that it did not touch Mannering's, and to ensure that it would not drip upon Mannering's overshoes, which were laid out beneath the coat-rack, each fitted with a shoe tree, and shined a handsome black. Then he plucked off his hat, somewhat gingerly.

'It's a pig of a day,' he said.

'Sit down, sit down,' said Mannering. 'You'll have a brandy?'

'I will, if you will,' said Frost, this being his policy in all expres-sions of appetite and thirst. He sat down, placing the palms of his hands upon his knees, and looked about him.

Mannering's office was located above the foyer of the Prince of Wales Opera House, and boasted a handsome view out over the theatre's striped awning to Revell-street, and beyond it to the open ocean, visible between the fronts of the facing houses as a band of bluish-grey, occasionally of green, and today, through the rain, as a whitish yellow—the water having taken on the colour of the sky.

The room had been designed as a testament to the wealth of its owner; for Mannering, in addition to managing the opera house, received income as a whoremonger, a card sharp, a shareholder, and a goldfields magnate. In all these professions he possessed a wonderful knack for profit, most especially the kind that can be made off the back of the trespasses of other men: this the room's furnishings made abundantly clear. The walls of his office were papered, and the cabinets oiled; there was a thick Turkish rug upon the floor; a ceramic bust, fashioned in the Roman style, served as a scowling bookend; under the window a specimen box displayed three black butterflies, each the size of a child's outspread hand. Behind Mannering's desk hung a sublime watercolour landscape, framed in gold: it showed a high cliff, slanting beams of sunlight, silhouetted foliage of a purplish hue, and, in the hazy distance, the pale wash of a rainbow, curving out of a cloud. Charlie Frost thought it a very fine piece of art, and one that commended Mannering's taste most favourably. He was always pleased when he thought up a reason to pay a call upon the older man, so that he might sit in this very chair, and gaze up at it, and imagine that he was somewhere very grand and far away.

'Yes: what a fortnight it's been,' Mannering was saying. 'And now my best whore has gone off and declared herself in mourning! Bloody pain in the neck, I'm telling you. Beginning to think she might be cracked. That's a blow. When it's your best whore. That's a blow. You know she was there with Emery, the night he disappeared.'

'Miss Wetherell—and Mr. Staines?' Frost had curled his hands around the scrolled arms of his chair, and was tracing the groove of the carving with the tips of his fingers.

Beauty, for Charlie Frost, was more or less synonymous with refinement. The ideal woman, in his mind, was one devoted to the project of her own enhancement, who was accomplished in the female arts of embroidery, piano-playing, pressing leaves, and the like; who sang sweetly, read quietly, and demurred to all opinion; who was a charming and priceless collectible; who loved, above all things, to be loved. Anna Wetherell had none of these qualities, but to admit that Anna did not at all resemble the fantastic shape of Frost's phantasmic ideal is not at all to say that the banker did not care for her, or that he did not take his satisfaction like the rest. Imagining Anna and Staines together now, he felt a twinge of discomfort—almost of distaste.

'Oh, yes,' said Mannering, plucking the crystal plug from the neck of the decanter, and swirling the liquid about. 'He bought her for the whole night, and b—er the constable, or whoever might come knocking! At his own house, too! No slag hotels for him! He was most particular: it had to be her, he said, not Kate, not Lizzie;

it had to be Anna. And then the next morning she's half dead and he's nowhere to be found. It's done my head in, Charlie. Of course *she's* no help. *She* says she can't remember a d—n thing before the moment she woke up in gaol—and by the stupid look on her face I'm inclined to believe her. She's my best whore, Charlie—but devil take that drug of hers; devil take it for his own. You'll have a cigar?'

Frost accepted a cigar from the box, and Mannering bent to hold a paper spill to the coals—but the spill was too short, and flared too quickly, and Mannering burned his fingers. He dropped the paper into the grate with an oath. He was obliged to fashion another spill out of a twist of blotting paper, and it was several moments before both their cigars were lit.

'But that's not to say a word of the troubles *you've* been going through,' Mannering added, as he sat down.

Frost looked pained. 'My troubles—as you call them—are under control,' he said.

'I should say they are *not*,' said Mannering. 'What with the widow arriving Thursday—and now the whole town's talking! I'll tell you what it looks like from where I'm standing. It looks an awful lot like you *knew* that gold was planted in the hermit's cottage, and once he died, you made d—ned sure the sale went through just as fast as could be.'

'That's not the truth of it,' said the banker.

'It looks like you're in it together, Charlie,' Mannering went on. 'You and Clinch: you look like partners, to the hilt. They'll bring in a judge, you know. They'll send someone from the High Court. This kind of thing doesn't just blow over. We'll all be drawn into it—where we were on the night of the fourteenth of January, all of that. We'd better get our stories straight before that happens. I'm not accusing you. I'm describing it from where I stand.'

There was often a touch of the sovereign address about Mannering's speech, for his self-perception was an unshakeable one, authoritarian and absolute. He could not view the world but from the perspective of commanding it, and he loved to declaim. In this he was the radical opposite of his guest—a difference that, in Mannering's case, caused him some irritation, for although he preferred deferential company, he was made peevish by those whom he considered unworthy of his attention. He was very generous to Charlie Frost, always sharing liquor and cigars with the young man, and gifting him gallery tickets to all the latest entertainment, but occasionally he found Frost's quiet reserve grating. Mannering tended to cast his followers into roles, labelling them as one labels a man by his profession, terming him 'the doctor' or 'the corporal'; his labels, internally made and never voiced aloud, described other men purely by way of their relation to him—which was how he saw everyone whom he encountered: as reflections of, or detractions from, his own authentic self.

Mannering, as has been already observed, was a very fat man. In his twenties he had been stout, and in his thirties, quite potbellied; by the time he reached his forties, his torso had acquired an almost spherical proportion, and he was obliged, to his private dismay, to request assistance in both mounting and dismounting his horse. Rather than admit that his girth had become an impediment to daily activity, Mannering blamed gout, a condition with which he had never been afflicted, but one that he felt had a soundly aristocratic ring. He very much liked to be mistaken for an aristocrat, an assumption that happened very often, for he had mutton-chop whiskers and a fair complexion, and he favoured expensive dress. That day his necktie was fastened with a gold stickpin, and his vest (the buttons of which were rather palpably strained) sported notched lapels.

'We're not in anything together,' said Frost. 'I'm sure I don't know what you mean.'

Mannering shook his head. 'I can see you're in a bind, Charlie— I can see it! You and Clinch both. If it comes to trial—it may come to trial, you know—then you'll have to explain why the sale of the cottage was put through so quickly. That will be the crucial point— the point on which you'll have to agree. I'm not suggesting perjury. I'm just saying your stories will have to square. What are you after—help? Do you need an alibi?'

'An alibi?' said Frost. 'Whatever for?'

'Come,' said Mannering, with a paternal wag of his finger.

'Don't tell me you weren't up to *something*. Just look at how fast the sale went through!'

Frost sipped at his brandy. 'We ought not to discuss it in such a casual manner. Not when there are other men involved.'

(This was another of his policies: always to appear reluctant to divulge.)

'Hang other men,' Mannering exclaimed. 'Hang "ought" and "ought not"! What's the story? Give it up!'

'I'll tell you; but there was nothing criminal about it,' Frost said—not without enjoyment, for he rather liked declaring that he was not at all to blame. 'The transaction was perfectly legal, and perfectly sound.'

'How do you explain it, then?'

'Explain what?'

'How it all *happened*!'

'It's perfectly explicable,' Frost said calmly. 'When Crosbie Wells died, Ben Löwenthal heard about it nearly straight away, because he went over to interview that political chap the very instant he got into town—so as to run a special in the paper the next morning. And the political chap—Lauderback's his name; Alistair Lauderback—well, *he* had just come from Wells's cottage; *he* was the one to find the fellow dead. Naturally he told Löwenthal all about it.'

'Crafty Jew,' said Mannering, with some relish. 'Always in the right place at the right time, aren't they?'

'I suppose,' Frost replied—for he did not wish to register an opinion one way or another. 'But as I was saying: Löwenthal found out about Wells's death before anybody. Before the coroner even arrived at the cottage.'

'But *he* didn't think to buy it up,' said Mannering. 'The land.'

'No; but he knew that Clinch was on the lookout to make an investment, and so he did him a good turn, and let him in on the news—that the Wells estate would soon be up for sale, I mean. Clinch came to me the next morning with his deposit, ready to buy. And that's all there is to it.'

'Oh no it isn't,' said Mannering.

'I assure you it is,' said Frost.

'I can read between the lines, Charlie,' said Mannering. '"Did him a good turn"? From the goodness of his charitable heart, eh? Not him—not Löwenthal! That's a tip-off, and it's a tip-off about a great bloody pile. They're in on it together—Löwenthal and Clinch. I'll bet my hat.'

'If they are,' said Frost, shrugging, 'I'm sure that I don't know about it. All that I'm telling you is that the sale of the cottage was perfectly legal.'

'Legal, the banker tells me! But you still haven't answered my question. Why did it have to happen so bloody *quickly*?'

Frost was unruffled. 'Simply because there was no paperwork in the way. Crosbie Wells had nothing: no debt, no insurance, nothing to resolve. No papers.'

'No papers?'

'Not in his cottage. Not a birth certificate, not a ticket, not a licence. Nothing.'

Mannering rolled his cigar in his fingers. 'No papers,' he said again. 'What do you make of that?'

'I don't know. Perhaps he lost them.'

'How do you lose your papers, though?'

'I don't know,' Frost said again. He did not like to be pressed to share his views.

'Perhaps someone burned them. Got rid of them.'

Frost frowned slightly. 'Who?'

'That political fellow,' said Mannering. 'Lauderback. He was the first upon the scene. Maybe *he's* mixed up in this business somehow. Maybe he told Löwenthal about the fortune hidden in the cottage. Maybe he saw the fortune—and told Löwenthal about it—and then Löwenthal told Clinch! But that's foolish,' he added, rebutting his own hypothesis. 'There's nothing in that for him, is there? And nothing for the Jew. Unless everyone's getting a cut, somewhere along the line . . .'

'Nobody got a cut,' said Frost. 'The fortune's being held in escrow at the bank. Nobody can touch it. At least not until the business with the widow gets straightened out.'

'Oh yes—the *widow*,' said Mannering, with relish. 'There's a

turn of events for you! What do you make of *her*? She's an acquaintance of mine, you know—an acquaintance. Greenway, that's her
maiden name. I never knew her as Mrs. Wells—the mistress
Greenway, she was to me. How do you like her, Charlie?'

Frost shrugged. 'She's got paperwork on her side,' he said. 'If the
marriage certificate turns out to be legal then the sale will be
revoked, and the fortune will be hers. That's in the hands of the
bureaucrats now.'

'But how do you like her, I said?'

Frost looked annoyed. 'She cuts a fine figure,' he said. 'I think
her very handsome.' He stuck his cigar in the side of his mouth,
and bit down upon it, lending to his expression the shadow of a
wince.

'She's handsome all right,' said Mannering happily. 'Oh, she's
handsome all right! Plays a man like a pianoforte, and what a
repertoire—indeed! I suppose that's what happened to poor old
Crosbie Wells: he got played, like all the rest of them.'

'I cannot make sense of their union at all,' Frost admitted. 'What
could an old man like Crosbie Wells have to offer—well, even a
plain woman, let alone a handsome one? I cannot make sense of
her attraction; though of course I can well imagine his.'

'You are forgetting his fortune,' Mannering said, wagging his
finger. 'The strongest aphrodisiac of all! Surely she married old
Crosbie for his money. And then he hoarded it up, and she had
nothing to do but wait for him to die. What else could explain it?
When she popped up so soon after his death—like she'd been planning it, you know. Oh, Lydia Wells is a canny soul! She keeps her
eyes on the pennies and her fingers on the pounds. She wouldn't
sign her name except to profit.'

Frost did not respond at once, for Mannering's response had
cued him to remember the reason for his visit, and he wished to
collect his thoughts before he announced his business; after a
moment, however, Mannering gave a bark of laughter, and
thumped his fist upon the desk.

'*There* it is!' he exclaimed, with much delight. 'I knew it! I knew
you were in a fix one way or another—and I knew I'd smoke you

out! What is it, then? What's your crime? What's the rub? You've given it away, Charlie; it's written all over you. It's something to do with that fortune, isn't it? Something about Crosbie Wells.'

Frost sipped his brandy. He had committed no crime, exactly—and yet there *was* a rub, and it *did* have to do with the fortune, and it *did* concern Crosbie Wells. His gaze slid over Mannering's shoulder to the window, and he paused a moment, in contemplation of the view, deciding how best to phrase the matter.

After the fortune discovered in Wells's cottage had been valued by the bank, Edgar Clinch had made Frost a very fine present, to acknowledge his role in facilitating the sale: a banknote made out to the sum of thirty pounds. The receipt of this banknote had a sudden and intoxicating effect upon Charlie Frost, whose income was devoted, in the main, to the upkeep of parents he never saw, and did not love. In a frenzy of excitement, unprecedented in his worldly experience, Frost determined to spend the entire sum of money, and at once. He would not inform his parents of the windfall, and he would spend every last penny on himself. He changed the note into thirty shining sovereigns, and with these he purchased a silk vest, a case of whisky, a set of leather-bound histories, a ruby lapel-pin, a box of fine imported candies, and a set of monogrammed handkerchiefs, his initials picked out against a rose.

Lydia Wells had arrived in Hokitika some days after this prodigal fit. Immediately upon her arrival she visited the Reserve Bank, announcing her intentions to revoke the sale of her late husband's cottage and effects. If this revocation proved successful, Frost would be obliged, he knew, to recover those thirty pounds in turn. He could not sell the vest back again, except as worn goods; the books and the lapel-pin he could pawn, but only at a fraction of their worth; he had opened the case of whisky; the candies were gone; and what fool would want to buy a handkerchief embroidered with another man's name? All in all he would be lucky to recover even half of the amount that he had spent. He would be forced to go to one of Hokitika's many usurers, and beg for credit; he would bear his debt for months, perhaps even for years; and worst of all, he would even have to confess the whole affair to his parents. The prospect made him sick.

But he had not come to Mannering to confess his humiliations. 'I am not in a fix,' he replied curtly, turning his gaze back to his host, 'but it is my guess that someone else very well might be. You see: I do not believe that fortune belonged to Crosbie Wells at all. I believe that it was stolen.' He leaned over to tap the ash of his cigar, and saw that the end had gone out.

'Well—from whom?' Mannering demanded.

'That is precisely what I wish to speak with you about,' the young banker said. There were lucifers in his vest pocket; he transferred his cigar to his right hand, to retrieve them. 'I had a notion just now, this afternoon, and I wanted to run it by you. It's about Emery Staines.'

'Oh—no doubt *he's* wrapped up in it all,' Mannering said, throwing himself back into his chair. (Frost set about lighting his cigar a second time.) 'Disappearing that very same day! No doubt he's connected. I don't hold out much hope for our friend Emery, I'm telling you that. We have a saying on the fields: it's unlucky to be lucky for long. Have you heard that one? Well, Emery Staines was the luckiest man I'm ever likely to know. He went from rags to riches, that boy, and all without a helping hand from any quarter. I'm wagering that he was murdered, Charlie. Murdered in the river—or on the beach—and his body washed away. No man likes to see a boy make his fortune. Not before he's thirty. And especially not when that fortune's clean. I'm wagering whoever killed him was twenty years his senior, on the inside. At least twenty years. How about that for a bet?'

'Forgive me,' Frost said, and shook his head very slightly.

'Oh yes,' Mannering said, disappointed. 'You don't place your money, do you? You're one of those sensible types. Never toss a coin except to lay it in your purse.'

Frost did not reply to this, having been put in mind, uncomfortably, of the thirty pounds he had recently squandered in such a profligate way; after a moment Mannering cried, 'But don't leave me waiting!'—feeling embarrassed, for his last remark had come out rather more as an insult than he had intended it to seem. 'Give it up! What's your notion?'

Charlie Frost explained what he had discovered that morning: that Frank Carver owned a half-share in the Aurora goldmine, and that he and Emery Staines were, to all intents and purposes, partners.

'Yes—I suppose I knew something about that,' Mannering said, vaguely. 'That's a long story, though, and Staines's own business. Why do you mention it?'

'Because the Aurora claim is connected to the Crosbie Wells debacle.'

Mannering frowned. 'How so?'

'I'll tell you.'

'Do.'

Frost puffed on his cigar a moment. 'The Wells fortune came through the bank,' he said at last. 'Came through me.'

'Yes?'

Dick Mannering could not bear to let another man hold the stage for long, and tended to interrupt frequently, most often to encourage his interlocutor to reach his own conclusion as quickly and concisely as he could.

Frost, however, was not to be hurried. 'Well,' he said, 'here's the curious thing. The gold had already been smelted, and not by a Company man. It had been done privately, by the looks of things.'

'Smelted—already!' said Mannering. 'I didn't hear about that.'

'No; you wouldn't have,' said Frost. 'Every piece of gold that comes over our counter has to be retorted, even if the process has been done before. It's to prevent any makeweights from slipping through, and to ensure a uniform quality. So Killarney did it all over again. He smelted Wells's colour before it was valued, and by the time anybody saw it, it had been poured into bars and stamped with the Reserve seal. Nobody outside the bank could have known that it had been retorted once before—save for the man who hid it in the first place, of course. Oh, and the commission merchant, who found it in the cottage, and brought it to the bank.'

'Who was that—Cochran?'

'Harald Nilssen. Of Nilssen & Co.'

Mannering frowned. 'Why not Cochran?'

Frost paused to draw on his cigar. 'I don't know,' he said at last.

'What's Clinch doing, dragging another body into the affair?' said Mannering. 'Surely he might have cleared the place himself. What's he doing, dragging Harald Nilssen into the mix?'

'I'm telling you: Clinch never dreamed there'd be anything of value in the cottage,' Frost said. 'He was flabbergasted when the fortune turned up.'

'Flabbergasted, was he?'

'Yes.'

'That your word, or his?'

'His.'

'*Flabbergasted*,' Mannering said again.

Frost continued. 'Well, it worked out famously for Nilssen. He was set to take home ten percent of the value of the goods in the cottage. Lucky day for him. He walked home with four hundred pounds!'

Mannering still wore a sceptical expression. 'Well, go on,' he said. 'Smelted. The gold had been smelted, you were saying.'

'So I had a look at it,' said Frost. 'We always write a short description of the ore—whether it's in flakes or whatnot—before it's smelted down. The practice is no different when the gold's been smelted already: we're still obliged to make a record of what the stuff looked like when it came in. For reasons of—' (Frost paused; he had been going to say 'security', but this did not exactly make sense) '—prudence,' he finished, rather lamely. 'Anyway, I examined the squares before Killarney put them in the crucible, and I saw that at the bottom of each square the smelter—whoever he was—had inscribed a word.'

He paused.

'Well, what was it?' said Mannering.

'Aurora,' said Frost.

'Aurora.'

'That's right.'

All of a sudden Mannering was looking very alert. 'But then

these squares—all of them—were retorted again,' he said. 'Pressed into bullion, by your man at the bank.'

Frost nodded. 'And then locked up in the vault, that very same day—once the commission merchant had taken his cut, and the estate taxes had been paid.'

'So there's no evidence of that name,' Mannering said. 'Do I have that right? That name is gone. That name has been smelted away.'

'Gone, yes,' said Frost. 'But I made a note of it, of course; it was officially recorded. Written down in my book, as I told you.'

Mannering set down his glass. 'All right, Charlie. How much to make that one page disappear—or your whole book, for that matter? How much for a little carelessness on your part? A touch of water, or a touch of fire?'

Frost was surprised. 'I don't understand,' he said.

'Just answer the question. Could you make that one page disappear?'

'I could,' Frost said, 'but I wasn't the only one to notice that inscription, you know. Killarney saw it. Mayhew did too. One of the buyers saw it; Jack Harmon, I think it was. He's off in Greymouth now. Any one of them might have mentioned it to any number of others. It was quite remarkable, of course—that inscription. Not something a man would easily forget.'

'D—n,' said Mannering. He struck the desk with his fist. 'D—n, d—n, d—n.'

'But I don't understand,' Frost said again. 'What's this all about?'

'What's the matter with you, Charlie?' Mannering burst out suddenly. 'Why—it's taken you *two bloody weeks* to front up to me about this! What have you been doing—sitting on your fingers? What?'

Frost drew back. 'I came to see you today because I thought this information might help recover Mr. Staines,' he said, with dignity. 'Given that this money very plainly belongs to *him*, and not to Crosbie Wells!'

'Rot. You might have done that two weeks ago. Or any day since.'

'But I only made the connexion to Staines this morning! How

was I to know about the Aurora? I don't keep a tally of every man's bankroll, and every man's claim. I had no reason—'

'You got a cut,' Mannering interrupted. He levelled a finger at Frost. 'You got a cut of that pile.'

Frost flushed. 'That's hardly pertinent.'

'Did you or did you not get a cut of Crosbie Wells's fortune?'

'Well—unofficially—'

Mannering swore. 'And you were just sitting tight, weren't you?' he said. He sat back, and with a disgusted flick of his wrist, threw the end of his cigar into the fire. 'Until the widow showed up, and you got backed in a corner. And *now* you're showing your cards— and making it look like charity! Well, I'll be d—ned, Charlie. I'll be God-d—ned.'

Frost had a wounded look. 'No,' he said. 'That's not the reason. I only put the pieces together this morning. Truly I did. Tom Balfour came by the bank with this cock-and-bull story about Francis Carver, and asked me to look up his shares profile, and I found out—'

'What?'

'—that Carver had taken out shares against Aurora, soon after Mr. Staines purchased it. I didn't know about that before this morning.'

'What's that about Tom Balfour?'

'And when Mr. Balfour left I looked up the Aurora's records, and I noticed that Aurora's profits started to fall away right around the time that Carver took out his shares, and *that's* when I remembered about the name in the smelting, and put it all together. Truly.'

Mannering raised his voice. 'What's Tom Balfour wanting with Francis Carver?'

'He's wanting to bring him to the law,' Frost said.

'On what account?'

'He said that Carver lifted a fortune from another man's claim, or something to that tune. But he was cagey about it, and he began with a lie.'

'Hm,' said the magnate.

'I brought the matter to you directly,' Frost went on, still hoping for praise. 'I left the bank early, to come to you directly. As soon as I put all the pieces together.'

'All the pieces!' Mannering exclaimed. 'You haven't *got* all the pieces, Charlie. You don't know what half the pieces look like.'

Frost was offended. 'What does that mean?'

But Mannering did not reply. 'Johnny Quee,' he said. 'Johnny bloody Quee.' He stood up so suddenly that the chair fell away behind him and struck the wall; the collie-dog leaped to her feet, overjoyed, and began to pant.

'Who?' said Charlie Frost, before he remembered: Quee was the name of the digger who worked the Aurora. His name had been written on the record at the bank.

'My Chinese problem—and now yours too, I'm afraid,' said Mannering, darkly. 'Are you with me, Charlie, or against me?'

Frost looked down at his cigar. 'With you, of course. I don't see why you have to ask questions like that.'

Mannering went to the back of the room. He opened a cabinet to reveal two carbines, sundry pistols, and an enormous belt that sported two buckskin holsters and a leather fringe. He began buckling this rather absurd accessory about his ample waist. 'You ought to be armed—or are you already?'

Frost coloured slightly. He leaned forward and crushed out his cigar—taking his time about it, stabbing the blunt end three times against the dish, and then again, grinding the ash to a fine black dust.

Mannering stamped his foot. 'Hi there! Are you armed, or are you not?'

'I am not,' said Frost, dropping the cigar butt at last. 'To be perfectly honest with you, Dick, I have never fired a gun.'

'Nothing to it,' said Mannering. 'Easy as breathing.' He returned to the cabinet, selecting two smart percussion revolvers from the rack.

Frost was watching him. 'I should be a very poor second,' he said presently, trying to keep his voice calm, 'if I do not know the subject of your quarrel, and I do not have the means to end it.'

'Never mind—never mind,' said Mannering, inspecting his revolvers. 'I was going to say I've got a Colt Army you could use, but now that I think of it . . . it takes a bloody age to load, and you don't want to bother with shot and powder. Not in this rain. Not if you haven't done it before. We'll make do. We'll make do.'

Frost looked at Mannering's belt.

'Outrageous, isn't it?' said Mannering, without smiling. He thrust the revolvers into his holsters, crossed the room to the coat-rack, and detached his greatcoat from its wooden hanger. 'Don't worry; see, when I put my coat on, and button it up, nobody will be any the wiser. I tell you, my blood is boiling, Charlie. That rotten chink! My blood is boiling.'

'I have no idea why,' said Frost.

'*He* knows why,' said Mannering.

'Stop a moment,' said Frost. 'Just let me—just tell me this. What is it exactly that you're planning?'

'We're going to give a Chinaman a scare,' said the magnate, thrusting his arms into his coat.

'What kind of a scare?' said Frost—who had registered the plural pronoun with trepidation. 'And on what score?'

'This Chinaman works the Aurora,' said Mannering. 'This is his work, Charlie: the smelting you're talking about.'

'But what's your grievance with him?'

'Less of a grievance; more of a grudge.'

'Oh!' said Frost suddenly. 'You don't suppose that *he* killed Mr. Staines?'

Mannering made a noise of impatience that sounded almost like a groan. He removed Frost's coat from the rack, and tossed it to him; the latter caught it, but made no move to put it on.

'Let's go,' said Mannering. 'Time's wasting.'

'For heaven's sake,' the other burst out, 'you might do me the courtesy of a plain speech. I'll need to have my story straight, if we're going to go storming in to bloody Chinatown!'

(Frost regretted this phrasing as soon as he spoke—for he did not want to storm into Chinatown under *any* conditions—with his story straight or otherwise.)

'There isn't time,' said Mannering. 'I'll tell you on the way. Put your coat on.'

'No,' said Charlie Frost—finding, to his surprise, that he could muster a delicate firmness, and hold his ground. 'You're not in a rush; you're only excited. Tell me now.'

Mannering dithered, his hat in his hands. 'This Chinese fellow worked for me,' he said at last. 'He dug the Aurora, before I sold it on to Staines.'

Frost blinked. 'The Aurora was yours?'

'And when Staines bought it,' Mannering said, nodding, 'the chink stayed on, and kept on digging. He's on a contract, you see. Johnny Quee is his name.'

'I didn't know the Aurora had been yours.'

'Half the land between here and the Grey has belonged to me at one stage or another,' said Mannering, throwing out his chest a little. 'But anyway. Before Staines came along, Quee and I had a bit of a quarrel. No: not exactly a quarrel. I have my way of doing things, that's all, and the chinks have theirs. Here's what happened. Every week I took the total of Quee's yield—after it had been counted, of course—and I fed it back into the claim.'

'You what?'

'I fed it back into the claim.'

'You were salting your own land!' said Frost, with a shocked expression.

Charlie Frost was no great observer of human nature, and as a consequence, felt betrayed by others very frequently. The air of cryptic strategy with which he most often spoke was not manufactured, though he was entirely sensible of its effects; it came, rather, out of a fundamental blindness to all experience exterior to his own. Frost did not know how to listen to himself as if he were somebody else; he did not know how to see the world from another man's eyes; he did not know how to contemplate another man's nature, except to compare it, either enviously or pitiably, to his own. He was a private hedonist, perennially wrapped in the cocoon of his own senses, mindful, always, of the things he already possessed, and the things he had yet to gain; his subjectivity was comprehensive, and complete. He was never forthright, and never declared his private motivations in a public sphere, and for this he was usually perceived to be a highly objective thinker, possessed of an impartial, equable mind. But this was not the case. The shock that he now expressed was not a show of indignation, and nor was it even disapproving in any real way: he was simply baffled, having failed to perceive Mannering as anything other than a man of enviable income and pitiable health, whose cigars were always of the finest quality, and whose decanter never seemed to run dry.

Mannering shrugged. 'I'm not the first man to want to make a profit, and I won't be the last,' he said.

'For shame,' said Frost.

But shame, for Mannering, was an emotion that attended only failure; he could not be made to feel compunction if he had not, in his own estimation, failed. He went on. 'All right—so you've got an opinion about it. Here's how it happened, though. The actual claim was useless. Little better than a tailing pile. After I bought it I buried maybe twenty pounds' worth of pure ore in the gravel, scattering it all about, then directed Quee to begin his digging. Quee finds it all right. At the end of the week he goes to have it weighed at the camp station like all the other fellows. This is before the gold escort, you remember. Back when the bankers had their stations along the river, and the buyers worked alone. So when my claim comes up, and my gold is weighed, the bankers ask me if I want to bank it right there. I say no, not yet; I'll take it back, pure. My story goes that I'm keeping it back for a private buyer who's going to export it altogether, as a lump sum. Or some such tale; I don't remember now. Well, after the stuff is weighed, and the value recorded, I gather it all back up again, wait for the cover of darkness, creep back to the claim, and shake it out a second time, over the gravel.'

'I can't believe you,' said Frost.

'Believe it or not, as you please,' said Mannering. 'Due credit to the Chinaman, of course: this happened maybe four or five times, and each week he came back with the exact same pile, more or less. He found it all, no matter how much I messed up the gravel, no matter how deep the grit settled, no matter the weather or what have you. Worked like a Trojan. That's one thing I'll say for the Chinese: when it comes to pure old-fashioned work, you can't fault them.'

'But you never told him what you were doing.'

Mannering was shocked. 'Of course not,' he said. 'Confess my sins? Of course I didn't! Anyway. To all appearances, it looked like the Aurora was pulling twenty pounds a week. Nobody knew it was the same twenty pounds, over and over! She just looked like a good, steady claim.'

Mannering had begun his tale in a posture of some exasperation, but his natural affinity for storytelling could not long be held in check, and it was enjoyable to him, to recount a proof of his own ingenuity. He relaxed into his narrative, thumping the brim of his stovepipe hat against his leg.

'But then Quee started to catch on,' he said. 'Must have been watching, or maybe he just figured me out. So what does he do? Cunning fox! He starts retorting the dust each week in a little crucible of his own. Then he brings it to the camp station already smelted, and done up in these one-pound blocks, about so big. There's no throwing *that* back among the stones!

'No matter, I thought. I had plenty of other claims for sale, and the other ones were pulling good dust. I could shuffle it around. So I started banking Quee's squares as returns against the Dream of England claim, and every week, I'd salt the Aurora just as before, only I'd use Dream of England dust, not Aurora dust—do you see? Aurora had been pulling twenty pounds a week until then; she had to maintain that same yield, or it would look like her profits had started to fall away—and I wouldn't get *my* profit, when I sold.

'But then Quee got wise to *that*,' Mannering went on, raising his voice in a final cadence, 'and the bloody devil starts carving the name of the plot—*Aurora*—into his little squares. I can't bank *that* against the Dream of England without raising a few eyebrows, can I? Would you believe it? The cheek of him!'

'I *don't* believe it,' said Frost, who was still feeling very much betrayed.

'Well, there it is, anyway,' said Mannering. 'That's the story. That's when Emery arrived.'

'And?'

'And what?'

'Well—what happened?'

'You know what happened. I sold him the Aurora.'

'But the claim was a duffer, you said!'

'Yes,' said Mannering.

'You sold him a duffer claim!'

'Yes.'

'But he's your friend,' said Charlie Frost, and even as he spoke the words he regretted them. How pathetic it sounded—to reprimand a man like Mannering about *friendship*! Mannering was in the august high noon of his life. He was prosperous, and well dressed, and he owned the largest and most handsome building on Revell-street. There were gold nuggets hanging from his watch chain. He ate meat at every meal. He had known a hundred women—maybe even a thousand—maybe more. What did he care about *friends*? Frost found that he was blushing.

Mannering studied the younger man for a moment, and then said, 'Here's the heart of it, Charlie. A four thousand-pound fortune—smelted, and every square of it stamped with the word *Aurora*—has turned up in a dead man's house. We don't know why, and we don't know how, but we do know who, and that "who" is my old friend Quee in Kaniere. All right? This is why we have to go to Chinatown. So as to ask him a question or two.'

Frost felt that Mannering was still concealing something from him. 'But the fortune itself,' he said. 'How do you account for it? If Aurora *is* a duffer, then where did all of that gold come from? And if Aurora's *not* a duffer, then who's cooking the books to make her appear as if she's worth nothing at all?'

The magnate put his hat on. 'All I know,' he said, running his finger and thumb around the brim and back again, 'is that I've got a score to settle. No man makes a fool of Dick Mannering more than once, and the way I see it, this johnny chink has had a jolly good try. Come along. Or are you turning yellow on me?'

No man likes to be called a coward—and least of all, a man who is feeling downright cowardly. In a cold voice Frost said, 'I'm not yellow in the least.'

'Good,' said Mannering. 'No hard feelings, then. Come along.'

Frost thrust his arms into his coat. 'I only hope it doesn't come to blows,' he said.

'We'll see about that,' said Mannering. 'We'll see about that. Come on, Holly—come on, girl! Giddyap! We've got business in the Hokitika gorge!'

Φ

As Frost and Mannering stepped out of the Prince of Wales Opera House, tugging down their hats against the rain, Thomas Balfour was turning into Weld-street, some three blocks to the south. Balfour had spent the last hour and a half at the Deutsches Gasthaus on Camp-street, where a pile of sauerkraut, sausage, and brown gravy, a seat before an open fire, and a period of uninterrupted contemplation had helped to refocus his mind upon Alistair Lauderback's affairs. He quit the Gasthaus refreshed, and made immediately for the office of the *West Coast Times*.

The shutters were drawn inside the box window, and the front door closed. Balfour tried the handle: it was locked. Curious, he stamped around to the rear of the building, to the small apartment where Benjamin Löwenthal, the paper's editor lived. He listened for a moment at the door, and, hearing nothing, cautiously turned the doorknob.

The door opened easily, and Balfour found himself face to face with Löwenthal himself, who was sitting at his table with his hands in his lap—quite as if he had been waiting for Balfour to startle him out of a trance. He stood up, in haste.

'Tom,' he said. 'What is it? Is something wrong? Why didn't you knock?'

The table at which he had been seated was properly a laboratory desk, the surface of which was pocked and worn, and mottled with spilled ink and chemicals; today, however, it had been swept clean of the detritus of Löwenthal's trade, and covered with an embroidered cloth. In the centre was a little plate upon which a fat candle was burning.

'Oh,' Balfour said. 'Sorry, Ben. Hello, there. Sorry. Sorry. Didn't mean to disturb your—I mean, I didn't mean to disturb you.'

'But you are most welcome!' said Löwenthal, perceiving that Balfour was not bearing ill tidings after all, but had simply dropped in for a chat. 'Come in, out of the rain.'

'Didn't mean to break your—'

'You haven't broken anything. Come in, come in—close the door!'

'It's not *business*, exactly,' Balfour said, by way of apology, knowing that Löwenthal's holy day was a day of rest. 'It's not *work*, exactly. I just wanted to talk with you about something.'

'It is never work, talking with you,' Löwenthal replied generously, and then, for the fourth time, 'But you must come in.'

At last Balfour stepped inside and closed the door. Löwenthal resumed his seat and folded his hands together. He said, 'I have long thought that, for the Jew, the newspaper business is the perfect occupation. No edition on Sunday, you see—and so the timing of the Shabbat is perfect. I have pity for my Christian competitors. They must spend their Sunday setting type, and spreading ink, ready for Monday; they cannot rest. When you came up the path just now, that was the subject of my thinking. Yes, hang up your coat. Do sit down.'

'I'm a Church of England man, myself,' said Balfour—who, like many men of that religion, was made very uncomfortable by icons of faith. He eyed Löwenthal's candle with some wariness, quite as if his host had laid out a hairshirt or a metal cilice.

'What is on your mind, Tom?'

Benjamin Löwenthal was not at all displeased that his weekly observances had been interrupted, for his religion was of a very confident variety, and it was not in his nature to be self-doubting. He often broke his Shabbat vows in small ways, and did not chastise himself for it—for he was sensible of the difference between duty that is dreaded, and duty that comes from love; he believed in the acuity of his own perception, and felt that whenever he broke the rules, he broke them for reasons that were right. He was also (it must be admitted) rather restless, after two hours of unmitigated prayer—for Löwenthal was an energetic spirit, and could not be without external stimulation for long.

'Listen,' Balfour said now, placing his fingertips on the table between them. 'I've just heard about Emery Staines.'

'Ah!' said Löwenthal, surprised. 'Only just now? Your head has been buried in the sand, perhaps!'

'I've been busy,' said Balfour, eyeing the candle a second time— for ever since he was a boy he had not been able to sit before a candle without wanting to touch it, to sweep his index finger through the flame until it blackened, to mould the soft edges where the wax was warm, to dip his fingertip into the pool of molten heat and then withdraw it, swiftly, so that the tallow formed a yellow cap over the pad of his finger which blanched and constricted as it cooled.

'Too busy for the news?' said Löwenthal, teasing him.

'I've got a fellow in town. A political fellow.'

'Oh yes: the honourable Lauderback,' said Löwenthal. He sat back in his chair. 'Well, I hope that *he* is reading my paper, even if you are not! He has featured in the pages enough.'

'Yes—featured,' said Balfour. 'But listen, Ben: I wanted to ask you a question. I stopped in at the bank this morning, and I heard someone's been putting up notices in the paper. On Mr. Staines's behalf—begging his return. Am I allowed to ask who placed them?'

'Certainly,' Löwenthal said. 'A notice is a public affair—and in any case, she left a box number at the bottom of the advertisement, as you might have seen; you only have to go to the post office, and look at the boxes, and you will see her name.'

'"She"?'

'Yes, you'll be surprised by this,' said Löwenthal. 'It was one of our ladies of the night! Will you guess which one?'

'Lizzie? Irish Lizzie?'

'Anna Wetherell.'

'Anna?' said Balfour.

'Yes!' said Löwenthal, now smiling broadly—for he had an

insider's sensibility, and enjoyed himself the most when he was permitted to occupy that role. 'You wouldn't have guessed *that*, would
you? She came to me not two days after Mr. Staines first disappeared. I tried to persuade her to wait until more time had
passed—it seemed wasteful to advertise for a man's return when he
was only two days' gone. He might have merely walked into the
gorge, I said, or ridden up the beach to the Grey. He might be back
to-morrow! So I told her. But she was adamant. She told me he had
not departed; he had vanished. She was very clear on that. She
used those very words.'

'Vanished,' echoed Balfour.

'The poor girl had been tried at the Courts that very morning,'
Löwenthal said. 'What rotten luck she has had, this year past. She's
a dear girl, Tom—very dear.'

Balfour frowned: he did not like to be told that Anna Wetherell
was a dear girl. 'Can't imagine it,' he said aloud, and shook his
head. 'Can't imagine it—the two of them. They're as chalk and
cheese.'

'Chalk and cheese,' echoed Löwenthal. He took pleasure in foreign idioms. 'Who is the chalk? Staines, I suppose—because of his
quarrying!'

Balfour did not seem to have heard him. 'Did Anna give you
any indication as to *why* she was asking after Staines? I mean—
why—'

'She was attempting to make contact with him, of course,'
Löwenthal said. 'But that is not your question, I think.'

'I just meant—' But Balfour did not go on.

Löwenthal was smiling. 'It is hardly a wonder, Tom! If that
fellow showed her the smallest ounce of affection—*well*.'

'What?'

The editor made a clucking noise. 'Well, you must admit it: next
to Mr. Staines, you and I are very grey indeed.'

Balfour scowled. What was a bit of greyness? Grey hair dignified
a man. 'Here's another question,' he said, changing the subject.
'What do you know about a man named Francis Carver?'

Löwenthal raised his eyebrows. 'Not a great deal,' he said. 'I've heard stories, of course. One is always hearing stories about men of his type.'

'Yes,' said Balfour.

'What do I know about Carver?' Löwenthal mused, turning the question over in his mind. 'Well, I know that he's got roots in Hong Kong. His father was a financier of some kind—something to do with merchant trading. But he and his father must have parted ways, because he is not associated with a parent firm any longer. He is a lone agent, is he not? A trader. Perhaps he and his father parted ways after he was convicted.'

'But what do you make of him?' Balfour pressed.

'I suppose that my impression of him is not an altogether good one. He is a rich man's son first and a convict second, but it might just as well be the other way about: I believe he shows the worst of both worlds. He's a thug, but he's conniving. Or, to put it another way, his life is lavish, but it's base.'

(This character summation was a quintessential one for Benjamin Löwenthal, who, in his thinking, tended always to position himself as the elucidating third party between opposing forces. In his evaluations of other men, Löwenthal first identified an essential disparity in their person, and then explained how the poles of this disparity could only be synthesised in theory, and by Löwenthal himself. He was fated to see the inherent duality in all things—even in his own appraisal of the duality of all things—and was obliged, as a consequence, to adopt a strict personal code of categorical imperatives, as a protective measure against what he perceived to be a world of discrepancy and flux. This personal code was phlegmatic, reflexive, and highly principled; it was the only fixed seat from which he could regard these never-ending dualities, and he depended upon it wholly. He tended to be relaxed in his daily schedule, humorous in his religion, and flexible in his business—but upon his imperatives, he could not be mistaken, and he would not yield.)

'Carver got me in a touch of hot water recently,' he went on. 'Around a fortnight ago, he left his mooring off-schedule—and in the middle of the night. Well, it was a Sunday, and so the shipping news had been published already, in Saturday's edition. But because *Godspeed* wasn't scheduled to leave that day, and because she left well after sundown, somehow her departure wasn't recorded in the customhouse log. Well, nobody told *me* anything about it, and so her departure was never recorded in the paper either. Quite as if the ship never left her mooring! The Harbourmaster was very upset about it.'

'Last Sunday?' said Balfour. 'That's the day Lauderback arrived.'

'I suppose it was. The fourteenth.'

'But Carver was in the Arahura Valley that very same night!'

Löwenthal looked up sharply. 'Who told you that?'

'A Maori fellow. Tay something, his name is. Youngish chap; wears a big green pendant. I spoke with him in the street this morning.'

'What is his authority?'

Balfour explained that Te Rau Tauwhare and Crosbie Wells had been great friends, and that Tauwhare had observed Francis Carver entering the cottage on the day of the hermit's death. As to whether Carver had been present in the cottage before or after Wells's death, Balfour did not know, but Tauwhare had assured him that Carver's arrival had occurred *before* Lauderback's—and Lauderback, by his own testimony, had arrived at the cottage not long after the event of the hermit's death, for when he entered the man's kettle had been boiling on the range, and had not yet run dry. It stood to reason, therefore, that Francis Carver had been present in the cottage *before* Crosbie Wells passed away, and perhaps (Balfour realised with a chill) had even witnessed his death.

Löwenthal stroked his moustache. 'This is very interesting news,' he said. '*Godspeed* sailed late that evening, well after sundown. So Carver must have come straight back to Hokitika from the Arahura Valley, made his way directly for the ship, and weighed anchor, all before the dawn. That is a very hasty departure, I think.'

'Rum to my eye,' said Balfour. He was thinking about his vanished shipping crate.

'And when one considers that Staines disappeared around the very same time—'

'And Anna,' said Balfour, cutting across him. 'That was the night of her collapse—because Lauderback found her, you remember, in the road.'

'Ah,' said Löwenthal. 'Another coincidence.'

'*You* might say only a weak mind puts faith in coincidence,' said Balfour, 'but I say—*I* say—a string of coincidences cannot be a coincidence. A string of them!'

'No indeed,' said Löwenthal, distantly.

Presently Balfour said, 'But young Staines. That's a perfect shame, that is. There's no use being soft about it, Ben—he's been murdered, surely. A man doesn't vanish. A poor man, maybe. But not a man of means.'

'Mm,' said Löwenthal—who was not thinking about Staines. 'I wonder what Carver was doing with Wells in the Arahura. And what he was running away from, for that matter. Or running towards.' The editor thought a moment more, and then exclaimed, 'I say: *Lauderback*'s not mixed up with Carver, is he?'

Balfour expelled a long breath. 'Well, that's the real question,' he said, with a show of great reluctance. 'But I'd be breaking Lauderback's confidence if I told you. I'd be breaking my word.' He looked again at the wick of the candle, hoping that his friend would prompt him to continue.

Unhappily for Balfour, however, Löwenthal's moral code did not accept the kind of violation that Balfour was proposing he indulge. After studying Balfour dispassionately for a moment, he sat back in his chair, and changed the subject. 'Do you know,' he said, speaking in a brisker tone, 'you are not the first man to come by my office and ask me about that notice in the paper—the one about Emery Staines.'

Balfour looked up, both disappointed and surprised. 'Why—who else?'

'A man came by in the middle of the week. Wednesday. Or perhaps it was Tuesday. Irish. A clergyman by profession—but not a Catholic; he was a Methodist, I think. He's to be the chaplain of the new gaol.'

'Free Methodist,' Balfour said. 'I met him this morning. Strange looking. Very unfortunate teeth. What was *his* interest on account of?'

'But I can't remember his name,' Löwenthal murmured, tapping his lip.

'Why was he interested in Staines?' Balfour asked again—for he did not know the chaplain's name, and could not offer it.

Löwenthal folded his hands together again, on the tabletop. 'Well, it was rather odd,' he said. 'Apparently he went along with the coroner to Crosbie Wells's cottage, to collect the man's remains.'

'Yes—and then buried him,' said Balfour, nodding. 'Dug the grave.'

'Devlin,' said Löwenthal, striking the table. 'That's his name: Devlin. But I haven't got the first name. Give me another moment.'

'But anyway,' said Balfour. 'As I was asking. What's *he* got to do with Staines?'

'I don't exactly know,' Löwenthal admitted. 'From our brief conversation I gathered that he needed to speak to Mr. Staines very urgently—either about the death of Crosbie Wells, or about something related to the death of Crosbie Wells. But I can't tell you any more than that. I didn't ask.'

'It's a shame you didn't,' said Balfour. 'That's a loose end, that is.'

'Why, Tom,' said Löwenthal, with a sudden smile, 'you are sounding like a detective!'

Balfour flushed. 'I'm not really,' he said. 'I'm only trying to figure something out.'

'Figure something out—for your friend Lauderback, who has sworn you to silence!'

Balfour remembered that the clergyman had also overheard Lauderback's story, that same morning, and this thought prompted a stirring of alarm: there was a *real* loose end, he thought. Really, Lauderback ought to have been more cautious, in speaking of such private matters in a public place! 'Well,' he said, bristling, 'isn't it odd? This chap—Devlin—'

'Cowell Devlin,' said Löwenthal. 'That's his name: I knew it would come to me. Cowell Devlin. Yes: unfortunate teeth.'

'Whoever he is, *I've* never seen him before,' Balfour said. 'Why's *he* so concerned about Emery Staines—out of nowhere? Doesn't it strike you as odd?'

'Oh, very odd,' Löwenthal said, still smiling. 'Very odd. But you're getting hot under your collar, Tom.'

Balfour had indeed become very flushed. 'It's Lauderback,' he began, but Löwenthal shook his head.

'No, no: I won't make you break your confidence,' he said. 'I was only teasing you. Let's change the subject. I won't ask.'

But Thomas Balfour was wishing very much that Löwenthal *would* ask. He was very ready to betray Alistair Lauderback's confidence, and he had rather hoped that by pretending that he could not possibly divulge the politician's secret, he could tempt Löwenthal to beg him to do exactly that. But evidently Löwenthal did not play this kind of game. (Perhaps he did not wish to, or perhaps he did not know that he might.) Balfour felt stifled. He wished that, at the outset, he had sat down and told the tale of Lauderback's blackmail and proposed revenge, frankly and in full. Now he would have to leave without really having learned anything—for he could hardly offer to narrate the story now, after the editor had assured him he did not need to know it!

We will interject to observe that this was a regrettable censorship; for if Balfour *had* recounted Lauderback's tale in full, the events of the 27th of January might have played out rather differently for him—and for a number of other men. Prompted by certain particulars of Lauderback's story, Löwenthal would have remembered an event that he had not had reason to remember for many months: a memory that would have been of great assistance to Balfour's investigations of Carver, helping to explain, in part at least, that man's mysterious assumption of the surname Wells.

As it happened, however, Balfour did not narrate Lauderback's tale, and Löwenthal's memory was not jogged, and presently Balfour, rising from the spattered table, had no choice but to thank his friend and bid him goodbye—feeling, as Löwenthal also did, that their conversation had been something of a disappointment, having served only to raise his hopes, and then frustrate them. Löwenthal returned to the quiet contemplation of his faith, and Balfour to the slush of Revell-street, where the bells were ringing half past three; the day rolled on.

But onward also rolls the outer sphere—the boundless present, which contains the bounded past. This story is being narrated, with much allusion and repeated emphasis, to Walter Moody—and Benjamin Löwenthal, who is also present in the smoking room of the Crown Hotel, is hearing parts of the tale for the very first time. Suddenly he is put in mind of an event that occurred some eight months prior. When Thomas Balfour pauses to drink, as he is doing now, Löwenthal steps forward, around the billiard table, and raises his hand to indicate that he wishes to interject. Balfour invites him to do so, and Löwenthal begins to narrate the memory that has so recently returned to him, speaking with the hushed gravity of one conveying very important news.

Here is his account.

One morning in the month of June, 1865, a dark-haired man with a scar on his cheek entered Löwenthal's small office on Weld-street and asked for a notice to be placed in the *West Coast Times*. Löwenthal agreed, took out his pen, and asked the man what he wished to advertise. The man replied that he had lost a shipping crate that contained items of great personal value. He would pay a sum of twenty pounds if the crate were to be returned to him— or fifty, if the crate were to be returned to him unopened. He did not say what was inside the crate, beyond the fact that its personal value was considerable; he spoke gruffly, and used very plain words. When Löwenthal asked his name, he did not answer. Instead he pulled a birth certificate from his pocket and laid it on the desk. Löwenthal copied down the name—Mr. Crosbie Francis Wells—and inquired, finally, where the man would like responders to be directed, if indeed his lost shipping crate was found. The man named an address on Gibson Quay. Löwenthal recorded this, filled out a receipt, collected his fee, and then bid the man good morning.

One might well ask (and indeed, Moody *did* ask) how Löwenthal could be so certain of the precise details of this event, given that the memory had only just returned to him, nearly eight months later, and he had not had any opportunity to verify its particulars. How could Löwenthal be sure, firstly, that the man who placed this advertisement did indeed have a scar upon his cheek; secondly, that this event had taken place in June of the previous year, and thirdly, that the name upon the birth certificate was, without a shadow of a doubt, Crosbie Francis Wells?

Löwenthal's reply was courteous, but rather lengthy. He explained to Moody that the *West Coast Times* had been founded in May of 1865, roughly one month after Löwenthal's first landing in New Zealand. At first printing, the newspaper's print run was a mere twenty copies, one each for Hokitika's eighteen hotels, one for the newly appointed magistrate, and one for Löwenthal himself. (Within a month, and following the purchase of a steam-powered press, Löwenthal's print run had expanded to two hundred; now, in January 1866, he was printing nearly a thousand copies of every edition, and he had hired a staff of two.) In order to advertise to his subscribers that the *Times* had been Hokitika's very first daily gazette, Löwenthal set the first edition of the paper behind glass and hung it in his front office. He therefore remembered the exact date of the newspaper's establishment (the 29th day of May, 1865), for he saw this framed edition every morning. The man in question, Löwenthal explained, had certainly arrived at some point in June, for Löwenthal's steam-powered press had been delivered on the first day of July, and he distinctly remembered processing the scarred man's advertisement on his old hand-powered machine.

How was it that his memory was so distinct upon this point? Well, upon setting the type, Löwenthal had discovered that two inches square (the standard size for a column advertisement, and the size for which the scarred man had paid) was not enough to contain the message: the advertisement was one word too long to fit in the column space available. Unless Löwenthal shuffled around his repeat notices and changed the format of the paper altogether, he would be forced to create what typographers call a 'widow': that is, the final word of the advertisement (which was 'Wells') would be marooned at the top of the third column, producing an undesirable and even confusing effect in the reader's mind. By the time Löwenthal discovered this, the scarred man had long since left his office, and Löwenthal was disinclined to venture out into the streets to find him. Instead he looked for a word to remove, finally deciding to excise the man's middle name, Francis. This omission would prevent the creation of a 'widow', and the format of his column would not be spoiled.

The *West Coast Times* was published early the following morning, and well before noon, the scarred man returned. He insisted— though he did not give a reason—that it was of the utmost importance that his middle name was included. He resented very much that Löwenthal had altered his advertisement without his knowledge, and expressed his displeasure with the same plain-spoken gruffness with which he had first entreated the editor's assistance. Löwenthal, apologising profusely, printed the notice again—and five times after that, for the man had paid for a week's worth of advertising, and Löwenthal thought it prudent, under the circumstances, to offer him a seventh printing for free.

Therefore, as Löwenthal explained to Moody, he was certain both of the date of the event, and of the man's full name, Crosbie Francis Wells. The event stood out in his mind: it is always his first mistake that an entrepreneur remembers, looking back upon the origins of his enterprise, and the displeasure of a patron is not easily forgotten, when one takes one's business to heart.

This only left the question of the man's description—for how could Löwenthal be sure that the man in question did in fact possess a scar upon his cheek, as the ex-convict known as Francis Carver certainly *did*, and as the hermit known as Crosbie Wells certainly did *not*? Upon this final point, Löwenthal conceded that he could not be sure. Perhaps in remembering the event he had over-laid a different memory of a scar-faced man. But he wished to add that his powers of recollection were typically strong, and he could picture this man very vividly in his mind; he remembered that the man had been holding a top hat, and that he had pressed it between his palms as he spoke, as if he meant to compress the thing to a single sheet of felt. This detail, surely, could not be false! Löwenthal declared that he would be willing to wager a decent sum of money that the man he remembered *had* indeed possessed a scar, shaped like a sickle, upon his cheek—and that he had possessed, also, a birth certificate that bore the name Crosbie Francis Wells. Löwenthal did

concede, however, that he had never known the hermit, Crosbie
Wells, in life, and had no way to imagine his features, because no
image or sketch of the dead man had survived him.

This new information, as one can well imagine, gave rise to a
veritable cacophony of interjection and supposition in the smoking room of the Crown Hotel, and the narrative did not resume for
some time. But we shall leave them in the present, and bear
onward, in the past.

Φ

The ferry service that ran between Kaniere and the mouth of the
Hokitika River had not been interrupted by the inclement weather,
though their custom had slowed; the ferrymen, with no one to escort
and no chores outstanding, were sitting about in the open warehouse adjacent to the quay, smoking cigarettes and playing at whist.
They looked none too happy to abandon their game and venture
out into the rain, and named a fare that reflected this displeasure.
Mannering agreed to the sum at once, however, and the ferrymen
were obliged to put away their cards, stub out their cigarettes, and
set about carrying the boat down the ramp to the water.

Kaniere was only some four miles upriver, a distance that would
be covered in no time at all on the return journey, when the oarsmen no longer had to pull against the current; the journey inland,
however, could easily take up to an hour, depending on the river's
motion, the wind, and the pull of the tide. Diggers travelling back
and forth between Kaniere and Hokitika usually covered that distance by coach, or on foot, but the coach had been and gone
already, and the weather disinclined them to walk.

Mannering paid the fare, and presently he and Frost were sitting
in the stern of a painted dinghy (in fact it was a lifeboat, salvaged
from a wreck) with the collie-dog Holly between them. The stroke-
side oarsmen pushed off from the bank with the blades of their
oars, and pulled strongly; soon the craft was on her way upstream.

Sitting with their backs against the stern, Frost and Mannering
found themselves face-to-face with the oarsmen, rather like a pair
of outsized, well-dressed coxswains; the distance between them

closed each time the oarsmen leaned forward to take another stroke. The two men therefore did not speak about the business they were about to perform, for to do so would have been to invite the oarsmen into their confidence. Instead Mannering kept up a steady flow of chatter about the weather, the Americas, soil, glass, breakfast, sluice mining, native timbers, the Baltic naval theatre, and life upon the fields. Frost, who was prone to seasickness, did not move at all, except to reach up periodically and wipe away the drips that formed beneath the brim of his hat. He responded to Mannering's chatter only with clenched noises of agreement.

In truth Frost was feeling very frightened—and progressively more frightened, as each stroke carried the craft closer and closer to the gorge. What in all heaven had come over him—in saying that he was not yellow, when he was as yellow as a man could be? He could easily have pretended that he was expected back at the bank! Now he was lurching around in three inches of brown water, shivering, unarmed, and unprepared—the ill-chosen second in another man's duel—and for what? What was *his* quarrel with the Chinaman Quee? What was *his* grudge? He had never laid eyes upon the man in all his life! Frost reached up to wipe the brim of his hat.

The Hokitika River threaded its way over gravel flats, the stones of which were uniformly round and worn. The banks of the river were fringed darkly with scrub, the foliage made still darker by the rain; the hills beyond them crawled with shifting cloud. One had the sense, peering up at them, that distance was measured in stages: the tall kahikatea, rising out of the scrub, were silhouetted green in the foreground, blue in the middle distance, and grey on the crest of the hills, where they merged with the colour of the mist. The Alps were shrouded, but on a fine day (as Mannering remarked) they would have been quite visible, as a sharp ridge of white against the sky.

The craft bore on. They were passed by one canoe, travelling swiftly downriver, conveying a bearded surveyor and a pair of Maori guides—who lifted their hats, cheerfully enough, and Mannering did likewise. (Frost could not risk the motion.) After that, there was nothing; only the riverbanks, jolting by; the rain lashing at the water.

The gulls that had followed them from the river mouth lost interest and fell back. Twenty minutes or so passed, and the craft turned a corner—and then, as a lamp suddenly illuminates a crowded room, there was noise and motion all around them.

The canvas settlement of Kaniere was stationed as a midpoint between Hokitika and the inland claims. The land around the settlement was fairly flat, rutted by a veritable lattice of gullies and streams, all of them bearing stones and gravel down from the Alps, towards the sea; the sound of moving water was ever-present here, as a distant roar, a click, a rush, a patter. As one early surveyor had put it, on the Coast, wherever there was water, there was gold— and there was water all about, water dripping from the ferns, water beading on the branches, water making fat the mosses that hung from the trees, water filling one's footsteps, welling up.

To Frost's eyes, the camp at Kaniere made for a very dismal picture. The diggers' tents, terraced in crooked rows, bowed low under the weight of endless rain; several had collapsed altogether. Ropes ran back and forth between them, heavy with flags and wet laundry. Several of the tents had been bricked with a makeshift siding made of schist and clay, and were faring better; one enterprising party had thought to hang a second sheet in the trees above them, as an auxiliary fly. Nailed to the tree-trunks were painted signs advertising every kind of entertainment and drink. (A man needed no more than a canvas fly and a bottle to open a grog-shanty on the diggings, though he would suffer a fine, and even a gaoling, were he to be sprung by the law; most of the liquor sold in this way had been fermented in the camp. Charlie Frost had once tried the Kaniere rotgut, only to spit out his mouthful in disgust. The liquor was oily, acidic in taste, and thick with strings of matter; it had smelled, he thought, very like a photographic emulsion.)

Frost marvelled that the rain had not driven the diggers indoors; their spirits, in fact, seemed quite undampened. They were clustered at the riverside, some of them panning, knee-deep in the water, others rattling their sluice boxes, still others cleaning their pots, bathing, soaping their laundry, plaiting rope, and darning on the shore. They all wore the digger's habitual costume of moleskin, serge, and twill. Some of them sported sashes about their waists, dyed the brightest scarlet, in the piratical fashion of the time, and most wore slouch hats with the brims turned down. They shouted back and forth to one another as they worked, seeming to take no notice of the rain. Behind this shouting, one could hear the conventional hubbub of industry—the ringing chop of an axe, laughter, whistling. Blue smoke hung in the air and dispersed over the river in lazy gusts. The sound of an accordion drifted up from deep in the trees, and from somewhere further off came a roar of applause.

'Quiet, isn't it?' said Mannering. 'Even for a Saturday.'

Frost did not think that it was quiet.

'Hardly a man out,' said Mannering.

Frost could see dozens of men—perhaps hundreds.

The panorama before them was Charlie Frost's very first impression of Kaniere—and indeed, his first impression of Hokitika's environs at large, for in the seven months since he had crossed the Hokitika bar, he had never once ventured inland, nor once along the beachfront further than the high terrace of Seaview. Although he frequently bemoaned the smallness of his circumstances, he knew, in his innermost heart, that his spirit was not well suited to adventure; now, as he watched a man haul a branch onto a puny fire at the river's edge, and deposit the thing bodily onto the dark bed of ashes, causing a *whuff* of smoke to engulf him, blackly, so that he began to cough in the terrible, lung-wracking way of a man not long for this world, Frost felt thoroughly justified in his conservatism. Kaniere, he told himself internally, was a wretched, God-forsaken place.

The ferry pulled into the shallows, and the lifeboat's keel ground on the stones. The forward oarsmen jumped out and dragged the boat clear of the water, so that Mannering and Frost could clamber out of the craft without wetting their boots—an unnecessary courtesy, for their boots were very wet already. The collie-dog leaped over the gunwale and flopped, belly-first, into the water.

'My word,' said Mannering, as he heaved himself onto the stones, and stretched his back. 'I ought to have changed my trousers. Not a day for fine dress—eh, Charlie? Makes a fool out of a dandy. My word!'

He had perceived that Frost was out of sorts, and was trying to be cheerful. For although he felt that it would do Frost a great deal of good to bear witness to a bit of rough and tumble (Frost's composure had a priggish quality that aggravated Mannering extremely) he wished to remain, all the same, in the boy's good opinion. Mannering was competitive by nature, and among the many hypothetical trophies for which he competed daily was one engraved with the names of every one of his associates. Were he ever to be forced to choose between another man's betterment and another man's compliance, he would choose the latter, no matter the cost. He would not go soft upon Frost, who was soft enough already, and he would ensure that the boy knew his place, but he was not too proud to extend a hand of kindness—not least because kindness was so patently desired.

But Frost did not respond. He was appalled to see an A-frame calico tent, barely big enough to fit three men lying side by side, sporting the hand-painted sign 'Hotel'; he was appalled still further to see a digger unbutton his trousers and relieve himself, in full view of his fellows, onto the stones at the riverside. He recoiled—and then, to his alarm, heard laughter. A pair of diggers, sitting beneath a timber-framed awning not ten yards from the ferry landing, had been observing the lifeboat's approach. They evidently found Frost's horror very amusing; one of them tipped his hat, and the other gave a mock salute.

'Come for a gander?'

'Naw, Bob—he's come to do his laundry in the river. Only problem, he forgot to get his clothes dirty first!'

The men laughed again—and Frost, red-faced, turned away. It was true that his life had been circumscribed by the twin compasses of duty and habit; it was true that he had not travelled, and would not speculate; it was true that his coat had been brushed that morning, and his vest was clean. He was not ashamed of these things. But Frost had spent his childhood in a place without other children, and he did not understand teasing. If another man made fun at his expense, he did not know how to respond. His face became hot, and his throat became tight, and he could only smile, unnaturally.

The oarsmen had lifted the lifeboat clear of the water. They agreed to transport the pair back to Hokitika in two hours' time (*two hours*, Frost thought, with a sinking heart), and then drew lots to determine which man would remain with the boat. The unlucky man sat down, disappointed; the rest, rattling their coins, disappeared into the trees.

The two men opposite were still laughing.

'Ask him for a pinch of snuff,' the first digger was saying to his mate.

'Ask him how often he writes home—to Mayfair.'

'Ask him if he knows how to roll up his sleeves past his elbow.'

'Ask him about his father's income. He'll be pleased about that.'

It was desperately unfair, Frost thought—when he had never even been to Mayfair—when his father was a poor man—when *he* was the New Zealander! (But the appellation sounded foolish; one did not say 'Englander'.) His own income was paltry when one considered the enormous portion of his wages that he diverted into his father's pocket every month. As for the suit he was currently wearing—he had bought it with his own wage; he had brushed the coat himself, that morning! And he very frequently rolled his sleeves above his elbows. His cuffs were buttoned, as were the diggers' own; he had purchased his shirt at the Hokitika outfitters, just as they had. Frost wanted to say all of this—but instead he knelt down and held out his hands, palm upward, for the collie-dog to lick.

'Can we move?' he said in an undertone to Mannering.

'In a moment.'

Having replaced his purse in his inner pocket, Mannering was now fussing over the buttons of his greatcoat—for he could not decide whether to leave all but the bottom button undone, which would give him the best ease of access to his pistols, or all but the topmost button undone, which would do best to conceal his pistols from sight.

Frost shot another nervous look around him—avoiding the gaze of the diggers beneath the awning. The track from the ferry landing forked away through the trees—one spoke bearing eastward, towards Lake Kaniere, and the other southeast, towards the Hokitika Gorge. Beyond the south bank of the river lay a rich patchwork of claims and mines that included, among others, the goldmine Aurora. Frost did not know any of this; in fact he could hardly have pointed north, had he been asked. He looked about for a sign that might direct them to Chinatown, but there was none. He could see no Chinese faces in the crowd.

'That way,' Mannering said, as if hearing his thoughts; he nodded his head to the east. 'Upriver. None too far.'

Frost had caught the dog between his knees; he now began kneading her wet fur, more for his own reassurance than for the dog's pleasure. 'Ought we to agree on—on a plan of some kind?' he ventured, squinting upward at the other man.

'No need,' said Mannering, buckling his belt a little higher.

'No need for a plan?'

'Quee doesn't have a pistol. I've got two. That's the only plan *I* need.'

Frost was not entirely soothed by this. He freed Holly—she bounded away from him immediately—and stood up. 'You're not going to shoot an unarmed man?'

Mannering had decided upon the top button. 'There,' he said. 'That's best.' He smoothed his coat over his body.

'Did you not hear me?'

'I heard you,' said Mannering. 'Stop fretting, Charlie. You'll only draw attention to yourself.'

'You might answer me, if you want to ease my fretting,' Frost said, in a voice that was rather shrill.

'Listen,' Mannering said, turning to face him at last. 'I've paid Chinamen to work my claims for the past five years, and if there's one thing I can tell you, it's this. They go after that smoke like a hatter for a whore, and no exceptions. By this time on a Saturday, every yellow man this side of the Alps will be laid out limp with the dragon in his eye. You could walk in to Chinatown and round up every one of them with one arm tied behind your back. All right? There'll be no need for violence. There'll be no need for any guns. They're only for show. It's all stacked to our advantage, Charlie. When a man's full of opium it's like he's made of water. Remember that. He's useless. He's a child.'

SUN IN CAPRICORN

*In which Gascoigne recalls his first encounter with the whore;
several seams are unpicked with a knife; exhaustion takes its
toll; and Anna Wetherell makes a request.*

Perceiving Anna and Gascoigne through the chink in the doorway,
Joseph Pritchard had seen only what he himself most craved—love,
and honest sympathy. Pritchard was lonely, and like most lonely
souls, he saw happy couples everywhere. In that moment—as
Anna's body folded against Gascoigne's chest, and he wrapped his
arms around her, and lifted her, and placed his cheek against her
hair—Pritchard, his hand cupped limp around the cold knob of the
door, would not have been consoled to know that Aubert Gascoigne
and Anna Wetherell were merely, and very simply, friends.
Loneliness cannot be reassured by proportion. Even friendship
would have seemed to Pritchard a feast behind a pane of glass; even
the smallest charity would have wet his lip, and left him wanting.

Pritchard's assumptions about Gascoigne had been formed on
very limited acquaintance—on one conversation only, as a matter
of fact. Judging from his haughty manner and the impeccable standard of his dress, Pritchard had supposed that Gascoigne occupied
a position of some influence at the Magistrate's Court, but in truth
the clerk's responsibilities there were very few. His chief duty lay in
the collection of bail each day from the gaol-house at the Police
Camp. Besides this task, his hours were spent recording fees, polic-
ing receipts for miner's rights, fielding complaints, and on occasion,

running errands on the Commissioner's behalf. It was a lowly position, but Gascoigne was new in town; he was content to be employed, and confident that he would not take home a lackey's wage for long.

Gascoigne had been in Hokitika for less than a month when he first encountered Anna Wetherell lying shackled on George Shepard's gaol-house floor. She was sitting with her back against the wall, and her hands in her lap. Her eyes were open, and shone with fever; her hair had come loose from its clasp and stuck damply to her cheek. Gascoigne knelt before her, and on impulse extended his hand. She gripped it and pulled him closer still, out of sight of the gaoler, who was sitting by the door with a rifle on his knees. She whispered, 'I can make my bail—I can raise it—but you have to trust me. And you can't tell him how.'

'Who?' Gascoigne's voice, too, had dropped to a whisper.

She nodded towards Governor Shepard, without taking her eyes from his. Her grip tightened, and she guided his hand to her breast. He was startled; he almost snatched his hand away—but then he felt what she was guiding him to feel. Something was packed around her ribcage, beneath the cloth. It felt, Gascoigne thought, like chainmail—but he had never touched a piece of chainmail.

'Gold,' she whispered. 'It's gold. Up and down the corset-bones, and in the lining, and all the way about.' Her dark eyes were searching his face, pleading with him. 'Gold,' she said. 'I don't know how it got there. It was there when I woke up—sewn in.'

Gascoigne frowned, trying to understand. 'You wish to pay your bail with gold?'

'I can't get it out,' she whispered. 'Not here. Not without a knife. It's been sewn in.'

Their faces were almost touching; he could smell the sweet aftertaste of opium, like a plummy shadow on her breath. He murmured, 'Is it yours?'

A desperate look flashed across her face. 'What's the difference? It's money, isn't it?'

Shepard's voice rang out from the corner. 'Does the whore detain you, Mr. Gascoigne?'

'Not at all,' Gascoigne said. She released him and he straightened, taking a step away from her. He pulled his purse from his pocket as a way of feigning nonchalance, feigning purpose. He weighed the pouch in his hand.

'You may remind Miss Wetherell that we do not take bail on promise,' Shepard said. 'Either she produces the money here and now, or she stays here until someone raises it for her.'

Gascoigne studied Anna. He had no reason to heed the woman's request, or to believe that the hard plating he had felt around her corset was, as she claimed, gold. He knew that he ought to report her to the gaoler immediately, on the grounds that she had attempted to distract him from his duty. He ought to break apart her corset with the hunting knife he carried in his boot—for if she was carrying pure gold about her person, it surely did not belong to her. She was a whore. She had been detained for public intoxication. Her dress was filthy. She stank of opium, and there were purple shadows underneath her eyes.

But Gascoigne surveyed her with compassion. His code was one of innate chivalry; he had a deep sympathy for people in desperate circumstances, and the wide-eyed anguish of her appeal had stirred both his compassion and his curiosity. Gascoigne believed that justice ought to be a synonym for mercy, not an alternative. He also believed that merciful action answered to instinct before it answered to any law. In a sudden rush of pity—for that emotion always came upon him as a flood—he was moved to meet the girl's request, and to protect her.

'Miss Wetherell,' he said (he had not known her name before the gaoler used it), 'your bail is set at one pound one shilling.' He was holding his purse in his left hand, and his ledger in his right; now he made as if to transfer the ledger to the other hand, and, using the latter object as a shield, extracted two coins from his purse and tucked them against his palm. Then he transferred both purse and ledger to his right hand and held out his left, palm upward, with his thumb crossed across the palm. 'Can you raise that sum from the money you have shown me in your corset?' He spoke loudly and clearly, as if addressing a halfwit or a child.

For a moment she didn't understand. Then she nodded, reached her fingers down between the bones of her corset, and drew out nothing. She pressed her pinched fingers into Gascoigne's hand; Gascoigne lifted his thumb, nodded, as if satisfied with the coins that had appeared there, and recorded the bail on the ledger. He dropped the coins audibly into his purse, and then moved on to the next prisoner.

This act of kindness, so unorthodox in George Shepard's gaol-house, was not a terribly unusual one for Gascoigne. It was his pleasure to strike up friendships within the servile classes, with children, with beggars, with animals, with plain women and forgotten men. His courtesies were always extended to those who did not expect courtesy: when he encountered a man whose station was beneath him, he was never rude. To the higher classes, however, he held himself apart. He was not ungracious, but his manner was jaded and wistful, even unimpressed—a practice that, though not a strategy in any real sense, tended to win him a great deal of respect, and earn him a place among the inheritors of land and fortune, quite as if he had set out to end up there.

In this way Aubert Gascoigne, born out of wedlock to an English governess, raised in the attics of Parisian row-houses, clothed always in cast-offs, forever banished to the coal scuttle, by turns admonished and ignored, had risen, over time, to become a personage of limited but respectable means. He had escaped his past—and yet he could be called neither an ambitious man, nor an unduly lucky one.

In his person Gascoigne showed a curious amalgam of classes, high and low. He had cultivated his mind with the same grave discipline with which he now maintained his toilette—which is to say, according to a method that was sophisticated, but somewhat out of date. He held the kind of passion for books and learning that only comes when one has pursued an education on one's very own—but it was a passion that, because its origins were both private and virtuous, tended towards piety and scorn. His temperament was deeply nostalgic, not for his own past, but for past ages; he was cynical of the present, fearful of the future, and profoundly regretful of the world's decay. As a whole, he put one in mind of a well-preserved old gentleman (in fact he was only thirty-four) in a period of comfortable, but perceptible, decline—a decline of which he was well aware, and which either amused him or turned him melancholy, depending on his moods.

For Gascoigne was extraordinarily moody. The wave of compassion that had compelled him to lie on Anna's behalf dissipated almost as soon as the whore was freed: it darkened to despair, a despair that his help might, after all, have been a vain one—misplaced, wrong, and worst of all, self-serving. Selfishness was Gascoigne's deepest fear. He loathed all signs of it in himself, quite as a competitive man loathes all traces of weakness that might keep him from his selfish goal. This was a feature of his personality of which he was extraordinarily proud, however, and about which he loved to moralise; whenever the irrationality of all this became too evident to ignore, he would fall into a very selfish bout of irritation.

Anna had followed him out of the gaol-house; in the street he suggested, almost brusquely, that she come to his quarters, so as to explain herself in private. Meekly she acquiesced, and they walked on together, through the rain. Gascoigne no longer pitied her. His compassion, quick to flare, had given way to worry and self-doubt—for she was a failed suicide, after all; and, as the gaoler had warned him as he signed the form for Anna's release, probably insane.

Now, two weeks later, in the Gridiron Hotel—with his arms about her, his hand splayed firmly in the hollow of her back, her forearms pressed against his chest, her breath dampening his collarbone—Gascoigne's thoughts again turned to the possibility that perhaps she had tried, a second time, to end her life. But where was the bullet that ought to have lodged in her breastbone? Had she known that the gun would misfire in such a peculiar way, when she pointed the muzzle at her own throat, and pulled the hammer down? How could she have known it?

'All men want their whores to be unhappy'—Anna herself had said that, the night she was released from gaol, after she followed him home to his quarters, and they took apart her gown at his kitchen table, with the rain beating down, and the paraffin lamp making soft the corners of the room. 'All men want their whores to be unhappy'—and how had he responded? Something curt, most likely, something terse. And now she had shot herself, or tried to. Gascoigne held her for a long time after Pritchard closed the door, gripping her tight, inhaling the salty smell of her hair. The smell was a comfort: he had been many years at sea.

And he had been married. Agathe Gascoigne—Agathe Prideaux, as he had known her first. Elfin, quick-witted, teasing, and consumptive—a fact he had known when he made his proposal, but which had somehow seemed immaterial, surmountable; more a proof of her delicacy than a promise of ill tidings to come. But her lungs would not heal. They had travelled south, in pursuit of the climate cure, and she had died on the open ocean, somewhere off the Indian coast—horrible, that he did not know exactly where. Horrible, how her body had bent when it had struck the surface of the water—that slapping sound. She had made him promise not to order a coffin, nor to have one approximated, should she die before they reached their port of call. If it happened, she said, it would happen in the mariners' way: sewn into a hammock with a double-backed seam. And because the hammock was hers, that bloom of scarlet, darkened now to brown—he'd knelt and kissed it, macabre though that was. After that, Gascoigne kept sailing. He stopped only when his money ran dry.

Anna was heavier than Agathe had been—more angular, more substantial; but then (he thought), perhaps the living always seem substantial to those whose thoughts are with the dead. He moved his hand across her back. With his fingers he traced the shape of her corset, the double seam of eyelets, laced with string.

After leaving the gaol-house they had detoured past the Magistrate's Court, so that Gascoigne could leave his bail purse in the deposit box there, and file the bail notices, ready for the morning. Anna watched him perform these tasks patiently and without curiosity: she seemed to accept that Gascoigne had done her a great favour, and she was content to obey him, and keep silent, in return. Out of habit she did not walk beside him in the street, but followed him at a distance of several yards—so that Gascoigne could claim not to know her, if they encountered an arm of the law.

When they reached Gascoigne's cottage (for he had a whole cottage to himself, though a small one; a one-roomed clapboard cabin, some hundred yards from the beach), Gascoigne directed Anna to wait beneath the awning of the porch while he split a log for kindling in the yard. He made short work of the log, feeling a little self-conscious with Anna's dark eyes fixed upon him as he chopped. Before the heartwood could dampen in the rain, he gathered the splintered fragments in his arms and dashed back to the doorway, where Anna stood aside to let him pass.

'It's no palace,' he said foolishly—though, by Hokitika standards, it was.

Anna made no comment as she passed under the lintel and into the dim fug of the cottage. Gascoigne dropped the kindling on the hearth and reached back to close the door. He lit the paraffin lamp, set it on the table, and knelt to build a fire—intensely aware, as he did so, of Anna's silent appraisal of the room. It was sparsely furnished. His one fine piece of furniture was a wingback armchair, upholstered in a thick fabric of pink and yellow stripes: this had been a present to himself, upon first taking possession of the place, and it stood pride of place in the centre of the room. Gascoigne wondered what assumptions she was forming, what picture was emerging from this scant constellation of his life. The narrow mattress, over which his blanket was folded thrice. The miniature of Agathe, hanging from a nail above the bedhead. The row of seashells along the window sill. The tin kettle on the range; his Bible, the pages mostly uncut except for Psalms and the epistles; the tartan biscuit tin, inside of which he kept his letters from his mother, his papers, and his pens. Beside his bed, the box of broken candles, the wax pieces held together by the string of their wicks.

'You keep a clean house,' was all she said.

'I live alone.' Gascoigne pointed with a stick to the trunk at the base of his bed. 'Open that.'

She loosed the clasps, and heaved open the top. He directed her to a swatch of dark linen, which she lifted up, and Agathe's dress slithered out over her knees—the black one, with the tatted collar, that he had so despised.

('People will think me an ascetic,' she had said cheerfully, 'but black is a sober colour; one ought to have a sober dress.'

It was to hide the bloodstains, the fine spray that peppered her cuffs; he knew it, but did not say so. He agreed, aloud, that one ought to have a sober dress.)

'Put it on,' Gascoigne said, watching as Anna smoothed the fabric over her knee. Agathe had been shorter; the hem would have to be let down. Even then, the whore would show three inches of her ankle, and maybe even the last hoop of her crinoline. It would be awful—but beggars could not be choosers, Gascoigne thought, and Anna was a beggar tonight. He turned back to the fire and shovelled ash.

It was the only dress of Agathe's that Gascoigne still possessed. The others, packed in their camphor-smelling cedar case, had been lost when the steamer ran aground—the berths first looted, then flooded, when the steamer fell at last upon her side, and the surf closed in. For Gascoigne the loss was a blessing. He had Agathe's miniature: that was all he wished to keep. He would pay her memory due respect, but he was a young man, and still hot-blooded, and he meant to begin again.

By the time Anna had changed, the fire was lit. Gascoigne glanced sideways at the dress. It looked just as ill upon her as it had upon his late wife. Anna saw him looking.

'Now I will be able to mourn,' she said. 'I never had a black dress before.'

Gascoigne did not ask her whom she was mourning, or how recent the death. He filled the kettle, and put it on the range.

Aubert Gascoigne preferred to initiate conversation, rather than fall in with another person's theme and tempo; he was content to be silent in company until he felt moved to speak. Anna Wetherell, with her whore's intuition, seemed to recognise this aspect of Gascoigne's character. She did not press him to converse, and she did not watch or shadow him as he went about the ordinary business of the evening: lighting candles, refilling his cigarette case, exchanging his muddy boots for indoor shoes. She gathered up the gold-lined dress and conveyed it across the room to spread on Gascoigne's table. It was heavy. The gold had added perhaps five pounds to the weight of the fabric, Anna guessed: she tried to calculate the value. The Crown would buy pure colour at a rate of around three sovereigns per ounce—and there were sixteen ounces in a pound of weight—and this was five pounds of weight, at least. How much did that total? She tried to imagine a column of sums in her mind, but the figures swam.

While Gascoigne banked the fire for the evening, and spooned tea leaves into a strainer, ready to steep, Anna examined her dress. Whoever had hidden the gold there evidently had experience with a needle and thread—either a woman or a sailor, she thought. They had sewn with care. The gold had been fitted up and down the bones of the corset, sewn into the flounces, and parcelled evenly around the hem—an extra weight she had not noticed earlier, for she often carried lead pellets around the bottom of her crinoline, to prevent the garment from blowing upward in the wind.

Gascoigne had come up behind her. He took out his bowie knife, to cut the corset free—but he began too like a butcher, and Anna made a noise of distress.

'Please,' she said. 'You don't know how—please let me.'

He hesitated, and then passed her the knife, and stood back to watch. She worked slowly, wanting to preserve the form and shape of the dress: first she took out the hem, then worked her way upward, along each flounce, snicking the threads with the point of the knife, and shaking the gold out of the seams. When she reached the corset, she made a little slice beneath each stay, and then reached up with her fingers to loose the gold from where it had been stuffed, in panels, between the bones. It was these lumpy parcels that had so reminded Gascoigne of chainmail, in the gaol-house.

The gold, shaken out of the folds, shone gloriously. Anna collected it in the centre of the table. She was careful not to let the dust scatter in the draught. Each time she added another handful of dust, or another nugget, she cupped her hands over the pile, as if to warm herself upon the shine. Gascoigne watched her. He was frowning.

At last she was done, and the dress was emptied.

'Here,' she said, taking up a nugget roughly the size of the last joint of Gascoigne's thumb. She pushed it across the table towards him. 'One pound one shilling: I haven't forgotten.'

'I will not touch this gold,' said Gascoigne.

'Plus payment for the mourning dress,' Anna said, flushing. 'I don't need charity.'

'You might,' said Gascoigne. He sat down on the edge of the bed and reached into his breast pocket for his cigarettes. He flipped open the silver case, plucked out a cigarette, and lit it with care; only after it was lit, and he had taken several lungfuls, did he turn to her, and say,

'Who do you work for, Miss Wetherell?'

'You mean—who runs the girls? Mannering.'

'I do not know him.'

'You would if you saw him. He's very fat. He owns the Prince of Wales.'

'I have seen a fat man.' Gascoigne sucked on his cigarette. 'Is he a fair employer?'

'He has a temper,' Anna said, 'but his terms are mostly fair.'

'Does he give you opium?'

'No.'

'Does he know you take it?'

'Yes.'

'Who sells you the stuff?'

'Ah Sook,' said Anna.

'Who is that?'

'He's just a chink. A hatter. He keeps the den at Kaniere.'

'A Chinese man who makes hats?'

'No,' Anna said. 'I was using local talk. A hatter is a man who digs alone.'

Gascoigne paused in his line of questioning to smoke.

'This hatter,' he said next. 'He keeps an opium den—at Kaniere.'
'Yes.'

'And you go to him.'

She narrowed her eyes. 'Yes.'

'Alone.' He spoke the word accusingly.

'Most often,' Anna said, squinting at him. 'Sometimes I buy a little extra, to take at home.'

'Where does *he* get it from? China, I suppose.'

She shook her head. 'Jo Pritchard sells it to him. He's the chemist. Has a drug hall on Collingwood-street.'

Gascoigne nodded. 'I know Mr. Pritchard,' he said. 'Well then, I am curious: why should you bother with Chinamen, if you could buy the stuff from Mr. Pritchard direct?'

Anna lifted her chin a little—or perhaps she merely shivered; Gascoigne could not tell. 'I don't know,' she said.

'You don't know,' said Gascoigne.

'No.'

'Kaniere is a long way to walk for a mouthful of smoke, I think.'
'I suppose.'

'And Mr. Pritchard's emporium is—what—not ten minutes' walk from the Gridiron. Still less if one walked at a pace.'

She shrugged.

'Why do you go to Kaniere Chinatown, Miss Wetherell?'

Gascoigne spoke acidly; he felt that he knew the probable answer to the question, and wanted her to say the words aloud.

Her face was stony. 'Maybe I like it there.'

'Ah,' he said. 'Maybe you like it there.'

(For goodness' sake! What had come over him? What did he care if the whore plied her trade with Chinamen or not? What did he care if she made the trip to Kaniere alone, or with an escort? She was a whore! He had met her for the first time that very evening! Gascoigne felt a rush of bewilderment, and then immediately, a stab of anger. He took refuge in his cigarette.)

'Mannering,' he said, when he had exhaled. 'The fat man. Could you leave him?'

'Once I clear my debt.'

'How much do you owe?'

'A hundred pounds,' said Anna. 'Maybe a little over.'

The empty dress lay between them, like a flayed corpse. Gascoigne looked at the pile, at its glimmer; Anna, following his line of sight, looked too.

'You will be tried at the courts, of course,' Gascoigne said, gazing at the gold.

'I was only tight in public,' said Anna. 'They'll fine me, that's all.'

'You will be tried,' Gascoigne said. 'For attempted suicide. The gaoler has confirmed it.'

She stared at him. 'Attempted *suicide*?'

'Did you not try and take your life?'

'No!' She leaped up. 'Who's saying that?'

'The duty sergeant who picked you up last night,' said Gascoigne.

'That's absurd.'

'I'm afraid it has been recorded,' said Gascoigne. 'You will have to plead, one way or another.'

Anna said nothing for a moment. Then she burst out, 'Every man wants his whore to be unhappy—every man!'

Gascoigne blew out a narrow jet of smoke. 'Most whores *are* unhappy,' he said. 'Forgive me: I only state a simple truth.'

'How could they charge me for attempted suicide, without first asking me whether I—? How could they? Where's the—'

'—Proof?'

Gascoigne studied her with pity. Anna's recent brush with death showed plainly in her face and body. Her complexion was waxy, her hair limp and heavy with grease. She was snatching compulsively at the sleeves of her dress with her fingers; as the clerk appraised her, she gave a shiver that racked her body like a wave.

'The gaoler fears that you are insane,' he said.

'I have never spoken one word to Gov. Shepard in all my months in Hokitika,' said Anna. 'We are perfect strangers.'

'He mentioned that you had recently lost a child.'

'*Lost*!' said Anna, in a voice full of disgust. '*Lost*! That's a sanitary word.'

'You would use a different one?'

'Yes.'

'Your child was taken from you?'

A hard look came across Anna's face. 'Kicked from my womb,' she said. 'And by—by the child's own father! But I suppose Gov. Shepard didn't tell you that.'

Gascoigne was silent. He had not yet finished his cigarette, but he dropped it, crushed the ember with the heel of his shoe, and lit another. Anna sat down again. She placed her hands upon the fabric of her dress, laid out upon the table. She began to stroke it. Gascoigne looked at the rafters, and Anna at the gold.

It was very unlike her to burst out in such a way. Anna's nature was watchful and receptive rather than declamatory, and she rarely spoke about herself. Her profession demanded modesty of the strictest sort, paradoxical though that sounded. She was obliged to behave sweetly, and with sympathy, even when sympathy was not owing, and sweetness was not deserved. The men with whom she plied her trade were rarely curious about her. If they spoke at all, they spoke about other women—the sweethearts they had lost, the wives they had abandoned, their mothers, their sisters, their daughters, their wards. They sought these women when they looked at Anna, but only partly, for they also sought themselves: she was a reflected darkness, just as she was a borrowed light. Her wretchedness was, she knew, extremely reassuring.

Anna reached out a finger to stroke one of the golden nuggets in the pile. She knew that she ought to thank Gascoigne in the conventional way, for paying her bail: he had taken a risk, in telling a falsehood to the gaoler, keeping her secret, and inviting her back to his home. She sensed that Gascoigne was expecting something. He was fidgeting strangely. His questions were abrupt and even rude—a sure sign that he was distracted by the hope of a reward—and when she spoke he glared at her, quickly, and then glanced away, as if her answers annoyed him very much. Anna picked up the nugget and rolled it around in her palm. Its surface was bubbled, even knot-holed, as if the metal had been partly melted in a forge.

'It appears to me,' Gascoigne said presently, 'that someone was waiting for you to smoke that pipe last night. They waited until you were unconscious, and then sewed this gold into your dress.'

She frowned—not at Gascoigne, but at the lump in her hand. 'Why?'

'I have no idea,' the Frenchman said. 'Who were you with last night, Miss Wetherell? And just how much was he willing to pay?'

'Listen, though,' Anna said, ignoring the question. 'You're saying that someone took this dress off me, sewed in all this dust so carefully, and then laced me back up—filled with gold—only to leave me in the middle of the road?'

'It does sound improbable,' Gascoigne agreed. He changed his tack. 'Well then: answer me this. How long have you had that garment?'

'Since the spring,' Anna said. 'I bought it salvage, from a vendor on Tancred-street.'

'How many others do you own?'

'Five—no; four,' said Anna. 'But the others aren't for whoring. This is my whoring gown—on account of its colour, you see. I had a separate frock for lying-in—but that was ruined, when—when the baby died.'

There was a moment of quiet between them.

'Was it sewed in all at once?' Gascoigne said presently. 'Or over a period? I suppose there's no way to tell.'

Anna did not respond. After a moment Gascoigne glanced up, and met her gaze.

'Who were you with last night, Miss Wetherell?' he asked again—and this time Anna could not ignore the question.

'I was with a man named Staines,' she said quietly.

'I do not know this man,' Gascoigne said. 'He was with you at the opium den?'

'No!' Anna said, sounding shocked. 'I wasn't at the den. I was at his house. In his—bed. I left in the night to take a pipe. That's the last thing I remember.'

'You left his house?'

'Yes—and came back to the Gridiron, where I have my lodging,' Anna said. 'It was a strange night, and I was feeling odd. I wanted a pipe. I remember lighting it. The next thing I remember, I was in gaol, and there was daylight.'

She gave a shiver, and suddenly clutched her arms across her body. She spoke, Gascoigne thought, with an exhilarated fatigue, the kind that comes after the first blush of love, when the self has lost its mooring, and, half-drowning, succumbs to a fearful tide. But addiction was not love; it could not be love. Gascoigne could not romanticise the purple shadows underneath her eyes, her wasted limbs, the dreamy disorientation with which she spoke; but even so, he thought, it was uncanny that the opium's ruin could mirror love's raptures with such fidelity.

'I see,' he said aloud. 'So you left the man sleeping?'

'Yes,' said Anna. 'He was asleep when I left—yes.'

'And you were wearing this dress.' He pointed at the orange tatters between them.

'It's my work dress,' Anna said. 'It's the one I always wear.'

'Always?'

'When I'm working,' Anna said.

Gascoigne did not reply, but narrowed his eyes very slightly, and pressed his lips together, to signify there was a question in his mind that he could not ask with decency. Anna sighed. She decided that she would not express her gratitude in the conventional way; she would repay the sum of her bail in coin, and in the morning.

'Look,' she said, 'It's just as I told you. We fell asleep, I woke up, I wanted a pipe, I left his house, I went home, I lit my pipe, and that's the last thing I remember.'

'Did you notice anything strange about your own rooms when you returned? Anything that might show that someone had been there, for example?'

'No,' Anna said. 'The door was locked, same as always. I opened it with my key, I walked in, I closed the door, I sat down, I lit my pipe, and that's the last thing I remember.'

It wearied her to recapitulate—and she would become still wearier in the days to come, once it transpired that Emery Staines had disappeared in the night, and had not been seen since, by anyone. Upon this point Anna Wetherell would be examined, and cross-examined, and scorned, and disbelieved; she would repeat her story until it ceased to be familiar, and she began to doubt herself.

Gascoigne did not know Staines, having arrived in Hokitika himself only very recently, but watching Anna now, he felt suddenly intensely curious about the man.

'Could Mr. Staines have wished you harm?' he said.

'No!' she said at once.

'Do you trust him?'

'Yes,' Anna said quietly. 'As much as—'

But she did not complete the comparison.

'He is a lover?' Gascoigne said, after a pause.

Anna blushed. 'He is the richest man in Hokitika,' she said. 'If you have not heard of him yet, you will presently. Emery Staines. He owns most things around town.'

Again Gascoigne's gaze drifted to the gleaming pile of gold on the table—but pointedly this time: to the richest man in Hokitika, this would seem, surely, like a very small pile. 'He is a lover?' he repeated. 'Or a client?'

Anna paused. 'A client,' she said at last, and in a smaller voice. Gascoigne inclined his head respectfully, as if Anna had just informed him that the man had passed away. She rushed on: 'He's a prospector. That's how he made his wealth. But he hails from New South Wales, as I do. In fact we were on the same ship across the Tasman, when we first arrived: the *Fortunate Wind*.'

'I see,' said Gascoigne. 'Well, then. If he is rich, perhaps this gold is his.'

'No,' Anna said, alarmed. 'He wouldn't.'

'He wouldn't what? Wouldn't lie to you?'

'Wouldn't—'

'Wouldn't use you as a beast of burden, to traffic this gold without your knowing?'

'Traffic it where?' said Anna. 'I'm not leaving. I'm not going anywhere.'

Gascoigne paused to drag upon his cigarette. Then he said, 'You left his bed in the night—did you not?'

'I meant to return,' Anna said. 'And sleep it off.'

'You left without his knowledge, I think.'

'But I meant to return.'

'And despite the fact—perhaps—that he had contracted you to remain until the morning.'

'I'm telling you,' Anna said, 'I only meant to be gone a little while.'

'But then you lost consciousness,' Gascoigne said.

'Perhaps I fainted.'

'You don't believe that.'

Anna chewed her lip. 'Oh, it doesn't make *sense*!' she exclaimed after a moment. 'The gold doesn't make sense; the opium doesn't make sense. Why would I end up *there*? Out cold, quite alone, and halfway to Arahura!'

'Surely much of what happens when you are under the effects of opium does not make sense.'

'Yes,' she said. 'Yes, all right.'

'But I would be happy to defer to you on that point,' Gascoigne said, 'having never touched the drug myself.'

The kettle began to whistle. Gascoigne stuck his cigarette in the corner of his mouth, wrapped his hand in a scrap of serge, and lifted it down from the range. As he poured the water over the tea leaves he said, 'What about your chink? He touched the opium, did he not?'

Anna rubbed her face—as a tired infant rubs its face: clumsily. 'I didn't see Ah Sook last night,' she said. 'I told you, I took a pipe at home.'

'A pipe filled with *his* opium!' Gascoigne set the kettle on a rack above the range.

'Yes—I suppose,' Anna said. 'But you might just as well call it Joseph Pritchard's.'

Gascoigne sat down again. 'Mr. Staines must be wondering what has happened to you, seeing as you left his bed so abruptly in the night, and did not return. Though I notice he did not come to make your bail today—neither he nor your employer.'

He spoke loudly, meaning to rouse Anna out of her fatigue; when he set out the saucers, he set Anna's down with a clatter, and pushed it across the table so it scraped.

'That's my business,' Anna said. 'I shall go and make my apologies, as soon as—'

'As soon as we are decided what to do with this pile,' Gascoigne finished for her. 'Yes: you ought to do that.'

Gascoigne's mood had changed again: suddenly, he was extremely vexed. No clear explanation had yet presented itself to him as to why Anna's dress had been filled with gold, or how she had ended up unconscious, or indeed whether these two events were connected in any way. He was vexed that he could not understand it—and so, to appease his own ill humour, he became scornful, an attitude that afforded him at least the semblance of control.

'How much is this worth?' said Anna now, moving to touch the pile again. 'As an estimate, I mean. I don't have an eye for such things.'

Gascoigne crushed the stub of his cigarette on his saucer. 'I think the question you ought to be asking, my dear,' he said, 'is not *how much*; it is *who*, and *why*. Whose gold is that? Whose claim did it come from? And where was it bound?'

Φ

They agreed, that first night, to hide the pile away. They agreed that if anyone asked Anna why she had exchanged her habitual gown for this new, more sombre one, she would reply, quite honestly, that she had wished to enter a belated period of mourning for the death of her unborn child, and she had procured the garment from a trunk that had washed up on the Hokitika spit. All of this was true. If anyone asked to see the old gown, or inquired as to where it was stored, then Anna was to inform Gascoigne immediately—for that person no doubt had knowledge of the gold that had been hidden in her flounces, and would therefore know about the gold's origin—and perhaps also its intended destination, wherever that was.

With this strategy having been decided, Gascoigne then emptied his tartan biscuit tin, and together they swept the gold into it, wrapped the tin in a blanket, and placed the entire bundle in a flour sack that Gascoigne tied with string. He requested, until they had further intelligence, that the sack be stowed at his quarters, beneath his bed. At first Anna was doubtful, but he persuaded her that the pile would be safest with him: he never entertained visitors, his cabin was locked during the day, and nobody had the slightest reason to think that he was harbouring a pile—after all, he was new in town, and had neither enemies nor friends.

The following fortnight seemed to pass in a blur. Anna returned to Staines's house to find that he had vanished completely; days later, she learned about the death of Crosbie Wells, and discovered that *that* event had also taken place during the hours of her unconsciousness. Soon after that she heard that an enormous fortune, the origins of which had yet to be determined, had been discovered hidden on Crosbie Wells's estate, which had since been purchased by the hotelier, Edgar Clinch—acting proprietor of the Gridiron Hotel, which was owned by Emery Staines, and the current residence of Anna herself.

Gascoigne had not spoken with Anna directly about any of these events, for she refused to be drawn on the subject of Emery Staines, and had nothing at all to say about Crosbie Wells, save that she had never known him. Gascoigne sensed that she was grieving Staines's disappearance, but he could not gauge whether she believed him to be alive or dead. In deference to her feelings Gascoigne dropped the subject altogether; when they spoke, they spoke of other things. From her high window on the upper floor of the Gridiron Hotel Anna watched the diggers struggle up and down Revell-street, through the rain. She kept to her room, and wore Agathe Gascoigne's black dress every day. No man inquired about Anna's change of costume; no man made any kind of intimation to suggest that he knew about the gold that had been hidden in her corset, now safely stowed under Gascoigne's bed. The responsible party was reluctant, for whatever reason, to come forward and show his hand.

On the day after Crosbie Wells's burial, Anna was tried for attempted suicide at the petty court, as Gascoigne had predicted she would be. She refused to plead, and in the end was fined a sum

of five pounds for her attempted felony—and then scolded roundly,
for having wasted the Magistrate's time.

Φ

All this was running through Gascoigne's mind as he stood in the
Gridiron Hotel with Anna Wetherell clasped against his chest, tracing the eyelets of her corset, up her back. He had held Agathe in
this way—exactly in this way, exactly so, with one hand splayed
beneath her shoulder blade, the other cupping the ball of her
shoulder, Agathe with her forearms against his chest, always—
having raised her arms to shield herself at the moment of
enclosure. How strange that he recalled her, now. One could know
a thousand women, Gascoigne thought; one could take a different
girl every night for years and years—but sooner or later, the new
lovers would do little more than call to mind the old, and one
would be forced to wander, lost, in that reflective maze of endless
comparison, forever disappointed, forever turning back.

Anna was still trembling from the shock of the misfire.
Gascoigne waited until her breathing was steady—some three or
four minutes after Pritchard's tread retreated down the stairs—and
then at last, when he felt her body regain some of its strength, he
murmured, 'What on earth got into you?'

But Anna only shook her head, burrowing against him.

'Was it a blank? A false cartridge?'

She shook her head again.

'Perhaps you and the chemist—perhaps you devised something
together.'

That roused her; she pushed away from him with the heels of
her hands, and said, in a voice full of disgust, 'With *Pritchard*?'

It pleased Gascoigne to see her brighten, even in anger. 'Well,
then: what was he wanting you for?' he said.

Anna almost told him the truth—but felt a sudden shame.
Gascoigne had been so kind to her, this past fortnight, and she
could not bear to tell him where the opium had gone. Just yesterday he had expressed happiness that she had ended her
enslavement to the pipe: he had marvelled at her strength, and

praised the clearness of her eyes, and admired her. She had not had the heart to disabuse him then, and she did not now.

'Old Jo Pritchard,' she said, looking away. 'He was lonely, that was all.'

Gascoigne pulled out his cigarette case, and found that he was trembling too. 'Have you any brandy left?' he said. 'I would like to sit a moment, if you don't mind. I need to gather myself.'

He laid the spent pistol carefully on the whatnot beside Anna's bed.

'Things keep *happening* to you,' he said. 'Things you can't explain. Things nobody seems to be able to explain. I'm not sure . . .'

But he trailed off. Anna went to the armoire to fetch the brandy, and Gascoigne sat down upon the bed to light his cigarette—and just for a moment they were fixed in a tableau, the kind rendered on a plate, and sold at a fair as an historical impression: he with his wrists on his knees, his head bowed, his cigarette dangling from his knuckles—she with her hand on her hip, her weight upon one leg, pouring him a measure. But they were not lovers, and it was not their room.

Gascoigne took another deep draught of his cigarette, and closed his eyes.

Meaning to cheer him, Anna said, 'I am very much looking forward to my surprise, Mr. Gascoigne.'

For she had not lied to Joseph Pritchard, when she informed him she had an appointment—going with a lady, to look at hats. Gascoigne had arranged a private consultation with a lady of fashion; apparently he had paid for the consultation himself, though he had insisted that the details of the arrangement, and the identity of the lady, remain a surprise. Anna had never been asked to wait for a surprise before, and the prospect had filled her with both elation and dread; she had thanked the Frenchman very prettily, however, for his consideration.

When Gascoigne did not respond, Anna tried to press him further. 'Is your woman downstairs, waiting?'

Gascoigne emerged from his reverie at last. He sighed. 'No: I am to fetch you and bring you to her. She's in the private parlour at the

Wayfarer—but she can wait ten minutes; she has waited ten minutes already.' He passed a hand over his face. 'Your hats can wait.'

'What are you not sure of?'

'What?'

'You just said, "I'm not sure", but you didn't finish your sentence.'

They had adopted an easy tone with one another, this past fortnight, as so often happens after a shared ordeal—though Anna still called him Mr. Gascoigne, and never Aubert. Gascoigne had not pressed her to use the more informal designation, for he rather liked shows of propriety, and it flattered him to hear his family name pronounced.

'I'm not sure what to make of it,' Gascoigne said at last. He took the glass from her, but did not drink: all of a sudden, he felt extraordinarily sad.

Aubert Gascoigne felt the pressure of anxiety rather more acutely than other men. When he was made anxious, as he had been by the inexplicable misfire of Anna's pistol, he tended to give himself over to bursts of powerful emotion—shock, despair, anger, sorrow: emotions which he seized upon because they channelled his anxiety outward, and in a sense regulated the pressure that he felt within. He had earned a reputation for being strong and level-headed at a time of crisis—as he had been, that afternoon—but he tended to unravel after the crisis had been weathered or forestalled. He was still trembling, an agitated motion that had only started when he released the whore from their embrace.

'There's something I need to speak with you about,' Anna said now.

Gascoigne rolled his brandy around his glass. 'Yes.'

Anna returned to the armoire and poured herself a measure also. 'I'm late on my rent. I owe three months. Edgar gave me notice this morning.'

Abruptly she stopped speaking, turned, and peered at him. Gascoigne had been taking a draught of his cigarette; he paused at the end of the intake, his chest expanded, and made a gesture with his hands to ask *how much*.

'It's ten shillings a week, with meals, and a bath every Sunday,' Anna said. (Gascoigne exhaled.) 'Over three months—that's—I don't know … six pounds.'

'Three months,' Gascoigne echoed.

'I was set back by that fine,' said Anna. 'Five pounds, to the Magistrate. That was a month of wages for me. It cleaned me out.'

She waited.

'Surely the whoremonger pays your rent,' Gascoigne said.

'No,' Anna said. 'He doesn't. I report direct to Edgar.'

'Your landlord.'

'Yes: Edgar Clinch.'

'Clinch?' Gascoigne looked up. 'That's the man who purchased Crosbie Wells's estate.'

'His cottage,' said Anna.

'But he's just come in on an enormous fortune! What does he care about six pounds?'

Anna shrugged. 'He just said to raise it. At once.'

'Perhaps he fears what will happen at the courthouse,' Gascoigne said. 'Perhaps he fears he will have to give it all back again, once the appeal is granted.'

'He didn't say why,' Anna said. (She had not yet heard about the sudden arrival, on Thursday afternoon, of the widow Wells, and so did not know that the sale of Crosbie Wells's estate was in danger of being revoked.) 'But he's not calling my bluff about it; he said he wasn't.'

'You can't—appease him somehow?' Gascoigne said.

'You can leave off the "somehow",' Anna said haughtily. 'I'm in mourning. My child is dead and I'm in mourning. I won't do that any more.'

'You could find another line of work.'

'There isn't one. The only thing I can do is needlework, and there's no call for it here. There aren't enough women.'

'There's mending,' Gascoigne said. 'Socks and buttons. Frayed collars. There's always mending, in a camp.'

'Mending doesn't pay,' said Anna.

She peered at him again—expectantly, Gascoigne thought, and

this interpretation gave rise to a flash of anger. He took refuge in another draught. It was not his responsibility that she had no money. She had not walked the streets once in the two weeks since her night in gaol, and whoring was her income: it stood to reason that she was out of pocket. As for this mourning business! Nobody had forced her into it. She was hardly impaired by grief—the child was three months dead, for heaven's sake. The frock was no real impediment either. She would make a shilling just as easily in Agathe's black dress as in her habitual orange one—for she had loyal custom in the Hokitika township, and whores were all too few along the Coast. Anyway, Gascoigne thought, what did it matter? One could not tell colours in the dark.

This burst of irritation was not for want of mercy. Gascoigne had known poverty, and since his youth he had been many times in debt. He would have helped Anna, and gladly, had she chosen to request his assistance in a different way. But like most extremely sensitive people, Gascoigne could not bear sensitivity in others: he required honesty and directness when he was asked a question—and he required it all the more desperately when he was vexed. He recognised that the whore was employing a strategy in order to get something. This strategy angered him because he could see it was a strategy—and also, because he knew exactly what Anna was about to ask for. He expelled a jet of smoke.

'Edgar's always been very kind to me,' Anna continued, when it became evident that Gascoigne was not going to speak. 'But lately he's been in a temper. I don't know what it is. I've tried pleading with him, but there's nothing doing.' She paused. 'If I could only—'

'No.'

'Only the smallest bit—that's all I'd need,' said Anna. 'Just one of the nuggets. I could tell him I found it in the creek, or on the road somewhere. Or I could tell him I'd been paid in pure—the diggers do that, sometimes. I could say it was from one of the foreign boys. I'm a good liar.'

Gascoigne shook his head. 'You cannot touch that gold.'

'But for how long?' Anna said. 'For how long?'

'Until you find out who sewed it into your corset!' Gascoigne snapped. 'And not a moment before!'

'But what am I to do about my rent, in the meantime?'

Gascoigne looked hard at her. 'Anna Wetherell,' he said, 'you are not my ward.'

This silenced her, though her eyes flashed in displeasure. She cast about for something to do, some mundane task with which to occupy herself. At last she knelt down to pick up her scattered trinkets, strewn by Pritchard on the floor—scooping them towards her angrily, and throwing them with some violence back into the empty dresser drawer.

'You are right: I am not your ward,' she said presently. 'But I will counter that the pile is not your gold—to be kept, and restricted, as you please!'

'Nor does that gold belong to you, Miss Wetherell.'

'It was in my dress,' she said. 'It was on my person. I bore the risk.'

'You would risk far more, in spending it.'

'So what do I do?' Anna cried. 'Once a whore, always a whore? That's the only option left me, I suppose!'

They glared at each other. *I would give you a gold sovereign*, Gascoigne was thinking, *if you plied your trade with me*. Aloud he said, 'How long do you have?'

Anna wound a scrap of ribbon into a vicious ball before answering. 'He didn't say. He said I had to raise the money or get out.'

'Would you like me to talk to him?' Gascoigne said—baiting her, because he knew this was not what she wanted at all.

'And say what?' Anna returned, throwing the balled ribbon into the drawer. 'Beg him to spare me for another week—another month—another quarter? What's the difference? I shall have to pay him sooner or later.'

'That,' said Gascoigne in an icy tone, 'is what characterises a debt, I'm afraid.'

'I wish that I had known *you* to be a creditor of this kind, two weeks ago,' Anna said now, and in a waspish tone. 'I should never have accepted your help, otherwise.'

'Perhaps your memory is faulty,' Gascoigne said. 'I will remind you that I gave help only because you asked for it.'

'*This*? This mouldy dress? This is "help"? I'd rather give you back the dress—and keep the gold!'

'I got you out of the gaol-house, Anna Wetherell, at great personal risk to myself—and that dress belonged to my late wife, in case you did not know it,' Gascoigne said. He dropped his cigarette onto the floor and ground it to nothing with his heel. Anna was opening her mouth to make a retort, and so he said, loudly: 'I'm afraid you are not in a fit state for my surprise.'

'I am perfectly fit, thank you.'

'A surprise,' Gascoigne said, raising his voice still further, 'that I organised for you for reasons of the purest charity and goodwill—'

'Mr. Gascoigne—'

'—for I felt that it might do you good, to get out and enjoy yourself a little,' Gascoigne concluded. His face was very white. 'I will inform my lady that your spirits are low, and that you won't be seen.'

'My spirits aren't low,' Anna said.

'I think that they are,' said Gascoigne. He drained his glass, and then set it on the nightstand next to Anna's pillow, the centre of which was still pierced by a single blackened hole. 'I will leave you now. I am sorry that your gun did not fire in the way that you intended, and I am sorry that your lifestyle exceeds your means to pay for it. Thank you for the brandy.'

MEDIUM COELI / IMUM COELI

In which Gascoigne raises the issue of Anna's debt, and Edgar Clinch does not confide in him.

As Gascoigne was crossing the foyer of the Gridiron Hotel, the door was wrenched open, and the hotelier, Mr. Edgar Clinch, entered at a pace. Gascoigne slowed in his step so that the two men would not have to pass too close to one another—an action that Clinch mistook for a different kind of hesitation. He stopped abruptly in the middle of the doorway, blocking Gascoigne's exit. Behind him, the door thudded shut.

'Can I help you?' he said.

'Thank you, no,' Gascoigne said politely—and hovered a moment, waiting for Clinch to move from the doorway so that he might leave without having to brush shoulders with the other man.

But the valet had been alerted by the slam of the door. 'Oi—you!' he called out to Gascoigne, coming forward from his cubicle beneath the stairs. 'What was the story behind those pistol shots? Jo Pritchard came downstairs like death incarnate. Like he'd seen a ghost.'

'It was a mistake,' said Gascoigne curtly. 'Just a mistake.'

'Pistol shots?' said Edgar Clinch—who had not moved from the doorway.

Clinch was a tall man, forty-three years of age, with sandy-coloured hair and a harmless, pleasant look. He wore an imperial moustache, greased at the tips, a handsome accessory that had not silvered at the same rate as his hair—which was likewise greased, parted in the middle, and cut to the level of his earlobes. He had apple-shaped cheeks, a reddish nose, and a blunted profile. His eyes were set so deep in his face that they seemed to shut altogether when he smiled, which he did often, as the crowfoot lines around his eyes could testify. At present, however, he was frowning.

'I was down here at the desk,' said the valet. 'This man, he was there—he saw it. He'd run up, on account of the shouting—the gun went off just after he walked in. After that there was another shot—a second. I'm about to go up, to investigate, but then Jo Pritchard comes down, and tells me not to worry. Tells me the whore was cleaning the piece, and it went off by accident—but that explanation only accounts for the first.'

Edgar Clinch slid his gaze back to Gascoigne.

'The second shot was mine,' Gascoigne said, speaking with ill-concealed annoyance; he did not like to be detained against his will. 'I fired the piece experimentally, once I could see that the first shot had fouled.'

'What was the shouting on account of?' asked the hotelier.

'That situation is now resolved.'

'Jo Pritchard—laying into her?'

'Sounded like that from here,' said the valet.

Gascoigne shot the valet a poisonous look, and then turned back to Clinch. 'There was no violence done to the whore,' he said. 'She is perfectly sound, and the situation is now resolved, as I have already told you.'

Clinch narrowed his eyes. 'Strange how many guns go off while being cleaned,' he said. 'Strange how many whores get it into their heads to clean their guns, when there's gentlemen about. Strange how many times that's happened, in my hotel.'

'I'm afraid I can't offer an opinion on that subject,' Gascoigne said.

'I think you can,' said Edgar Clinch. He planted his feet a little wider apart, and folded his arms across his chest.

Gascoigne sighed. He was in no mood for bullish displays of proprietorship.

'What happened?' Clinch said. 'Did something happen to Anna?'

'I suggest you ask her yourself,' Gascoigne said, 'and save us both some time. You can do that very easily, you know: she's right upstairs.'

'I don't appreciate being made a fool in my own hotel.'

'I wasn't aware that I was making you a fool.'

Clinch's moustache twitched dangerously. 'What's your quarrel?'

'I'm not sure that I have one,' said Gascoigne. 'What's yours?'

'Pritchard.' He spat out the name.

'You needn't bring that to *me*,' Gascoigne said. 'Pritchard's not *my* man.' He felt trapped. It was useless pretending to reason with a man whose mind was already fixed, and Edgar Clinch, by the looks of things, was spoiling for a fight.

'That's a true fact,' put in the valet, coming to Gascoigne's rescue. He had also observed that his employer was out of sorts. The hotelier's face was very red, and his trouser leg was twitching, as though he were bouncing his weight up and down upon his heel—a sure sign that he was angry. The valet explained, in soothing tones, that Gascoigne had only interrupted the argument between Pritchard and Anna; he had not been present for its origin.

Clinch did not cut a terribly intimidating figure, even when poised in fighting stance, as he currently was: he seemed fretful rather than fearsome. His anger, though palpable, seemed to render him somehow powerless. He was occupied *by* his emotion; he was its servant, not its liege. Watching him, Gascoigne was put more in mind of a child preparing for a tantrum than a fighter preparing for a brawl—though of course the former was no less dangerous, when the provocation was the same. Clinch was still blocking the door. It was clear that he would not be rational—but perhaps, Gascoigne thought, he could be calmed.

'What has Pritchard done to you, Mr. Clinch?' he said—thinking that if he gave the man a chance to speak, his anger might run its course, and he might calm himself that way.

Clinch's reply was strangled and inarticulate. 'To *Anna*!' he cried. 'Feeds her the very drug that's killing her—sells it!'

This was hardly explanation enough: there must be more. To coax him, Gascoigne said, lightly, 'Yes—but when a man's a drunk, do you blame the publican?'

Clinch ignored this piece of rhetoric. 'Joseph *Pritchard*,' he said. 'He'd feed it to her if he could, like a babe at suck; he'd do that. *You* agree with me, Mr. Gascoigne.'

'Ah—you know me!' said Gascoigne, in a tone of relief, and then, 'I do?'

'Your sermon in yesterday's *Times*. A d—n fine sentiment, by the bye; a d—n fine piece,' said Clinch. (Paying a compliment appeared to soothe him—but then his features darkened again.) '*He* might have done well to read it. Do you know where he gets it from? That filthy muck? The resin? Do you know? Francis Carver, that's who!'

Gascoigne shrugged; the name meant nothing to him.

'Francis bloody Carver, who kicked her—*kicked* her, beat her— and it was his baby! His baby in her belly! Killed his own spawn!'

Clinch was almost shouting—and Gascoigne was suddenly very interested. 'What's that you're saying?' he said, stepping forward. Anna had confided to him that her unborn baby had been killed by its own father—and now it appeared that this same man was connected to the opium by which she herself had nearly perished!

But Clinch had rounded on his valet. '*You*,' he said. 'If Pritchard comes by again, and I'm not here, it's *you* I'm counting on to turn him back. Do you hear me?'

He was very upset.

'Who is Francis Carver?' said Gascoigne.

Clinch hawked and spat on the floor. 'Piece of filth,' he said. 'Piece of murderous filth. Jo Pritchard—*he's* just a reprobate. Carver—*he's* the devil himself; *he's* the one.'

'They are friends?'

'Not *friends*,' said Clinch. 'Not *friends*.' He jabbed his finger at the valet. 'Did you hear me? If Jo Pritchard sets foot on that staircase— the *bottom stair*—you're out on your own!'

Evidently the hotelier no longer regarded Gascoigne as a threat—for he moved from the doorway, snatching his hat from his head; Gascoigne was now free to exit, as he pleased. He did not move, however; instead he waited for the hotelier to elaborate, which, after slicking his hair back with the palm of his hand, and hanging his hat upon the hatstand, he did.

'Francis Carver's a trafficker,' he said. '*Godspeed*—that's his ship; you might have seen her at anchor. A barque—three-masted.'

'What's his connexion to Pritchard?'

'Opium, of course!' said Edgar Clinch, with impatience. He evidently did not take well to being questioned; he frowned anew at Gascoigne, and it seemed that a new wave of suspicion came over him. 'What were you doing in Anna's room?'

Gascoigne said, in a tone of polite surprise, 'I was not aware that Anna Wetherell is in your employ, Mr. Clinch.'

'She's in my care,' said Clinch. He slicked back his hair a second time. 'She lodges here—it's part of the arrangement—and I have a right to know her business, if it happens on my province, and there are pistols involved. You can go: you've got ten minutes'—this last to the valet, who scuttled off to the dining room, to take his lunch.

Gascoigne took hold of his lapels. 'I suppose you think she's lucky, living here, with you to watch over her,' he said.

'You're wrong,' said Clinch. 'I don't think that.'

Gascoigne paused, surprised. Then he said, delicately, 'Do you care for many girls like her?'

'Only three right now,' Clinch said. 'Dick—he's got an eye for them. Only the class acts—and he doesn't drop his standard; he holds to it. You want a shilling whore, you go down to Clap Alley, and see what you catch. There's no spending your loose change with him. It's pounds or nothing. Dick, he put you on to Anna?'

This must be Dick Mannering, Anna Wetherell's employer. Gascoigne made a vague murmur instead of answering. He did not care to narrate the story of how he and Anna had come to meet.

'Well, you ought to go to him, if you want a poke at one of the others,' Clinch went on. 'Kate, the plump one; Sal, with the curly hair; Lizzie, with the freckles. It's no use asking me. I don't do all of that—the bookings and whatnot. They just sleep here.' He saw that his choice of verb had provoked some disbelief in the other, and so he added, 'Sleep is what I mean, you know: I wasn't mincing. I can't have night-callers. I'd lose my licence. You want the whole night, you take it on your own head—in your own room.'

'This is a fine establishment,' said Gascoigne politely, with a sweep of his hand.

'It isn't *mine*,' said Clinch, with a scornful look. 'I'm renting. Up and down the street—from Weld to Stafford, it's all rented. This place belongs to a fellow named Staines.'

Gascoigne was surprised. 'Emery Staines?'

'Odd,' Clinch said. 'Odd to be renting from a man who's half my age. But that's the modern way: all of us upended, each man for his own.'

It seemed to Gascoigne that there was a forced quality to the way that Clinch spoke: his phrases seemed borrowed, and he uttered them unnaturally. He was guarded in his tone, even anxious, and seemed to be protecting himself against Gascoigne's poor opinion, impossible project though that was. *He does not trust me*, Gascoigne thought, and then, *well, I do not trust him, either.*

'What will happen to this place if Mr. Staines doesn't return, I wonder?' he said aloud.

'I'll stay on,' said Clinch. 'I'll buy it, maybe.' He fumbled a moment with a drawer beneath the desk, and then said, 'Listen: you'll think me a bore for asking again—but what were you doing in Anna's room?'

He looked almost pleading.

'We exchanged some words about money,' Gascoigne said. 'She is out of pocket. But I believe you know that already.'

'Out of *pocket*!' Clinch scoffed. 'There's a word! She has pockets enough, believe me.'

Was this a cryptic reference to the gold that had been sewn into Anna's dress? Or simply a crass allusion to the girl's profession? Gascoigne felt suddenly alert. 'Why should I believe you—above Anna?' he said. 'By *her* account, she hasn't a penny to her name—and yet you think it right, to demand six pounds of her, paid up at once!'

Clinch's eyes widened. So Anna had confided in Gascoigne

about the rent she owed. So she had complained about him—and
bitterly, judging by the Frenchman's hostile tone. The thought was
hurtful. Clinch did not like the thought of Anna speaking about
him to other men. Quietly he said, 'That isn't your business.'

'On the contrary,' Gascoigne said. 'Anna brought the matter to
my attention. She begged me.'

'Why?' said Clinch. 'Why, though?'

'I imagine because she trusts me,' Gascoigne said, with a touch
of cruelty.

'I meant, what's the use in begging *you*?'

'So that I might help her,' Gascoigne said.

'But why *you*, though?' Clinch said again.

'What do you mean, why *me*?'

Clinch was almost shouting. 'What's Anna doing asking *you*?'

Gascoigne's eyes flashed. 'I suppose you are asking me to define
the precise state of relations between us.'

'I don't need to ask *that*,' said Clinch, with a hoarse laugh. 'I
know the answer to *that*!'

Gascoigne felt a swell of fury. 'You are impertinent, Mr. Clinch,'
he said.

'Impertinent!' said Clinch. 'Who's impertinent? The whore's in
mourning—that's all—and you can't deny it!'

'The fact that she is in mourning is the very reason why she
cannot repay her present debts. And yet you persist in abusing her.'

'*Abusing*—!'

'I got the impression,' Gascoigne said coldly, 'that Anna is very
much afraid of you'—which was not at all true.

'She isn't afraid of me,' said the hotelier, looking shocked.

'What do you care about six pounds? What do you care if Anna
pays up to-morrow or next year? You've just landed yourself a
homeward-bounder. You've got thousands of pounds in the bank!
And here you are splitting hairs over a whore's rental, like a
Limehouse profiteer!'

Clinch bristled. 'A debt's a debt.'

'Rot,' said Gascoigne. 'A grudge is a grudge, more like.'

'What's that supposed to mean?'

'I don't yet know,' said Gascoigne. 'But I'm beginning to think, for Anna's sake, that I ought to try and find out.'

Clinch turned red again. 'You ought not to talk to me like that,' he said. 'You oughtn't—in my own hotel!'

'You talk as if you were her keeper! Where were you this afternoon, when she was in danger?' said Gascoigne—who was beginning to feel a little reckless. 'And where were you when she turned up near-dead in the middle of the Christchurch-road?'

But this time Clinch did not cower beneath the accusation, as he had done before. Instead he seemed to harden. He looked back at Gascoigne with his jaw newly set. 'I won't be schooled about Anna,' he said. 'You don't know what she is to me. I won't be schooled.'

The two men stared at each other, as two fighting dogs across a pit—and then each expressed his recognition of the other, and conceded, tacitly, that he had met his match. For Gascoigne and Clinch were not so very dissimilar in temperament, and even in their differences, showed a harmony of sorts—with Gascoigne as the upper octave, the clearer, brighter sound, and Clinch as the bass-note, thrumming.

Edgar Clinch had something of a circular nature. He was both solicitous and self-doubting—attributes that, because they opposed one another, tended to engender in him a state of constant, anxious flux. He provided for those whom he loved only to demand their fullest approbation for his care—a demand which, in turn, shamed him, for he was sensitive to the nuances of his own actions, and doubtful of their worth; consequently, he retracted the demand, doubled his provision, and began again, only to find that his need for approbation had doubled also. In this way he remained perpetually in motion, as a woman is perpetually in motion, harnessed to the rhythms of the moon.

His relationship with Anna Wetherell had begun in just this way. When Anna had first arrived from Dunedin, Clinch had been all but overcome: she was the rarest and most troubled creature he had ever known, and he swore that he would not rest until she was beloved. He secured his best room for her, and pampered her in all the ways that he was able, but he became very hurt when she did not notice the efforts he had made—and when she did not notice his hurt, he became angry. His anger was both unsustainable and unsustaining; it did not nourish him, as men are sometimes nourished by their own rage. Instead the emotion only diminished him, leaving him all the emptier—and, therefore, all the more ready to love.

When Anna first arrived in Hokitika she was with child, though her belly had not yet begun to wax, and her figure did not yet betray the secret of her condition. Clinch met her upon Gibson Quay, to which place she had been conveyed by lighter, the barque *Godspeed* having dropped its anchor some hundred yards or so off-shore. The day was clear and bright with cold. The mouth of the river shone brilliantly; there was birdsong in the air. Even now Clinch felt that he could recollect every detail. He could see the wide halo of her bonnet, and the ends of her ribbons, flapping in the wind; he could see her ankle-boots, her buttoned gloves, her reticule. He could see the purple shimmer of her gown—which had been hired, as he later discovered, from the impresario Dick Mannering, to whom Anna would pay a daily rental until she could afford to make a purchase of her own. The garish colour did not suit her: it turned her complexion sallow, and drained the life from her eyes. Edgar Clinch thought her radiant. Beaming, he enclosed her thin hand in both of his own, and shook it vigorously. He welcomed her to Hokitika, offered her his elbow, and proposed a stroll, which she accepted. After directing the porters to have her trunk delivered to the Gridiron Hotel, Clinch threw out his chest and walked Anna Wetherell down Revell-street like a consort escorting a queen.

At that time Edgar Clinch had been in Hokitika less than a month. He did not yet know Dick Mannering, though he had heard the latter's name; he had met Anna's boat that afternoon quite without prearrangement with either the magnate or the whore. (Mannering had been detained in Dunedin, and would not arrive in Hokitika until the following week; in any case, he pre-ferred to travel by steamship than by sail.) On fine days Clinch often stood upon the spit and greeted the diggers as they disembarked onto the sand. He shook their hands, smiled, and invited each man to take his lodgings at the Gridiron Hotel—remarking, casually, that he could offer a handsomely discounted price, but only to those men who accepted it within the next half-hour.

During the short walk from Gibson Quay Clinch became very aware of the delicate pressure of Anna's hand upon his elbow; by the time they reached the Gridiron's front door, he found that he all but depended on it. He begged to treat the young woman to luncheon in the dining room; she accepted, prompting in his breast a paroxysm of redemptive feeling, as a result of which he offered her his very best, and very largest, room.

Anna paid for her lodging with a promissory note from Dick Mannering, which Clinch, in his sudden flood of generosity, accepted without question. By the time it dawned upon him that she must be a member of the old profession, his affections had been securely, and irrevocably, bestowed. When Mannering arrived in Hokitika one week later, he introduced himself to Clinch as Anna's employer, and thereafter negotiated an agreement under which the whore would receive, in exchange for a weekly fee, the benefits of protection, discreet surveillance, two meals a day, and a weekly bath. This last item was an expensive luxury, and one that would be rescinded (as Mannering confidentially explained) once the girl was well established in the town. Over the first few weeks of her employment, however, it was necessary to pander to her sense of opulence, and to satisfy her tastes.

Clinch was more than happy to fill the copper bathtub every Sunday, laborious though that duty was. He loved to glimpse Anna upon the landing, wet-haired and freshly clean; he loved to pass her in the dining room on Sunday evenings, and catch the milky scent of soap upon her skin. He loved to pour the spent bathwater, clouded with dirt, into the gutter at the edge of the road, and hope, as the white water seeped away, that Anna was looking down upon him from her window on the floor above.

Clinch's efforts in love were always of a mothering sort, for it is a feature of human nature to give what we most wish to receive, and it was a mother that Edgar Clinch most craved—his own having died in his infancy, and since then been resurrected as a goddess of shining virtue in his mind, a goddess whose face was as a blurred shape, seen through a window on a night of fog. There was an ill-fated aspect to all of his love's labours, however, for they required of their object a delicacy of intuition that he himself did not possess. Edgar Clinch was a hopeless romantic, but in all the ordinary senses, he was an unsuccessful one: despite his daily ministrations, Anna Wetherell remained entirely ignorant of the fact that the hotelier loved her with the passion of a lonely and desperate heart. She was courteous to him, and kept her rooms in decent order, but she never solicited his company, and she restricted their conversation to the most trivial of themes. Needless to say, her indifference only warmed the coals of the man's infatuation—and banked them higher, so that they burned longer, and with a redder light. When Mannering suggested, after a month, that the extravagance of Anna's weekly bath ought to be discontinued, Clinch only ceased to itemise this service on Anna's monthly bill. Every Sunday he set out the copper tub, and laid out the linens, and drew the water as before.

It seemed, in those first few months, that nothing at all could dampen Clinch's adoration for Anna. He was not repelled by the fact of her profession, though it did distress him to know that she was so frequently in danger of harm. When he learned that she was an opium eater, and took the drug nearly every day, he was likewise only grieved and fearful, rather than repulsed. (He reasoned that the drug was very fashionable, and that he himself took laudanum whenever he could not sleep; why, what was the difference, between opium that had been turned into a tincture, and opium that had been burned into a smoke?) The sorrier aspects of Anna's life, far from driving Clinch away, only caused him sadness, and as a consequence he longed for her happiness all the more.

When it became apparent that Anna was expecting another man's child, however, Clinch's sadness acquired an edge of alarm. He began to wonder whether he ought now to make his feelings known to her. Perhaps he should make an offer of marriage.

Perhaps, when the babe was born, he might adopt the little thing as his own, and care for it; perhaps they could become a family, of a kind.

Clinch was pondering this very question one midwinter afternoon when he heard a thud upon the hotel's veranda, and a muted cry. He opened the sash window (he had been lighting the fires in the upstairs rooms) and peered down to see that Anna had stumbled on the short flight of stairs that led to the front door. As he watched, she lifted her arm, slowly, and began to cast about for the rail.

Clinch descended the stairs, crossed the foyer, and opened the door to admit her—in which time Anna had hauled herself upright and crossed the veranda. When Clinch stepped out, Anna, who had been upon the point of reaching for the latch herself, fell against him, and, to stop herself from falling, she reached up and wrapped her heavy arms around his neck. She turned her face into his collar, so that her nose and mouth were pressed against the skin of his throat; she seemed to sag against him. Clinch gave a murmur of surprise—and then he was very still. He felt that if he spoke, or moved too quickly, the moment might be shattered, and the whore might flee. He looked out, over her shoulder. It was a pale, bright Sunday afternoon, and the street was quiet. No one could see them. No one was watching. Clinch cupped Anna's waist between his palms, and breathed, and breathed again—and then, in one swift movement, he folded Anna against him, lifted her up, and crushed his mouth against her cheek. He stayed there for a long moment, his lips against her jaw. Then he hoisted her higher, retreated back into the foyer, shut the door with the edge of his foot, turned the key in the lock, and carried her upstairs.

Anna's bath had been set out in the room opposite the landing, and iron pots of water were waiting, covered, on the ledge beside the fire. Clinch, still with Anna in his arms, lowered himself down upon the sofa next to the bath. His heart was beating very fast. He drew back, to look at her. Her eyes were closed; her limbs were loose and syrupy.

Many months had passed since Anna had returned the rented

purple dress to Dick Mannering, having purchased, in place of it, several dresses that were better suited to her frame. Today, however, she was not wearing the bustled orange gown with which she habitually advertised her trade—for the whores in Hokitika wore bright colours when they were working, and muted tones when they were not. She was dressed, instead, in a cream-coloured muslin frock, the bust of which was cut in the style of a riding jacket, and buttoned to her throat. Around her shoulders she wore a blue three-cornered shawl. From these clues, and from the fact that she was all but insensible from the effects of opium, Edgar Clinch deduced that she had just been in Chinatown: when she travelled to that place, she travelled incognito, in her dull-coloured clothes.

With shaking fingers Clinch eased the shawl from Anna's shoulders and let it fall upon the floor. He then untied the bow at the back of her dress and loosed the strings of her corset, moving slowly and in stages. His fingers found her covered buttons, one by one, and unhooked the loops that secured them. She was compliant in his arms, and when he moved to ease the dress off her shoulders, she lifted her arms like a very small child. Next he detached her crinoline, and lifted her out of the uppermost hoop, so that the frame fell away, hitting the floor in a rattle of buckles and wood. He eased her down upon the sofa again—she was now undressed to her slip—and folded her shawl over her body. Then he stood, and began to fill the bath. She lay with her cheek against the back of her hand, her breast rising and falling with the fitful breath of sleep. When the water was ready Clinch returned to her, murmuring phrases of reassurance; he drew her slip over her head, gathered her naked body up, knelt, and lowered her into the tub.

Anna made a cooing noise when her body touched the water, but she did not open her eyes. Clinch arranged her so that the copper lip of the tub sat snug against the nape of her neck, ensuring that she could not slither down, and drown herself. He smoothed her hair from her cheek, and ran his thumb around her jaw. He had wet his sleeves up to the shoulders, in lowering her into the water; now he stood back, and held his dripping sleeves apart from his body, and looked down at her. He felt very lonely and very contented at once.

After a moment the hotelier knelt and picked up the muslin dress from the ground, meaning to shake it straight, and fold it over the back of the sofa. The dress was heavier than he would have imagined—why, it was only muslin and thread, now that the crinoline had been detached, and the bloomers and petticoats discarded! Why was the thing so very burdensome? He pinched the fabric, and as he did so, felt something strange beneath his hands. He turned the dress over—what was that, some kind of weight, spaced along the seam? It felt like a row of stones. He eased his finger beneath a thread and felt it snap, then wormed his finger and thumb into the tunnel of the hem. Perhaps it had been stuffed with something. He withdrew, to his astonishment, a pinch of pure gold.

Anna was still sleeping, her cheek against the lip of the bath. Clinch, his heartbeat racing, felt along the seams of the gown, and up the flounces to the bust. There were ounces and ounces—perhaps pounds—concealed within the fabric. And all of it pure! What had Anna been doing in Chinatown, to return half-addled with opium, her dress stitched up with ore? She must be trafficking the stuff somewhere—smuggling it, by the looks of things. Taking it *into* Chinatown? That did not make sense. She must be taking it *out*. In exchange for opium, perhaps! Clinch's mind was moving very fast. He recalled now that concealing gold in the lining of one's clothing was a common method of evading duty at the customhouse, though it was a risky business, for if one were caught, one faced heavy fines, and even time in gaol. But Anna herself was not a digger—she was a woman, for heaven's sake!—and the gold could not be hers. Someone must have trusted Anna enough to hide this gold in her clothing. And Anna must have trusted that man enough to bear the risk on his behalf.

Then it came to him: *Mannering*. Dick Mannering owned nearly every Chinaman in Kaniere; they all worked his claims, in exchange for a salary of a kind. Mannering was also Anna's employer. Why, of course! Mannering was known to be a dirty dealer—what whoremonger was not? And had he not declared, over and over, that Anna Wetherell was the very best of whores?

Clinch turned back to Anna, and was startled to see that her eyes were open, and she was staring at him.

'How's the water?' he said stupidly, shaking out the fold of the dress so that the pinch of gold in his fingers was concealed.

She hummed her pleasure—but she shifted her knee for the sake of modesty, and crossed her arms across her breasts. Her distended belly was a perfect sphere, buoyed high in the cloudy water like an apple in a pail.

'Did you walk back—all the way from Kaniere?' Clinch asked. Surely she had not just walked four miles—not when she could hardly hold her head up! Not when she could hardly stand!

She hummed again, breaking the tone in two pieces, to indicate a negative.

'How then?' Clinch said.

'Dick was passing through,' she mumbled. The words were like treacle in her mouth.

Clinch stepped closer. 'Dick Mannering—passing through Chinatown?'

'Mm.' She closed her eyes again.

'Gave you a lift, did he?'

But Anna did not answer. She had passed back into sleep. Her head lolled back against the lip of the tub, and her crossed arms fell away from her bosom, struck the surface of the water, sank, and rose again.

Clinch was still holding the pinch of gold in his fingers. Carefully he laid the dress over the back of the chair and then dropped the pinch of gold into his pocket, rubbing his thumb and forefinger together to release the flakes, as if he were salting a stew.

'I'll leave you to your bath,' he said, and withdrew from the room.

But instead of returning downstairs he walked swiftly across the hallway, to Anna's quarters, and fitted his master key easily into her lock. He entered her room and strode across to the armoire, where she kept her clothes. Anna had five dresses, all of them purchased salvage, from a cargo steamer that had been wrecked upon the bar. Clinch turned to the whoring dress first. With swiftly tapping fingers he moved along every seam, and felt inside the bustle. Like the muslin, this too was veritably stuffed with gold! He turned to the next—and the next—and the next; each dress was the same. Why, Clinch thought, doing some calculation in his head, between these five dresses, Anna Wetherell was hoarding a veritable fortune.

He sat down upon her bed.

Anna never wore the orange dress in Chinatown—Clinch knew that with certainty—and yet that gown was packed with gold, just like the others. So this was not just an agreement with the Orientals, as he had first believed! This was an operation that went beyond the bounds of Chinatown. Beyond the bounds of Hokitika, perhaps. Someone, Clinch thought, was preparing a heist of the first degree.

He considered the alternatives. Could Mannering be using Anna as a mule, to traffic ore out of the gorge *without* her knowledge? Why, Clinch thought, that task would be easy enough: one only needed to feed her a pipe of opium, and wait for her to drift into sleep, and thereafter the gold could be sewn into her dress, one pinch at a time. Perhaps ... but no: it was absurd to think that Mannering would court such a colossal risk without the security of the whore's own discretion. She was bearing hundreds of pounds on her person, for heaven's sake—perhaps thousands. She *must* know about it. Mannering was not a fool when it came to money. He would never place a fortune in the custody of a common whore without insurance. Anna must have provided him with some kind of security—some debt, Clinch thought, some obligation. But what could she possibly have to give, that might serve as a surety on a fortune in pure?

Suddenly furious, Clinch punched the quilt with the heels of his hands. *Mannering!* The presumption of him—to engineer a deception of this kind, when Anna was living under Clinch's roof, and supping at Clinch's table! What if the duty sergeants had come calling—what if they had searched her room? Who would bear the responsibility then? Why, Clinch thought, *he* ought to have been given a cut of the profit, at the very least—he ought to have been told! And the Chinamen were in on the secret, no doubt. That was galling. Perhaps all of Hokitika knew. Clinch uttered an oath. Dick Mannering, he thought sourly, could be d—ned in hell.

He heard splashing in the room next door—Anna must have roused herself—and wondered, quickly, whether he ought to confiscate the dresses from the wardrobe. He could hold them as ransom against Mannering, perhaps. He could wait until Anna had regained her senses, and question her about the matter. He could force a confession—an apology. But his courage failed him. Edgar Clinch was always stymied by ill feeling; his grievances, though acutely felt, rarely developed beyond their unvoiced expression in his mind. With a heavy heart, he left Anna's room, returned downstairs, and unlocked the foyer door.

'Please accept my sincere apologies,' said Gascoigne.

Clinch blinked. 'What for?'

'For insinuating that you had anything other than Miss Wetherell's very best interests at heart.'

'Oh,' said Clinch. 'Yes. Well, thanks.'

'Goodbye,' said Gascoigne.

Clinch received this farewell with disappointment. He had rather hoped that Gascoigne would stay a moment longer—at least until his valet returned from lunch—and talk the issue over. It always pained him to leave a conversation on a less than civil note, and in fact he *did* want to discuss the issue of Anna's debt with Gascoigne, however hostile he had been at its first mention. He had not meant to lose his temper with Anna the previous afternoon. But she had lied to him—saying she had not a shilling to call her own, when there were hundreds, even thousands, sewn into the dresses in her wardrobe! The dresses were still there; he checked them periodically, to make sure that the ore had not been removed. Why should *he* foot the bill for her daily expenses, when she had access to such extraordinary wealth? Why should *he* be the one to soothe her troubles, when she was conspiring against him, and even telling falsehoods to his face? Months of silence had made him very bitter, and his bitterness had ripened, in an instant, into spite.

He stepped forward, and even put out his hand, meaning to delay Gascoigne's departure. He wanted to beg him not to leave;

he wanted, suddenly, desperately, not to be alone. But what reason could he give, to persuade Gascoigne to stay? Stalling for time, he said, 'Where are you off to?'

The question rankled Gascoigne. How dreary frontier living could be! Every man was asked to share his private business; it was not like Paris, or London, where one felt the luxury of strangeness on every corner; where one could really be alone.

'I have an appointment,' he said curtly.

'Who's your appointment? What's it all about?'

Gascoigne sighed. It was so dull to be asked. Clinch was looking almost sulky—as if Gascoigne's departure was vexing to him! Why, they had only met ten minutes before.

'I'm going with a lady,' he said, 'to look at hats.'

TRUE NODE IN VIRGO

In which Quee Long is interrupted thrice; Charlie Frost holds his ground; and Sook Yongsheng names a suspect, to everyone's surprise.

At the very moment that Gascoigne took his leave of Edgar Clinch, slamming the Gridiron's front door rather discourteously behind him, Dick Mannering and Charlie Frost were disembarking from the ferry onto the stones at the riverbank at Kaniere. The commission merchant Harald Nilssen was also rapidly approaching that place on foot; he had just passed the wooden marker announcing he was one half-mile distant from the settlement, an encouragement that had induced him to increase his pace considerably, though he continued to swipe the wet grasses at the roadside with his stick. The object of all three men was, of course, to reach Kaniere Chinatown, and there demand an interview with the Chinese goldsmith Quee Long—who had just been startled, as presently he would be again, by the arrival of a very unexpected guest.

'Chinatown' was something of a misleading name for the small clutch of tents and stone cabins some few hundred yards upriver from the Kaniere claims, for although every man hailed from Canton, and most from Kwangchow, together they could hardly be said to comprise a township: 'Chinatown' was home, at that time, to only fifteen Chinese men. Of this small cluster, Quee Long's dwelling was notable for its handsome chimney, made of fired clay.

The brick oven from which this chimney issued had been constructed as a miniature forge, fitted with a cast-iron chamber beneath a raised clay shelf, and positioned in the centre of the dwelling's only room; it was upon this clay shelf that Quee Long slept at night, warmed by the bricks that still held the heat of that day's fire. When he was smelting his weekly yield in ore, he filled the firebox with charcoal, for although that fuel was costly, it burned hotter than coke; today, however, his crucible and bellows had been set aside, and the firebox was stacked with a lattice of slow-burning wood.

Quee Long was a barrel-chested man of capable proportions and a practical strength. His eyes were rounded in their inner corners, but came to a point at his cheeks; the shape of his face was almost square. When he smiled, he revealed a very incomplete set of teeth: he had lost two incisors, as well as his foremost molars in his lower jaw. The gaps in his smile tended to put one in mind of a child whose milk teeth were falling away—a comparison that Quee Long might well have made himself, for he had a critical eye, a quick wit, and a flair for caustic deprecation, most especially when that deprecation was self-imposed. He painted a very feeble picture whenever he spoke about himself, a practice that was humorously meant, but that belied, nevertheless, an excessively vulnerable self-conception. For Quee Long measured all his actions by a private standard of perfection, and laboured in service of this standard: as a consequence he was never really satisfied with any of his efforts, or with their results, and tended, in general, towards defeatism. These nuances of his character were lost upon the subjects of the British Crown, with whom Quee Long shared but eighty or a hundred words, but to his compatriots, he was renowned for his cynical humour, his melancholy spirit, and his dogged perseverance in the service of untouchable ideals.

He had travelled to New Zealand under contract. In exchange for the cost of his return passage from Kwangchow, Quee Long agreed to surrender the majority percentage of his earnings on the goldfield to a corporate purse. Quee Long was made very poor by the conditions of his indenture, which were neither flexible nor charitable; but he remained a diligent worker nonetheless. His dream—an unlikely one, alas—was to return to Kwangchow with seven hundred and sixty-eight shillings in his pocket: upon this, he had decided, he would live out his days. (This particular sum had been chosen both for auspicious reasons—for, when spoken in Cantonese, it sounded like the phrase 'perennial fortune'; and also for reasons of partiality—for Quee Long worked best when he could envision the fulfilment of a goal.)

Quee Long's father, Quee Zuang, had worked in Kwangchow as a city watchman. He had spent his working life marching up and down the city wall, supervising the opening and closing of doors, and ensuring that the porters' rotation was executed correctly. It was an important occupation, if a routine one, and as a boy Quee Long had been not unduly proud of his father's station. In the trade wars of recent years, however, the relative prestige of Quee Zuang's position had paled. When Kwangchow was stormed in 1841, the city looked to its fortifications—only to despair. British soldiers swarmed the forts in numbers that far exceeded the forces of the Qing, and the Chinese defences were overrun. The British took the city, and Quee Zuang, along with hundreds of his fellows, was captured—to be released on the condition that Kwangchow agreed to open her port to trade.

The natural shame that Quee Long felt for his city's repeated surrender (for Kwangchow would be captured by British soldiers no less than four times in the coming score of years) was amplified a hundredfold by the shame he felt on his father's behalf. Quee Zuang was all but broken by the ignominy he suffered. The old man died soon after the conclusion of the second war; by the time of his death, he had faced down the barrel of a British rifle three times.

Quee Long did not like to imagine what his father might think, were he to look upon him now. Quee Zuang had given his honour and his life in defending China from Britain's unreasonable demands—and now, not eight years after his death, Quee Long was here, in New Zealand, profiting from the very circumstance that his father—and his country—had attempted, vainly, to forestall. He was sleeping on foreign soil, digging for gold (for *gold*, not silver), and conceding the bigger portion of his daily earnings to a British-owned firm, the governing ranks of which he would never be entitled to join. His discomfort, when he tallied up these betrayals, was characterised less by filial shame than by a pervasive kind of disenfranchisement. Looking back upon the long crisis of his own life (for so he perceived it, as if his selfhood was balanced, always, upon the point of choice—but what choice, he did not know, for this ambivalence was without a real beginning, and without a perceptible end) Quee Long felt only disassociated: from his own work, from his father's wishes, from the circumstances under which his country, and his family, had been shamed. He felt that he did not know how to feel.

But there was one point upon which Quee Long remained loyal to his father's shade. He would not take opium, and would not suffer it to be taken in his presence, or by the ones he loved. The drug, for Quee Long, was a symbol, signifying the unforgivable depths of Western barbarism towards his civilisation, and the contempt with which the Chinese life was held, in the face of the lifeless Western goals of profit and greed. Opium was China's warning. It was the shadow-side of Western expansion—its dark complement, as a yin to a yang. Quee Long often said that a man with no memory was a man with no foresight—to which he added, humorously, that he had quoted this maxim many times before, and he was determined to keep quoting it, without alteration. Any Chinese man who took a pipe in his hands was, in Quee Long's estimation, both a traitor and a fool. Whenever he passed the opium den at Kaniere, he turned his head, and spat upon the ground.

It will come as some surprise, then, when we identify the man with whom Quee Long was currently talking as none other than Sook Yongsheng—the man who operated the opium den at Kaniere, and who had sold Anna Wetherell the lump of opium by which she had so nearly perished, two weeks prior to the present day. (Quee Long's forbidding code did not extend to Anna Wetherell, who often visited him after she had taken her pipe at the

Kaniere den, when her body had become limp and supple with the drug, and she could not speak above a moan. But Quee Long never saw the instruments of her addiction, though he profited greatly from its effects; had she ever produced the drug in his presence, he would have knocked it from her hand. So he told himself, at least. Beneath this vague assertion ran another, more inarticulate belief: that a cosmic justice, in the case of Anna's pitiful addiction, had somehow been served.)

Sook Yongsheng and Quee Long were not friends. When the former had knocked upon Quee Long's door earlier that afternoon, begging his compatriot's help and hospitality, the latter had received him with no small sense of trepidation. The two men, as far as Quee Long knew, shared only three things in common: a birthplace, a language, and a fondness for a Western whore. Quee Long guessed that it was concerning this third article of connexion that Sook Yongsheng desired to speak, for Anna Wetherell had been a topic of much speculation and opinion in recent days; he was further surprised, therefore, when his guest announced that his information pertained to two men: one named Francis Carver, the other, Crosbie Wells.

Sook Yongsheng was perhaps ten years younger then Quee Long. His eyebrows were very faint, and sloped in such a way as to express gentle surprise. His eyes were large, his nose broad, and his lips finely formed in a Cupid's bow. Though he spoke with much animation, he tended to keep his face very still when he was listening, and because of this habit he was often perceived to be wise. He too was clean-shaven, and also wore a pigtail—though in fact Sook Yongsheng harboured strong anti-Manchu sentiments, and cared little for the empire of the Qing; his hairstyle was not a token of affiliation, but one of habit, carried over from the days of his youth. He was wearing, again like his host, a grey cotton shift and simple trousers, over which he had belted a black woollen coat.

Quee Long had never heard of either Francis Carver or Crosbie Wells, but he nodded gravely, stood aside, and welcomed the other man into his home, insisting that Sook Yongsheng seat himself in pride of place nearest the fire. He set out the choicest selection of food that he could offer, filled a pot of water for tea, and apologised for the poverty of his offerings. The opium dealer waited in silence until his host had completed these tasks. He then bowed deeply, praised Ah Quee's excellent generosity, and tasted each one of the dishes that had been set before him, commending every one. With these formalities discharged, Sook Yongsheng began to explain the real purpose of his visit—speaking, as he always did, in a style that was vital, poetically exaggerated, and accented by proverbs, the meaning of which was always beautiful, but not always particularly clear.

He began speaking, for example, by observing that upon a big tree there are always dead branches; that the best soldiers are never warlike; and that even good firewood can ruin a stove—sentiments which, because they came in very quick succession, and lacked any kind of stabilising context, rather bewildered Quee Long. The latter, impelled to exercise his wit, retaliated with the rather acidic observation that a steelyard always goes with the weights—implying, with the aid of yet another proverb, that his guest had not begun speaking with consistency.

We shall therefore intervene, and render Sook Yongsheng's story in a way that is accurate to the events he wished to disclose, rather than to the style of his narration.

Φ

Ah Sook rarely ventured into Hokitika proper. He kept, in the main, to his hut in Kaniere, which was fitted like a salon, with sofa-beds against every wall, and cushions strewn about, and fabrics pinned up to conserve and subdue the heavy smoke that coiled up from the pipes, the chafing dishes, the spirit lamps, the stove. The opium den had an air of stout impregnability about it, an impression compounded by the warm fug of its close atmosphere, and this was a comfort upon which Ah Sook had come to depend. Over the course of the past fortnight, however, he had made the journey to the river mouth no less than five times.

Upon the morning of the 14th of January (some twelve hours prior to Anna Wetherell's near-death), Ah Sook had received word from Joseph Pritchard that a long-awaited shipment of opium had just been delivered to his drug emporium, and was available for purchase. Ah Sook's own supplies of the drug were very low. He donned his hat, and made for Hokitika at once.

At Pritchard's emporium he purchased a half-pound block of resin and paid for it in pure. In the street, with the paper-wrapped block stowed safely in the bottom of his satchel, he felt a rush of summery possibility, the likes of which a Hokitika morning rarely produced in him. The sun was shining, and the Tasman wind lent a briny sharpness to the air. The crowds in the street seemed very gay, and as he stepped across the gutter, a passing digger tipped his hat, and smiled at him. Emboldened by this incidental gesture, Ah Sook resolved to delay his return to Kaniere. He would spend an hour or so browsing the salvage crates on Tancred-street, as a special present to himself. After that, he thought, he might even purchase a joint of meat from the butcher's, and take it home to make a soup.

But on the corner of Tancred-street he came up short: his festive mood dissolved at once. Standing at the far end of the street was a man whom Ah Sook had not seen in over a decade, and whom Ah Sook had believed, prior to that moment, he would never see again.

His old acquaintance was very much changed since their last encounter. His proud face was much disfigured, and a decade in gaol had lent a muscled bulk to his chest and arms. His posture was familiar, however: he was standing with his shoulders slightly rounded, and the backs of his hands against his hips, as in the days of old. (How strange, Ah Sook thought later, that one's gestures remain the same, even as the body changes, weathers, and gives itself over to age—as though the gestures were the real vessel, the vase to the body's flower. For it was Francis Carver through and through, to stand with his hips cocked slightly forward, and his shoulders hunched—a posture that would have been slovenly in another man. But Carver's presence, grave, dark, and imposing, was such that he could afford to neglect those rules of carriage that other men were obliged, by virtue of their very mediocrity, to observe.) Carver half-turned to cast his gaze down the street, and Ah Sook leaped sideways, out of view. He leaned against the rough pine of the grocery store wall and waited there a moment until the beating of his heart had slowed.

The full account of Sook Yongsheng's history with Francis Carver was not yet known to Quee Long, but Ah Sook did not recount the full particulars of the story at this time. He explained to his host only that Francis Carver was a murderer, and that he, Sook Yongsheng, had sworn to take Carver's life as an act of vengeance. He gave this information almost carelessly, as though it were altogether commonplace to swear vengeance upon one's foes; in truth, however, the source of this carelessness was pain, for he did not like to dwell upon the unhappy details of his private past. Ah Quee, sensing that this was not the time to interrupt, only nodded—but he stored the pertinent facts away, resolving to remember them.

Ah Sook continued his tale.

He remained for several seconds with his forehead pressed against the rough cladding of the grocery store wall. When his breathing was steady, he edged back to the corner of the building to look at Carver again—for to look at last upon the face that one has conjured in one's most vengeful dreams is a pleasure of the most rare and passionate sort, and Ah Sook had conjured Carver's image in his sleep for nigh on fifteen years. His hatred of the man needed no renewal, but he felt, upon perceiving Carver now, a surge of sudden fury, unfamiliar, uncontrolled: he had never hated the man more than he did at that instant. If he had a pistol he would have shot him at once, and in the back.

Carver was speaking to a young Maori man, though from their respective postures Ah Sook guessed they were not familiar: they were standing slightly apart from one another, as affiliates rather than as friends. He could not quite hear their conversation, but from its rapidly staccato nature he guessed that they were bartering; the Maori man was gesticulating very firmly, and kept shaking his head. At length it seemed that a fixed price had been agreed, and Carver, taking out his purse, counted several coins into the

Maori man's open hand. He had evidently purchased information of some kind, for now the Maori man began to speak at length, and with exaggerated motions. Carver repeated back the information, to fix it in his mind. The Maori man nodded his assent, and spoke a little more. Presently they shook hands and parted ways, the Maori man eastward, towards the mountains, and Carver westward, towards the mouth of the river, and the quays.

Ah Sook considered pursuing Carver at a safe distance, but decided against it: he did not wish to force a reunion with the man until he was prepared for such an event. At present he was unarmed, and he guessed that Carver had at least a knife about his person, and possibly also a firearm of some kind: it would be folly to accost him when at a disadvantage. Instead Ah Sook set off in pursuit of the Maori man—who was on his way back to the Arahura Valley to build a bird trap, having purchased from the Hokitika Dry Goods several yards of strong fishing line, and a small loaf of hardtack to crumble into bait.

Ah Sook caught up with him in the next block, and caught his sleeve. He begged to know the import of the man's conversation with Carver, and produced a coin to show that he would pay for the information if necessary. Te Rau Tauwhare looked at him inscrutably for a moment, and then shrugged, took the coin, and gave his explanation.

Many months prior to the present day, Tauwhare said, Francis Carver had offered him a monetary reward for any news of a man named Crosbie Wells. Soon after this offer was made, Carver returned to Dunedin, and Tauwhare to Greymouth; the two men did not cross paths again. But as chance would have it, Tauwhare did then meet the very man for whom Carver was searching, and Crosbie Wells had since become his very good friend. Mr. Wells, Tauwhare added, lived in the Arahura Valley; he was a former prospector, and had given his life over, more recently, to the project of building a mill.

(Tauwhare spoke slowly, and with much gesticulation; he was evidently well used to communicating with his hands and his expressions, and paused after every clause to make sure that he was accurately understood. Ah Sook found that he could understand his meaning very clearly, though English was neither man's native tongue. He whispered the names to himself: Arahura Valley, Te Rau Tauwhare, Crosbie Wells.)

Tauwhare explained that he had not seen Carver again until that very morning—the morning of the 14th of January. He had spied Carver upon the Hokitika waterfront less than half an hour before, and, remembering the offer the captain had made many months ago, he saw an opportunity to make an easy profit. He approached Carver and announced that he could offer news of Crosbie Wells at a price, if Carver's offer was still valid—which, evidently, it was. They agreed upon the fee (two shillings) and once the coins were in his hand, Tauwhare told the other man where Crosbie Wells was living.

Ah Sook, in what he had understood of Tauwhare's narrative, had discovered nothing that was of immediate use to him; however, he thanked the man very courteously for his information, and bid him goodbye. He then returned to Kaniere—where he found Anna Wetherell sitting in a patch of sunshine beyond his front door, waiting for him. Feeling suddenly tender towards her (any reminder of the troubles of his past life tended to furnish Ah Sook with a wealth of redemptive feeling about his present) he made her a present of a fresh half-ounce, cut from the new block of resin that he had purchased from Pritchard that morning. She wrapped the gift in a square of cheesecloth, and stuck it into the band of her hat. Ah Sook then lit his lamp, and they lay down together, waking only when the air began to cool with the coming of the dusk, whereupon Anna took her leave of him, and Ah Sook turned his mind to supper.

The goldsmith Ah Quee, to whom this was being narrated at a great pace, found that his impression of his guest was rapidly changing. Ah Quee had never cherished a very great regard for Ah Sook, who was clothed always in the conjured shadows of his reeking smoke, who shunned the company of other men, who squandered his meagre profits at the gambling house, where he rolled his dice in silence, and spat with little grace upon the floor. Perceiving Ah

Sook now, however, Ah Quee felt that he had been mistaken, to repudiate the hatter's character so completely. The man who sat before him now seemed—what? Virtuous? Principled? The words were not quite right. His speech was ardent, and there was a sweetness to this ardour, almost a naïvety. Ah Quee realised, to his surprise, that he did not at all dislike him. He was flattered that Ah Sook had sought his company—and his confidence—that afternoon, and this pleasure disposed him to be sympathetic; what was more, he had not yet guessed the purpose of the other man's visit, and therefore was very much enthralled in his tale. He had forgotten, for the moment, his disapproval of the other man's trade, and the sickly smell of the smoke, which he had brought with him, on his clothing, in his hair.

Ah Sook had paused to eat a mouthful of curd. He praised the dish a second time, and then resumed his tale.

On the night of the 14th of January, directly following Francis Carver's rendezvous with Crosbie Wells, *Godspeed* weighed anchor— a fact about which Ah Sook would remain ignorant for some days. He remained in Kaniere, where he was occupied with planning the logistics of his impending crime. He had a keen sense of ceremony, and he desired very much that Carver's death should happen in the proper way; however, he did not possess a pistol, and to his knowledge nor did any one of his compatriots. He would have to purchase one, discreetly, and learn to use it on his own. He had just spent the sum total of his dust upon the opium he had purchased from Pritchard's emporium, and he had no more money at his disposal. Ought he to ask one of his fellows for a loan? He was pondering this problem when there came another unexpected tiding from Hokitika: Anna Wetherell had tried, and failed, to end her life.

Ah Sook was very distressed by this intelligence—though he found, upon reflection, that he did not believe it to be true. He decided instead that Pritchard's latest shipment of opium must have been poisoned. Anna's constitution was well accustomed to the drug, and a fraction of an ounce was hardly enough to cause her to lose consciousness for many hours, such that she could not be revived. Ah Sook returned to Hokitika the following morning and requested an immediate interview with Pritchard's shipping agent, Thomas Balfour.

It so happened that this morning (the 16th of January) was the very morning that Balfour discovered that the shipping crate containing Alistair Lauderback's personal effects had disappeared from the Hokitika waterfront; as a consequence of this, the shipping agent was curt, and very much distracted. Yes, Balfour Shipping had Pritchard's contract; Balfour had little to do with the cargo itself, however. Perhaps Ah Sook might do better to contact Pritchard's supplier, who was a rather brutish-seeming man, thick-set, with a scarred cheek and a gruff nature. His name was Francis Carver. Was Ah Sook at all acquainted with this man?

Ah Sook controlled his shock as best he could. He asked how long Carver and Pritchard had been partners in business. Balfour replied that he did not know, but since Carver had been an infrequent face in Hokitika since the spring of the previous year, he imagined that the two men had conducted their relationship for at least that long. It was strange, Balfour went on, that Ah Sook had never encountered Carver, if they were known to one another! (For such was very obvious, from the expression on Ah Sook's face.) But perhaps not that strange, seeing as Carver so seldom ventured inland, and Ah Sook so seldom ventured into town. Was Carver known to him from his years in Canton? Yes? Well, in that case, it was certainly a shame that they had missed each other! Yes, missed each other: Mr. Carver had recently set sail. Two days ago, in fact. What a pity! For the man had most likely sailed for Canton, in which case he was not likely to return to Hokitika for some time.

Ah Sook had reached this point in his narrative when the kettle began to boil. Ah Quee lifted it down from the range and poured the water over their tea, to steep. Ah Sook paused, watching the tea leaves float to the bottom of his bowl and gather there. After a long moment, he resumed.

Taking Balfour's supposition—that Carver had left Hokitika for Canton, and would not return for some months—as the truth, Ah Sook again returned to Kaniere to ponder his next move. He knew from the Maori man, Tauwhare, that Francis Carver had been

seeking news of a man named Crosbie Wells just prior to his departure. Perhaps he could contact this Crosbie Wells himself, and
question him. He remembered, from his brief conversation with
Tauwhare, that Wells lived in the Arahura Valley, some few miles
upriver from the coast. He journeyed there, and discovered, to his
even greater disappointment, that the cottage was empty: the
hermit was dead.

In the week that followed, Ah Sook followed the story of the
Wells fortune very closely—believing, not unreasonably, that the
hermit's death was in some way related to Carver's departure. This
project had consumed him for nigh on eight days—until that very
morning, in fact, the 27th of January, when he had made two discoveries that had surprised him very much indeed.

Ah Sook was just about to announce the reason for his visit when
a pistol-crack rent the air—he started in shock—and there came
shouting from the clearing beyond Ah Quee's door.

'Come out of there, you rotten chink! You come out of there
and stand up like a man!'

Ah Sook's eyes found Ah Quee's. *Who?* he asked silently, and Ah
Quee pinched his mouth to indicate distaste: *Mannering.* But his eyes
were fearful.

In the next moment the hessian curtain was wrenched aside, and
Mannering filled the doorway. He had his pistol in his hand.
'Sitting around the forge, are you—scheming, are you? Both of you
in it together? I'd have thought better of *you*, Johnny Sook! To dirty
yourself in muck such as this! Yellow peril—by God!'

He strode into the cabin—rather less threateningly than he
would have liked, for the stud was very low, and he was obliged to
stoop—and caught Ah Quee around his body with one strong arm.
He placed the muzzle of his Smith & Wesson against the man's
temple, and at once Ah Quee became very still.

'All right,' Mannering said. 'I'm listening. What's your business
with Crosbie Wells?'

For a moment Ah Quee did not move at all. Then he shook his
head—minutely, for he was conscious of the muzzle's pressure
against his skull. He did not know a man named Crosbie Wells,

beyond what Ah Sook had just narrated to him, which was simply
that the man had been a hermit, had lived in the Arahura Valley,
and had recently died. Behind Mannering a white-faced Charlie
Frost slipped into the room—and then, moments later, the collie-
dog Holly bounded in behind him. Her coat was very wet. She
trotted the perimeter of the small room, panting gloriously, and
uttered several hoarse barks that nobody bothered to hush.

'Well then,' Mannering said, when Ah Quee did not respond,
'I'll ask it the other way around, shall I? Tell me this, Johnny Quee.
What was Crosbie Wells doing with four thousand pounds of
Aurora gold?'

Ah Quee made a noise of confusion. *Aurora gold?* he thought.
There was no Aurora gold! Aurora was a duffer claim. Mannering,
of all people, knew that!

'Stuffed into the flour canister,' Mannering snarled. 'Wedged
into the bellows. Inside the teapot. In the meat safe. Do you understand me? *Four thousand pounds' worth of pure!*'

Ah Quee was frowning: his understanding of English was very
limited, but he knew 'gold', and he knew 'Aurora', and he knew
'thousand', and it was very plain to him that Mannering wished to
recover something that was lost. He must be referring to the gold
from Anna's dresses, Ah Quee thought—the gold that he had come
upon, one afternoon, lifting a flounce of her skirt and finding it
heavy, mineral, weighted with stones; the gold that he had
siphoned, week by week, taking out the threads, a seam at a time,
while she lay sleeping atop the brick bed of this very range, the
waxing half-sphere of her pregnancy rising and falling with every
breath, murmuring only when the snick of his needle touched her
skin. He had smelted that metal, over the weeks and months following his discovery, and he had stamped each square with the
name of the claim to which he was indentured—the *Aurora*—
before taking it to the camp station at Kaniere ...

'Four thousand pounds!' Mannering shouted. (Holly began to
bark.) 'The Aurora is a bloody duffer—she's a bloody tailing pile!
I know that! Staines knows that! Aurora's dry and always has been.
You tell me the truth. Did you strike it rich on the Aurora? Did you

find a seam? Did you find a seam and retort the gold and hide it at Crosbie Wells's cottage? *Tell* me, d—n you! *Quiet*, Holly! *Quiet!*'

It was the Aurora mine to which Ah Quee was exclusively indentured; his contract would not allow him to make a profit, except from ore lifted from that plot of land. After smelting the gold from Anna's dresses, and inscribing each smelted block with the word *Aurora*, he had delivered the ore to the camp station to be banked and weighed. When the Aurora's quarterly return was published in the first week of January, however, Ah Quee had discovered, to his shock, that the gold had not been banked against the claim at all. Somebody had stolen it from the camp station vault.

Mannering shoved the gun harder into Ah Quee's temple, and again instructed him to speak, uttering several profanities too vulgar to set down here.

Ah Quee wet his lips. He did not have enough English to articulate a full confession; he cast about for the few English words he knew. 'Unlucky,' he said at last. 'Very unlucky.'

'D—ned right you're unlucky,' Mannering shouted. 'And you're about to become unluckier still.' He struck Ah Quee's cheek with the butt of his revolver, and then shoved the muzzle into his temple again, pushing the man's head painfully to the side. 'You had better start thinking about your luck, Johnny Quee. You had better start thinking about how to turn your luck around. I will shoot you. I will put a hole in your head, with two men to witness. I will.'

But Charlie Frost had become very agitated, and it was he who spoke. 'You stop that,' he said.

'Hush up, Charlie.'

'I won't hush up,' Frost said. 'You put down that gun.'

'Not for Africa.'

'You're confusing him!'

'Rot.'

'You are!'

'I'm speaking the only language he can understand.'

'You've got your pocketbook!'

This was very true. After a moment, as if in concession, Mannering took the revolver away from Ah Quee's temple. But he did not return the weapon to its holster. He paused a moment, weighing the piece in his hand, and then he raised it again, and levelled it—not at Ah Quee, but at Ah Sook, who, of the two men, had the better English. With the muzzle pointed directly at Ah Sook's face, Mannering said, 'I want to know whether the Aurora turned up a bonanza, and I want the truth. Ask him.'

Ah Sook relayed Mannering's question to Ah Quee in Cantonese, who responded at length. The goldsmith recounted the full history of the Aurora goldmine, salted by Mannering, since purchased by Staines; he explained the reason why he had first chosen to retort his weekly earnings, and later, to inscribe the blocks with the name of the mine to which he was indentured; he assured Ah Sook that the Aurora, to the best of his knowledge, was worth nothing at all—having barely turned up pay dirt for six months. Mannering shifted from foot to foot, scowling. All the while Holly was circling the room, her mouth in a grin, her wide tail thumping. Charlie Frost put his hand down for her to lick.

'No nugget,' Ah Sook translated, when Ah Quee was done. 'No bonanza. Ah Quee say Aurora is duffer claim.'

'Then he's a God-d—ned liar,' Mannering said.

'Dick!' said Frost. 'You said yourself that the Aurora's a duffer!'

'Of course it is!' shouted Mannering. 'So where in hell did all that gold come from—all of it smelted by *this* filthy heathen—and in *this* very room? Is he in league with Crosbie Wells? Ask him!'

He shook his pistol at Ah Sook, who said, after confirming the answer with Ah Quee, 'He not know Crosbie Wells.'

Ah Sook could easily have shared his own intelligence with Mannering—the intelligence that had brought him to Ah Quee's hut that very afternoon, seeking the other man's advice—but he did not approve of Mannering's interrogative technique, and he felt that the magnate did not deserve a helpful answer.

'What about Staines, then?' said Mannering to Ah Sook. His fury was acquiring a desperate edge. 'What about Emery Staines? Aha: you know *that* name, don't you, Johnny Quee—of course you do! Go on: where is *he*?'

This question was relayed from Ah Sook to Ah Quee, as before.

'He not know,' said Ah Sook again, when Ah Quee was done.

Mannering exploded with annoyance. 'He not know? He not know? He not know a lot of things, Johnny Sook, wouldn't you say?'

'He won't answer if you ask him like that!' Frost cried.

'You hush, Charlie.'

'I won't hush!'

'This isn't your business, d—n it. You're getting in the way.'

'It'll be my business if any blood gets spilled,' Frost said. 'Put down your gun.'

But Mannering only thrust it once again at Ah Sook. 'Well?' he snarled. 'And you can wipe that stupid look off your face, or I'll wipe it off for you. I'm asking *you*, now—not him, not Johnny Quee. I'm asking *you*, Sook. What do *you* know about Staines?'

Ah Quee's eyes were moving back and forth between them.

'Mr. Staines very nice man,' said Ah Sook pleasantly.

'Nice man, is he? Care to say where the nice man might have disappeared to?'

'He leave,' said Ah Sook.

'Did he, now?' Mannering said. 'Just upped his sticks, did he? Left all his claims behind? Walked out on everyone he knows?'

'Yes,' said Ah Sook. 'It was in the paper.'

'Tell me why,' said Mannering. 'Why would he do that?'

'I not know,' said Ah Sook.

'You are playing a very stupid hand—both of you,' said Mannering. 'I'll ask you one last time, and I'll spell it out slowly, so you understand. A very large fortune has recently come into play. Hidden in a dead man's house. All of it—every last flake of it—had been smelted and stamped with the word *Aurora*. That's the signature of my old friend Quee here and if he denies it he can rot in hell. Now, what I want to know is this. Did that gold really come from the Aurora, or did it not? You ask him that. Yes or no.'

Ah Sook put this question to Ah Quee, who decided, given the gravity of the circumstances, to respond with the truth. Yes, he had found a bonanza, and no, it had not come from the Aurora, though when he smelted the gold he had stamped it with the goldmine's name, in order to ensure that the profits, at least in part, would return to him. He explained that, strange as it sounded, he had found the gold on Anna Wetherell's person, sewn into the seams of her gown. He had first discovered it nearly six months ago, and had deduced, after some thought, that Anna must be trafficking the metal on behalf of someone else. He knew that Anna Wetherell was Mannering's girl; he also knew that Mannering had falsified his own financial records before. It was reasonable to conclude, therefore, that Mannering was using Anna Wetherell as a method of transporting gold out of the gorge, in order to evade duty at the bank.

'What's he saying?' said Mannering. 'What's his answer?'

'He's telling a frightfully long story,' said Frost.

He was—and it was Ah Sook's turn to be enthralled. Anna Wetherell had been concealing a *bonanza*? Anna, whom Mannering would not permit to carry even a purse upon her person, for fear of thieves? He could not believe it!

Ah Quee continued.

He could not forget his earlier grievance with Dick Mannering, for it was explicitly by Mannering's hand that he was now forced to remain indentured to a duffer claim. Here was a chance both to get his revenge, and earn his freedom. Ah Quee began inviting Anna Wetherell back to his hut each week, always when she was addled with opium, for upon leaving Ah Sook's hut she was always very sleepy and stupid; most often she fell asleep within moments after her arrival, lulled by the heat of Ah Quee's stove. This suited Ah Quee. Once Anna was arranged comfortably upon the brick bed of his stove, he took her dress apart with a needle and thread. He replaced the tiny nuggets around her hem with leaden makeweights, so that she would not notice the sudden lightness of the fabric when she woke; if she stirred in her sleep, he held a cup of strong liquor to her lips, and encouraged her to drink it down.

Ah Quee tried to describe how the gold had been hidden in the flounces of Anna's gowns, but with Mannering's arm still around his body, he could not supplement his description with gestures, and therefore turned to metaphor in order to describe how the metal had been sewn into her corset and around her bustle—'like a suit of armour,' he said, and Ah Sook, who was always pleased by poetic expressions, smiled. Anna had four dresses in all, Ah Quee said, each containing, in his estimation, roughly a thousand pounds' worth of pure ore. Ah Quee worked until each dress was empty, smelting every last flake of the dust into his signature blocks, and inscribing each one with the name of the claim to which he was bound—quite as though he had come upon it honestly, and legally, in the gravel pit of the Aurora. For a time, he added, he was very happy: once his surety had been repaid, he could return to Kwangchow at last, and as a wealthy man.

'Well?' Mannering said to Ah Sook, stamping his foot with impatience. 'What's the story? What's he saying?'

But Ah Sook had forgotten his role as translator. He was gazing at Ah Quee in wonderment. The story was incredible to him! Thousands of pounds … Anna had been concealing *thousands* of pounds about her person, for months! That was a fortune large enough to retire a dozen men, if not more, in luxury. Anna might have purchased the entire beachfront with that kind of sum … and even then, she would have money to spare! But where was that fortune now?

In the next moment Ah Sook understood.

'*Sei qin*,' he breathed. So the fortune that Ah Quee had lifted from Anna's dresses had ended up, by some caprice or misdirection, in the possession of the hermit, Crosbie Wells. But what was this misdirection in aid of—and who was to blame?

'Speak English!' Mannering shouted. 'Speak *English*, d—n you!'

Suddenly very excited, Ah Sook asked Ah Quee how the fortune might have come to end up hidden in Wells's cottage. Ah Quee replied, bitterly, that he did not know. He had never heard the name Crosbie Wells before that afternoon. As far as he knew, the last person to touch the retorted fortune was the Aurora's current owner, Emery Staines—and Staines, of course, was nowhere to be found. Ah Quee explained that it was Staines who took the Aurora's returns from the camp station to the Reserve Bank at the end of every month—a duty that had plainly not been carried out.

'All I'm hearing is noise and nonsense,' said Mannering. 'If you don't tell me what it's all about, Johnny Sook—I'm telling you—'

'They've finished talking,' said Frost. 'Just wait.'

Ah Sook was frowning. Did Emery Staines really steal from his own vault, only to stash the smelted fortune in a hermit's cottage, twelve miles away? Where was the method in that? Why would Staines steal his own fortune, only to gift it to another man?

'I'll give you the count of five,' Mannering said. His face was purple. 'Five!'

Ah Sook looked at Mannering at last, and sighed.

'Four!'

'I tell you,' Ah Sook said, holding up his palms. But what a lot there was to tell . . . and how few words he possessed, to contain the explanation! He thought for a moment, trying to remember the English word for 'armour', in order to preserve the poetic metaphor that Ah Quee had used. At last he cleared his throat, and said,

'Bonanza not from Aurora. Anna wear secret armoury, made of gold. Quee Long find secret gold armoury that Anna wear. Quee Long try to bank armoury gold as Aurora gold. Then Staines thief from Quee Long.'

Dick Mannering, naturally enough, misunderstood this.

'So the bonanza wasn't from anywhere in the Aurora,' he repeated. 'Emery made a strike somewhere—but he kept it secret—until Quee here discovered it. Then Quee tried to bank Emery's gold against the Aurora, so Mr. Staines took it back.'

That was confounding! Ah Sook began talking rapidly to Ah Quee in Cantonese—which Mannering, evidently, interpreted as a sign of assent. 'Where is Mr. Staines now?' he demanded. 'Stop with your other questions. Ask him that. Where is Mr. Staines now?'

Obediently Ah Sook broke off, and relayed the question. This time Ah Quee responded in a tone of patent distress. He said that he had not spoken with Emery Staines since December, but he was very desirous to see him again, for it had not been until the Aurora's quarterly return was published in early January that he had realised that he had been cheated. The fortune he had found in Anna's dresses had not been banked against the Aurora as he had intended it to be, and Ah Quee was certain that Mr. Staines was responsible for this error. By the time he figured this out, however, Mr. Staines had disappeared. As to where he might have disappeared to, Ah Quee had no idea.

Ah Sook turned back to Mannering, and said, for the second time, 'He not know.'

'Did you hear that, Dick?' said Charlie Frost, from the corner. 'He doesn't know.'

Mannering ignored him. He kept his revolver levelled at Ah Sook's face, and said, 'You tell him that unless he plays fair with me, I'm going to kill you.' He twitched the gun, to emphasise his point. 'You tell him that: either Johnny Quee talks, or Johnny Sook dies. Tell him that. Tell him now.'

Ah Sook dutifully relayed this threat to Ah Quee, who made no answer. There was a pause, in which every man seemed to be expecting one of the others to speak—and then suddenly Mannering made a lightning motion with his right hand, knocked Ah Quee forward, grabbed a fistful of his pigtail, and jerked his head violently back. His pistol was still pointed at Ah Sook. Ah Quee did not make a sound, but his eyes filled instantly with tears.

'Nobody misses a Chinaman,' Mannering said to Ah Sook. 'In Hokitika least of all. How would your friend here explain it to the Commissioner, I wonder? "Unlucky," he'd say. "Sook die—valley unlucky." And what would the Commissioner say?' Mannering gave a vicious wrench to Ah Quee's pigtail. 'He'd say—"Johnny Sook? He's the hatter with the smoke, is he not? Laid out most afternoons with the dragon in his eye? Selling poisoned tar to chinks and useless whores? He's *dead*? Well, then! Why in heaven would you assume I care?"'

This venom was unprecedented, as Mannering and Ah Sook had always been on equable terms; but if Ah Sook was angry, or insulted, he did not show it. He gazed back at Mannering with a glassy expression, and did not blink or break his gaze. Ah Quee, whose neck was still bent backwards, so that the muscles of his throat showed against his skin, was likewise still.

'Not poison,' Ah Sook said after a moment. 'I not poison Anna.'

'I'll tell you this,' Mannering said. 'You poison Anna every day.'

'Dick,' Frost said desperately. 'This is hardly on point—'

'*On point?*' Mannering shouted. He aimed his revolver about a foot away from Ah Sook's head and fired. There was a clap—Ah Sook cried out in shock, and flung up his arm—and then a pattering noise, as the powdered rubble ran away from the hole. 'Here's on point,' Mannering shouted. 'Anna Wetherell is laid out flat at *this* man's filthy joint' (he pointed the revolver at Ah Sook) 'six days out of seven. *This* man' (he gave Ah Quee's scalp a furious wrench) 'calls Staines a thief. He apparently uncovered some secret that has something to do with gold, and something to do with a bonanza. I know for a fact that Anna Wetherell was *with* Emery Staines the night he disappeared—which was *also* the night, by the way, that a bonanza showed up in a *very* peculiar location, and Anna lost her bloody mind! D—n it, Charlie, don't tell me to talk *on point!*'

In the next moment all four men spoke at once.

Ah Quee said, '*Li goh sih hai ngh wiuh*—'

Frost said, 'If you're so sure about the Aurora—'

Ah Sook said, '*Ngor moh zou chor yeh*—'

Mannering said, '*Somebody* gave that gold to Crosbie Wells!'

And then from behind Charlie Frost came another voice: 'What in all heaven is going on?'

It was the commission merchant, Harald Nilssen. He ducked under the low lintel of the hut and looked around him, astonished. The collie-dog leaped upon him, sniffing at the hem of his jacket and his cuffs. Nilssen reached down and caught her behind the ears. 'What is going on?' he repeated. 'For heaven's sake, Dick—I could hear your voice from fifty paces! The celestials are all staring out of their windows!'

Mannering tightened his grip on Ah Quee's pigtail. 'Harald Nilssen,' he cried. 'Witness to the prosecution! You're just the man to lend a hand.'

'Quiet down,' Nilssen said, lowering Holly to the floor and placing his hand upon her head, to calm her. 'Quiet! You'll bring in the sergeant in another moment. What are you doing?'

'*You* went to Crosbie's cottage,' Mannering continued, without lowering his voice. '*You* saw that the gold had been retorted—did you not? This yellow devil's playing us for fools!'

'Yes,' Nilssen said. Somewhat absurdly, he was attempting to brush the rain from his coat. 'I saw that the gold had been retorted. That, in fact, is the reason why I'm here. But you might have asked me quietly. You've an audience, you know!'

'See?' Mannering was saying to Ah Quee. 'Here's another man, come to make you talk! Here's another man to hold a pistol to your head!'

'Excuse me,' Nilssen said. 'I did *not* come to hold a pistol to anybody's head. And I wouldn't mind asking again what it is that you are doing. It looks ugly, whatever it is.'

'He won't hear any kind of reason,' said Frost, who was anxious not to be implicated in this ugliness.

'Let a man speak for himself!' Nilssen snapped. 'What's going on?'

We shall omit Mannering's answer to this question, which was both inaccurate and inflammatory; we shall omit, also, the ensuing discussion, during which Mannering and Nilssen discovered that their purpose in journeying to Chinatown was one and the same, and Frost, who could intuit quite plainly that the commission merchant was holding him in some suspicion over the sale of the Wells estate, maintained a rather sullen silence. The clarifications took some time, and it was nearly ten minutes later that the conversation turned, at last, to the goldsmith Ah Quee, who was still being held by the nape of his neck in a posture of much discomfort and indignity. Mannering suggested that his pigtail be cut off altogether, in order to impress upon the man the urgency of the matter at hand; he tugged at Ah Quee's head as he said it, taking evident pleasure in the motion, as if weighing a spoil. Nilssen's code of ethics did not permit humiliation, however, just as his code of aesthetics did not permit ugliness; again he made his disapproval known, prompting a quarrel with Mannering that delayed Ah Quee's release still further, and excited Holly to the point of riotous and irrepressible joy.

Finally Charlie Frost, who had been hitherto very successfully ignored, suggested that perhaps the Chinese men had simply not understood Mannering's line of questioning. He proposed instead that the questions be put to Ah Sook again, and this time in writing: that way, he said, they could be sure that nothing had been lost in the act of translation. Nilssen saw the sense in this idea, and approved of it. Mannering was disappointed—but he was in the minority, and presently he was forced to agree. He released Ah Quee, returned his revolver to its holster, and retrieved his pocket-book from his vest, in order to compose a question in Chinese script.

Mannering's pocketbook was an artefact about which he was not unreasonably proud. The pages of the book had been laid out rather like an alphabet primer, with the Chinese characters written beneath their English meanings; Mannering had devised an index by which the characters could be placed together, to form longer words. There was no phonetic translation, and for this reason the pocketbook occasionally caused more confusion than it allayed, but on the whole it was an ingenious and helpful conversational tool. Mannering set the tip of his tongue in the corner of his mouth, as he always did when he was reading or writing, and began thumbing through the book.

But before Mannering found his question, Ah Sook answered it. The hatter stood up from where he had been seated, next to the forge—the hut seemed very small indeed, once he too was standing—and cleared his throat.

'I know secret of Crosbie Wells,' he said.

This was what he had discovered in Kaniere that very morning; this was what he had come to Ah Quee's dwelling to discuss.

'What?' Mannering said. 'What?'

'He was in Dunstan,' Ah Sook said. 'Otago field.'

Mannering collapsed in disappointment. 'What's the use of *that?*' he snapped. 'What's secret about *that?* Crosbie Wells—in *Dunstan!* When was Dunstan? Two years ago—three years ago! Why—*I* was in Dunstan! All of Hokitika was in Dunstan!'

Nilssen said to Mannering, 'You didn't encounter Wells there— did you?'

'No,' said Mannering. 'Never knew him. I knew his wife, though. From Dunedin days.'

Nilssen looked surprised. 'You knew his wife? The widow?'

'Yes,' Mannering said shortly, not caring to elaborate. He turned a page. 'But never Crosbie. They were estranged. Now hush up, all of you: I can't hear myself think without a patch of quiet.'

Φ

'Dunstan,' said Walter Moody. He was stroking his chin with his finger and thumb.

'It's an Otago field.'

'Central Otago.'

'Past its prime now, Dunstan. It's all company dredges these days. But she was a shiner in her time.'

'That is the second time this particular goldfield has been referenced this evening,' Moody said. 'Am I right?'

'You are quite right, Mr. Moody.'

'Steady on. How is he quite right?'

'The gold that was used to blackmail Mr. Lauderback hailed from a Dunstan field. Lauderback said so.'

'Lauderback said so: precisely,' Moody said. He nodded. 'I am wondering whether I trust Mr. Lauderback's intentions, in referencing the name of that goldfield so casually to Mr. Balfour this morning.'

'What do you mean by that, Mr. Moody?'

'Don't you trust him—Lauderback, I mean?'

'It would be most irrational if I mistrusted Mr. Lauderback,' Moody said, 'seeing as I have never met the man in my life. I am very conscious of the fact that the pertinent facts of this tale are being relayed to me second-hand—and, in some cases, third-hand. Take the mention of the Dunstan goldfield, for example. Francis Carver apparently mentioned the name of that field to Mr. Lauderback, who in turn narrated that encounter to Mr. Balfour, who in turn relayed *that* conversation to me, tonight! You will all agree that I would be a fool to take Mr. Balfour's words to be true.'

But Moody had misjudged his audience, in questioning so sensitive a subject as the truth. There was an explosion of indignation around the room.

'What—you don't trust a man to tell his own story?'

'This is all as true as I can make it, Mr. Moody!'

'What else can he tell you, except what he was told?'

Moody was taken aback. 'I do not believe that any part of your story has been altered or withheld,' he replied, more carefully this time. He looked from face to face. 'I only wished to remark that one should never take another man's truth for one's own.'

'Why not?' This question came from several quarters at once.

Moody paused a moment, thinking. 'In a court of law,' he said at last, 'a witness takes his oath to speak the truth: his own truth, that is. He agrees to two parameters. His testimony must be the *whole* truth, and his testimony must be *nothing but* the truth. Only the second of these parameters is a true limit. The first, of course, is largely a matter of discretion. When we say *the whole truth* we mean, more precisely, all the facts and impressions that are pertinent to the matter at hand. All that is impertinent is not only immaterial; it is, in many cases, deliberately misleading. Gentlemen,' (though this collective address sat oddly, considering the mixed company in the room) 'I contend that there are no whole truths, there are only pertinent truths—and pertinence, you must agree, is always a matter of perspective. I do not believe that any one of you has perjured himself in any way tonight. I trust that you have given me the truth, and nothing but the truth. But your perspectives are very many, and you will forgive me if I do not take your tale for something whole.'

There was a silence at this, and Moody saw that he had offended. 'Of course,' he added, more quietly, 'I speak importunately; for you have not yet finished your story.' He looked from man to man. 'I ought not to have interrupted. I repeat that I meant no slight to anyone. Please: go on.'

Φ

Charlie Frost was looking at Ah Sook curiously. 'Why did you say that, Mr. Sook?' he said. 'Why did you say that you knew a secret about Crosbie Wells?'

Ah Sook turned his gaze on Frost and appraised him. 'Crosbie

Wells strike big in Dunstan,' he said. 'Many very big nugget. Very lucky man.'

Nilssen turned. 'Crosbie Wells made a *strike*?'

Mannering had also looked up. 'What?' he said. 'A strike? How much?'

'In Dunstan,' Sook Yongsheng said again, still gazing at Frost. 'Very lucky man. Big bonanza. Very rich.'

Nilssen stepped forward—which rather annoyed Frost, for he had been the one to introduce this new line of questioning, after all. But Nilssen and Mannering both seemed to have forgotten that Frost was there.

'How long ago?' Nilssen demanded. 'When?'

'Two.' Ah Sook held up two fingers.

'Two years ago!' said Mannering.

'How much? How much colour?' said Nilssen.

'Many thousand.'

'How much—four?' Nilssen held up four fingers. 'Four thousand?'

Ah Sook shrugged; he did not know.

'How do you know this, Mr. Sook?' said Frost. 'How do you know that Mr. Wells struck a 'bounder at Dunstan?'

'I ask escort,' said Ah Sook.

'Didn't trust the bank!' said Mannering. 'What do you think of that, Charlie? Didn't trust the bank!'

'Which escort—Gilligan's? Or Gracewood and Spears?' said Nilssen.

'Gracewood and Spears.'

'So Crosbie Wells made a strike at Dunstan, and then hired Gracewood and Spears to ship the bonanza from the field?' said Frost.

'Yes,' said Ah Sook. 'Very good.'

'Then Wells was sitting on a fortune—all along!' said Nilssen, shaking his head. 'The money was his very own! None of us believed it.'

Mannering pointed at Ah Quee. 'What about him?' he said. 'He knew about this?'

'No,' said Ah Sook.

Mannering exploded with irritation. 'Then why in hell does any of it matter? This is *his* work, remember—*his* work, in Crosbie's cottage! Smelted by Johnny Quee's own hand!'

'Perhaps Crosbie Wells was in league with him,' said Frost.

'Was that it?' said Nilssen. He pointed at Ah Quee, and said, 'Was he in league with Crosbie Wells?'

'He not know Crosbie Wells,' said Ah Sook.

'Oh, for the love of Christ,' said Mannering.

Harald Nilssen was looking from one Chinese face to the other—searchingly, as if their countenances might betray some evidence of their collusion. Nilssen was very suspicious of Chinese men, having never known one personally; his were the kind of beliefs that did not depend upon empirical fact, and indeed, were often flatly disproved by it, though no disproof was ever enough to change his mind. He had decided, long ago, that Chinese men were duplicitous, and so they would be, whatever disproof he might encounter. Gazing at Ah Quee now, Nilssen recalled the theory of conspiracy that Joseph Pritchard had put to him earlier that afternoon: 'If *we* are being framed, then perhaps *he* is, too.'

'Someone else is behind this,' he said. 'There's someone else involved.'

'Yes,' said Ah Sook.

'Who?' said Nilssen, eagerly.

'You won't get a grain of sense out of him,' said Mannering. 'It's not worth your breath, I'm telling you.'

But the hatter did reply, and his answer surprised every man in the room. 'Te Rau Tauwhare,' he said.

VENUS IN CAPRICORN

In which the widow shares her philosophy of fortune;
Gascoigne's hopes are dashed; and we learn something new
about Crosbie Wells.

Upon quitting the Gridiron, Aubert Gascoigne had crossed directly
to the Wayfarer Hotel—so identified by a painted sign which hung
on two short chains from a protruding spar. The sign boasted no
words at all, but showed, instead, the painted silhouette of a man
walking, his chin held high, his elbows cocked, and a Dick
Whittington bundle on his shoulder. From the jaunty cut of the silhouette, it would not be unreasonable to assume that this was a
male-only lodging house; indeed, the establishment as a whole
seemed to suggest a marked absence of the feminine, as communicated by the brass spittoon on the veranda, the lean-to privy in
the alley, and the deficiency of drapes. But in fact these were the
tokens of thrift rather than of regulation: the Wayfarer Hotel did
not discriminate between the sexes, having made a firm policy of
asking no questions of its lodgers, promising them nothing, and
charging them only the very smallest of tariffs for their nightly
board. Under these conditions, one was naturally prepared to put
up with a very great deal—or so Mrs. Lydia Wells, current resident,
had reasoned, having no small genius for thrift.

Lydia Wells always seemed to arrange herself in postures of
luxury, so that she might be startled out of them, laughing, when
someone approached. In the parlour of the Wayfarer Hotel

Gascoigne discovered her stretched out on the sofa with her slipper dangling free from her toe, one arm flung wide, and her head thrown back against a pillow; she was clasping a pocket-sized novel in her other hand, quite as if the book were an accessory to a faint. Her rouged cheeks and titillated aspect had been manufactured in the moments prior to Gascoigne's entrance, though the latter did not know it. They suggested to him, as was the woman's intention, that the narrative in which she had been engrossed was a very licentious one.

When Gascoigne rapped upon the doorframe (as a courtesy only, for the door was open) Lydia Wells roused herself, opened her eyes wide, and gave a tinkling laugh. She closed the book with a snap—but then tossed it onto the ottoman, so that its cover and title were in the man's full view.

Gascoigne bowed. Rising from the bow, he let his gaze linger upon her, relishing the sight—for Lydia Wells was a woman of ample beauty, and a pleasure to behold. She was perhaps forty years of age, though she might have been a mature-seeming thirty, or a youthful fifty; the precise figure she would not disclose. She had entered that indeterminate period of middle age that always seems to call attention to its own indeterminacy, for when Lydia was girlish, that girlishness was made all the more visible by the fact of her age, and when she was wise, her wisdom was all the more impressive for having been produced in one so young. There was a vixen-like quality to her features: her eyes slanted slightly and her nose curved upward in a way that called to mind some alert and inquisitive creature. Her lips were full; her teeth, when she showed them, were delicately shaped, and spaced evenly. Her hair was a bright copper, that colour called 'red' by men and 'auburn' by women, that darkens with movement, like a flame. Currently it was pulled back into a chignon made of braids, an elaborate contour that covered both the nape and the crown of Lydia's head. She was wearing a striped gown made of grey silk—a sombre hue, and yet it could not quite be called a mourning dress, just as Lydia's expression could neither be called the expression of a woman, nor really, the expression of a girl. The dress sported a high buttoned collar, a ruffled bustle, and puffed leg-o'-mutton sleeves, ballooning shapes which served to accent Lydia's ample bosom, and diminish her waist. At the ends of these enormous sleeves, her hands—clasped together now, to convey her rapture at the sight of Gascoigne standing in the doorway—seemed very small and very fragile, like the hands of a doll.

'Monsieur Gascoigne,' she said, relishing the name, drawing it out. 'But you are alone!'

'I convey regrets,' Gascoigne said.

'You convey regrets—and cause them, deeply.' Lydia looked him up and down. 'Let me guess: a headache?'

Gascoigne shook his head, and recounted as briefly as he was able the tale of Anna's gun misfiring in her hand. He told the truth. Lydia made noises of alarm, and pressed him with questions, which he answered thoroughly, but with a deep exhaustion that showed as a tremor in his throat. At last she took pity on him, and offered him a chair and a drink, both of which he accepted readily, and with relief.

'I only have gin, I'm afraid,' she said.

'Gin-and-water will do fine.' Gascoigne sat down in the armchair nearest the sofa.

'It's putrid stuff,' said Lydia, with relish. 'You'll have to grin and bear it. I ought to have brought a case of something with me from Dunedin—foolish, in hindsight. I've not yet found a dram of decent liquor in this town.'

'Anna keeps a bottle of Spanish brandy in her room.'

'Spanish?' Lydia looked interested.

'Jerez de la Frontera,' said Gascoigne. 'Andalusia.'

'I am sure that I would adore Spanish brandy,' said Lydia Wells. 'I wonder how she came by the bottle.'

'I am sorry that she could not be here to tell you herself,' Gascoigne said, rather automatically—but as Lydia eased her foot back into her slipper, lifting her skirts to show the stockinged plumpness of her calves, Gascoigne reflected that he was not, in fact, particularly sorry.

'Yes: we would have had the most delicious time together,' said

Lydia. 'But the expedition is easily postponed, and I love to look forward to an outing. Unless you would like to come shopping in Anna's place? Perhaps you cherish a passion for women's hats!'

'I could feign a passion,' said Gascoigne, and Lydia laughed again.

'Passion,' she said, in a low voice, 'is not to be feigned.' She rose from the sofa and went to the sideboard, where a plain bottle and three glasses were set out on a wooden tray. 'I'm not surprised, you know,' she added, turning two of the glasses right side up, and leaving the third upended.

'You mean—about the pistol? You're not surprised she tried to take her life again?'

'Oh heavens, no—not that.' Lydia paused, the bottle in her hand. 'I am not surprised to see you here alone.'

Gascoigne flushed. 'I did as you asked,' he said. 'I did not give your name; I told her it was a surprise. Going with a woman to look at hats, I said. She was pleased by the idea. She would have come. It was only this business with the pistol. She was shaken by it—and she wasn't in a fit state, afterwards.'

He felt that he was gabbling. What a fine woman she was—the widow Wells! How smartly the ruffled bustle curved away from her!

'You have been ever so kind to humour my silliness,' said Lydia Wells, soothing him. 'I tell you: when a woman approaches my age, she likes to play the fairy godmother, once in a while. She likes to wave her wand about, and make magic, for the betterment of younger girls. No, no—I knew that you had not spoiled my surprise. I simply had a premonition that Anna would not come. I have premonitions, Aubert.'

She brought Gascoigne his glass, carrying with her the sharp-and-cloudy scent of fresh-cut lemons—for she had bleached her skin and nails with lemon juice that morning.

'I did not break your confidence, as I swore I would not,' Gascoigne repeated. He wanted, for some obscure reason, her continued approbation.

'Of course,' Lydia agreed. 'Of course! You wouldn't have!'

'But I am sure that if she had known that it was *you*—'

'She would have rallied—in a heartbeat!'

'She would have rallied.'

(This conviction, rather weakly echoed, was formed on Lydia's assurance, repeatedly made, that she and Anna had once been the best of friends. It was on the strength of this assurance that Gascoigne had agreed to engineer Lydia's 'surprise', whereby the two women would reunite, and renew their intimacy at once—an offer that was an atypical one for Gascoigne. It was rare for him to perform tasks for others that they might just as well have done themselves, and social manoeuvring of any kind generally made him uncomfortable: he preferred to be manoeuvred than to move. But Gascoigne was, as will now be fairly evident, somewhat in love with Lydia Wells—a foolishness that was powerful enough to drive him not only to act against his inclinations, but also, to alter them.)

'Poor Anna Wetherell,' said Lydia Wells. 'That girl is the very picture of ill luck.'

'Governor Shepard thinks that she has lost her mind.'

'Gov. Shepard!' said Lydia Wells, and laughed gaily. 'Well, on *that* subject he is a veritable expert. Perhaps he's right.'

Gascoigne had no real opinion about Governor Shepard, whom he did not really know, or his lunatic wife, whom he did not know at all. His thoughts turned back to Anna. He was already regretting the sharp tone he had taken with her just now, in her room at the Gridiron Hotel. Gascoigne could never stay vexed for long: even the shortest of intermissions was always sufficient to engender self-reproach. 'Poor Anna,' he agreed aloud. 'You are right: she is a wretched picture. She cannot make rent, and her landlord is to cast her out. But she will not violate her code of mourning by returning to the streets. She will not disrespect the memory of her poor late child—and so, you see, she is in a bind. A wretched picture.'

Gascoigne spoke with admiration and pity.

Lydia leaped up. 'Oh, but she must come live with me—she *must*!' she cried, speaking as if she had been impressing this notion upon Gascoigne for some time, instead of having only just proposed it. 'She can sleep in my bed, as a sister—perhaps she has a sister, somewhere far away; perhaps she misses her. Oh, Aubert, she *must*. Do be the one to beg her.'

'Would she want it, do you think?'

'Poor Anna *adores* me,' Lydia said firmly. 'We are the closest of friends. We are as two doves—or we were, at least, in Dunedin last year. But time and distance is nothing in the face of true affinity: we shall find each other once again. We *must* arrange it. You *must* make her come.'

'Your generosity is most admirable—but also, perhaps, excessive,' said Gascoigne, smiling indulgently at her. 'You know Anna's trade. She would bring that trade with her, you know, if only by way of her sullied reputation. Besides, she has no money.'

'Oh, tosh: there's always money to be made, upon a goldfield,' said Lydia Wells. 'She can work for me. I long for a maid. For a *companion*, as the ladies say. In three weeks the diggers will forget she'd ever been a whore! You won't change my mind, Aubert—you won't! I can be very mulish, when I have set my mind on something, and I have set my mind on this.'

'Well.' Gascoigne looked down at his glass, feeling weary. 'Shall I walk back across the thoroughfare—to ask her?'

She purred. 'You shall do nothing unless you perfectly desire it. I will go myself. I'll go tonight.'

'But then there will be no surprise,' said Gascoigne. 'You were so looking forward to your surprise.'

Lydia pressed his sleeve. 'No,' she said firmly. 'The poor dear has been surprised enough. It's high time she was given reason to relax; high time she was cared for. I shall take her under my wing. I shall spoil her!'

'Are you this good to all your charges?' Gascoigne said, smiling. 'I have a vision of you: the lady with the lamp, moving from bedside to bedside, ministering kindness—'

'It is well you spoke that word,' Lydia said.

'Kindness?'

'No: vision. Oh, Aubert, I am *bursting* with news.'

'News about the estate?' Gascoigne said. 'So soon!'

Gascoigne did not rightly understand the state of relations

between Lydia Wells and her late husband, Crosbie. It was strange
to him that the two had lived so many hundreds of miles apart—
Lydia in Dunedin, and Crosbie in the depths of the Arahura Valley,
a place that Lydia Wells never once visited, until now, nearly two
weeks after the event of her husband's death. It was only for very
superficial reasons of propriety that Gascoigne had not questioned
Lydia directly about her marriage—for he was curious, and Lydia
did not appear to be grieving in any visible sense. She became
vague and foolish whenever Crosbie's name was mentioned.

But Lydia was shaking her head. 'No, no, no,' she said. 'Nothing
to do with that! You must ask me what I have been doing since I
saw you last—what I have been doing this very morning, in fact. I
have been aching for you to ask. I cannot believe that you haven't
asked.'

'Tell me, do.'

Lydia sat erect, and opened her grey eyes very wide, so that they
sparkled. 'I have bought an hotel,' she said.

'An hotel!' Gascoigne said, marvelling. 'Which hotel?'

'This one.'

'This—?'

'You think me capricious!' She clapped her hands together.

'I think you enterprising, and brave, and very beautiful,' said
Gascoigne. 'And a thousand other things. Tell me why you have
bought this whole hotel.'

'I intend to convert the place!' Lydia said. 'You know I am a
worldly woman: I owned a business in Dunedin for almost ten
years, and in Sydney before that. I am quite the entrepreneur,
Aubert! You have not yet seen me in my element. You will think me
very enterprising, when you do.'

Gascoigne looked about him. 'What conversions will you
make?'

'We come at last to my "vision",' Lydia said. She leaned forward.
'Did you see the *séance* advertised in this morning's paper—with the
date and location yet to be confirmed?'

'Oh, come—no!'

Lydia raised her eyebrows. 'Oh come no what?'

'Table-turning and spirits?' Gascoigne smiled. 'A *séance* is an amusing foolishness—but it is not a business! You ought not to try to profit from a parlour trick! Folk get very angry when they suppose they are being cheated out of honest pay. And besides,' he added, 'the Church is disapproving.'

'You speak as if the art were not an art! As if the whole business were nothing more than a swindle,' said Lydia Wells—who was made very bored by the disapproval of the Church. 'The realm of the paranormal is not a *trick*, Aubert. The ether is not a *cheat*.'

'Now, come,' Gascoigne said again. 'This is entertainment you're speaking of, not prophecy: let's not go talking about realms.'

'So you are a cynic!' She pretended to be disappointed. 'I would never have picked *that*—disillusioned, maybe; disbelieving, maybe; but tender underneath.'

'If I am a cynic, I am a discerning cynic,' Gascoigne said loftily. 'I have been to several *séances*, Mrs. Wells; if I dismiss them as foolish superstition, I do not do it out of hand.'

She hesitated—and then her plump hand shot out, and pressed his sleeve.

'But I am being uncourteous: the subject is of some fascination to you,' Gascoigne said, remembering himself.

'It's not that.' She stroked the fabric of his cuff a moment, and then withdrew her hand just as quickly. 'You are not to call me Mrs. Wells—not for very much longer.'

Gascoigne bowed his head. 'You wish to be addressed now by your maiden name?' he asked, thinking privately that if this was true, it was a very improper wish indeed.

'No, no.' Lydia bit her lip, and then leaned in close and whispered, 'I am to be married.'

'Married?'

'Yes—as soon as I dare; but it is a secret.'

'A secret—from me?'

'From everyone.'

'I am not to know the name of your beloved?'

'No: not you, nor anyone. It is my clandestine love affair,' Lydia said. She giggled. 'Look at me—like a girl of thirteen years, preparing to elope! I dare not even wear his ring—though it is a fine one: a Dunstan ruby, set in a band of Dunstan gold.'

'I suppose I ought to offer my congratulations,' Gascoigne said—cordially enough, but with a new reservation, for his hopes had been somewhat dashed by this news.

He felt that a shaft of possibility had closed: a light had been extinguished; a door had slammed. Virtually since he first laid eyes upon the woman, Gascoigne had fantasised that Lydia Wells might one day become *his* lover. He had conjured her in his cottage, had seen her shaking out her russet locks at his bedside, had watched her stoking his range in the morning, wrapped in a flannel robe; he had imagined the heady days of their early courtship, the construction of the house that they would share together, the passing years. Gascoigne dreamed all of this without shame or embarrassment, and even without conscious awareness that his mind was straying so. It had seemed, simply, natural: she was a widow, and he was a widower. They were both strangers in an unfamiliar town, and they had struck up a cordial acquaintance. It was not so very unlikely, that they might fall in love.

But now that he knew that Lydia Wells was betrothed, Gascoigne was forced to relinquish his fantasy—and to relinquish his fantasy, he had to acknowledge it, and see it for the foolishness it was. At first he felt sorry for himself, but as soon as he turned his mind upon this sorrow, he found that its shallowness amused him.

'I am happiness itself,' the widow said.

Gascoigne smiled. 'What am I to call you, then, if I cannot call you Mrs. Wells?'

'Oh, Aubert,' said the widow. 'We are the very best of friends. You do not have to ask. Of course, you must call me Lydia.'

(We will briefly interject with the correction that Aubert Gascoigne and Lydia Wells were not at all the very best of friends: in fact, they had known each other only three days. Gascoigne had first encountered the widow on Thursday afternoon, when the latter arrived at the Magistrate's Court to inquire after her late husband's fortune—a fortune that had already been found, and banked, by other men. Gascoigne filed Mrs. Wells's request to have the sale of the cottage revoked, and over the course of this transaction, the pair fell to talking. The widow returned to the courthouse again on Friday morning, and Gascoigne, emboldened by the evident interest with which she appeared to regard him, begged to escort her to luncheon. She accepted this invitation with a coquettish astonishment, and Gascoigne, holding her parasol, accompanied her across the thoroughfare to Maxwell's dining hall, where he ordered two plates of barley soup, the whitest bread on offer, and a small carafe of dry sherry—and then seated her in pride of place, next to the window.

It quickly transpired that Lydia Wells and Aubert Gascoigne had much to talk about, and much in common. Mrs. Wells was very curious to learn all that had happened since her late husband's passing, a subject that naturally led Gascoigne to Anna Wetherell, and her strange brush with death in the Kaniere-road. Lydia Wells was further astonished by this—for, as she explained, Anna Wetherell was known to her. The girl had stayed some weeks at her lodging house in Dunedin, before she struck out to make her living on the Hokitika fields the previous year, and over this period the pair had become very close. It was at this point in the conversation that Lydia devised her 'surprise'. Directly after their luncheon was cleared away, she dispatched Gascoigne to the Gridiron, where he informed Anna Wetherell that she was to be treated to a mystery shopping expedition the following afternoon, at two o'clock.)

'If you have a fiancé—and a new enterprise,' said Gascoigne now, 'then perhaps I am right to hope that your sojourn in Hokitika will not be a short one?'

'One is always right to hope,' said Lydia Wells—who had a fine store of rhetorical set pieces just like this one, and liked to pause dramatically after uttering them.

'Am I right to guess that your investment was made with the help of your fiancé? Perhaps he is a magnate of some kind!'

But the widow laughed. 'Aubert,' she said, 'you will not draw me out!'

'I rather thought you expected me to try.'

'Yes—but only to *try*,' the widow said. 'Not to succeed!'

'I fancy that is a feminine motif,' Gascoigne said dryly.

'Perhaps,' the widow returned, with a little laugh. 'But we are a discriminating sex—and *I* fancy that you would not have it any other way.'

What followed was a rather saccharine exchange of compliments, a game in which both the widow and the widower found themselves extremely well matched. Rather than transcribe this sentimental interchange, we will choose to talk above it, and instead describe in better detail what otherwise might be mistaken for a profound weakness in character on the Frenchman's part.

Gascoigne was enraptured by Lydia Wells, and much admiring of the refined flamboyance of that woman's speech and manner—but he had not put his faith in her. He had not betrayed Anna Wetherell's confidence, and in his narration of the latter's story to Lydia, he had made no mention of the gold that had been discovered in Anna's orange dress the previous week, which was now wrapped in a flour sack and stowed beneath his bed. Gascoigne had also described the events of the 14th of January as if he believed that Anna had, indeed, attempted to take her life—sensing that, until a better explanation could be reached, it was prudent not to call attention to the evening's many mysteries. He knew very well that Anna had no notion of where on earth those midnight hours had gone—or, to phrase the matter a different way, of who on earth had stolen them—and he did not wish to place her in any kind of danger. Gascoigne therefore adhered to the 'official' story, which was that Anna was a would-be suicide, found insensate and wretched on the side of the road. He had adopted this perspective when discussing the event with other men, and it required no great effort to maintain it here.

That Gascoigne *was* enraptured by Lydia Wells, and not instantly suspicious of her many caprices, is a point we cannot so easily defend. We do observe that the attraction had been formed before he even knew Lydia's reason for inquiring at the Courthouse; it had been formed, in fact, before the widow even spoke her name. But now Gascoigne knew that Lydia bore a very mysterious relation to her late husband; now he knew that the mysterious fortune that had been discovered in the dead man's cottage was currently in dispute. He knew that he ought not to trust her—

and he knew that when he was with her, a pure and liquid adoration filled the chambers of his heart. Reason is no match for desire: when desire is purely and powerfully felt, it becomes a kind of reason of its own. Lydia's was a rare and old-world glamour—and Gascoigne knew it, just as if the fact had been logically proved. He knew that her sleekly feline features had been lifted, intact, from an older, better age. He knew that the shape of her wrist and ankle were without compare, and that her voice—

But our point has already been made; we ought to return to the scene at hand.

Gascoigne had set down his glass. 'I think,' he was saying, 'that it is well you are to be married. You are far too charming to be a widow.'

'But perhaps,' said Lydia Wells, 'perhaps I am far too charming to be another man's wife?'

'Not at all,' Gascoigne returned. 'You are exactly as charming as another man's wife ought to be: it is only thanks to the likes of you that men get married at all. You make the idea of marriage seem very tolerable.'

'Aubert,' she said. 'You flatterer.'

'I should like to flatter you further, by inviting you to speak upon the subject of your expertise, that I so inadvertently depreciated just now,' the Frenchman said. 'Come, Lydia: tell me about spirits, and about the forces of the ether, and I shall try my very best to be naïve and hopeful, and not sceptical in the slightest.'

How very lovely she was, with the muted light of the afternoon falling over her shoulder like a veil! How gorgeously the shadow filled that notch beneath her lip!

'Firstly,' said Lydia Wells, drawing herself up, 'you are mistaken to think that common folk will not pay to have their fortunes told. Men get very superstitious when the stakes are high, and a goldfield is a place of great risk and great reward. Diggers will always pay good money for a tip—why, the word "fortune" is on their lips almost every day! They'll try their luck at anything, if they think it might give them an edge upon the field. What is a speculator, anyway, but a gypsy wearing different clothes?'

Gascoigne laughed. 'I doubt many speculators would appreciate that comparison,' he said, 'but, yes, I take your point, Miss Lydia: men are always happy to pay for advice. But will they trust in the efficacy of your advice—the practical efficacy, I mean? I fear it will be an extraordinary pressure—for you will have to bear up beneath the burden of proof! How will you ensure you won't lead any one of them astray?'

'What a terrifically dreary question,' said Lydia Wells. 'You doubt my affinity to my subject, I suppose.'

Gascoigne did; but he chose to dissemble for the sake of politeness. 'I don't doubt it,' he said, 'but I am ignorant of it. I am intrigued.'

'I have owned a gambling house for a decade,' the widow said. 'My gambling wheel has stopped upon the jackpot only once in all that time, and that was because the pin jammed in the pivot, on account of grit. I had the wheel weighted in such a way that the prize nearest the jackpot always fell against the arrow. As a secondary precaution, the pegs on either side of the number were greased. The arrow always slid past, at the final moment—but so barely, and so tantalisingly, that the men could not help but clamber up and throw down their shillings for another spin.'

'Why, Miss Lydia,' said Gascoigne, 'that is devilishly unfair!'

'Not at all,' said Lydia.

'Of course it is!' said Gascoigne. 'It's cheating!'

'Answer me this,' said Lydia Wells. 'Do you call a grocer a cheat, for placing the choicest apples at the back of the cart, so the blemished fruits will get chosen first?'

'It hardly compares,' said Gascoigne.

'Tosh: it compares perfectly,' said the widow. 'The grocer is making sure of his income: for if he placed the choicest apples in front, the blemished fruits would not be bought until they had gone over to mould, and they would have to be discarded. He ensures a steady income for himself by encouraging each one of his customers to settle for a piece of fruit that is slightly—ever so slightly—defective. I must also make sure of my income, if I am to remain in business, and I do it in exactly this same way. When a

gambler goes home with only a small reward—say five pounds—
and a sense that he came within a hair's breadth of a perfectly
enormous fortune, it is as if he has gone home with a blemished
apple. He has a modest reward, a pleasant memory of a very fine
evening, and the sense of having just fallen short of something
absolutely extraordinary. He's happy—more or less. And so am I.'

Gascoigne laughed again. 'But gambling is a vice,' he said. 'A
blemished apple is not a vice. Forgive me: I do not mean to be
dreary, but it seems that your example—like your gambling wheel—
is heavily weighted to favour your own position.'

'Of course gambling is a *vice*,' said the widow scornfully. 'Of
course it's a terrible sin and a scourge and it ruins men and all the
rest of it. What do I care about that? Try telling a grocer that you
do not care for apples! No matter, he'll tell you—there are plenty
of others who like them just fine!'

Gascoigne saluted her in the military style. 'I am persuaded of
your ability to persuade,' he said. 'You are a force to be reckoned
with, Miss Lydia! I pity that poor fellow who won that jackpot—
who had to come to you afterwards, and demand his winnings.'

'Oh, yes . . . But I never paid out,' said Lydia Wells.

Gascoigne was incredulous. 'You defaulted—on your own jackpot?'

She tossed her head. 'Who's defaulting?' she said. 'I only gave
him a second option. I told him that he could have the one hundred pounds in pure, or he could have me. Not as a *whore*,' she
said, seeing the look on Gascoigne's face. 'As a wife, silly. That
was Crosbie. He made his choice. And you know which way he
chose!'

Gascoigne's mouth had fallen open. 'Crosbie Wells.'

'Yes,' said the widow. 'We were married before the night was
over. What, Aubert? I certainly didn't have one hundred pounds to
give away. I never dreamed the wheel would ever come to rest upon
the bonanza—I had weighted it so that would never happen! I
could hardly have made good. I would have ruined myself altogether. I would have been bankrupted. You cannot be *shocked*!'

'I confess I am, a little,' Gascoigne said—though his shock was of a most admiring kind. 'Why—were you at all acquainted with the man?'

'Of course not,' said Lydia Wells. 'What modern notions you have.'

Gascoigne blushed. 'I did not mean that,' he said, and then, rushing on, 'Of course, if you were preventing your own financial ruin, as you say . . .'

'We were terribly ill suited, of course, and within the month we could not stand the sight of one another. It was to be expected. Yes: it was the best that either of us could have expected, given the circumstances.'

Gascoigne was wondering why the pair had not arranged a divorce, but he could not ask this question without offending the widow's propriety, and merely nodded.

'You see I am very modern about *that*,' Lydia added. 'You must agree with my circumspection on that score—to insist upon a separation, above a divorce! *You* have been married, Mr. Gascoigne.'

He noticed the coquettish use of his family name, and smiled at her. 'Yes,' he said. 'But let us not talk of the past; let us talk of the present, and the future, and all that lies ahead. Tell me about the conversions you will make to this hotel.'

Lydia was pleased to be given the stage. She leaped to her feet, and, clasping her hands together in the pose of a chorister, stepped forward around the ottoman. Turning on her heel, she cast her gaze around the parlour—at the mullioned window; the thinly plastered walls; the threadbare Union Jack, no doubt salvaged from a wreck, which was tacked vertically to the wall that faced the window.

'I will change the name, of course,' she said. 'It will no longer be the Wayfarer: it will be the Wayfarer's Fortune.'

'There's a music in that.'

This satisfied her. She took a few steps away from the sofa, and spread her arms. 'I will have drapes—I cannot abide a room without drapes—and fainting-couches, in the modern style. In the drawing room there will be a cubicle with saloon doors, rather like a confessional—*very* like a confessional. The front parlour will be a waiting room of sorts. The *séances* I will conduct here, of course.

Oh, I have every kind of idea. I will read fortunes, and draw up cosmic birth-charts, and play out the patterns of the Tarot. Upstairs ... but what is this? You are still sceptical, Aubert!'

'I am no longer a sceptic! I have recanted,' said Gascoigne, reaching out to clasp her hand—a movement that was spurred partly because he was trying to smother a smile. (He *was* a sceptic, through and through, and he could not hear her roll the *r* of Tarot without wanting to burst with laughter.) Squeezing her hand, he added, 'I should very much like to be rewarded for recanting.'

'In this matter I am the expert, and you are the layman,' said Lydia Wells. 'You ought to remember that—no matter your poor opinion of realms.'

Her arm was extended between them limply, as a lady extends her rings to be kissed, and Gascoigne repressed the urge to snatch it up, and kiss it.

'You are right,' he said, squeezing her hand again. 'You are quite right.'

He released her, and she moved away to the mantel.

'I will reward you with a fact,' she said, 'but on the condition that you must take me very seriously—quite as seriously as you would take any other man.'

'Of course,' Gascoigne murmured, becoming solemn. He sat back.

'Here it is,' said Lydia Wells. 'Next month will be a month without a moon.'

'Dear me!' said Gascoigne.

'It will never wax completely full, is what I mean. February is a short month. There will be a full moon just prior to the first, and another just after the twenty-eighth—and so, no full moon in February.'

Gascoigne smiled at her. 'And does it fall so—every year?'

'Not at all,' said Lydia. 'The phenomenon is very rare.' She ran her finger along the plaster moulding.

'Rare implies a value, does it not? Or a danger—?'

'It happens only once every score of years,' Lydia continued, straightening the carriage clock.

'And what does it prophesy, Miss Lydia—a month without a moon?'

Lydia Wells turned to him, and placed her hands upon her hips. 'If you give me a shilling,' she said, 'I'll tell you.'

Gascoigne laughed. 'Not yet,' he said. 'I don't yet have proof of your expertise. I shall have to test you before I part with any money, or anything else that belongs to *this* realm. The cloud will be down tonight—but I will check the Monday papers, and look up the tides.'

The widow gazed at him, impenetrably. 'I'm not mistaken,' she said. 'I've an almanac, and I am very skilled at reading it. The moon is waxing now, above the cloud. It will be full by Monday night, and on Tuesday it will begin to wane. Next month will be a month without a moon.'

CONJUNCTIONS

In which poor impressions are restored; the invitations multiply; and the past rolls forward to touch the present hour.

The Reverend Cowell Devlin had remained in the dining room of the Palace Hotel until the middle hours of the afternoon, whereupon he began to feel thick-headed and slow, and his reading ceased to be profitable. Judging himself to be in need of fresh air, he drained his coffee, stowed his pamphlets, paid his bill, turned his collar up against the rain, and set off along the beachfront, heading north. The afternoon sun was bright above the cloud, lending to the scene a silvery glow that leached the sea of colour and picked out points of white light in the sand. The very raindrops seemed to shimmer in the air; the wind, blowing chill from the ocean, carried with it a pleasant, rusty smell. All this did much to dispel Devlin's torpor, and in very little time at all he was red-cheeked and smiling, his wide-brimmed hat clamped tight to his head with the palm of his hand. He decided to make the most of his perambulation, and return to Hokitika via the high terrace of Seaview: the site of the future Hokitika Gaol, and Devlin's own future residence.

Upon gaining the crest of the hill he turned, panting slightly, and was surprised to see that he was being pursued. A young man, clad only in a twill shirt and trousers, both of which were plastered wetly to his body, was ascending the track to the terrace at a great pace.

The man's head was down, and he was not immediately identifiable; it was not until he came within twenty yards of Devlin that the latter recognised him. Why, he thought, it was the man from the Arahura Valley: the Maori man, friend of the late Crosbie Wells.

Cowell Devlin had not trained as a missionary, and had not journeyed to New Zealand for that purpose. It had been quite to his surprise when he discovered that the New Testament had been translated into Maori some twenty years prior to his arrival; he was even more astonished to learn that the translation was available for public purchase at the stationer's on George-street in Dunedin, at a very reasonable price. Turning the pages of the translated document, Devlin had wondered how the holy message had been simplified, and at what cost. The unfamiliar words in their truncated alphabet seemed infantile to him, composed of repeating syllables and babble—unrecognisable, like the nonsense of a child. But in the next moment Devlin chastised himself; for what was *his* own Bible, but a translation of another kind? He ought not to be so hasty, or so prideful. In penance for his unvoiced doubt he took out his pocketbook and made a careful note of some key verses from the Maori text. *He aroha te Atua. E Aroha ana tatou ki a ia, no te ea ko ia kua matua aroha ki a tatou. Ko Ahau te huarahi, te pono, te ora. Hone 14:6*, he wrote, and then, marvelling, *from the epistles of Paora.* The translator had even changed the names.

The Maori man looked up; seeing Devlin standing on the ridge above him, he stopped, and from a distance of several yards they regarded each other, saying nothing.

A sudden gust of wind flattened the tussock around where Devlin stood, blowing his hair back from his temples. 'Good afternoon,' he called.

'Good afternoon,' returned the other, squinting slightly.

'I see that we are neither of us deterred by a spot of foul weather!'

'Yes.'

'The view is rather compromised; that's the only shame,' Devlin added, throwing out his arm to include the shrouded vista before them. 'It seems that we might be anywhere on earth, when the clouds come down—do you not think? I fancy that when they clear again, we shall find ourselves in an altogether different place!'

The terrace of Seaview, aptly named, had a singular prospect of the ocean, which, from this height, was a featureless expanse, a fat band of uniform colour, with the sky a lighter shade of the same. The shoreline was not visible from the terrace, owing to the steepness of the cliff below—the edge gave out abruptly into a scree of loose stones and clay—and the blankness of this vista, trisected into earth, water, air, with no trees to interrupt the level, and no contour to soften the shape of the land, alarmed one's senses to the point that one was soon compelled to turn one's back upon the ocean altogether, and to face the eastern mountains instead—which were obscured, today, by a shifting curtain of white cloud. Below the terrace, the clustered roofs of Hokitika gave way to the wide brown plain of the Hokitika River and the grey curve of the spit; beyond the river, the coastline bore away southward, blurring with haze and distance until it was swallowed absolutely by the mist.

'It is a good vantage,' said the Maori man.

'It most certainly is; though I must say that I have yet to come across a view I did not like, in this country.' Devlin descended several steps, thrusting out his hand. 'Here: my name is Cowell Devlin. I'm afraid I don't remember yours.'

'Te Rau Tauwhare.'

'Te Rau Tauwhare,' Devlin repeated solemnly. 'How do you do.'

Tauwhare was not familiar with this idiom, and paused to puzzle over it; while he was doing so, Devlin went on. 'You were a very good friend of Crosbie Wells, I remember.'

'His only friend,' Tauwhare corrected.

'Ah: but even to have one good friend, a man should count himself lucky.'

Tauwhare did not respond to this at once. After a moment he said, 'I taught him *korero* Maori.'

Devlin nodded. 'You shared your language. You shared the stories of your people. It is a fine friendship that is built from that kind of stone.'

'Yes.'

'You called Crosbie Wells your brother,' Devlin went on. 'I remember it: you spoke the very word, that night at the Police Camp—the night before his body was interred.'

'It is a figure of speech.'

'Yes, it is—but the sentiment behind it is very fine. Why did you say it, if not to say, simply, that you cared for the man, and loved him, as you would love your own? "Brother" is another word for love, I think. The love we choose to give—and gladly.'

Tauwhare thought about this, and then said, 'Some brothers you cannot choose.'

'Ah,' said Devlin. 'No indeed. We cannot choose our blood, can we? We cannot choose our families. Yes: you draw a nice distinction there. Very nice.'

'And within a family,' Tauwhare went on, encouraged by this praise, 'two brothers can be very different men.'

Devlin laughed. 'Right again,' he said. 'Brothers can be very unalike. I had only sisters, you know. Four sisters—and all of them older. They made quite a pet of me.' He paused, meaning to give Tauwhare the opportunity to volunteer information about his own family, but Tauwhare only repeated his observation about brothers a second time, seeming well pleased with his own perspicacity.

'I wonder, Te Rau, if I might ask you something about Crosbie Wells,' said Devlin suddenly.

For he had not forgotten the story that he had overheard, that morning, in the dining room of the Palace Hotel. The politician Alistair Lauderback had been convinced, for some mysterious reason, that the late Crosbie Wells and the blackmailer Francis Carver had been brothers, despite the fact that they did not appear to share a name; *why* Lauderback believed this, however, he had refused to say. Perhaps Tauwhare, as Wells's great friend, knew something about it.

Tauwhare was frowning. 'Do not ask me about the fortune,' he said. 'I know nothing of the fortune. I have been questioned already, by the Magistrate, and by the police, and by the keeper of the gaol. I do not want to give my answers another time.'

'Oh no—I'm not interested in the fortune,' Devlin said. 'I wanted to ask you about a man named Carver. Francis Carver.'

Tauwhare stiffened. 'Why?'

'I heard that he was an old acquaintance of Mr. Wells's. Apparently there's some unfinished business between the two of them. Something—criminal.'

Tauwhare said nothing. His eyes were narrowed.

'Do you know anything about it?' Devlin said.

When, on the morning of the 14th of January, Te Rau Tauwhare had told Francis Carver, for a price of two shillings, where Crosbie Wells was living, he had not felt as though he were placing his friend in any kind of danger. The offer itself was not unusual, and nor was the manner of its expression. Men often offered rewards for news of fellows who had been lost upon the goldfields: not only brothers, but fathers, uncles, sons, debtors, partners, and mates. There was the missing persons page in the newspaper, of course, but not every digger could read, and still fewer had the time or the inclination to keep abreast of the daily news. It was cheaper, and sometimes more efficient, to offer a reward by word of mouth instead. Tauwhare collected his two shillings quite happily; when, later that same evening, he saw Carver approach Wells's cottage, knock, and enter, it did not occur to him to be suspicious. He decided that he would sleep the night on the ridge beside his snares, so that Carver and Wells might conduct their reunion in private. He assumed that Carver was an old associate from Wells's years in Dunedin, and did not speculate beyond this assumption.

The following morning, however, Wells was found dead; on the day of his funeral, a phial of laudanum was discovered under his cot; some days after that, it was revealed that Carver's ship, the *Godspeed*, had departed on the night of the 14th of January, off schedule, and under the cover of darkness. Tauwhare was horrified. All evidence seemed to point to the fact that Francis Carver had played a part in the hermit's death—and if this was true, then it was Te Rau Tauwhare who had equipped him with the means to do so, by telling him explicitly where Wells could be found! Still more horrible: he had received payment for his betrayal.

Tauwhare's sense of self-mastery, integral to his self-conception, did not permit unwitting action. The knowledge that he had betrayed his friend for money was deeply shaming to him, and this shame manifested as a disgusted outrage that was directed both inward and outward at once. He spent the days following Wells's burial in a very black humour, grinding his teeth, pulling on his forelock, and cursing Francis Carver with every step.

Devlin's inquiry prompted a renewal of this ill humour. Tauwhare's eyes flashed, and his chin lifted. 'If there is unfinished business between them,' he said angrily, 'it is finished now.'

'Of course,' Devlin said, raising his palms to pacify the other man's temper, 'but here: I heard a rumour somewhere that they were brothers. Crosbie Wells and Carver. It might only be a figure of speech, as you put it, but I wanted to make sure.'

Tauwhare was bewildered by this; to cover his bewilderment, he scowled at the chaplain very darkly.

'Do you know anything about it?'

'No,' Tauwhare said, spitting out the word.

'Wells never mentioned a man named Carver to you?'

'No.'

Devlin, perceiving that Tauwhare's mood had soured, decided to try a different approach. 'How did Crosbie Wells get on, then—learning Maori?'

'Not as good as my English,' said Tauwhare.

'That I do not doubt! Your English is extremely good.'

Tauwhare lifted his chin. 'I have travelled with surveyors. I have led many men over the mountains.'

Devlin smiled. 'Do you know,' he said, 'I believe I feel a touch of the kindred spirit in you, Te Rau. I think that we are not so very different, you and I—sharing our stories, sharing our language, finding brothers in other men. I think that we are not so very different at all.'

Here Devlin spoke whimsically rather than perceptively. His years as a clergyman had taught him that it was prudent always to begin upon a point of connexion, or to forge one, if a connexion did not yet exist. This practice was not dishonest exactly, but it was true that, if pressed, Devlin would not have been able to describe this apparent similarity in any great detail, before devolving into generality.

'I am not a man of God,' said Tauwhare, frowning.

'And yet there is much of God in you,' Devlin replied. 'I believe you must have an instinct for prayer, Te Rau—to have come here today. To pay respects at your dear friend's grave—to pray over him, indeed.'

Tauwhare shook his head. 'I don't pray for Crosbie. I remember him.'

'That's all right,' Devlin said. 'That's fine. Remembering is a very good place to start.' Smiling slightly, he pressed the pads of his fingers together, and then tilted both hands downward—his clerical pose. 'Prayers often begin as memories. When we remember those whom we have loved, and miss them, naturally we hope for their safety and their happiness, wherever they might be. That hope turns into a wish, and whenever a wish is voiced, even silently, even without words, it becomes a supplication. Perhaps we don't know to whom we're speaking; perhaps we ask before we truly know who's listening, or before we even believe that listener exists. But I judge it a very fine beginning, to make a practice of remembering those people we have loved. When we remember others fondly, we wish them health and happiness and all good things. These are the prayers of a Christian man. The Christian man looks outward, Te Rau; he loves others first, himself second. This is why the Christian man has many brothers. Alike and unalike. For none of us are so dissimilar—would you not agree?—when perceived from a collective point of view.'

(We do perceive, from the advantage of this collective point of view, that Te Rau Tauwhare and Cowell Devlin are indeed very similar in a great many ways; the most pertinent of these, however, are to go both unobserved and unremarked. Neither man possesses curiosity enough to disturb the other's prideful equanimity, nor truly to draw him out: they are to stand forever proximal, one the act of his own self-expression, the other, the proof of it.)

'A prayer needn't always be a supplication, of course,' Devlin added. 'Some prayers are expressions of gladness; some are expressions of thanks. But there is hope in all good feeling, Te Rau, even in feelings that remember the past. The prayerful man, the good man, is always hopeful; he is always an optimist. A man is made hopeful by his prayers.'

Tauwhare, who had received this sermon doubtfully, only nodded. 'These are wise words,' he added, feeling pity for his interlocutor.

In general Tauwhare's conception of prayer was restricted to the most ritualised and oratorical sort. The ordered obeisance of the *whaikorero* produced in him, as did all rituals of speech and ceremony, a feeling of centrality and calm, the likes of which he could not manufacture alone, and nor did he wish to. The sensation was quite distinct from the love he felt for his family, which he experienced as a private leaping in his breast, and distinct, too, from the pride he felt in himself, which he felt as a pressurised excitement, an elated certainty that no man would ever match him, and no man would ever dare to try. It ran deeper than the natural goodness that he felt, watching his mother shuck mussels and pile the slippery meat into a wide-mouthed flax basket on the shore, and knowing, as he watched her, that his love was good, and wholly pure; it ran deeper than the virtuous exhaustion he felt after a day stacking the *rua kumara*, or hauling timber, or plaiting *harakeke* until the ends of his fingers were pricked and raw. Te Rau Tauwhare was a man for whom the act of love was the true religion, and the altar of this religion was one in place of which no idols could be made.

'Shall we go to the grave together?' Devlin said.

The wooden headstone that marked Crosbie Wells's grave had surrendered already to the coastal climate. Two weeks following the hermit's death, the wooden plaque was already swollen, the face already spotted with a rime of black mould. The indentation of the cooper's engraving had softened, and the thin accent of paint had faded from white to a murky yellow-grey, giving the impression, not altogether dispelled by the stated year of his death, that the man had been deceased for a very long time. The plot was yet unseeded by lichen or grass, and, despite the rain, had a barren look—not of earth recently turned, but of earth that had settled, and would not be turned again.

The favoured epitaphs here were chiefly beatitudes from Matthew, or oft-quoted verses from the Psalms. Injunctions to sleep and be at peace did not reassure, however, as they might have done in some hedged and cobbled parish, ten thousand miles away. It was in the company of the lost and the drowned that Crosbie Wells lay at his eternal rest, for there were yet only a hand-ful of headstones in the plot at Seaview, and most of them were memorials erected in honour of vessels that had been wrecked, or lost at sea: the *Glasgow*, the *City of Dunedin*, the *New Zealand*—as though entire cities, entire nations, had been bound for the Coast, only to run aground, or sink, or disappear. On the hermit's right was a memorial to the brigantine *Oak*, the first ship to founder at the mouth of the Hokitika River, a fact engraved with forbidding premonition upon the greenish stone; on Wells's left was a wooden headstone barely larger than a plaque, which bore no name at all, only a verse, unattributed: MY TIMES ARE IN YOUR HAND. None too far from the cemetery was the site of George Shepard's future gaol-house, the foundations of which had been paced and meas-ured out already, the dimensions marked in white lead paint upon the soil.

It was the first time that Tauwhare had ventured to Seaview since Wells's interment, a ceremony that had taken place before a small and perfunctory audience, and despite very heavy rain. In these aspects, and in the general speed with which the conventional blessings were dispatched, Wells's funeral had seemed to embody every kind of inconvenience, and every kind of dreariness. Needless to say Te Rau Tauwhare had not been invited to con-tribute to the proceedings; in fact George Shepard had specifically enjoined him, with an ominous wag of his large-knuckled finger, to keep silent during all but the chaplain's 'Amen'—a chorus to which Tauwhare did not, in the event, add his voice, for Devlin's bene-diction was quite swallowed in the downpour. He was permitted to assist in lowering Wells's coffin down into the mud of the hole, however, and in depositing thirty, forty, fifty shovelfuls of wet earth after it. He should have liked to do this alone, for the party made short work of filling the hole, and it seemed to Tauwhare that everything was over far too soon. The men, pulling their collars up about their ears, buttoned their coats, took up their earth-spattered tools, and trooped single-file back down the muddy switchback to the warmth and light of Hokitika proper, where they shucked their greatcoats, and wiped their faces dry, and changed their sodden boots for indoor shoes.

Tauwhare came silently upon the grave of his friend, Devlin following, his hands folded, his expression peaceful. Tauwhare halted some five or six feet from the wooden headstone, and looked upon the plot as though upon a deathbed from a chamber doorway—as though fearing to step, bodily, into the room.

Tauwhare had never seen Crosbie Wells beyond the Arahura Valley. He had certainly never seen him here, upon this forsaken terrace, ravaged by the sky. Had the man not said countless times that it was in the solitary Arahura that he wished to end his days? It was senseless that he should have been laid to rest here, among men who were not his brethren, upon soil he had not worked, and did not love—while his dear old cottage stood empty and abandoned, some dozen miles away! It was *that* soil that ought to have claimed him. It was *that* earth that ought to have turned his death to fertile life. It was in the Arahura, Tauwhare thought, that he ought to have been buried, in the end. At the edge of the clearing, perhaps ... or by the plot of his tiny garden ... or on the north-facing side of the cottage, in a patch of sun.

Te Rau Tauwhare came closer—into the phantom chamber, to the foot of the phantom bed. A wave of guilt overcame him. Ought he to confess to the chaplain after all—that he, Tauwhare, had led Crosbie to his death? Yes: he would make his confession; and Devlin would pray for him, as though for a Christian man. Tauwhare squatted down upon his haunches, placed a careful palm over the wet earth that covered Crosbie's heart, and held it there.

'Weeping may endure for the night, but joy cometh in the morning,' Devlin said.

'*Whatu ngarongaro he tangata, toitu he whenua.*'

'May the Lord keep him; may the Lord keep us, as we pray for him.'

Tauwhare's palm had made an indentation in the soil; seeing this, he lifted his hand a little, and with his fingertips, smoothed the print away.

Φ

At the *West Coast Times* office on Weld-street, Benjamin Löwenthal's Shabbat was just coming to an end. Charlie Frost found him sitting at his kitchen table, finishing his supper.

Löwenthal was rather less pleased to see Frost than he had been to see Thomas Balfour earlier that afternoon, for he guessed, rightly, that Frost was come to speak about the estate of Crosbie Wells—a subject of which he had long since tired. He welcomed Frost into his kitchen courteously, however, and invited the young banker to take a seat.

Frost, for his part, did not apologise for interrupting Löwenthal's devotions, for he was not worldly, and he did not know them to be devotions. He sat down at the ink-stained table, thinking it very strange that Löwenthal had cooked himself such an elaborate supper, only to partake of it alone. The candle he took for an eccentricity; he glanced at it only once.

'It's about the estate,' he said.

Löwenthal sighed. 'Bad news, then,' he said. 'I might have guessed it.'

Frost gave a brief summary of what had transpired in Chinatown that afternoon, describing Mannering's former grievances with Ah Quee in some detail.

'Where's the bad news?' Löwenthal said, when he was done.

'I'm afraid your name came up,' said Frost, speaking delicately.

'In what context?'

'It was suggested'—even more delicately—'that perhaps this fellow Lauderback used you as a pawn, on the night of the four-teenth. In coming straight to you, I mean, on the night of the hermit's death, and telling you all about it. Maybe—just possibly—he came to you by some sort of design.'

'That's absurd,' Löwenthal said. 'How was Lauderback to know that I'd go straight to Edgar Clinch? I certainly never mentioned

Edgar's name to him ... and he said nothing out of the ordinary to me.'

Frost spread his hands. 'Well, we're making a list of suspects, that's all, and Mr. Lauderback is on that list.'

'Who else is on your list?'

'A man named Francis Carver.'

'Ah,' said Löwenthal. 'Who else?'

'The widow Wells, of course.'

'Of course. Who else?'

'Miss Wetherell,' said Frost, 'and Mr. Staines.'

Löwenthal's face was inscrutable. 'A broad taxonomy,' he said. 'Continue.'

Frost explained that a small group of men were meeting at the Crown Hotel after nightfall, in order to pool their information, and discuss the matter at length. The group was to include every man who had been present in Quee Long's hut that afternoon, Edgar Clinch, the purchaser of Wells's estate, and Joseph Pritchard, whose laudanum had been found in the hermit's cottage following the event of Wells's death. Harald Nilssen had vouched for Pritchard's character; he, Frost, had vouched for Clinch.

'You vouched for Clinch?' said Löwenthal.

Frost confirmed this, and added that he would be happy to vouch for Löwenthal, too, if Löwenthal was desirous to attend.

Löwenthal pushed his chair back from the table. 'I will attend,' he said, standing, and moving to fetch a box of matches from the shelf beside the door. 'But there's someone else I think ought to be present also.'

Frost looked alarmed. 'Who is that?'

Löwenthal selected a match, and struck it against the doorjamb. 'Thomas Balfour,' he said, tilting the match, and watching the small flame climb along the shaft. 'I believe that his information may be of considerable value to the project of our discussion—if he is willing to share it, of course.' He lowered the match, carefully, into the sconce above the table.

'Thomas Balfour,' Frost repeated.

'Thomas Balfour, the shipping agent,' Löwenthal said. He

turned the dial to widen the aperture: there was a hiss, and the globe flared orange-red. 'He came to you this morning, did he not? I think he mentioned that he had seen you at the bank.'

Frost was frowning. 'Yes, he did,' he said. 'But he asked some mighty strange questions, and I wasn't altogether sure of his purpose, to tell you the truth.'

'That's just it,' Löwenthal said, shaking out the match. 'There's another dimension to this whole business, and Tom knows about it. He told me this afternoon that Alistair Lauderback is sitting on a secret—something big. He might be unwilling to break Lauderback's confidence, of course (he kept his peace with me) but if I put the matter to him in the context of this assembly . . . well, he can be the master of his own choice. He can make up his own mind. Perhaps, once everyone else has shared his own piece, he might be moved to speak.'

'To speak,' Frost repeated. 'All right. But can he be trusted—to listen?'

Löwenthal paused, pinching the charred match between his finger and his thumb. 'Please correct me if I am mistaken,' he said coldly, 'but I understood from your invitation that this is to be an assembly of innocent men—not of schemers, or conspirators, or felons of any kind.'

'That's right,' said Frost. 'But even so—'

'And yet you ask whether Tom can be trusted to listen,' Löwenthal went on. 'Surely *you* are not in possession of any information that might indict you? Surely you know nothing that you would not want to share aloud, and freely, with a company of innocents united by a common cause?'

'Of course not,' said Frost, blushing. 'But we still need to be cautious—'

'Cautious?' Löwenthal said. He dropped the match into the woodpile, and rubbed his fingertips together. 'I am beginning to doubt your better interests, Mr. Frost. I am beginning to wonder whether this is not a kind of conspiracy after all.'

They looked at each other for a long moment, but Frost's will was not equal to Löwenthal's; he ducked his head, his cheeks flaming, and nodded once.

'You should invite Mr. Balfour—certainly,' he said. 'Certainly you should.'

Löwenthal clucked his tongue. His manner could be very school-masterly when his code of ethics was aggrieved: his reprimands were always stern, and always effective. He gazed at the younger man now with a very sorrowful expression, causing Frost to blush still more furiously, like a schoolboy who has been caught doing violence to a book.

Wishing to redeem himself, Frost said, somewhat wildly, 'And yet there *are* things about the sale of the cottage that are not yet public knowledge—that Mr. Clinch would not like to be made public, I mean.'

Löwenthal's look was almost smouldering. 'Let me make this very clear,' he said. 'I trust in your discretion, just as you trust in mine, and just as we both trust in the discretion of Mr. Clinch. But discretion is a far cry from secrecy, Mr. Frost. I do not consider that any of us is withholding information in the legal sense. Do you?'

In a voice that pretended to be casual Frost said, 'Well, I suppose we can only hope that Mr. Clinch is of your mind'—meaning, somewhat foolishly, to curry Löwenthal's favour by applauding his rationale. But Löwenthal shook his head.

'Mr. Frost,' he said. 'You are indiscreet. I do not advise it.'

Benjamin Löwenthal hailed from Hanover, a city that, since his departure from Europe, had fallen under Prussian rule. (With his walrus moustache and severely receded hairline Löwenthal was not unlike Otto von Bismarck, but the correlation was not an imitative one: imitation was not a form of self-styling that Löwenthal had ever thought to adopt.) He was the elder son of a textiles merchant, a man whose life's ambition had centred wholly upon giving both his sons an education. This aspiration, to the old man's immeasurable gratification, he achieved. Soon after the boys' studies were completed, however, both parents contracted influenza. They died, as Löwenthal was later informed, upon the very day that the Jewish people were granted formal emancipation by the Hanoverian state.

This event was young Löwenthal's watershed. Although he was

not superstitious, and so attached no real value to the fact that
these events happened contemporaneously, they were nevertheless
linked in his mind: he felt a profound sense of detachment from
either circumstance, by virtue of their happening on the very same
day. At that time he had just been offered a newspaperman's
apprenticeship at *Die Henne* in Ilmenau, an opportunity that both
his parents would surely have encouraged him to seize—but
because the state of Thuringia had not yet formally emancipated
its Jewish citizens, he felt that it would be disrespectful to his parents' memory to accept. He was torn. Löwenthal cherished an
outsized fear of catastrophe, and was prone to over-analysis in self-
contemplation; his reasons for his actions were always many, and
rationalised in the extreme. We shall pass over these reasons why,
and remark only that Löwenthal chose neither to move to Ilmenau
nor to remain in Hanover. Immediately following his parents'
deaths, he left Europe altogether, never to return. His brother
Heinrich took over their father's business in Hanover, and
Benjamin Löwenthal, degree in hand, sailed across the Atlantic,
to America—where, for the months and years and decades after
that, he recounted this very history to himself, in exactly these
words, in exactly this way.

Repetition is a fortification like no other. Over time Löwenthal's
conception of the story of his past had become fixed and (by virtue
of its fixity) unassailable. He lost the capacity to talk about his life
in any other terms but those he had prescribed: that he was a moral
man; that he was a man confronted with paradox; that he was a
man who had done the right thing, who did the right thing, who
would do the right thing. All of his choices, in his mind, had been
moral choices. He ceased to be able to distinguish between personal preference and moral imperative, and he ceased to accept
that such a distinction was possible. It was as a consequence of all
of this that he chastised Charlie Frost so freely now.

Frost's eyes were lowered. 'I can be discreet,' he said quietly. 'You
needn't worry about me.'

'I will go and speak to Tom myself,' Löwenthal said, crossing the
room in two strides, and holding open the door for the banker to

leave. 'I thank you for the invitation. I shall see you tonight, at the Crown.'

Φ

Dick Mannering, upon returning from Kaniere, had gone at once to the Gridiron Hotel, where he found Edgar Clinch alone in his private office, sitting at his desk. The magnate sat down without invitation, talked for some time about the afternoon's occurrences, and very swiftly described the proposed conference that was to take place that evening. The men had decided, for reasons of prudence, to meet upon neutral ground, and the smoking room of the Crown Hotel, as the least attractive room of the least popular establishment in all of Hokitika, had seemed to all the assembled company to be a very sensible choice. Mannering talked with great exuberance, for he liked the idea of a secret council very much; he had always longed to be a member of a guild, the kind possessed of arcane histories, and feudal rankings, and a code. Presently he became aware, however, that the hotelier did not appear to be listening very closely. Clinch had placed both palms of his hands flat on the desk before him, as though to steady himself against a wind, and during Mannering's long speech he had not once altered his posture, though his gaze darted anxiously around the room. His usually florid face was very pale, and his moustache was twitching.

'*You* look as if something's on your mind—I declare it,' said Mannering at last, and in a rather sulky tone, for he was sure that whatever this preoccupation was, it could hardly be as exciting as his afternoon in Chinatown, or the prospect of a secret conference to discuss the perplexing disappearance of a very wealthy man.

'The widow was here,' said Edgar Clinch, hollowly. 'She had business with Anna, she said. She went upstairs—and not half an hour later, she was back down again, with Anna in tow.'

'Lydia Wells?'

'Lydia Wells,' Clinch echoed. In his mouth her name was like a curse.

'When?'

'Just now,' said Clinch. 'They left together, the very moment before you got here.' He fell silent again.

Mannering made an impatient noise. 'Don't make me beg you for it.'

'They know each other!' Clinch burst out. 'They *know* each other—Lydia and Anna! They're the best of friends!'

This revelation was not news to Mannering, who was a frequent patron of the House of Many Wishes in Dunedin, and had seen the two women together at that place before: in fact it was at the House of Many Wishes that Mannering had first engaged Anna Wetherell to work for him. He shrugged. 'All right,' he said. 'What's the problem?'

'Thick as thieves,' Clinch said mournfully. 'And thieves is right, Dick. Thieves is what I mean.'

'Who's a thief?'

'They're in on it together!' Clinch cried.

Really, Mannering thought, Clinch could be terribly irksome when he was vexed; he became altogether unintelligible. Aloud he said, 'Is this about the widow's appeal?'

'*You* know what I'm talking about,' Clinch said. '*You* know.'

'What?' Mannering said. 'Is it about the fortune? What?'

'Not the Wells fortune. The *other* fortune.'

'What other fortune?'

'You know!'

'On the contrary: I have not the least idea.'

'*I'm talking about Anna's dresses!*'

This was the first time Clinch had ever mentioned the gold he had discovered in Anna's dress the previous winter—when he carried her upstairs, and lowered her into the bath, and he picked up her gown, and felt a heaviness along the seam, and broke the thread of the hem, and withdrew, in his fingers, a shining pinch of it. The pressure of a long-time concealment lent an almost crazed aspect to his outburst now; for he was still convinced that the magnate was embroiled in a scheme of some kind, although he had never figured out, exactly, what this scheme might properly entail.

But Mannering only looked confused. 'What?' he said. 'What's all this about?'

Clinch was scowling. 'Don't play stupid.'

'Excuse me: I am doing no such thing,' Mannering said. 'What are you talking about, Edgar? What do a whore's fashions have to do with the price of anything at all?'

Studying him, Edgar Clinch felt a tremor of doubt. Mannering's bewilderment seemed perfectly genuine. He was not behaving like a man exposed. Could that mean that he had *not* known about the gold hidden in Anna's gowns? Could Anna have been colluding with quite another man—behind *Mannering's* back? Clinch felt bewildered also. He decided to change the subject.

'I meant that mourning gown,' he said, clumsily. 'The one with the stupid collar that she's taken to wearing this past fortnight.'

Mannering waved his hand. 'She's just being pious,' he said. 'Giving herself airs. It'll blow over.'

'I'm not so sure,' Clinch said. 'Last week, you see, I told her she had to make good her debts before she quit walking the streets— and we had words, and I suppose I got angry, and I threatened to turn her out of the hotel.'

'What's that got to do with Lydia Wells?' said Mannering impatiently. 'So you lost your temper. What's that got to do with anything?'

'Lydia Wells just paid Anna's debt,' Clinch said. At last he lifted his hands from the desk: beneath them, slightly damp from the pressure of his palms, lay a crisp banknote, made out for a sum of six pounds. 'Anna's gone over to the Wayfarer. Indefinitely. Got a new profession, she says. Won't answer to the name of whore.'

Mannering looked at the banknote, and did not speak for a moment.

'But that's her debt to *you*,' he said at last. 'That's just for rent. She owes *me* a hundred pounds—and then some! She's in the red— and she's in it deep—and she answers to *me*, d—n it! Not to you, and certainly not to Lydia bloody Wells! But what do you mean— won't answer to the name of whore?'

'Just that,' said Edgar Clinch. 'She's done with the profession. So she says.'

Mannering's face had turned purple. 'You can't just walk out on your own job. I don't care if you're a whore or a butcher or a bloody baker! You can't just walk out—not when there's a debt outstanding!'

'That's the—'

'In mourning, she said!' Mannering cried, leaping up. 'For a time, she said! Give a girl an inch and she takes a bloody mile! Not on my watch, all right! Not with a hundred pounds against her name! No indeed!'

Clinch was looking at the magnate coldly. 'She said to tell you that Aubert Gascoigne has the money for you,' he said. 'She said to tell you that it's hidden underneath his bed.'

'Who in hell is Obur Gaskwon?'

'He's a clerk at the Magistrate's Court,' Clinch said. 'He filed the widow's appeal on Crosbie Wells's fortune.'

'Aha!' said Mannering. 'So we're coming back around to *that*, are we? I'll be God-d—ned!'

'There's another thing,' Clinch said. 'Mr. Gascoigne was up in Anna's room this afternoon, and shots were fired. Two shots. I asked him about it afterwards—and he countered by mentioning the debt. I went up to look. There's a hole in Anna's pillow. Right through the middle. The stuffing came out.'

'Two holes?'

'Just one.'

'And the widow saw it,' Mannering said.

'No,' Clinch said. 'She came later. But when Mr. Gascoigne left, he *did* say that he was going to talk to a lady ... and then she showed up about two hours after that.'

'What's the other fortune?' Mannering said suddenly. 'You said there was another fortune.'

'I thought—' Clinch dropped his gaze. 'No. It doesn't matter. I made a mistake. Forget it.'

Mannering was frowning. 'What obligation does Lydia Wells have, to pay off Anna's debt?' he said. 'Where's her profit there?'

'I don't know,' Clinch said. 'But the two of them seemed very intimate this afternoon.'

'Intimate—that's not a profit.'

'I don't know,' Clinch said again.

'They were on each others' arms? They were in good spirits? What?'

'Yes,' said Clinch. 'They were linked at the elbow—and when the widow spoke, Anna leaned in close.'

He fell silent, dwelling on the memory.

'And you let her go!' Mannering barked suddenly. 'You let her go—without asking me—without calling me over? She's my best girl, Edgar! You know *that* without me telling you! The others aren't a patch on Anna!'

'I could hardly have detained her,' Clinch said, looking sour. 'What would I have done—locked her up? And anyway, you were in Kaniere.'

Mannering leaped up from his chair.

'So Chinaman's Ann is no longer *any* man's Ann!' He thumped his hat on his leg. 'She makes it seem altogether simple—does she not? Quitting her profession! As if we could all just wake up one morning, and decide ... !'

But Edgar Clinch did not care to pursue this rhetorical line. He was meditating, sorrowfully, upon the fact that to-morrow was Sunday, and the first Sunday in many months when he did not have the drawing of Anna's bath to look forward to. Aloud he said, 'Maybe you ought to go and speak to Mr. Gascoigne about that money.'

'Do you know what makes me angry, Edgar?' Mannering said. 'Second-hand news makes me angry. Picking up after other men makes me angry. Hearing all this from you—it makes me angry. What does Anna want me to do? Knock on the door of a man I barely know? What would I say? "Excuse me, sir, I believe there's a great deal of money under your bed, and Anna Wetherell owes it to me!" It's disrespectful. Disrespectful is what it is. No: as far as I'm concerned, that girl is still in my employ. She is still very much a whore, and her debt to me is still very much unpaid.'

Clinch nodded. His energy had dissipated, and he wanted now to be alone. He picked up the banknote, folded it, and placed it inside his wallet, against his heart. 'What time did you say, for the meeting tonight?'

'Sundown,' said Mannering. 'Only you might want to arrive before or after, so we're not all trooping in at once. You'll find a fair clutch of men have come out of this business feeling like there's someone to blame.'

'Can't say I care for the Crown,' said Clinch, half to himself. 'They skimped on glass, I think. The frontage windows ought to be wider—and there ought to be a roof over the porch.'

'Well, it'll be quiet, and that's all that matters.'

'Yes.'

Mannering put his hat on. 'If you'd asked me last week who was to blame for all of this madness, I would have guessed the Jew. If you'd asked me yesterday, I would have guessed the widow. This afternoon, I would have told you Chinamen. And now? Well, Edgar, I'm d—ned if I don't lay my money on that whore. You mark my words: Anna Wetherell knows exactly why that money turned up at Crosbie Wells's, and she knows exactly what happened to Emery Staines—God rest his soul, though I do speak prematurely. Attempted suicide, my hat. Mourning dress, my hat. She's in to the teeth with Lydia Wells—and together, they're up to something.'

Φ

Sook Yongsheng and Quee Long stamped down the Kaniere-road towards Hokitika, identically clad in wide-brimmed felt hats, woollen capes, and canvas overshoes. Dusk was falling, bringing with it a rapid drop in temperature, and turning the standing water at the roadside from brown to glossy blue. There was little traffic save for the infrequent cart or lone rider making for the warmth and light of the town ahead—still some two miles distant, though one could hear the roar of the ocean already, a dull, pitchless sound, and above it, the infrequent cry of a sea-bird, the call floating thin and weightless above the sound of the rain.

The two men were conversing in Cantonese.

'There is no gold in the Aurora,' Ah Quee was saying.

'Can you be certain?'

'The claim is barren. It is as if the earth has been already turned.'

'Turned earth can be surprising,' replied Ah Sook. 'I know of many men who make their livings out of tailing piles.'

'You know of many Chinese men who make their livings out of tailing piles,' Ah Quee corrected. 'And then they are beaten, even killed, by those men whose eyes were not as sharp.'

'Money is a burden,' said Ah Sook. This was a proverb he quoted often.

'A burden that is felt most keenly by the poor,' said Ah Quee. He glanced sidelong at the other man. 'Your trade has also been slow, of late.'

'It has,' said Ah Sook, evenly.

'The whore has lost her taste for the smoke.'

'Yes. I cannot account for it.'

'Perhaps she has found an alternate supplier.'

'Perhaps.'

'You do not believe that.'

'I do not know what to believe.'

'You are suspicious of the chemist.'

'Yes; among other men.'

Ah Quee mused a moment, and then said, 'I do not think that the fortune I uncovered ever belonged to Anna herself.'

'No,' Ah Sook agreed. 'That is likely. After all, she did not remark its theft.'

Ah Quee glanced at him. 'Do you think of my action as a theft?'

'I do not wish to impugn your honour,' Ah Sook began, but then he hesitated.

'Your implication goes against your wish, Sook Yongsheng.'

Ah Sook ducked his head. 'Forgive me. I am ignorant, and my ignorance shines brighter than my intent.'

'Even ignorant men have opinions,' said Ah Quee. 'Tell me. Am I a thief to you?'

'It is the wish for secrecy that defines a theft,' the hatter said at last, somewhat lamely.

'In saying so, you impugn the honour of more men than me!'

'If I speak untruly, I will swallow back my words.'

'You speak untruly,' Ah Quee snapped. 'When a man finds a nugget on the goldfields, he does not proclaim it. He hides it, and speaks nothing to his fellows. Here on the goldfields, every man has a wish for secrecy. Only a fool speaks of his discoveries aloud. You would be no different, Sook Yongsheng, if you came upon a pile.'

'But the gold you speak of was not discovered on the field,' Ah Sook said. 'You found your fortune in a woman's pocket; you took it from her person, not from the ground.'

'The woman had no knowledge of what she carried! She was like a man who camps beside a river rich in gold, and sees nothing, suspects nothing.'

'But the gold in a river does not belong to anyone; nor does it belong to the river.'

'You have said yourself that the gold could not have belonged to Anna!'

'Not to Anna; but what of the tailor's claim upon it? What of the tailor's purpose, in hiding such a sum in the folds of a woman's gown?'

'I had no knowledge of the tailor,' said Ah Quee hotly. 'When you come upon a silver penny, do you ask who forged it? No: you ask only who touched that penny last! I am not a thief, for taking something that was lost.'

'Lost?'

'*Lost*,' said Ah Quee. 'That fortune had been claimed by no one. It had been stolen before me, and it has been stolen since.'

'Forgive me,' said Ah Sook. 'I stand corrected.'

'A whore is not a concubine,' said Ah Quee. He was getting worked up; evidently this was a subject on which he had desired to defend himself for some time. 'A whore cannot become respectable. A whore cannot become rich. All the prestige and all the profit belong to the whoremonger, never to the whore. Yes: the only one who truly profits from her trade is the man who stands behind her, purse in one hand, pistol in the other. I did not steal from Anna!

What could I have stolen? She owns nothing. That gold was never hers.'

They heard hoof beats behind them, and turned: a pair of riders, both sitting very low in the saddle, were heading for Hokitika at a canter; both horses were in a lather, and both riders were making very free with their crops, to urge them still faster. The Chinese men stood aside to let them pass.

'Forgive me,' said Ah Sook again, when they were gone. 'I was mistaken. You are not a thief, Quee Long.'

They resumed walking. 'Mr. Staines is the true thief,' said the goldsmith. 'He stole with intent, and then fled without compunction. I was foolish to place my trust in him.'

'Staines is in league with Francis Carver,' said Ah Sook. 'The Aurora's records prove as much. That alliance is reason enough to doubt his worth.'

Ah Quee glanced across at his companion. 'I do not know your Francis Carver,' he said. 'I have never heard his name before today.'

'He is a merchant trader,' said Ah Sook, without expression. 'I knew him in Guangzhou, as a boy. He betrayed my family, and I have sworn to take his life.'

'This much I know already,' said Ah Quee. 'I should like to know more.'

'It is a pitiful story.'

'Then I will listen with compassion. A betrayal of any of my countrymen is a betrayal of me.'

Ah Sook frowned at this. 'The betrayal is mine to avenge,' he said.

'I meant only that we must help each other, Sook Yongsheng.'

'Why do you say "must"?'

'Chinese life is cheap in this country.'

'All life is cheap, upon a goldfield.'

'You are wrong,' said Ah Quee. 'Today you saw a man strike me, pull my hair, insult me, and threaten me with death—all without consequence. And there will be no consequence. Every man in Hokitika would sooner take Mannering's part than mine, and why? Because I am Chinese and he is not Chinese. You and I *must* help each other, Ah Sook. We must. The law is united against us; we must have the means to unite against the law.'

This was a sentiment that Ah Sook had never heard expressed; he was silent for a time, digesting it. Ah Quee took off his hat, struck it several times with his palm, and replaced it on his head. Somewhere in the bush nearby a bellbird gave its lusty, open-throated cry; the call was taken up by another, and another, and for a moment the trees around them were alive with song.

It was by preference, and not by necessity, that Sook Yongsheng lived and worked alone. He was not surly by temperament, and in fact did not find it difficult to form friendships, nor to allow those friendships to deepen, once they had been formed; he simply preferred to answer to himself. He disliked all burdens of responsibility, most especially when those responsibilities were expected, or enforced—and friendship, in his experience, nearly always devolved into matters of debt, guilt, and expectation. Those men he did choose to call his intimates were those who demanded nothing, and gave much; as a consequence, there were many charitable figures in Ah Sook's past, and very few upon whom he had expressly doted. He had the sensibility of a social vanguard, unattached, full of conviction, and, in his own perception at least, almost universally misunderstood. The sense of being constantly undervalued by the world at large would develop, over time, into a kind of private demagoguery; he was certain of the comprehensive scope of his own vision, and rarely thought it necessary to explain himself to other men. In general his beliefs were projections of a simpler, better world, in which he liked, fantastically, to dwell—for he preferred the immaculate fervour of his own solitude to all other social obligations, and tended, when in company, to hold himself aloof. Of this propensity, he was not at all unaware, for he was highly reflexive, and given to extensive self-analysis of the most rigorous and contemplative kind. But he analysed his own mind as a prophet analyses his own strange visions—that is, with reverence, and believing always that he was destined to be the herald of a cosmic raison d'être, a universal plan.

'My history with Francis Carver,' he said at last, 'is a story with many beginnings; but I hope that it will only have one end.'

'Tell it,' said Ah Quee.

Φ

Harald Nilssen closed the door of his quayside office, sat down at his desk, and without first removing his hat or his coat, penned a hasty note to Joseph Pritchard. The tone of his letter was frantic, even slovenly, but Nilssen did not care to revise it. Without re-reading his words, he blotted the page, folded the paper, and stamped the sealing wax with the circular matrix of Nilssen & Co. He then summoned Albert, and instructed the boy to deliver the note to Pritchard's drug emporium on Collingwood-street post-haste.

Once Albert had departed Nilssen hung up his hat, exchanged his rain-soaked coat for a dry robe, and reached for his pipe—but even after the tobacco was lit, and he had sat down, put up his feet, and crossed his ankles, he did not feel reassured. He felt chilly. His skin was damp to the touch, and the rhythm of his heart would not slow. He stuck the pipe in the corner of his mouth, as he liked to do, and turned his attention to the subject of his disquiet: the promise he had made, earlier that day, to George Shepard, Governor of the Hokitika Gaol.

Nilssen wondered whether he ought to break his vow of silence and share the details of Shepard's proposition with the assembly that evening. The matter was certainly relevant to their prospective discussion, principally for the reason that it concerned a percentage of Crosbie Wells's fortune, but also because, Nilssen suspected, Shepard's antipathy towards the politician Lauderback was not just a matter of convict labour, gaol-houses, and roads. When one considered that the politician Alistair Lauderback had been the first to encounter Crosbie Wells's dead body—well, Nilssen thought, it was clear that Governor Shepard was as mixed up in the Crosbie Wells conspiracy as the rest of them! But how much did Shepard know—and whom was he serving, beyond his own self-interest? Had he known about the fortune hidden in Crosbie Wells's cottage? Had *Lauderback* known about it, for that matter? Brooding, Nilssen recrossed his ankles, and repositioned his pipe in his mouth, cupping the bowl between the crook of his index finger and the pad of his thumb. Whichever way one looked at it, he thought, there was no denying that George Shepard knew a great deal more than he was letting on.

Harald Nilssen was used to commanding public attention, an authority he achieved through the use of wit, declamation, and comical self-styling. He became very quickly bored when he was required, for whatever reason, to inhabit the periphery of a crowded room. His vanity required constant stimulation, and constant proof that the ongoing creation of his selfhood was a project that he himself controlled. He was vexed, now, to think that he had been played as a fool, not because he believed himself undeserving of such treatment (Nilssen knew very well that he was an impressionable type, and often joked about this very fact) but because he could not perceive Shepard's motivation in having treated him so.

He puffed at his pipe, conjuring in his mind the prospective gaol-house, the asylum, the scaffold of the gallows, built high above the drop. All of it would be built with his commission, and by his leave. *Hang Governor Shepard*, he thought suddenly. He had no real obligation to keep Shepard's secret—why, he did not even know, exactly, what that secret really *was*! He would share Shepard's request with the assembly that evening, and he would share his own suspicions about the man, to boot. He was not yet contractually bound to keep his silence. He had not yet signed his name to any document. What did that matter, anyway? A gaol-house was not a private property. It belonged to all of Hokitika. A gaol-house was built by the government—and on behalf of the adherents of the law.

Presently Nilssen heard the door in the outer office open and close. He leaped up. It was Albert, returning from Joseph Pritchard's drug hall. His jacket was very wet, and when he stepped into Nilssen's office, he carried with him the earthy smell of rain.

'Did he burn the letter?' Nilssen said anxiously. 'Did you watch him burn it? What's that you've got there?'

'Pritchard's reply,' said Albert. He held up a folded piece of paper.

'I said there wasn't to be a reply! I said that!'

'Yes,' said Albert, 'and I told him—but he penned one anyway.'

Nilssen eyed the document in Albert's hand. 'Did he burn my letter, at least?'

'Yes,' Albert said, but then he hesitated.

'What? What?'

'Well,' Albert said, 'when I said he had to burn it—he laughed.'

Nilssen narrowed his eyes. 'Why did he laugh?'

'I don't know,' said Albert. 'But I thought I should tell you that he did. Maybe it doesn't matter.'

The muscle beneath Nilssen's eye began to pulse. 'He laughed when he read the letter? When he read the words?'

'No,' said Albert. 'He only laughed before. When I said he had to burn it.'

'He found it amusing, did he?'

'That you'd told him to burn it,' said Albert, nodding. He was fingering the edges of the letter in his hand. He wanted very much to ask his employer what all of this to-do was on account of, but he did not know how to ask without risking a rebuke. Aloud he said, 'Do you want to read the reply?'

Nilssen held out his hand. 'Here,' he said. '*You* didn't read it, did you?'

'No,' Albert said, looking wounded. 'It's sealed.'

'Oh, yes, so it is,' said Nilssen. He took the note from Albert's hand, turned it over, and broke apart the seal with his fingers. 'What are you waiting for?' he said, before he unfolded the paper. 'You can go.'

'Home?' said Albert, in a voice of great regret.

'Yes—home, you idiot,' said Nilssen. 'And you can leave the key on the desk before you do.'

But the boy lingered. 'On the way back,' he said, 'when I passed the Prince of Wales, I saw there's a new show opening tonight: a foreign spectacle. Mr. Mannering's giving away tickets for free—on account of the opening—and I got one for you.' He had spoken all of this very quickly; now he screwed up his face, and looked away.

Nilssen had not yet unfolded Pritchard's letter. 'What?' he said.

'*Sensations from the Orient*,' the boy said. 'It's a gallery ticket—front and centre. The best. I asked for it special.'

'You use it yourself,' Nilssen said. 'You go yourself. I don't want a ticket to the theatre. Get along, now.'

The boy scuffed his shoe upon the boards. 'I got myself one too,' he said. 'I thought—seeing as it's Saturday—and the races have been postponed—'

Nilssen shook his head. 'I can't go to the theatre tonight,' he said.

'Oh,' said Albert. 'Why?'

'I'm feeling poorly.'

'Just for the first act,' the boy said. 'There's supposed to be champagne. Champagne's good if you're feeling poorly.'

'Take Henry Fuller with you.'

'By the players' door I saw a lady with a parasol.'

'Take Henry.'

'She was Japanese,' said Albert, mournfully. 'It didn't look like greasepaint. It looked like she was really Japanese. Henry Fuller's up the beach. Why won't you come?'

'I'm very ill.'

'You don't look ill. You're smoking.'

'I'm sure you can find someone to go along with you,' Nilssen said, with mounting irritation. 'Go down to the Star and wave that ticket around. How about that?'

Albert stared at the floorboards for a moment and worked his mouth. At length he sighed and said, 'Well, I expect I'll see you on Monday, Mr. Nilssen.'

'Yes, I expect you will, Albert.'

'Goodbye.'

'Goodbye. You'll have to tell me all about the show. All right?'

'Maybe we can go again,' Albert said. 'Only the ticket's for tonight. But maybe we can go again.'

'Yes,' Nilssen said. 'Next week, perhaps. After I recover.'

He waited until the disappointed subordinate had padded from the room, and closed the door quietly behind him. Then he unfolded Pritchard's letter, and stepped towards the window, for a better light.

H.—Can confirm. But listen: something odd happened this afternoon at Anna's. Pistols involved. Will explain in full in person. Event witnessed by A.G. courthouse clerk. Perhaps you should speak to him, if you're playing the detective. Whatever Anna's mixed up in, I'm sure that A.G. knows about it. Do you trust him? Can't say that I do: well, the jury's still out, as the saying goes. Destroy this letter!—J.S.P.

Φ

Thomas Balfour had returned, in the late afternoon, to the Palace Hotel, with the intention of finding Cowell Devlin—the chaplain who had overheard his conversation with Lauderback that morning. He wished to apologise for his earlier rudeness, but also (and rather more urgently) to ask the chaplain about his connexion to the vanished prospector, Emery Staines. He was sure that Devlin's inquiry at the office of the *West Coast Times* was connected, somehow, to the Crosbie Wells affair.

Devlin was not at the Palace Hotel, however; the kitchen staff informed Balfour that he had left the dining room several hours before. He was not in his tent upon the beachfront, nor at the Police Camp gaol-house, nor in any of the churches; he was not in any of the stores or billiard-halls, and he was not on the quay. Balfour wandered about Hokitika for several hours, dejected, and was about to give up and go home when he spied Devlin at last. The chaplain was walking down Revell-street, his hat and coat quite saturated; walking next to him was another man, a good deal taller and larger than he. Balfour crossed the street. He was already raising his arm to flag the other down when he recognised Devlin's companion: it was the Maori man with whom he had also spoken, earlier that day, and to whom he had also been rather unforgivably rude.

'Hi there,' he called. 'Reverend Devlin. Would you believe it! The very man I was looking to find! Hello, Ted: I'm glad to see you again, too.'

Tauwhare did not offer a greeting; Devlin, however, smiled. 'I see that you have found out my surname,' he said. 'I'm afraid I still do not know yours.'

Balfour thrust out his hand. 'Tom Balfour,' he said, beaming, and they shook hands. 'Yes: I went to see Ben Löwenthal, over at the *Times*, and we had some words about you. Matter of fact I've been trying to track you down these past few hours. To ask you something.'

'Then our meeting is doubly fortuitous,' said Devlin.

'It's a question about Emery Staines,' Balfour said, interrupting him. 'I hear you've been asking after him, you see. Wanting to know who placed that notice in the paper, advertising his return. Ben told me that you'd been by. I'm wanting to know why you're asking after him—Staines, I mean—and what's your connexion to the man.'

Cowell Devlin hesitated. The truth, of course, was that Emery Staines was one of the three names written upon the deed of gift that he had taken from the ash-drawer of Crosbie Wells's range, the day after the hermit's death. He had not showed that deed to anyone, however, and he had resolved not to do so, until he knew a little more about the people it concerned. Ought he to lie to Balfour? He did not like to utter falsehoods, but perhaps he could tell a partial truth. He bit his lip.

Balfour had perceived the chaplain's hesitation, and had mistaken it for reproof. He put up his hands. 'Hark at me,' he exclaimed, 'asking questions in the street—and in the weather—when we're getting wetter all the time! Look here. How about we share a meal together? Something hot. There's no sense in talking out of doors—not when there are warm hotels on either side of us, and good cheer to be had.'

Devlin glanced at Tauwhare, who, despite his dislike of Balfour, had brightened considerably at the prospect of a meal.

Balfour coughed, and then thumped his chest with his fist, wincing. 'I wasn't myself this morning—out of sorts; I wasn't myself. I'm sorry for it—and I mean to make it up—to both of you. I'll stand us all a plate of something, and we'll have a drink together—as friends. Come: let a man say he's sorry, when he asks.'

The threesome was soon established at a corner table at Maxwell's. Balfour, who was always very happy to play the role of the munificent host, ordered three bowls of clear soup, a round of bread, a fat black pudding, a hard cheese, sardines in oil, hot buttered carrots, a pot of stewed oysters, and a demijohn of stout. He had the prescience to delay any talk of Crosbie Wells or Emery Staines until both his guests were sated with food and drink, and talked instead of whaling, a subject of which all three men had a most romantic conception, and much to share. When Benjamin Löwenthal found them some three-quarters of an hour later, they were a very merry party.

'Ben!' cried Balfour, when he saw Löwenthal approaching. 'But what about your Sabbath?'

He had become, for the second time that day, rather drunk.

'Ends at starlight,' Löwenthal said shortly. To Tauwhare he said, 'I believe that we have not yet been introduced. I am Benjamin Löwenthal; I publish the *West Coast Times.*'

'Te Rau Tauwhare,' the Maori man replied, and shook his hand very firmly.

'He also goes by Ted,' said Balfour. 'Very good friend of Crosbie Wells.'

'Were you?' said Löwenthal to Tauwhare.

'His finest friend,' said Devlin.

'Better than brothers,' said Balfour.

'Well, in that case,' said Löwenthal, 'my business concerns all three of you.'

Benjamin Löwenthal had no authority to widen the invitation to the Crown Hotel council to include Devlin and Tauwhare. But as we have observed already, Löwenthal could be very forbidding when his ethical code was affronted, and Charlie Frost had affronted him, that afternoon, by suggesting that the Crown assembly ought to be restricted to an exclusive few. Löwenthal felt the need to rectify what he perceived to have been Frost's moral error, and he extended the invitation to Tauwhare and Devlin now as an obscure act of reproach.

'Capital,' Balfour said. 'Pull up a chair.'

Löwenthal sat down, placed the palms of his hands together, and, in a low voice, explained the purpose of the meeting that evening—to which Balfour acquiesced immediately, Tauwhare gravely, and Cowell Devlin after a long, judicious pause. The chaplain was thinking about the deed of gift that he had taken from the hermit's stove, currently stored in his Bible, between the Old Testament and the New. He resolved to bring his Bible with him to the council that evening, and to produce the deed, if the occasion moved him, and the timing was right.

Φ

There was smoke issuing from Gascoigne's chimney, and upon Mannering's knock, the door opened promptly, and Gascoigne peered out. He was holding a freshly lit cigarette, and had exchanged his formal jacket for shirtsleeves and a woollen vest.

'Yes?' he said.

'I have it on good information that you're holding on to some money,' Dick Mannering said. 'That money's mine, and I've come to collect it.'

Aubert Gascoigne looked at him, then put his cigarette to his lips, inhaled, and blew a stream of smoke over Mannering's shoulder, into the rain. 'Who is the source of your good information?' he said mildly.

'Miss Anna Wetherell, by way of Mr. Edgar Clinch,' Mannering said.

Gascoigne leaned against the doorframe. 'And how did Miss Anna Wetherell, by way of Mr. Edgar Clinch, imagine that you would act, upon receiving this good information?'

'Don't play clever with me,' Mannering said. 'Don't do it. I'll only tell you once: I don't like cleverness one bit. She says the money's hidden under your bed.'

Gascoigne shrugged. 'Well, if I am holding a fortune for Anna,' he said, 'I am doing it on promise, and see no reason why I should break that promise, and hand the money over to another man— just because he claims the money belongs to him. She certainly did not tell me to expect a visitor.'

'It does belong to me.'

'How so?'

'It's a debt,' Mannering said. 'She owes me.'

'A debt is a private business,' Gascoigne said.

'A debt can be made public very easily. How would you like it if I spread the word that you were holding on to more than a hundred pounds in pure? Let me tell you. By midnight your door would be beaten down, by dawn the thief would be fifty miles away, and by this time to-morrow, you would be dead. Why, there'd be nothing easier—when you've no allegiances to speak of, and you live alone.'

Gascoigne's expression darkened. 'I am the custodian of that gold, and I will not hand it over without Miss Wetherell's consent.'

Mannering smiled. 'I'm going to take that as an admission of guilt.'

'And I'm going to take *that* as proof of your logical inadequacy,' Gascoigne said. 'Good night. If Anna wants her money, she can come for it herself.'

He made to close the door, but Mannering stepped forward and put out his hand, halting him.

'Strange, isn't it?' he said.

Gascoigne scowled. 'What is strange?'

'Strange how a common whore suddenly fronts up with gold enough to pay the sum total of her obligations—and then hides that sum total beneath the bed of a man who's been in Hokitika barely long enough to learn her name.'

'It is excessively strange.'

'Perhaps I ought to introduce myself.'

'I know who you are,' Gascoigne said. 'And I know what you do.'

Mannering unbuttoned his coat to reveal his pistols. 'Do you know what these are? And do you know what they do?'

'Yes,' said Gascoigne coolly. 'Those are percussion revolvers, and they can each fire six rounds in six seconds flat.'

'Seven rounds, actually,' said Mannering. 'Second issue Smith & Wessons. Seven rounds each. But six seconds is right.'

Gascoigne took another draught of his cigarette.

Mannering placed his hands upon his holsters, smiling. 'I must ask you to invite me into your home, Mr. Gascoigne.'

The Frenchman did not reply, but after a moment he crushed

the end of his cigarette on the doorframe, dropped it, stepped to the side, and gestured with exaggerated courtesy for Mannering to enter. Mannering glanced to the corners of the room, letting his gaze linger pointedly on Gascoigne's bed. Once Gascoigne had closed the door behind him, he rounded on his host and said,

'Who has your loyalty?'

'I am not sure I understand the question,' Gascoigne said. 'You wish me to make a list of my friends?'

Mannering glared at him. 'Here's my question,' he said. 'Does Anna have your loyalty?'

'Yes,' Gascoigne said. 'Up to a point, of course.' He sat down in his striped wingback armchair, but made no gesture to offer his guest a seat.

Mannering locked his hands behind his back. 'So if you knew that she was mixed up in something, you wouldn't tell me.'

'Well, it would depend on the situation, of course,' Gascoigne said. 'What kind of "something" are you talking about?'

'Are you lying on her behalf?'

'I agreed to conceal a pile of money on her behalf,' Gascoigne said. 'I hid it underneath my bed. But you already know all about that. So I suppose the answer is no.'

'Why does she have your loyalty? Up to a point?'

Gascoigne's wrists were limp upon the armrests; he had arranged himself casually, like a king in a throne. He explained that he had cared for Anna when she was released from gaol two weeks prior, and had thereafter courted her friendship. He pitied her, for he believed that someone was using her for ill, but he could not say that he enjoyed any special intimacy with her, and had never paid to enjoy her company. The black dress, he added, had belonged to his late wife. He had given it to the whore as a gesture of charity, for her whoring gown had been ruined during her sojourn in gaol. He had not expected that she would enter a period of mourning, upon acquiring the dress, and in truth had been rather disappointed by this eventuation, for he thought her a very fine specimen of her sex, and would have very much liked to have taken his pleasure in the conventional way.

'Your story doesn't account for that gold underneath your bed,' Mannering said.

Gascoigne shrugged. He felt too tired, and too angry, to lie. 'The morning after Crosbie Wells died,' he said, 'Anna woke up in gaol with a great quantity of gold stashed about her person. The metal had been sewn around her corset. She had no idea how she had come to be in possession of such a sum, and was, naturally, quite frightened. She requested my help. I thought it best to hide it, for we did not know who had hidden the gold on her body, or for what purpose. We have not yet had it valued, but I would hazard its total worth at well over a hundred pounds—and in all likelihood, a great deal more. That, Mr. Mannering, is the whole truth—at least as far as *I* am concerned.'

Mannering was quiet. This explanation did not make any sense to him at all.

'I must say,' Gascoigne added, 'you do me a great disservice by assuming my guilt before you have queried me on the subject of my innocence. I resent very much that you have trespassed upon my time and my privacy in such a belligerent way.'

'You can leave off with that kind of talk,' Mannering said. 'Belligerent! Have I pointed a firearm in your face? Have I threatened you with violence?'

'You have not—and yet I would be happier if you were to take off your belt.'

'Take it off?' Mannering looked contemptuous. 'And lay it down in the middle of the table, I suppose—with each of us an equal distance away—until you make a move for it, and I'm too slow! I won't fall for it: I've seen *that* trick before.'

'Then I will make another request,' Gascoigne said. 'I request that your presence in my house is of as short a duration as possible. If you have further questions, you ought to make them now—but I have told you everything I know about that gold.'

'Listen,' Mannering said firmly. (He was rather bewildered that he had so swiftly lost the upper hand.) 'I didn't mean for us to start on the wrong foot.'

'Certainly you meant it,' said Gascoigne. 'Perhaps now you regret it, but you meant it.'

Mannering swore. 'I don't regret anything!' he cried. 'I don't regret anything at all!'

'That accounts for your serenity.'

'Let me tell you something,' Mannering said—but he was prevented from saying anything further: just at that moment came a smart rap upon the door.

Gascoigne stood immediately. Mannering, who looked suddenly alarmed, stepped back several paces and withdrew one of his pistols from its holster. He held it against his thigh, to conceal it from view, and nodded for Gascoigne to lift the latch.

On the threshold, standing with his stick set at a rather rakish angle from his body and his hat tipped back from his brow, was Harald Nilssen. He bowed, and was just about to make his introduction to Gascoigne when he perceived, over the latter's shoulder, Dick Mannering, standing awkwardly, with one arm held stiff at his side. Nilssen burst out laughing.

'*Well*,' he said. 'Seems I'm two steps behind you, Dick. Everywhere I go today—there you are, and you got there first! Hello, Mr. Gascoigne. My name's Harald Nilssen. I'm very pleased to make your acquaintance. I do hope I'm not interrupting anything.'

Gascoigne bowed courteously, though his expression remained cold. 'Not at all,' he said. 'Do come in.'

'I *had* come to talk with you about Anna Wetherell,' Nilssen said cheerfully, wiping his boots, 'but I see I've been pipped at the post!'

Gascoigne closed the door and said, 'What about Anna?'

At the same time, Mannering said, 'Steady up, Mr. Nilssen.'

Nilssen answered Gascoigne. 'Well, it concerns something rather peculiar,' he said. 'So perhaps it's not for all ears. But listen: I don't want to interrupt you. I can easily come back when you're not otherwise engaged.'

'No, please,' Gascoigne said. 'Mr. Mannering was just leaving; he just told me so himself.'

It vexed Mannering to be excluded in this way. 'What's it all about?' he said to Nilssen.

Nilssen made a short bow. 'It is a very delicate situation; I do apologise.'

'Hang *delicate*,' Mannering said. 'You needn't conceal anything from *me*, for God's sake: we're in this together! Is this about the widow? Or about the gold?'

Nilssen was uncomprehending. 'The Wells fortune?' He turned to Gascoigne. 'Are you mixed up in *that*, then?'

Gascoigne was looking very amused all of a sudden. 'It seems I am being interrogated from all quarters at once,' he said. 'Are you also wearing pistols, Mr Nilssen? You really ought to confess them, if you are.'

'I'm not wearing pistols,' Nilssen said. He glanced at Mannering, and saw the revolver in his hand. 'What's that for? What are you doing?'

But Mannering did not answer: he was caught, momentarily, between all that he wished to conceal from Nilssen, and all that he wished to conceal from Gascoigne. He hesitated, wishing that he had not already mentioned the widow and the gold.

'Mr. Mannering was just showing me his second-issue Smith and Wesson,' Gascoigne said conversationally. 'That cylinder takes seven cartridges, apparently.'

'Oh,' Nilssen said—but he looked suspicious. 'What for?'

Again Mannering's explanation stalled in his throat. He did not wish Nilssen to know about the gold hidden beneath Gascoigne's bed . . . but he did not wish Gascoigne to know about the Crosbie Wells debacle, and Ah Quee, and Ah Sook, and opium, and all that was to be discussed at the Crown Hotel that very evening.

'It's a delicate situation,' Gascoigne said, putting in for the older man. He leaned towards Nilssen. 'All I can tell you is that Mr. Mannering here has a source of very good information in Miss Anna Wetherell, and the information comes by way of Mr. Edgar Clinch.'

'That's enough out of you,' said Mannering, finding his tongue at last. 'Nilssen. What's your news about Anna? What's your business?'

But Nilssen misunderstood Mannering's intention, in pressing him to speak upon this subject in front of Gascoigne. He remembered that Pritchard's letter had mentioned pistols, and Anna, and indirectly, Edgar Clinch—for Pritchard had said a strange event had taken place in Anna's rooms at the Gridiron Hotel that very afternoon. *Of course!* Nilssen thought suddenly. Their 'delicate situations' must be one and the same.

'Look here,' he said, holding up his hand. 'I believe we're talking about the same thing after all. If Mr. Gascoigne's in on the secret, then we may as well wait until everyone's assembled at the council, and share our stories then. Save telling everything twice. Shall I see you both at the Crown?'

Mannering exhaled.

'I am afraid,' Gascoigne said presently, 'that I am not in on the secret, and I have not been invited to a council at the Crown.'

There was a silence. Gascoigne looked at Nilssen, and then at Mannering. Mannering looked at Gascoigne, and then at Nilssen. Nilssen was looking at Mannering. He had a very apologetic expression upon his face.

'Now you've done it,' the magnate said. He uttered an oath, put away his pistol, and then levelled his finger at Gascoigne. 'All right,' he said. 'There's nothing for it—though I'm d—ned if your presence is welcome, and I'll be d—ned if I don't keep you in my sights until the evening's over, and beyond. Put your coat on. You're coming along.'

MERCURY IN SAGITTARIUS

In which Walter Moody meditates upon the mystery at hand;
we learn what happened on his journey from Dunedin; and
a messenger brings unexpected news.

There was a silence in the smoking room of the Crown Hotel—a silence that, for a moment, seemed to still the breath of every man, and still the smoke that rose in coils from the pipes, the cigarettes, the cheroots, and the cigars.

It was past midnight. The darkness had rounded the corners of the room, and the cones of light cast by the spirit lamps now seemed robust and warming, where before they had been faint and chill. Strains of Saturday night filtered in from the street—an accordion, distant shouting, an infrequent whoop, hoof beats. It had stopped raining, though the cloud had not yet cleared, and the gibbous moon showed only as a squarish patch of light in the lowering sky.

'That's it,' said Thomas Balfour. 'That's it. That's where we'd got to.'

Moody blinked and looked around him. Balfour's narrative, disjunctive and chaotic as it was, had indeed accounted for the presence of every man in the room. There by the window was the Maori carver, Te Rau Tauwhare, who had been Crosbie's loyal friend in life, though he had unwittingly betrayed him at the last. There in the farthest corner was Charlie Frost, the banker who had engineered the sale of Wells's house and land, and opposite him, the newspaperman Benjamin Löwenthal, who had heard about the death within mere hours of its occurrence. Edgar Clinch, purchaser of Wells's estate, was sitting on the sofa beside the billiard table, smoothing his moustache with his finger and thumb. There by the fire was Dick Mannering, whoremonger, theatre owner, and close associate of Emery Staines; there behind him was Ah Quee, his enemy. There with a cue in his hand was the commission merchant, Harald Nilssen, who had discovered in Crosbie Wells's cottage not only an enormous fortune, but a corked phial of laudanum, half empty, which had been purchased at Joseph Pritchard's drug hall. The latter, of course, was sitting nearest Moody; on his other side was Thomas Balfour, lackey to the politician Lauderback, whose shipping crate had lately disappeared. There in the wingback arm-chair next to Balfour was Aubert Gascoigne, who had paid Anna Wetherell's bail, and had uncovered another, smaller fortune hoarded in her orange whoring gown. Behind him was Ah Sook, peddler of opium, keeper of the den at Kaniere, and former associate of Francis Carver, who had discovered, that very afternoon, that Crosbie Wells had once been rich. And there, finally, leaning against the billiard table with his arms folded across his chest, was the chaplain Cowell Devlin, who had committed the hermit's body to its final resting place upon the terrace at Seaview.

It was, in Moody's estimation, a confoundedly peripheral gathering. The twelve men were united only by their association to the events of the 14th of January, upon which night Anna Wetherell had nearly died, Crosbie Wells *had* died, Emery Staines had vanished, Francis Carver had sailed away, and Alistair Lauderback had arrived in town. It struck Moody that none of *these* people were present. The gaol warden, Governor Shepard, was likewise absent, as was the crafty widow, Lydia Wells.

Another thought struck Moody: the night of the 14th of January was the very evening that he himself had first set foot upon New Zealand soil. Disembarking the packet steamer that had conveyed him from Liverpool to Dunedin, he had cast his gaze skyward, and had felt for the first time the strangeness of where he was. The skies were inverted, the patterns unfamiliar, the Pole Star beneath his feet, quite swallowed. At first he searched for it, stupidly, wanting to measure his present latitude from the incline of his rigid arm, as he had done as a boy, on the other side of the earth. He found Orion—upended, his quiver beneath him, his sword hanging upward from his belt; Canis Major—hanging like a dead dog from a butcher's hook. There was something very sad about it, Moody thought. It was as if the ancient patterns had no meaning here. At length he found the Southern Crux, and tried to recall the rule for locating the pole, for there was no equivalent star to mark it, here in the black of the antipodes, where everything was upended and unformed. Did one use the crossbar of the thing? Or the spar? He could not remember. There was some kind of formula: the length of a knuckle, some equation. A matter of inches. It had bothered him extremely that there was no star to mark the pole.

Moody gazed into the fire, the coals of which had long since gone to ash. Thomas Balfour had not told his tale at all chronologically, and his narrative had been further convoluted by countless inter-ruptions, clarifications, and echoes—all chasing one another, as endless circles, going round. What a convoluted picture it was—and how difficult to see, in its entirety! Moody turned his mind to all that he had heard that evening. He tried to place the recounted events into the order in which they had actually occurred.

Roughly nine months prior to the present day, the former con-vict Francis Carver had successfully cheated Alistair Lauderback out of his ship, the *Godspeed*. At some point thereafter, and by an unknown complication, he had then lost the shipping crate by which he had forced the politician's hand. Inside this shipping crate was a trunk containing approximately four thousand pounds in pure gold, a fortune that had been meticulously sewn into the lining of five dresses. The seamstress was a woman named Lydia Wells, who was, at that time, posing as Francis Carver's wife.

Four thousand pounds was a great deal of money, and Carver, naturally, wished to recover it, once he discovered that the thing had been lost. He sailed to Hokitika, presumably guessing that the crate had been delivered there by mistake, and placed an adver-tisement in the *West Coast Times*, offering a large reward for the crate's safe return. He placed this advertisement under the name of Crosbie Francis Wells—producing a birth certificate to confirm this identity—though he was known, both beforehand and thereafter, by the name of Francis Carver. It was yet unknown why Carver's blackmail of Lauderback had required him (or inspired him) to assume an alias. It was also unknown why Crosbie Wells's birth certificate, if indeed genuine, had been in Carver's possession at that time.

The real Crosbie Wells (or perhaps, Moody thought, *another* Crosbie Wells) lived alone in the Arahura Valley, some miles north of Hokitika. Wells was not a notorious personage, and his acquaintance was small; before his death he was little known in Hokitika, and those who did know him did not suspect him to be a person of any wealth or consequence. It was Ah Sook, investigating the circumstances of his death nine months later, who discovered that Wells had made a strike on the fields at Dunstan several years before, pulling in a fortune of thousands of pounds. Evidently Wells had desired, for some reason, to keep this information a secret.

Francis Carver placed his advertisement in the *Times* in early June (the precise month having been confirmed by Benjamin Löwenthal). While in Hokitika he offered Te Rau Tauwhare a private reward for any news of a man named Crosbie Wells. Tauwhare did not know a man of that name or description, however, and the shipping crate was not found; Carver returned to Dunedin empty-handed.

Anna Wetherell had also arrived in Hokitika upon the *Godspeed*, clad in a purple working gown rented from her new employer, Dick Mannering. When she learned, some weeks after her arrival, that a trunk containing women's dresses had been salvaged from a wreck, she purchased all five.

It was not unreasonable to presume that Anna was ignorant of the fortune these gowns contained, and ignorant, also, of their origin. She had never spoken of the hidden gold to any man, and she had never attempted in any visible way to remove it. Moody considered this. Was total ignorance really possible? As an opium eater, perhaps she had not noticed the added weight about her person as a sober woman might; then again, she was, as Gascoigne had attested, a former acquaintance of Lydia Wells's, and perhaps she had recognised the garments as Lydia's. Well, Moody thought, whatever the case, Anna had been wearing that entire fortune—a portion at a time, of course—ever since then, save for a month-long period in September and October, when the advanced stage of her pregnancy had compelled her to wear, instead, a frock designed for lying-in.

When Anna's landlord, Edgar Clinch, discovered the fortune hidden in the gowns, he concluded that the whoremonger Dick Mannering must be using Anna to smuggle raw ore off the gold-fields, as a way of evading duty at the bank. The thought of this collusion grieved Clinch extremely, but he had no reason to press the matter with either party, and did not do so.

Clinch was not the only man to chance upon the hidden fortune in Anna's gowns, however, and he was not the only man to mis-apprehend its likely meaning. The digger Quee Long had also uncovered the secrets hidden in Anna's seams—around much the same time, in fact—and had leaped to the very same conclusion as Clinch. Ah Quee knew first-hand that Mannering was more than capable of fraud, for he had been cheated by the magnate once before. Ah Quee decided to beat Mannering at his own game. He began siphoning the gold out of Anna's dresses, retorting the dust into squares, and stamping these squares with the name of the goldmine Aurora—so as to ensure that the profit would be banked against his own claim, which by this time had been purchased by a young prospector named Emery Staines.

The project of removing the gold from Anna's dress took several months. Whenever Anna visited Ah Quee's hut in Kaniere Chinatown, she was all but senseless with opium; Ah Quee was therefore able to remove the gold with his thread and needle with-out her knowledge, while she slept. Anna did not wear her orange whoring dress when she travelled to Chinatown. For this reason, the orange dress had remained filled with gold, long after Ah Quee had stripped the other four of their fortune.

Nobody knew how, or why, Ah Quee's retorted fortune had been stolen from the vault at the camp station. The most probable thief, given the information currently available, was the vanished prospector, Staines—who, significantly, lacked a motivation. The young man was colossally rich, and, by popular opinion at least, colossally fortunate. Why should he desire to steal from his own indentured worker? And why should he choose to stash the gold in another man's cottage, so far from his own claims? Well, whatever the young man's reasons, Moody thought, at least one thing was certain: Staines had never banked Ah Quee's earnings against the Aurora as he was legally obliged to do. This was very perplexing, for the retorted gold, if banked, would have transformed the Aurora gold-mine from a duffer into a homeward-bounder overnight.

Emery Staines was also very strangely implicated by the deed of gift that Cowell Devlin had discovered in Crosbie Wells's stove—which, though it did not bear his signature, bore his name. This deed seemed to imply that Emery Staines and Crosbie Wells had been associates of some kind, and that the hoarded fortune had been intended, for some reason, as a gift from Emery Staines to Anna Wetherell. But this was even more confounding, for whichever way one looked at it, the gold was not Staines's to give away!

Anna had been carrying a child—Carver's child—since before she arrived in Hokitika, and in the springtime she began at last to show. Her condition was never to fully ripen into birth, however: in mid-October, Carver returned to Hokitika, confronted Anna, and beat her severely. The unborn child did not survive this encounter. Anna's later intimation, when she described the scene to Edgar Clinch, was that Carver had killed the child in cold blood.

Moody paused in his chronology to dwell upon this unhappy event. Although the child's death had been referenced in passing several times that evening, it did not seem as though any man present was entirely clear about how this fatal altercation had come about. It was for reasons of natural delicacy that Moody had not pressed the men for further information, but he wondered now how Anna's relations with Carver fitted in to the scheme of the story at large. He wondered whether the child's death had truly been intended, and, if so, what might have motivated Francis

Carver to commit such a heinous act. None of the twelve men currently present could answer this question with any kind of objective certainty, of course; they could only describe what they had been told to be true.

(How opaque, the minds of absent men and women! And how elusive, motivation! For Francis Carver might have killed his child in cold repudiation, as an act of loathing, as a brutal prophylactic, or quite by accident: short of asking the man directly, there was no way to tell. Even Anna Wetherell, who had named Carver as the murderer, might have had any number of reasons to lie.)

Having reflected upon this, Moody continued.

Te Rau Tauwhare, encountering Carver by chance on the morning of the 14th of January, had remembered the offer that the man had made him the previous year. For a price of two shillings, Tauwhare offered to tell Carver where Crosbie Wells was living. The men shook hands, Tauwhare gave directions, and Carver made for the Arahura Valley that very same day—a night that was to be Wells's last. Perhaps Carver had witnessed the hermit's death, or perhaps he had left moments before its occurrence, but in either case, he had arrived at the cottage with a phial of laudanum, traces of which were later discovered in Crosbie Wells's stomach during his post-mortem. Following their encounter, Carver returned to Hokitika, manned the *Godspeed*, and weighed anchor, leaving well before the dawn. From Hokitika Carver had travelled not to Canton (as Balfour had speculated he might) but to Dunedin, a fact that Moody himself could corroborate, for it was at Port Chalmers that Moody had boarded the very same craft, twelve days later.

Alistair Lauderback, arriving at Wells's cottage soon after Carver departed it, found the hermit dead at his kitchen table, his head resting on his arms. He journeyed on to Hokitika, where he was interviewed by the editor Benjamin Löwenthal, who was intending to run a political special in Monday's edition of the *Times*. Löwenthal, hearing from Lauderback that Crosbie Wells was dead, deduced that Wells's property would presently be put up for sale. The next morning he informed the hotelier Edgar Clinch of this probable eventuation, knowing that Clinch was looking to make an investment in land. Clinch immediately took his deposit to the bank, where the banker Charlie Frost facilitated his purchase of the dead man's estate.

Clinch then commissioned Harald Nilssen to clear the dead man's cottage and dispose of his effects. Nilssen did so—and discovered, to his astonishment, a perfect fortune, hidden in every conceivable hiding place around the dwelling's single room. The ore, once it had been purified by the bank, was valued at a little over four thousand pounds. Nilssen was paid his ten percent commission, leaving a little over thirty-six hundred; out of this had been paid sundry death taxes, fees, and incidentals, which included a present of thirty pounds to the banker, Charlie Frost. The remainder—still a certifiable fortune—was currently being held in escrow at the Reserve Bank. Clinch was not likely to see a single penny of the sum, however: Lydia Wells, arriving mysteriously from Dunedin some days after the hermit's funeral, had since appealed to revoke Clinch's purchase, on the grounds that his property and effects legally belonged to her.

Of course, the gold found in Crosbie's cottage did not represent the sum total of the fortune at play. Ah Quee had only stripped four out of Anna's five gowns. The final portion, sewn into the folds of Anna's orange whoring dress, had been discovered by Anna Wetherell herself but two weeks ago, when she woke up in gaol following the crisis of her overdose. She had assumed, reasonably enough, that the gold had only just been planted on her person— for she had no memory of what had happened to her in the twelve hours prior to her arrest, and was in a state of considerable confusion. She entreated Gascoigne's help, and together they excavated the metal from the orange gown and hid it in a flour sack under Gascoigne's bed.

When Anna then returned to the Gridiron Hotel, wearing the black dress that had belonged to Gascoigne's late wife, Edgar Clinch's old suspicions were renewed. He felt sure—rightly this time—that Anna's change of dress had something to do with the hidden gold, and he noted with bitterness that her orange whoring gown had now disappeared. He resented very much that she claimed to be unable to pay her debts to him, when he knew full well that she was flush with colour; letting his resentment get the better of him, he spoke to her cruelly, and gave her notice to leave.

But Clinch's threat did not have the consequence he was expecting. Anna Wetherell had since paid her debt to him in full, but not with the gold in her gowns, and not with her legal earnings either. The debt had been paid out that very afternoon by way of a six-pound loan from Crosbie's widow, Lydia Wells; her debt to Mannering, which by the magnate's reckoning was well over a hundred pounds, would be more than covered by the gold she and Gascoigne had excavated from the orange gown. Anna had since quit the Gridiron for good. She had been invited, henceforth, to take her lodging with Lydia Wells at the Wayfarer's Fortune, where she would no longer call herself a whore.

Did Lydia Wells know that Carver's missing shipping crate had ended up in Hokitika, and that the dresses had been purchased by Anna, and that the fortune at Crosbie Wells's cottage was one and the same as the fortune with which Carver had blackmailed the politician Lauderback, some ten months ago? Such a question depended entirely upon Anna. How much did Anna know about her own involvement in this very circular affair? And how much, for that matter, was she willing to reveal to Lydia Wells? It was very possible that Anna did *not* know the dresses had once been Lydia's. In this case, Mrs. Wells would remain ignorant of this fact also, for Anna was still wearing the black dress that had once belonged to Gascoigne's late wife, and she had vowed to remain in mourning for some time. Of course, Moody thought, Anna would only need to have opened the wardrobe in her room for the widow to have recognised the dresses ... but given that the gowns were currently lined with leaden makeweights, placed there as a decoy by the goldsmith Quee, Mrs. Wells might not have realised, at first glance or first touch, that the original fortune had been replaced by a worthless replica. Clinch had been fooled to this effect already. Moody wondered whether it was upon this false surety that the widow had paid Anna's debt that afternoon.

If Anna *did* know that the five dresses had once belonged to

Lydia Wells, however, then she surely must have known about their concealed fortune all along, and therefore, about Lauderback's blackmail, and the forced sale of the *Godspeed*, ten months prior. In light of this, Moody thought, the circumstance under which Anna's baby had been killed suddenly seemed *very* pertinent to the mysteries at hand, for Anna's relation to Francis Carver, like her relation to Lydia Wells, was a matter about which no man present knew anything at all.

Moody ran his finger absent-mindedly around the rim of his glass. There had to be a better explanation for all of this than merely the correlative accident of circumstance. What had Balfour said, hours ago? 'A string of coincidences is not a coincidence'? And what was a coincidence, Moody thought, but a stilled moment in a sequence that had yet to be explained?

'That's our part in it, at least,' Balfour added, in a tone of some apology. 'It's not much of an answer, Mr. Moody—but it accounts for what got us here tonight; the cause, as I said, of our assembly.'

'A little more than he bargained for, perhaps,' said Dick Mannering.

'It's always that—when it's the truth,' replied Balfour.

Moody looked from face to face. No one man could really be called 'guilty', just as no one man could really be called 'innocent'. They were—associated? Involved? Entangled? Moody frowned. He felt that he did not possess the right word to describe their interrelation. Pritchard had used the word 'conspiracy' ... but the term was hardly applicable, when each man's involvement was so incidental, and each man's relation to the events in question so palpably different. No: the real agents, and the real conspirators, were surely those men and women who were *not* present—who each had a secret that he or she was trying to hide!

Moody considered the absentees.

Francis Carver, as had been asserted many times that evening, was certainly 'behind' something. By Lauderback's account at least, Carver was an inveterate schemer with a taste for blackmail; what's more, he had visited Crosbie Wells on the day of his death, and perhaps had even watched him die. This reputation ought not to be forgotten, but it ought not to be given undue credence either,

Moody thought: Carver could not be 'behind' everything at once, and he certainly could not have engineered a plot of such elaborate proportion as to simultaneously indict twelve men.

Then there was Lydia Wells, the alleged wife of *both* Wells *and* Carver, the erstwhile mistress of Alistair Lauderback, and now (as she had recently confided to Gascoigne) the clandestine fiancée of an unnamed man. Like Carver, Mrs. Wells had shown herself to be capable of the most ruthless blackmail, and the most elaborate lies. She had also acted in partnership with Carver once before. The validity of her claim upon Crosbie Wells's fortune would be determined by the law in due course. . . though even if her claim *was* valid, Moody thought, the method of her claiming it was at best discourteous, and at worst, downright heartless. He felt that he distrusted Lydia Wells rather more than he distrusted Francis Carver—though of course this was unreasonable, for he had never met her, nor laid eyes upon her; he knew her only by report, and by a most disjointed and multifarious report at that.

Moody turned now to the other couple, Anna Wetherell and Emery Staines—who had been together on the night of the 14th of January, hours before Anna lapsed into unconsciousness, and Emery disappeared. What had really happened on that night, and what role had they played, whether witting or unwitting, in the Crosbie Wells affair? On the surface of things, it rather seemed as though Emery Staines had all the luck, and Anna, none of it—and yet Anna had survived her brush with death, and Staines, presumably, had not. It struck Moody that every man present, in his own way, was terribly envious of Staines, and terribly jealous of Anna. Staines's luck as a prospector was shared by no one, and Anna, as a camp whore, was a common property, shared by them all.

He was left with the politician and the gaoler. Moody considered them together. Alistair Lauderback, like his antagonist George Shepard, was a delegator, a man who was protected from the fullest consequences of his actions for the reason that his whims were most often performed and carried out by other men. There were other parallels too. Lauderback was soon to stand for the seat of

Westland; Shepard was soon to begin building his gaol-house and asylum on the terrace at Seaview. Lauderback had a personal history with Lydia Wells, his former mistress at the gambling house, just as Shepard had a personal history with Francis Carver, his former prisoner at the Sydney gaol.

In his mind Moody had arranged these external figures into three pairs: the widow and the trafficker; the politician and the gaoler; the prospector and the whore. This realisation pleased him—for Moody's mind was an orderly one, and he was reassured by patterns of any kind. Almost whimsically he wondered what role he himself played, in this strange tangle of association, yet to be solved. He wondered if he, too, had an opposite. Crosbie Wells, perhaps? Was his counterpart a dead man? Moody recalled, all of a sudden, the apparition upon the barque *Godspeed*, and he gave an involuntary shiver.

'Penny for your thoughts,' said Harald Nilssen, and Moody became aware that the men in the room had been waiting for him to speak for some time. They were gazing at him with more or less the same expression of hopeful expectation—the emotion betrayed, restrained, or displayed, according to the temper of the man. So I am to be the unraveller, Moody thought. The detective: that is the role I am to play.

'Don't rush him,' Harald Nilssen added, addressing the room at large—though it had been he who had encouraged Moody to break his silence. 'Let him speak on his own time.'

But Moody found he could not speak. He looked from face to face, at a loss for what to say.

After another moment, Pritchard leaned in and placed a long finger on the arm of Moody's chair. 'Look here,' he said. 'You said you had found something in the cargo of the *Godspeed*, Mr. Moody—something that made you doubt her errand was an honest one. What was it?'

'The shipping crate, maybe?' said Balfour.

'Opium?' said Mannering. 'Something to do with opium?'

'Don't rush him,' Nilssen said again. 'Let him answer as he will.'

Walter Moody had entered the smoking room that evening with

no intention of divulging what had happened on his journey from Dunedin. He had barely been able to acknowledge what he had witnessed to himself, let alone make sense of it for other men to hear and understand. In the context of the story that had just been related to him, however, he could see that his recent experience presented an explanation of a kind.

'Gentlemen,' he said at last. 'I have been honoured to enter your confidence this evening, and I thank you for your story. I have a tale to offer in return. There are several points upon which I think my story will be of interest to you, though I am afraid I will be doing little more than exchanging your present questions for different ones.'

'Yes, yes,' said Balfour. 'Have the stage, Mr. Moody; have at it.'

Obediently Moody got to his feet, and turned his back to the fire; immediately upon doing so, however, he felt very foolish, and wished that he had remained seated. He clasped his hands behind his back, and rocked forward several times on his heels before speaking.

'I should like to tell you all at the outset,' he said at last, 'that I believe I have news about Emery Staines.'

'Good or bad?' said Mannering. 'He's alive? You've seen him?'

Aubert Gascoigne was looking progressively sourer each time Mannering opened his mouth: he had not yet forgiven the magnate for his rudeness that afternoon, and nor was he likely to do so. Gascoigne bore humiliation extremely ill, and he could hold a grudge for a very long time. At this interruption he hissed audibly through his teeth, in disapproval.

'I cannot say for certain,' Moody replied. 'I must warn you, Mr. Mannering, as I must warn you all, that my story contains several particulars that do not (how shall I put it?) lead me to an immediately rational conclusion. I hope you will forgive me for not disclosing the full narrative of my journey earlier this evening; I confess, I knew not what to make of it myself.'

The room had become very still.

'You will recall,' Moody said, 'that my passage from Dunedin to the Coast was a very rough one; you will also recall, I hope, that the

ticket I had so hastily purchased did not buy me a berth in any real
sense, but only a small space in steerage. This space was pitch-dark,
foul-smelling, and completely unfit for human habitation. When
the storm struck, gentlemen, I was on deck, as I had been for
almost the entire journey.

'At first the storm seemed little more than a touch of bad
weather, merely a lash of wind and rain. As it gathered strength,
however, I became progressively more and more alarmed. I had
been warned that the seas off the West Coast were very rough, and
that upon every journey to the diggings, Death would roll her dice
against the lady Nightmare. I began to feel afraid.

'I had my suitcase with me. I wished to return it to the hold, so
that if I were to be washed overboard then my documents would
survive me, and I might have a proper funeral service, with my
proper name. To the sailors upon the docks I had given a false
name, as you will remember: I had shown them identity papers that
belonged to another man. The thought of having a false name
spoken at my funeral—'

'Horrible,' said Clinch.

Moody bowed. 'You understand. Well, I struggled up the deck,
clasping my case against me, and opened the forward hatch with
considerable difficulty, for the wind was gusting and the boat was
pitching all about. I managed finally to heave the thing open, and
threw my case into the hole ... but my aim was poor. The clasp
struck on the edge of the deck below; the case opened, and the contents burst out. My belongings were now strewn about the cargo
hold, and I was obliged to shimmy down the ladder after them.

'It took me some time to descend the ladder. The hold was very
dark; however, with each jibe and yaw, the ray of light through the
open hatch would roll about the cargo hold, as a roving glance.
There was a diabolical smell. The cases were groaning against their
straps and chains with a noise that was positively infernal. There
were several crates of geese in the hold, and many goats. These
poor animals were braying and honking and sounding their distress
in every possible way. I set about gathering my belongings as effi-
ciently as I was able, as I did not wish to spend any longer in that

place than was absolutely necessary. Through all the cacophony, however, I became aware of another sound.

'A kind of knocking was ensuing from inside the shipping crate nearest me—a furious knocking, loud enough to be heard over all the other din.'

Balfour was looking very alert.

'It sounded,' Moody went on, 'as if a man were trapped in there, and thrashing with all his limbs. I shouted hello and staggered over—the ship was pitching awfully—and from within heard a single name shouted over and over: *Magdalena, Magdalena, Magdalena.* I knew then that it was a man inside, and not a rat or beast of any other kind. I moved to pry the tacks from the lid of the case, working as fast as I could, and in due course managed to lever the lid open. I believe this was around two o'clock in the afternoon,' Moody added, with delicate emphasis. 'It was some four or five hours before we landed at Hokitika, in any case.'

'Magdalena,' said Mannering. 'That's Anna.'

Gascoigne looked furious.

Moody looked at Mannering. 'Forgive me,' he said. 'I'm afraid I don't follow. Is Magdalena Miss Wetherell's middle name?'

'It's a name to give a whore,' Mannering explained.

Moody shook his head, to indicate that he still did not understand.

'As every dog is called Fido, and every cow is called Bess.'

'Ah—yes, I see,' said Moody, thinking privately that the man might have produced two more attractive examples, when he was in the whoring business himself.

'Perhaps,' said Benjamin Löwenthal slowly, 'perhaps we can say—with reasonable doubt, of course—that the man inside that shipping crate was Emery Staines.'

'He took a particular shine to Anna, that's for sure,' Mannering agreed.

'Staines vanishes the very day Carver weighs anchor!' Balfour said, sitting forward. 'And the very day my crate goes missing! Of course: there it is! Staines goes into the crate—Carver swipes the crate—Carver sails away!'

'But for what purpose?' Pritchard said.

'You didn't happen to get a look at the docking slip, by any chance? The bill of lading?'

'No, I did not,' said Moody shortly. He had not yet finished his story, and he did not like being interrupted in mid-performance. But the rapt audience in the room had dissolved, for the umpteenth time that evening, into a murmuring rabble, as each man voiced his suppositions, and expressed his surprise.

'Emery Staines—on Carver's ship!' Mannering was saying. 'Question is, of course, whether he stowed himself away—that's one option; whether he was brought on board by accident—that's another; or whether Carver captured him, and chose to lock him in a shipping crate, in full knowledge—that's a third.'

Nilssen shook his head. 'What did he say, though—that the lid was tacked down! You can't do *that* from the inside!'

'You may as well call it a coffin. How's the man to breathe?'

'There are slats in the pine—gaps—'

'Not enough to breathe, surely!'

'Tom: your shipping crate. Was there room enough inside it for a grown man?'

'How big is a shipping crate, anyway?'

'Don't forget that Carver and Staines are business partners.'

'About the size of a dray-cart. You'll have seen them, stacked along the quay. A man could lie inside quite comfortably.'

'Business partners on a duffer claim!'

'Strange, though, that he's still in the crate on the way *back* from Dunedin. Isn't that strange? Seems almost to point to the fact that Carver didn't know he was there.'

'We ought to let Mr. Moody finish.'

'*That's* a way to treat your business partner—lock him up to die!'

The only men who had not joined this rabble of supposition were the two Chinese men, Quee Long and Sook Yongsheng, who were sitting very erect, with their eyes fixed very solemnly upon Moody—as they had been for the duration of the evening. Moody met Ah Sook's gaze—and though the latter's expression did not alter, it seemed to Moody that he conveyed a kind of sympathy, as though to say that he understood Moody's feeling of impatience very well.

The lack of a common language had prevented Ah Sook from articulating the full story of his dealings with Francis Carver to the assembly that evening, and as a result, the English-speaking company remained quite ignorant of the particulars of this former association, beyond the fact that Carver had committed a murder, and Ah Sook had resolved to avenge it. Moody regarded him now, holding Ah Sook's dark gaze in his pale one. He wondered at the history the two men had shared. Ah Sook had confided only that he had known Carver as a boy; he had divulged nothing else. Moody guessed that Ah Sook was around forty-five in age, which would mean he had been born in the early twenties; perhaps, then, he and Carver had known one another during the Chinese wars.

'Mr. Moody,' said Cowell Devlin. 'Let us put the question to you. Do *you* believe the man inside the shipping case could have been Emery Staines?'

The room fell quiet at once.

'I have never met Mr. Staines, and so would not recognise him,' Moody said stiffly, 'but yes, that is my guess.'

Pritchard was doing some calculation in his head. 'If Staines had been inside that shipping case since Carver left for Dunedin,' he said, 'that makes thirteen days without water or air.'

'Unlucky number,' somebody muttered, and Moody was struck by the thought that thirteen was also the number of men currently assembled in the smoking room—and that he himself was the thirteenth man.

'Is that possible—thirteen days?' said Gascoigne.

'Without water? Barely.' Pritchard stroked his chin. 'But without air, of course . . . impossible.'

'But he might not have been in there since leaving Hokitika,' Balfour pointed out. 'He might have been put into the case in Dunedin—though whether by his own volition, or by force—'

'I have not yet finished my story,' Moody said.

'Yes,' said Mannering. 'Quite right! He hasn't finished. Hold your tongues.'

The supposition ceased. Moody rocked on his heels again, and after a moment, resumed.

'Once I had determined that the thing inside the crate was indeed a man,' he said, 'I helped him out—with difficulty, for he was very weak, and not breathing at all well. He seemed to have spent all of his strength upon the knocking. I loosed his collar—he was wearing a cravat—and just as I did so, his chest began to bleed.'

'You cut him somehow?' said Nilssen.

But this time Moody did not answer; he closed his eyes and continued, as if in a trance. 'The blood was welling up—bubbling, as from a pump; the man clutched at his chest, trying to staunch the flow, all the while sobbing that name, *Magdalena, Magdalena* ... I watched him in horror, gentlemen. I could not speak. The volume—'

'He scratched himself on the crate?' Nilssen said again, persistently.

'The blood was veritably pumping from his body,' Moody said, opening his eyes. 'It was most definitely not a scratch wound, sir. *I* could hardly have scratched him, except perhaps with a fingernail, and I keep my nails very close, as you can observe. And I repeat, the blood began to pump well *after* he was out of the crate, and seated upright. I thought perhaps there had been a stickpin in his cravat—but he was not wearing a stickpin. His cravat had been tied in a bow.'

Pritchard was frowning. 'He must have been already injured, then,' he said. 'Before you opened the crate. Perhaps he cut himself—before you arrived on the scene.'

'Perhaps,' said Moody, without conviction. 'I'm afraid my understanding of the event is rather less ...'

'What?'

'Well,' Moody said, gathering himself, 'let me put it this way. The injury did not seem—natural.'

'Not natural?' Mannering said.

Moody looked embarrassed. He had faith in the analytic properties of reason: he believed in logic with the same calm conviction with which he believed in his ability to perceive it. Truth, for him, could be perfected, and a perfect truth was always utterly beautiful and entirely clear. We have mentioned already that Moody had no religion—and therefore did not perceive truth in mystery, in the inexplicable and the unexplained, in those mists that clouded one's scientific perception as the material cloud now obscured the Hokitika sky.

'I know this sounds very odd,' he said, 'but I am not altogether sure that the man inside the shipping case was even alive. By the light in the hold—and the shadows—' He trailed off, and then said, in a harsher voice, 'Let me say this. I am not sure if I would even call the thing a man.'

'What else?' said Balfour. 'What else, if not a man?'

'An apparition,' Moody replied. 'A vision of some kind. A ghost. It sounds very foolish; I know that. Perhaps Lydia Wells would be able to describe it better than I.'

There was a brief moment of quiet.

'What happened next, Mr. Moody?' said Frost.

Moody turned to address the banker. 'My next action, I'm afraid, was a cowardly one. I turned, grabbed my valise, and swarmed back up the ladder. I left him there—still bleeding.'

'I don't suppose you saw the bill of lading—on the crate?' said Balfour again, but Moody did not answer him.

'Was that your last encounter with the man?' said Löwenthal.

'Yes,' said Moody heavily. 'I did not venture down into the hold again—and when we arrived at Hokitika, the passengers were conveyed by lighter to the shore. If the man in question was indeed *real*—if he *was* Emery Staines—then he is still aboard the *Godspeed* as we speak . . . as is Francis Carver, of course. They are both offshore, just beyond the river mouth, waiting for the tide. But perhaps I imagined it. The man, the blood, all of it. I have never suffered from hallucinations before, but . . . well; you see that I am very undecided. At the time, however, I was sure that I had seen a ghost.'

'Perhaps you had,' said Devlin.

'Perhaps I had,' Moody said, bowing his head. 'I will accept that explanation as the truth, if there is compelling proof enough. But you will forgive me for admitting that the explanation is, to my mind, a fantastic one.'

'Ghost or no ghost, it seems that we are facing some kind of a solution at last,' said Löwenthal—who was looking very tired. 'To-morrow morning, when Mr. Moody goes to the wharf to collect his trunk—'

But Löwenthal was interrupted. The door of the smoking room suddenly swung to and struck the wall with such violence that every man in the room started in surprise. As one they turned—and saw, in the doorway, Mannering's boy, breathless, and clutching a stitch in his side.

'The lights,' he gasped.

'What is it?' said Mannering, levering himself up. 'What lights? What's wrong?'

'The lights on the spit,' the boy said, still clutching his side—for his breath was coming in gasps.

'Out with it!'

'I can't—' He began to cough.

'Why on earth have you been running?' Mannering shouted. 'You were supposed to be standing right outside! Standing *still*, d—n you! I don't pay your wage so you can take your bloody constitutional!'

'It's the *Godspeed*,' the boy managed.

All of a sudden the room was very still.

'The *Godspeed*?' Mannering barked, his eyes bulging. 'What about it? Talk, you idiot!'

'The nav lights on the spit,' the boy said. 'They went out—in the wind, and—the tide—'

'What *happened*?'

'*Godspeed*'s run aground,' the boy said. 'Foundered on the bar—she rolled, not ten minutes ago.' He drew a ragged breath. 'Her mainmast cracked—and then she rolled again—and then the surf came through the hatches and pulled her down. She's a goner, sir. She's a goner. She's wrecked.'

PART TWO

Auguries
18 February 1866
42° 43' 0" S ∫ 170° 58' 0" E

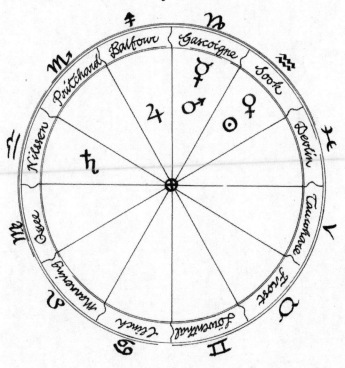

ECLIPTIC

In which our allegiances have shifted, as our countenance makes clear.

Three weeks have passed since Walter Moody first set foot upon the sand, since the council at the Crown convened in stealth, and since the barque *Godspeed* was added to the wrecks upon the bar. When the twelve men greet each other now, it is with a special under-standing—as when a mason meets a member of his guild, in daylight, and shares a glance that is eloquent and grave. Dick Mannering has nodded to Cowell Devlin in the Kaniere thor-oughfare; Harald Nilssen has twice raised his hat to Thomas Balfour; Charlie Frost has exchanged the morning's greetings with Joseph Pritchard while in line for breakfast at the sixpenny saloon. A secret always has a strengthening effect upon a newborn friend-ship, as does the shared impression that an external figure is to blame: the men of the Crown have become united less by their shared beliefs, we observe, than by their shared misgivings—which are, in the main, externally directed. In their analyses, variously made, of Alistair Lauderback, George Shepard, Lydia Wells, Francis Carver, Anna Wetherell, and Emery Staines, the Crown men have become more and more suggestive, despite the fact that nothing has been proven, no body has been tried, and no new information has come to light. Their beliefs have become more fan-ciful, their hypotheses less practical, their counsel less germane.

Unconfirmed suspicion tends, over time, to become wilful, falla-cious, and prey to the vicissitudes of mood—it acquires all the qualities of common superstition—and the men of the Crown Hotel, whose nexus of allegiance is stitched, after all, in the bright thread of time and motion, have, like all men, no immunity to influence.

For the planets have changed places against the wheeling canvas of the stars. The Sun has advanced one-twelfth along the tilted wheel of her ecliptic path, and with that motion comes a new world order, a new perspective on the whole. With the Sun in Capricorn we were reserved, exacting, and lofty in our distance. When we looked upon Man, we sought to fix him: we mourned his failures and measured his gifts. We could not imagine what he might have been, had he been tempted to betray his very nature—or had he betrayed himself without temptation, better still. But there is no truth except truth in relation, and heavenly relation is composed of wheels in motion, tilting axes, turning dials; it is a clockwork orches-tration that alters every minute, never repeating, never still. We are no longer sheltered in a cloistered reminiscence of the past. We now look outward, through the phantasm of our own convictions: we see the world as we wish to perfect it, and we imagine dwelling there.

In which Te Rau Tauwhare goes in search of employment and Löwenthal's suggestions are rebuffed.

At the newspaper office on Weld-street, Te Rau Tauwhare found the door propped open with a hatstand, and the sound of whistling issuing from within. He entered without knocking, and passed through the shop to the workroom at the rear, where the paper's editor, Benjamin Löwenthal, was sitting at his workbench, setting the type for Monday's edition of the *West Coast Times*.

In his left hand Löwenthal held a steel composing stick, roughly the size of a schoolboy's rule; with his right, he selected and deftly fitted tiny blocks of type, their nicks facing outward, onto the square edge of the stick—a task that required him to read not only right-to-left, but also back-to-front, for the galley text was both mirrored and reversed. Once the line was set, he would slide it into the forme, a flat steel tray a little larger than a newspaper broadsheet; beneath each line he slotted thin straps of lead, to create a space between the lines, and occasionally, a raised brass rule, to produce a solid underscore. When he had slid the last line of text into the forme, he fitted wooden quoins around the edge of the tray, tapping them with a mallet to ensure that every block was snug; then he planed the surface of the galley with a piece of two-by-four to ensure each block of type sat at a uniform height. Finally, he dipped his hand-roller in a tray of ink, and coated the entire galley in a thin film of glossy black—working swiftly, so the ink did not have time to dry—and laid a trembling sheet of newsprint over it. Löwenthal always printed his first proof by hand, so as to check it for errors before committing the galley to the press—though he made few errors of an accidental or careless sort, being, by nature, something of a stickler for perfection.

He greeted Tauwhare very warmly. 'I'm sure I haven't seen you since the night *Godspeed* came to ground, Mr. Tauwhare,' he said. 'Can that be true?'

'Yes,' Tauwhare said, indifferently. 'I have been in the north.' He cast his eye over the other man's workbench: cases of type, pots of ink and lye, brushes, tweezers, mallets, assorted blocks of lead and brass, a bowl of spotted apples, a paring knife.

'Just arrived back, have you?'

'This morning.'

'Well then, I am sure I can guess why you've returned.'

Tauwhare frowned. 'How can you guess?'

'Why—for the widow's *séance*! Do I not hit upon it?'

Tauwhare said nothing for a moment, still frowning. Then he said, with a tone of suspicion, 'What is a *séance*?'

Löwenthal chuckled. He put down his composing stick, crossed the room, and took up Saturday's paper from where it lay folded on the side of the washstand. 'Here,' he said. He unfolded it to the second page, tapped an advertisement with his ink-stained finger, and passed the paper to Tauwhare. 'You ought to come along. Not to the *séance* itself—you need a special ticket for that—but to the party beforehand.'

The advertisement ran over two columns. It had been printed in a bold eighteen-point type that Löwenthal typically reserved for mastheads and historic headlines only, and it was bordered thickly in black. The Wayfarer's Fortune, owned and operated by Mrs. Lydia Wells, late of the city of Dunedin, widow to Crosbie, was to open to the public for the first time that very evening. In honour of this occasion Mrs. Wells, a celebrated medium, would condescend to host Hokitika's inaugural *séance*. This *séance* would be restricted to an elite audience, with tickets allocated according to the principle 'first to come, first to be served'; the occasion would be prefaced, however, by an evening of 'drinks and speculation', open to the discerning public—who was encouraged, collectively, to come with an open mind.

This last injunction was perhaps easier said than done, for as the paper had it, the purpose of the *séance* was to locate, via the extraordinarily sensitive instrument of Mrs. Wells herself, certain tremors of spirit, the investigation of which would open a channel between this realm and the next, and thereby establish some kind of a rapport with the dead. Within the broad category of the dead, Mrs. Wells had been both excessively particular and excessively confident in making her selection: she planned to summon the shade of Mr. Emery Staines, who had not yet returned to Hokitika, and whose body, after five weeks of absence, had not yet been found.

The widow had not made clear what she planned to ask the shade of Mr. Staines, but it was universally assumed that, if nothing else, she would surely request to know the manner of his death. Any medium worth her salt will tell you that a spirit who has been murdered is far more loquacious than a spirit who has left this world in peace—and Lydia Wells, we need hardly remark, was worth every grain of hers.

'What is a *séance*?' said Tauwhare again.

'It is a piece of utter foolishness,' said Löwenthal cheerfully. 'Lydia Wells has announced to all of Hokitika that she is going to commune with the spirit of Emery Staines, and more than half of Hokitika has taken her at her word. The *séance* itself is just a performance. She will go into a trance—as though she's having a fit, or a seizure—and then she'll say a few words in a man's voice, or make the curtains move in some unexpected fashion, or pay a boy a penny to climb up the chimney and call down the pipe. It's a piece of cheap theatre. Of course every man will go home believing he's made contact with a ghost. Where did you say you've been?'

'Mawhera,' said Tauwhare. 'Greymouth.' He was still frowning at the paper.

'No word of Mr. Staines up there, I suppose.'

'No.'

'Nor here. We're rather losing hope, I'm sorry to say. But perhaps we'll get a clue of some kind this evening. The real cause for suspicion, you see, is Mrs. Wells's certainty that Mr. Staines really is dead. If she knows that much, then what else does she know, and how does she know it? Oh: tongues have been wagging, Mr. Tauwhare, this fortnight past. I wouldn't miss this party for the world. How I wish that I'd got my hands on a ticket.'

For the widow had chosen to limit her *séance* to only seven souls— seven being a number of magical allusion, possessed of a darkly mysterious ring—and Löwenthal, arriving at the Wayfarer's Fortune some fifteen minutes before nine in the morning, discovered, to his immense regret, that these seven places had already been filled. (Of the Crown men, only Charlie Frost and Harald Nilssen had been successful in securing a ticket.) Löwenthal, along with scores of other disappointed men, would have to content himself with attending the preliminary 'drinks and speculation', and leaving before the *séance* was officially conducted. He attempted to buy a ticket at double price from one of the lucky seven, but to no avail. Frost and Nilssen both refused his offer outright, though Nilssen promised to describe the event in a high degree of detail, after the fact, and Frost suggested that Löwenthal might like to assist him in developing a strategy of reconnaissance, beforehand.

'It'll be three shillings on the door,' Löwenthal supplied, in case Tauwhare could not read, and was disguising his lack of ability.

'Three shillings?' Tauwhare said, glancing up. That was an extraordinary sum, for one evening's entertainment. 'What for?'

Löwenthal shrugged. 'She knows that she can charge what she likes, and she's going to do just that. It might pay for your brandy if you drink quick enough: she's doing bottomless cups, you see, not drink-for-drink. But you're right—it's a robbery. Of course every second man is champing at the bit to get a word with Anna. She's the real attraction—the real draw! You know she's barely been seen beyond the Wayfarer's front door in three weeks. Goodness only knows what's been happening inside.'

'I wish to place a notice in your paper,' Tauwhare said. He tossed the paper down onto the desk, somewhat rudely, so that it skidded over Löwenthal's forme.

'Certainly,' said Löwenthal, with disapproval. He reached for his pencil. 'Do you have an advertisement prepared?'

'"Maori guide, very experienced, fluent in English, locally knowledgeable, offers services to surveyors, diggers, explorers and the like. Success and safety guaranteed."'

'Surveyors, diggers, explorers,' repeated Löwenthal, as he wrote. 'Success and safety. Yes, very good. And then I'll put your name, shall I?'

'Yes.'

'I'll need an address as well. Are you stopping off in town?'

Tauwhare hesitated. He had planned to return to the Arahura Valley that night, and spend the night in Crosbie Wells's deserted cottage; he did not wish to disclose this fact to Löwenthal, however, given Löwenthal's close acquaintance with Edgar Clinch, the man to whom the dwelling now legally belonged.

Edgar Clinch had been the frequent object of Tauwhare's meditations ever since the assembly at the Crown Hotel three weeks ago, for despite all the transactions between Maori and Pakeha that had occurred over the past decade, Te Rau Tauwhare still looked upon the Arahura Valley as his own, and he was made very angry whenever any tract of Te Tai Poutini land was bought for profit rather than for use. As far as Tauwhare knew, Clinch had not spent any length of time in the Arahura prior to the sale; since the purchase, he had not even troubled himself to walk the perimeter of the acreage that now belonged to him by law. What had been the point of the purchase? Did Clinch mean to settle there? Did he mean to till the soil? Fell the native timbers? Dam the river? Drop a shaft, perhaps, and mine for gold? Certainly he had not done a thing to Crosbie's cottage beyond stripping it of all that he could sell—and even that he had done by proxy. It was a hollow dividend that required no skill, no love, and no hours of patient industry: such a dividend could only be wasted, for it was borne from waste, and to waste it would return. Tauwhare could not respect a man who treated land as though it was just another kind of currency.

Land could not be minted! Land could only be lived upon, and
loved.

In this Te Rau Tauwhare was no hypocrite. He had travelled
every inch of the West Coast, on foot, by cart, on horseback, and
by canoe. He could picture the entire length of it, as though upon
a richly illustrated map: in the far north, Mohikinui and Karamea,
where the mosses were fat and damp, where the leaves were waxy,
where the bush was an earthy-smelling tangle, where the Nikau
fronds, shed from the trunks of the palms, lay upon the ground as
huge and heavy as the flukes of whales; further south, the bronze
lacquer of the Taramakau, the crenulated towers at Punakaiki, the
marshy flats north of Hokitika, always crawling with the smoky
mist of not-quite-rain; then the cradled lakes; then the silent valleys, thick with green; then the twisting flanks of the glaciers,
rippled blue and grey; then the comb of the high Alps; then, at last,
Okahu and Mahitahi in the far South—wide, shingled beaches littered with the bones of mighty trees, where the surf was a ceaseless
battery, and the wind a ceaseless roar. After Okahu the coastline
became sheer and impassable. Beyond it, Tauwhare knew, lay the
deep waterways of the southern fjords, where the sun set early
behind the sudden peaks, so that the water took on the blackened
look of tarnished silver, and the shadows pooled like oil. Tauwhare
had never seen Piopiotahi, but he had heard tell of it, and he loved
it because it was Te Tai Poutini land.

Thus the ribbon of the Coast—and there at the heart of it all,
the Arahura River, *taonga, wahi tapu, he matahiapo i te iwi*! If the
Arahura was Tauwhare's equator, dividing the land of Te Tai
Poutini into halves, then Crosbie's cottage, situated in the valley
more or less halfway between the mountains and the ocean, was his
meridian. And yet he could not claim it; his hapu could not claim
it; his iwi could not claim it. Before Crosbie Wells's body had been
committed to the ground, those hundred rolling acres in the
Arahura Valley had been purchased by a profit-hungry Pakeha,
who had sworn, upon his honour, that he had come by the land
honestly: there had been no foul play of any kind, he had said, and
he certainly had not broken any laws.

'A hotel?' said Löwenthal. 'Or a doss house? Just the name will do.'

'I do not have an address,' Tauwhare said.

'Well, here,' said Löwenthal, coming to his aid. 'I'll write "inquiries care of the editor, Weld-street". How about that? You can come to me later this week and ask if anyone has inquired.'

'That's fine,' said Tauwhare.

Löwenthal waited for an expression of gratitude, but none came. 'Very good,' he said, after a pause. His voice was cold. 'It's sixpence, for a week in the columns. Ten pence for a fortnight, and a shilling sixpence for a month. In advance, of course.'

'A week,' Tauwhare said, shaking the contents of his purse carefully onto his palm. The small pile of pennies and farthings showed plainly that he was in need of work. His only income since the night at the Crown had been a silver shilling, won on a game of strength two weeks ago. Once he had paid Löwenthal for the advertisement, he would barely have enough to cover the following day's meals.

Löwenthal watched him count pennies a moment, and then said, in a kinder voice, 'I say, Mr. Tauwhare: if you're short of ready money, you might please yourself to head down to the spit. There's a call for hands on Gibson Quay. You might not have heard it—the bell sounded an hour ago. *Godspeed*'s out of the water at long last, you see, and they need men to clear the cargo.'

Over the past three weeks the barque had been shunted into shallower waters by two large tugboats; from there her hull had been lifted onto rollers, laid flush with the shore; finally, at low tide that morning, she had been hauled clear of the surf by a team of harnessed Clydesdales and a winch. She was now dry upon the spit—seeming, in her shattered enormity, less like a beached creature of the water than like a fallen creature of the air. Löwenthal had detoured past the spit that morning; he had fancied that the ship had plunged from a great height, and had perished, where she fell. All three of her masts had broken off at the base, and without her sails and rigging she seemed almost shorn. He had gazed at her for a long moment before moving on. Once her cargo had been cleared and her fixings removed she would be dismantled and sold, piecemeal, for salvage and repair.

'Now that I mention it,' he went on, 'we might do very well to have one of our own men on hand, while the cargo's being cleared. On account of Tom's shipping crate, I mean—and whatever it was that Mr. Moody thought he saw, below. You can be our eyes and ears, Mr. Tauwhare. You have the perfect excuse, if you're short on cash, and in need of honest work. Nobody will ask you how or why.'

But Tauwhare shook his head. He had pledged, privately, never to transact with Francis Carver again, under any circumstances. 'I do not do odd jobs,' he said, placing six pennies on the countertop.

'Go on down to the *Godspeed*,' Löwenthal insisted. 'Nobody's going to ask you any questions. You have the perfect excuse.'

But Tauwhare did not like to take advice from other men, however well intentioned. 'I will wait for surveying work,' he said.

'You might be waiting a good long time.'

He shrugged. 'Perhaps.'

Löwenthal was becoming annoyed. 'You aren't seeing sense,' he said. 'Here's a chance for you to do us all a good turn, and yourself besides. You won't be able to attend the widow's party without a ticket, and you won't be able to buy a ticket if you've got an empty purse. Go on down to Gibson Quay, and put in a day's work, and do us all a favour.'

'I do not want to attend the party.'

Löwenthal was incredulous. 'Why on earth not?'

'You said it would be foolish. A piece of theatre.'

A moment of quiet passed between them. Then Löwenthal said, 'Did you know they've brought in a barrister? A Mr. John Fellowes, from the Greymouth Police. He's been assigned to straighten out the Crosbie Wells affair.'

Tauwhare shrugged.

'He's doing his research as we speak,' Löwenthal continued, 'in order to find out if this business warrants an inquiry. He's making a report for a Supreme Court judge. Supreme Court means murder, Mr. Tauwhare. A murder trial.'

'I have had no part in murder,' said Tauwhare.

'Perhaps not—but we both know that you're as mixed up in this business as the rest of us. Come! Mr. Moody saw something in the hold of the *Godspeed*, and you have a perfect chance to find out what he saw.'

But Tauwhare did not care what Mr. Moody saw, or did not see. 'I will wait for honest work,' he said again.

'You might show a little loyalty.'

Tauwhare flared at this. 'I have not broken my oath,' he said.

Löwenthal reached across the workbench, put his hand over the pile of pennies, and swept them into his apron pocket. 'I don't mean to the Crown lot,' he said. 'I mean to your old friend Wells. This is his widow we're talking about, after all. His widow, and his inheritance, and his memory. You'll do as you please, of course. But if I were you, I'd make it my business to attend the party tonight.'

'Why?' Tauwhare spat out the word contemptuously.

'Why?' said Löwenthal, picking up his composing stick again. 'Why show loyalty to your good friend Wells? Only that I would have thought you owed it to the man, after selling him out to Francis Carver.'

JUPITER IN SAGITTARIUS

In which Thomas Balfour suffers a lapse of discretion; old subjects are revived; and Alistair Lauderback pens a letter of complaint.

Alistair Lauderback had not been in Hokitika since Wednesday morning, chiefly for the reason that the wreck of the *Godspeed* was wholly visible from his suite of rooms on the upper floor of the Palace Hotel, and the sight of it caused him no end of bitterness. When he was offered the chance to give an address at the Greymouth Town Hall, and to cut a ribbon on a shaft mine near Kumara, he accepted both invitations heartily, and at once. At the moment we join him—the moment Tauwhare took his leave of Löwenthal—Lauderback was making his way across the Kumara wetlands at a great pace, with a Sharps sporting rifle propped against his shoulder, and a satchel full of shot in his hand. Beside him was his friend Thomas Balfour, similarly armed, and similarly flushed with virtuous exertion. The two had spent the morning shooting at game, and they were now returning to their horses, which were tethered at the edge of the valley, visible from this distance as a small patch of white and a small patch of black against the sky.

'Hell of a day,' Lauderback exclaimed, as much to himself as to Balfour. 'It's a glorious hell of a day! Why, it almost makes one forgive the rain, does it not—when the sun comes out like this, at the end of it all.'

Balfour laughed. 'Forgiven, maybe,' he said, 'but not forgotten. Not by me.'

'It's a grand country,' said Lauderback. 'Look at those colours! Those are New Zealand colours, rinsed by New Zealand rain.'

'And we are New Zealand patriots,' said Balfour. 'The view's all ours, Mr. Lauderback. There for the taking.'

'Yes indeed,' said Lauderback. 'Nature's patriots!'

'No need for a flag,' said Balfour.

'How lucky we are,' said Lauderback. 'Think how few men have laid eyes upon this view. Think how few men have walked this soil.'

'More than we expect, I don't doubt,' said Balfour, 'if the birds have learned to scatter at the sight of us.'

'You give them too much credit, Tom,' said Lauderback. 'Birds are very stupid.'

'I shall remember that, next time you come home with a brace of duck and a long account of how you snared them.'

'You do that: but I shall make you hear the story all the same.'

For Thomas Balfour this good-humoured exchange was very welcome. Over the past three weeks Lauderback had been excessively bad company, and Balfour had long since tired of his capricious moods, which alternated brittle, vicious, and sour. Lauderback tended to revert to childish modes of behaviour whenever his hopes were dashed, and the wreck of the *Godspeed* had wrought an unbecoming change in him. He had become very jealous of the company of crowds, needing always to be surrounded and attended; he would not spend any length of time alone, and protested if he was required to do so. His public manner was unchanged—he was exuberant and convincing when speaking from a pulpit—but his private manner had become altogether peevish. He flew into a temper at the slightest provocation, and was openly scornful of his two devoted aides, who chalked these vicissitudes of humour up to the taxing nature of political life, and did not protest them. That Sunday they had been granted a reprieve from Lauderback's company, owing to a shortage of rifles, and, equally, to Lauderback's disinclination to share; instead they would spend the period of their master's absence at the Kumara chapel, contemplating, at Lauderback's instruction, their sins.

Alistair Lauderback was an intensely superstitious man, and he felt that he could date the sudden change in his fortune to the night of his arrival in Hokitika, when he came upon the body of the hermit, Crosbie Wells. When he dwelled upon all the misfortunes he had suffered since that day—the wreck of the *Godspeed* in particular—he felt soured towards all of Westland, as though the whole forsaken district had been complicit in the project of embarrassing his successes, and frustrating his desires. The ruin of the *Godspeed* was proof, in his mind, that the very place was cursed against him. (This belief was not as irrational as might be supposed, for the shifty movement of the Hokitika bar owed, in the large part, to the silt and gravel that was carried down the Hokitika River from the claims upstream, and now clotted the river mouth, invisibly, in ever-changing patterns that answered only to the tide: in essence, the *Godspeed* had met her end upon the tailings of a thousand claims, and for that, every man in Hokitika could be said to be partially to blame for the wreck.)

Some days after *Godspeed*'s ruin Thomas Balfour had confessed to Lauderback that, in fact, the shipping crate containing Lauderback's documents and personal effects had disappeared from Gibson Quay, due to a mistake of lading for which no one man seemed to be accountable. Lauderback received this information dispiritedly, but without real interest. Now that the *Godspeed* was ruined, he had no reason to blackmail Francis Carver, the purpose of which had only been to win his beloved ship back again: the barque's bill of sale, stowed in his trunk among his personal possessions, was no longer of any use to him as leverage.

Lauderback had recently taken to playing dice in the evenings, for gambling was a weakness to which he periodically fell prey whenever he felt shamed, or out of luck. He demanded, naturally, that Jock and Augustus Smith take up this vice also, for he could not endure to sit at the table alone. They dutifully complied, though their bets were always very cautious, and they bowed out early. Lauderback placed his bets with the grim determination of a man for whom winning would mean inordinately much, and he was as chary of his tokens as he was of his whisky, which he drank very slowly, to make the evening last until the dawn.

'You weren't going to ride back this afternoon, were you?' he said to Balfour now, with an emphasis that suggested regret.

'I was,' Balfour said. 'That is—I am. I mean to be in Hokitika by tea-time.'

'Put it off a day,' Lauderback entreated. 'Come along to the Guernsey tonight for craps. No sense to ride back on your own. I have to stay on to cut a ribbon in the morning—but I'll be back in Hokitika by to-morrow noontime. Noontime on the inside.'

But Balfour shook his head. 'Can't do it. I've a shipment coming first thing to-morrow morning. Monday sharp.'

'Surely you don't need to be present—for a *shipment*!'

'Oh—but I need the time to tally up my finances,' Balfour said with a grin. 'I'm twelve pounds redder than I was on Wednesday—and that's twelve pounds into *your* pocket, you know. One pound for every face of the dice.'

(Balfour concealed the real reason for his haste, which was that he wished to attend the widow's 'drinks and speculation' in the front room of the Wayfarer's Fortune that evening. He had not spoken of Mrs. Wells to Lauderback since the politician made his confession in the dining room of the Palace Hotel, having judged it prudent to let Lauderback introduce the subject himself, and on his own terms. Lauderback, however, had also avoided any mention of her, though Balfour felt that his silence was of a taut and even desperate quality, as though at any moment he might burst out, and cry her name.)

'That takes me back to my schooling days,' Lauderback said. 'We got one lash for every pip of the dice—if they caught us. Twenty-one pips on a single die. There's a trivial fact I've never forgotten.'

'I won't stay until I'm down twenty-one pounds, if that's your angle.'

'You ought to stay,' Lauderback persisted. 'Just one more night. You ought to.'

'Look at that marvellous fern,' said Balfour—and indeed it was marvellous: furled perfectly, like the scroll of a violin. Balfour touched it with the muzzle of his gun.

The recent alteration in Lauderback's humour had had a very injurious effect upon his friendship with Thomas Balfour. Balfour was certain that Lauderback had not told him the whole truth about his former dealings with Francis Carver and Crosbie Wells, and this exclusion left him very disinclined to pander to him. When Lauderback expressed his dissatisfaction on the subject of Westland, and sandbars, and cold-cut dinners, and disposable collars, and imitation, and German mustard, and the Premier, and bones in fish, and ostentation, and ill-made boots, and the rain, Balfour responded with less energy and admiration than he might have done but one month prior. Lauderback, to put it plainly, had lost his advantage, and both men knew this to be so. The politician was loath to admit that their friendship had cooled, however; he persisted in speaking to Balfour exactly as he always had done—that is, in a tone that was occasionally supercilious, always declamatory, and very rarely humble—and Balfour, who could be very supercilious himself if only he put his mind to the task, persisted in resenting him.

Presently they retrieved their horses, saddled up, and set off for Kumara at a slow trot. After they had been riding for a short while, Lauderback took up the thread again.

'We had talked of stopping off at Seaview together—on the return journey,' he said. 'To take a look at the foundations for the gaol-house.'

'Yes,' said Balfour. 'You'll have to tell me all about it.'

'I suppose I'll have to go alone.'

'Alone—with Jock and Augustus! Alone in a party of three!'

Lauderback shifted on his saddle, seeming very disgruntled. Presently he said, 'What's the gaoler's name again—Sheffield?'

Balfour glanced at him sharply. 'Shepard. George Shepard.'

'Shepard, yes. I wonder if he's angling for a shot at Magistrate. He's done very well on the Commissioner's budget—to get everything moving so smartly. He's done very well indeed.'

'I suppose he has. Hark at *that* one!' Balfour pointed with the end of his crop at another fern frond, more orange than the first, and furrier. 'What a pleasant shape it is,' he added. 'The motion of it—eh? As though it's stilled in motion. There's a thought!'

But Lauderback was not to be distracted by the pleasant shape of ferns. 'He's right in the Commissioner's pocket, of course,' he said, still referring to George Shepard. 'And I gather he's the Magistrate's old friend.'

'Perhaps they'll keep it in the family then.'

'Smacks of ambition. Don't you think? The gaol-house, I mean. His devotion to the project. His devotion to the whole affair. He's done very well about it.'

Lauderback, as an ambitious man, was very much the kind to be suspicious of ambition in others. Balfour, however, only snorted.

'What?' said Lauderback.

'Nothing,' said Balfour. (But it was not nothing! He detested it when a man received moral credit—however distantly—for something undeserved.)

'What?' said Lauderback again. 'You made a noise.'

'Well, tally it all up,' Balfour said. 'Timber for the gallows. Iron for the fencing. Stone for the foundation. Twenty navvies on a daily wage.'

'What?'

'Commissioner's budget my hat!' Balfour cried. 'That money must be coming in from another quarter—from another source! Tally it up in your head!'

Lauderback looked across at him. 'A private investment? Is that what you mean?'

Balfour shrugged. He knew full well that George Shepard had funded the construction of the gaol-house with Harald Nilssen's commission on Crosbie Wells's estate—but he had vowed to keep the secret, at the council of the Crown Hotel, and he did not like to break his promises.

'Private investment, you said?' Lauderback persisted.

'Listen,' said Balfour. 'I don't want to break any oaths. I don't want to tread on any toes. But I will say this: if you stop in at Seaview, you ought to sniff around a bit. That's all I'm saying. Sniff around, and you might come up with something.'

'Is that why you're heading home early?' Lauderback demanded. 'To avoid Shepard? Is this something between the two of you?'

'No!' Balfour said. 'No, no. I was tipped off, that's all.'

'Tipped off? By whom?'

'I can't say.'

'Come on, Tom! Don't go proud on me. What did you mean by that?'

Balfour thought for a moment, squinting over the valley floor towards the rumpled slopes in the East. His horse was slightly shorter than Lauderback's black mare, and because he was a shorter man than Lauderback, his shoulders were a clear foot below the other man's—even when he squared them, which he did now. 'It's just common sense, isn't it?' he said. 'Twenty navvies on the foundation at once? All the materials paid up in cash? That's not the way that Council funding gets paid out. You know that yourself! Shepard must be dealing ready money.'

'Which one is it?' said Lauderback. 'Common sense—or a tip-off?'

'Common sense!'

'So you weren't tipped off.'

'Yes, I was,' Balfour said hotly. 'But I might just as well have figured it out. That's what I'm saying: I might just as well have figured it out on my own.'

'So what was the point in it?'

'In what?'

'Tipping you off!'

Balfour was scowling. 'I don't know what you're saying,' he said. 'You're not making any sense.'

But Lauderback was making perfect sense, and Balfour knew it. 'What doesn't make sense, Tom,' he said, 'is that *you're* the one tipped off about a gaol-house! What does Balfour Shipping care about public funding, and how it's spent? What do *you* care about a private investment—unless it's wrapped up in something else?'

Balfour shook his head. 'You've got me wrong,' he said.

'Something to do with one of the felons maybe,' Lauderback said. 'A private investment—in exchange for—'

'No, no,' Balfour said. 'Nothing like that.'

'What then?'

When Balfour did not immediately respond, Lauderback added, 'Listen: if it has to do with private funding, that's a campaign matter, and I need to know. Anything that gets rushed over the Commissioner's desk right before an election is worth looking at— and clearly this man Shepard is rushing something. Looks to me as though he's got political designs, and I want to know what they are. If it's all a matter of common sense, then why don't you just tell me what you know—and if anyone asks me, I'll pretend I worked it out on my own.'

This seemed reasonable enough to Balfour. His affection for Lauderback had not dissolved altogether over the course of the last month, and he wanted to remain in the politician's good opinion, despite any new opinions he might have developed, in his turn. It could not hurt to tell him where Shepard's money was coming from—not if Lauderback could pretend to have worked it out on his own!

Balfour was pleased, also, by the sudden sharpness of Lauderback's expression, and the eagerness with which the older man was pressing him for news. He disliked it when Lauderback was broody, and this sudden change in the politician's humour put Balfour in mind of the old Lauderback, the Lauderback of Dunedin days, who spoke like a general, and walked like a king; who made his fortune, and then doubled it; who rubbed shoulders with the Premier; who would never dare to beg a man to stay on one extra night in Kumara, so that he would not have to take his sorrows to the gambling house alone. Balfour was sympathetic to this old Lauderback, of whom he was still very fond, and it flattered him to be begged for news.

And so, after a long pause, Balfour told his old acquaintance what he knew about the gaol-house: that the construction had been funded by a cut of the fortune discovered in Crosbie Wells's cottage. He did not say why, or how, this arrangement had come about, and he did not say who had tipped him off about the situation. He did say that the investment had occurred at George

Shepard's instigation, two weeks after Crosbie Wells's death, and that the gaoler was very anxious to keep it quiet.

But Lauderback's legal training had not been for nothing: he was a canny inquisitor, and never more than when he knew that he was being told a partial truth. He asked the value of the cut, and Balfour replied that the investment totalled a little over four hundred pounds. Lauderback was quick to ask the reason why the investment comprised ten percent of the total value discovered in the cottage, and when Balfour remained silent, he guessed, with even more alarming quickness, that ten percent was the standard rate of commission, and perhaps this investment represented the commission merchant's fee.

Balfour was appalled that Lauderback had figured this out so quickly, and protested that it wasn't Harald Nilssen's fault.

Lauderback laughed. 'He consented! He gave his commission away!'

'Shepard had him in a corner. He's not to blame. It was an inch short of blackmail, the way it played out—really. You oughtn't make a meal of it. You oughtn't, for Mr. Nilssen's sake.'

'A private investment, upon the eleventh hour!' Lauderback exclaimed. (He was not particularly interested in Harald Nilssen, whom he had met only once at the Star Hotel in Hokitika, over a month ago. Nilssen had struck him as a very provincial type, rather too accustomed to a loyal audience of three or four, and rather too garrulous when drinking; Lauderback had written him off as bore, who was self-satisfied, and would never amount to anything at all.) He stood up on his stirrups. 'This is politics, Tom—oh, this is politics, all right! Do you know what Shepard's trying to do? He's trying to get the gaol-house underway before Westland gets her seat, and he's using a private investment to spur the enterprise along. Oh-ho! I shall have something to say about *this* in the *Times*—rest assured!'

But Balfour was not particularly assured by this, and nor did he feel inclined to rest. He protested, and after a short negotiation Lauderback agreed to leave Nilssen's name out of it—'Though I shan't spare George Shepard the same courtesy,' he added, and laughed again.

'I take it you don't fancy him as Magistrate,' Balfour said—wondering whether Lauderback had designs upon that eminent position himself.

'I don't give two shakes about the Magistrate's seat!' Lauderback returned. 'It's the principle of the thing: that's what I shall stand upon.'

'Where's the principle?' Balfour said, with momentary confusion: Lauderback *did* care about the Magistrate's seat. He had begun by mentioning it, and in a very surly humour at that.

'The man's a thief!' Lauderback cried. 'That money belongs to Crosbie Wells—dead *or* alive. George Shepard has no right to spend another man's money as he pleases, and I don't care what for!'

Balfour was quiet. Until this moment Lauderback had never once mentioned the fortune that had been discovered in Wells's cottage, or expressed interest in how it was to be deployed. Nor had he once mentioned the legal debacle that revolved around the widow's claim upon her late husband's estate. Balfour had assumed that this silence owed to the fact of Lydia Wells's involvement, for Lauderback was still too embarrassed of his past disgraces to mention her name. But now it seemed almost as though Lauderback had leaped to Crosbie Wells's defence. It seemed as though the issue of Crosbie Wells's fortune was an issue about which Lauderback cherished a very raw opinion. Balfour glanced at the other man, and then away. Had Lauderback guessed that the fortune discovered in Wells's cottage was the very same fortune by which he had been blackmailed the year before? Balfour's interest was whetted. He decided to provoke the other man.

'What does it really matter?' he said lightly. 'Why, most likely that fortune had already been stolen from somebody else; it certainly didn't belong to Crosbie Wells. What's a man like *him* doing with four thousand pounds? It's no secret that he was a wastrel, and the step from a wastrel to a thief is short indeed.'

'There's no proof of that,' Lauderback began, but Balfour interrupted him.

'So what does it really matter, if someone steals it back after he's

dead and gone? That's my question. Chances are it was dirty
money in the first place.'

'What does it *matter*?' Lauderback exploded. 'It's the principle of
the thing—it's as I say: the principle of it! You do not solve a crime
by committing another. Thieving from a thief—it's still a crime,
whichever way you try and dress it! Don't be absurd.'

So Lauderback was Crosbie Wells's defender—and a very sore
defender, by the looks of things. This was interesting.

'But you are getting the almshouse you wanted,' Balfour said—
still speaking lightly, as though they were discussing something very
trivial. 'The money is not to be squandered. It is to be used for the
erection of a public works.'

'I don't care whether Governor Shepard is lining his pockets or
building an altar,' Lauderback snapped. 'That's an excuse, that is—
using the end to justify the means. I don't deal in that kind of logic.'

'And not just *any* public works,' Balfour continued, as if Lauderback
had not spoken. 'You will get your asylum after all! Come; do you not
remember our conversation at the Palace? "Where's a woman to go"?
"One clean shot at another kind of a life"—all of that? Well: we are
soon to have that one clean shot! George Shepard has made it so!'

Lauderback looked furious. He remembered very well what he
had said about the merits of asylum three weeks ago, but he did not
like his own words to be quoted back to him unless the purpose of
the reference was commendation alone.

'It is disrespectful to the dead,' he said shortly, 'and that is all I
will say about it.'

But Balfour was not so easily dissuaded. 'I say,' he exclaimed, as
though the thought had just occurred to him, 'the gold that Francis
Carver put up against your *Godspeed*—that had been sewn into the
lining of—'

'What about it?'

'Well—you never saw it again, did you? Nor heard tell of it. And
then the very same sum—more or less—turns up in Crosbie Wells's
cottage, barely a year later. A little over four thousand pounds.
Perhaps it's the very same pile.'

'Very possible,' said Lauderback.

'One wonders how it got there,' said Balfour.

'Indeed one does,' said Lauderback.

At the Golden Lion they parted ways—Lauderback having evidently given up on his wish that Balfour remain in Kumara a second day, for he bid his friend goodbye very curtly, and without regret.

Balfour set off for Hokitika in a state of considerable discomfort. He had promised to keep Nilssen's confidence, as he had on behalf of each one of the men of the Crown, and he had broken that promise. And for what? What had he gained, by reneging on his oath, and breaking his word? Disgusted with himself, Balfour dug his heels into his mare's flanks, spurring her to a canter; he kept her at that pace until he reached the Arahura River, where he was obliged to dismount, walk the creature down to the beach, and lead her carefully across the shallows at the place where the torrent of fresh water fanned out over the sand.

Lauderback had not stayed to watch his friend ride off. He had already begun forming his letter in his mind: his lips were pursed in concentration, and there was a furrow in his brow. He led his horse to the stables, pressed a sixpence into the groom's hand, and then retired at once to his rooms upstairs. Once alone, he locked the door, dragged his writing desk into the diamond-shaped patch of light beneath the window, fetched a chair, sat down, and pulled out a fresh sheet of paper; after some final moments' contemplation with his pen against his lips, he shook out his cuff, leaned forward, and wrote:

A POSTHUMOUS INVESTMENT?—To the Editor of
the West Coast Times.

18 February 1866

Sir—

It is desirable for Mr. GEORGE SHEPHERD to publish in these pages a list of names of persons appointed to the construction of the Hokitika gaol-house upon the terrace at Seaview; also to transmit a statement of works contracted for, and entered into; to reveal the amount of

*money voted for all such works, the subsidies of sums advanced to date,
and the extra amounts required (if any) for their completion, or to render
them more serviceable.*

*Such a publication may serve to ameliorate what the undersigned
believes to have been a gross breach of conduct on Mr. Shepherd's part:
that the preliminary construction of the Hokitika gaol-house was funded
by a private donation made without the consent of the Provincial Council,
the Westland Public Works Committee, the Municipal Board, or indeed,
the investor himself—for the investment was made some two weeks after
the man's own death! I allude here to Mr. CROSBIE WELLS whose
estate has been the subject of much speculation in these pages. It is my
understanding that the endowment (such as it might be termed) was
extracted from Mr. Wells's dwelling posthumously, and later apportioned,
without public knowledge, to the erection of the future gaol. If this
understanding is a false one I shall stand corrected; in the meantime I
request immediate clarification from Mr. Shepherd himself.*

*I hold that the transparency of Mr. Shepherd's conduct in this affair is
desirable not least because of the nature of the institution he wishes to
build, and the origin of the sum in question; but also for the reason that
financial transparency in the management of public funds is of paramount
importance given that this undeveloped region of our province is so rich in
gold and therefore so sadly prey to the primitive temptations of corruption.*

*I maintain a high regard for Mr. Shepherd's intentions, &c., in the
instigation of this project, as I am sure he acts in the interests of the
common settler and with due respect for colonial law. I beg only to restate
my belief that all private endorsements of public works must be made
transparent for the benefit of all, and to assure you, Sir, and all of the
province of Westland that I am*

Yours, &c.,

*Mr. ALISTAIR LAUDERBACK, PROVINCIAL
COUNCILMAN, M.P.*

He sat back and read the document through aloud, and in ringing tones, as if in rehearsal for an important public address; then,
satisfied, he folded the paper, slid it into an envelope, and addressed
the envelope to the editor of the *West Coast Times*, marking it as

both 'to be read upon receipt', and 'urgent'. When the thing was sealed he reached into his vest, and checked the time: it was almost two o'clock. If Augustus Smith rode direct for Hokitika now, he could reach Löwenthal before the Monday morning edition of the *Times* had gone to proof. Better sooner than later, Lauderback thought, and went in search of his aide.

In which Gascoigne repeats his theories, and Moody speaks of death.

Walter Moody was finishing his luncheon at Maxwell's dining hall when he received a message that the cargo of the *Godspeed* had at last been cleared, and his trunk had been delivered to his room at the Crown Hotel.

'Well!' he exclaimed, as he passed the messenger a twopenny bit, and the boy scampered away. 'That puts paid to my so-called apparition at last—does it not? If Emery Staines *was* on board, they would have surely found his corpse among the cargo.'

'I doubt it would have been so neat as all that,' said Gascoigne.

'You mean his corpse might not have been reported?'

'I mean his corpse might not have been found,' Gascoigne said. 'A man—even an injured man—could fight his way towards a hatch ... and the wreck was not entirely submerged. I think it far more likely that he was swept away.'

Over the past three weeks Moody had struck up a very cordial acquaintance with Aubert Gascoigne, having discovered that the latter's character improved very much in successive interviews—for Gascoigne was very skilled at adapting himself to every kind of social situation, and could court another man's favour with great success if only he put his mind to the task. Gascoigne had determined that he would befriend Moody with a force of ambition that, if known, might have caused the latter some alarm; as it was, however, Moody thought him a very sophisticated personage, and was pleased to have an intellectual equal with whom he could comfortably converse. They took luncheon together nearly every day, and smoked cigars at the Star and Garter in the evenings, where they played partners at whist.

'You are persisting with your original theory,' Moody observed. 'Jetsam, not flotsam.'

'Either that, or his remains have been destroyed,' Gascoigne said. 'Perhaps he called to be rescued, only to be killed, tied to something heavy, and then dropped into the sea. Carver has rowed out to the wreck a fair few times, as you know—and there has been ample opportunity for drowning.'

'That is also possible,' Moody said, folding the delivered message into halves, and then quarters, and running his thumbnail along each fold. 'But the problem remains that we cannot know for certain one way or another, and if you are right that Staines *has* drowned, whether by chance or by design, then we shall never know at all. What a poor crime this is—when we have no body, and no murderer!'

'It is a very poor crime,' Gascoigne agreed.

'And we are very poor detectives,' Moody said, meaning this as a closing statement of a kind, but Gascoigne was reaching for the gravy boat, and showed no sign at all of wishing to conclude their discussion.

'I dare say we shall feel excessively foolish,' he said, pouring gravy over the remainder of his meal, 'when Staines is found in the bottom of a gully, with a broken neck, and not a sign of harm upon him.'

Moody pushed his knife a little closer to his fork. 'I am afraid that we all rather *want* Mr. Staines to have been murdered—even you and I, who have never met the man in our lives. We would not be contented with a broken neck.'

Moody's jacket was hanging over the back of his chair. He knew that it would be impolite to reach back and put it on, when his friend had not yet finished his luncheon . . . but now that he knew his trunk had been recovered at last, he was very anxious to leave, and go to it. Not only did he not yet know whether his belongings had survived the wreck, he had not changed his jacket and trousers in three weeks.

Gascoigne chuckled. 'Poor Mr. Staines,' he agreed. 'And how Mrs. Wells is making sport of him! If my shade were summoned to a shilling *séance* . . . why, I should be aghast, you know. I should not know how to take the invitation.'

'If mine were summoned, I should be relieved; I should accept at once,' Moody said. 'I daresay the afterlife is a very dreary place.'

'How do you conceive it so?'

'We spend our entire lives thinking about death. Without that project to divert us, I expect we would all be dreadfully bored. We would have nothing to evade, and nothing to forestall, and nothing to wonder about. Time would have no consequence.'

'And yet it would be entertaining, to spy upon the living,' Gascoigne said.

'On the contrary, I should consider that a very lonely prospect,' Moody said. 'Looking down on the world, unable to touch it, unable to alter it, knowing everything that had been, and everything that was.'

Gascoigne was salting his plate. 'I have heard that in the New Zealand native tradition, the soul, when it dies, becomes a star.'

'That is the best recommendation I have yet heard, to go native.'

'Will you get your face tattooed—and wear a skirt made of grass?'

'Perhaps I will.'

'I would like to see that,' Gascoigne said, picking up his fork again. 'I would like to see that even more than I should like to see you don your slouch hat and knee-boots, and fossick for gold! I have yet to believe even *that*, you know.'

Moody had purchased a swag, a cradle, and a digger's costume of moleskin and serge, but apart from a few indifferent forays into Kaniere, he had not really applied his mind to the prospect of panning for gold. He did not yet feel ready to begin his new life as a digger, and had resolved not to do so until the case pertaining to Emery Staines and Crosbie Wells was finally closed—a resolution that he had made under the pretence of necessity, but in reality there was nothing at all for him to do except to wait for new information, and, like Gascoigne, to continue to speculate upon the information he already possessed.

He had twice extended his board at the Crown Hotel, and on the afternoon of the 18th of February, was about to do so for a third time. Edgar Clinch had invited him to transfer to the Gridiron, suggesting that he might like to take up the room formerly occupied by Anna Wetherell, which now stood empty. The handsome view over the Hokitika rooftops to the snow-clad Alps in the East would be wasted on a common digger, and Moody, as a gentleman, would find pleasure in the harmonies of nature that other men would likely miss. But Moody had respectfully declined: he had grown rather fond of the Crown, shabby though the establishment was, and in any case he did not like to mingle too closely with Edgar Clinch, for there was still a very good chance that the case of Crosbie Wells's hoarded fortune would go to trial, in which event Clinch—along with Nilssen, and Frost, and sundry other men—would certainly be called in to be questioned. The thirteen men had sworn, each upon his honour, to keep the secret of the council at the Crown, but Moody did not like to rely on another man's honour, having little confidence in any expression of integrity save his own; he expected, in time, that at least one of the other twelve would break his word, and he had determined, in anticipation of that event, to remain aloof from them.

Moody had introduced himself to Alistair Lauderback, having discovered, through their mutual background in the law, that they shared several acquaintances in common: lawyers and judges in London whom Lauderback variously exalted, decried, and dismissed, in a recitation of confident opinion that brokered neither interruption nor reply. Moody listened to him politely, but the impression he formed was an unfavourable one, and he had left the scene of their first acquaintance with no intention of repeating it. He saw that Lauderback was the kind of man who did not care to court the good opinion of any man whose connexions could not benefit his own.

This had been quite contrary to his expectation; in fact Moody had been very surprised to discover that his natural sympathies aligned far more closely with the gaol's governor, George Shepard, than they did with the politician Lauderback. Moody had met Shepard only in passing, at a Public Assembly in Revell-street, but he admired the gaoler as a man who kept himself in check, and who was unfailingly courteous, however cold and rigid the expression of his courtesy might be. The summation of Shepard's character by the council at the Crown Hotel had been as critical as Lauderback's had been sympathetic—which only showed, Moody thought, that a man ought never to trust another man's evaluation of a third man's disposition. For human temperament was a volatile compound of perception and circumstance; Moody saw now that he could no more have extracted the true Shepard from Nilssen's account of him than he could have extracted the true Nilssen from his portrayal of Shepard.

'Do you know,' he said now, tapping the folded message with his finger, 'until this afternoon, I half-believed that Staines was still alive. Perhaps I was foolish ... but I did believe that he was aboard that wreck, and I did believe that he would be found.'

'Yes,' Gascoigne said.

'But now it seems that he can only be dead.' Moody tapped his fingers, brooding. 'And gone forever, no doubt. Hang not knowing! I would give any money for a seat at the widow's *séance* tonight.'

'Not just the widow's,' Gascoigne said. 'Don't forget that she is to be assisted.'

Moody shook his head. 'I hardly think this business is Miss Wetherell's doing.'

'She was mentioned in the paper by name,' Gascoigne pointed out. 'And not only by name: her role was specifically indicated. She is to be the widow's aide.'

'Well, her apprenticeship has been extraordinarily short,' Moody said, with some acidity. 'It makes one rather doubt the quality of the training—or the quality of the subject.'

Gascoigne grinned at this. 'Is a whore's praxis not the original arcana?' he said. 'Perhaps she has been in training all her life.'

Moody was always embarrassed by conversation of this kind. 'Her former praxis *is* arcane, in the proper sense of the word,' he conceded, drawing himself up, 'but the female arts are natural; they cannot be compared to the conjuration of the dead.'

'Oh, I am sure that the tricks of both professions are more or less the same,' Gascoigne said. 'A whore is the very mistress of persuasion, just as a sibyl must be persuasive, if she is to be believed … and you must not forget that beauty and conviction are always persuasive, whatever the context in which they appear. Why, the shape of Anna's fortunes is not so very greatly changed. You may as well keep calling her Magdalena!'

'Mary Magdalene was no clairvoyant,' Moody said stiffly.

'No,' Gascoigne agreed, still grinning, 'but she was the first to come upon the open tomb. She was the one to swear that the stone had been rolled away. It bears mention, that the news of the ascension first came as a woman's oath—and that at first the oath was disbelieved.'

'Well, tonight Anna Wetherell will make her oath upon another man's tomb,' Moody said. 'And we will not be there to disbelieve it.' He twitched his knife and fork still straighter, wishing that the waiter would come and clear his plate away.

'We have the party beforehand to look forward to,' said Gascoigne, but the cheer had gone from his voice. He too had been excessively disappointed by his exclusion from the widow's impending communion with the dead. The exclusion rankled him rather more bitterly than it did Moody, for he felt, as the first friend Lydia Wells had made in Hokitika, that a place ought properly to have been reserved for him. But Lydia Wells had not once paid a call upon him, since the afternoon of the 27th of January, and nor had she once received him, even for tea.

Moody had not yet met either woman formally. He had glimpsed them hanging drapes in the front windows of the former hotel, silhouetted darkly, like paper dolls against the glass. Perceiving them, he felt a rather strange thrill of longing—unusual for him, for it was not his habit to envy the relations that women conduct with other women, nor really, to think about them with any great interest at all. But as he walked past the shadowed frontage of the Wayfarer's Fortune and saw their bodies shifting behind the contorting pane he wished very much that he could hear what they were saying. He wished to know what caused Anna to redden, and bite her lip, and move the heel of her hand to her cheekbone, as if to test it for heat; he wished to know what caused Lydia to smile, and dust her hands, and turn away—leaving Anna with her arms full of fabric, and her dress-front stuck all over with pins.

'I think that you are right to doubt Anna's part in all this—or at least, to wonder at it,' Gascoigne went on. 'I got the impression, when I first spoke to her about Staines, that she held the boy in rather high esteem; I even fancied that she might care for him. And now by all appearances she is seeking to profit from his death!'

'We cannot be certain of the degree of Miss Wetherell's complicity,' Moody said. 'It depends entirely upon her knowledge of the fortune hidden in the gowns—and therefore, of Mr. Lauderback's blackmail.'

'There has been no mention of the orange gown—from any quarter,' said Gascoigne. 'One would think Mrs. Wells might have been more active in its recovery, had Anna told her that it was stowed beneath my bed.'

'Presumably Miss Wetherell believes the gold was paid out to Mr. Mannering, as she instructed.'

'Yes—presumably,' Gascoigne said, 'but wouldn't you suppose that in that case, Mrs. Wells would pay a call upon Mannering, to see about recovering it? There's no want of love between *them*: she and Mannering are old friends from gambling days. No: I think it far more possible that Mrs. Wells remains entirely ignorant about the orange gown—*and* about all the others.'

'Hm,' said Moody.

'Mannering won't touch it,' Gascoigne said, 'for fear of what will happen down the line—and I'm certainly not going to take it to the bank. So there it stays. Under my bed.'

'Have you had it valued?'

'Yes, though unofficially: Mr. Frost came by to look it over.

Somewhere in the neighbourhood of a hundred and twenty pounds, he thought.'

'Well, I hope for Miss Wetherell's sake that she has not confided in Mrs. Wells,' Moody said. 'I dread to think how Mrs. Wells might respond to such a revelation, behind closed doors. She would only blame Anna for the loss of the fortune—I am sure of it.'

Suddenly Gascoigne put down his fork. 'I've just had a thought,' he said. 'The money in the dresses *became* the money in the cottage. So if the widow's appeal goes through, and she receives the fortune as her inheritance, she'll get it all back—less the money in the orange gown, of course. She'll end up where she started, after all.'

'In my experience people are rarely contented to end up where they started,' Moody said. 'If my impression of Lydia Wells is accurate, I think that she will feel very bitter about Anna's having been in possession of those dresses, no matter what Anna's intentions might have been, and no matter what the outcome.'

'But we're fairly certain that Anna did not even know about the gold she was carrying—at least, not until very recently.'

'Mr. Gascoigne,' Moody said, holding up his hand, 'despite my youth, I possess a certain store of wisdom about the fairer sex, and I can tell you categorically that women do not like it when other women wear their clothes without their asking.'

Gascoigne laughed. Cheered by this joke, he applied himself to finishing his luncheon with a renewed energy, and a good humour.

The truth of Moody's observation notwithstanding, it must be owned that his store of wisdom, as he had termed it, could be called empirical only in that it had been formed upon the close observation of his late mother, his stepmother, and his two maternal aunts: to put it plainly, Moody had never taken a lover, and did not know a great deal about women, save for how to address them properly, and how to dote upon them as a nephew and as a son. It was not despite the natural partialities of youth that the compass of Moody's worldly experience was scarcely larger than a keyhole, through which he had perceived, metaphorically speaking, only glimpses of the shadowed chamber of adulthood that lay beyond. In fact he had met with ample opportunity to widen this aperture, and indeed, to unlock the door altogether, and pass through it, into that most private and solitary of rooms ... but he had declined these opportunities with quite the same discomfort and stiff propriety with which he fielded Gascoigne's rhetorical teases now.

When he was one-and-twenty a late night of carousing in London had led him, by the usual methods and channels, to a lamplit courtyard not far from Smithfield Market. This courtyard, by the authority of Moody's college chums, was frequented by the most fashionable of whores—so identifiable for their red Garibaldi jackets, brass-buttoned, that were the height of Parisian fashion at the time, and alarming to English ladies for that reason. Although the military style of their jackets gave the women a deliberate and brazen look, they pretended at shyness, turning away so they might look at the men over the rounded curve of their shoulders, and feint, and titter, and point their toes. Moody, watching them, felt suddenly sad. He could not help but think of his father—for how many times, over the years of Moody's youth, had he come across the man in some dark corner of the house, to perceive, upon his father's lap, a perfect stranger? She would be gasping unnaturally, or squealing like a pig, or speaking in a high-pitched voice that was not her own, and she would leave behind her, always, that same greasy musk: the smell of the theatre. Moody's college chums were pooling their sovereigns and cutting straws to draw for the first pick; silently, he withdrew from the courtyard, hailed a hansom, and retired to bed. It was a point of pride for him, thereafter, that he would not do as his father had done; that he would not fall prey to his father's vices; that he would be the better man. And yet how easy it might have been—to contribute his sovereign, and select his straw, and choose one of the red-shirted ladies to follow into the cobbled alcove on the dark side of the church! His college chums supposed him to have set his sights upon a clerical vocation. They were surprised, some years later, when Moody enrolled at Inner Temple, and began to study for the Bar.

It was therefore with a very well-concealed ignorance that Moody played interlocutor to Gascoigne, and Clinch, and Mannering, and Pritchard, and all the others, when they spoke of Anna Wetherell, and the esteem in which they held her, as a whore. Moody's well-timed murmurs of 'naturally' and 'of course' and 'exactly so', combined with a general rigidity of posture whenever Anna's name was mentioned, implied to these men merely that Moody was made uncomfortable by the more candid truths of human nature, and that he preferred, like most men of exalted social rank, to keep his earthly business to himself. We observe that one of the great attributes of discretion is that it can mask ignorance of all the most common and lowly varieties, and Walter Moody was nothing if not excessively discreet. The truth was that he had never spoken two words together to a woman of Anna Wetherell's profession or experience, and would hardly know how to address her—or upon what subject—should the chance arise.

'And of course,' he said now, 'we ought to be cheered by the fact that Miss Wetherell's trunk did not follow her to the Wayfarer's Fortune.'

'Did it not?' said Gascoigne, in surprise.

'No. The lead-lined dresses remain at the Gridiron, along with her pipe, and her opium lamp, and other miscellaneous items; she never sent for them.'

'And Mr. Clinch has not raised the issue?'

'No,' said Moody. 'It is cheering, I think: whatever role Miss Wetherell played in Mr. Staines's disappearance, and whatever role she is to play in the ridiculous *séance* this evening, we can at least be fairly certain that she has not confided in Mrs. Wells absolutely. I take heart in that.'

He looked about for the waiter, for Gascoigne had finished eating, and he wished to settle his account as soon as possible, so that he might return to the Crown, and unpack his trunk at long last.

'You are anxious to depart,' Gascoigne observed, wiping his mouth with his table napkin.

'Forgive my rudeness,' Moody said. 'I am not tired of your company—but I *am* rather anxious to be reunited with my possessions. I have not changed my jacket in some weeks, and I do not yet know the degree to which my trunk survived the storm. It is possible that all my clothes and documents were ruined.'

'What are we waiting for? Let us go, at once,' said Gascoigne, for whom this explanation was not only entirely reasonable, but also something of a relief. Gascoigne feared very much that his own society was tiring, and he was made very anxious whenever a man he respected showed boredom in his company. He insisted upon settling the cheque himself, shooing away Moody in the manner of an indulgent governess; once this was done, the two friends stepped out into the noisy rush of Revell-street, where a party of diggers was swarming cheerfully past. Behind them came a shout from a surveyor on horseback, reining in, and above them, the solitary bell in the Wesleyan chapel, which was striking the hour, once, twice. Raising their voices above this noise—the creaking wheels of a gig, the snap of canvas, laughter, hammering, the shrill voice of a woman calling to a man—the two friends bid one another good afternoon, and shook hands very warmly as they parted ways.

THE LESSER MALEFIC

In which certain key facts are disputed; Francis Carver is discourteous; and Löwenthal is provoked to speak his mind.

It was Löwenthal's practice, when a letter of inflammatory accusation was delivered to the *West Coast Times*, to contact all parties concerned before the paper went to press. He judged it right to give fair warning to any man about to be lambasted, for the court of public opinion in Hokitika was a court of severe adjudication, and a reputation could be ruined overnight; to every man so threatened, he extended the invitation to pen a reply.

Alistair Lauderback's long-winded and rather haphazard address on the subject of Governor Shepard's professional dereliction was no exception to this rule, and upon reading it through, Löwenthal sat down at once to make a copy of the document. The copy he would set into type; the original he would take to the Police Camp, to show to the gaoler himself—for Shepard would certainly wish to defend himself upon several counts, and it was still early enough in the day that his reply could be included, as a response to Lauderback's, in the Monday edition of the *Times*.

Löwenthal was frowning as he set out his writing implements. He knew that the information about Shepard's private investment could only have been leaked by one of the twelve men of the Crown, which meant that someone—sadly—had broken his vow of silence. As far as Löwenthal knew, the only man who had any kind of acquaintance with Alistair Lauderback was his friend, Thomas Balfour. It was with a heavy heart that the newspaperman pulled out a fresh sheet of paper, unscrewed the cap on his inkwell, and dipped his nib. *Tom*, he thought, with admonition, *Tom*. He shook his head, and sighed.

Löwenthal was copying out Lauderback's final paragraph when he was roused by the sound of the bell. Immediately he stood, laid his pen upon his blotter, and walked through to the shop, his face already relaxing into a smile of welcome—which froze, ever so slightly, when he saw who was standing in the doorway.

The incomer wore a long grey coat with velvet-faced lapels and turned velvet cuffs; the coat was made of a tight weave of some shiny, sealskin-like variety that turned an oily colour when he moved. His cravat was piled high at his throat, and the lapels of his shawl-collared waistcoat were turned up at the sides, lending an added bulk to his shoulders, and an added thickness to his neck. There was a heavy quality to his features, as though they had been hewn from some kind of mineral: something elemental and coarsely grained that would not polish, and that weighed a great deal. His mouth was wide, and his nose flattened; his brow protruded squarely. Upon his left cheek was a thin scar, silvery in colour, which curved from the outer corner of his eye down to his jaw.

Löwenthal's hesitation was only momentary. In the next instant he was bustling forward, wiping his hands on his apron, and smiling very broadly; when his hands were clean, he extended both his palms to his guest, and said, 'Mr. Wells! How good to see you again. Welcome back to Hokitika.'

Francis Carver narrowed his eyes, but did not take the bait. 'I want to place an advertisement,' he said. He did not step into the bounds of the other man's reach; he remained by the door, keeping eight feet of distance between them.

'Certainly, certainly,' said Löwenthal. 'And may I say: I am both honoured and gratified that you have sought my paper's services a second time. I should have been very sorry to lose any man's custom through an error of my own.'

Again Carver said nothing. He had not removed his hat, and made no move to do so.

But the newspaperman was not intimidated by Carver's insolence. Smiling very brightly, he said, 'But let us not talk of former days, Mr. Wells; let us talk of today! You must tell me what I can do for you.'

A flash of irritation darkened Carver's face at last. 'Carver,' he corrected. 'My name's not Wells.'

Satisfied, Löwenthal folded his hands. The first two fingers of his right hand were stained very darkly with ink, which created a curiously striped effect when he laced his fingers together—as though his two hands belonged to two different creatures, one black, the other fawn.

'Perhaps my memory is faulty,' he said, 'but I feel I do recall you very vividly. You were here nearly a year ago, were you not? You had a birth certificate. You placed an advertisement about a missing shipping crate—for which you were offering some kind of a reward. There was some confusion regarding your name, I remember. I made a mistake in the printing—omitting your middle name—and you returned the following morning, to identify the error. I believe your birth certificate was made out as Crosbie Francis Wells. But please—have I mistaken you for another man?'

Again Carver did not reply.

'I have always been told,' Löwenthal added after a moment, 'that I have a remarkably good memory.'

He was taking a risk, in speaking impertinently . . . but perhaps Carver would be drawn. Löwenthal's expression remained pleasantly impassive. He waited for the other man to speak.

Löwenthal knew that Carver was lodging at the Palace Hotel, from which place he conducted the unhappy business of arranging for the wreck of the *Godspeed* to be hauled ashore. This was a project that would surely have been undertaken slyly, and with much restriction, had Carver been taking pains to conceal a murdered man aboard the foundered ship. But by all reports—including that of the shipping agent, Thomas Balfour—Carver had been most forthcoming in his business. He had submitted a cargo inventory to the Harbourmaster; he had met with delegates from each of Hokitika's shipping firms, in order to settle their accounts; and he had several times rowed out to the wreck himself, in the company of shipwrights, salvage vendors, and the like.

'My name's not Wells,' Carver said at last. 'That was on behalf of someone else. It doesn't matter now.'

'I beg your pardon,' Löwenthal said smoothly. 'So Mr. Crosbie Wells had lost a shipping crate—and you were helping him retrieve it.'

A pause, then, 'Yes.'

'Well then, I do hope you were successful in that project! I trust the crate was eventually returned to him?'

Carver jerked his head in annoyance. 'It doesn't matter,' he said. 'I told you.'

'But I would be remiss,' Löwenthal said, 'if I did not offer my condolences to you, Mr. Carver.'

Carver studied him.

'I was very saddened to learn of Mr. Wells's death,' Löwenthal continued. 'I never had the pleasure of meeting him, but by all accounts he was a decent citizen. Oh—I do hope I'm not the man to break the news to you—that your acquaintance is deceased.'

'No,' Carver said again.

'I am glad of that. How did you know one another?'

The flash of irritation returned. 'Old friends.'

'From Dunedin, perhaps? Or further back?'

Carver did not look inclined to answer this, so Löwenthal went on, 'Well, I expect it must be a great comfort to you, to know that he died peacefully.'

Carver's mouth twisted. After a moment he burst out, 'What's *peaceful*?'

'To die in our sleep—in our own homes? I dare say it is the best that any of us can hope for.' Löwenthal felt that he had gained some ground. He added, 'Though it was a great pity his wife was not present at his passing.'

Carver shrugged. Whatever sudden fire had prompted his last

outburst had been smothered just as suddenly. 'A marriage is a man's own business,' he said.

'I couldn't agree with you more,' Löwenthal said. He smiled. 'Are you at all acquainted with Mrs. Wells?'

Carver made an inscrutable noise.

'I have had the pleasure of meeting her, but only briefly,' Löwenthal went on, undeterred. 'I had intended to go along to the Wayfarer's Fortune this evening—as a sceptic, of course, but with an open mind. Can I expect to see you there?'

'No,' Carver said, 'you can't.'

'Perhaps your scepticism about *séances* exceeds even mine!'

'I don't have an opinion about *séances*,' Carver said. 'I might be there or I might not.'

'In any case, I expect Mrs. Wells welcomed your return to Hokitika *very* gladly,' said Löwenthal—whose conversational gambits were becoming tenuous indeed. 'Yes: I am sure she must have been *very* pleased, to know that you had returned!'

Carver was now looking openly annoyed. 'Why?' he said.

'Why?' said Löwenthal. 'Because of all the fuss over his estate, of course! Because the legal proceedings have been halted precisely on account of Wells's birth certificate! It's nowhere to be found!'

Löwenthal's voice rang out rather more loudly than he had intended, and he worried briefly that perhaps he had overplayed his hand. What he had said was perfectly true, and what's more, it was public knowledge: Mrs. Wells's appeal to revoke the sale of Wells's estate had not yet been heard by the Magistrate's Court because no documentation had survived the dead man that might have served as proof of his true identity. Lydia Wells had arrived in Hokitika several days after her late husband had been buried, and therefore had not identified his body; short of digging his body up (the Magistrate begged the widow's pardon) there was, it seemed, no way of proving that the hermit who had died in the Arahura Valley and the Mr. Crosbie Wells who had signed Mrs. Wells's marriage certificate were the same man. Given the enormity of the inheritance in question, the Magistrate thought it prudent to delay the Court proceedings until a more definite conclusion could be reached—for which pronouncement Mrs. Wells thanked him very nicely. She assured him that her patience was of the most stalwart female variety, and that she would wait for as long as necessary for the outstanding debt (so she conceived of the inheritance) to be paid out to her.

But Carver was not provoked; he only looked the editor up and down, and then said, in a voice of surly indifference, 'I want to place a notice in the *Times*.'

'Yes, of course,' Löwenthal said. His heart was beating fast. Drawing a sheet of paper towards him, he said, 'What is it that you are wishing to sell?'

Carver explained that the hull of the *Godspeed* would shortly be dismantled, and in advance of this event, he wished to sell her parts at auction on Friday, care of Glasson & Rowley Salvage. He gave his instructions very curtly. No part was to be sold prior to auction. No privilege would be given, and no correspondence entered into. All inquiries were to be directed, by post, to Mr. Francis Carver, at the Palace Hotel.

'You see I am making careful note of it,' Löwenthal said. 'I will not make the mistake of omitting any part of your name—not this time! Say—I don't suppose that you and Crosbie were related?'

Carver's mouth twisted again. 'No.'

'It's true that Francis is a very common name,' Löwenthal said, nodding. He was still making note of the name of Carver's hotel, and did not look up for several seconds; when he did, however, he found that Carver's expression had soured still further.

'What's *your* name?' Carver demanded, accenting the fact that he had not bothered to use it before. When Löwenthal replied, Carver nodded slowly, as if committing the name to heart. Then he said, 'You'll shut your f—ing mouth.'

Löwenthal was shocked. He received the payment for the advertisement and wrote up Carver's receipt in silence—penning the words very slowly and carefully, but with a steady hand. This was the first time he had ever been insulted in his own office, and his shock was such that he could not immediately respond. He felt an exhilaration building within him; a pressure; an exultant, roaring

sound. Löwenthal was the kind of man who became almost glad-
iatorial when he was shamed. He felt a martial stirring in his breast
that was triumphal, even glad, as if a long-awaited call to arms had
sounded somewhere close at hand, and he alone had felt its private
resonation, drumming in his ribcage, drumming in his blood.

Carver had taken up the receipt. He turned, and made to leave
the shop without either thanking Löwenthal or bidding him goodbye—a discourtesy that released a surge of outrage in Löwenthal's
breast: he could contain himself no longer. He burst out, 'You've
got a lot to answer for, showing your face around here!'

Carver stopped, his hand upon the doorknob.

'After what you did to Anna,' Löwenthal said. 'I was the one to
find her, you know. All bloody. It's not a way to treat a woman. I
don't care who she is. It's not a way to treat a woman—still less
when she's expecting, and so close to being due!'

Carver did not answer.

'It was a hair short of a double murder. Do you know that?'
Löwenthal felt his anger mounting into fury. 'Do you know what
she looked like? Did you see her when the bruises were going
down? Did you know that she had to use a cane for two weeks? Just
to be able to *walk*! Did you know that?'

At last Carver said, 'Her hands weren't clean.'

Löwenthal almost laughed. 'What—she left *you* in a bloody pool,
then? She boxed *you* senseless? What is the phrase—an eye for an
eye?'

'I didn't say that.'

'She killed your child? She killed your child—so you killed hers?'
Löwenthal was almost shouting. 'Say the words, man! Say them!'

But Carver was unmoved. 'I meant she's no blushing flower.'

'Blushing *flower*! Now I expect you're going to tell me she brought
it all upon herself—that she deserved it!'

'Yes,' said Francis Carver. 'She got what she was owed.'

'You are short on friends in Hokitika, Mr. Carver,' said
Löwenthal, levelling his ink-blackened finger at the other man.
'Anna Wetherell may be a common whore but she is treasured by
more men in this town than you can hold off, armed or no, and you

ought not to forget that. If any harm should come to her—let me warn you—if any harm—'

'Not by my hand,' Carver said. 'I've got nothing more to do with her. I've settled my dues.'

'Your *dues*!' Löwenthal spat on the floor. 'You mean the baby? Your own child—dead, before its own first breath! That's what you call *dues*!'

But suddenly Carver was looking at him with a very amused expression.

'My own child?' he repeated.

'I'll tell you, though you haven't asked,' Löwenthal shouted. 'Your baby's dead. Do you hear me? Your own child—dead, before its first breath! And by your hand!'

And Carver laughed—harshly, as though clearing something foul from his throat. 'That whore carried no baby of *mine*,' he said. 'Who told you that?'

'Anna herself,' Löwenthal said, feeling a flash of trepidation for the first time. 'Do you deny it?'

Carver laughed again. 'I wouldn't touch that girl with a boathook,' he said, and before Löwenthal could reply, he was gone.

In which Sook Yongsheng pays another unexpected call; Lydia Wells has a most prophetic notion; and Anna finds herself alone.

Anna Wetherell had not visited the opium den in Kaniere since the afternoon of the 14th of January. The half-ounce of fresh resin that Sook Yongsheng had gifted her that afternoon ought to have lasted no more than two weeks, by Anna's habitual rate of consumption. But now over a month had passed, and Anna had not once returned to Kaniere to share a pipe with her old companion, or to replenish her supply—an absence for which Ah Sook could not produce any kind of reasonable explanation.

The hatter missed the whore's visits very much. Every afternoon he waited, in vain, for her to appear at the edge of the clearing beyond the bounds of Kaniere Chinatown, her bonnet hanging down her back, and every afternoon he was disappointed. He guessed that she must have ceased to take opium altogether: either that, or she had decided to source the drug from the chemist directly. This latter alternative ought to have been the more hurtful to Ah Sook, for he still suspected that Joseph Pritchard had played a part in engineering Anna's overdose, on the night of the 14th: he still believed, despite many assurances to the contrary, that Pritchard had tried for some reason to end Anna's life. But in fact it was the former alternative that was the more difficult for Ah Sook to bear. He simply could not believe—did not *want* to believe—that Anna had managed to rid herself, once and for all, of her addiction.

Ah Sook was very fond of Anna, and he believed that she was fond of him also. He knew, however, that the intimacy that they enjoyed together was less a togetherness than it was a shared isolation—for there is no relationship as private as that between the addict and his drug, and they both felt that isolation very keenly. Ah Sook loathed his own enslavement to opium, and the more he loathed it, the more his craving for the drug strengthened, taking a disgusted shape in his heart and mind. Anna, too, had loathed the habit in herself. She had loathed it all the more when she began to swell with child, and her trade in Hokitika dwindled, and she was left with days and weeks of twilit smoke, an acreage of time, that softened at the edges, and blurred, until the baby died, and Anna's dependence acquired a desperation that even Ah Sook did not attempt to understand. He did not know how the baby came to perish, and had not asked.

They never spoke in the Kaniere den—not as they lit the lamp, not as they lay back, not as they waited for the resin to soften and bubble in the bowl. Sometimes Anna filled Ah Sook's pipe first, and held it for him as he took the smoke into his body, and breathed, and slipped away—only to wake, later, and find her stretched out beside him, supple and clammy, her hair plastered wet against her cheek. It was important to the lighting of the pipe that no words were ever spoken, and Ah Sook was pleased that they had adopted this practice without any kind of negotiation or request. As the conjugal act cannot be spoken of aloud for reasons both sacred and profane, the ritual of the pipe was, for the pair of them, a holy ritual that was unspeakable and mortified, just as it was ecstatic and divine: its sacredness lay in its very profanity, and its profanity, in its sacred form. For what a solemn joy it was, to wait in silence for the resin to melt; to ache for it, shamefully, wondrously, as the sweet scent of it reached one's nose; to pull the needle through the tar; to cut the flame, and lie back, and take the smoke into one's body, and feel it, miraculous, rushing to one's very extremities, one's fingers, one's toes, the top of one's head! And how tenderly he looked upon her, when they woke.

On the afternoon of the widow's *séance* (it was a Sunday—a provocative scheduling on Mrs. Wells's part, and one of which she was very well aware) Ah Sook was sitting in the rectangular patch of sunshine that fell through the doorway of his hut, scraping clean the bowl of his opium pipe, humming through his teeth, and thinking about Anna. This had been his occupation for the better part of an hour, and the bowl was long since clean. His knife no longer turned up the reddish powder left by the burnt opium gum; the long chamber of the pipe was clear. But the redundant motion matched the redundancy of his repeating thoughts, and helped to reassure him.

'*Ah Quee faat sang me si aa?*'

Tong Wei, a smooth-faced young man of thirty, was watching him from the other side of the clearing. Ah Sook did not respond. He had pledged not to speak of the council at the Crown Hotel, or the events that preceded it, to any man.

The lad persisted. '*Keoi hai mai bei yan daa gip aa?*'

Still Ah Sook said nothing, and presently Tong Wei gave up, muttering his displeasure, and sloped off in the direction of the river.

Ah Sook sat still for a long while after the lad's departure, and then all of a sudden he sat back, uttered an oath, and folded his knife away. It was hell to spend his days waiting for her, thinking about her, wondering. He would not endure it. He would journey to Hokitika that very afternoon, and demand an audience with her. He would go at once. He rolled up his pipe and tools, stood, and went inside to fetch his coat.

Ah Sook had only understood part of what was discussed in the smoking room of the Crown Hotel three weeks prior. In his confusions he had received no aid from his compatriot, for Ah Quee's English was even more severely limited than his own, and none from the remaining men of the Crown, whose collective patience was worn very thin by any request for clarification from Chinese men. Balfour's narration had been much too swift and poetically accented to be readily understood by a foreign ear, and both Ah Sook and Ah Quee had left the assembly at the Crown with only a partial understanding of all that had been discussed.

The crucial points of ignorance were these. Ah Sook did not know that Anna Wetherell had quit her lodgings at the Gridiron Hotel, and had taken up instead with Lydia Wells. He also did not know that Francis Carver was the master of the ship *Godspeed*, the craft that had foundered on the Hokitika bar. When the assembly at the Crown broke up, soon after midnight, Ah Sook had not followed the other men to the Hokitika spit to look over the wreck: shipping misadventures did not interest him, and he did not like to be on the Hokitika streets after dark. He had returned, instead, to Kaniere, where he had remained ever since. As a consequence, he still believed that Francis Carver had departed nearly a month ago for Canton, and would not be due back in Hokitika for some time. Thomas Balfour, who had quite forgotten imparting this piece of misinformation to Ah Sook in the first place, had not thought to disabuse him.

By the time the bells rang out half past three, Ah Sook was mounting the steps to the veranda of the Gridiron Hotel. At the front desk, he requested an audience with Anna Wetherell, pronouncing her name with both gravity and satisfaction, as though the meeting had been scheduled many months in advance. He produced a shilling, to show that he was willing to pay for the privilege of the whore's conversation, and then bowed very deeply, as a gesture of respect. He remembered Edgar Clinch from the secret council, and had judged him, then, to be a decent and reasonable man.

Clinch, however, only shook his head. He gestured, repeatedly, towards the newly washed Wayfarer's Fortune, on Revell-street's opposite side, and spoke a flurry of words; when Ah Sook did not understand, Clinch brought him outside by the elbow, pointed at the hotel opposite, and explained, more slowly, that Anna now took her lodging there. Eventually Ah Sook spied a thrust of movement in the front window of the former hotel, and perceived that the figure behind the glass was Anna; satisfied, he bowed to Clinch a second time, retrieved his shilling from the other man's palm, and pocketed it. He then crossed the thoroughfare, mounted the steps to the Wayfarer's veranda, and rapped smartly upon the door.

Anna must have been in the foyer, for she answered the door within seconds. She appeared, as was her habit of late, in the distracted posture of a lady's maid, full of annoyance and disapproval, keeping one hand upon the doorframe, so as to be ready to close the door at once. (Over the past three weeks she had received a great many callers: wistful diggers, for the most part, who missed her presence at the Dust and Nugget in the evenings. They begged to buy her a glass of champagne, or brandy, or small beer, and to 'shoot the bull' at one of the brightly lit saloons along Revell-street—but their pleading had no effect: Anna only shook her head, and shut the door.) When she saw who was on the threshold, however, she pulled the door open wide, and made an exclamation of surprise.

Ah Sook was surprised also; for a moment he simply stared. After so many weeks of recalling her shape to his mind—here she was! Was she truly so altered? Or was his memory so imperfect, that she seemed, standing in the doorway, to be a wholly different woman than the one with whom he had passed so many luxurious afternoons, with the cold light of winter falling slantwise through the square of the window, and the smoke winding about their bodies, in coils? Her dress was a new one: black, and cut very severely. But this was not merely a new dress, Ah Sook thought. This was a different woman altogether.

She was sober. Her cheeks held a new lustre, and her eyes were brighter, larger, and more alert. The syrupy quality to her movements was gone—and gone, too, was the slightly dreamy gauze that had always overlaid her features, like a veil of lawn. Gone was the vague half-smile, the trembling corner of her mouth, the awed confusion— as though she were privy, always, to some small bewilderment that no one else could see. In the next moment Ah Sook's astonishment had given way to bitterness. So it was true. Anna had rid herself of opium's dragon. She had cured herself—when he had tried for over a decade to do the same, remaining, always, that shapeless creature's slave.

Anna made a little snatching motion with her hand, as though wishing to steady herself upon the frame of the door. In a whisper she said, 'But you can't come in—you can't come in, Ah Sook.'

Ah Sook waited a moment before he made his bow, for he trusted his own first impressions, and he wished to make this impression last. She was much thinner than he remembered: he could see the bones of her wrist quite plainly, and her cheeks were sunken in.

'Good afternoon,' he said.

'What do you want?' Anna whispered. 'Yes—good afternoon. You know I'm not taking opium any more. Did you know that?'

He peered at her.

'Three weeks,' she added, as if to persuade him. 'I haven't had a pipe in three weeks.'

'How?' said Ah Sook.

She shook her head. 'You have to understand it: I'm not the same as I was.'

'Why you come no more to Kaniere?' Ah Sook said. He did not know how to say that he missed her; that each afternoon before her arrival he used to arrange the cushions on the daybed just so, and tidy his belongings, and make sure his clothes were neat and his pigtail tied; that as he watched her sleep he had often been near-choked with joy; that he had sometimes reached out his hand and let it hover within an inch of her breast, as though he could feel the softness of her skin in that smoky space between his flesh and hers; that sometimes after she took her pipe he would wait some time before taking his own, so that he could watch her, and fix her image in his mind, to remember.

'I can't come to see you any more,' Anna said. 'You mustn't be here. I can't come.'

Ah Sook studied her sadly. 'No more smoke?'

'No more,' Anna said. 'No more smoke, and no more Kaniere.'

'Why?'

'I can't explain it—not here. I've stopped, Ah Sook. I've stopped it altogether.'

'No more money?' said Ah Sook, trying to understand. He knew that Anna had laboured under an enormous debt. She owed a great deal of money to Dick Mannering, and the debt mounted every day. Perhaps she could no longer afford the drug. Or perhaps she could no longer afford the time to make the journey, to take it.

'It's not money,' Anna said.

Just then a female voice called out Anna's name, from deep in the well of the house, and asked, in a tone of impatient condescension, to know the name and business of the caller at the door.

Anna turned her chin to the side but did not move her eyes from Ah Sook's face. 'It's just a chink I used to know,' she called. 'It's nothing.'

'Well, what does he want?'

'Nothing,' Anna called again. 'He's only trying to sell me something.'

There was a silence.

'I bring to you—here?' said Ah Sook. He cupped his hands together and proffered them to her, indicating that he was willing to deliver the resin himself.

'No,' Anna whispered. 'No, you can't do that. It's no use. I just— the thing is—I can't feel it any more.'

Ah Sook did not understand this. 'Last piece,' he said, meaning the ounce he had gifted her on the afternoon of her near-death. 'Last piece—unlucky?'

'No,' Anna began, but before she could speak further there were quick steps in the passage, and in the next moment a second woman had appeared at Anna's side.

'Good afternoon,' she said. 'What is it that you are selling? That will do, Anna'—and at once Anna melted back from the doorway.

Ah Sook had also taken a step backwards—but in shock rather than submission, for this was the first he had seen of Lydia Greenway in nearly thirteen years. The last time that he had laid eyes upon her was—when?—at the Sydney courthouse, she in the gallery, he in the dock; she red-faced, fanning herself with an embroidered sandalwood fan, the scent of which had floated down to reach him, recalling, in a rush of emotion, his family's warehouse on the Kwangchow waterfront, and the sandalwood boxes in which the merchants packed their bolts of silk, before the wars. She had been wearing a gown of pale green—this he remembered well— and a bonnet covered in lace; she had kept her face perfectly grave, throughout the trial. Her testimony, when she gave it, had been short and to the point. Ah Sook had not understood a word of it, save for when she pointed directly at him, evidently to identify him to the court. When Ah Sook was acquitted of the murder she had betrayed no emotion of any kind: she had only risen, mutely, and left the courtroom without a backward glance. Over twelve years had passed since that day! Over twelve years—and yet here she was, monstrously present, monstrously unchanged! Her copper hair was as bright as ever; her skin was fresh, and hardly lined. She was as plump and buxom as Anna was gaunt.

In the next moment her features also slackened—which was unusual, for Lydia's expressions were typically very artfully mani-cured, and she did not like to show surprise—and her eyes became wide.

'I know this man,' she said, in a tone of astonishment. She brought her hand up to her throat. 'I know him.'

Anna looked from Ah Sook to Mrs. Wells, and then back again. 'How?' she said. 'Not from Kaniere!'

Ah Sook had acquired a film of perspiration on his upper lip. He said nothing, however, and merely bowed; perhaps they would think that he could not understand them. He turned back to Anna, feeling that if he kept eye contact with Lydia Greenway for even a moment longer, she would recall where they had met before. He could still feel her in the periphery of his eye, watching him.

Anna was frowning too. 'Perhaps you're thinking of a different man,' she said to Mrs. Wells. 'It's often hard to tell Chinamen apart.'

'Yes—perhaps,' said Mrs. Wells. But she was still staring at Ah Sook. Whether she had placed him already or not, he could not tell. He cast about for something to say to Anna, but his mind was blank.

'What do you want, Ah Sook?' said Anna. She did not speak unkindly, but with longing; there was a pleading, almost fearful look in her eye.

'What did you call him?' said the older woman, quickly.

'Ah Sook,' Anna said. 'Mister Sook, I suppose. He's the dealer at Kaniere.'

'Ah!' Her gaze sharpened immediately. 'Opium!'

So she had placed him. She had remembered who he was.

At once, Ah Sook changed his tack. He turned to Anna and announced, 'I buy you. Top price.'

The widow laughed.

'Oh,' Anna said. She had flushed very red. 'No. You can't do that. I suppose nobody told you. I'm done with whoring now. I'm not a whore any longer. No selling. Not for sale.'

'What you now?' said Ah Sook.

'Miss Wetherell is my assistant,' said Mrs. Wells—but Ah Sook did not know the word. 'She lives here now.'

'I live here now,' Anna echoed. 'I don't take opium any more. Do you understand? No more smoke. I—I've given it up.'

Ah Sook was bewildered.

'Well, goodbye,' Anna said. 'Thank you for calling.'

Suddenly Mrs. Wells's wrist shot out. She grabbed Ah Sook's forearm in her milky hand, and squeezed it tight. 'You must come to the *séance* this evening,' she said.

'He doesn't have a ticket,' Anna said.

'An Oriental presence,' said Mrs. Wells, ignoring her. 'It will be just the thing! What did you call him again?'

'Ah Sook,' said Anna.

'Oh *yes*,' said Mrs. Wells. 'Just think of it: an Oriental presence, at this evening's *séance*!'

'Is a *séance* an Oriental practice?' Anna said, doubtfully.

Ah Sook did not know the word—but he knew Oriental, and guessed that he was the subject of their discussion, and the cause, presumably, of Lydia's sudden look of greed. It was astonishing to him that she could have changed so little over the course of a decade, when Anna, over the course of a month, had altered so very much. Looking down at her hand, wrapped tight around his forearm, he was surprised to see a band of gold upon her finger.

'Mrs. Carver,' he said, and pointed to the ring.

The woman smiled—more broadly this time. 'I fancy he has a touch of the prophet in him,' she said to Anna. 'How is that for a notion?'

'What do you mean, Mrs. Carver?' Anna said to Ah Sook. She was frowning.

'Wife of Carver,' said Ah Sook, unhelpfully.

'He thinks you're Carver's wife,' said Anna.

'He's only guessing,' said Mrs. Wells. To Ah Sook she said, 'Not Mrs. Carver. My husband is dead. I am a widow now.'

'Not Mrs. Carver?'

'Mrs. Wells.'

Ah Sook's eyes widened. 'Mrs. *Wells*,' he repeated.

'It is very well his English is so limited,' the widow said to Anna, conversationally. 'That way he will not get distracted. His composure will not falter. Isn't he handsome! He will do us very well, I think.'

'He knows Carver,' Anna said.

'I'm sure he does,' said Mrs. Wells, with a breezy tone. 'Captain Carver has a great many Oriental connexions. I expect they've done business with each other here in Hokitika. Come into the parlour, Ah Sook.' She gripped his arm tighter. 'Come along. Just for a moment. Don't be a baby; I'm not going to *hurt* you! Come inside.'

'Francis Carver—in Guangdong?' said Ah Sook.

'In Canton; yes, it's very likely,' said Mrs. Wells, mistaking Ah Sook's question for a statement. 'Captain Carver was based in Canton. He was based there for many years. Come along into the parlour.'

She shepherded Ah Sook into the parlour, pointing to the far corner of the room. 'You will sit upon a cushion—there,' she said. 'You will observe the faces around you, and contribute a cool air of judgment to our mystical *séance*. We shall call you the Eastern Oracle—or the Living Statue of the Orient—or the Dynastic Spirit—or some such thing. Which do you prefer, Anna? The Statue—or the Oracle?'

Anna did not have a preference. It was clear to her that Lydia Wells and Ah Sook recognised each other, and that their shared history had something to do with Francis Carver, and that the widow did not wish to speak of it aloud. She knew better than to press the point, however, and asked, 'What will be his purpose?'

'Merely to observe us!'

'Yes, but to what end?'

The widow waved her hand. 'Didn't you see the spectacle at the Prince of Wales? Nothing sells tickets like an Oriental touch.'

'He's not unknown in Hokitika, you know,' Anna said. 'He'll be recognised.'

'As will you!' Mrs. Wells pointed out. 'That won't matter a jot.'

'I don't know,' said Anna. 'I'm not sure.'

'Anna *Wetherell*,' said Mrs. Wells, with pretended annoyance. 'Do you remember last Thursday, when I proposed hanging the sketch of the Bagatto at the top of the stairs, and you protested, claiming that the print would be shadowed by the attic landing, and then I hung it anyway, and the light was quite as perfect as I promised it would be?'

'Yes,' Anna said.

'Well—*there*,' said Mrs. Wells, and laughed.

Ah Sook had not understood a word of this. He turned to Anna and frowned very slightly, to show her that she needed to explain.

'A *séance*,' Anna said, uselessly.

Ah Sook shook his head. He did not know the word.

'Let's try it,' said Mrs. Wells. 'Come—come to the corner—Anna, get the man a cushion to sit upon. Or would a stool be more ascetic? No, a cushion: then he can fold his legs as the Eastern men do. Yes, come here—further—further. There.'

She pushed Ah Sook down upon the cushion, and took several quick steps backwards, to appraise him from the other side of the room. She nodded with delight.

'Yes,' she said. 'Do you see, Anna? Do you not think it fine? How solemn he is! I wonder if we might ask him to smoke a pipe of some kind—for the curling smoke around his head would be rather nice indeed. But smoke indoors makes me ill.'

'He has not yet given his consent,' Anna observed.

Mrs. Wells looked faintly irritated; she did not protest this observation, however, but advanced upon Ah Sook, smiled, and peered down at him, her hands on her hips. 'Do you know Emery

Staines?' she said, enunciating clearly. 'Emery Staines? Do you
know him?'

Ah Sook nodded. He knew Emery Staines.

'Well,' the woman said, 'we are going to bring him here.
Tonight. And speak with him. Emery Staines—here.' She pointed
at the floorboards with a lemon-scented hand.

A ray of understanding passed over Ah Sook's face. Excellent:
the prospector must have been found at last—and found alive! This
was good news.

'Very good,' he said.

'Tonight,' said Mrs. Wells. 'Here, at the Wayfarer's Fortune. In
this room. The party will begin at seven; the *séance*, at ten.'

'Tonight,' said Ah Sook, staring at her.

'Precisely. You will be here. You will come. You will sit, as you are
sitting now. Yes? Oh, Anna—does he understand? I can hardly tell;
his face is such a perfect statue. You see what gave me the idea—
the Living Statue!'

Slowly, Anna explained to Ah Sook that Lydia was requesting his
presence, that evening, at a meeting with Emery Staines. She used
the word *séance* several times; Ah Sook, who had no reason to have
ever learned that word, deduced by context that it was a gathering
or meeting of some scripted kind, which Emery Staines had been
invited to attend. He nodded to show that he understood. Anna
then explained that Ah Sook was invited to return, that evening,
and take his place upon the cushion in the corner, exactly as he was
sitting now. Other men had also been invited. They would sit in a
circle, and Emery Staines would stand in the centre of the room.

'Does he understand it?' said Mrs. Wells. 'Does he understand?'

'Yes,' said Ah Sook, and then, to show her: 'A *séance* with Emery
Staines, tonight.'

'*Excellent*,' said Mrs. Wells, smiling down at him in the same way
that one might smile at a precocious child after the recitation of a
sonnet—which is to say, with an admiration that was a little dis-
trustful, and somewhat contrived.

'A whore in mourning and an Eastern mystic,' she went on. 'It
is quite perfect; I am chilled simply thinking of it! Of course a *séance*

is not an Oriental *tradition*'—in response to Anna's earlier question—'but have I not said every day this fortnight that in this
business, the ambience is half the battle? Ah Sook will do us *very*
well.'

Anna looked away, and said, lightly, 'Of course he must be
recompensed.'

The widow turned upon Anna with a very chilly look, but Anna
was not looking at her, and could not receive it; in the next
moment, her expression cleared again. Carelessly she said, 'Of
course! But you ought to ask him how much he thinks he deserves
for such easy work. Ask him, Anna; seeing as you are his *special*
friend.'

Anna did so, explaining to Ah Sook that the widow was willing
to pay him a fee for his contribution to the *séance* that evening. Ah
Sook, who had not yet understood that Emery Staines was going
to be present in spirit only, thought this a wonderful proposition.
He was rightly very suspicious of the offer, and made his suspicion
known. A rather absurd negotiation followed, and at length Ah
Sook agreed, more for her sake than for his own, to receive a fee
of one shilling.

Ah Sook was no fool. He knew very well that he had not really
comprehended what was to happen that evening. It was very
strange to him that Anna had placed such a high emphasis upon
the fact that Emery Staines would stand in the very centre of the
room, with all the others ranged around him, and it was even
stranger still that the widow was willing to pay him a wage for
doing nothing at all. He concluded that he was to play a part in a
scripted drama of some kind (in which guess, of course, he hit very
close upon the mark) and reasoned that whatever humiliation he
might suffer as a consequence, it was surely worth it, to get a
chance to speak to Mr. Staines. He accepted the widow's invitation,
and her promise of payment, in the certainty that his uncertainties
would resolve themselves in time.

With this, their negotiations were concluded. Ah Sook looked at
Anna. They held one another's gaze a moment, Ah Sook steadily,
and Anna—it seemed—with a cool detachment that the hatter did

not recognise at all. But was that even detachment? Or was he simply unused to the clarity of her expression, now that her features were not overlaid by opium's thick veil? She was so changed. If he had not known her better he might have almost called her expression haughty—as though she fancied herself a cut above Chinese society, now that she was no longer a whore.

Ah Sook decided to take her cool expression as a cue to leave, and rose from his cushion. He had calculated that he had time enough to walk to Kaniere and back again before the sun went down, and he wished to inform his compatriot Quee Long that Emery Staines would be present, that very evening, at the Wayfarer's Fortune on Revell-street. He knew that Ah Quee had long desired an audience with Staines, wishing to interrogate the young prospector upon the matter of the Aurora gold; he would be very pleased to discover that Staines was alive.

Ah Sook bowed to the widow, and then to Anna. Anna returned his bow with a shallow curtsey, the kind that bespoke neither longing nor regret, and then turned away at once, to straighten the lace on the arm of the sofa.

'You'll be back tonight—for the *séance*. Tonight,' said Lydia Wells. 'Say six o'clock.'

'Six o'clock,' Ah Sook echoed, and pointed at the cushion he had just vacated, to show that he understood. He glanced one last time at Anna, and then Lydia Wells gripped his arm and ushered him into the foyer. She reached around him and opened the door, flooding the space with the sudden light of the day.

'Goodbye,' said Ah Sook, and stepped over the lintel.

But the widow did not close the door behind him, as he had expected; instead she reached for her shawl, wrapped it around her shoulders, and followed Ah Sook out on to the veranda. To Anna she said, 'I am going out for a spell; I'll be back in an hour or so.'

Anna, from the parlour, looked up in astonishment. Then her expression closed. She nodded woodenly, crossed the parlour, and came to the door to latch it in Mrs. Wells's wake.

'Good afternoon, Mrs. Wells,' she said, her hand on the frame. 'Good afternoon, Ah Sook.'

They descended the steps to the street, where they parted ways: Ah Sook to the south, towards the river, and Lydia Wells to the north. After several steps Mrs. Wells cast a look over her shoulder, as if to appraise the building from the street, and Anna hurriedly moved to close the door.

She kept her hand upon the knob, however, and did not turn it; after a moment she opened it again, very quietly and carefully, and put her eye to the crack. Lydia was walking swiftly now; she had not turned, as Anna had expected she might, to pursue Ah Sook, and demand a private audience with him. Anna pulled the door open a little wider. Would she double back? Surely that was why she had left so abruptly—to talk in private with the man she so very plainly recognised! But presently Ah Sook rounded the corner on Gibson Quay and disappeared, and Lydia Wells, at almost the same moment, stepped over the ditch at the side of the road, and mounted the steps of—Anna squinted—which establishment? A two-storeyed building—beside Tiegreen's Hardware and Supply. One of the saloons, perhaps? Evidently there was someone on the porch, for Lydia Wells lingered for a moment, exchanging words, before she opened the door of the establishment, and disappeared inside—and as the door swung to, Anna caught a flash of pale blue paint, and recognised the building. So Lydia Wells had gone to pay a *social* call. But upon whom? Anna shook her head in wonderment. Well, she thought, whoever it was, he was not a common digger by any measure. He must be a man of some consequence, for he was lodging at the Palace Hotel.

SATURN IN LIBRA

In which Harald Nilssen reneges upon a contract; the holy book is opened; Cowell Devlin is confounded; and George Shepard forms a plan.

Harald Nilssen had just brewed and steeped his four-o'clock pot of tea, and was sitting down to a plate of sugared biscuits and a book, when he received a summons in the penny post. It was from George Shepard, and marked 'urgent', though the gaoler did not specify a reason why. Doubtless it concerned some detail of infinitesimal consequence, Nilssen thought, with irritation: some piece of gravel in the gaol-house foundation, some drop of coffee on the gaol-house plans. Sighing, he fitted a quilted cosy around his teapot, exchanged his jersey for a jacket, and reached for his stick. It was jolly bad form to bother a man on a Sunday afternoon. Why, he had been working six days out of seven. He deserved a day of rest, without George Shepard plaguing him for receipts, or wage records, or quotes on salvage. The penny post was an added insult—for Shepard could not even trouble himself to walk the five short blocks from the Police Camp to Gibson Quay; instead he insisted that Nilssen come to *him*, as a servant to a liege! Nilssen was in a very bad temper as he locked the door of his office behind him, and strode off down Revell-street with his hat set at an angle and his coat-tails flared.

At the Police Camp Mrs. George answered the door. She directed Nilssen, with a very sorry aspect, into the dining room, and then fled before Nilssen could speak any words of politeness, pulling the door so firmly closed behind her that the calico wall gave a shudder, and Nilssen had the fleeting sensation of being at sea.

The gaoler was sitting at the head of the table, where he was making short work of a cold meal composed of jellied meats, various cold puddings of homogenous consistency, and a dense bread of some dark, large-crumbed kind. He held himself very straight as he stacked his fork, and did not offer Nilssen a chair.

'So,' he said, when the door had closed, and he had swallowed his mouthful. 'You told somebody about our agreement; you broke your word. Whom did you tell?'

'What?' said Nilssen.

Shepard repeated his question; Nilssen, after a pause, repeated his bewilderment, at a slightly higher pitch.

Shepard's expression was cold. 'Do not lie to me, Mr. Nilssen. Alistair Lauderback is to publish a letter in the *Times* to-morrow morning, lambasting my character. He claims that a percentage of the fortune discovered on Crosbie Wells's estate was invested in the Hokitika gaol-house. I do not know how he came upon this information, and I wish to know. At once.'

Nilssen faltered. How was it possible that *Alistair Lauderback* knew about his commission? One of the Crown men must have broken his word! Balfour, perhaps? Balfour and Lauderback were close familiars, and Nilssen had never seen Lauderback in the company of any of the rest. But what reason could Balfour have, to betray him? Nilssen had never wished him any kind of harm. Could it have been Löwenthal? Perhaps—if the letter was to be published in the paper. But Nilssen could not believe that Löwenthal had broken his word any more than he could believe it of Balfour. He watched Shepard assemble a forkful of jellied meats, pickled cucumber, and hash, and inexplicably (for Nilssen was not at all hungry) his own mouth began to water.

'Whom did you tell?' Shepard said. 'Please mark this moment as the end of my patience: I will not ask you again.' He put his mouth over his assembled forkful, slid the food off the fork, and chewed.

Nilssen did not know how to respond. The truth, of course, was that he had told twelve men—Walter Moody, plus the eleven others who had been summoned to the smoking room of the Crown. He could hardly admit to having betrayed Shepard's secret to *twelve men*! Ought he to pretend that he had told no one at all? But it was obvious that he had broken his confidence to someone—if Lauderback knew! His mind was racing.

'I can't think how it might have happened,' he said, in desperation. 'I can't think.'

Shepard was busy stacking another mouthful on the back of his fork. 'Did you go to Lauderback yourself?' he said, his eyes fixed intently upon his dinner. 'Or did you go to another man—who went to Lauderback in his turn?'

'I haven't spoken five words to Lauderback in all my life,' Harald Nilssen said, with much indignation.

'Who, then?' Shepard looked up, his utensils loose in his hands. Nilssen said nothing. He had begun to perspire.

'You are keeping a digger's honour, I see,' Shepard said with disapproval. 'Well, at least someone has your loyalty, Mr. Nilssen.'

He turned back to his dinner, and did not speak for what Nilssen felt was a very long while. Shepard was dressed in his Sunday suit of black; he had flung his coat-tails to the sides of his chair so that they would not be creased beneath him while he ate. His high-waisted trousers and collarless vest had a disapproving, funereal look, and his wide cravat—somewhat out of fashion, Nilssen noticed with a touch of condescension; his own cravat was thin and loosely tied, following the style of the day—seemed to accent the gaoler's aspect of admonishment still further. Even his cold supper was abstemious in its plainness. Nilssen himself had dined upon half a boiled chicken, served with mashed buttered turnip and a great deal of white sauce; he had drunk half a pitcher of a very nice wine, besides.

From elsewhere in the house, a clock sounded the quarter hour. Mrs. George moved beyond the flimsy walls, padding from room to room. Shepard remained fixated on his meal. Nilssen waited until Shepard had cleaned his plate of every last crumb, hoping that once his meal was concluded, the gaoler might begin to speak. When it became evident that this hope was a false one, he said, somewhat feebly, 'Well—what are you going to do?'

'My first action,' Shepard replied, daubing his mouth with a table napkin, 'will be to relieve you of all duties pertaining to the construction of the gaol-house. I will not be served by a man who breaks his word.'

'The investment will be returned to me?' said Nilssen.

'Not at all,' said Shepard. He tossed the table napkin onto his plate. 'In fact I consider that a most unreasonable request, given that the work is already well underway.'

Nilssen worked his mouth. At length he said, 'I understand.'

'You will not break your digger's code.'

'No.'

'Incredible.'

'I am sorry.'

Shepard pushed his plate away, becoming brisk. 'Mr. Lauderback's letter will be published to-morrow in the *Times*; I have an advance copy here.'

Nilssen saw that there was an opened letter on the table next to the gaoler's plate. He stepped forward, putting out his hand. 'May I—?'

But Shepard ignored him. 'The letter,' he went on, raising his voice slightly, 'does not refer to you by name. You should know that I will be writing to the editor myself tonight, in order to correct that omission. My response will be published below Mr. Lauderback's, as a formal reply.'

Nilssen tried again. 'May I read it?'

'You may read it to-morrow in the paper, along with every other man in Westland.' Shepard uttered the phrase with a dangerous emphasis.

'All right,' Nilssen said. He withdrew his hand. 'I take your meaning.'

Shepard paused before adding, 'Unless, of course, there's something that you'd like to tell me.'

In a voice of loathsome dejection, Nilssen said, 'Yes.'

'Yes?'

'Yes—there's something.'

Poor Harald Nilssen! Thinking that he might regain the gaoler's trust by means of a second transgression, as though by committing a second disloyalty, he might reverse the fact of the first! He had conceded in a panic—for it crushed Nilssen's spirit to be held in low esteem by other men. He could not bear to know that he was disliked, for to him there was no real difference between being disliked, and being dislikeable; every injury he sustained was an injury to his very selfhood. It was for reasons of self-protection that Nilssen dressed in the latest fashions, and spoke with affectation, and placed himself as the central character of every tale: he built his persona as a shield around his person, because he knew very well how little his person could withstand.

'Pray continue,' Shepard said.

'It's about—' (Nilssen cast about wildly) '—Mrs. Wells.'

'Indeed,' Shepard said. 'How so?'

'She was Lauderback's mistress.'

Shepard raised his eyebrows. 'Alistair Lauderback was cuckolding Crosbie Wells?'

Nilssen thought about it. 'Yes, I suppose he was. Well, it would depend on when Crosbie and Lydia got married, of course.'

'Go on,' Shepard said.

'The thing is—the thing is—he was blackmailed—Lauderback, I mean—and Crosbie Wells took home the ransom. That's the fortune, you see—in Crosbie's cottage.'

'How did this blackmail happen? And how do you know about it?'

Nilssen hesitated. He did not trust the gaoler's expression, which had suddenly become very greedy and intense.

'How do you know about it?' Shepard demanded.

'Somebody told me.'

'Who?'

'Mr. Staines,' said Nilssen—settling upon the man to whom he could do the least damage, in the short term at least.

'Was he the blackmailer—Staines?'

'I don't know,' said Nilssen, momentarily confused. 'I mean, yes, maybe.'

'Are you with him, or against him?'

'I—I don't know.'

Shepard looked annoyed. 'What have you got on him, then?' he said. 'You must have something on the man, if you're not sure about your allegiance.'

'There was a deed of gift,' Nilssen said miserably. 'In Crosbie Wells's stove—partly burned, as though someone tried to destroy it. The chaplain found it. When he went to the cottage to collect the body, the day after his death. He didn't tell you about it; he kept it for himself. He didn't tell Dr. Gillies either.'

Shepard betrayed no flicker of emotion at all. 'What kind of a deed of gift?'

Nilssen briefly detailed the particulars of the contract. He kept his eyes upon a spot some three feet to the left of the gaoler's face, and squinted oddly—for a bubble of despair was growing in his chest, pushing out against his breastbone. He had meant to reassure the gaoler of his loyalty by betraying this secret; now he saw that he had only confirmed his disloyalty, and his worthlessness. And yet—despite his misery—there was something terribly relieving about speaking of the Crown conspiracy aloud. He felt that a great weight was being lifted off his shoulders, just as he felt that a terrible weightlessness was settling in its place. He glanced at the gaoler quickly, and then away.

'Is Devlin your man?' Shepard said. 'Did you tell Devlin about this investment—and did he tell Lauderback?'

'Yes,' Nilssen said. 'That's right.' (What kind of wretched man was he—to accuse a *clergyman*? But of course it was only half a lie ... and better to accuse one man than all twelve.) 'I mean,' he added, 'I only suppose he told Lauderback. I don't know. I've never spoken to Lauderback about anything at all—as I told you.'

'So Devlin is Lauderback's man,' Shepard said.

'I don't know about that,' said Nilssen. 'I don't know about that at all.'

Shepard nodded. 'Well, Mr. Nilssen,' he said, rising from the table. 'That concludes our discussion, I think.'

It panicked Nilssen still further to be dismissed. 'The part about the deed,' he said. 'It's just—if you're going to mention it to the Reverend—'

'I imagine that I will, yes.'

'Well—can you leave my name out of it?' said Nilssen, with a look of pure misery on his face. 'You see: I can tell you where he's keeping it—the deed, I mean—and that way you can come upon it yourself, and there's no bridges broken on my end. Will you do that?'

Shepard studied him without pity. 'Where does he keep it?'

'I won't tell you until you give your word,' said Nilssen.

Shepard shrugged. 'All right.'

'Do you give your word?'

'Upon my honour, I will not speak your name to the chaplain of the gaol,' Shepard snapped. 'Where does he keep it?'

'In his Bible,' said Nilssen, very sadly. 'In his Bible, between the Old Testament, and the New.'

Φ

Since the construction of the gaol-house had begun in earnest Cowell Devlin and George Shepard had not seen a great deal of one another, save for in the evenings when Shepard returned from the construction site at Seaview to write his letters and tally his accounts. Devlin, who found the atmosphere of the temporary Police Camp much improved in Shepard's absence, had not pursued a deeper intimacy with the other man. Had he been pressed to pass judgment on the gaoler's character, he might, after a long pause, have conceded that he pitied Shepard's rigidity, and mourned the evident displeasure with which Shepard seemed to regard the world around him; after another pause, he might have added that he wished Shepard well, but did not expect the relations between them to develop beyond their present capacity, which was strictly professional, and none too warm.

That day was a Sunday, however, and construction on the terrace had halted for the day. Shepard had spent the morning at chapel, and the afternoon in his study at the Police Camp, from which place Harald Nilssen was now very rapidly departing; Devlin, who had recently returned from the Kaniere camp, was in the temporary gaol-house, preaching to the felons on the subject of rote prayer. He had brought his battered Bible with him, as he always did whenever he left his tent, though the nature of that day's sermon was such that he had had no cause to open it that afternoon; when Shepard stepped into the gaol-house it was lying, closed, upon a chair at Devlin's side.

Shepard waited for a lull in the conversation, which came about within moments, owing to his imposing presence in the room. Devlin turned an inquiring face up at him, and Shepard said, 'Good afternoon, Reverend. Hand me your Bible, would you please?'

Devlin frowned. 'My Bible?'

'If you wouldn't mind.'

The chaplain placed his palm over the book. 'Perhaps you might simply ask me what it is you seek,' he said. 'I pride myself that I do know my scriptures rather well.'

'I do not doubt it; and yet browsing is a pleasure to me,' Shepard replied.

'But of course you have a Bible of your own!'

'Of course,' Shepard agreed. 'However, it is the hour of my wife's devotions, and I do not like to disturb her.'

For a moment Devlin considered extracting the purloined deed himself—but its charred aspect would surely not escape the gaoler's comment, and in any case, he was surrounded by felons; where would he hide the thing?

'What is it that you are looking for, exactly?' he said. 'A verse— or an allusion—?'

'You are very chary of your Bible, for a man of God,' Shepard snapped. 'Heavens, man! I only wish to look through the pages! You will deny me that?'

And Devlin was obliged to surrender it. Shepard, thanking him, took the book back to his private residence, and closed the door.

Devlin's sermon on rote prayer was perversely applicable to the ensuing half hour, for it was with a ritual circularity that his attention kept straying to the gaoler's study, where the man would be seated behind his desk, turning the thin pages of the book in his great white hands. Devlin did not guess that Shepard might have known about the deed that he had concealed between the testaments, for his nature was not a suspicious one, and he did not take pleasure, as some men did, in believing himself to have been betrayed. He hoped, as the minutes dragged by, that Shepard would restrict his reading to the more ancient parts of the text; he hoped that the book would be returned to him with the charred deed undiscovered and untouched. Devlin knew very well that Shepard's faith was of a staunchly Levitican variety; it was not unreasonable to hope that he might confine his browsing to the Pentateuch, or to Chronicles and Kings. He was hardly likely to favour the minor prophets ... but the Gospels were standard fare, most especially for a Sunday. He was very likely to turn there, whatever his persuasion, and in that case he would almost certainly come across the hidden page.

Finally the afternoon's discussion came to an end, and Devlin, in a posture of some dread, took his leave of the felons in his spiritual charge. The duty sergeant nodded goodbye, stifling a yawn; Devlin let himself out; a hush fell over the gaol-house. He crossed the courtyard, mounted the steps to the porch of the gaoler's cottage, and knocked upon the door.

From within Shepard's deep voice bid him to enter; Devlin did so, and crossed the calico hallway to the gaoler's study. The door was open; Devlin saw at once that his Bible lay open on the gaoler's desk, with the charred slip of paper on top of it, in full view.

On this 11th day of October 1865 a sum of two thousand pounds is to be given to MISS ANNA WETHERELL, formerly of New South Wales, by MR. EMERY STAINES, formerly of New South Wales, as witnessed by MR. CROSBIE WELLS, presiding.

Shepard folded his hands and waited for his guest to speak.

'Something I found,' Devlin said. 'But it's no use to anyone.'

'No use to anyone?' Shepard queried, pleasantly. 'Why on earth do you say that?'

'It's invalid,' Devlin said. 'The principal hasn't signed. Therefore it's not legal.'

Cowell Devlin, like all men who will not admit fault to themselves, was loath to admit fault to any other man. He became very arch and condescending whenever he was accused of doing ill.

'No indeed,' said Shepard. 'It's not legal.'

'It's not *binding*—that's what I meant,' Devlin said, with a slight frown. 'It's not binding, in the legal sense.'

Shepard did not blink. 'Which is rather a shame, wouldn't you say?'

'Why is that?'

'If only Emery Staines *had* signed it—why, half of the fortune discovered at Crosbie Wells's cottage would belong to Anna Wetherell! That would be a turn of events, would it not?'

'But the fortune in the hermit's cottage never belonged to Emery Staines.'

'No?' Shepard said. 'Forgive me: you seem to be rather more certain of that fact than I am.'

Cowell Devlin knew very well that the gold in Crosbie Wells's cottage had originated from four gowns, sewn up by Lydia Wells, purchased by Anna Wetherell; he knew that the gold had been siphoned and then retorted by the goldsmith Ah Quee, only to be stolen by Staines, and concealed in Wells's cottage at some point thereafter. He could not say any of this to Shepard, however; instead he said, 'There is no reason to think that the fortune belonged to Mr. Staines.'

'Beyond the fact that Mr. Staines vanished upon the day of Mr. Wells's death, and Mr. Wells was not, to popular understanding, a man of means.' Shepard stabbed the deed with his index finger. 'This certainly seems pertinent, Reverend, to our case at hand. This document appears to indicate that the fortune originated with Staines—and that Staines meant to give half of it—*exactly* half— to a common prostitute. I would hazard to guess that Crosbie Wells, as his witness, was keeping the fortune for him, when he died.'

This was a reasonable hypothesis. Perhaps Shepard was right upon the latter point, Devlin thought, though of course he was mistaken upon the former. Aloud he said, 'You are right that it seems pertinent; however, as I have told you already, the contract is not valid. Mr. Staines has not signed his name.'

'I presume that you found this deed in Crosbie Wells's cottage, the day you went to collect his remains.'

'That is correct,' Devlin said.

'If you have kept such careful custody of it,' Shepard said, 'then I dare say it occurred to you how very valuable this deed might be. To certain persons. To Anna Wetherell, for instance. By this paper's authority, she could become the richest woman this side of the Southern Alps!'

'She could not,' Devlin said. 'The deed is unsigned.'

'If it were to be signed,' Shepard said.

'Emery Staines is dead,' Devlin said.

'Is he?' Shepard said. 'Dear me. Another certainty that we do not share.'

But Cowell Devlin was not easily intimidated. 'The promise of great riches is a dangerous thing,' he said, folding his hands across his navel in the clerical way. 'It is a temptation like no other, for it is the temptation of great influence and great opportunity, and these are things we all desire. If Miss Wetherell were to be told about this deed, her hopes would be falsely raised. She would start dreaming of great influence and great opportunity; she would no longer be contented with the life she led before. This was a circumstance I feared. I therefore resolved to keep the information to myself, at least until Emery Staines was either recovered, or found to be dead. If he *is* found dead, I will destroy the deed. But if he lives, I shall go to him, and show him the paper, and ask him whether he wishes to sign it. The choice would be his own.'

'And what if Staines is never found?' the gaoler said. 'What then?'

'I made my decision with compassion, Mr. Shepard,' Devlin said firmly. 'I feared very much what would happen to poor Miss Wetherell, should that deed of gift be made public, or should it fall into the wrong hands. If Mr. Staines is never found, then no hopes will be dashed, and no blood spilled, and no faith lost. I judge that to be no small mercy. Don't you?'

Shepard's pale eyes had become wet: a sign that he was thinking hard. 'As witnessed by Crosbie Wells,' he murmured, 'presiding.'

'In any case,' Devlin added, 'it's hardly likely that a man would give such a great deal of money to a prostitute. Most likely it is a joke or deceit of some kind.'

Shepard looked suddenly amused. 'You doubt the woman's talents?'

'You mistake me,' Devlin said calmly. 'I only meant that for a man to give two thousand pounds to a whore is a very unlikely situation. As a gift, I mean—and all at once.'

Abruptly Shepard shut the Bible with a snap, trapping the purloined document between the pages. He handed the book back to the chaplain, already reaching with his other hand for his pen, as though the affair was no longer of any interest to him.

'Thank you for the loan of your Bible,' he said, and nodded to indicate that Devlin was free to leave. He then bent over his ledger, and began to tally up his columns.

Devlin hovered uncertainly for a moment, the Bible in his hand. The charred document protruded from one edge, dividing the profile of the book into unequal halves.

'But what do you think?' he said at last. 'What do you make of it?'

Shepard did not pause in his writing. 'What do I make of what?'

'The contract!'

'I imagine you are right: it must be a joke or deceit of some kind,' Shepard said. He placed a finger on his ledger, to hold his place, and then reached over to dip his pen into his inkwell.

'Oh,' said Devlin. 'Yes.'

'The contract is invalid, as you say,' Shepard said conversationally. He tapped the nib of the pen against the rim of the inkwell.

'Yes.'

'The witness is certainly dead, and the principal almost certainly so.'

'Yes.'

'But if you want an answer from the horse's mouth, then perhaps you ought to go along to the Wayfarer's Fortune tonight, with all the other heathens.'

'To speak with Mr. Staines?'

'To speak with Anna,' the gaoler said, with pointed disapproval. 'Now, if you don't mind, Reverend, I have rather a lot of work to do.'

After Devlin had closed the door behind him, Shepard laid down his pen, went to his bookcase, and pulled out a file, out of which he extracted a single sheet of paper: the only copy of the contract he had made, three weeks ago, with Harald Nilssen, under which the commission merchant had promised not to speak of his four-hundred pound investment to any other man. Shepard struck a match on the side of the cabinet and touched it to the piece of paper, holding it lightly by one corner and tilting it until the document was aflame, and the signatures obscured. When he could hold it no longer he tossed it to the floor, watched it shrink to a grey nothing, and kicked the ashes aside with the toe of his boot.

Sitting back down at his desk, he pulled a fresh sheet of paper from beneath his ledger, took up his pen, and dipped his nib. Then, in a slow, measured hand, he wrote:

A GIFT OF CONSCIENCE—To the Editor of the West Coast Times.

18 February 1866

Sir—

I write in response to Mr. ALISTAIR LAUDERBACK, Provincial Councilman, M.P., who casts damaging aspersions upon the undersigned, and therefore, upon all his associates, including the Westland Public Works Committee, the Municipal Council, the Office of the Commissioner, the Hokitika Board, &c. It is my duty to correct Mr. Lauderback's errors: of propriety, of decency, and of fact.

Indeed the construction of the future Hokitika Gaol-House was aided in the large part by a donation made by a Westland man. Mr. Harald Nilssen, of Nilssen & Co., donated to the Council a sum of approximately four hundred pounds, to be used, as per his personal instruction, for public good. This sum represented the commission received by him as payment for honest employment. It was, as Mr. Lauderback attests, a portion of the fortune discovered on Mr Crosbie Wells's estate, to which Mr. Nilssen, commission merchant, was legally entitled, as payment for services satisfactorily rendered. Mr. Lauderback will be pleased to recall that, in legal phrasing, a 'donation' is distinct from an 'investment' in that a donation does not create a relationship of the debtor-

creditor variety; in plain language, a donation does not have to be repaid.
In understanding that Mr. Nilssen's donation was an act of charity of the
most virtuous and selfless order, Mr. Lauderback will further acknowledge
that no laws have been broken and no regulations breached.

I hold that the profoundest and most enduring testament to progress in
civilisation is the creation of public works, and I am satisfied that the
Hokitika Gaol-House will bear up under this definition in every respect.
Should Mr. Lauderback find this explanation insufficiently transparent for
his tastes, I cordially invite him to disclose to the voting public what he
has hitherto concealed: that he has enjoyed a formerly intimate relation
with Mrs. Lydia Wells, widow to Crosbie. I anticipate Mr. Lauderback's
full disclosure upon this matter, and remain,

Yours &c,

GEORGE M. SHEPARD

When he was done Shepard blotted the page, reached for a
clean sheet of paper, and transcribed the letter in full—creating a
replica so exact, in fact, that one would have to compare them for
quite some time before one perceived the smallest difference. He
then folded both pages, sealed them, and wrote two addresses in his
laborious hand. Once the wax was dry, he rang the bell for Mrs.
George, and asked her to summon the penny postman for the
second time that day. This instruction was promptly carried out.

The penny postman was a freckled thing with a mass of yellow
curls.

'This one to Löwenthal at the *Times*,' Shepard said. 'This gets
delivered first. And this one goes to Harald Nilssen at the Auction
Yards on Gibson Quay. All right?'

'Is there a message?' said the young man, pocketing the letters.

'Only for Mr. Nilssen,' said Shepard. 'You tell Mr. Nilssen that
he's expected at work to-morrow morning. Can you remember
that? Tell him no complaints, no hard feelings, and no questions
asked.'

MARS IN CAPRICORN

*In which Gascoigne finds common ground with Francis
Carver; Sook Yongsheng acts upon a false impression; and
Quee Long gives the avenger some advice.*

Aubert Gascoigne had what one might call a lubber's love of ships.
In the last three weeks he had ventured to the Hokitika spit several
times, in order to meditate upon the fractured hull of the *Godspeed*,
and to chart her progress as she was shunted, by degrees, closer and
closer to the shore. Now that the wreck had at last been hauled
onto the sand, he had a much better opportunity to look her over,
and to gauge, with his lubber's eye, the extent of the damage that
she had sustained. It was here that he had come, upon taking his
leave of Moody—having no other occupation, that Sunday afternoon, for he had read the papers already, and he was not thirsty,
and the day was much too bright and cheerful to remain indoors.

He had been sitting with his back against the beacon for some
hours, watching the progress of the ship's recovery, and turning a
green-flecked stone in his hands; beside him he had constructed a
little castle, the ramparts made of stacks of flattened pebbles,
pressed into mounds of sand. When, some time after five, the wind
suddenly changed direction, blowing his collar against his neck,
and sending a damp chill down his spine, Gascoigne decided to
retire. He stood, dusting himself down, and was wondering
whether he ought to kick his castle apart or leave it intact when he
perceived that a man was standing some fifty yards away. The

man's feet were planted rather far apart, and his arms were folded, as though in disapproval; his posture in general communicated an implacability of the most humourless kind, as did his dress, which was sombre. He turned his head slightly, and Gascoigne caught, for a brief moment, the glassy shine of a scar.

Gascoigne and Francis Carver had never formally met, though of course the latter's reputation was well known to Gascoigne, coloured chiefly by the report that Anna Wetherell had given more than a month ago on the subject of the murder of her unborn child. Such a report was more than sufficient provocation to avoid the former captain altogether, but Gascoigne's ill-feeling was of the kind that needed private affirmation, rather than public display: he gained a real pleasure in befriending a man whom he privately had cause to despise, for he liked very much the feeling that his regard for others was a private font, a well, that he could muddy, or drink from, at his own discreet pleasure, and on his own time.

He walked up to Carver, already raising his hat.

'Excuse me, sir—are you the captain of this craft?'

Francis Carver eyed him, and then, after a moment, nodded. 'I was.'

The white scar on his cheek was slightly puckered at one end, as when a seamstress leaves the needle in the fabric, before she quits for the day; this phantom needle lay just beyond the edge of his mouth, and seemed to tug it upward, as if trying to coax his stern expression—unsuccessfully—into a smile.

'If I could introduce myself: Aubert Gascoigne,' Gascoigne said, putting out his hand. 'I am a clerk at the Magistrate's Court.'

'A clerk?' Carver eyed him again. 'What kind?' Rather reluctantly, he shook Gascoigne's hand—showing his reluctance by way of a grip that was limp and very brief.

'Very low-level,' Gascoigne said, without condescension. 'Petty claims, mostly—nothing too large—but there is the occasional insurance claim that comes across our desks. *That* craft, for example.' He pointed to the wreck of a steamer, lying on its side just beyond the river mouth, some fifty yards from where they were standing. 'We managed to scrape even on that one, though barely.

The master was very well pleased; he had been facing down a five-hundred-pound debt.'

'Insurance,' said Carver.

'Among other things, yes. I have some personal acquaintance with the subject also,' Gascoigne added, pulling out his cigarette case, 'for my late wife's father was a maritime insurer.'

'Which firm?' said Carver.

'Lloyd's—of London.' Gascoigne snapped open the silver case. 'I have been charting *Godspeed*'s progress, these past few weeks. I am gratified to see that she has been hauled clear of the surf at last. What a project it has been! A monumental effort, if I may praise the work of the crew ... and *your* work, sir, in commandeering it.'

Carver watched him for a moment, and then turned his gaze back to the deck of the *Godspeed*. With his eyes fixed on his foundered craft, he said, 'What do you want?'

'Certainly not to offend you,' Gascoigne said, holding his cigarette lightly between his fingers, and pausing a moment, his palms upturned. 'I am sure I do not mean to intrude upon your privacy in any way. I have been watching the progress of the ship's recovery, that's all. It is rather a rare privilege, to see such a craft upon dry land. One really gets a sense of her.'

Carver kept his eyes on the ship. 'I meant: are you set to sell me something?'

Gascoigne was lighting his cigarette, and took a moment to answer. 'Not at all,' he said at last, blowing a white puff of smoke over his shoulder. 'I'm not affiliated with any insurance firms. This is a personal interest, you might say. A curiosity.'

Carver said nothing.

'I like to sit on the beach on Sundays,' Gascoigne added, 'when the weather is nice. But you must tell me if my private interest offends you.'

Carver jerked his head. 'Didn't mean to be uncivil.'

Gascoigne waved the apology away. 'One hates to see a fine ship come to ground.'

'She's fine all right.'

'Marvellous. A frigate, is she not?'

'A barque.'

Gascoigne murmured his appreciation. 'British-made?'

He nodded. 'That's copper sheathing you can see.'

Gascoigne nodded absently. 'Yes, a fine craft ... I do hope she was insured.'

'You can't drop anchor at a port without insurance,' Carver said. 'Same for every vessel. Without it they won't let you land. Thought you'd know that, if you know anything about insurance at all.'

He spoke in a voice that was flat and full of contempt, seeming not to care how his words might be interpreted, or remembered, or used.

'Of course, of course,' Gascoigne said airily. 'I mean to say that I am glad that you are not out of pocket—for your sake.'

Carver snorted. 'I'll be a thousand pounds down when all is said and done,' he said. 'Everything that you can see right now is costing money—and out of my pocket.'

Gascoigne paused a moment before asking, 'What about P&I?'

'Don't know.'

'Protection and indemnity,' Gascoigne explained. 'Against extraordinary liabilities.'

'Don't know,' Carver said again.

'You don't belong to a shipowners' association?'

'No.'

Gascoigne inclined his head gravely. 'Ah,' he said. 'So you'll have been liable for all this'—indicating, with a sweep of his hand, the beached hull before him, the screw jacks, the horses, the tugboats, the rollers, and the winch.

'Yes,' said Carver, still without emotion. 'Everything you can see. And I'm bound to pay every man a guinea more than he's worth, for standing about and tying his shoelaces—and untying them—and conferencing about conferencing, until everyone's out of breath, and I'm a thousand pounds down.'

'I am sorry,' Gascoigne said. 'Would you like a cigarette?'

Carver eyed his silver case. 'No,' he said after a moment. 'Thanks. Don't care for them.'

Gascoigne drew deeply on his own cigarette and stood for a moment, thinking.

'You certainly seem set to sell me something,' Carver said again.

'A cigarette?' Gascoigne laughed. 'That was offered quite free of charge.'

'I reckon I'm still freer for having turned it down,' said Carver, and Gascoigne laughed again.

'Tell me,' he said. 'How long ago did you purchase this ship?'

'You've got a lot of questions,' Carver said. 'What's your business asking them?'

'Well, I suppose it doesn't really matter,' Gascoigne said. 'It would only matter if you made the purchase less than a year ago. Never mind.'

But he had snagged Carver's interest. The other man looked over at him and then said, 'I've had her ten months. Since May.'

'Ah!' Gascoigne said. 'Well. That's very interesting. That could work in your favour, you know.'

'How?'

But Gascoigne didn't answer at once; instead he squinted his eyes, and pretended to brood. 'The man who sold it to you. Did he pass on conventional cover? That is to say: did you inherit an extant policy, or did you take out a policy on your own account?'

'I didn't take out anything,' Carver said.

'Was the vendor a shipowner in the professional sense? Did he own more than just *Godspeed*, for example?'

'He had a couple of others,' Carver said. 'Clipper ships. Charters.'

'Not steam?'

'Sail,' said Carver. 'Why?'

'And where did you say you were coming from, when you ran aground?'

'Dunedin. Are you going to tell me where all these questions are headed?'

'Only from Dunedin,' Gascoigne said, nodding. 'Yes. Now, if you'll forgive my impertinence once last time, I wonder if I might ask about the circumstances of the wreck itself. I trust there was no dereliction of duty, or anything of that kind, that caused the ship to founder?'

Carver shook his head. 'Tide was low, but we were well offshore,' he said. 'I dropped sixty-five feet of chain and she caught, so I dropped two anchors and another twenty feet of chain. I made the call to keep her on a reasonable leash and wait until the morning. Next thing we knew, we were broadside on the spit. It was raining, and the moon was clouded over. The wind blew out the beacons. Wasn't anything anyone could have done. Nothing that might be called dereliction. Not under my command.'

This, for Francis Carver, was a very long speech; at its conclusion he folded his arms across his chest, and his expression closed. He frowned at Gascoigne.

'Listen,' he said. 'What's your interest on account of? You'd do well to tell me plain: I don't like a slippery dealer.'

Gascoigne remembered that the man had murdered his own child. The thought was strangely thrilling. Lightly he said, 'I've thought of something that might be of some help to you.'

Carver's scowl deepened. 'Who says I need help?'

'You're right,' said Gascoigne. 'I am impertinent.'

'Say it, though,' said Carver.

'Well, here,' said Gascoigne. 'As I mentioned before, my late wife's father worked in shipping insurance. His speciality was P&I—protection and indemnity.'

'I told you I don't have that.'

'Yes,' Gascoigne said, 'but there's a good chance that the man who sold you this ship—what was his name?'

'Lauderback,' said Carver.

Gascoigne paused in a show of surprise. 'Not the politician!'

'Yes.'

'Alistair Lauderback? But he's in Hokitika now—running for the Westland seat!'

'Go on with what you were saying. P&I.'

'Yes,' Gascoigne said, shaking his head. 'Well. There's a good chance that Mr. Lauderback, if he owned several ships, belonged to some sort of a shipowners' association. There's a good chance that he paid a yearly fee into a mutual fund, called P&I, as an additional insurance that was of a slightly different nature than what you and I might think of as conventional cover.'

'To protect the cargo?'

'No,' said Gascoigne. 'P&I works more like a mutual pool, into which all the shipowners pay a yearly fee, and out of which they can then draw down funds if they find themselves liable for any damages that regular insurers refuse to touch. Liabilities of the kind that you're facing now. Wreck removal, for instance. It's possible that *Godspeed* could remain protected, even though the ownership of the ship has changed.'

'How?' He spoke the word without curiosity.

'Well, if P&I was taken out some years ago, and this is the first significant accident that this particular ship has sustained, then Mr. Lauderback might be in credit against *Godspeed*. You see, P&I doesn't work like regular insurance—there aren't any shareholders, and no company, really: nobody's looking to make a profit off anyone else. Instead it's a co-operative body of men, all of them shipowners themselves. Every man pays his dues every year, until there's enough in the pool to cover them all. After that, the ships stay covered—at least, until something goes wrong, and then somebody has to dip into the pool for some reason. The notion of being "in credit" applies very nearly.'

'Like a private account,' Carver said. 'For *Godspeed*.'

'Exactly.'

Carver thought about this. 'How would I know about it?'

Gascoigne shrugged. 'You could ask around. The association would have to be registered, and the shipowners would have to be listed by name. This is assuming that Lauderback indeed belongs to such a group, of course—but I would venture to say that it's very likely that he does.'

In fact this was more than likely: it was certain. Alistair Lauderback *did* have protection and indemnity against all his crafts, and each ship *was* in credit to the tune of nearly a thousand pounds, and Carver *was* legally entitled to draw down these funds to help pay for the removal of the wreck from the Hokitika spit, so long as he filed his appeal before the middle of May—whereupon a year would have passed since the sale of the craft, and Lauderback's legal obligation to *Godspeed* would cease. Gascoigne knew all this for certain because he had made the inquiries himself, first in the offices of Balfour Shipping, and then in the news archives of the *Times*, and then at the Harbourmaster's office, and then at the Reserve Bank. He knew that Lauderback belonged to a small co-operative of shipowners called the Garrity Group, so named for its most prominent member, John Hincher Garrity, who was (as Gascoigne had discovered) an enthusiastic champion of the Age of Sail, the imminent twilight of that era notwithstanding, and who was also, it transpired, the incumbent Member of Parliament for the electorate of Heathcote in the East, and Lauderback's very good friend.

We ought to clarify that Gascoigne had made these inquiries in the service of a separate investigation—one that was not concerned with maritime insurance, or with John Hincher Garrity, in the slightest. Since the night of the 27th of January he had spent long hours in the Harbourmaster's office, poring over old logs and old pages of the shipping news; he had worked with Löwenthal to examine all the old political bulletins in the *Leader*, the *Otago Witness*, the *Daily Southern Cross*, and the *Lyttelton Times*; and he had skimmed through all the archives at the Courthouse that pertained to George Shepard's appointment, the temporary Police Camp, and the future gaol. He had been looking for something very particular: one thread of evidence to connect Shepard to Lauderback, or Lauderback to Crosbie Wells, or Crosbie Wells to Shepard—or perhaps, to connect all three. Gascoigne felt very sure that at least one of these possible connexions was significant to the mystery at hand. So far, however, his research had turned up nothing useful at all.

The discovery that *Godspeed* was insured against extraordinary damages was no exception to this 'nothing useful', for Lauderback's insurance history had no bearing upon the case of Crosbie Wells, and nor was it connected in any way to George Shepard, or to the gaol-house currently under construction. But Gascoigne *did* have some experience in the field of maritime insurance, as he had admitted to Francis Carver, and he had not lied in saying that the subject was of some curiosity to him, being the profession of his former father-in-law, and therefore the subject of much drawing-room conversation over years past. He had made a note of Lauderback's affiliation to the Garrity Group with interest, filing it away in his mind as something to be examined in better detail at a later time.

Aubert Gascoigne knew that Francis Carver was a brute, and he did not care to court his friendship; he felt, however, that to get Carver on his side would be somehow valuable, and he had solicited the other man's attention on the spit that afternoon with that purpose in mind.

Carver was still thinking about protection and indemnity. 'I suppose I'd need Lauderback's consent,' he said. 'To lay claim to that cover. I suppose I'd need him to sign something.'

'Perhaps you would,' Gascoigne replied, 'but the fact that only ten months have passed since *Godspeed* changed hands might be worth something. That might be a loophole.' (Indeed it was.) 'And the fact that you inherited a standard policy from Lauderback might be worth something, too: why, if you inherit the whole, you inherit its parts, do you not?' (Indeed you do.) With a flourish Gascoigne concluded, 'You were sailing in New Zealand waters, and if there was no dereliction on your part, as you say, then it's very possible that you will be entitled to lay claim to those funds.'

He had done his research well. Carver nodded, seeming impressed.

'Anyway,' Gascoigne said, sensing that the seeds of curiosity had been adequately sowed, 'you ought to look into it. You might save yourself a great deal of money.' He turned his cigarette over in his hand, examining its ember, to give Carver a chance to look him over unobserved.

'What's your stake in this?' said Carver presently.

'None whatsoever,' said Gascoigne. 'As I told you, I work for the Magistrate's Court.'

'You've got a friend in P&I, maybe.'

'No,' Gascoigne said. 'I don't. That's not the way it works—as I've told you.' He flicked the end of his cigarette onto the rocks below the beacon.

'You're just a man who tells another man about loopholes.'

'I suppose I am,' Gascoigne said.

'And then strolls away.'

Gascoigne lifted his hat. 'I shall take that as my cue,' he said. 'Good afternoon—Captain . . .?'

'Carver,' said the former captain, shaking Gascoigne's hand very firmly this time. 'Frank Carver's my name.'

'And I'm Aubert Gascoigne,' Gascoigne reminded him, with a pleasant smile. 'I can be found at the Courthouse, should you ever need me. Well—good luck with *Godspeed*.'

'All right,' Carver said.

'She really is a marvellous craft.'

Gascoigne, strolling away, felt a kind of dawning wonder at himself. He kept his face forward, and did not look back—knowing that Carver's dark eyes had followed him down the spit, and around the edge of the quay, and all the way to the southern end of Revell-street, where he turned the corner, and disappeared from view.

Φ

Sook Yongsheng, en route to Kaniere to seek an interview with his compatriot Quee Long, was at that moment very deep in thought, his hands locked behind his back, his eyes fixed sightlessly upon the ground before him. He hardly registered the figures he passed along the roadside, nor the laden dray-carts that clattered by, nor the infrequent riders making for the gorge—every man hatless and in shirtsleeves, enjoying the pale summer sun that seemed, for its rarity, to shine with a providential, good-hearted light. The mood along the Kaniere-road was merry; through the trees there came, occasionally, a snatch of a hymn, sung unaccompanied and in unison, from one of the makeshift chapels at the inland camps. Ah Sook paid no attention. His reunion that morning with Lydia Greenway—now Lydia Wells—had deeply unsettled him, and as a kind of conciliation to his unrest he was replaying his own history in his mind—narrating the very same tale, in fact, that he had related to Ah Quee three weeks ago.

When Francis Carver had first made his introduction to the

Sook family he had been but one-and-twenty, and Ah Sook, as a boy of twelve, had very naturally looked up to him. Carver was a terse and brooding young man, born in Hong Kong to a British merchant trader, and raised at sea. He was fluent in Cantonese, though he cherished no love for China, and meant to leave that place as soon as he acquired a ship of his own—an ambition he referenced very frequently. He worked for the Kwangchow branch of the merchant firm Dent & Co., of which his father was a high-ranking official, and he was responsible for overseeing the transfer of Chinese wares to and from the export warehouses along the Pearl River. One of these warehouses was owned by Sook Yongsheng's father, Sook Chun-Yuen.

Sook Yongsheng understood very little about the financial operations of his father's business. He knew that the Sook warehouse served as a liaison point for buyers, the majority of which were British merchant firms. He knew that Dent & Co. was by far the most illustrious and well connected of these firms, and that his father was very proud of this association. He knew that his father's clients all paid for their wares in silver ore, and that this was a further point of pride for Sook Chun-Yuen; he knew also that his father hated opium, and that he held the imperial commissioner, Lin Tse-Hsu, in very high esteem. Ah Sook did not know the significance of any of these particulars; but he was a loyal son, and he accepted his father's beliefs without comment, trusting them to be both virtuous and wise.

In February 1839, the Sook warehouse was targeted for an imperial investigation—a fairly routine procedure, but a dangerous one, for under Commissioner Lin's decree, any Chinese merchants harbouring opium faced the penalty of death. Sook Chun-Yuen welcomed the imperial forces into his warehouse cordially—where they discovered, hidden amongst the tea, some thirty or forty crates of opium resin, each weighing roughly fifty pounds. Sook Chun-Yuen's protestations came to nothing. He was executed without trial, and at once.

Ah Sook did not know what to believe. His natural trust in his father's honesty prompted him to believe that the man had been framed, and his natural trust in his father's acumen made him doubt that the man *could* have been framed. He was in two minds—but he had no time to contemplate the matter, for within a week of the execution, war broke out in Kwangchow. Fearing for his own safety, and for the safety of his mother, who had been driven near to madness with grief, Ah Sook turned to the only man he knew to trust: the young delegate from Dent & Co., Francis Carver.

It transpired that Mr. Carver was more than happy to take on the Sook family business as a holding, and to accept all burdens of organisation and management upon himself—at least, he said, until Ah Sook's grief had run its course, and the civil wars had quieted, or resolved themselves. In a show of kindness to the boy, Carver suggested that he might like to continue working in the export trade, in order to honour the memory of his late father, disgraced though that memory now was. If Ah Sook wished it, Carver could find work for him packing merchandise—a decent, honourable job, if menial, which would see him through the war. This proposition gratified Ah Sook extremely. Within hours of this conversation he had become Francis Carver's employee.

For the next fifteen years Ah Sook packed chaff around specimens of porcelain and china, wrapped bolts of printed silk in paper, stacked caddies of tea into boxes, loaded and unloaded packages, hammered the lids of shipping crates, pasted labels onto cartons, and itemised those finely wrought and purposeless objects that were termed, upon the merchandise inventories, *Chinoiserie*. He saw Carver only infrequently over this period, for the latter was often at sea, but their interactions, when they happened, were always cordial: it was their custom to sit upon the wharf together and share a bottle of liquor, gazing out over the estuary as the water turned from brown to blue to silver, and finally to black, whereupon Carver would rise, clap his hand upon Ah Sook's shoulder, toss the empty bottle into the river, and depart.

In the summer of 1854 Carver returned to Kwangchow after several months' absence, and informed Ah Sook—now a man of nearly thirty years—that their agreement was finally to come to an end. His lifelong ambition to one day command a trade vessel had at last been realised: Dent & Co. was to establish a trade run to Sydney and the Victorian goldfields, and his father had chartered a handsome clipper ship, the *Palmerston*, on his behalf. It was a fine promotion, and one that Carver could not ignore. He had come, he said, to bid the Sook family, and this era of his life, goodbye.

Ah Sook received Carver's farewell with sadness. By this time his mother was dead, and the opium wars had given way to a new rebellion in Kwangchow—one that was bloody, and incensed: it promised war, and perhaps even the end of empire. Change was in the air. Once Carver was gone, the warehouse sold, and the relationship with Dent & Co. dissolved, Ah Sook would be severed from his former life completely. On impulse, he begged to be taken along. He could try his hand on the Victoria goldfields, to which place many of his countrymen had already sailed; perhaps, he said, he could forge a new life for himself there, as they had done. There was nothing left for him in China.

Carver acquiesced to his suggestion without enthusiasm. He supposed that Ah Sook could come along, though he would be required to pay for his own ticket, and keep well out of the way. The *Palmerston* was scheduled to break her journey in Sydney, spending two weeks loading and unloading cargo at Port Jackson before continuing on to Melbourne in the south; during these two weeks, Ah Sook must keep to himself, and not bother Carver— henceforth styled 'Captain'—in any way. When the *Palmerston* landed at Port Phillip, they would part as amicable strangers, owing nothing, expecting nothing; thenceforth, they would never see each other again. Ah Sook agreed. In a frenzy of sudden excitement, he relinquished his few possessions, changed his meagre savings into pounds, and purchased a standard ticket in the highest class of berth that Carver would permit him to occupy (third). He was, he soon discovered, the ship's only passenger.

The journey to Sydney passed without incident; looking back, Ah Sook remembered it only as a static, nauseated haze, slowly brightening, like the onset of a migraine. As the craft made her long approach into the wide, low throat of the harbour, Ah Sook, weak and malnourished after many weeks at sea, struggled from his berth at last, and ventured topside. The quality of the light seemed very strange to him; he felt that in China the light was thinner, whiter, cleaner. The Australian light was very yellow, and there was a thickened quality to its brightness, as though the sun were always on the point of setting, even in the morning, or at noon.

Upon reaching the mooring at Darling Harbour, the ship's captain hardly paused to exchange his sea legs for a steadier gait: he walked down the *Palmerston*'s gangway, along the quay, and into a dockside brothel, without so much as a backward glance. His crew was fast upon his heels; in no time at all, therefore, Ah Sook found himself alone. He left the ship, committing the location of its mooring to memory, and promptly set off inland—resolving, somewhat naïvely, to get a measure of the country in which he was to live.

Ah Sook's English was very poor, simply for the reason that he and Carver had always conducted their conversations in Cantonese, and he was not acquainted with any other English-speaking men. He looked for Chinese faces on the docks, in vain; venturing further inland, he walked the streets for hours, looking for a painted sign—even a single character—that he could understand. He found nothing. Presently he ventured to the customhouse, where he produced one of the banknotes that he had folded inside the band of his hat, and held it up: perhaps the money could speak where he could not. The customhouse official raised his eyebrows—but before he said a word, Ah Sook's hat was wrenched from his hand. He wheeled about and saw a boy, barefoot, running at speed away from him. Outraged, Ah Sook yelled, and gave chase, but the boy was fast, and knew the warren of the docks familiarly; within minutes, he was gone.

Ah Sook searched for the boy until well after nightfall. When finally he gave up and returned to the customhouse, the customs officials only shook their heads and spread their hands. They pointed inland, and spoke a volley of words. Ah Sook did not know what they were pointing at, or what they were saying. He felt a sob rising in his throat. His hatband had contained all the money he owned, save for the single banknote that he had been holding in his

other hand: he was now all but destitute. Distraught, he removed
his boot, placed this last banknote in the worn hollow beneath his
heel, replaced his boot, and returned to the *Palmerston*. At least, he
thought, there was one man in Sydney who could speak Cantonese.

Ah Sook approached the brothel cautiously. From within he
could hear the sound of a piano—the timbre unfamiliar to him: he
felt that it had a squarish, comfortable sound. He was lingering on
the threshold, wondering whether he should knock, when the door
was wrenched open, and a man appeared in the doorway.

Ah Sook bowed. He attempted to explain, as courteously as he
was able, that he wished to speak to a man named Carver, captain
of the *Palmerston*. The man in the doorway responded with a string
of unintelligible sounds. Ah Sook persisted, repeating Carver's name
very slowly and carefully. He received the same response. Next he
tried to indicate with the flat of his hand that he wished to step
around the man, and venture inside, so that he might speak to
Carver himself. This was a mistake. The man grabbed Ah Sook's
shirt collar with one enormous hand, picked him up, and threw him
bodily into the street. Ah Sook fell painfully, jarring his wrist and his
hip. The man pushed up his shirtsleeves and advanced down the
stairs. He took one final drag of his cigar before throwing it, with a
flick of his wrist, sideways into the quay. Then, grinning, he put up
his fists. Ah Sook became very anxious. He put up his hands also,
to indicate that he did not wish to fight, and begged for mercy. The
man called something over his shoulder—perhaps an instruction—
and within moments a second man, his face much thinner, his nose
more hooked, had appeared at the doorway of the brothel. This
second man darted around behind Ah Sook, hauled him to his feet,
and pinned his hands behind his back—a pose that left his face and
torso undefended. The pair exchanged words. Ah Sook struggled,
but he could not wrench his wrists free. The first man, raising his
forearms in front of his face, shifted his weight lightly from foot to
foot. He approached and then retreated several times, stepping very
lightly, and then darted forward and began to batter Ah Sook's face
and stomach with his fists. The man behind him crowed something.
The first grunted in return and fell back, only to advance again in

the same style, and release a second flurry of blows. Soon the revellers inside the brothel were roused. They spilled into the street, bringing the noise of their party with them.

Francis Carver appeared in the doorway of the brothel. He had removed his jacket; he was in ruffled shirtsleeves and a blue necktie, tied with a sloppy four-in-hand knot. His placed his hands loosely upon his hips and surveyed the fight with an irritated look. Ah Sook met his eyes.

'*Mh goi bong ngoh,*' he cried through a mouthful of blood. '*Mh goi bong ngoh!*'

Francis Carver seemed to look right through him. He made no sign that he could understand Ah Sook at all. One of the other revellers said something, and Carver responded in English, shifting his gaze away.

'*Pang yao! Ho pang yao!*'

But Carver did not look at him again. A copper-haired woman appeared next to him in the doorway, snaking beneath his arm; he caught her around the waist, and pulled her body close to his own. He murmured something into her hair. She laughed, and they went back inside.

Soon the second man could not support the dead weight of Ah Sook's body; he dropped him, complaining, evidently, of the blood that had spattered on his jacket and his cuffs. The first man began to kick Ah Sook where he lay, but evidently this was not as entertaining as his former sport, and soon the crowd lost interest and dispersed. The first man gave Ah Sook a final kick in the ribs with the toe of his boot, and then returned inside also. When he re-entered the brothel there was a rising wave of laughter, and then the piano struck up a new tune.

Using his elbows and his knees, Ah Sook dragged his broken body to the alley, out of sight. He lay in the shadow, feeling a sharp pain each time he drew a breath. He watched the masts of the ships move back and forth. The sun went down. After a time he heard the lamplighter's tread upon the quay, and near him, the hiss and thump as the gas lamp was ignited. The darkness turned grey. He feared that all his ribs were broken. He could feel a sticky wetness, like a sponge, above his hairline. His left eye had closed. He did not know if he had strength enough to stand.

Presently the rear door of the brothel opened, spilling yellow light onto the stones. Quick steps padded into the alley. Ah Sook heard the clink of a tin bowl being set down upon the cobbles, and then felt a cool touch of a hand upon his brow. He opened his right eye. A young woman with a thinly pointed face and buck-teeth was kneeling before him. Murmuring phrases he did not understand, she dipped a square of cloth in warm water, and began to daub the blood from his face. He let her voice wash over him. She was wearing a starched apron, in the manner of a barmaid: she must work inside, he thought. This guess was confirmed when, after a moment, there came a shouted summons from within, and, muttering, she put the cloth down and darted away.

Several hours passed. The piano player ceased, and the noises from within began to dwindle. Ah Sook slept a while, and awoke to find that all was very quiet, and the barmaid had returned. This time she was carrying a caddy under one arm, several implements rolled in cloth, and a spirit lantern. She knelt beside him, placing the lantern carefully upon the cobbles, and twisting the dial so the globe flared white. Ah Sook turned his head, as gently as he was able, and saw, with some surprise, that the caddy she was carrying bore his own family name, stamped in Chinese. He gave a start, which the woman interpreted strangely; she smiled and nodded, and placed her finger against her lips, to signify a secret. She then opened the caddy, fished around amongst the tea leaves, and withdrew from the interior a small square package, wrapped in paper. She smiled at him. Ah Sook was confused. He turned his head painfully to the right, so as to see the implements the woman had unrolled from her bundle—and saw a short, inelegant pipe, laid out next to a needle, a knife, and a tin bowl. He turned back to her, questioningly, but she was busy adjusting the wick of the lamp, assembling the pipe, and preparing the resin. When at last the opium was bubbling, and a tendril of white smoke escaped the thin aperture of the bowl, she pressed the mouthpiece of the pipe to Ah Sook's lips. He was too exhausted to decline. He took the vapour into his mouth, and held it there.

There came a dawn in his chest, a liquid light. A perfect calm flooded through his body. The pain in his head and chest drained out of him, as simply and suddenly as water seeping through a piece of silk. Opium, he thought, dully. Opium. It was extraordinary. The drug was extraordinary. It was a miracle, a cure. She passed him the pipe again and he supped from its end greedily, like a beggar supping from a spoon. He did not remember passing out of consciousness, but when he next opened his eyes it was daylight, and the barmaid was gone. He was lying propped between two slop-crates at the back of the building, with a blanket spread over his body, and another folded beneath his cheek. Someone—the barmaid, perhaps?—must have dragged him there. Or had he come here of his own accord? Ah Sook could not remember. He had a terrible headache, and the pain in his ribcage had returned. From within the building he could hear splashing water and the sound of knives.

Then he remembered the can of opium, buried in the middle of the box of tea. Dent & Co. had been paying for their wares in *opium*—for Britain had no more silver, and China had no need for gold. How could he have been so stupid? Francis Carver had been smuggling the drug *into* China, using the Sook family warehouse as a liaison point. Francis Carver had betrayed his father. Francis Carver had turned away from him, and pretended not to understand his cry. Ah Sook lay on his side in the alley without moving. A deadly conviction was swelling in his chest.

Over the course of the next week the buck-toothed woman kept him fed, watered and sedated. She checked upon him several times daily, always under the pretence of feeding the pig, emptying the dishwater, or taking the laundry to the buckled line; after nightfall, she came with the pipe, and fed him smoke until the pain lessened, and he fell asleep. She conducted these ministrations in silence, and Ah Sook, as he watched her, was quiet too. He wondered about her. One night she came out with her own eye blackened. He raised his hand to touch it, but she frowned, and turned away.

Within a few days Ah Sook could stand, though it was painful to do so, and within the week he could walk slowly around the yard.

He knew that the *Palmerston* had only scheduled a fortnight's stopover in Sydney; soon it would be departing for the Victorian goldfields, in the south. Ah Sook no longer cared whether he continued on to Melbourne. He wanted only to confront Carver before the clipper sailed.

Since the *Palmerston* had reached her mooring Carver had not spent a single night aboard: he spent his nights at the dockside brothel, in the company of the woman with copper-coloured hair. Ah Sook saw him approaching every evening, striding along the quay with his arms swinging and his coat-tails flared. He did not leave the brothel until the early hours of the afternoon, and very often the copper-haired woman accompanied him to the alley doorway to bid him a private goodbye. Ah Sook had twice glimpsed the pair walking along the docks together, well after sundown. They spoke as intimates. Each leaned in close to listen when the other spoke, and the woman's hand was always in the crook of Carver's elbow, pressing close.

The eighth night after Ah Sook's assault was a Sunday, and the carousing at the brothel quit well before midnight, in accordance with curfew. Ah Sook crept around to the front of the place and saw Carver silhouetted in the central window of the upper floor, leaning his forearm against the lintel and looking down into the dark. As Ah Sook watched the red-haired woman came up behind him, caught his sleeve in her hand, and pulled him back out of sight, into the depths of the room. Keeping to the shadows, Ah Sook crept back to the sash window above the kitchen cutting-board, and slid it open. He climbed inside. The room was deserted. He looked around for a weapon, selecting, finally, a bone-handled cleaver from the rack above the board. He had never wielded a weapon of any kind against another man, but it gave him confidence, to feel the thing heavy in his hand. He moved to find the staircase in the gloom.

There were three doors at the top of the staircase, all of them closed. He listened at the first (only silence) and then the second (muted scuffling) and then the third, behind which he could hear the rumble of a man's voice, the creak of a chair, and then a woman's low reply. Ah Sook tried to estimate the distance from the

edge of the house to the upper window at which he had seen
Carver standing moments before. Could this third door lead to that
central room—did it square? Yes: for he was ten feet from the edge
of the landing, and if he imagined the brothel's frontage in his
mind, the window was easily twelve feet from the building's edge.
Unless the second door led to a larger room, of course, and this
third door led to a small one. Ah Sook put his ear to the door. He
heard the man raise his voice and speak several words in English—
sharply, and with a terse accent, as though he were very displeased.
It must be Carver, Ah Sook thought. It could only be Carver. Full
of sudden fury, he wrenched the door open—but it was not Carver.
It was the man who had beaten him, little more than a week earlier. He had the buck-toothed woman on his lap, one hand
encircling her throat, the other spread flat across her breast. Ah
Sook stepped back in surprise—and the man, roaring his displeasure, threw the woman from his lap, and leaped to his feet.

He uttered a string of syllables that Ah Sook did not understand,
and reached for his revolver, which was lying on a nightstand next
to the bed. In the same instant, the buck-toothed woman reached
into her bosom and withdrew a muff pistol. The man levelled his
gun and pulled the hammer—Ah Sook flinched—but the mechanism jammed; there was a spent casing in the breech. By the time
the man had tipped his revolver up to release the spent casing, the
woman had rushed upon him and shoved the muzzle of her pistol
into his temple. Distracted, he tried to push her away—and there
was a clap—and the man crumpled. His revolver fell from his
hand, and thudded upon the floor. Ah Sook had not moved. The
buck-toothed woman darted forward, removed the revolver from
the dead man's hand, and fitted her own muff pistol in place of it.
She then thrust the heavy revolver upon Ah Sook, closed his fingers
over the barrel, and motioned for him to leave, and leave quickly.
Bewildered, he turned on his heel, revolver in one hand, cleaver in
the other. She grabbed his shoulders, yanked him back, and
directed him, instead, to the servants' stairwell on the other side of
the hall—down which he vanished, hearing footsteps, and clamour,
on the main stair.

Outside Ah Sook tossed both weapons into the water and watched them sink rapidly out of view. There came screaming from inside, and muffled shouts. He turned and began to run. Before he reached the end of the quay he heard footsteps behind him. Then something struck him on the back, and he fell face-first upon the ground. He gave a grunt of pain—his ribs were still very tender—and felt his hands being cuffed, roughly, behind him. He did not protest as he was hoisted to his feet, marched to the horse post, and shoved against it; his captor then cuffed him, with a second pair of handcuffs, to the iron ring, where he remained until the policeman's wagon arrived to take him to gaol.

Ah Sook could not make head or tail of the questions that were put to him in English, and at length his interrogators despaired of him. He was not afforded the courtesy of a translator, and when he said the name 'Carver' the policemen only shook their heads. He was placed in cramped custody with five other men. In due course the case was heard, and judged to warrant a trial, which was sched-uled to take place some six weeks later. By this time the *Palmerston* must have long since departed; Carver, in all likelihood, was gone for good. Ah Sook passed the next six weeks in a state of great anx-iety and dejection, and awoke on the morning of his trial as if upon the day of his very execution. How could he hope to defend him-self? He would be convicted, and hanged before the month was out.

The case was heard in English, and Ah Sook, from the dock, understood virtually none of it. He was surprised when, after sev-eral hours of speeches and swearings-in, Francis Carver was brought to the stand in handcuffs. Ah Sook wondered why this wit-ness was the only one to have been restrained. He stood up as Carver approached the stand, and called out to him in Cantonese. Their gaze met—and in the sudden stillness, Ah Sook, speaking calmly and distinctly, promised to avenge his father's death. Carver, to his dishonour, was the first to look away.

It was only much later that Ah Sook learned the nature of what transpired during the trial. The name of the man he was accused of having murdered, as he later discovered, was Jeremy Shepard, and the buck-toothed woman who had nursed Ah Sook back to health was his wife, Margaret. The copper-haired woman was Lydia Greenway; she was the proprietrix of the Darling Harbour brothel, which was known as the White Horse Saloon. At the time of his trial, Ah Sook knew no names at all; it was not until the morning after his acquittal that he found a copy of the *Sydney Herald* and was able to pay a Cantonese trader to translate the account given in the courthouse pages—which, owing to its sensational nature, ran over three columns, nearly filling an entire page.

The case of the prosecutor, according to the *Sydney Herald*, rested upon three points: firstly, that Ah Sook had a very good reason to bear a grudge against Jeremy Shepard, given that the latter had beaten him senseless the week before; secondly, that Ah Sook had been apprehended fleeing the White Horse Saloon in the moments after the shot was fired, which naturally made him the most likely suspect; and thirdly, that Chinese men, in general, could not be trusted, and indeed bore an inherent malice against all white men.

The defence, in the face of these charges, was lackadaisical. The lawyer reasoned that it was unlikely that Ah Sook, being but a fraction of Shepard's height and weight, could have got close enough to place the muzzle of the pistol against the other man's temple; for this reason, the possibility of suicide ought not to be ruled out. When the prosecutor interjected to assert that the act of suicide was, by the testimony of his friends, vehemently against Jeremy Shepard's nature, the defence ventured the opinion that no man on earth was wholly incapable of suicide—a surmise that received a sharp reprimand from the judge. Begging the judge's pardon, the lawyer concluded his argument by suggesting, as a kind of general summation, that perhaps Sook Yongsheng had only fled the White Horse in alarm: a shot had just been fired, after all. When he sat down the prosecutor made no effort to hide his smirk, and the judge sighed very audibly.

At last the prosecutor called for the testimony of Margaret Shepard, Jeremy Shepard's widow—and it was here that the trial took a startling turn. Upon the stand, Margaret Shepard flatly refused to corroborate with the prosecutor's line of questioning. She insisted that Sook Yongsheng had not murdered her husband.

She knew this to be true for a very simple reason: she had witnessed his suicide herself.

This startling confession gave rise to such an uproar in the court that the judge was obliged to call for order. Ah Sook, to whom these events would only be translated long after the fact, never dreamed that the woman was risking her own safety in order to save his life. When Margaret Shepard's questioning was allowed to continue, the prosecutor inquired as to why she had hitherto concealed this very vital information, to which Margaret Shepard replied that she had lived in great fear of her husband, for he abused her daily, as more than one witness could attest. Her spirit was all but broken; she had only just mustered the courage to speak of the incident aloud. After this poignant testimony, the trial dissolved. The judge had no choice but to acquit Ah Sook of the crime of murder, and to release him. Jeremy Shepard, it was decreed, had committed suicide, may God rest his soul—though *that* prospect was, theologically speaking, very unlikely.

Ah Sook's first action, upon his release from gaol, was to seek news of Francis Carver. He learned, to his surprise, that in fact the *Palmerston* had been apprehended in the Sydney Harbour some weeks ago, following a routine search. Francis Carver had been found in breach of the law on charges of smuggling, breach of customs, and evasion of duty: according to the report given to the maritime police, there were sixteen young women from Kwangchow in the ship's hold, all of them severely malnourished, and frightened in the extreme. The *Palmerston* had been seized, the women had been sent back to China, Carver had been remanded in gaol, and Carver's relationship with Dent & Co. had been formally dissolved. He had been sentenced to ten years of penal servitude at the penitentiary upon Cockatoo Island, effective instant.

There was nothing to do but wait for Carver's sentence to elapse. Ah Sook sailed to Victoria, and began to dig the ground; he acquired some facility in English, apprenticed himself to various trades, and dreamed, with increasing lucidity, of avenging his father's murder by taking Carver's life. In July 1864 he sent a written inquiry to Cockatoo Island requesting to know where Carver had gone upon his liberation. He received an answer three months later, informing him that Carver had sailed to Dunedin, New Zealand, upon the steamer *Sparta*. Ah Sook bought a ticket there also—and in Dunedin, the trail suddenly went cold. He searched and searched—and found nothing. At last, defeated, Ah Sook gave up the case as lost. He bought a miner's right and a one-way ticket to the West Coast—where, eight months later, he chanced upon him: standing in the street, his face newly scarred, his chest newly thickened, counting coins into Te Rau Tauwhare's hand.

Φ

Ah Sook found Ah Quee sitting cross-legged on a shelf of gravel, some few feet from the boundary peg that marked the Aurora's southeast corner. The goldsmith held a prospector's dish in both hands, and he was shaking the dish rhythmically, flicking out his wrists in the confident motion of a man long-practised in a single skill. There was a lit cigarette in the corner of his mouth, but he did not appear to be smoking it: the ash shredded finely down his tunic as he moved. Before him was a wooden trough of water, and beside him, an iron crucible with a flattened spout.

His rhythm followed a circular pattern. First he shook the largest stones and clods out of his dish, keeping to a persistent tempo, so that the finer sands tumbled, by degrees, to the bottom of the pan; then he leaned forward, dipped the far edge of the pan into the clouded water, and with a sharp movement tilted the pan back towards his body, swirling the liquid carefully clockwise, to create a vortex in the dish. Gold was heavier than stone, and sank to the bottom: once he skimmed the wet gravel from the surface, the pure metal would be left behind, shining wetly, tiny points of light against the dark. Ah Quee plucked out these glistering flakes with his fingers, and transferred them carefully to his crucible; he then refilled his dish with earth and stones, and repeated the procedure, with no variation whatsoever, until the sun sank below the treetops to the west.

The Aurora was a good distance from both the river and the sea, an inconvenience that accounted, in part, for its undesirability as

a goldmine. It was necessary for Ah Quee to transport his own river
water to the claim every morning, for without water, his task was
all but impossible; once the water was clouded with dirt and silt,
however, it was very hard to see the gold, and he was obliged to
tramp back to the river, in order to fill his buckets again. A tailrace
might have been constructed from the Hokitika River, or a shaft
might have been dropped for a well, but the goldmine's owner had
made it clear from the outset that he would spare the Aurora no
resources at all. There was no point. The two acres that comprised
the Aurora was only barely payable ground: it was only a dull patch
of stones, treeless. The tailing pile at Ah Quee's back, testament to
long hours of solitary industry, was long and low; a burial mound,
under which no body had been interred.

Ah Quee looked up as Ah Sook approached.

'*Neih hou.*'

'*Neih hou, neih hou.*'

The two men regarded each other with neither hostility nor
kindness, but the gaze they shared was long. After a moment Ah
Quee plucked the last of the cigarette from his mouth, and flicked
it away over the stones.

'The yield is small today,' he said in Cantonese.

'A thousand sympathies,' replied Ah Sook, speaking in his native
language also.

'The yield is small every day.'

'You deserve better.'

'Do I?' said Ah Quee, who was in an irritable temper.

'Yes,' said Ah Sook. 'Diligence deserves to be rewarded.'

'In what proportion? And in what currency? These are empty
words.'

Ah Sook placed the palms of his hands together. 'I come bearing good news.'

'Good news and flattery,' Ah Quee observed.

The hatter took no notice of this correction. 'Emery Staines has
returned,' he said.

Ah Quee stiffened. 'Oh,' he said. 'You have seen him?'

'Not yet,' said Ah Sook. 'I am told that he will be in Hokitika tonight, at a hotel upon Revell-street where a celebration has been planned to welcome his return. I have been invited, and as a gesture of my good faith, I extend my invitation to you.'

'Who is your host?'

'Anna Wetherell—and the widow of the dead man, Crosbie Wells.'

'Two women,' said Ah Quee, sceptically.

'Yes,' said Ah Sook. He hesitated, and then admitted what he had discovered that morning: that in fact Crosbie's widow was the very same woman who had operated the White Horse Saloon in Darling Harbour, who had testified against Ah Sook at his own trial, and who had once been the lover of his enemy, Francis Carver. Formerly Lydia Greenway, her name was now Lydia Wells.

Ah Quee took a moment to digest this information. 'This is a trap,' he said at last.

'No,' said Ah Sook. 'I came here of my own accord, not under instruction.'

'This is a trap to capture *you*,' said Ah Quee. 'I am sure of it. Why else would your presence be so specifically requested at the celebration tonight? You have no connexion to Mr. Staines. What purpose can you serve, in a party to welcome his return?'

'I am to play a part in a staged drama. I am to sit on a cushion, and pretend to be a statue.' This sounded foolish even to Ah Sook. He rushed on: 'It is a kind of theatre. I shall be paid a fee for my participation.'

'You shall be paid?'

'Yes; as a performer.'

Ah Quee studied him. 'What if the woman Greenway is still in league with Francis Carver? They were lovers once. Perhaps she has already sent word to him, that you will be present at the party tonight.'

'Carver is at sea.'

'Even so, she will notify him as soon as she can.'

'When that happens, I will be ready.'

'How will you be ready?'

'I will be ready,' Ah Sook said, stubbornly. 'It does not matter yet. Carver is at sea.'

'The woman's allegiance is with him—and you have sworn to avenge yourself upon him, as she must remember. She cannot wish you well.'

'I will be on my guard.'

Ah Quee sighed. He stood, brushing himself down, and then he paused, inhaling sharply through his nose. He advanced several steps upon Ah Sook, and gripped his shoulders in both hands.

'You reek with it,' he said. 'You are reeling on your feet, Sook Yongsheng. I can smell the stink of it from twenty paces!'

Ah Sook had indeed detoured past his den at Kaniere, to smoke his late-afternoon pipe, of which the effects were very plainly visible; but he did not like to be chastised. He wrestled himself from Ah Quee's grasp, saying sourly, 'I have a weakness.'

'A weakness!' Ah Quee cried. He spat into the dirt. 'It is not weakness: it is hypocrisy. You ought to be ashamed of yourself.'

'Do not speak to me as to a child.'

'A man addicted is a childish man.'

'Then I am a childish man,' said Ah Sook. 'It is not of consequence to you.'

'It is of great consequence to me, if I am to accompany you tonight.'

'I have no need of your protection.'

'If that is what you believe, you are deluded,' said Ah Quee.

'Deluded—and a hypocrite!' said Ah Sook, feigning astonishment. 'Two insults, when I have been nothing but courteous to you!'

'You deserve to be insulted,' said Ah Quee. 'You indulge the very drug that killed your father—and you have the audacity to style yourself his defender! You insist he was betrayed—and yet *you* betray him, every time you light your lamp!'

'Francis Carver killed my father,' said Ah Sook, stepping back.

'Opium killed your father,' said Ah Quee. '*Look* at yourself'—for Ah Sook had stumbled against a root, and partly fallen. 'You are a fine avenger, Sook Yongsheng; one who cannot even stand on his own two feet!'

Furious, Ah Sook put a hand out to steady himself, hauled himself upright, and rounded on Ah Quee, his pupils dark and soft.

'You know my history,' he said. 'I was first given the drug as a medicine. I did not take it of my own accord. I cannot help its power
over me.'

'You had ample time to shake your addiction,' said Ah Quee.
'You were imprisoned for weeks before your trial, were you not?'

'That interval was not sufficient to rid me of the craving.'

'The *craving*!' said Ah Quee, full of contempt. 'What a pathetic
word that is. No wonder it has no place in the history you
recounted to me. No wonder you prefer such grand words as *honour*,
and *duty*, and *betrayal*, and *revenge*.'

'My history—'

'Your history, as you tell it, dwells far longer on your own injus-
tices than on the shame that was brought upon your family. Tell
me, Sook Yongsheng. Are you avenging yourself upon the man
who killed your father, or the man who refused to come to your aid
outside the White Horse Saloon?'

Ah Sook was shocked. 'You doubt my motives,' he said.

'Your motives are not your own,' said Ah Quee. 'They cannot be
your own! Look at yourself. You can hardly stand.'

There was a silence between them. From the adjacent valley
there came a muffled crack of gunshot, and then a distant cry.

Finally Ah Sook nodded. 'Goodbye,' he said.

'Why do you farewell me?'

'You have made your opinions clear,' said Ah Sook. 'You disap-
prove of me; you are disgusted by me. I will go to the widow's
celebration tonight regardless.'

Though Ah Quee's temper was quick to flare, he could not bear
to be made the villain in any dispute. He shook his head, breathing hard through his nose, and said, 'I will come with you. I want
very much to speak to Mr. Staines.'

'I know,' said Ah Sook. 'I came here on good faith, Quee Long.'

When Ah Quee spoke again, his voice was quiet. 'A man knows
his own heart. I was wrong to doubt your motivation.'

Ah Sook closed his eyes briefly. 'By the time we reach Hokitika,'
he said, opening them again, 'I will be sober.'

Ah Quee nodded. 'You will need to be,' he said.

CARDINAL EARTH

*In which Walter Moody makes a startling discovery; several
confusions are put to rest; and a symmetry presents itself.*

Walter Moody, upon taking his leave of Gascoigne, had returned
at once to the Crown Hotel, to which place his trunk had been
delivered. He wrenched the door open, crossed the foyer at a
pace, and took the stairs to the upper landing two by two; when
he reached the door at the top of the stairs, he fumbled with his
key in the keyhole, and cursed aloud. He was suddenly absurdly
impatient to lay eyes upon his possessions—feeling that his
reunion with the treasured items of his former life would somehow repair a connexion that, since the wreck of the *Godspeed*, had
seemed very unreal.

Of late Moody's thoughts had been drifting, with increasing frequency, back to his reunion with his father in Dunedin. He found
that he regretted the haste with which he had quitted the unhappy
scene. It was true that his father had betrayed him. It was true that
his brother had betrayed him. But even so, he might have been for-
giving; he might have stayed on, and heard Frederick's part in the
story. He had not seen his brother while in Dunedin, for he had fled
the scene of reunion with his father before Frederick could be summoned, and so he did not know whether Frederick was well, or
married, or happy; he did not know what Frederick had made of
Otago, and whether he meant to live out his days in New Zealand;

he did not know whether his father and brother had dug the ground as a party, or whether they had gone mates with other men, or whether they had prospected alone. Whenever Moody dwelled upon these uncertainties, he felt sad. He ought to have sought an audience with his brother. But would Frederick have desired such a thing? Even that Moody did not know. Since arriving in Hokitika he had thrice sat down to write to him, but after penning the salutation and the date, sat motionless.

At last the key turned in the lock. Moody shoved open the door, strode into the room—and stopped. There was indeed a trunk in the middle of the room, but it was a trunk he had never seen before. His own trunk was painted red, and was rectangular in its dimensions. This one was black, with iron straps, and a long square hasp through which a horizontal bar had been thrust to keep it closed; its lid was domed, and slatted like a barrel that had been laid upon its side. There were several baggage labels plastered to the half-barrel of the lid, one marked 'Southampton', one marked 'Lyttelton', and the standard 'Not Wanted On Voyage'. Moody could tell at once that the trunk's owner had always travelled first class.

Instead of ringing the bell to inform the maid of the mistake, Moody closed the door behind him, locked it, and moved forward to kneel before the unfamiliar chest. He unfastened the hasp, and heaved open the lid—and saw, pasted to the underside, a square of paper that read:

PROPERTY OF MR. ALISTAIR LAUDERBACK,
PROVINCIAL COUNCILMAN, M.P.

Moody exhaled, and sat back on his heels. Now *this* was a misunderstanding! So Lauderback's trunk had been aboard *Godspeed*, as Balfour had suspected: the shipping crate must indeed have been wrongly taken from the Hokitika quay. Moody's trunk, like Lauderback's, was not engraved with the name of its owner, and bore no particular marks of identification save for on the interior, where his name and address had been stamped into a square of leather and sewn into the lining of the lid. Presumably the two trunks had been switched: Moody's trunk had been delivered to Lauderback's rooms at the Palace Hotel, and Lauderback's, to the Crown.

Moody thought for a moment. Lauderback was not currently in Hokitika: according to the *West Coast Times*, he was campaigning in the north, and was not due to return until to-morrow afternoon. Suddenly decisive, Moody shucked off his jacket, leaned forward on his knees, and began to go through Lauderback's belongings.

Walter Moody did not chastise himself for intrusions upon other people's privacy, and nor did he see any reason to confess them. His mind was of a most phlegmatic sort, cool in its private applications, quick, and excessively rational; he possessed a fault common to those of high intelligence, however, which was that he tended to regard the gift of his intellect as a licence of a kind, by whose rarefied authority he was protected, in all circumstances, from ever behaving ill. He considered his moral obligations to be of an altogether different class than those of lesser men, and so rarely felt shame or compunction, except in very general terms.

He went through Lauderback's chest swiftly and methodically, handling each item and then replacing it exactly as he found it. The trunk contained largely items of stationery—letter-sets, seals, ledgers, books of law, and all the necessities that might furnish the desk of a Member of Parliament. Lauderback's clothing and personal effects had presumably been packed elsewhere, for the only item of clothing in this cedar chest was a woollen scarf, which had been wrapped around a rather ugly brass paperweight in the shape of a pig. The trunk carried with it the smell of the sea—a briny odour, less salty than sour—but its contents were hardly even damp; mercifully for Lauderback, the trunk must have been spared a full immersion.

At the bottom of the trunk was a leather briefcase. Moody opened it and withdrew a sheaf of papers, all of them contracts, receipts, and bills of sale. After several minutes' searching he found the deed for the sale of the barque *Godspeed*, and pulled that document free of the others—handling it carefully, so that the legal seal did not crumble, or pull away.

The contract had been signed, as Lauderback had attested to Balfour three weeks ago, by a Mr. Francis Wells. The date of the sale also corroborated with the politician's story: the ship had changed ownership in May of 1865, nine months prior to the present day.

Moody bent closer to look at the purchaser's signature. 'Francis Wells' had signed his false name expansively. The inscriber had made a huge looping flourish on the left-hand side of the capital 'F', so large that it might have been a letter of its own. Moody squinted at it sideways. Why, he thought: in fact that flourish might have easily been a C, cursively joined to the next letter. He peered closer. There was even a dot of ink between the C and the F—a dot that one might have taken for a spatter, if one glanced at the paper carelessly—which seemed to suggest that Carver had signed the name deliberately ambiguously, so that it might read either 'Francis Wells' merely, *or* 'C. Francis Wells'. The penmanship was rather shaky, as often happens when one writes very slowly, wishing to ensure a particular effect.

Moody was frowning. In June of the previous year, Francis Carver had been in possession of Crosbie Wells's birth certificate, a document that proved (as Benjamin Löwenthal had attested) that Crosbie Wells's middle name was Francis. Why, Moody thought, it was plain enough: Francis Carver had stolen Crosbie Wells's birth certificate with the intention of posing as the other man. The ambiguities of this bill of sale must surely be deliberate. If Carver were brought to court on the charge of false impersonation, he could deny that he had ever signed it.

Was the shared name, Francis, merely a happy coincidence? Or could Wells's birth certificate have been falsified after the fact? A middle name would be very easy to add to any document, Moody thought, and one could easily use a lighter shade of ink, or fade the word somehow, to mask the fact of the later addition. But why should Carver have *wanted* to falsify his own identity—most especially, upon a bill of sale? How could it have been to his advantage, to use another man's name?

Moody reviewed what he knew about the matter. Francis Carver had used Crosbie Wells's identity when speaking to Benjamin

Löwenthal in the office of the *West Coast Times* in June ... but he had *not* used Crosbie Wells's identity when confronting Alistair Lauderback, the month before. To Lauderback he had called himself Francis Wells ... and then he had signed his name with deliberate ambiguity. Bearing in mind Lauderback's mysterious belief that Crosbie Wells and Carver had been brothers, Moody could only assume that Carver had posed as Crosbie Wells's brother in his dealings with Lauderback. As to why he might have done such a thing, however, Moody had no idea.

He scrutinised the bill of sale for a long moment, committing its particulars to memory, and then returned it to the briefcase, slotted the briefcase back into the trunk, and continued with his methodical investigation.

At length he was satisfied that the trunk contained no more clues that were of use to him, and, in a gesture that was partly idle, ran his fingers around the edge of the lid. All of a sudden he gave a murmur of surprise. A slim package, squarish in shape, had been slipped beneath the calico lining, so that it lay, concealed, between the cedar and the cloth. He bent closer, and his fingers found a neat slit in the fabric, roughly the size of the span of his hand, and delicately hemmed so that it would not fray. The calico lining was stamped with a tartan pattern, and the slit in the cloth was cleverly disguised against the vertical stripes of the tartan, which ran flush with the edge of the trunk. Moody wormed his fingers into the cavity and withdrew the squarish object that his fingers had located. It was a wad of letters, tied with string.

There were around fifteen letters in total, each addressed to Lauderback in a plain and unsophisticated hand. Moody took a moment to memorise the look of the knot, and the length of the strings of the bow. He then untied the ends, tossed the string to one side, and smoothed the folded letters over his knee. He could see from their postmarks that they were arranged in reverse chronological order, with the most recent letter first; he shuffled to the back of the pile, selected the very first letter that Lauderback had received, and began to read it. In the next moment his heart jumped into his throat.

Dunedin. March 1852

Sir you are my brother though you do not know me. Your father sired a bastard I am that bastard. I was raised CROSBIE WELLS taking the surname of my parish priest not knowing my father but knowing myself a whoreson. I passed my childhood in the Newington whorehouse THE JEWEL. I have lived a modest life such as I am able as a man of little means. I have not suffered. However I desired always to see my father just to know his shape & voice. Finally these prayers were answered with a letter from the man himself. He had always known of me he wrote. He expected he would soon be gone & confessed he would not identify me in his will for fear of tarnishing his name but he enclosed me £20 & blessings. He did not sign his name but I made inquiries about the servant who had brought the note & tracked his carriage though it was a rented one to GLEN HOUSE your father's house & yours. I bought a coat I shaved I took a gig to your father's house but sir I could not ring the bell. I returned home distraught & cowed & then I made a blunder seeing in the shipping news that ALASTAIR LAUDERBACK lawyer was departing for the colonies next tide. I believed it was my father I did not know he had a son I did not think that son might share his name. That ship departed but I was sharp upon the next. I landed at Dunedin & began to make inquiries as my fortunes would allow. I attended your public address the one conducted in the rain upon the wharf where the Harbour Master made you a present of a pocket watch & you seemed very well pleased. When I saw you I knew at once that I had erred & you were not my father but my brother. I was too anguished to confront you then & now you are in Lyttelton a place to which I cannot afford to sail. Sir I write with a request a prayer. I have spent my father's £20 on this journey & other necessaries & I have not the means to return home. I have sold my coat but it fetched little more than half the price I paid for the broker did not believe it was a fine one. I have now but pennies to my name. You are a dignitary sir a man of politics philosophy & law I do not need to meet you but I beseech you for your charity believing you a good & Christian man & because I will remain always

  Your brother
  CROSBIE WELLS

There was a forwarding address beneath his name, a post-office box in Dunedin.

Moody put down the letter with a beating heart. So *Lauderback* and Crosbie Wells were brothers. That was a turn of events indeed! But Lauderback had not mentioned this connexion to the magistrate, when he admitted to having arrived at Crosbie Wells's deathbed half an hour too late; nor had he confessed it to his friend, the shipping agent Thomas Balfour. What reason did he have to conceal his brother's illegitimate parentage? Shame, perhaps? Or something else?

Moody took up the bundle and moved to the window, where there was more light. He unfolded the next letter and tilted it towards the glass.

Dunedin. September 1852

Sir six months have passed since I first wrote & I fear by your silence that I have offended you. I cannot recall my phrasing exactly but I do recall that in my last address I styled myself your brother & perhaps that caused you grief. I imagine that it pains you to know that your father was a less than perfect man. I imagine that you wish it otherwise. If the above is true then I beg forgiveness. Sir in these past months my fortunes have fallen further still. I assure you that as a whoreson I am not unaccustomed to the beggar's life but to beg a man a second time is shame indeed. Nonetheless I write in desperation. You are a man of means the cost of a third-class ticket is all I ask & thenceforth you needn't hear of me again. Here in Dunedin I save my pennies as I can. I have tried my hand at navvy work but find myself ill suited to the trade. I have been laid very low by 'chill-blains' & fever & other ills pertaining to the cold. I have not worked as steadily as I should have liked to do. My desire to meet our father Alastair Lauderback Senior has not diminished & I am conscious of the passing days for as I told you he confessed to me in writing that he was very close to death. I should like to speak to him but once before that sad event just so that we might lay eyes on one another & speak as men. Please sir I ask you on my knees to buy my passage home. You would not hear of me again I swear. I am nothing more than

Your grateful friend,
CROSBIE WELLS

Moody hardly paused before turning to the next; with his free hand, he fumbled for a chair, and sank into it, still reading.

Dunedin. January 1853

Sir how ought I read this silence that is the question on my mind. I believe you are in receipt of my correspondence but for some reason of principle you decline to answer or to extend a scrap of charity to your father's bastard child. These letters did not take dictation. This is mine own hand sir & I can read as well & though I flatter myself I shall tell you that my parish priest Father Wells remarked more than once that I was an uncommonly bright boy. I state all this to make it clear I am no scoundrel though my station is a low one. Perhaps you wish for proof of my bastardy. Perhaps you think this an attempted swindle. I say on my honour it is not. Since I wrote to you last my needs and wishes are unchanged. I do not want to be in this country sir I never sought this life. For £20 I would return to England and never speak your name again.

Yours truly,
CROSBIE WELLS

Dunedin. May 1853

Sir I know from the provincial papers that you have taken up the post of Superintendent of the proud province of Canterbury. You took the post & offered up your honorarium for charity a noble gesture sir but one I observed with sadness. I wondered if you thought of me as you gave that £100 away. I have not the means to travel to Lyttelton where you are much less back home. I have never felt more alone than I do in this forsaken land surely you will understand this as a British man yourself. We have creeping damp and frost in-doors I wake most mornings with a rime of ice across my legs. I am not suited to the hard frontier & mourn my circumstances daily. Sir in this year past I have saved only £2 10s. 4d & I have now spent 4d upon these pages and postage. I beg of you to help

A man in need
CROSBIE WELLS

Dunedin. October 1853

Sir I write in great dejection. I am certain now that you will never write back to me & even I a whoreson am too proud to beg again. I am a sinner like our father the apple falling never far as the common saying goes. But in my youth I was taught that charity is a primary virtue & one to be practised most especially when that virtue is not due. You sir are not behaving as a Christian man. I do believe that if our respective circumstances were reversed I would not maintain the cruel silence that you keep with me. Rest assured I will not beg your charity again but I wish to make my dejection known to you. I have been following your career in the pages of the 'Otago Witness' & I know you are a man of no small means & much opinion. I have neither privilege but notwithstanding my abject position I am proud to call myself a Christian man & if you were in need sir I should turn my pockets out to help you as your brother. I do not expect that you will reply and perhaps I will die soon and you will never hear from me again. Even in the likelihood of that event I am proud to remain

Yours very sincerely
CROSBIE WELLS

Dunedin. January 1854

Sir I must apologise for the letter I wrote you last as it was written bitterly & with the purpose of insulting you. My mother warned me never to touch a pen when in a temper & now I see the wisdom in her words. My mother you have never known of course but she was quite a beauty in her time. SUE BUTCHER was her name in life God rest her soul though she also went by other names better suited to her line of work & liked to invent new ones at her pleasure. She was our father's particular favourite a preference that was formed she said upon the handsome colour of her eyes. I do not resemble her except in pieces. She always said that I bore my father's likeness though my father never returned to the whorehouse after I was born & as you know I never met him. I have been told that prostitution is a social ill composed of male licentiousness on the one hand & female depravity on the other & although I know this to be the opinion of wiser men than I nevertheless it does not make sense of how I remember my mother in my mind. She had 'fine pipes' & loved to sing all manner of

*hymns in the morning a practice that I also loved. I believe she was kind
& hardworking & although she was known to be a flirt she was a very
good one. How strange that we have separate mothers but share a father. I
suppose it means that we are only half alike. But forgive these idle
meditations & please accept my apologies & my assurance that I remain*
    Yours
    CROSBIE WELLS

                                        Dunedin. June 1854
*Sir perhaps it is right you do not reply. You are acting only as a man of
your high station can & you have a reputation to consider. I think I have
become contented with your silence strange though that might sound. I have
secured a modest wage & decent lodgings & I am 'settling down' as they
term it here. I find Dunedin much changed in the summer months. The
sun is bright on the hills & on the water & I can bear the briskness very
well. How odd it is that I should find myself on the contrary face of the
world. I believe that I am as far from England as any man could be. You
will be surprised to learn that I am not to return home after all. I have
resolved to make New Zealand the land in which I will be buried.
Perhaps you wonder what spurred this change of heart & so I shall tell
you. You see in New Zealand every man has left his former life behind &
every man is equal in his way. Of course the flockmasters of Otago are
barons here just as they were barons in the Scottish Highlands but for men
like me there is a chance to rise. I find this very cheering. It is not
uncommon for men to tip their hats to one another in the street regardless
of their station. For you perhaps this is not a strange occurrence but for me
it is a wondrous one. The frontier I think makes brothers of us all & in
making this remark I shall remain*
    Yours very truly
    CROSBIE WELLS

                                      Dunedin. August 1854
*Sir you will I hope forgive these letters I have no other correspondents &
thoughts of you consume my days. I have been waxing philosophical*

*myself in thinking what might have happened if you knew me sooner or if
I knew you. I do not know your age so I do not know if you are the elder
or if I am the elder. In my mind the difference signifies & because I am
the bastard I imagine myself younger but of course that might not be the
case. There were other children in the whorehouse several girls who grew
up whoring & one boy who died of smallpox when I was very young but
I was the eldest always & I should have liked a brother to admire. I have
been thinking with much sadness upon the fact that I do not know whether
you have sisters & brothers or if there are other bastards or if your father
ever spoke of me to you. If I were in London I would be taking every
chance to walk to Glen House & look in through the railings & spy my
father whom you remember I have never seen. I have his letter still it says
he knew of me & watched me and I wonder what he thought of me &
what he might think about the life I lead here. But perhaps he is no longer
living. You wish not to be my brother you have made that clear but perhaps
you are as my priest with our correspondence as confession. I am heartened
by this notion for I say with pride that I was properly confirmed. But I
expect you are a Church of England man.*

    Yours,
    CROSBIE WELLS

                      Dunedin. November 1854

*Sir do you feel as if you know me or could pick me from a crowd? It
struck me lately that I know your likeness though you do not know mine.
We are not so dissimilar in our physique though I am slighter I think &
my hair is darker than yours & folk would likely say that yours is the
kinder face because my expression is too often sullen. I wonder if you walk
about & think of me & if you search for fragments of my features in
other people's faces or their bodies when they pass you by. That is what I
did every day while I was young & dreaming always of my father &
trying to piece him from all the faces I had known. How comforting to
think of all that unites us as brothers living at the end of the world. You
are the subject of my repeating thoughts today.*

    Sincerely,
    CROSBIE WELLS

The next letter in the sequence was much crisper, and the ink much brighter. Moody looked at the date, and noticed that nearly a decade had elapsed since Crosbie Wells's last correspondence.

Dunedin. June 1862

Sir I will renew my correspondence to inform you very proudly that I write this as a married man. The courtship was a very short one though I believe the script followed conventional themes. In recent months I have been digging the gullies at Lawrence & though I have amassed a 'competence' I am yet to truly strike. Mrs. Wells as I must call her now is a fine specimen of the female sex & one I shall be very proud to carry on my arm. I suppose she is your sister now. I should like to know if you have a sister already or if Mrs. Wells is your very first. You shall not hear from me for some time after this for I must return to Dunstan in order to provide for my wife. What are your thoughts on the gold rush I wonder. Recently I heard a politician speak who called the gold a moral scourge. It is true that on the diggings I have seen much degradation but there was degradation prior to the strike as well. I fancy that it is the thought of men like me becoming rich that has most politicos afraid.

  Cordially,
  CROSBIE WELLS

Kawarau. November 1862

Sir I read in the papers that you are recently married for which I offer my heartiest congratulations. I have not seen a picture of your wife CAROLINE née GOUGH but she is reported to be a very fine match. I am happy when I think that we will both spend our Christmases as married men. I will journey back from Lawrence to spend the season with my wife who keeps her lodging in Dunedin & does not come to the diggings as she cannot bear the mud. I have never become used to Christmas in the summertime & feel the tradition as a whole is suited best to the colder months. Perhaps I blaspheme to talk of Christmas so but I esteem that there is much that does not retain its meaning here in New Zealand seeming instead like a faded relic from another time. I think of you receiving this letter & sitting down beside the fire perhaps or leaning close into the lamplight to make out the words. Permit me to invent these details it is a great pleasure always for me to think of you I assure you that I remain, from afar,

   Yours very truly,
   CROSBIE WELLS

                                                    Dunstan. April 1863
Sir I have passed this week in a melancholy humour wondering if Alistair Lauderback our father is yet deceased as I expect he is. London seems but a dream to me now. I recall the smoke & fog & cannot trust my own memory at all. As an experiment last week I sat down & tried to draw a map of Southwark in the dirt. I hardly could remember the shape of the Thames & no street names returned to me. Is it the same for you I wonder? I read in the 'Otago Witness' with some astonishment that you now style yourself a proud Cantabrian. I feel English through and through.

   Yours,
   CROSBIE WELLS

                                                Kawarau. November 1863
Sir I like to think that you receive my words with pleasure but am content with the more probable event that you do not read them at all. In either case writing is a comfort to me and gives shape to my days. I read with interest that you have resigned the Superintendency. The word upon the diggings here is that Canterbury is soon to have her rush in gold following Otago's fade & I rather wonder whether such a discovery would make you regret your decision to step down from that eminent position. The reward offered for a payable goldfield has excited more than one man upon the fields here at Kawarau. The land is steep & the sky very blinding here. I have been sun-burned so often that the shape of my collar has been branded into my neck & though this is painful I do not look forward to the winter months which in this high country will be bitter indeed. If gold is discovered in Canterbury will you run for the Super again? I do not mean that as an interrogative in the proper sense just as an expression of

*my curiosity in the course of your days. It is in this spirit that I sign
myself*

Sincerely,
CROSBIE WELLS

                                        Kawarau. March 1864

*Sir I write with most important and indeed astonishing news. I have been
in Dunstan where I hit upon some extraordinary luck a claim veritably
shining with the colour! I am now a wealthy man though I have not spent
a penny of it having seen too many fellows spend their dust on hats &
coats only to return those items to the pawnbroker's when their fortunes
change again. I will not tell you the amount for fear this message is
intercepted but I will say that even by your handsome salary it is an
enormous sum & I fancy that now I am the richer brother of us two at
least in terms of ready money. What a lark that is. With this fortune I
could return to London & set up a shop but I will continue to prospect as
I believe my luck has not yet run dry. I have not yet declared the ore and
have chosen to export it from the goldfields via a private escort which I am
told is the safest route. Notwithstanding the alteration of my fortune I am,
as ever,*

Yours,
CROSBIE WELLS

                                    West Canterbury. June 1865

*Sir you will notice from my postmark that I am no longer a resident of the
province of Otago but have 'upped my sticks' as the saying goes. You most
likely have had little cause to venture west of the mountains so I shall tell
you that West Canterbury is a world apart from the grasses of the South.
The sunrise over the coastline is a scarlet marvel & the snowy peaks hold
the colour of the sky. The bush is wet & tangled & the water very white.
It is a lonely place though not quiet for the birdsong is constant & very
pleasant for its constancy. As you may have guessed already I have put my
former life behind me. I am estranged from my wife. I ought to tell you
that I concealed much in my correspondence with you fearing that if you*

knew the bitter truth about my marriage you might think less of me. I shall not trouble you with the details of my escape to this place for it is a sorry tale & one that saddens me to recall. I am twice bitten three times shy which is a less admirable ratio than other men can boast but suffice to say that I have learned my lesson. Enough upon that subject instead I shall speak about the present & the future. I mean to dig for gold no longer though West Canterbury is flush with colour & men are making fortunes every day. No I will not prospect & have my fortune stolen once again. Instead I shall try my hand at the timber trade. I have made a fine acquaintance of a Maori man Terou Tow-Faray. This name in his native tongue means 'The Hundred House of Years'. What poor names we British fellows have compared to these! I fancy it might be a line from a poem. Tow-Faray is a noble savage of the first degree & we are fast becoming friends. I confess it lifts my spirits to be in the companionship of men again.

Yours &c,
CROSBIE WELLS

West Canterbury. August 1865

Sir I read in the papers that Westland is to have a seat in Parliament & you are running for that seat. I am proud to say I am now a voting man sir for my cottage in the Arahura Valley is not leasehold it is my very own & as you know the ownership of land affords a man a vote. I will place my ballot in your favour & drink to your success. In the meantime I spend my days felling 'totara' with a thousand blows of my humble axe. You are a landed man sir you have Glen House in London and also I presume your electoral lodgings in handsome Akaroa. But I have never owned a scrap before. I have been with Mrs. Wells in name if not in deed for nigh on three years but all that time I was on the fields & without a fixed address while she remained in town. Although my present solitude suits me very well it is the stationary life to which I am unaccustomed. Perhaps we will meet or see each other while you are in Hokitika on your campaign. You must not fear that I will harm you or that I will betray the secret of our father's wrong. I have told no man & only my estranged wife & her temperament is such that when she cannot profit from the knowledge she *loses interest in the news. You must not fear me. You need only to send an X on paper to this return address if you make your mark in this way I will know that you do not wish to meet & I should keep away & stop writing & cease my wondering. I would do that gladly & anything else you ask of me because I am,*

   Yours very truly,
CROSBIE WELLS

                West Canterbury. October 1865
Sir I have not received a letter X from you for which I thank you. Today I am heartened by your silence, though the very same has caused me grief before. I remain, as ever,

   Yours,
CROSBIE WELLS

                West Canterbury. December 1865
Sir I observe in the 'West Coast Times' that you mean to make the passage to Hokitika overland & therefore will pass through the Arahura Valley lest you make some deliberately circuitous route. I am a voting man and as such I would be honoured to welcome a politician at my home humble though the dwelling is. I shall describe it so that you might approach or direct your course away as you see fit. The house is roofed in iron & set back thirty yards from the banks of the Arahura on that river's Southern side. There is a clearing of some thirty yards on either side of the cottage & the sawmill is some twenty yards further to the Southeast. The dwelling is a small one with a window & a chimney made of clay-fired brick. It is clad in the usual way. Perhaps even if you do not stop I shall see you riding by. I shall not expect it nor hope for it but I wish you a pleasant journey Westward and a triumphant campaign and I assure you that I remain,

   With the deepest admiration,
CROSBIE WELLS

This was the final letter. It was dated a little over two months prior to the present day—and less than a month before Wells's own death.

Moody threw down the page and sat a moment without moving. He did not habitually smoke alone, and so rarely kept tobacco about his person; right now, however, he wanted very much to be occupied by some compulsive and repeated motion, and briefly wondered whether he ought to ring the bell for a cigarette or a cigar. But he could not bear the thought of speaking to another person, even to deliver a command, and contented himself instead with the task of reshuffling the letters, and returning them to their original order, with the most recent letter placed on top.

It was clear from Crosbie Wells's repeated allusions to Lauderback's silence that the politician had never once responded to these letters from his bastard half-brother, his father's whoreson child. Alistair Lauderback had kept his silence for *thirteen years*! Moody shook his head. Thirteen years! When Crosbie's letters were so yearning, and so candid; when the bastard so plainly desired to meet his brother, and to look upon him, even once. Would it have so harmed Lauderback—the honourable Lauderback—to pen a few words in response? To send a banknote, and buy the poor man's passage home? It was extraordinarily callous, never to reply! And yet (Moody conceded) Lauderback had kept Wells's letters—he had kept them, and read them, and reread them, for the oldest were very worn, and had been folded, and refolded, many times. And he *had* journeyed to Crosbie Wells's cottage in the Arahura Valley—arriving, in the last, just half an hour too late.

But then Moody remembered something else. Lauderback had taken Lydia Wells as his mistress! He had taken *his brother's wife* as his mistress! 'Unconscionable,' Moody said aloud. He leaped up and began to pace. It was extraordinarily callous! It was inhuman! He made the calculations in his head. Crosbie Wells had been on the fields at Dunstan, and at Kawarau … and all the while the brother he so desired to meet was in Dunedin, making him a cuckold! Could Lauderback have been truly ignorant of this connexion? That was hardly likely, for Lydia Wells had taken her husband's surname!

Moody stopped. No, he thought. Lauderback had told Balfour explicitly that he had *not* known that Lydia Wells was married throughout the course of their affair. In all of their dealings with one another, she had used her maiden name, Greenway. It was not until Francis Carver returned from gaol—calling himself Francis *Wells*—that Lauderback discovered that Lydia was married, and that her name was properly Lydia Wells, and that he, Lauderback, had been cuckolding her husband. Moody rifled back through the pile of letters until he found the one dated August of the previous year. Yes: Crosbie Wells had made it explicitly clear that he *had* shared the details of his illegitimate parentage with his wife. So Lydia Wells had known about Lauderback's illegitimate brother from the very beginning of their love affair—and she had known, furthermore, that this was a matter about which Lauderback presumably cherished a very raw and private feeling, for he had never replied to Crosbie's letters, even once. Perhaps, Moody thought, she had even sought out Lauderback with the express purpose of exploiting that connexion.

Why—the woman was nothing better than a profiteer! To have used *both* brothers—to have ruined them both! For another thing was now clear: the fortune by which Lauderback had been blackmailed had *not* originated from Carver's own claim at all. The sum total had been stolen from Crosbie Wells; *he* had been the one to make a strike on the fields at Dunstan, as his correspondence had attested! So Lydia Wells had betrayed Wells's secret to Francis Carver, with whose help she had then devised a plan to steal Wells's fortune and blackmail Lauderback, leaving the pair of them rich, *and* the proud possessors of the barque *Godspeed*, into the bargain. Lauderback was plainly ashamed of his illegitimate relation, as Mrs. Wells, as his mistress, must have known first-hand; clearly, she had devised a scheme to use that shame as leverage.

Suddenly Moody's heart gave a lurch. This was the twinkle—the private information by which Francis Carver had blackmailed Lauderback, and guaranteed his silence on the sale of the *Godspeed*. For Carver had called himself Francis Wells, leading Lauderback to believe that he and Crosbie were brothers: fellow whoresons, brought up in the same whorehouse … born, perhaps, to the same *mother*! Crosbie Wells's surname had been given to him by assignation, and it was not implausible that Crosbie Wells might have had other siblings on his mother's side, if his mother was a prostitute. What a way to play on Lauderback's sympathies, and force his hand!

Crosbie Lauderback, Moody thought suddenly, feeling a rush of empathy for the man. He thought of Wells dead in his cottage in the Arahura, one hand curled around the base of an empty bottle, his cheek against the table, his eyes closed. How coldly the wheels of fortune turned. How steely Lauderback's heart must have been, to maintain his silence, in the face of these impassioned appeals! And how pitiful, that Crosbie Wells had watched his brother's ascension, over the course of a decade, through the ranks of the Provincial Council into the very House of Parliament itself—while the bastard struggled in the damp and frost, alone.

And yet Moody could not repudiate Lauderback altogether. The politician *had* visited his brother, in the end. . . . though with what intention, Moody did not know. Perhaps the politician meant to make up for thirteen years of silence. Perhaps he had intended to apologise to his half-brother, or merely, to look upon him, and speak his name, and shake his hand.

There were tears in Moody's eyes. He swore, though without conviction, drew the back of his hand roughly across his face— feeling a bitter kinship with the hermit, a man whom he had never seen, and would never know. For there was a terrible resemblance between Crosbie Wells's situation and his own. Crosbie Wells had been abandoned by his father, as had Moody. Crosbie Wells had been betrayed by his brother, as had Moody. Crosbie Wells had relocated to the southern face of the world in pursuit of his brother, as had Moody—and there he had been spurned, and ruined, only to live out his days alone.

Moody squared the edges of the letters in his hands. He ought to have rung the bell for the maid an hour ago, and demanded the trunk be removed from his room; he would invite suspicion if he delayed any further. He wondered what he should do. There was not enough time to make copies of the entire correspondence. Ought he to return the letters to the lining of the trunk? Ought he to steal them? Surrender them to a relevant authority here in Hokitika? They were certainly pertinent to the case at hand, and in the event that a Supreme Court judge was summoned, they would be very valuable indeed.

He crossed the room and sat down upon the edge of his bed, thinking. He could send the letters to Löwenthal, with instructions that they were all to be published, in sequence and in full, in the *West Coast Times*. He could send them to George Shepard, the gaol warden, begging the latter's advice. He could show them to his friend Gascoigne, in confidence. He could summon the twelve men of the Crown, and solicit their opinion. He could send them to the goldfields Commissioner—or better yet, to the Magistrate. But to what end? What would come of it? Who would profit from the news? He tapped his fingertips together, and sighed.

At length Moody gathered up the letter-bundle, tied the bow exactly as it had been tied, and replaced the bundle in the lining of the trunk. He fitted the bar back into the hasp, wiped the lid of the trunk, and stood back to make sure everything looked exactly as he had found it. Then he put his hat and coat back on—as though he had only just returned home from Maxwell's dining hall—and rang the bell. The maid stamped upstairs in due course, and in a tone of deep exasperation he told her that the wrong trunk had been delivered to his rooms. He had taken the liberty of opening the trunk, and of reading the name inscribed on the interior: it belonged to Mr. Alistair Lauderback, a man whom he had never met, who was certainly not lodging at the Crown Hotel, and whose name bore no resemblance at all to his own. Presumably *his* own trunk had been sent to Mr. Lauderback's hotel—wherever *that* was. He intended to spend the afternoon at the billiard hall on Stafford-street, and expected that the mistake would be corrected during the hours of his absence, for it was of the utmost importance that he was reunited with his possessions at the earliest convenience: he planned to attend the widow's 'drinks and speculation' at the Wayfarer's Fortune that evening, and he wished to do so in appropriate attire. He added, before taking his leave, that he was most severely displeased.

A MONTH WITHOUT A MOON

In which the Wayfarer's Fortune opens to the public at long last.

The hanging sign outside the Wayfarer's Fortune had been repainted so that the jaunty silhouette with his Dick Whittington bundle was now walking beneath a starry sky. If the stars formed a constellation above the painted figure's head, Mannering did not recognise it. He glanced up at the sign only briefly as he mounted the steps to the veranda, noting, as he did so, that the knocker had been polished, the windows washed, the doormat replaced, and a fresh card fitted into the plate beside the door:

MRS. LYDIA WELLS, MEDIUM, SPIRITIST
SECRETS UNCOVERED FORTUNES TOLD

At his knock he heard female voices, and then quick footsteps on the stairs, ascending. He waited, hoping that it would be Anna who received him.

There was a rattling sound as the chain was unhooked. Mannering touched the knot of his necktie with his fingers, and stood a little straighter, looking at his faint reflection in the glass.

The door opened.

'Dick Mannering!'

Mannering was disappointed, but he did not show it. 'Mrs. Wells,' he exclaimed. 'A very good evening to you.'

'I certainly hope it will be; but it is not the evening yet.' She smiled. 'I would expect you of all people to know that it is dreadfully unfashionable to arrive early to a party. What would my mother call it? A barbarism.'

'Am I early?' Mannering said, reaching for his pocket watch in a pretence of surprise. He knew very well that he was early: he had desired to arrive before the others, so as to get a chance to speak with Anna alone. 'Oh yes—look at that,' he added, squinting at the watch. He shrugged and tucked it back into the pocket of his vest. 'I must have forgotten to wind it this morning. Well, I'm here now—and so are you. Dressed for the occasion. Very handsome. Very handsome indeed.'

She was wearing widow's weeds, though her costume had been 'enhanced', as she might have phrased it, in various small ways, and these enhancements belied its sombre tone. The black bodice had been embroidered with vines and roses, stitched in a glossy thread, so that the designs winked and flashed upon her breast; she wore another black rose upon a band of black that was fitted, as a cuff, around the plump whiteness of her forearm, and a third black rose in her hair, pinned into the hollow behind her ear.

She was still smiling. 'What am I to do now?' she said. 'You have put me in a dreadful position, Mr. Mannering. I cannot invite you in. To do so would only encourage you to arrive early on other occasions; before long, you would be inconveniencing men and women of society all over town. But I cannot turn you out into the street either—for then you and I will *both* be barbarians. You for your impudence, and me for my inhospitality.'

'Seems there's a third option,' said Mannering. 'Let me stand on the porch all night, while you mull it over—and by the time you make up your mind, I'll be right on time.'

'There's another barbarism,' said Mrs. Wells. 'Your temper.'

'You've never seen my temper, Mrs. Wells.'

'Have I not?'

'Never. With you, I'm a civilised man.'

'With whom are you uncivilised, one wonders.'

'It's not a matter of with whom,' said Mannering. 'It's a matter of how far.'

There was a brief pause.

'How grand that must have felt,' said Mrs. Wells presently.

'When?'

'Just then,' said Mrs. Wells. 'What you just said. It must have felt grand.'

'There's a certain style about you, Mrs. Wells. I'd forgotten it.'

'Is there?'

'Yes—a certain style.' Mannering reached into his pocket. 'Here's the tariff. Daylight robbery, by the way. You can't charge three shillings in Hokitika for an evening's entertainment—not if you're calling up Helen of Troy. The fellows won't stand for it. Though I oughtn't to be giving you advice. As of this evening, you and I are direct competitors. Don't think that I don't know it: it'll be the Prince of Wales or the Wayfarer's Fortune, when the boys turn out their pockets of a Saturday night. I'm a man who takes notice of my competition—and I'm here tonight to take notice of you.'

'A woman likes to be noticed,' said Mrs. Wells. She accepted the coins, and then pulled the door wide. 'Anyway,' she added, as Mannering stepped into the hall, 'you're a rotten liar. If you'd forgotten to wind your watch, you wouldn't have been early, you'd have been late.'

She shut the door behind him, and set the chain.

'You're in black,' Mannering observed.

'Naturally,' she returned. 'I am recently widowed, and therefore in mourning.'

'Here's a fact,' Mannering said. 'The colour black is invisible to spirits. I'll make a bet that you didn't know that—did you, now! It's why we wear black at funerals: if we dressed in colour we'd attract the attention of the dead. Wearing black, they can't make us out.'

'What a charming piece of trivia,' said Mrs. Wells.

'Do you know what it means, though? It means that Mr. Staines won't be able to see you. Not in that gown. You'll be quite invisible to him.'

She laughed. 'Dear me. Well, there's nothing to be done, I suppose. Not at this late stage. I shall have to call the whole evening off.'

'And Anna,' said Mannering. 'What colour will she be wearing, tonight?'

'Black, as a matter of fact,' said Mrs. Wells, 'for she is in mourning also.'

'You're scuppered,' said Mannering. 'The whole enterprise. And all on account of your gowns. How's that for a stick in a wheel? Thwarted—by your own gowns!'

Mrs. Wells was no longer smiling. 'You are irreverent,' she said, 'to make sport of the tokens of bereavement.'

'You and I both, Mrs. Wells.'

They looked at each other for a moment, each searching the other's expression.

'I have the greatest respect for swindlers,' said Mannering presently. 'I ought to—seeing as I count myself among them! But fortune telling—that's a poor swindle, Mrs. Wells. I'm sorry to say it plain, but there it is.'

Her expression was still cautious; lightly she said, 'How so?'

'It's nothing better than a falsehood,' said Mannering, stoutly. 'Tell me the name of the next man to bet against me. Buy me into my next game of brag. Give me the winner of next week's races. You wouldn't do it, would you? No, you wouldn't—because you can't.'

'I see that you like to doubt, Mr. Mannering.'

'I'm an old hand at this game, that's why.'

'Yes,' said the widow, still gazing at him. 'You relish doubting.'

'Give me the winner of next week's races, and I'll never doubt again.'

'I cannot.'

Mannering spread his hands. 'There you have it.'

'I cannot; because in asking me for such a thing, you are not asking me to tell your fortune. You are asking me to give you an incontrovertible proof of my own ability. That is what I cannot do. I am a fortune-teller, not a logician.'

'Poor fortune-teller, though, if you can't see ahead to next Sunday.'

'One of the first lessons one learns, in this discipline, is that nothing about the future is incontrovertible,' said Mrs. Wells. 'The reason is very simple: a person's fortune always changes in the telling of it.'

'You're feathering your own nest, with that argument.'

She lifted her chin slightly. 'If you were a jockey in next week's horse race, and you came to me and asked to know if your fortune was likely good—well, that would be a different story. If I pronounced that your fortune was very gloomy, you would likely ride poorly, because you would be dejected; if I made a favourable forecast, you would likely ride with confidence, and thus do well.'

'All right—I'm not a jockey,' said Mannering, 'but I *am* a punter with five pounds riding on a mare called Irish—that's the truth— and I'm asking you to tell my fortune, good or bad. What's my forecast?'

She smiled. 'I doubt your fortunes would be very much altered by the loss or gain of five pounds, Mr. Mannering; and in any case, you are still seeking proof. Come through into the parlour.'

The interior of the Wayfarer's Fortune hardly recalled the grimy establishment at which Mrs. Wells had received Aubert Gascoigne three weeks prior. The widow had ordered drapes, a new suite of furniture, and a dozen rolls of paper in a striking rose-and-thorn design; she had set a number of exotic prints behind glass, painted the stairwell, washed the windows, and papered both front rooms. She had found a lectern, upon which to place her almanac, and several shawled lamps, which she had placed in various situations around the former hotel's front rooms in order to create a more mystical atmosphere. Mannering opened his mouth to comment upon the transformation—and came up short.

'Why—it's Mr. Sook,' he said, in astonishment. 'And Mr. Quee!'

The two Chinese men stared back at him. They were sitting cross-legged on either side of the hearth, their faces painted very thickly with grease.

'Do you know these men?' said Lydia Wells.

Mannering remembered himself. 'Only to look at them,' he said. 'I do a fair patch of business with the Chinamen, you know—and these boys are familiar faces in Kaniere. How do you do, fellows?'

'Good evening,' said Ah Sook. Ah Quee said nothing. Their expressions were all but indistinguishable beneath the greasepaint, which exaggerated their features, lengthening the corners of their eyes, emphasising the roundness of their cheeks.

Mannering turned to Mrs. Wells. 'What—they have a part in the *séance*, do they? In your employ?'

'This one came by this afternoon,' Mrs. Wells explained, pointing at Ah Sook, 'and I had the idea that his presence might add a certain flavour to the *séance* this evening. He agreed to return, and in the event, he did me one better: he brought his friend along. You must agree that two is a good deal better than one. I like an axis of symmetry in a room.'

'Where is Anna?' said Mannering.

'Oh—upstairs,' said Mrs. Wells. 'In fact it was you, Mr. Mannering, who gave me the idea. Your *Sensations from the Orient*. Nothing sells tickets like an Oriental touch! I saw it twice—once from the gallery, and once from the stalls.'

Mannering was frowning. 'When is she coming down?'

'Not until the *séance*,' said Mrs. Wells.

He started. 'What—not for the party? She won't be here for the party?'

Mrs. Wells turned away to arrange the glasses on the sideboard. 'No.'

'Why ever not?' said Mannering. 'You know there are a dozen men champing at the bit to get a word in with her. They're shelling out a week's wages just to get in the door—and it's all on account of Anna. You'd be mad to keep her upstairs.'

'She must prepare herself for the *séance*. I cannot have her equilibrium disturbed.'

'Poppycock,' said Mannering.

'Pardon me?' said Mrs. Wells, turning.

'I said that's poppycock. You're keeping her back—for a reason.'

'What do you imply?'

'I lost my best girl in Anna Wetherell,' said Mannering. 'I've kept my distance for three weeks, out of respect for God knows what, and now I want a chance to speak with her. There's no such thing as equilibrium disturbed and we both know it.'

'I feel I must remind you that this is a field in which you lack expertise.'

'Expertise!' said Mannering, contemptuously. 'Three weeks ago Anna didn't know equilibrium from her own elbow. This is poppycock, Mrs. Wells. Call her down.'

Mrs. Wells drew back. 'I must *also* remind you, Mr. Mannering, that you are a guest in my home.'

'This isn't a home; it's a place of business. I've paid you three shillings on the surety that Anna would be here.'

'In fact no such surety was given.'

'Hear this!' said Mannering—who was becoming very angry. 'I'll give you another piece of advice, Mrs. Wells, and I'll give it to you free: in show business, you give an audience exactly what they've paid for, and if you don't, you'll suffer the consequences of their unrest. It said in the paper that Anna would be here.'

'It said in the paper that she would be present at the *séance*, as my assistant.'

'What have you got on her?'

'I'm sure I don't know what you mean.'

'Why did she agree to it? To stay upstairs—alone, and in the dark?'

Mrs. Wells ignored this question. 'Miss Wetherell,' she said, 'has been learning to play out the patterns of the Tarot, an art at which she has proven to be something of an adept. Once I am satisfied that she has achieved mastery, she will advertise her services in the *West Coast Times*, and at that time you will be very welcome, as will all the citizens of Hokitika, to make an appointment with her.'

'And I'll be paying through the nose for the privilege, will I?'

'But of course,' said Mrs. Wells. 'I wonder that you expected otherwise.'

Ah Sook was looking at Mrs. Wells, Ah Quee, at Mannering.

'This is an outrage,' Mannering said.

'Perhaps you no longer wish to attend the party,' said Mrs. Wells. 'If that is the case, you need only say so; I shall repay your tariff in full.'

'What's the point of it? Keeping her upstairs.'

The widow laughed. 'Come, Mr. Mannering! We are in the same business, as you have already pointed out; I don't need to spell it out for you.'

'No. Spell it out,' said Mannering. 'Go on. Spell it out.'

Mrs. Wells did not, however; she gazed at him a moment, and then said, 'Why did you come to the party tonight?'

'To speak with Anna. And to get a measure of my competition. You.'

'The first of your ambitions will not be realised, as I have now made clear, and you surely must have achieved the second by now. This being the case, I do not see that there is any reason for you to remain.'

'I'm staying,' Mannering said.

'Why?'

'To keep an eye on you, that's why.'

'I see.' Mrs. Wells gazed at him. 'I think that there is another reason why you decided to attend the party tonight—a reason that you have not hitherto shared with me.'

'Oh? And what might that be?' said Mannering.

'I'm afraid I can only guess,' said Mrs. Wells.

'Well, go on—make your prediction. That's your game, isn't it? Tell my fortune.'

She put her head to the side, appraising him. Then she said, suddenly decisive, 'No; this time I believe I shall keep my prediction to myself.'

Mannering faltered, and after a moment Mrs. Wells gave her tinkling laugh, and drew herself upright, clasping her hands together over her bosom. Begging Mannering's leave to depart, she explained that she had hired two barmaids from the Star and Garter to wait on her guests that evening, and the girls had not yet been briefed: they were waiting in the kitchen, very patiently, and she would not suffer them to wait a moment longer. She invited

Mannering to pour himself a drink from the decanters set out upon the sideboard, and to make himself very much at home—and with that, she swept from the room, leaving Mannering staring after her, red-faced.

Once the door had closed behind her, he rounded on Ah Sook. 'What have *you* got to say for yourself, then?'

'To see Emery Staines,' said Ah Sook.

'You've got some questions for *him*, I suppose.'

'Yes.'

'Dead or alive,' said Mannering. 'It's one or the other, isn't it, Mr. Sook? It's one or the other, at this stage.'

He stamped to the sideboard and poured himself a very stiff drink.

Φ

Mrs. Wells had hired a two-man orchestra, comprising a fiddle and a flute, from the Catholic Friendly Society on Collingwood-street. The musicians arrived a little before seven, their instruments rolled in velvet, and Mrs. Wells directed them to the end of the hallway where two chairs had been set up facing the door. The only songs they knew were jigs and hornpipes, but Mrs. Wells had lit upon the idea that they might play their repertoire at a quarter time, or as slowly as their breath and co-ordination would permit, in order to be more in keeping with the tenor of the evening. Played slowly, the jigs turned sinister, and the hornpipes became sad; even Mannering, whose bad temper had not been assuaged by two fingers of brandy and the cheerful ministration of the Star and Garter barmaids, had to admit that the effect was very striking. When the first guests knocked upon the door, 'Sixpenny Money' was sounding at an aching drawl—putting one in mind not of dancing and celebration, but of funerals, sickness, and very bad news.

By eight o'clock the former hotel had reached capacity, and the air was thick with smoke.

'Have you ever watched a magician at a market? Have you ever seen a cup-and-ball man at work? Well, it's all in the art of diversion, Mr. Frost. They have ways of making you look away, by means of a joke or a noise or something unexpected, and while your head is turned, that's when the cups get swapped, or filled, or emptied, or what have you. I don't need to tell you that no diversion's as good as a woman, and tonight, you'll be contending with two.'

Frost glanced at Pritchard, uncomfortably, and then away: he was a little afraid of the chemist, and he did not like the way that Pritchard was looming over him—standing so close that when he spoke Frost could feel the heat of his breath. 'How do you propose I am not diverted?' he said.

'You keep both eyes open,' Pritchard said. 'Nilssen watches Anna. You watch the widow. Between the two of you, you've got them covered, you see? You watch Lydia Wells no matter what. If she invites you to close your eyes or look elsewhere—they often do that, you know—well, don't.'

Frost felt a twinge of irritation at this. He wondered what right Joseph Pritchard had, to allocate duties of surveillance at a séance to which he did not hold an invitation. And why was he assigned to the widow, when Nilssen got Anna? He did not voice these complaints aloud, however, for a barmaid was approaching with a decanter on a tray. Both men filled their glasses, thanked her, and watched her move away through the crowd.

As soon as she had left Pritchard resumed, with the same intensity. 'Staines has got to be *somewhere*,' he insisted. 'A man doesn't just vanish without a trace. What do we know for sure? Let us catalogue it. We know that Anna was the very last to see him alive. We know that she was lying about that opium—saying she'd eaten that ounce herself, when I saw for myself that that was a plain-faced lie. And we know that now she's fixing to call him up from the dead.'

It occurred to Frost suddenly that Pritchard's jacket fit him very ill, and that his necktie had not been pressed, and that his shirt was all but threadbare. Why, and his razor must be very blunt, Frost thought, to produce so uneven and patchy a shave. This criticism, internally voiced, gave him a sudden confidence. He said,

'You don't trust Anna very much, do you, Mr. Pritchard?'

Pritchard seemed taken aback by the assumption. 'There is

ample reason not to trust her,' he said coldly. 'As I have just chron-
icled for you.'

'But personally,' Frost said. 'As a woman. I gather that your
impression of her integrity is very low.'

'You talk of a whore's integrity!' Pritchard burst out, but he did
not go on.

After a moment Frost added, 'I wonder what you think of her.
That's all.'

Pritchard stared at Frost with a vacant expression. 'No,' he said,
at last. 'I don't trust Anna. I don't trust her a straw. I don't even love
her. But I wish I did. Isn't that a curious thing? I wish I did.'

Frost was uncomfortable. 'Hardly worth three shillings, is it?' he
said, referring to the party. 'I must say I expected more.'

Pritchard seemed embarrassed also. 'Just remember,' he said,
'during the *séance*, keep both eyes on Mrs. Wells.'

They turned away from one another, pretending to scan the
faces of the crowd, and for a moment the two men shared the
very same expression: the distant, slightly disappointed aspect of
one who is comparing the scene around him, unfavourably, to
other scenes, both real and imagined, that have happened, and
are happening, elsewhere.

Φ

'Mr. Balfour. May I speak with you a moment alone?'

Balfour glanced up: it was Harald Nilssen, looking characteris-
tically dapper in a vest of imperial blue. He saw on Nilssen's face
the hardened expression of a man who is resolved to ask a difficult
question, and his heart became heavy in his chest. 'Of course—
naturally, naturally,' he said. 'You can speak to me—of course you
can speak to me! Naturally!'

What fools men became, he thought, when they knew they were
about to be shamed. He followed Nilssen through the crowd.

When they were out of earshot of the parlour, Nilssen stopped
abruptly. 'I'll get right to it,' he said, turning on his heel.

'Yes,' said Balfour. 'Get right to it. That's always best. How do
you like the party?'

From the sitting room came a roar of laughter, and a woman's indignant squeal.

'I like it very well,' said Nilssen.

'No sign of Anna, though.'

'No.'

'And three shillings,' said Balfour. 'That's a price! We'll be drinking our money's worth—won't we?' He looked into his glass.

'I'll get right to it,' Nilssen said again.

'Yes,' said Balfour. 'Do.'

'Somehow,' Nilssen began, 'Mr. Lauderback knows about my commission. He's publishing a letter in the paper about it, to-morrow. Lambasting Shepard's character and so forth. I haven't seen it yet.'

'Oh dear,' Balfour said. 'Oh dear—yes, I see. I see.' He nodded vigorously, though not at Nilssen. They were standing almost side-by-side. Nilssen was directing his speech at a framed print upon the wall, and Balfour, at the wainscot.

'Governor Shepard penned a reply,' Nilssen went on, still addressing the print, 'which is to appear directly underneath Lauderback's, in to-morrow's paper. I've seen the reply: Shepard sent me a copy this afternoon.'

He gave a brief account of Shepard's response—causing Balfour's anxiety to dissolve, in a moment, into pure astonishment.

'Well,' he said, looking squarely at Nilssen for the first time, 'I'm blowed. That's a shark in shallow water, all right. Fancy Gov. Shepard coming up with something like *that*. Saying it's all *your* instigation—the investment—as a donation! I'm blowed! He's got you in a corner, hasn't he? What a confident devil that man is! What a snake!'

'Did you tell Mr. Lauderback about my commission?' Nilssen said.

'No!' said Balfour.

'You didn't even mention it—off-hand?'

'No!' said Balfour. 'Not a bit!'

'All right,' Nilssen said heavily. 'Thanks. I'm sorry to have troubled you. I suppose it has to be one of the others.'

Balfour started. 'One of the others? You mean—one of the fellows from the Crown?'

'Yes,' Nilssen said. 'Somebody must have broken his oath. *I* certainly didn't tell Mr. Lauderback anything—and I'm certain that nobody else knows about the investment, beyond the twelve who swore.'

Balfour was looking panicked. 'What about your boy?' he said.

Nilssen shook his head. 'He doesn't know.'

'Someone at the bank, maybe.'

'No: it was a private agreement—and Shepard has the only copy of the deed.' Nilssen sighed. 'Listen,' he said. 'I'm sorry for having sprung it on you—for having asked, you know—and doubted you. But I knew you were Lauderback's man—and, well, I had to make sure.'

'Naturally you did! Of course!'

Nilssen nodded gloomily. He looked through the drawing-room doorway to the crowd beyond—to Pritchard, who stood a clear head taller than any other man in the room—to Devlin, who stood in conversation with Clinch—to Löwenthal, who was talking to Frost—to Mannering, who was refilling his glass from the decanter on the sideboard, and laughing very freely at another man's joke.

'Hang tight,' said Balfour suddenly. 'You said that Shepard's letter mentioned Lauderback and Lydia Wells.'

'Yes,' said Nilssen, uncomfortably. 'He's made their affair all but public knowledge—saying that Lauderback must come clean about her. That's the—'

Balfour interrupted him. 'But how in all heaven does Shepard know about the affair in the first place? I hardly think that Lauderback would have—'

'I told him,' Nilssen burst out. 'I broke my oath. Oh, Mr. Balfour—he had me in a corner—and he knew I was hiding something—and I buckled. I couldn't think fast enough. You've every right to be furious with me. You've every right. I don't mind.'

'Not at all,' said Balfour—to whom this confession had come as a strange relief.

'Now Lauderback will know you didn't keep his confidence,'

Nilssen went on, miserably, 'and by to-morrow morning all of Westland will know that he took a mistress in Mrs. Wells, and perhaps he'll lose the seat in Parliament, and it's all my fault. I'm ever so sorry—truly, I am.'

'What else did you tell him?' Balfour said. 'About Anna—and the blackmail—and the gowns?'

'No!' said Nilssen, looking shocked. 'And nothing about Carver, either. All I said was that Mrs. Wells had been Lauderback's mistress. That was all. But now Governor Shepard's gone and said as much—in the paper.'

'Well, that's quite all right,' said Balfour, clapping Nilssen on the shoulder. 'That's quite all right! Governor Shepard might have found that out from anywhere. If Lauderback asks, I'll tell him that I've never spoken two words to Shepard in all my life, and that will be the truth.'

'I'm dreadfully sorry,' said Nilssen.

'Not a bit,' said Balfour, patting him. 'Not a bit of it.'

'Well, you're very kind to say so,' said Nilssen.

'Happy to help,' said Balfour.

'I still don't know who sold me out to Lauderback in the first place,' Nilssen said, after a moment. 'I'll have to keep asking, I suppose.'

He sighed, and turned again to scan the faces of the crowd.

'I say, Mr. Nilssen,' Balfour said, 'I've thought of something. Apropos of ... of ... well, of nothing at all really. Here. Next time I have some commission work—next time something comes across my desk, you know—I might not go to Mr. Cochran after all. You know he's had my business for a long time—but, well, I wonder if it might be time for a change. I'll wager we'll all come out of this business looking for a man to lean on. Looking for a man to trust. As I say—you'll have it—my business—in the future.'

He did not look at Nilssen; he began to fish in his jacket pocket for a cigar.

'That's very kind of you,' said Nilssen. He watched Balfour for a moment longer, and then, nodding slowly, turned away. Balfour found a cigar, unwrapped it, bit off its end, and placed it between his teeth; then he struck his match, angled it so the flame caught, and held the flame to the square end of the cigar. He puffed at it three times, blowing out his cheeks; then he shook out the match, plucked the cigar from his mouth, and turned it around, to make sure that the tobacco was burning.

Φ

'Mr. Clinch.'

'Yes,' said Clinch. 'What is it?'

'I have a question,' Tauwhare said.

'Well then—ask.'

'Why did you buy the cottage of Crosbie Wells?'

The hotelier groaned. 'Not that,' he said. 'Let's not talk about that. Not tonight.'

'Why?'

'Just leave it,' Clinch snapped. 'I'm out of humour. I'm not discussing Crosbie bloody Wells.'

He was watching the widow as she moved from guest to guest. Her crinoline was so wide that she parted the crowd wherever she walked, leaving an aisle of space behind her.

'She has a cruel face,' Tauwhare observed.

'Yes,' Clinch said, 'I think so, too.'

'Not a friend of Maori.'

'No, I expect not. Nor of the Chinese—as we can very well see. Nor of any man in this room, I don't doubt.' Clinch drained his glass. 'I'm out of humour, Mr. Tauwhare,' he said again. 'When I am out of humour, do you know what I like to do? I like to drink.'

'That's good,' Tauwhare said.

Clinch reached for the decanter. 'You'll have another?'

'Yes.'

He refilled both their glasses. 'Anyway,' he said, as he returned the decanter to the sideboard, 'the appeal will go through, and the sale will be revoked, and I'll get my deposit back, and that will be that. The cottage won't belong to me any longer: it will belong to Mrs. Wells.'

'Why did you buy?' Tauwhare persisted.

Clinch exhaled heavily. 'It wasn't even my idea,' he said. 'It was Charlie Frost's idea. Buy up some land, he said: that way nobody will ask any questions.'

Tauwhare said nothing, waiting for Clinch to go on; presently he did.

'Here's the argument,' he said. 'You don't need a miner's right if the land's your very own, do you? And if you find a piece of gold on your own land, it's yours, isn't it? That was the idea—his idea, I mean: it wasn't mine. I couldn't take the gowns to the bank—not without a miner's right. They'd ask where it came from, and then I'd be stuck. But if I had a piece of land for my very own, then nobody asks anything at all. I never knew about Johnny Quee, you see. I thought the gold had been in the dresses all along—still pure. So I saved up for a deposit. Charlie, he said to wait for either a deceased estate or a subdivision: either the one or the other, he said, for the sake of staying clean. So when the Wells tract came up for sale, I bought it first thing, thinking that—well, I don't know. It was stupid. Settling there, with—I don't know. Of course, Anna comes home from gaol in a different dress, the very next day—and then, after she quits the place, I find out the other dresses have been stripped. It was the leaden makeweights that I was feeling. The whole plan's gone to custard. I've got a piece of land I don't want, and no money to call my own, and Anna—well. You know about her.'

Tauwhare was frowning. 'The Arahura is a very sacred place,' he began.

'Yes, well,' said Clinch, waving a hand to silence him, 'the law's the law. If you want to buy the cottage back again, you're more than welcome; but it's not me you should be talking to. It's her.'

They gazed across the room at Mrs. Wells.

'The problem with beautiful women,' Clinch said presently, 'is that they always know it, and the knowing turns them proud. I like a woman who doesn't know her own beauty.'

'A stupid woman,' Tauwhare said.

'Not stupid,' Clinch said. 'Modest. Unassuming.'

'I do not know those words.'

Clinch waved a hand. 'Doesn't say too much. Doesn't speak about herself. Knows when to keep quiet, and knows when to speak.'

'Cunning?' said Tauwhare.

'Not cunning.' Clinch shook his head. 'Not cunning, and not stupid either. Just—careful, and quiet. And innocent.'

'Who is this woman?' said Tauwhare slyly.

'No: this isn't a real woman,' said Clinch. He scowled. 'Never mind.'

'Hi—Edgar. Do you have a moment?'

Löwenthal had come up behind them.

'By all means,' said Clinch. 'Excuse me, Mr. Tauwhare.'

Löwenthal blinked, seeing Tauwhare for the first time. 'You must have gone down to the wreck,' he said. 'Find anything?'

Tauwhare did not like to be addressed with condescension, as though he belonged to a servile class; nor could he forgive Löwenthal for having shamed him earlier that day.

'No,' he replied, scornfully. 'Nothing.'

'Pity,' said Löwenthal, already turning away.

'What's on your mind, Ben?' said Clinch, when they were alone.

'It's an indelicate question, I'm afraid,' said Löwenthal. 'About the child of Anna's—the baby that never came to term.'

'All right,' said Clinch, cautiously.

'You recall the night I found her—after the dust-up with Carver.'

'Of course.'

'That was the night she confessed that Carver was the child's father.'

'Yes—I remember.'

'I would like to know whether you knew that fact already, or whether, like me, you heard that confession for the first time that evening,' Löwenthal said. 'You will please forgive my indelicacy— and the impertinence of the subject in question.'

Clinch was silent for a long time. 'No,' he said at last. 'That was the first time she spoke of it. She kept mum on the subject until that night.'

'But did you have an inkling?' Löwenthal pressed. 'Some idea?

Were you of the opinion, perhaps, that Carver might have been the—ah—the sire?'

Clinch looked uncomfortable. 'It was some fellow from Dunedin days,' he said. 'That's all I knew. It wasn't a Hokitika chap: the months didn't match up.'

'And Carver knew Anna in Dunedin.'

'She came over on *Godspeed*,' Clinch said shortly. 'Beyond that, I couldn't tell you. What's this in aid of?'

Löwenthal explained what had happened in the office of the *West Coast Times* that afternoon. 'Anna might not have been telling the truth, you see. She might have been spinning us a line. Of course we never had reason to doubt her word—until now.'

Clinch scowled. 'But who else could it be—if not Carver?'

Löwenthal pursed his lips. 'I don't know,' he said. 'Any number of men, I suppose. Perhaps it's no one we know.'

'This is just Carver's word against Anna's,' Clinch said hotly. 'You aren't taking Carver's part—on the strength of a single declaration? Any man can deny a thing, you know; it doesn't cost a man a penny, to deny a thing!'

'I'm not taking either part—yet,' Löwenthal said. 'But I do think that the timing of Anna's confession could be significant. Perhaps.'

Frowning, Clinch reached up to stroke the side of his face. As he did so Löwenthal caught the spice of his cologne and realised that Clinch must have paid for a scented shave at the barbershop, rather than the penny lather that was the standing order of most Hokitika men—a guess that was further confirmed when Clinch moved his hand, and Löwenthal saw a reddish spray of irritation upon the man's soft cheeks. Discreetly, Löwenthal looked the hotelier up and down. Clinch's jacket had been brushed, and his collar starched; the shirt he was wearing seemed very white, and the toes of his boots were freshly blackened. *Oh*, Löwenthal thought, with pity: *he made himself handsome, for Anna.*

'So she only named the father after the child was dead,' Clinch said at last, and in a very harsh voice. 'That's a whore's honour— that's all that is.'

'Perhaps you're right,' Löwenthal said, more kindly. 'Let's drop the subject.'

Φ

'Mr. Walter Moody—Mrs. Lydia Wells,' said Gascoigne. 'Mr. Moody is come to Hokitika from Scotland, Mrs. Wells, to make his fortune in the gorge; Mrs. Wells, as you will know, Mr. Moody, is the mistress of this establishment, and a great enthusiast of realms.'

Lydia made a very pretty curtsey, and Moody a short but respectful bow. Moody then paid the necessary compliments to his hostess, thanking her very nicely for the evening's entertainment, and praising her renovations of the old hotel. Despite his best efforts, the compliments came out very flat: when he looked at her, he thought only of Lauderback, and Crosbie Wells.

When he had finished speaking she said, 'Do you have an interest in the occult, Mr. Moody?'—a question which Moody could not answer honestly without risking offence.

He paused only a moment, however, before replying, 'There are many things that are yet arcane to me, Mrs. Wells, and I hope that I am a curious man; if I am interested in those truths that are yet unknown, it is only so that they might, in time, be made known—or, to put it more plainly, so that in time, I might come to know them.'

'You are wonderfully free with one verb, I notice,' the widow returned. 'What does it mean for you, Mr. Moody, to *know* something? I fancy you put rather a lot of stock in *knowing*—judging from the way you speak.'

Moody smiled. 'Why,' he said, 'I suppose that to know a thing is to see it from all sides.'

'To see it from all sides,' the widow repeated.

'But I confess you catch me off guard; I have not spent any time working on the definition, and should not like to hear it quoted back to me—at least not until I have spent some time thinking about how I might defend it.'

'No,' the widow agreed, 'your definition leaves much to be desired. There are so many exceptions to the rule! How could one possibly see a *spirit* from all sides, for example? The notion is incredible.'

Moody gave another short bow. 'You are quite right to name that as an exception, Mrs. Wells. But I am afraid I do not believe a spirit can be known at all—by anyone—and I certainly do not believe a spirit can be seen. I do not mean to impugn your talents in the slightest—but there it is: I do not believe in spirits, categorically.'

'And yet you applied for a ticket to the *séance* this evening,' the widow pointed out.

'My curiosity was piqued.'

'By the particular spirit in question, perhaps?'

'Mr. Staines?' Moody shrugged. 'I have never met the man. I arrived in Hokitika some fortnight after he disappeared. But since then I have heard his name many times, of course.'

'Mr. Gascoigne says that you have come to Hokitika to make your fortune.'

'Yes: so I hope.'

'And how will you make it?'

'By dint of hard work and good planning, I expect.'

'Of course, there are many rich men who work little, and plan nothing at all.'

'Those men are lucky,' Moody said.

'Do you not wish to be lucky also?'

'I wish to be able to call myself deserving of my lot,' Moody said carefully. 'Luck is by nature undeserved.'

'What an honourable answer,' said Lydia Wells.

'And a truthful one, I hope,' said Moody.

'Aha,' said the widow. 'We are back to "truth" again.'

Gascoigne had been watching Lydia Wells. 'You see how her mind is working,' he said to Moody. 'She will swoop down in a moment, and savage your argument. Prepare yourself.'

'I hardly know how to prepare to be savaged,' Moody said.

Gascoigne was right. The widow lifted her chin and said, 'Are you a man of religion, Mr. Moody?'

'I am a man of philosophy,' he rejoined. 'Those aspects of

religion that can be called philosophy, interest me extremely; those that cannot, do not.'

'I see,' said Lydia Wells. 'I am afraid that in my case it is quite the reverse: it is only those philosophies that can be called religions that hold any interest for me.'

Gascoigne laughed outright at this. 'Very good,' he said, wagging his finger. 'That is very good.'

Moody was amused, despite himself, by the widow's acuity, but he was determined not to let her take the upper hand. 'It seems that we have little in common, Mrs. Wells,' he said. 'I hope that this lack of common ground will not be an impediment to friendship.'

'We disagree upon the validity of spirits: we have established that much,' said Lydia Wells. 'But let me put the contrary question to you. What about a soul—a living soul? Do you believe that you can "know" a person who is living, if you cannot "know" a person who is dead?'

Moody considered this, smiling. After a moment, the widow went on:

'Do you feel that you could ever truly "know" your friend Mr. Gascoigne, for example? Can you see *him* from all sides?'

Gascoigne looked very peeved for having been used as a rhetorical example, and said so aloud; the widow shushed him, and put the question to Moody a second time.

Moody looked at Gascoigne. In fact he had anatomised Gascoigne's character to a very fine degree of detail, over the three weeks of their acquaintance. He felt that he understood the scope and limits of the man's intelligence, the quality of his sentiment, and the tenor of his many expressions and habits. He felt, as a whole, that he could summarise the man's character very accurately. But he knew that Lydia Wells was intending to trap him, and in the end he chose to reply very blandly indeed, repeating that he had only arrived in Hokitika but three weeks ago, and could not hope to form an accurate assessment of Gascoigne's soul in such a time. That project, he added, would require more than three weeks of observation.

'Mr. Moody was Mr. Carver's passenger,' Gascoigne put in. 'He arrived on the *Godspeed* the very night she came to ground.'

Moody felt a stirring of unease at this disclosure. He had used a false name while booking his passage upon *Godspeed*, and he did not like to advertise the fact that he had arrived in Hokitika upon that craft, given the nature of what he had witnessed—or imagined that he had witnessed—in the hours before the ship had foundered. He looked at the widow, seeking, in her face, some flicker of doubt or recognition that might show that she had known about the bloody phantom in *Godspeed*'s hold.

But Lydia Wells was smiling. 'Did he?' she said, looking Moody up and down. 'Then I'm afraid Mr. Moody is a very common specimen of a man indeed.'

'How so?' Moody said stiffly.

The widow laughed. 'You are a lucky man who is scornful of the notion of luck,' she said. 'I am afraid, Mr. Moody, that I have met a great many men like you.'

Before Moody could think of a reply to this, she picked up a small silver bell, rang it sharply, and announced, in a voice that was no less penetrating for its husky half-whisper, that all those without tickets were to make their departures at once, for the *séance* was about to begin.

*In which Sook Yongsheng forgets his shilling; Lydia Wells
becomes hysterical; and we receive an answer from the realm
of the dead.*

What a different gathering this was to the clandestine council that
had assembled in the Crown Hotel three weeks ago! The Crown
had played host to a party of twelve, which, following Moody's
arrival, became a party of thirteen; here, in the front room of the
Wayfarer's Fortune, they were a party of eleven seeking to summon
a twelfth.

Charlie Frost, under Joseph Pritchard's instruction, kept his eyes
fixed upon Lydia Wells as the widow led the seven ticket holders
into the parlour where Ah Sook and Ah Quee, shining with greasepaint, sat cross-legged on either side of the hearth. The drapes had
been drawn over the parlour windows, and all but one of the paraffin lamps had been doused, giving the room a pinkish glow. Above
this last lamp a tin dish of attar had been placed on a metal stand,
and the liquid, gently heated by the warmth of the flame, filled the
room with the pleasant scent of roses.

Mrs. Wells invited the men to take their seats, which, in the interval while the other guests departed the Wayfarer's Fortune and
dispersed into the night, had been arranged in a circle in the
middle of the room. There was much embarrassment and nerv-
ousness in the room as the seven guests were seated. One man kept
emitting a high-pitched giggle; others grinned and elbowed their

mates in the ribs. Mrs. Wells paid these disturbances no notice. She was busy arranging five candles in a star pattern upon a plate, and lighting them, one by one. When the candles were lit, and the paper spill extinguished, Lydia Wells seated herself at last, and remarked, in a voice that was suddenly hushed and conspiratorial, that Anna Wetherell, these hours past, had been preparing her mind for the impending communion with the dead. She was not to be spoken to, when she made her entrance in the parlour, for even the smallest disturbance could disrupt her state of mind, which in turn would disrupt the widow's own transmissions. Did the present company consent to ignore her?

The present company consented.

Did the present company consent to assist the widow's transmissions further, by maintaining a state of mental receptivity for the duration of the event? Would every man agree to keep his mind cool and open, his limbs relaxed, his breathing deep and rhythmic, and his attention focused absolutely, like that of a monk at prayer?

This was assured.

'I cannot tell you what will happen in this room tonight,' the widow went on, still speaking in a voice of conspiracy. 'Perhaps the furniture will move about. Perhaps we will feel breezes—the breath of the underworld, some might call it—as the spirits around us are disturbed. Perhaps the dead will speak through the mouths of the living. Or perhaps they will reveal themselves by the presentation of a token.'

'What do you mean, a token?' one of the diggers said.

Lydia Wells turned her calm gaze upon the speaker. 'Sometimes,' she said quietly, 'and for reasons unknown to us, the dead are unable to speak. When this happens, they choose to communicate in other ways. I was party to a *séance* in Sydney where this occurred.'

'What happened?'

Mrs. Wells became glazed. 'A woman had been killed in her own home,' she said, 'under circumstances that were a touch mysterious—and some months following her death, a select group of spiritists convened at her house, to contact her.'

'How was she killed?'

'The family dog went savage,' said Lydia Wells. 'Quite out of character, the beast attacked her—and ripped out her throat.'

'Hideous.'

'Ghastly.'

'The circumstances of her death were suspicious,' the widow continued, 'not the least because the dog was shot before its true nature could be established by the law. But the case was closed, and the woman's husband, wild with grief, quit the house and sailed away. Some months later, a servant who had been employed in the house brought the matter to a medium's attention. We arranged for a *séance* to be held in the very room in which this woman had been killed.

'A gentleman in our group—not the medium, but another spiritist of high renown—happened to be wearing a pocket watch that evening. The watch was tucked inside his vest pocket, with the chain pinned to his breast. He had wound it, he assured us afterwards, before he arrived at the house, and the piece kept very good time. Well, that night—during the *séance*—there came a queer little whirring noise from his vest. We all heard it, though we did not know what it was. He retrieved the piece, and found to his astonishment that the dial now read three minutes past one. He insisted that he had wound the watch at six o'clock, and it was not yet nine. There was no way that the hands could have moved so far on their own accord, and he could hardly have turned the knob by accident! He tried the knob—and found that it had stuck. It was broken. In fact the piece never worked again.'

'But what did it mean?' someone said. 'Three minutes past one?'

The widow's voice became low. 'We could only assume,' she said, 'that the spirit of the dead woman was trying to tell us something, very urgently. The time of her death, perhaps? Or was she delivering a warning? A death that was yet to come?'

Charlie Frost found that he was breathing shallowly.

'What happened next?' Nilssen whispered.

'We decided to stay in the drawing room until three minutes past one in the morning,' said Lydia Wells. 'Perhaps, we thought, the spirit was inviting us to stay until that time—at which point something was to happen. We waited until the hour struck one; we waited in silence for one minute—two minutes—three—and then, exactly at that moment, there was a terrible crash: a painting tumbled from its hook upon the wall. We all turned, and saw, behind it, a hole in the plaster. The painting had been put up, you see, to mask the hole.

'Well, the women in the group were screaming; there was noise all about; you can imagine the commotion. Someone found a knife, and cut out the piece of plaster—and lo and behold, lodged into the plaster, there was a ball of shot.'

Frost and Nilssen exchanged a quick glance. The widow's story had reminded them both of the bullet that had vanished from Anna Wetherell's bedchamber, in the upper room of the Gridiron Hotel.

'Was the case ever solved?' somebody said.

'Oh, yes,' the widow said. 'I shan't go into the details—there are too many—but you can look it all up in the papers if you're curious. You see, the woman was never savaged by a dog at all. She had been murdered by her own husband—and he'd shot the dog, and slashed her throat himself, to cover it up.'

There were murmurs of distress around the room.

'Yes,' said Lydia Wells. 'Tragic, the whole story. Elizabeth something, the woman's name was. I forget the last name. Well, the good news was that when the case reopened, they had two clues on their side: first, that she had been killed by a ball from a Colt Army handgun ... and second, that the precise time of her death was three minutes past one.'

The widow was quiet for a moment, and then she laughed. 'But you aren't here tonight to hear me tell tales!' She rose from her chair. Several of the assembled men made to rise also, out of politeness, but the widow put up her hand, stalling them. 'I regret to say that the sceptics of the world are very many,' she said, 'and for every good-hearted man, there are ten more who are not good at all. There may be men among you who will attempt to deny whatever happens tonight, or who will attempt to discredit me. I invite you all to look around you, now, and to reassure yourselves that this room contains no tricks or deceits or follies of any kind. I know as well as you that there are many pretenders in the art of fortune telling, but you may rest assured that *I* am not one of them.' She spread her arms and said, 'You can see that I am concealing nothing on my person. Don't worry—you are free to look.'

There was tittering at this, and much shuffling as the men looked around them, examining the ceiling, the chairs, the paraffin lamp on the table, the candles, the rug upon the floor. Charlie Frost kept his eyes on Lydia Wells. She did not look tense. She twirled around, revealing that she was hiding nothing in her skirts, and then seated herself very easily, smiling at the room at large. She picked at a loose thread upon her sleeve and waited until the men were still.

'Excellent,' she said, when the collective attention had focused upon her once again. 'Now that we are all happy, and ready, I shall cut the lights, and await Anna's arrival.'

She leaned forward and doused the paraffin lamp, plunging them all into the gloom of candlelight. After several seconds of quiet, there came three knocks at the parlour door behind them, and Lydia Wells, still fussing over the lamp, called, 'Come!'

The door opened, and the seven men turned. Frost, forgetting Pritchard's instruction for a moment, looked too.

Anna was standing in the doorway with an expression of ghostly vacancy upon her face. She was still wearing the mourning dress she had been gifted by Aubert Gascoigne, but if the dress had been ill fitting once, it looked wretched on her now. The gown hung from her shoulders as though from a rail. The waist, though plainly cinched, was loose, and the tatted collar masked an almost concave breast. Her face was very pale, her expression sombre. She did not look at the faces of the assembled crowd. With her eyes fixed upon the middle distance, she came forward, slowly, and sank into the vacant armchair facing Lydia Wells.

Why, thought Frost, as she sat down, *she is starving*! He glanced at Nilssen, meaning to catch the other man's eye, but Nilssen was frowning at Anna, an expression of grave perplexity upon his face. Too late, Frost remembered his own assignation, and turned back to the widow—who, in the brief moment while every man's head was turned towards the door, had *done* something. Yes: she had done something, certainly, for she was smoothing down her dress in a self-conscious, satisfied way, and her expression had suddenly become brisk. What had she done? What had she altered? In the dim light he could not tell. Frost cursed himself for having looked away. This was just the kind of subterfuge that Pritchard had predicted. He vowed that he would not look away a second time.

The corners of the room had now vanished entirely into black. The only light came from the flickering glow of the candles in the centre of the group, and around it the eleven faces had a greying, ghostly look. Without taking his eyes from the widow's face, Frost noted that in fact the circle of chairs was not perfectly circular: it was more nearly an ellipsis, placed with its longest axis pointing to the door, and Lydia seated at its farthest end. By placing the seats in this configuration, she had been able to ensure that every man's head would turn towards the door—and away from *her*—when Anna arrived. Well, Frost thought, the Chinese men, at least, must have seen the sleight of hand that she had performed in that quick instant when Anna appeared in the doorway. He made a second mental note: to question them once the *séance* was over.

The group now joined hands, at the widow's instruction; and then, in the fluttering light of the candles, Lydia Wells heaved a great sigh, smiled, and closed her eyes.

The widow's visitation took a very long time coming. The group sat in perfect silence for nigh on twenty minutes, each man holding himself very still, breathing rhythmically, and waiting for a sign. Charlie Frost kept his eyes on Mrs. Wells. At length she set up a humming sound, low at the back of her throat. The humming thickened, acquired pitch; soon one could make out words, some nonsensical, some recognisable only by their shapes, their syllables. These too thickened into phrases, entreaties, commands: finally Mrs. Wells, arching her back, made her request of the world of the dead: to give up the shade of Emery Staines.

Later, Frost would describe the scene that followed as, variously, a 'fit', a 'seizure', and a 'prolonged convulsion'. He knew that none of these explanations was quite right, for none conveyed, accurately, either the elaborate theatrics of Lydia Wells's performance, or Frost's acute embarrassment, in witnessing them. Mrs. Wells called out Staines's name, again and again, intoning the words with a lover's dying fall—and when no answer came, she became agitated. She suffered paroxysms. She repeated syllables, like a babbling child. Her head lolled against her chest, reared back, lolled again. Presently her convulsions began approaching a kind of climax. Her breathing became faster and faster—and then suddenly quelled. Her eyes snapped open.

Charlie Frost felt a cold jolt of unease: Lydia Wells was staring directly at him, and the expression on her face was unlike any he had seen her wear before: it was rigid, bloodless, fierce. But then the flames from the candles ducked and leaped and he saw that Lydia Wells was not looking at him, but past him, over his shoulder, to where Ah Sook sat in the corner in his Oriental pose. Frost did not blink; he did not look away. Then Lydia Wells gave a strange sound. Her eyes rolled back in her head. The muscles in her throat began to pulse. Her mouth moved strangely, as though she were chewing on the air. And then in a voice that did not belong to her she said:

'*Ngor yeu nei wai mut haak ngor dei gaa zuk ge ming sing tung wai waai ngor ge sing yu fu zaak. Mou leon nei hai bin, dang ngor co yun gaam cut lai, ngor yat ding wui wan dou nei. Ngor yeu wan nei bou sou*—'

And she gave a great shudder, and pitched sideways, onto the floor. In the very same moment (Frost would discuss this inexplicable event with Nilssen for weeks to come) the paraffin lamp on the table lurched violently to the side, coming down upon the plate of candles that had been set out next to it. This was a mistake that ought to have been very easily righted, for the glass globe of the lamp did not shatter, and the paraffin did not spill—but there was a colossal *whoosh* of flame, and the circle of men was suddenly illuminated: the entire surface of the table was burning.

In the next moment everyone burst into life. Someone shouted to cover the fire. One of the diggers pulled the widow to safety, and two others cleared the sofa; the fire was doused with shawls and blankets; the lamp was knocked away; everyone was talking at once. Charlie Frost, wheeling round in the sudden darkness, saw that Anna Wetherell had not moved, and her expression had not changed. The sudden blaze of the fire did not seem to have alarmed her in the slightest.

Someone lit the lamp.

'Was that it? Was that what was supposed to happen?'

'What did she say?'

'Clear a space, would you?'

'Coo—to see us all lit up like that!'

'Some kind of primitive—'

'Make sure she's breathing.'

'Have to admit, I didn't expect—'

'Did it mean anything, do you think? What she said? Or was it—'

'That wasn't Emery Staines, sure as I'm—'

'Another spirit? Working through—'

'The way the lamp moved of its own accord like that!'

'We ought to ask the johnnies. Hi! Was that Chinese?'

'Does he understand?'

'Was that Chinese, that she was speaking just now?'

But Ah Quee did not appear to understand the question. One of the diggers leaned over and tapped him on the shoulder.

'What was that, eh?' he said. 'What was it that she said? Was it Chinese, what she was saying? Or some other tongue?'

Ah Quee returned his gaze without understanding, and did not speak. It was Ah Sook who answered.

'Lydia Wells speak Cantonese,' he said.

'Yes?' Nilssen said eagerly, swivelling about. 'And what did she say?'

Ah Sook studied him. '"One day I come back and kill you. You kill a man. He die—so you die. I come back and kill you, one day."'

Nilssen's eyes went wide; his next question died on his lips. He turned to Anna—who was looking at Ah Sook, her expression faintly perplexed. Charlie Frost was frowning.

'Where's Staines in all of that?' demanded one of the diggers.

Ah Sook shook his head. 'Not Staines,' he said quietly. He got up from his cushion suddenly, and walked to the window, folding his arms.

'Not Staines?' said the digger. 'Who then?'

'Francis Carver,' said Ah Sook.

There was an explosion of outrage around the room.

'Francis Carver? How's that for a *séance*—when he isn't even dead? Why—I could talk to Carver myself; I'd only have to knock upon his door!'

'But he's at the Palace,' said another. 'That's fifty yards away from where we are.'

'That's not the point.'

'I mean you can't deny that *something* strange—'

'I could have talked to Carver myself,' the digger repeated, stubbornly. 'I don't need a medium for that.'

'What about the lamp, though? How do you account for the lamp?'

'It jumped across the room!'

'It *levitated*.'

Ah Sook had stiffened. 'Francis Carver,' he said, directing his question to Harald Nilssen. 'At the Palace Hotel?'

Nilssen frowned—surely Ah Sook knew this already! 'Yes, Carver's staying at the Palace,' he said. 'On Revell-street. The building with the blue edging, you know. Next to the hardware store.'

'How long?' said Ah Sook.

Nilssen looked even more confused. 'He's been here for three weeks,' he said, lowering his voice. 'Since the night—I mean, since the *Godspeed* came to ground.'

The other men were still arguing.

'It's not a *séance* unless it's talking with the dead.'

'No—when you talk to Carver, it's *you* who ends up dead!'

They laughed at this, and then the digger's mate said, 'Rum do, you're thinking? Some kind of a hoax?'

The stubborn digger looked inclined to agree, but he cast a glance over at Lydia Wells. The widow was still unconscious, and her face was very pale. Her mouth was partly open, showing the glint of a molar and a dry tongue, and her eyes were fluttering weakly beneath the lids. If she was shamming, the digger thought, then she was shamming extraordinarily well. But he had paid for a communion with Emery Staines. He had not paid to hear a string of Chinese syllables and then watch a woman fall into a faint. Why, how could he be sure that the words were even Chinese? She might have been speaking gibberish! The Chinese fellow might be in on the secret, and she might have paid him a fee, to corroborate the lie.

But the digger had a cowardly temperament; he did not voice these opinions aloud. 'Wouldn't want to say,' he said at last, but he still looked surly.

'Well, we'll ask her, when she comes around.'

'Frank Carver speaks *Chinese*?' one of the others said, in a voice of incredulity.

'He goes back and forth from Canton, does he not?'

'Born in Hong Kong.'

'Yes, but to *speak* the language—as they do!'

'Makes you think different of the man.'

At this point the digger who had been discharged to the kitchen returned with a glass of water, and threw it across Lydia's face. Gasping, she revived. The men crowded closer, asking in an anxious chorus after her health and safety, so that it was some moments before the widow had a chance to respond. Lydia Wells looked from face to face in some confusion; after a moment, she even managed a weak laugh. But her laughter was without its usual surety, and as she accepted a glass of Andalusian brandy from the man at her elbow her hand visibly trembled.

She drank, and in the moments that followed, all manner of questions were put to her—what had she seen? What could she remember? Whom had she channelled? Had she made any contact with Emery Staines?

Her answers were disappointing. She could remember nothing at all from the point she fell into her trance—which was unusual, she said, for usually she could recall her 'visions' very well indeed. The men prompted her, but without success; she simply could not remember anything at all. When it was revealed to her that she had spoken in a foreign tongue, quite fluently and for some time, she looked genuinely puzzled.

'But I don't know a word of Chinese,' she said. 'Are you sure? And the johnnies confirmed it? Real Chinese? You're really sure?'

This was confirmed, with much perplexity and excitement.

'And what is all *this* mess?' She gestured weakly at the scorched table and the remains of the fire.

'The lamp just fell,' said one of the diggers. 'It just fell, of its own accord.'

'It did more than fall: it *levitated*!'

Lydia looked at the paraffin lamp a moment, and then seemed to rouse herself. '*Well*!' She raised herself a little higher on the sofa. 'So I channelled the ghost of a Chinaman!'

'Interference wasn't what I paid for,' the stubborn digger said.

'No,' said Lydia Wells, soothingly, 'no—of course it wasn't. Of course we must refund the cost of *all* your tickets ... but tell me: what were the very words I spoke?'

'Something to do with a murder,' said Frost, who was still watching her very closely. 'Something to do with revenge.'

'Indeed!' said Mrs. Wells. She seemed impressed.

'Ah Sook said it had something to do with Francis Carver,' said Frost.

Mrs. Wells went pale; she started forward. 'What were the very words—the exact words?'

The diggers looked around them, but perceived only Ah Quee, who returned their gaze stonily, and did not speak.

'He doesn't have English.'

'Where's the other one?'

'Where did he go?'

Ah Sook had extracted himself from the group some minutes before, padding from the room and into the foyer so quietly that nobody had noticed his departure. The revelation that Francis Carver had returned to Hokitika—that he had been in Hokitika for *three weeks*—had caused a flood of private emotion in his breast, and he desired, all of a sudden, to be alone.

He leaned against the rail of the porch and looked out, down the long arm of Revell-street, towards the quay. The long row of hanging lanterns formed a doubled seam of light that came together, in a haze of yellow, some two hundred yards to the south; their brightness was so intense that upon the camber of the street it might have been high noon, and the shadows of the alleys were made all the blacker, by contrast. A pair of drunks staggered past him, clutching one another around the waist. A whore passed in the other direction, her skirts gathered high above her knees. She looked at him curiously, and Ah Sook, after a moment of blankness, remembered that his face was still heavily painted, the corners of his eyes lengthened with kohl, his cheeks rounded with white. She called out to him, but he shook his head, and she walked on. From somewhere nearby there came a sudden roar of laughter and applause.

Ah Sook sucked his lips between his teeth. So Francis Carver had returned to Hokitika once again. He surely was not aware that his old associate was living in a hut at Kaniere, less than five miles away! Carver was not a man to bear a risk if he could remove the threat of that risk altogether. In that case, Ah Sook thought, perhaps he, Ah Sook, had the advantage. He sucked again at his teeth, and then, after a moment, shook his head: no. Lydia Wells had recognised him that morning. She would surely have relayed the news to Carver at once.

Inside, the conversation had returned to the subject of the paraffin lamp—a trick that Ah Sook had already dismissed out of hand. Lydia Wells had merely slipped a loop of thread over the knob of the lamp, at the moment she doused it. The thread was the same colour as her dress, and the other end of it was affixed to the inside of her wrist. One sharp twitch of her right hand, and the lamp would fall over the candles. The small table upon which the candles were burning had been coated with paraffin oil, which had the virtues of being both odourless and colourless, such that, to an outsider, the table might have seemed merely clean; at first contact with a naked flame, however, the surface of the table was sure to ignite. It was all a charade, a sham. Mrs. Wells had not made any kind of communion with the realm of the dead, and the words that she had spoken were not the words of a dead man. Ah Sook knew this because the words were his own.

The whore had lingered in the thoroughfare; she now called out to the men on the veranda opposite, and lifted the flounces of her skirt a little higher. The men called back in response, and one leaped up to caper. Ah Sook watched them with a distant expression. He marvelled at the strange power of feminine hysteria—that Lydia Wells might have remembered his very words, perfectly, over all these years. She did not speak Cantonese. However could she have recalled his speech, and his intonation, so exactly? *That* was uncanny, Ah Sook thought. For he might have taken her, by her 'visitation', for a true native of Canton.

In the street the men were pooling their shillings, while the streetwalker stood by. There came a whistle-blast from near the quays, and then a shout of warning from the duty sergeant, and then running footsteps, approaching. Ah Sook watched the men scatter and formed his resolution in his mind.

He would return to Kaniere that very evening, clear all his belongings from his cottage, and make for the hills. There he would apply himself wholly to the task of turning the ground. He would save every flake of dust he came upon, and live as simply as he was able, until he had amassed a total of five ounces. He would not take opium until he held five ounces in his hand; he would not drink; he would not gamble; he would eat only the cheapest and plainest of foods. But the very moment that he reached this target he would return to Hokitika. He would change the metal at the Grey and Buller Bank. He would walk across the thoroughfare to Tiegreen's Hardware and Supply. He would lay his paper note upon the counter-top. He would purchase a store of shot, a tin of black powder, and a gun. Then he would walk to the Palace Hotel, climb the stairs, open Carver's door, and take his life. And after that? Ah Sook exhaled again. After that, nothing. After that his life would come full circle, and he could rest, at last.

PART THREE

The House of Self-undoing

20 March 1866

42° 43' 0" S ∫ 170° 58' 0" E

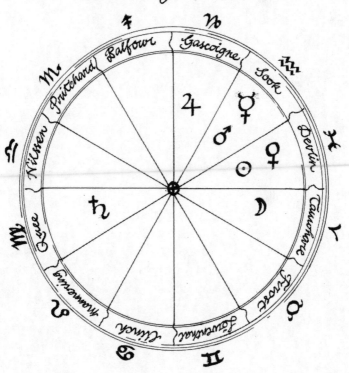

MERCURY IN AQUARIUS

In which Moody passes on some vital information, and Sook
Yongsheng presents him with a gift.

On the morning of the 20th of March Walter Moody rose before
the dawn, rang for hot water, and washed standing at the window,
looking over the rooftops as the navy pre-dawn sky faded to grey,
then pale blue, then the splendid yellow of a fresh yolk—by which
time he was dressed, and descending the stairs, and calling for his
toast to be buttered, and his eggs boiled hard. En route to the
dining room he lingered in the hallway, leaning his ear towards
the door of a locked chamber at the foot of the stairs. After listening a moment he perceived a grainy, rhythmic sound, and
continued on, satisfied that the room's inhabitant was still very
sound asleep.

The Crown dining room was empty save for the intermittent
presence of the cook, who stifled a yawn as he brought Moody's
pot of tea, and another as he delivered the morning edition of the
West Coast Times, the pages slightly damp from the chill of the night.
Moody scanned the paper as he ate. The front page was composed
chiefly of repeat notices. The banks offered competing terms of
interest, each promising the very best price for gold. The hoteliers
boasted the various distinctions of their hotels. The grocers and
warehousemen listed a full inventory of their wares, and the shipping news reported which passengers had lately departed, and

which passengers had lately arrived. The second page of the paper was taken over by a long and rather spiteful review of the latest show at the Prince of Wales ('so poor in quality as to defy—because it is beneath—criticism'), and several gossipy correspondences from goldfield speculators in the north. Moody turned to the social notices as he finished his second egg, and his eyes came to rest upon a pair of names he recognised. A modest ceremony had been planned. No date had yet been determined. There would be no honeymoon. Cards and other expressions of congratulation could be addressed care of the prospective groom, who took his nightly lodging at the Palace Hotel.

Moody was frowning as he folded the paper, wiped his mouth, and rose from the table—but it was not the engagement, nor the fact of its announcement, that preoccupied his thinking as he returned upstairs to fetch his hat and coat. It was the matter of the forwarding address.

For Moody knew very well that Francis Carver no longer lodged at the Palace Hotel. His rooms at the Palace stood as before, with his frockcoat hanging in the armoire, his trunk set out at the foot of the bed, and his bedclothes mussed and strewn about. He still broke his fast in the Palace dining room every morning, and drank whisky in the Palace parlour every night. He still paid his weekly board to the Palace proprietor—who, as far as Moody had been able to ascertain, remained quite unaware that his most notorious guest was paying two pounds weekly for an unoccupied room. The fact of Carver's nightly relocation was not commonly known, and were it not for the accident of their conjunction, Moody might have also remained ignorant of the fact that Carver had slept every night since the night of the widow's *séance* at the Crown, in a small room next to the kitchen that afforded an unobstructed view up the rutted length of the Kaniere-road.

By seven-thirty Moody was striding eastward along Gibson Quay, dressed in a grey slouch hat, yellow moleskin trousers, leather knee-boots, and a dark woollen coat over a shirt of grey serge. He now donned this costume six days out of seven, much to the amusement of Gascoigne, who had asked him more than once why he had chosen to leave off the piratical red sash, which might have finished off the ensemble very nicely.

Moody had staked a claim close enough to Hokitika to permit his continued board at the Crown Hotel. This arrangement cut into his weekly earnings rather severely, but he preferred it to sleeping in a tent beneath the open sky, something he had attempted only once, to his great discomfort. It took him an hour and twenty minutes to walk to his claim from Hokitika; before the clock struck nine every morning, therefore, he was at his cradle at the creekside, hauling pails of water, whistling, and shovelling sand.

Moody was not, truth be told, a terribly skilful prospector: he was hoping for nuggets rather than panning for dust. Too often the ore-bearing gravel slipped through the netting at the bottom of the cradle, only to be washed away; sometimes he emptied his cradle twice over without finding any flakes at all. He was making what the diggers called 'pay dirt', meaning that the sum total of his weekly income was more or less equal to the sum total of his weekly expenditure, but it was a holding pattern he could not sustain. He knew that he ought to heed popular advice, and go mates with another man, or with a party. The chance of striking rich was doubled in a partnership, and the chances multiplied still further in a party of five, or seven, or nine. But his pride would not permit it. He persevered alone, visualising, every hour, the nugget with which he would buy his future life. His dreams at night began to glister, and he began to see flashes of light in the most unlikely places, such that he had to look again, and blink, or close his eyes.

Stepping across the small creek that formed the northern boundary of his claim, Moody was surprised to see the pale silhouette of a tent through the scrub, and beside it, the remains of a fire. He came up short. The Hokitika diggers typically spent their weekends in town, not returning to the field until mid-morning on Monday at the very earliest. Why had this digger not joined his fellows? And what was he doing on another man's patch of land?

'Hello there,' Moody called, meaning to rouse the tent's inhabitant. 'Hello.'

At once there came a grunt, and a flurry of motion inside the tent. 'Sorry,' someone said. 'Very sorry—very sorry—'

A Chinese face appeared at the opening, blurred with sleep.

'No trouble,' he said. 'Very sorry.'

'Mr. Sook?' said Moody.

Ah Sook squinted up at him.

'I'm Walter Moody,' Moody said, placing his hand over his heart. 'Do you—ah—do you remember me?'

'Yes, yes.' Ah Sook knuckled his eyes with his fist.

'I'm so glad,' said Moody. 'This is my claim, you see: from this creek here to those yellow pegs on the southern side.'

'Very sorry,' Ah Sook said. 'No harm done.'

'No: of course,' Moody said. 'In any case, Ah Sook, I'm pleased to see you. Your absence from Kaniere has been noted by a great many people. Myself included. I am very pleased to see you—very pleased, not angry at all. We feared that something had happened to you.'

'No trouble,' the hatter said. 'Tent only. No trouble.' He disappeared from sight.

'I can see you're not causing trouble,' Moody said. 'It's all right, Mr. Sook: I'm not worried about you making camp! I'm not worried about that at all.'

Ah Sook clambered out of the tent, pulling his tunic down as he did so. 'I will go,' he said. 'Five minutes.' He held up five fingers.

'It's all right,' Moody said. 'You can sleep here if you like; it's of no consequence to me.'

'Last night only,' said Ah Sook.

'Yes; but if you want to tent here tonight also, I don't mind a bit,' said Moody. His manner was alternating between bluff cheer and clumsy condescension, as it might if he were speaking to someone else's child.

'Not tonight,' said Ah Sook. He began to strike his tent. Hauling the canvas fly, still wet with dew, from the rope over which it had been draped, he revealed the flattened square of earth where he had spent the night: the woollen blanket, twisted, and pressed flat with the tangled imprint of his body; a pot, filled with sand; his leather purse; a panning dish; a string bag containing tea and flour and several wrinkled potatoes; a standard-issue swag. Moody, casting his eye over this meagre inventory, was oddly touched.

'I say,' he said, 'but where have you been, Mr. Sook, this month past? It's been a full month since the *séance*—and no one's heard a word from you!'

'Digging,' said Ah Sook, flattening the canvas fly across his chest.

'You vanished so soon after the *séance*,' Moody continued, 'we rather thought you'd gone the same way as poor old Mr. Staines! No one could make heads or tails of it, you disappearing like that.'

Ah Sook had been folding the fly into quarters; now he paused. 'Mr. Staines come back?'

'I'm afraid not,' Moody said. 'He's still missing.'

'And Francis Carver?'

'Carver's still in Hokitika.'

Ah Sook nodded. 'At the Palace Hotel.'

'Well, in actual fact, no,' said Moody, pleased to be given an opportunity to conspire. 'He's begun sleeping at the Crown Hotel. In secret. Nobody knows he's staying there: he's kept up the pretence that he's staying at the Palace, and he still pays rent to the Palace proprietor—and keeps his rooms, just as before. But he sleeps every night at the Crown. He arrives well after nightfall, and leaves very early. I only know because I rent the room above.'

Ah Sook had fixed him with a penetrating look. 'Where?'

'Carver's room? Or mine?'

'Carver.'

'He sleeps in the room next to the kitchen, on the ground floor,' said Moody. 'It faces east. Very near the smoking room—where you and I first met.'

'A humble room,' said Ah Sook.

'Very humble,' Moody agreed, 'but he's got a vantage down the length of the Kaniere-road. He's keeping watch, you see. He's watching out for you.'

Walter Moody knew virtually nothing about Ah Sook's history with Francis Carver, for Ah Sook had not had the opportunity, at the Crown Hotel, to narrate the tale in any detail, and had not been seen since, save for his appearance at the Wayfarer's Fortune one month ago. Moody wished very much to know the full particulars, but despite his best efforts of surveillance and inquiry—he had become an adept at turning idle conversation, discreetly, to provocative themes—his understanding had not developed beyond what he had learned in the smoking room of the Crown, which was that the history concerned opium, murder, and a declaration of revenge. Ah Quee was the only man to whom Ah Sook had narrated the tale in full, and he did not, alas, possess language enough to share it with any English-speaking man.

'Every night, at the Crown Hotel?' said Ah Sook. 'Tonight?'

'Yes, he'll be there tonight,' said Moody. 'Though not until well after dark, as I've told you.'

'Not the Palace.'

'No, not the Palace,' said Moody. 'He changed hotels.'

'Yes,' said Ah Sook gravely. 'I understand.' He went to loose the knot of his guy-rope from the fork of a tree.

'Who was he?' said Moody. 'The murdered man.'

'My father,' said Ah Sook.

'Your *father*,' said Moody. After a moment, he said, 'How was he killed? I mean—forgive me, but—what happened?'

'A long time ago,' said Ah Sook. 'Before the war.'

'The opium wars,' said Moody, prompting him.

'Yes,' said Ah Sook, but he did not go on. He began to reel in the guy-rope, using his forearm as a spool.

'What happened?' said Moody.

'Profit,' said Ah Sook, giving his explanation flatly.

'Profit of what kind?'

Clearly Ah Sook thought this was a very stupid question; perceiving this, Moody rushed on to ask another. 'I mean—was your father—was he in the opium business, as you are?'

Ah Sook said nothing. He withdrew his forearm from the loop of rope, twisted it into a figure-eight, and secured it onto his swag. Once it was affixed, he sat back on his haunches, regarded Moody coolly for a moment, and then leaned over and spat, very deliberately, into the dirt.

Moody drew back. 'Forgive me,' he murmured. 'I ought not to pry.'

Walter Moody had told nobody at all that Crosbie Wells was the bastard brother of the politician Lauderback. He had decided, in the hours following this discovery, that the intelligence was not his to share. His reasons for this concealment were deeply felt, but vaguely articulated. A man should not be made to answer for his family. It was wrong to expose a man's private correspondence without his consent. He did not want to perform this exposure himself. But these reasons, even when taken together, did not quite comprise the whole truth, which was that Moody had compared himself to both men many times over the past month, and felt a profound kinship with each of them, though in very different ways: with the bastard, for his desperation; with the politician, for his pride. This double comparison had become the habitual project of his meditations every day, as he stood in the chill water and ran clods of earth and metal through his hands.

Ah Sook stuffed the last of his possessions into his swag, and then sat down upon it to lace his boots.

Moody could not bear it any longer. He burst out, 'You know you will be hanged. If you take Carver's life, you will be hanged. They'll take your life, Mr. Sook, if you take his, no matter what your provocation.'

'Yes,' said Ah Sook. 'I understand.'

'It will not be a fair trial—not for you.'

'No,' Ah Sook agreed. The prospect did not appear to distress him. He knelt by the fire, picked up a twig, and stirred the damp earth that he had placed over the embers the night before. Below the earth the coals were still warm, dark as matted blood.

'What are you going to do?' said Moody, watching him. 'Shoot him down?'

'Yes,' said Ah Sook.

'When?' said Moody.

'Tonight,' said Ah Sook. 'At the Crown Hotel.' He appeared to be digging for something beneath the coals. Presently his stick struck something hard. Using the end as a lever, he flipped the object out onto the grass: it was a little tin tea caddy, black with soot. The box was evidently still hot: he wrapped his sleeve around his hand before he picked it up.

'Show us your arms,' said Moody.

Ah Sook looked up.

'Go on and show us your arms,' said Moody, suddenly flushed. 'There are pistols and there are pistols, Mr. Sook: you have to know your powder, as my own father used to say.'

It was rare he quoted his father in company, Adrian Moody's habitual phrases being, in general, unsuitable to civil conversation, and Walter Moody being, in general, disinclined to reference him.

'I buy a pistol,' said Ah Sook.

'Good,' said Moody. 'Where is it?'

'Not yet,' said Ah Sook.

'You haven't bought it yet?'

'Today,' said Ah Sook. He opened the caddy, and poured a handful of golden flakes into his palm. Moody realised that he must have buried the box in the earth beneath his fire, in case he was robbed during the night.

'What kind of pistol are you going to buy?'

'From Tiegreen's.' With his free hand he reached for his purse.

'What manufacturer, I meant. What kind.'

'Tiegreen's,' said Ah Sook again. He opened the mouth of the purse one-handed, to transfer the gold into it.

'That's the name of the store,' Moody said. 'What *kind* of pistol are you going to buy? Are you a weapons man?'

'To shoot Francis Carver,' said Ah Sook.

'Tiegreen's won't do for you,' Moody said, shaking his head. 'You might go there to buy a fowling piece ... or a rifle of some kind ... but they won't furnish you with a pistol. A military weapon is what you want. Not every ball of shot will kill a man, you see, and the last thing you want is to do the job by halves. Heavens, Mr. Sook! A pistol is not just a piece of hardware—just as a horse is not merely a ... mode of transport,' he said, rounding off this comparison rather lamely.

Ah Sook did not reply. He had chosen Tiegreen's Hardware

and Supply for two reasons: firstly, because the store was located beside the Palace Hotel, and secondly, because the shopkeeper was sympathetic to Chinese men. The first consideration no longer mattered, of course, but the second consideration was an important one: Ah Sook had planned to ask Mr. Tiegreen to load the piece for him, in the store, so that the deed could be carried out the very same day. He had never fired a pistol. He knew the basic principles behind the design, however, and he guessed it was not a skill that required a great deal of practice.

'Go to the outfitters on Camp-street,' Moody said. 'Right beside the Deutsches Gasthaus. The building that shows the peak of the roof behind the sham. The sign isn't painted yet, but the proprietors are Brunton, Solomon & Barnes, and the door should be open. When you get there, ask for a Kerr Patent. Don't let them sell you anything else: it's a British military piece, very sound, and it will do the job. The cost for a Kerr Patent is five pounds even. Any more than five pounds, and they're robbing you.'

'Five pounds?' Ah Sook looked down at the gold in his purse. He had had no idea that a pistol could be got for such a reasonable sum! He had been quoted a figure twice that much. 'Kerr Patent,' he repeated, to remember it. 'Camp-street. Thank you, Mr. Moody.'

'What are you going to do,' Moody said, 'when the deed is done? When Carver's dead? Will you turn yourself in? Will you try to make a run for it?' All of a sudden he felt absurdly excited.

But Ah Sook only shook his head. He closed the mouth of his purse and then wrapped the purse tightly in a square of cloth. At last he rose, swinging his swag onto his back as he did so, and tucking the bundled object very carefully into his pocket.

'This claim,' he said, gesturing. 'Pay dirt only. Very small gold.'

Moody waved his hand. 'Yes. I know.'

'No 'bounders here,' said Ah Sook.

'No homeward-bounders,' said Moody, nodding. 'You needn't spell it out, Mr. Sook: I know the truth of it.'

Ah Sook peered at him. 'Go north,' he said. 'Black sands. Very lucky in the north. No nuggets here. Too close to town.'

'Charleston,' said Moody. 'Yes. There's fortunes to be made, in Charleston.'

Ah Sook nodded. 'Black sands,' he said. He stepped forward, and Moody saw that he was holding the soot-blackened tea caddy in both hands. He proffered it, and Moody, surprised, extended his own hands to receive it. Ah Sook did not release the gift at once: he bowed low over it, and Moody, copying him, bowed also.

'*Juk neih houwahn*,' said Ah Sook, but he provided no translation, and Moody did not ask for one. He straightened, tin box in hand, and watched the hatter walk away.

SUN IN PISCES

In which Anna Wetherell is twice surprised; Cowell Devlin grows suspicious; and the deed of gift acquires a new significance.

What was glimpsed in Aquarius—what was envisioned, believed in, prophesied, predicted, doubted, and forewarned—is made, in Pisces, manifest. Those solitary visions that, but a month ago, belonged only to the dreamer, will now acquire the form and substance of the real. We were of our own making, and we shall be our own end.

And after Pisces? Out of the womb, the bloody birth. We do not follow: we cannot cross from last to first. Aries will not admit a collective point of view, and Taurus will not relinquish the subjective. Gemini's code is an exclusive one. Cancer seeks a source, Leo, a purpose, and Virgo, a design; but these are projects undertaken singly. Only in the zodiac's second act will we begin to show ourselves: in Libra, as a notion, in Scorpio, as a quality, and in Sagittarius, as a voice. In Capricorn we will gain memory, and in Aquarius, vision; it is only in Pisces, the last and oldest of the zodiacal signs, that we acquire a kind of selfhood, something whole. But the doubled fish of Pisces, that mirrored womb of self and self-awareness, is an ourobouros of mind—both the will of fate, and the fated will—and the house of self-undoing is a prison built by prisoners, airless, doorless, and mortared from within.

These alterations come upon us irrevocably, as the hands of the clock-face come upon the hour.

Φ

Lydia Wells had not hosted a *séance* a second time. She was well apprised of the charlatan's motto that one must never repeat the very same trick to the very same crowd—but when she was accused, because of this, of being a charlatan herself, she only laughed. She had admitted, in an open letter in the *West Coast Times*, that her attempt to communicate with the shade of Mr. Staines had been unsuccessful. This failure, as she reported, was unprecedented in her professional experience, an anomaly that suggested to her that the afterlife had been unable, rather than unwilling, to produce him. From this, she wrote, one could only conclude that Mr. Staines was not dead after all, and she signed off expressing her confident anticipation of the young man's eventual return.

This statement confounded the men of the Crown considerably; it had the effect, however (common to all of the widow's strategies), of enhancing the value of her enterprise, and following its publication the Wayfarer's Fortune began to do a very good trade. The establishment was open every evening between the hours of seven and ten, offering cut-price brandy and conversation of the speculative sort. Fortune telling happened in the afternoons, by private appointment only, and Anna Wetherell, in continuance with former policy, was not seen.

Anna only left the Wayfarer's Fortune to take her daily exercise, in which she was accompanied, invariably, by Mrs. Wells, who was not insensible of the myriad benefits of daily perambulation, and who often said that there was nothing she liked better than a stroll. Together, arm in arm, the two women walked the length of Revell-street every morning, setting out to the north, and returning down the opposite side. They examined the contents of each window box as they passed, purchased milk and sugar, when milk and sugar could be got, and greeted the Hokitika regulars very blandly and impassively indeed.

That morning they had taken their daily walk earlier than usual, for Lydia Wells had an appointment at the Hokitika Courthouse at nine. She had been summoned to appear before the Magistrate about a legal matter pertaining to the estate of her late husband, Crosbie Wells, and the wording of the summons had intimated that the news was likely good: at ten minutes before nine, the front door of the Wayfarer's Fortune opened, and Lydia Wells, her copper hair shining splendidly against a gown of midnight blue, stepped out into the sunshine.

Cowell Devlin watched Mrs. Wells exit the hotel and descend the steps to the street, drawing her shawl tightly around her shoulders, and smiling at the men who paused in their daily business to stare at her. He waited until she had disappeared into the throng of the crowd, and then waited five minutes more, to be safe. Then he crossed the street to the Wayfarer's Fortune, mounted the steps to the veranda, and, after glancing back at the blank façade of the Courthouse, knocked upon the door. He was holding his battered Bible against his chest.

The door opened almost at once.

'Miss Wetherell,' Devlin said, removing his hat with his free hand. 'Please allow me to introduce myself. My name is Cowell Devlin; I am the resident chaplain of the Hokitika Gaol. I have in my possession a document that I expect will be of great interest to you, and I hope to gain a private audience with you, in order to discuss it.'

'I remember you,' said Anna. 'You were there when I woke up in gaol after my blackout.'

'Yes,' Devlin said.

'You prayed for me.'

'And I have prayed for you many times since.'

She looked surprised. 'Have you?'

'Fervently,' the chaplain replied.

'What did you say you wanted?'

Devlin repeated his intentions.

'What do you mean, a document?'

'I would prefer not to produce it here. May I come in?'

She hesitated. 'Mrs. Wells is out.'

'Yes, I know,' Devlin said. 'In fact I saw her entering the Courthouse just now, and hastened here with the precise hope that I might speak with you alone. I confess I have been waiting for just such an opportunity for some time. May I come in?'

'I'm not supposed to receive guests when she's not here.'

'I have but one item of business to speak with you about,' Devlin said calmly, 'and I am a member of the clergy, and this is a respectable hour. Would your mistress deny you so little?'

Anna's mistress would certainly her deny so little, and a great deal more—it being against the widow's policy ever to admit exceptions to the regulations she imposed at whim. But in a moment Anna decided to be reckless.

'Come through into the kitchen,' she said, 'and I'll make us a pot of tea.'

'You are most kind.'

Devlin followed her down the corridor to the kitchen at the rear of the house, where he waited, still standing, for Anna to fill the kettle and place it on the stove. She had certainly become extraordinarily thin. Her cheeks were hollow, and her skin had a waxy sheen; her wasted carriage bespoke malnourishment, and when she moved, it was with a trembling exhaustion, as though she had not eaten a decent meal in weeks. Devlin glanced quickly around the kitchen. On the washboard the plates from breakfast had been stacked to dry, and he counted two of everything, including two ceramic egg cups, printed with a raised blackberry design. Unless Lydia Wells had had a guest to dine early that morning—which was doubtful—then Anna must have eaten breakfast, at least. There was a half-round of bread on the breadboard, wrapped in a linen cloth, and the butter dish had not yet been put away.

'Will you have a biscuit with your tea?'

'You are most kind,' Devlin said again, and then, embarrassed at having repeated the platitude, he rushed on: 'I was gratified, Miss Wetherell, to learn that you had conquered your dependence upon the Chinese drug.'

'Mrs. Wells won't permit it in the house,' Anna said, swiping a strand of hair from her face. She fetched the biscuit tin from the pantry shelf.

'She is right to be strict,' Devlin said, 'but it is you who deserves congratulation. You must have shown great fortitude, in throwing off your dependency. I have known grown men who have not managed such a feat.'

Whenever Devlin was nervous, his speech became very formal and correct.

'I just stopped,' Anna said.

'Yes,' Devlin said, nodding, 'an abrupt cessation is the only way, of course. But you must have battled every kind of temptation, in the days and weeks afterward.'

'No,' Anna said. 'I just didn't need it any more.'

'You are too modest.'

'I'm not mincing,' Anna said. 'I kept going, for a while—until the lump ran out. I ate all of it. But I just couldn't feel it any more.'

Devlin appraised her with a calculating look. 'Have you found that your health has much improved, since your cessation?'

'I expect it has,' Anna said, fanning the biscuits in an arc over the plate. 'I'm well enough.'

'I am sorry to contradict you, Miss Wetherell, but you do not seem at all well.'

'You mean I'm too thin.'

'You are very thin, my dear.'

'I'm cold,' said Anna. 'I'm always cold these days.'

'I expect that is on account of your being very thin.'

'Yes,' she said. 'I expect so too.'

'I have observed,' Devlin said after a moment, 'in persons of low morale—particularly those who have contemplated suicide—that the loss of appetite is a common symptom.'

'I have an appetite,' she said. 'I *eat*. I just can't seem to keep the weight on.'

'Do you eat every day?'

'Three meals,' she said, 'two of them hot. I manage the cooking for both of us.'

'Mrs. Wells must be very grateful,' Devlin said, speaking in a tone that made it clear he did not entirely believe her.

'Yes,' she said, vaguely. She turned away to fetch cups and saucers from the rack above the washboard.

'Will you continue in your present circumstances after Mrs. Wells is married?' Devlin inquired.

'I expect so.'

'I imagine that Mr. Carver will take up residence here.'

'Yes, I believe he means to.'

'Their engagement was announced in the *West Coast Times* this morning. It was a very modest announcement; even, one might have said, subdued. But a wedding is always a happy event.'

'I love a wedding,' Anna said.

'Yes,' said Devlin. 'A happy event—no matter what the circumstances.'

It had been suggested, following the scandal precipitated by George Shepard's letter to the editor of the *West Coast Times* one month ago, that only remarriage could ameliorate the damage the widow's reputation had sustained. Mrs. Wells's claim upon Crosbie Wells's inheritance had been considerably weakened by the revelation that she had made him a cuckold in the years before his death, and her position had been weakened still further by the fact that Alistair Lauderback had made a full and very frank confession. In a public reply to George Shepard, Lauderback admitted that he had concealed the fact of the affair from the voting public, to whom he offered his sincere apologies. He wrote that he had never been more ashamed of himself, and that he accepted full responsibility for all consequences, and that until the day he died he would regret that he had arrived at Mr. Wells's cottage half an hour too late to beg the man's forgiveness. The confession had its desired effect; indeed, by the outpouring of sympathy and admiration that followed it, some even supposed Lauderback's reputation to have been improved.

Anna had finished arranging the saucers. 'Let us go into the parlour,' she said. 'I'll hear the kettle when it boils.'

She left the tray, and padded back down the corridor to the

parlour, which was set up for the widow's afternoon appointments, with the two largest armchairs drawn very close to one another, and the curtains closed. Devlin waited for Anna to sit before he did so himself, and then he opened his Bible and withdrew the charred deed of gift from between its pages. He handed it to her without a word.

> *On this 11th day of October 1865 a sum of two thousand pounds is to be given to MISS ANNA WETHERELL, formerly of New South Wales, by MR. EMERY STAINES, formerly of New South Wales, as witnessed by MR. CROSBIE WELLS, presiding.*

Anna took up the deed with a rather glazed look: she was all but illiterate, and did not expect to make sense of the words in a single glance. She knew her alphabet, and could sound out a line of print if she worked very slowly and in a very good light; it was a laborious task, however, and she made many errors. But in the next moment she snatched it up, and, with an exclamation of surprise, held it close to her eyes.

'I can read this,' she said, speaking almost in a whisper.

Devlin did not know that Anna had never learned to read, and this pronouncement was not remarkable to him. 'I found this document in the bottom of Crosbie Wells's stove the day after his death,' he said. 'As you can see, it is an extraordinary sum of money—still more because the sum is intended as a bequest—and I confess I do not know quite what to make of it. I must warn you at the outset that, in terms of legality, the document is not good. Mr. Staines did not sign his name, which, in turn, makes Mr. Wells's signature invalid. The witness cannot sign before the principal.'

Anna said nothing. She was still looking at the paper.

'Have you ever seen this document before?'

'No,' she said.

'Did you know of its existence?'

'No!'

Devlin was alarmed: she had almost shouted the word. 'What is it?' he said.

'I just—' Her hand went to her throat. 'May I ask you something?'

'Of course.'

'Have you ever—I mean, in your experience—' She stopped herself, bit her lip, and began again. 'Do you know why I can read this?'

His eyes were searching hers. 'I'm afraid I don't understand.'

'I never learned to read,' Anna explained, 'not properly. I mean—I can sound out a line of letters—and I know labels and signs; but that's more like remembering than reading, because I see them every day. I could never read a paper. Not front to back. It would take me hours and hours. But this—I can read it. Without any effort, I mean. Quick as thinking.'

'Read it out loud.'

She did, fluently.

Devlin was frowning. 'Are you quite sure that you have never seen this document before?'

'Quite sure,' Anna said.

'Did you know already that Mr. Staines intended to give you two thousand pounds?'

'No,' she said.

'What about Mr. Wells? Did you ever speak with Mr. Wells about it?'

'No,' she said. 'I'm telling you: it's the first I've seen of it.'

'Perhaps,' Devlin said, 'if you had been told about it—but you had forgotten . . .'

'I wouldn't forget a dirty great fortune,' said Anna.

Devlin paused, watching her. Then he said, 'One hears stories of children with Continental nannies, waking up one day, and speaking fluent Dutch, or French, or German, or whatever it is—'

'I never had a nanny.'

'—but I have never heard of a person suddenly acquiring the ability to read,' he finished. 'That is most peculiar.'

There was a sceptical accent in his voice.

'I never had a nanny,' Anna said again.

Devlin sat forward. 'Miss Wetherell,' he said, 'your name is associated with a great many unsolved crimes, including a possible murder, and I am sure that I do not need to impress upon you the gravity of a Supreme Court trial. Let us talk frankly—and in confidence.' He pointed at the deed in Anna's hand. 'This bequest was written three months before Mr. Staines disappeared. It represents exactly half of the Wells inheritance. Mr. Wells died the very day that Mr. Staines vanished, and on the morning after his death I found this paper in the stove. The events are clearly related, and a lawyer will be able to join the dots, even if I cannot. If you are in a difficult position, I may be able to help you; but I cannot help you if you do not trust me. I am asking you to take me into your confidence, and tell me what you know.'

Anna was frowning. 'This paper doesn't have anything to do with the Wells inheritance,' she said. 'This is about Emery's money, not Crosbie's.'

'You are right; but it is doubtful that the gold discovered in Mr. Wells's cottage ever belonged to Mr. Wells,' Devlin said. 'You see, the ore was not discovered pure: it had been smelted by a goldsmith, and pressed into a kind of bullion. The smelting bears a signature, and by this signature the bank has been able to trace the gold back to a goldmine belonging to Mr. Staines. The Aurora.'

'The what?' said Anna.

'The Aurora,' Devlin said. 'That's the name of the goldmine.'

'Oh,' she said. She was clearly confused; feeling pity for her, Devlin explained it all again, more slowly. This time she understood. 'So the fortune was Emery's, all along?'

'Perhaps,' said Devlin, cautiously.

'And he meant to give exactly half of it to me!'

'This document certainly seems to imply that Mr. Staines meant to give you two thousand pounds—and that Mr. Wells, as of the night of the eleventh of October, knew about this intention, and possibly even endorsed it. But as I have already told you, the document is not valid: Mr. Staines never signed.'

'What if he did sign it?'

'Until Mr. Staines is found,' Devlin said, 'I'm afraid there's nothing to be done.' He watched her for a moment, and then said, 'It has taken me a very long time to bring this document to your attention, Miss Wetherell, and for that I ask your forgiveness. The reason is simply that I have been waiting for a chance to speak with you alone; as you know, those chances have been very hard to come by.'

'Who knows about this?' she said suddenly. 'Besides you and me.'

Devlin hesitated. 'Governor Shepard,' he said, deciding to tell the truth, but not the whole truth. 'I spoke with him about the matter perhaps a month ago.'

'What did he say?'

'He imagined that it must have been a joke of some kind.'

'A joke?' She looked crestfallen. 'What kind of a joke?'

Devlin reached forward to take her hand, crushing her fingers slightly in his sympathy. 'Don't be disappointed, my dear. It is the poor in spirit who are blessed, and every one of us awaits a much greater inheritance than any that can be gifted in gold.'

There came a shrill piping from the kitchen, and a hiss as the hot water spouted onto the cast-iron plate.

'There's our kettle,' said Devlin, smiling at her.

'Reverend,' Anna said, withdrawing her hand from his grip, 'would you mind very much if I asked you to pour out the tea? I'm feeling a little strange, and I would like some time alone.'

'Certainly,' said Cowell Devlin with courtesy, and he left the room.

As soon as he was gone Anna rose and crossed the parlour in two quick steps, the charred deed of gift still in her hand. Her heart was beating fast. She stood unmoving for a moment, gathering confidence, and then, in one fluid motion, she went to the widow's writing desk, laid the deed of gift upon the table, uncorked a pot of ink, picked up Mrs. Wells's pen, wet the nib in the inkwell, leaned forward, and wrote:

Emery Staines

Anna had never seen Emery Staines's signature before, but she knew without a doubt that she had replicated the form of it exactly. The letters of Staines's last name followed a careless diminution, and the letters of his first were cheerfully illegible; the signature was confidently sloppy, and underlined with a casual relish, as if to say that the shape had been formed so many times before as not to be disproved by any minor variation. There was a doubled curlicue preceding the E—a personal touch—and the S had a slightly flattened quality.

'What have you done?'

Devlin was standing in the doorway with the tea tray in his hands and an expression of fearsome admonition on his face. He set the tray upon the sideboard with a clatter and advanced upon her, holding out his hand. Mutely, Anna passed the document to him, and he snatched it up. For a moment, his outrage was such that he could not speak; then he controlled himself, and said, very quietly,

'This is an act of fraud.'

'Maybe,' said Anna.

'*What?*' Devlin shouted, suddenly furious. He rounded on her. '*What* did you say?'

He had expected her to cower, but she did not. 'That's his signature,' she said. 'The deed is good.'

'That is not his signature,' Devlin said.

'It is,' said Anna.

'That is a forgery,' Devlin snapped. 'You have just committed forgery.'

'Maybe I don't know what you're talking about,' said Anna.

'Your insolence is unbecoming,' Devlin said. 'Will you add the crime of perjury to the crime of fraud?'

'Maybe I don't know anything about fraud.'

'The truth will bear out,' said Devlin. 'There are analysts, Miss Wetherell, who can tell a forgery at sight.'

'Not this one,' Anna said.

'Do not delude yourself,' Devlin said. 'Shame on you.'

But Anna was feeling quite without delusion, and quite without shame; she was feeling, in fact, sharper than she had felt in many months. Now that Emery Staines's signature was upon the deed of gift, it was no longer invalid. By the authority of this document, two thousand pounds *must* be given, as a present, to Miss Anna Wetherell, by Mr. Emery Staines; the deed had been signed, and witnessed, and the signature of the donor was a good one. Who could fault her word, when one of the signatories had vanished, and the other was dead?

'Can I look at it again?' she said, and Devlin, red-faced with anger, handed the deed back to her. Once it was in her hand, Anna darted away, loosed the bodice of Agathe Gascoigne's dress, and slipped the paper between the buttons, so that it lay against her skin. Placing her hands over her bodice, she stood a moment, panting, her eyes searching Devlin's—who had not moved. There was ten feet of space between them.

'For shame,' Devlin said quietly. 'Explain yourself.'

'I want a second opinion, that's all.'

'You have just falsified that deed, Miss Wetherell.'

'That can't be proved.'

'By my oath, it can.'

'What's to stop me swearing an oath against you?'

'That would be a falsehood,' Devlin said. 'And it would be a very grave falsehood, if you swore to it in court, which you would certainly be forced to do. Don't be foolish.'

'I'll get a second opinion,' she said again. 'I'll go to the Courthouse and ask.'

'Miss Wetherell,' Devlin said. 'Calm yourself. Think. It would be the word of a minister against the word of a whore.'

'I'm not whoring any more.'

'A former whore,' said Devlin. 'Forgive me.'

He took a step towards her, and Anna retreated. Her hand was still pressed flat over her breast.

'If you come one step closer,' she said, 'I'll scream, and I'll rip my bodice open, and say you did it. They'll hear me from the street. They'll rush in.'

Devlin had never before been threatened in this way. 'I will come no closer,' he said, with dignity. 'I will retreat, in fact, and at once.' He returned to the chair he had formerly occupied, and sat down. 'I do not wish to brawl with you,' he said, speaking quietly now. 'I do wish to ask you several questions, however.'

'Go on,' said Anna, still breathing hard. 'Ask.'

Devlin decided upon a direct approach. 'Did you know that the gowns you purchased salvage last winter had once belonged to Lydia Wells?'

Anna gaped at him.

'Kindly answer the question,' Devlin said. 'I am referring to the five gowns which Mrs. Wells used to blackmail Mr. Alistair Lauderback, with Francis Carver's help.'

'What?' she said.

'The gowns,' Devlin went on, 'which each contained a small fortune in pure ore, stitched into the lining, around the bodice, and around the hem. One of these dresses was made of orange silk; the other four were muslin, and coloured cream, grey, pale blue, and striped pink. These four are currently stowed in a box beneath the stairs at the Gridiron Hotel; the orange gown is in the possession of Mr. Aubert Gascoigne, at his private residence.'

He had her full attention now. 'How do you know this?' she whispered.

'I have made it my business to find out a good deal about you,' said Devlin. 'Now answer the question.'

Her face was pale. 'Only the orange gown had gold,' she said. 'The other four had makeweights—made of lead.'

'Did you know that they had once belonged to Lydia Wells?'

'No,' Anna said. 'Not for sure.'

'But you suspected it.'

'I—I'd heard something,' she said. 'Months ago.'

'When did you first discover what the gowns contained?'

'The night after Emery disappeared.'

'After you were gaoled for attempted suicide.'

'Yes.'

'And Mr. Gascoigne paid your bail, on promise, and together you took apart the orange gown at his cottage on Revell-street, and hid the tatters under his bed, thereafter.'

'How—?' she whispered. She looked terrified.

Devlin did not pause. 'Presumably, after you returned to the Gridiron that evening, your first move was to go back to your wardrobe and check the four remaining gowns.'

'Yes,' said Anna. 'But I didn't cut them open. I only felt along the seams. I didn't know that it was lead that I was feeling: I thought it was more colour.'

'In that case,' Devlin said, 'you must have believed that you were suddenly extraordinarily rich.'

'Yes.'

'But you did not open the hems of those dresses, in order to use that gold to repay your debt to Edgar Clinch.'

'Later, I did,' said Anna. 'The following week. That's when I found the makeweights.'

'But even then,' Devlin said, 'you did not tell Mr. Gascoigne what you surmised. Instead, you pretended helplessness and ignorance, claimed to have no money, and begged him for aid!'

'How do you know all this?' Anna said.

'I will ask the questions, thank you,' Devlin said. 'What were you intending to do with that gold?'

'I wanted to keep it back,' Anna said. 'As a nest egg. And I didn't have anywhere to hide the metal. I thought I might ask Emery about it. There was no one else I trusted. But by then he was gone.'

'What about Lydia Wells?' Devlin said. 'What about Lydia Wells, who came to the Gridiron that same afternoon—who paid your debt to Mr. Clinch—and who has shown you every kind of hospitality ever since?'

'No.' Anna's voice had become very small.

'You never told her about those gowns?'

'No.'

'Because you suspected they had once belonged to her.'

'I'd heard something,' Anna said. 'I never knew—not for certain—but I knew that there was something—and she was desirous to get them back.'

Devlin folded his arms. Anna was plainly fearful of how much he knew about her situation, and how he had come to know it. This pained him, but he reflected that, given the circumstances, it was better to keep her frightened, than to risk her becoming bold. It would not do, to have her flapping that forged signature about.

'Where is Mr. Staines?' he said next.

'I don't know.'

'I think you do.'

'No,' she said.

'I shall remind you that you have committed serious fraud by forging a signature in a dead man's hand.'

'He's not dead.'

Devlin nodded; he had been hoping for a definite answer. 'How do you know that?'

Anna did not reply, so Devlin said again, more sharply, 'How do you know that, Miss Wetherell?'

'I've been getting messages,' Anna said at last.

'From Mr. Staines?'

'Yes.'

'What kind of messages?'

'They're private.'

'How does he communicate them?'

'Not with words,' said Anna.

'How then?'

'I just feel him.'

'You feel him?'

'Inside my head.'

Devlin exhaled.

'I suppose you doubt my word now,' Anna said.

'I most certainly do,' Devlin said. 'It goes rather hand in hand with your being a fraudster, I'm afraid.'

Anna thumped a hand over the paper hidden in her breast. 'You held onto *this* for a mighty long time,' she said.

Devlin glared at her. He opened his mouth to make a retort, but before he could find the words, he heard brisk steps upon the porch, and the rattle of the door handle, and the sudden noise of the street as the front door swung inwards, and someone walked in. Anna looked at Devlin with frightened eyes. The widow had returned from the Courthouse, and she was calling Anna's name.

SATURN IN VIRGO

*In which George Shepard does not appoint a deputy; Quee
Long is mistaken for another man; and Dick Mannering
draws the line.*

George Shepard had spent the morning of the 20th of March supervising various deliveries of materials and hardware to the site of the
future gaol-house at Seaview—which, two months into the project
of its construction, was looking more and more imposing every day.
The walls had gone up, the chimneys had been bricked, and inside
the main residence the fortified doors had all been fitted and hung
in their steel frames. There were still many details to be ironed out,
of course—the lamps had yet to be delivered; the gaol-house kitchen
still lacked a stove; there was still no glass in the gaoler's cottage windows; the pit beneath the gallows had not yet been dug—but all in
all everything had moved splendidly quickly, thanks to Harald
Nilssen's four-hundred pound 'donation', and additional funding,
finally paid out, from the Westland Public Works Committee, the
Hokitika Council, and the Municipal Board. Shepard had predicted
that the felons could be moved from the Police Camp before the end
of April, and several of them already spent their nights upon the
Seaview premises, watched over by Shepard, who preferred, now
that the prison was so near completion, to sleep there also, and to
take his suppers cold.

When the bell in the Wesleyan chapel rang out noon Shepard
was in the future asylum, digging an alternate pit for the latrine. As

the sound of the bell drifted up from the town below the foreman called for the felons to break. Shepard put down his spade, wiped his forehead with his shirtsleeve, and clambered bodily out of the hole—perceiving as he did so that a young ginger-haired man was standing on the far side of the iron gate, peering through the bars, and evidently waiting for an interview.

'Mr. Everard,' Shepard said, striding forward.

'Gov. Shepard.'

'What brings you up to Seaview this morning? Not idle curiosity, I think.'

'I'd hoped to beg an audience with you, sir.'

'I trust you haven't been waiting long.'

'Not at all.'

'Do you wish to come in? I can call for the gate to be unlocked.' Shepard was still perspiring from his recent exertion: he mopped his forehead a second time with his sleeve.

'It's all right,' the man said. 'I've only got a message.'

'Deliver it,' said Shepard. He placed his hands on his hips.

'I've come on behalf of Mr. Barnes. Of Brunton, Solomon and Barnes.'

'I do not know any of those men.'

'They're outfitters. They've a new warehouse,' said Everard. 'On Camp-street. Only the sign hasn't been painted yet. Sir,' he added hastily.

'Continue,' Shepard said, still with his hands on his hips.

'A couple months back you made it known that you'd be very grateful for a watch to be placed on a certain Chinaman.'

Shepard's expression sharpened at once. 'You remember rightly.'

'I'm here to report to you that a Chinaman bought a pistol this morning,' the young man said.

'From Mr. Barnes's establishment, I presume.'

'Yes, sir.'

'Where is this Chinaman now?'

'I couldn't tell you that,' said Everard. 'I saw Barnes just now, and he said he'd sold a Kerr Patent to a Chinaman this morning, and I came straight to you. I don't know if the Chinaman in question is your man or not . . . but I thought it would do well to advise you, either way.'

Shepard offered neither thanks nor congratulation for this. 'How long ago did the sale occur?'

'Two hours ago at least. Perhaps more. Barnes said that the fellow must have acted on a tip: he wouldn't lay down any more than five pounds for the Kerr. Five pounds even, he kept saying, like he'd been tipped. He knew not to be overcharged.'

'How did he pay for it?'

'With a paper note.'

'Anything else?'

'Yes,' said Everard. 'He loaded the piece in the store.'

'Who loaded it?'

'Barnes. On the Chinaman's behalf.'

Shepard nodded. 'Very good,' he said. 'Now. Listen closely. You go back to Hokitika, Mr. Everard, and you tell every man you see that George Shepard is on the lookout for a Chinaman called Sook. Let it be known that if anybody sees Johnny Sook in town today, no matter what for and no matter where, I'm to be sent for, at once.'

'Shall you offer a reward for the man's capture?'

'Don't say anything about a reward, but don't deny it either, if anyone asks.'

The young man drew himself up. 'Am I to be your deputy?'

Shepard did not answer at once. 'If you come upon Johnny Sook,' he said at last, 'and you find a way to apprehend him without a great deal of fuss, then I shall turn a blind eye to whatever your method of capture might have been. That's as much as I will say.'

'I understand you, sir.'

'There's another thing you can do for me,' said Shepard. 'Do you know a man named Francis Carver by sight?'

'The man with the scar on his face.'

'Yes,' said Shepard. 'I want you to take him a message for me. You'll find him at the Palace Hotel.'

'What's it to be, sir?'

'Tell him exactly what you just told me,' said Shepard. 'And then tell him to buckle on his holsters.'

Everard sagged a little. 'Is he your deputy, then?'

'I don't have a deputy,' Shepard said. 'Go on now. We'll speak later.'

'All right.'

Shepard raised his arms and placed his hands on the bars of the gate; he watched the youth's retreating form. Then he called, 'Mr. Everard!'

The young man stopped and turned. 'Yes, sir.'

'Do you want to be a lawman?'

He brightened. 'One day, I hope, sir.'

'The best lawmen can enforce the law without a badge,' Shepard said, gazing at him coolly through the bars of the gate. 'Remember that.'

Φ

Emery Staines had now been absent for over eight weeks, an interval judged by the Magistrate to be sufficient to nullify ownership of all gold-bearing ground. By the Magistrate's ruling, all mines and claims owned by Mr. Staines had been returned to the Crown, a repossession that had taken effect on Friday of the previous week. The Aurora, naturally, was one of the many claims surrendered, and as a consequence of this surrender, Quee Long had been released, at long last, from his fruitless obligation to that barren patch of ground. He made for Hokitika first thing Monday, in order to inquire where he was to be indentured next, and to whom.

Ah Quee disliked going to the Company offices very much, for he was never treated courteously while he was there, and he was always made to wait. He bore the officials' jeers with equanimity, however, and pretended not to notice as their junior clerks flicked him with pellets made of spit and paper, and held their noses whenever they passed the chair in which he sat. At length he was invited forward to explain his purpose to the bureaucrat at the front desk. After another long delay, the purpose of which was not explained to him, he was allocated another claim in Kaniere, given a receipt of the transfer, and sent on his way—by which time the ginger-haired Mr. Everard had reached Hokitika proper, and was dispensing George Shepard's message left and right.

As Ah Quee exited the Company offices on Weld-street, clutching the paper proof of his indenture in his hand, he heard somebody shout. He looked up, confused, and saw to his alarm that he was being rushed at from both sides. He cried out, and flung up his arm. In the next moment he was on the ground.

'Where's the pistol, Johnny Sook?'

'Where's the pistol?'

'Check in his waistband.'

There were hands on his body, patting and punching. Somebody aimed a kick at his ribs and he gasped.

'Stashed it, most likely.'

'What's that you've got? Coolie papers?'

His indenture was wrenched from his hand, scanned briefly, and tossed aside.

'Now what?'

'Now what have you got to say for yourself, Johnny Sook?'

'Ah Quee,' said Ah Quee, managing to speak at last.

'Got a tongue in his head, does he?'

'You'll speak in English if you speak at all.'

Another kick in the ribs. Ah Quee gave a grunt of pain and doubled up.

'He's not the right one,' said one of his attackers.

'What's the difference?' responded the other. 'He's still a Chinaman. He still stinks.'

'He doesn't have a pistol,' the first man pointed out.

'He'll give us Sook. They're all in thick.'

Ah Quee was kicked again, in the buttocks this time; the toe of the man's boot caught his tailbone and shot a jolt of pain up his spine to his jaw.

'You know Johnny Sook?'

'You know Johnny Sook?'

'You seen him?'

'We want to talk to Johnny Sook.'

Ah Quee grunted. He attempted to raise himself up onto his hands, and fell back.

'He's not going to spill,' observed the first man.

'Here. Move away a bit—'

The second man danced away on light feet and then ran at Ah Quee like a kicker hoping to make a conversion. Ah Quee felt him coming at the last moment, and rolled fast towards him, to cushion the blow. The pain in his ribs was excruciating. He could only breathe with the topmost part of his lung. The men were laughing now. Their voices had receded into a throbbing haze of sound.

Then a voice thundered out over the street:

'You've got the wrong man, my friends.'

The attackers turned. Standing in the open doorway of the Weld-street coffee house, his arms folded across his chest, was the magnate Dick Mannering. His bulk quite filled the doorway: he made for an imposing presence, despite the fact that he was unarmed, and at the sight of him the two men shrank away from Quee Long at once.

'We're under instructions to apprehend a Chinaman with the name of Johnny Sook,' said the first man, sticking his hands into his pockets, like a boy.

'That man's name is Johnny Quee,' said Mannering.

'We didn't know that, did we?' said the second man, his hands stealing into his pockets also.

'Instructions from the gaoler,' said the first man.

'The chink called Johnny Sook is on the loose,' said the second.

'He's got a pistol.'

'Armed and dangerous.'

'Well, you've got the wrong man,' said Mannering, descending the stairs to the street. 'You know that because I'm telling you, and I'm telling you for the last time. This man's name is Johnny Quee.'

Mannering seemed rather more menacing for the fact that he was advancing upon them, and at his approach the men finally balked.

'Didn't mean any trouble,' the first man muttered. 'Had to make sure.'

'Yellow-lover,' muttered the other, but quietly, so that Mannering didn't hear.

Mannering waited until they had departed, and then looked down at Ah Quee, who rolled onto his side, checked his ribs for breakage, and clambered laboriously to his feet, picking up his trampled certificate of indenture as he did so, and brushing it clean of dust. His throat was very tight.

'Thank you,' he said, when he could breathe at last.

Mannering seemed annoyed by this expression of gratitude. He frowned, looking Ah Quee up and down, and said, 'What's this about Johnny Sook and a pistol?'

'Don't know,' said Ah Quee.

'Where is he?'

'Don't know.'

'Have you seen him? Anywhere at all?'

Ah Quee had not seen Ah Sook since the night of the widow's *séance*, one month prior: late that night he had returned from the Wayfarer's Fortune to find Ah Sook packing his few belongings and vanishing, with a grim efficiency, into the rustle of the night. 'No,' he said.

Mannering sighed. 'I suppose you've been reassigned, now that Aurora's gone back to the bank,' he said after a moment. 'Let's have a look at your paper, then. Let's see where they've placed you. Hand it over.'

He held out his hand for the certificate. The document was brief, and had been written without consultation with Ah Quee: it provided his 'apparent age' instead of his actual age; the origin of the ship he had arrived on, rather than his actual birthplace in Canton; and a brief list of his attributes as a worker. It was heralded with the numeral five, indicating that the length of his indenture was five years, and had been stamped with the Company seal. Mannering cast his eye down the document. In the box marked 'present site of employment' the word *Aurora* had been recently scratched out, and replaced with the words *Dream of England*.

'Can't get a bit of luck, can you?' Mannering said. 'That claim belongs to me! One of mine. Belongs to me.' He tapped himself on the chest. 'You're working for me again, Johnny Quee. Just like the good old days. Back when you were running rings around me with your bloody crucible, and bleeding Anna Magdalena for dust.'

'You,' said Ah Quee, massaging his ribs.

'Together again,' said Mannering grimly. 'Dream of England, my eye. English Nightmare, more like.'

'Unlucky,' said Ah Quee.

'Unlucky for you or unlucky for me?'

Ah Quee did not reply to this, having not understood the question, and all of a sudden Mannering laughed and shook his head. 'It's the nature of indenture, I'm afraid, that you sign away your luck. Every chance to get lucky, you sign away. It's the nature of any contract. A contract's got to be fulfilled, you see: it's got to come around on itself, sooner or later. A lucky man, I've always said, is a man who was lucky once, and after that, he learned a thing or two about investment. Luck only happens once and it's always an accident when it does. It's contracts that come back around. It's investments and obligations; it's paperwork; it's business. I'll tell you another thing I like to say. If a man wants any shot at making his fortune then he'll never sign his name to any piece of paper that he didn't write himself. I've done that, Johnny Quee. I've never signed my name to any contract that I didn't write myself.'

'Very good,' said Ah Quee.

Mannering glared at him. 'I don't suppose you'd be so stupid as to try and run something funny past me again. That's twice now that you've tried to bet against me: once on the Aurora, and once on Anna. I'm a man who knows how to count.'

'Very good,' said Ah Quee again.

Mannering passed the indenture back to him. 'Well, you'll be pleased to turn your back upon Aurora, I don't doubt—and you needn't worry about Dream of England. She's as sound as a drum.'

'Not a duffer?' said Ah Quee, slyly.

'Not this one,' said Mannering. 'I'll give you my word on that. You'll do all right on Dream of England. She's been raked for nuggets, of course, but there's plenty of dust in the tailings. Perfect for a man like you. Someone with two eyes in his head. You won't make a fortune on her, Johnny Quee, but who among you ever does?'

Ah Quee nodded.

'Get yourself back to Kaniere,' said Mannering at last, and returned inside.

VENUS IN PISCES

In which the chaplain loses his temper, and the widow loses a fight.

'But who is this?' said Lydia Wells. 'A man of God?'

She stood in the doorway, half-smiling, plucking at each of her fingertips in turn, to ease off her gloves; Anna and Devlin looked back at her in mute horror, as though apprehended in some gross act of fornication—though Anna was by the window, her palm still pressed flat against her breast, and Devlin was seated at the sofa, from which he now leaped up, blushing horribly.

'Goodness me,' said Lydia Wells, easing one milky hand out of her glove, and tucking it under her elbow to begin plucking off the other. 'What a pair of sheep.'

'Good morning, Mrs. Wells,' said Devlin, finding his tongue at last. 'My name is Cowell Devlin. I am the chaplain of the prospective gaol-house at Seaview.'

'A charming introduction,' said Lydia Wells. 'What are you doing in my parlour?'

'We were having a—theological discussion,' said Devlin. 'Over tea.'

'You appear to have forgotten the tea.'

'It's still steeping,' said Anna.

'So it is,' said Lydia Wells, without glancing at the tray. 'Well, in that case, my arrival has been fortuitously timed! Anna, run and fetch another cup. I'll join you. I have a great fondness for theological debate.'

With a desperate look at Devlin, Anna nodded, ducked her head, and slipped out of the room.

'Mrs. Wells,' whispered Devlin quickly, as Anna's footsteps receded down the hallway, 'may I ask you a very odd question, while we are alone?'

Lydia Wells smiled at him. 'I make my living answering odd questions,' she said, 'and you of all people should know that we are hardly alone.'

'Well, yes,' said Devlin, feeling uncomfortable. 'But here's the question. Does Miss Wetherell know how to read?'

Lydia Wells raised her eyebrows. 'That *is* a very odd question,' she replied, 'though not because of its answer. I wonder what prompted the asking.'

Anna returned with a cup and saucer, and set it beside the others on the tray.

'What is the answer?' Devlin said quietly.

'You play mother, Anna,' said Lydia Wells, her voice ringing out. 'Reverend: be seated, please. There you are. How nice, to have a clergyman to tea! It makes one feel quite civilised. I will have a biscuit, I think, and sugar too.'

Devlin sat.

'The answer, to the best of my knowledge, is no,' the widow said, sitting down herself also. 'And now I have an odd question of my own. Is it a different class of falsehood, when a minister of God tells a lie?'

He balked. 'I do not see the pertinence of your question.'

'But Reverend, you are not playing fair,' the widow said. 'I answered *your* question without begging to know the reason why; will you not now do the same for me?'

'What was his question?' said Anna, looking around—but she was ignored.

'Is it a different class of falsehood, I ask,' the widow went on, 'when the liar is a minister of God?'

Devlin sighed. 'It would be a different class of falsehood,' he said, 'only if the minister was using the authority of his office for ill. So long as the falsehood did not pertain to his office, there would be no difference. We are equal in the eyes of God.'

'Ah,' said the widow. 'Thank you. Now. You said just now that you were talking of theology, Reverend. Would you care to count me in to the debate?'

Devlin flushed. He opened his mouth—and faltered: he did not have an alibi prepared.

Anna came to his rescue. 'When I woke up in gaol,' she said, 'the Reverend Devlin was there. He prayed for me, and he has been praying ever since.'

'Then you have been talking about prayer?' the widow said, still addressing Devlin.

The chaplain recovered his composure. 'Among other things,' he said. 'We have also been discussing acts of great providence, and unexpected gifts.'

'Fascinating,' said Lydia Wells. 'And do you make it your habit, Reverend, to drop in on young women when their guardians are otherwise engaged, in order to discuss, without a chaperone, matters of theology?'

Devlin was offended by the accusation. 'You are hardly Miss Wetherell's guardian,' he said. 'She lived alone for months until you arrived in Hokitika; what sudden need has she of a guardian?'

'A very great one, I should judge,' said Lydia Wells, 'given the degree to which she has been formerly exploited in this town.'

'I wonder at your adverb, Mrs. Wells! You mean to say that she is exploited no longer?'

Lydia Wells seemed to stiffen. 'Perhaps you do not think it a gladness,' she said coldly, 'that this young woman is no longer prostituting her body every night, and risking every kind of violence, and concussing herself daily with a contemptible drug. Perhaps you wish that she had her former life back again.'

'Don't perhaps *me*,' Devlin said, flaring up. 'That's cheap rhetoric. It's nothing better than bullying, and I won't stand for a bully; I won't.'

'I am astonished by your accusation,' said Lydia Wells. 'In what way am I a bully?'

'The girl has no freedoms, for heaven's sake! She was brought here against her will, and you keep her on the shortest leash imaginable!'

'Anna,' said Lydia Wells, still addressing Devlin. 'Did you come to the Wayfarer's Fortune against your will?'

'No, ma'am,' Anna said.

'Why did you come and take up lodgings here?'

'Because you made me an offer, and I accepted it.'

'What was my offer?'

'You offered to pay my debt to Mr. Clinch up front, and you said that I could come and live with you as your companion, so long as I helped you on the business end.'

'Did I keep my end of the bargain?'

'Yes,' Anna said, miserably.

'Thank you,' the widow said. She had not taken her eyes from Devlin's, and nor had she touched her cup of tea. 'As for the length of the girl's leash, I find it very wonderful that you should protest a life of virtue and austerity, in favour of—what did you call them—"freedoms"? Freedoms to do what, exactly? Freedom to fraternise with those very men who once defiled and abused her? Freedom to smoke herself senseless in a Chinaman's saloon?'

Devlin could not resist countering this. 'But *why* did you make your offer, Mrs. Wells? *Why* did you offer to repay Miss Wetherell's debts?'

'Out of concern for the girl, naturally.'

'Moonshine,' said Devlin.

'Pardon me,' said Lydia Wells. 'I have ample concern for Anna's welfare.'

'Look at her! The poor girl's half the size she was a month ago; you can't deny *that*. She's starving. You're starving her.'

'Anna,' said Lydia Wells, spitting out the girl's name. 'Do I starve you?'

'No,' said Anna.

'Are you, in your own opinion, starving?'

'No,' Anna said again.

'You can spare me the pantomime,' said Devlin, who was

becoming angry. 'You don't care two straws for that girl. You've no more concern for her than you do for anyone—and from what I have heard about you, that's a paltry kind of concern indeed.'

'Another terrible accusation,' said Lydia Wells. 'And from the chaplain of a prison, no less! I suppose I ought to try to clear my name. Anna, tell the good Reverend what you did while you were in Dunedin.'

There was a pause. Devlin glanced at Anna, his confidence faltering.

'Tell him what you did,' said Lydia Wells again.

'I played the serpent in your household,' said Anna.

'Meaning what, precisely? Tell him *exactly* what it was you did.'

'I lay down with your husband.'

'Yes,' said Lydia Wells. 'You seduced my husband, Mr. Wells. Now tell the good Reverend this. What did *I* do, in retaliation?'

'You sent me away,' Anna said. 'To Hokitika.'

'In what condition?'

'With child.'

'With whose child, please?'

'With your husband's child,' Anna whispered. 'Crosbie's child.'

Devlin was astonished.

'So I sent you away,' the widow said, nodding. 'Do I still maintain that my reaction was the right one?'

'No,' Anna said. 'You have repented. You have begged for my forgiveness. More than once.'

'Are you quite sure?' said Mrs. Wells, feigning astonishment. 'According to our good Reverend here, I have no concern at all for the welfare of others, and presumably still less for those who have played temptress beneath my roof! Are you quite sure that I am even capable of begging your forgiveness?'

'Enough,' said Devlin. He raised his hands. 'Enough.'

'It's true,' Anna said. 'It's true that she has asked for my forgiveness.'

'*Enough.*'

'Now that you have insulted my integrity in virtually every way imaginable,' said the widow, picking up her teacup at last, 'would you mind telling me, without falsehood this time, what you are doing in my parlour?'

'I was delivering a private message to Miss Wetherell,' Devlin said.

The widow turned to Anna. 'What was it?'

'You don't have to tell her,' Devlin said quickly. 'Not if you don't want to. You don't have to say a single word to her.'

'Anna,' said Lydia Wells, dangerously. 'What was the message?'

'The Reverend showed me a document,' Anna said, 'by the authority of which, half of that fortune in Crosbie's cottage belongs to me.'

'Indeed,' said Lydia Wells—and although she spoke coolly Devlin thought he saw a flash of panic in her eye. 'To whom does the other half belong?'

'Mr. Emery Staines,' said Anna.

'Where is this document?'

'I hid it,' said Anna.

'Well, go and fetch it out,' Lydia snapped.

'Don't,' Devlin said quickly.

'I won't,' said Anna. She made no move to touch her bodice.

'You might at least do me the courtesy of telling me the whole truth,' Lydia said. 'Both of you.'

'I'm afraid we can't do that,' Devlin said, speaking before Anna could have a chance. 'This information, you see, pertains to a crime that has not yet been fully investigated. It concerns, among other things, the blackmail of a certain Mr. Alistair Lauderback.'

'Pardon me?' said Lydia Wells.

'What?' said Anna.

'I'm afraid I can't disclose anything further,' Devlin said— observing, to his great satisfaction, that the widow had become very pale. 'Anna, if you wish to go to the Courthouse directly, I will escort you there myself.'

'You will?' Anna said, peering at him.

'Yes,' Devlin said.

'What on earth do you think you'll be doing at the Courthouse?' said Lydia Wells.

'Seeking legal counsel,' said Anna. 'As is my civil right.'

Mrs. Wells fixed Anna with an impenetrable look. 'I consider this a very poor way to repay my kindness,' she said at last, and in a quiet voice.

Anna went to Devlin's side, and took his arm. 'Mrs. Wells,' she said, 'it is not your kindness that I mean to repay.'

JUPITER IN CAPRICORN

*In which Aubert Gascoigne is very much amused; Cowell
Devlin abdicates responsibility; and Anna Wetherell makes
a mistake.*

The Hokitika Courthouse, home of the Resident Magistrate's
Court, was a scene of robust but much-approximated ceremony.
The courtroom had been cordoned with ropes, rather like a shear-
ing yard. District officials sat behind a row of desks that protected
them from the milling crowd; when the court was in session, these
desks would form a kind of barricade between the figures of the
court and the public, who was required to stand. The magistrate's
seat, currently vacant, was only a captain's chair on a raised dais,
though the chair had been draped with sheepskins to give it a more
dignified aspect. Beside it stood an outsize Union Jack, hung on a
stand that was rather too short for the size of the flag. The flag
might have pooled on the dusty ground, had an enterprising soul
not thought to place an empty wine cask beneath the bottom of the
stand—a detail that served to diminish, rather than enhance, the
flag's effect.

It had been a busy morning in the petty courts. Mrs. Wells's
appeal to revoke the sale of Crosbie Wells's estate had been
approved at last, which meant that the Wells fortune, formerly held
in escrow at the Reserve Bank, had been surrendered to the
Magistrate's purse. Harald Nilssen's four-hundred-pound commission had not likewise been revoked, for two reasons: firstly,

because the sum constituted his legal payment for a service adequately rendered; and secondly, because the commission had since been donated, in its entirety, to assist in the erection of the new gaol-house at Seaview. It was unseemly, the Magistrate declared, to revoke a gift of charity, especially when the gift was such a handsome and selfless one; he commended Nilssen, in absentia, for his benevolence.

There were sundry other legal expenses to be itemised, most of which reflected the many hours the Magistrate's office had spent on the project of trying to find the late Mr. Wells's birth certificate. These expenses would come out of Mrs. Wells's inheritance also— which, less the estate taxes and fees, and after these many corrections had been made, now totalled a little over £3500. This sum was to be made payable to Mrs. Wells as soon as the fortune had been cleared by the Reserve Bank, in whatever form of currency the widow desired. Did Mrs. Wells have anything to say? No, she did not—but she gave Aubert Gascoigne a very broad smile as she swept away from the Courthouse, and he saw that her eyes were shining.

'Oi—Gascoigne!'

Gascoigne had been staring into the middle distance. He blinked. 'Yes?'

His colleague Burke was in the doorway, a fat paper envelope in his hand. 'Jimmy Shaw tells me you've a flair for maritime insurance.'

'That's right,' said Gascoigne.

'Do you mind taking on another job? Something's just come in.'

Gascoigne frowned at the envelope. 'What kind of a "something"?'

'Letter from a John Hincher Garrity,' said the other, holding it up. 'Regarding one of the wrecks on the bar. *Godspeed* is the name of the craft.'

Gascoigne held out his hand. 'I'll take a look at it.'

'Good man.'

The envelope had been postmarked in Wellington, and slit already. Gascoigne opened it and withdrew its contents. The first document enclosed was a short letter from John Hincher Garrity, M.P. for the electoral district of Heathcote in Canterbury. The politician authorised a representative of the Hokitika Courthouse to act as his agent in drawing down funds from the Garrity Group's private account at the Bank of New Zealand. He trusted that the enclosed documents would explain the matter sufficiently, and thanked the representative in advance for his efforts. Gascoigne put this letter aside and turned to the next document. It was also a letter, forwarded by Garrity; it had been addressed to the Garrity Group.

Hokitika, 25 Feb. 66

Sirs—

I write to inform you of the regrettable wreck of the barque Godspeed, *of which I was until very recently the operating master, upon the treacherous Hokitika Bar. The shipowner, Mr. Crosbie F. Wells, is recently deceased, and I am settling matters as his proxy. I understand that in purchasing* Godspeed *Mr. Crosbie F. Wells inherited all extant policies from former owner A. Lauderback, member of the Garrity Group, and therefore, that* Godspeed *is protected and indemnified by said authority. I seek now to draw down all funds designated by Mr. Lauderback for this purpose in order to facilitate the removal of the wreck. I enclose the full record of all expenses, deeds of sale, receipts, quotes, inventories, &c., and remain,*

Yours,

Francis W. R. Carver

Gascoigne frowned. What did Carver mean by this? Crosbie Wells had certainly not purchased *Godspeed*; Carver had purchased the craft himself, using the alias Wells. Gascoigne shuffled through the remaining pages, which had evidently been forwarded by Carver to Mr. Garrity as evidence of the validity of his claim. He passed over the harbourmaster's assessment of the wreck, a balance sheet of all the debts incurred, and sundry receipts and testimonials, until he found, at the bottom of the pile, a copy—presumably Carver's personal copy—of *Godspeed*'s bill of sale. Gascoigne took up this last item and looked at the signature closely. It had been signed by a Francis Wells! What was Carver playing at? Looking at the signature a moment longer, however, Gascoigne perceived that the large loop on the side of the F could easily have been a C ... why, yes! There was even a dot of ink, fortuitously placed, between the C and the F. The longer Gascoigne looked at it, the more the ambiguity became clear to him: Carver must have signed the false name with this future purpose in mind. Gascoigne shook his head, and then, after a moment, laughed aloud.

'What's tickled you?' said Burke, looking up.

'Oh,' said Gascoigne, 'nothing of consequence.'

'You just laughed,' said Burke. 'What's the joke?'

'There is no joke,' said Gascoigne. 'I was expressing my appreciation, that's all.'

'Appreciation? What for?'

'A job well done,' said Gascoigne. He returned the letters to the envelope and stood, intending to take John Hincher Garrity's letter of authorisation to the bank at once—but just as he did so the foyer door opened, and Alistair Lauderback walked in, shadowed at his heels by Jock and Augustus Smith.

'Ah,' said Lauderback, perceiving the letter in Gascoigne's hand. 'I'm just in time, then. Yes: I had a message from Garrity myself this morning. There's been a mix-up, and I'm here to set it straight.'

'Mr. Lauderback, I presume,' said Gascoigne dryly.

'I want a private interview with the Magistrate,' Lauderback said. 'It's urgent.'

'The Magistrate is taking his luncheon at present.'

'Where does he take it?'

'I'm afraid I don't know,' said Gascoigne. 'The afternoon sessions begin at two o'clock; you are welcome to wait until then. Excuse me, gentlemen.'

'Hold up,' said Lauderback, as Gascoigne bowed, and made to exit. 'Where do you think you're going with that letter?'

'To the bank,' said Gascoigne—who could not bear officious rudeness of the kind that Lauderback had just displayed. 'I have been deputised by Mr. Garrity to facilitate a transaction on his behalf. I beg you to excuse me.'

Again he made to leave.

'Hold up a moment,' said Lauderback. 'Just hold up a moment! It's on account of this very business that I want an audience here; you're not to go off to the bank, before I've said my piece!'

Gascoigne stared at him coolly. Lauderback seemed to realise that he had begun on the wrong foot, and said, 'Hear me out, would you? What's your name?'

'Gascoigne.'

'Gascoigne, is it? Yes, I had you for a Frenchman.'

Lauderback held out his hand, and Gascoigne shook it.

'I'll speak to you, then,' Lauderback said. 'If I can't get the Magistrate.'

'I imagine you would prefer to do so in private,' said Gascoigne, still without warmth.

'Yes, good.' Lauderback turned to his aides. 'You wait here,' he said. 'I'll be ten minutes.'

Gascoigne led him into the Magistrate's office, and closed the door behind him. They sat down on the Windsor chairs that faced the Magistrate's desk.

'All right, Mr. Gascoigne,' said Lauderback at once, sitting forward, 'here's the long and short of it. This whole business is a set-up. I never sold *Godspeed* to a man named Crosbie Wells. I sold it to a man who told me that his name was Francis Wells. But the name was an alias. I didn't know it at the time. This man. Francis Carver. It was him. *He* took the alias—Francis Wells—and I sold the ship to *him*, under that name. You see he kept his Christian name. Only the surname changed. The point is this: he signed the deed with a false name, and that's against the law!'

'Let me see if I understand you correctly,' Gascoigne said, pretending to be bemused. 'Francis Carver claims that a man named Crosbie Wells purchased *Godspeed* ... and you claim that this is a lie.'

'It is a lie!' said Lauderback. 'It's an out-and-out fabrication! I sold the ship to a man named Francis Wells.'

'Who doesn't exist.'

'It was an alias,' said Lauderback. 'His real name is Carver. But he told me that his name was Wells.'

'*Francis* Wells,' Gascoigne pointed out, 'and Crosbie Wells's middle name was Francis, and Crosbie Wells does exist—at least, he did. So perhaps you were mistaken about the purchaser's identity. The difference between Francis Wells and C. Francis Wells is not very great, I observe.'

'What's this about a C?' said Lauderback.

'I have examined the forwarded copy of the deed of sale,' Gascoigne said. 'It was signed by a C. Francis Wells.'

'It most certainly was *not*!'

'I'm afraid it was,' said Gascoigne.

'Then it's been doctored,' said Lauderback. 'It's been doctored after the fact.'

Gascoigne opened the envelope in his hand, and extracted the bill of sale. 'On first inspection, I believed that it read merely "Francis Wells". It was only on leaning closer that I saw the other letter, cursively linked to the F.'

Lauderback looked at it, frowned, and looked closer—and then a deep blush spread across his cheeks and neck. 'Cursive or no cursive,' he said, 'C or no C, that deed of sale was signed by the blackguard Francis Carver. I saw him sign it with my own two eyes!'

'Was the transaction witnessed?'

Lauderback said nothing.

'If the transaction was not witnessed, then it will be your word against his, Mr. Lauderback.'

'It'll be the truth against a lie!'

Gascoigne declined to answer this. He returned the contract to the envelope, and smoothed it flat over his knee.

'It's a set-up,' Lauderback said. 'I'll take him to court. I'll have him flayed.'

'On what charge?'

'False pretences, of course,' Lauderback said. 'Impersonation. Fraud.'

'I'm afraid that the evidence will bear out against you.'

'Oh—you're afraid of that, are you?'

'The law has no grounds to doubt this signature,' Gascoigne said, smoothing the envelope a second time, 'because no other documentation survives Mr. Crosbie Wells, official or otherwise, that might serve as proof of his hand.'

Lauderback opened his mouth; he seemed about to say something, but then he shut it again, shaking his head. 'It was a set-up,' he said. 'It was a set-up all along!'

'Why do you think Mr. Carver saw the need to take an alias with you?'

The politician's answer was surprising. 'I've done some digging on Carver,' he said. 'His father was a prominent figure in one of the British merchant trading firms—Dent & Co. You might have heard of him. William Rochfort Carver. No? Well, anyway. Some time in the early fifties he gives his son a clipper ship—the *Palmerston*—and the son starts trading Chinese wares back and forth from Canton, under the banner of Dent & Co. Carver's still a young man. He's being coddled, really, becoming master of a ship so young. Well, here's what I found out. In the spring of 1854 the *Palmerston* gets searched when it's leaving the Sydney harbour—just a routine job— and Carver's found to be foul of the law on several counts. Evading duty, and failing to declare, and a pile of other misdemeanours. Each small enough that a judge might turn a blind eye, but the charges come in all at once; when they're stacked up like that, the law has to come down. He's given ten years at Cockatoo, and that's ten years of penal servitude, no less. A real dishonour. The father's furious. Revokes the ship, disinherits the son, and as a final touch, makes sure to tarnish his name at every dock and shipyard in the South Pacific. By the time Francis Carver gets out of gaol, he has about as good a character as Captain Kidd—in seafaring circles at least. No shipowner's going to lease a ship to him, and no crew's going to take him on.'

'And so he assumed an alias.'

'Exactly,' said Lauderback, sitting back.

'I am curious to know why he only assumed an alias with *you*,' Gascoigne said lightly. 'He does not seem to have assumed the name Wells in any other context, save for when he purchased this ship. He introduced himself to *me*, for example, as Mr. Francis Carver.'

Lauderback glared at him. 'You read the papers,' he said. 'Don't make me spell it out to you. I've made my apology in public: I won't do it again.'

Gascoigne inclined his head. 'Ah,' he said. 'Carver assumed the alias Francis Wells in order to exploit your former entanglement with Mrs. Wells.'

'That's it,' said Lauderback. 'He said that he was Crosbie's brother. Told me he was settling a score on Crosbie's behalf—on account of my having made a bad woman of his wife. It was an intimidation tactic, and it worked.'

'I see,' said Gascoigne, wondering why Lauderback had not explained this so sensibly to Thomas Balfour two months ago.

'Look,' said Lauderback, 'I'm playing straight with you, Mr. Gascoigne, and I'm telling you that the law is my side. Carver's break with his father is commonly known. He had a thousand provocations to assume an alias. Why, I could call in the father's testimony, if need be. How would Carver like *that*?'

'Not very well, I should imagine.'

'No,' cried Lauderback. 'Not very well at all!'

Gascoigne was annoyed by this. 'Well, I wish you luck, Mr. Lauderback, in bringing Mr. Carver to justice,' he said.

'Spare the bromide,' Lauderback snapped. 'Talk to me plain.'

'As you wish,' Gascoigne said, shrugging. 'You know without my telling you that proof of provocation is not evidence. A man cannot be convicted simply because it can be proved that he had good reason to commit the crime in question.'

Lauderback bristled. 'Do you doubt my word?'

'No indeed,' said Gascoigne.

'You just think my case is weak. You think I don't have a leg to stand on.'

'Yes. I think it would be very unwise to take this matter to court,' said Gascoigne. 'I am sorry to speak so bluntly. You have my compassion for your troubles, of course.'

But Gascoigne felt no compassion whatsoever for Alistair

Lauderback. He tended to reserve that emotion for persons less privileged than himself, and although he could acknowledge that Lauderback's current situation was pitiable, he considered the politician's wealth and eminence to be ample consolation for whatever inconveniences the man might be encountering in the short term. In fact, enduring a spot of injustice might do Lauderback a bit of good! It might improve him as a politician, thought Gascoigne—who was, in his private adjudications at least, something of an autocrat.

'I'll wait for the Magistrate,' said Lauderback. 'He'll see sense.'

Gascoigne tucked the envelope into his jacket, next to his cigarettes. 'I understand that Carver is now attempting to draw down funds from your protection and indemnity scheme, in order to finance the debts that he incurred in disposing of the shipwreck.'

'That is correct.'

'And you wish to refuse him access to this money.'

'Also correct.'

'On what grounds?'

Lauderback turned very red. 'On what grounds?' he cried. 'The man has stiffed me, Mr. Gascoigne! He was planning this from the outset! You're a fool if you think I'll take it lying down! Is that what you're telling me? To take it lying down?'

'Mr. Lauderback,' Gascoigne said, 'I do not presume to give you any kind of advice at all. What I am observing is that no laws appear to have been broken. In his letter to Mr. Garrity, Mr. Carver made it very plain that he is acting on Mr. Wells's behalf—for Mr. Wells, as you know, is dead. To all appearances Carver is merely doing the charitable thing, in settling matters as the shipowner's proxy, because the shipowner is not able to do the job himself. I do not see that you have any evidence to disprove this.'

'But it's not *true*!' Lauderback exploded. 'Crosbie Wells never bought that ship! Francis Carver signed that bloody contract in another man's name! It's a case of forgery, pure and simple!'

'I'm afraid that will be very difficult to prove,' said Gascoigne.

'Why?' said Lauderback.

'Because, as I have already told you, there is no proof of Crosbie

Wells's true signature,' said Gascoigne. 'There were no papers of any kind in his cottage, and his birth certificate and his miner's right are nowhere to be found.'

Lauderback opened his mouth to make a retort, and again seemed to change his mind.

'Oh,' said Gascoigne, suddenly. 'I've just thought of something.'

'What?' said Lauderback.

'His marriage certificate,' said Gascoigne. 'That would bear his signature, would it not?'

'Ah,' said Lauderback. 'Yes.'

'But no,' said Gascoigne, changing his mind, 'it wouldn't be enough: to prove a forgery of a dead man's hand, you would need more than one example of his signature.'

'How many would you need?' said Lauderback.

Gascoigne shrugged. 'I am not familiar with the law,' he said, 'but I would imagine that you would need several examples of his true signature in order to prove the abberations in the false one.'

'Several examples,' Lauderback echoed.

'Well,' said Gascoigne, rising, 'I hope for your sake that you find something, Mr. Lauderback; but in the meantime, I'm afraid that I am legally obliged to carry out Mr. Garrity's instruction, and take these papers to the bank.'

Φ

Upon quitting the Wayfarer's Fortune the chaplain had not escorted Anna Wetherell directly to the Courthouse. He took her instead into the Garrick's Head Hotel, where he ordered one portion of fish pie—the perennial lunchtime special—and one glass of lemon cordial. He directed Anna to be seated, placed the plate of food in front of her, and bid her to eat, which she did obediently, and in silence. Once her plate was clean, he pushed the sugared drink across the table towards her, and said,

'Where is Mr. Staines?'

Anna did not seem surprised by the question. She picked up the glass, sipped at it, winced at the sweetness, and then sat for a moment, watching him.

'Inland,' she said at last. 'Somewhere inland. I don't know exactly where.'

'North or south of here?'

'I don't know.'

'Is he being held against his will?'

'I don't know.'

'You *do* know,' said Devlin.

'I don't,' Anna said. 'I haven't seen him since January, and I've no idea why he vanished like he did. I only know that he's still alive, and he's somewhere inland.'

'Because you've been getting messages. Inside your head.'

'Messages wasn't the right way to describe it,' Anna said. 'That wasn't right. It's more like ... a feeling. Like when you're trying to remember a dream that you had, and you can remember the shape of it, the sense of it, but no details, nothing sure. And the more you try and remember, the more hazy it becomes.'

Devlin was frowning. 'So you have a "feeling".'

'Yes,' Anna said.

'You have a feeling that Mr. Staines is somewhere inland, and that he is alive.'

'Yes,' said Anna. 'I can't give you any details. I know it's somewhere muddy. Or leafy. Somewhere near water, only it isn't the beach. The water's quick-moving. Over stones ... You see: as soon as I try and put it into words, it trips away from me.'

'This all sounds very vague, my dear.'

'It's not vague,' Anna said. 'I'm certain of it. Just as when you're certain you did have a dream ... you *knew* you dreamed ... but you can't remember any of the details.'

'How long have you been having these "feelings"? These dreams?'

'Only since I stopped whoring,' Anna said. 'Since my blackout.'

'Since Staines disappeared, in other words.'

'The fourteenth of January,' said Anna. 'That was the date.'

'Is it always the same—the water, the mud? The same dream?'

'No.'

She did not elaborate, and to prompt her Devlin said, 'Well, what else?'

'Oh,' she said, embarrassed. 'Just sensations, really. Snatches. Impressions.'

'Impressions of what?'

She looked away from him. 'Impressions of me,' she said.

'I'm afraid I don't understand you.'

She turned her hand over. 'What he thinks of me. Mr. Staines, I mean. What he dreams about, when he imagines me.'

'You see yourself—but through his eyes.'

'Yes,' Anna said. 'Exactly.'

'Ought I to infer that Mr. Staines holds you in high esteem?'

'He loves me,' she said, and then after a moment, she said it again. 'He loves me.'

Devlin studied her critically. 'I see,' he said. 'Has he made an avowal of his love?'

'No,' Anna said. 'He doesn't need to. I know it, just the same.'

'Do you get these feelings frequently?'

'Very frequently,' she said. 'He thinks of me all the time.'

Devlin nodded. The situation was at last becoming clear to him, and with this dawning clarity his heart was sinking in his chest. 'Are you in love with Mr. Staines, Miss Wetherell?'

'We spoke of it,' she said. 'The night he vanished. We were talking nonsense, and I said something silly about unrequited love, and he became very serious, and he stopped me, and he said that unrequited love was not possible; that it was not love. He said that love must be freely given, and freely taken, such that the lovers, in joining, make the equal halves of something whole.'

'A passionate sentiment,' Devlin said.

This seemed to please her. 'Yes,' she said.

'But he did not declare his love for you, after all that.'

'He didn't make any vows. I said that.'

'And nor did you.'

'I never got another chance,' she said. 'That was the night he disappeared.'

Cowell Devin sighed. Yes, he understood Anna Wetherell at long last, but it was not a happy understanding. Devlin had known many women of poor prospects and limited means, whose only transport out of the miserable cage of their unhappy circumstance was the flight of the fantastic. Such fantasies were invariably magical—angelic patronage, invitations into paradise—and Anna's story, touching though it was, showed the same strain of the impossible. Why, it was painfully clear! The most eligible bachelor of Anna's acquaintance possessed a love so deep and pure that all respective differences between them were rendered immaterial? He was not dead—he was only missing? He was sending her 'messages' that proved the depth of his love—and these were messages that only *she* could hear? It was a fantasy, Devlin thought. It was a fantasy of the girl's own devising. The boy could only be dead.

'You want Mr. Staines to love you very much, don't you, Miss Wetherell?'

Anna seemed offended by his implication. 'He does love me.'

'That wasn't my question.'

She squinted at him. 'Everyone wants to be loved.'

'That's very true,' Devlin said, sadly. 'We all want to be loved—and need to be loved, I think. Without love, we cannot be ourselves.'

'You're of a mind with Mr. Staines.'

'Am I?'

'Yes,' Anna said. 'That is precisely the sort of thing that he would say.'

'Your Mr. Staines is quite the philosopher, Miss Wetherell.'

'Why, Reverend,' Anna said, smiling suddenly, 'I believe you've just paid yourself a compliment.'

They did not speak for a moment. Anna sipped again at her sugared drink, and Devlin, brooding, looked out across the hotel dining room. After a moment Anna's hand went to her bosom, where the forged deed of gift still lay against her skin.

Devlin looked sharply at her. 'You have ample time to reconsider,' he said.

'I only want a legal opinion.'

'You have my clerical opinion.'

'Yes,' Anna said. '"Blessed are the meek".'

She seemed to regret this impudence immediately; a violent blush spread across her face and neck, and she turned away.

Suddenly Devlin wanted nothing more to do with her. He pushed his chair back from the table, and placed his hands on his knees.

'I will accompany you to the Courthouse door and no further,' he said. 'What you do with the document in your possession is no longer my business. Know that I will not lie to protect you. I will certainly not lie in a court of law. If anyone asks, I shall not hesi-tate to tell them the truth, which is that you forged that signature with your own hand.'

'All right,' said Anna, rising. 'Thank you very much for the pie. And the cordial. And thank you for all that you said to Mrs. Wells.'

Devlin rose also. 'You oughtn't to thank me for that,' he said. 'I let my temper get the better of me there, I'm afraid. I wasn't at my best.'

'You were marvellous,' Anna said, and she stepped forward, and put her hands on his shoulders, and kissed him very nicely on the cheek.

Φ

By the time Anna Wetherell arrived at the Hokitika Courthouse, Aubert Gascoigne had already departed for the Reserve Bank, the envelope from John Hincher Garrity snug in the inside pocket of his jacket; Alistair Lauderback had likewise long since left the build-ing. Anna was received by a red-faced solicitor named Fellowes, whom she did not know. He directed her into an alcove at the far side of the hall, where they sat down on either side of a plain deal table. Anna handed him the charred document without a word. The lawyer placed it on the table before him, squaring it with the edge of the desk, and then cupped his hands around his eyes to read it.

'Where did you get this?' Fellowes said at last, looking up.

'It was given to me,' Anna said. 'Anonymously.'

'When?'

'This morning.'

'Given how?'

'Someone slipped it under the door,' Anna lied. 'While Mrs. Wells was down here at the Courthouse.'

'Down here at the Courthouse, receiving the news that her appeal has been revoked at last,' Fellowes said, with a sceptical emphasis. He turned back to the document. 'Crosbie Wells . . . and Staines is the fellow whom nobody's heard from . . . and Miss Wetherell is you. Strange. Any idea who dropped it off?'

'No.'

'Or why?'

'No,' Anna said. 'I suppose someone wanted to do me a good turn.'

'Anyone in mind? Care to speculate?'

'No,' Anna said. 'I only want to know whether it's good.'

'It seems all right,' said Fellowes, peering at it. 'But it's not exactly a cash cheque, is it? Not with things being as they are—eight weeks on, and Mr. Staines still missing.'

'I don't understand.'

'Well. Even *if* this deed is valid, our good friend Mr. Staines no longer has two thousand pounds to give away. All of his assets have been seized, on account of his absence. Effective last Friday. He'd be lucky to scrape together a few hundred from what he's got left.'

'But the deed is binding,' Anna said. 'Even so.'

The lawyer shook his head. 'What I'm saying to you, my girl, is that our Mr. Staines *can't* give you two thousand pounds—unless by some miracle he's found alive, with a great deal of cash money on his person. His claims have been given over. Bought by other men.'

'But the deed is binding,' Anna said again. 'It has to be.'

Mr. Fellowes smiled. 'I'm afraid the law doesn't quite work that way. Think on this. I could write you a cheque right now for a million pounds, but that doesn't mean you're a million pounds up, does it, if I've nothing in my pocket, and nobody to act as my surety? Money always has to come out of someone's pocket, and if everyone's pockets are empty . . . well, that's that, no matter what anyone might claim.'

'Mr. Staines has two thousand pounds,' Anna said.

'Yes—well, if he did, that would be a different story.'

'No,' Anna said. 'I'm telling you. Mr. Staines has two thousand pounds.'

'How's that?'

'The gold in Crosbie Wells's cottage belonged to him.'

Fellowes paused. He stared at her for several seconds, and then, in quite a different voice, he said, 'Can that be proven?'

Anna repeated what Devlin had told her that morning: that the gold was found retorted, and bearing a signature that identified the origin of the gold.

'Which mine?'

'I can't remember the name,' Anna said.

'What's your source?'

She hesitated. 'I'd rather not say.'

Fellowes was looking interested. 'We could check the truth of it. The fortune was a component part of Wells's estate, after all, so there should be a record somewhere at the bank. I wonder why it hasn't come up before. Someone at the bank is keeping it back, perhaps.'

'If it's true,' Anna said, 'that means the fortune's mine, does it not? Two thousand pounds of it belongs to me. By the authority of this piece of paper here.'

'Miss Wetherell,' Fellowes said, 'this kind of money does not change hands so easily. I'm afraid it is never as simple as drawing down a cheque. But I will say that your coming here today is fortuitously timed. Mrs. Wells's appeal has just been granted, and the share apportioned her is in the process of being released. I can place a hold on her claim very easily, while we figure out what to do with this paper of yours.'

'Yes,' Anna said. 'Will you do that?'

'If you will consent to take me on as your solicitor, I will do all that I can to help,' Fellowes said, sitting back. 'My retainer is two pounds weekly, with expenses. I charge in advance, of course.'

She shook her head. 'I can't pay you in advance. I don't have any money.'

'Perhaps you might draw down a loan of some kind,' Fellowes said delicately, shifting his gaze away. 'I'm afraid that I am very strict on all matters of finance; I make no exceptions, and take nothing on promise. It's nothing personal; it comes with the training, that's all.'

'I can't pay you in advance,' Anna said again, 'but if you do this for me, I can pay you treble your retainer, when the money comes in.'

'Treble?' Fellowes smiled gently. 'Legal processes often take a very long time, Miss Wetherell, and sometimes without results: there is no guarantee that the money would come in at all. Mrs. Wells's appeal took two months to verify, and as you've shown very well, that business is not over yet!'

'Treble, up to a ceiling of one hundred pounds,' Anna said firmly, 'but if you clear the funds for me within the fortnight, I'll pay you two hundred, in cash money.'

Fellowes raised his eyebrows. 'Dear me,' he said. 'This is very bold.'

'It comes with the training,' Anna said.

But here Anna Wetherell made a misstep. Mr. Fellowes' eyes widened, and he shrank away. Why, she was a *whore*, he thought—and then it all came back to him. This was the very whore who had tried to end her life in the Kaniere-road, the very day of Staines's disappearance, and Wells's death! Fellowes was new to Hokitika: he did not know Anna Wetherell by sight, and had not immediately recognised her name. It was only at her brazen remark that he suddenly knew her.

Anna had mistaken his discomfiture for simple hesitation. 'Do you consent to my terms, Mr. Fellowes?'

Fellowes looked her up and down. 'I shall inquire at the Reserve Bank about this alleged retortion,' he said. His voice was cold. 'If the rumour you heard was a good one, then we will draw up a contract; if it was not, then I'm afraid I cannot help you.'

'You are very kind,' Anna said.

'None of that,' said Fellowes, roughly. 'Where might I find you, say in three hours' time?'

Anna hesitated. She could not return to the Wayfarer's Fortune that afternoon. She had no money on her person, but perhaps she could ask an old acquaintance to stand her a drink at one of the saloons along Revell-street.

'I'll just come back,' she said. 'I'll just come back and meet you here.'

'As you wish,' Fellowes said. 'Let us err on the side of caution and say five o'clock.'

'Five o'clock,' Anna said. She held out her hand for the charred document, but Fellowes was already opening his wallet, to slip the piece of paper inside.

'I think I'll hold onto this,' he said. 'Just for the meantime.'

MOON IN ARIES, CRESCENT

In which Te Rau Tauwhare makes a startling discovery.

Te Rau Tauwhare was feeling very pleased as he leaped from stone
to stone through the shallows of the Arahura River, making his way
downriver towards the beach. He had spent the past month with
a party of surveyors in the Deception Valley, and his purse was full;
what's more, that morning he had come upon a marvellous slab of
kahurangi pounamu, the weight of which was causing his satchel to
thump against his back with every step.

Back at Mawhera it would be time to dig the crop of kumara
from the ground: Tauwhare knew it from the appearance of
Whanui in the northern sky, the star low on the horizon, dawning well after midnight, and setting well before the dawn. His
people called this month *Pou-tu-te-rangi*—the post that lifted up
the sky—for at nights *Te Ikaroa* formed a milky arch that ran
north to south across the black dome of the heavens. It hung
between *Whanui*, in the north, and *Autahi*, in the south, and it
passed through the red jewel of *Rehua*, directly overhead: for a
moment, every night, the sky became a perfect compass, its
needle a dusty stripe of stars. At the dawning of *Whanui* the
crops would be unearthed from the ground; after this was *Paenga-
wha-wha*, when the tubers would be piled upon the margins of
the fields to be classified and counted, and then taken to the store
pits and storehouses, to be stacked for the winter months ahead.

After *Paenga-wha-wha*, the year came to an end—or, as the *tohunga* phrased, it, 'to a death'.

He rounded a bend in the river, left the shallows, and mounted the bank. Crosbie Wells's cottage was looking more forlorn with each passing day. The iron roof had rusted to a flaming orange, and the mortar had turned from white to vivid green; the small garden that Wells had planted had long since gone to seed. Tauwhare strode up the path, taking sorrowful note of these tokens of decay—and then halted suddenly.

There was somebody inside.

Slowly, Tauwhare came closer, peering through the open doorway into the gloom of the interior. The figure in question was curled on the floor, either dead or asleep. He was lying on his hip, with his knees angled close to his chest and his face turned away from the door. Tauwhare came closer still. He saw that the man was dressed in a jacket and trousers rather than digger's moleskin, and as Tauwhare watched, the fabric over his rib moved very slightly, rising and falling with the motion of a breath. Asleep, then.

Tauwhare passed through the doorway, taking care that his shadow did not fall across the man's body, and wake him. Moving softly, he edged around the wall behind him, to look down upon the sleeper's face. The man was very young. His hair was darkly matted with dirt and grease; the skin of his face seemed almost white by contrast. His face would have been handsome had it not been so plainly ravaged by privation. The lids of his eyes were mottled purple, and there were deep shadows in the hollows beneath them. His breath was fretful and inconstant. Tauwhare cast his eye over the boy's body. His dress had been worn almost to tatters, and apparently had not been changed in many weeks, for it was thick with mud and dust of all varieties. The coat had once been fine, however—that was plain—and the cravat, stiff with mud, was likewise of a fashionable cut.

'Mr. Staines?' Tauwhare whispered.

The boy's eyes opened.

'Hello,' he said. 'Hello, there.'

'Mr. Staines?'

'Yes, that's me,' the boy said, speaking in a voice that was high and very bright. He lifted his head. 'Excuse me. Excuse me. Is this Maori land?'

'No,' said Tauwhare. 'How long have you been here?'

'It's not Maori land?'

'No.'

'I need to be on Maori land,' the boy said, struggling up into a sitting position. He was holding his left arm oddly across his chest.

'Why?' Tauwhare said.

'I buried something,' said Staines. 'By a tree. But all the trees look the same to me and I'm afraid I've got myself into a bit of a muddle. Thank heavens you've come along—I'm ever so grateful.'

'You disappeared,' Tauwhare said.

'Three days, perhaps,' said the boy, sinking back again. 'I think it was three days ago. I've been mixing up my days: I can't seem to keep them in any sort of order. One forgets to mark the hours, when one's alone. I say: will you have a look at this, please?'

He pulled down the neck of his shirt and Tauwhare saw that the soiled darkness on his cravat was in fact the sticky tar of old blood. There was a wound just above his collarbone, and even from his distance of several feet Tauwhare could see that it was a very grave one. It had begun to putrefy. The centre of the wound was black, and fingers of red speared away from it in rays. Tauwhare could see black speckles of powder-burn, dark against the white of his chest, and deduced that it could only be a gunshot wound. Evidently somebody had shot Emery Staines at very close range, some time ago.

'You need medicine,' he said.

'Exactly,' said Staines. 'Exactly right. Will you fetch it for me? I'd be most exceedingly obliged. But I'm afraid I don't know your name.'

'My name is Te Rau Tauwhare.'

'You're a Maori fellow!' said Staines, blinking, as though seeing him for the first time. His eyes crossed, and then focused again. 'Is this Maori land?'

Tauwhare pointed east. 'Up there is Maori land,' he said.

'Up there?' Staines looked where Tauwhare pointed. 'Why are you down here, then, if your patch is up there?'

'This is the house of my friend,' said Tauwhare. 'Crosbie Wells.'

'Crosbie, Crosbie,' said Staines, closing his eyes. 'He was euchred, wasn't he? Lord, how that man can drink. Hollow legs, both of them. Where is he, then? Gone fossicking?'

'He's dead,' said Tauwhare.

'I'm exceedingly sorry to hear that,' Staines mumbled. 'What a terrible blow. And you were his friend—his very good friend! And Anna ... You'll accept my condolences, I hope ... But I've forgotten your name already.'

'It's Te Rau,' said Tauwhare.

'So it is,' said Staines. 'So it is.' He paused a moment, wretched with exhaustion, and then said, 'You wouldn't mind taking me there, would you, old fellow? You wouldn't mind it?'

'Where?'

'To the Maori land,' said Staines, closing his eyes again. 'You see, I've buried a great deal of gold on Maori land, and if you help me, I wouldn't be averse to giving you a pinch of it. I'll stand you whatever you like. Whatever you like. I remember the place exactly: there's a tree. The gold's underneath the tree.' He opened his eyes again and gave Tauwhare a beseeching, blurry look.

Tauwhare tried again. 'Where have you been, Mr. Staines?'

'I've been looking for my bonanza,' said Staines. 'I know it's on Maori land ... but there's nothing to mark Maori land, is there? No kind of fence to mark it. They always said a man could never get lost on the West Coast, because there's always mountains on one side, and ocean on the other ... but I seem to have got myself a little muddled, Te Rau. It's Te Rau, isn't it? Yes. Yes. I've been lost.'

Tauwhare came forward and knelt. Up close the man's wound looked even worse. In the centre of the blackness was a thick crust, showing through it the glint of yellow. He reached out his hand and touched the skin of Staines's cheek, feeling his temperature. 'You are sick with fever,' he said. 'This wound is very bad.'

'Never saw it coming,' said Staines, staring at him. 'Fresh off the boat, I was, and green with it. Nothing shows like greenness, on a man. Never saw it coming. Heavens, you *are* a sight for sore eyes! I'm terribly sorry about this muddle. I'm terribly sorry about your mate Crosbie. I really am. What kind of medicine did you say you had about you?'

'I shall bring it to you,' said Tauwhare. 'You wait here.' He did not feel hopeful. The boy was not speaking sense, and he was much too sick to walk to Hokitika on his own; he would need to be carried there on a litter or a cart, and Tauwhare had seen enough of the Hokitika hospital to know that men went there to die, not to be cured. The place was canvas-roofed, and walled only with the simplest clapboard; the bitter Tasman wind blew through the cracks in the planking, giving rise to a new cacophony of coughing and wheezing with each gust. It stank of filth and disease. There was no fresh water, and no clean linen, and only one ward. The patients were forced to sleep in close quarters with one another, and sometimes even to share a bed.

'Half-shares,' the boy was saying. 'Seemed fair enough to me. Half for you, half for me. What about it, he says. Going mates.'

Tauwhare was calculating the distance in his mind. He could make for Hokitika at a pace, alert Dr. Gillies, hire a cart or a trap of some kind, and be back, at the very earliest, within three hours ... but would three hours be soon enough? Would the boy survive? Tauwhare's sister had died of fever, and in her final days she had been very like the way that Staines was now—bright-eyed, both sharp and limp at once, full of nonsense and tumbling words. If he left, he risked the boy's death. But what could he do, if he stayed? Suddenly decisive, he bowed his head to say a *karakia* for the boy's recovery.

'*Tutakina i te iwi,*' he said, '*tutakina i te toto. Tutakina i te iko. Tutakina i te uaua. Tutakina kia u. Tutakina kia mau. Tenei te rangi ka tutaki. Tenei te rangi ka ruruku. Tenei te papa ka wheuka. E rangi e, awhitia. E papa e, awhitia. Nau ka awhi, ka awhi.*'

He raised his head.

'Was that a poem?' said Staines, staring. 'What does it mean?'

'I asked for your wound to heal,' Tauwhare said. 'Now I shall bring medicine.' He took off his satchel, pulled out his flask, and pressed it into the boy's hands.

'Is it the smoke?' the boy said, shivering slightly. 'I've never touched the stuff, myself, but how it claws at one . . . like a thorn in every one of your fingers, and a string around your heart . . . and one feels it always. Nagging. Nagging. You'd stand me a mouthful of smoke. I believe you would. You're a decent fellow.'

Tauwhare shucked his woollen coat, and draped it across the boy's legs.

'Just until I find this tree on Maori land,' the boy went on. 'You can have as many ounces as you please. Only it's the good stuff I'm after. Are you going to the druggist? Pritchard's got my account. Pritchard's all right. Ask him. I've never touched a pipe before.'

'This is water,' said Tauwhare, pointing at the flask. 'Drink it.'

'How extraordinarily kind,' said the boy, closing his eyes again.

'You stay here,' Tauwhare said firmly. He stood. 'I go to Hokitika and tell others where you are. I shall come back very soon.'

'Just a bit of the good stuff,' said Staines, as Tauwhare left the cottage. His eyes were still closed. 'And after you come back we'll go and have a nose around for all that gold. Or we'll start with the smoke—yes. Do it properly. What an unrequited love it is, this thirst! But is it love, when it is unrequited? Good Lord. Medicine, he says. And him a Maori fellow!'

MARS IN AQUARIUS

In which Sook Yongsheng pays a call upon a very old acquaintance, and Francis Carver dispenses some advice.

Sook Yongsheng, after making his five-pound purchase at Brunton, Solomon & Barnes that morning, had immediately gone into hiding. The shopkeeper who loaded the pistol had been very plainly suspicious of his intentions, though he had accepted Ah Sook's paper note without complaint: he had followed Ah Sook to the door of his establishment, to see him off, and Ah Sook twice looked over his shoulder to see him standing, arms folded, scowling after him. A Chinaman purchasing a revolver with cash money, laying down that cash money all at once, refusing to pay more than five pounds even for the item, and requesting that the piece be loaded in the store? This was not the kind of suspicion that one kept to oneself. Ah Sook knew very well that by the time he reached the corner of Weld- and Tancred-streets the rumour mill would have begun to turn, and swiftly. He needed to find a place to hide until sundown, whereupon he would venture, under the cover of darkness, to the rearmost bedroom on the ground floor of the Crown Hotel.

There was no one in Hokitika Ah Sook trusted enough to ask for aid. Certainly not Anna: not any more. Nor Mannering. Nor Pritchard. He was not on speaking terms with any of the other men from the council at the Crown, except Ah Quee, who, of course, would be in Kaniere, digging the ground. For a moment he considered taking a room at one of the more disreputable hotels on the eastern side of town, perhaps even paying for the week in advance, to disguise his motivation ... but even there he could not guarantee anonymity; he could not guarantee that the proprietors would not talk. His presence in Hokitika on a Monday morning was conspicuous enough, even without wagging tongues. Better not to trust in the discretion of other men, he thought. He resolved instead to take his pistol into the alley that ran in parallel between Revell-street and Tancred-street. The alley formed a rutted thoroughfare between the rear allotments of the Revell-street warehouses and hotels, which faced west, and the rear allotments of the Tancred-street cabins, which faced east. There was ample opportunity for camouflage, and the alley was central enough to allow points of entry and exit from all sides. Best of all, the space was frequented only intermittently, by the tradesmen and penny-postmen who serviced the hotels.

In the allotment behind a wine and spirit merchant's Ah Sook found a place to hide. A piece of corrugated iron had been propped against an outhouse, creating a kind of lean-to, open at both ends. It was shielded from the alley by a large flax bush, and from the rear of the merchant warehouse by the outhouse pump. Ah Sook crawled into the triangular space, and sat down, cross-legged. He was still sitting in this way three hours later, when Mr. Everard came running down Revell-street, shouting the news to the bellmen that George Shepard had taken out a warrant for a Chinaman's arrest.

At Mr. Everard's words a thrill ran through Ah Sook's body. Now he could be certain that Francis Carver had been forewarned. But Ah Sook had an advantage Carver did not—*could* not—suspect: thanks to Walter Moody's confidence, he knew exactly where to find Carver, and when. Warrant or no warrant, George Shepard had not arrested him yet! Ah Sook listened until the cry up and down Revell-street had faded, and then, smiling slightly, he closed his eyes.

'What are you doing down there?'

Ah Sook started. Standing over him, his hand on the outhouse door, was a dirty youth of perhaps five-and-twenty, wearing a sack coat and a collarless shirt.

'You're not allowed to squat here, you know,' the youth said, frowning. 'This is private land. It belongs to Mr. Chesney. You can't just hole up where you please.'

Another voice, from the warehouse: 'Who's that you're talking to, Ed?'

'There's a chink—just sitting here. Beside the outhouse.'

'A what?'

'A Chinaman.'

'He's using the outhouse?'

'No,' called the youth. 'He's just sitting beside it.'

'Well, tell him to get a move on.'

'Get on with you,' said the youth, giving Ah Sook a gentle nudge with the toe of his boot. 'Get on with you. You can't stay here.'

The voice from the warehouse called again. 'What did you say he was doing there, Ed?'

'Nothing,' the youth called back. 'Just sitting. He's got a pistol.'

'A what?'

'He's got a pistol, I said.'

'What's he doing with it?'

'Nothing. He's not making any trouble, as far as I can see.'

A pause. Then, 'Is he gone?'

'Get on with you,' Ed said again to Ah Sook, motioning. 'Go *on*.'

Roused to motion at last, Ah Sook slipped out from beneath the corrugated iron, and hurried away—feeling the puzzled eyes of the youth on his back, as he did so. He ducked behind a laundry line, and into the oaty-smelling stables at the rear of the Hotel Imperial, keeping his head down and his pistol clasped tight to his chest. Above the whickering and stamping of the horses he could hear that the two men were still calling back and forth, discussing him. He knew that before long he would be pursued; he needed to hide himself, and quickly, before someone sounded the alarm. Ah Sook ran to the end of the stalls and peered over the half-door. He looked along the row of allotments, at the lean-to kitchens beyond them, the baize doors for the tradesmen, the privies, the pits for waste. Where would he be safest? His gaze came to rest upon the small cluster of buildings that formed the Police Camp, and among them, the wooden cottage in which George Shepard lived. His heart gave a sudden lurch. *Well, why not?* he thought, suddenly bold. *It is the last place in Hokitika that anyone would think to find me.*

He crossed the small track between the stables and the Police Camp fence, walked up to George Shepard's kitchen door, and rapped smartly upon it. While he was waiting for a response he looked furtively about him, but the alley was quite empty, and there was nobody in the yards on either side of where he stood. Unless someone was watching from inside one of the hotels—which was very possible, the cockled glass shielding all view of the interior— then nobody could see him, standing in the shadow of George Shepard's lean-to, pistol in hand.

'Who is it?' came a woman's voice, through the door. 'Who is it?'

'For Margaret,' said Sook Yongsheng, leaning his mouth close to the wood.

'Who?'

'For Margaret Shepard.'

'But who is it? Who's calling?'

It seemed to him that her mouth was very close to the wood also; perhaps she was leaning close, on the other side.

'Sook Yongsheng,' he said. And then, into the ensuing silence, 'Please.'

The door opened, and there she was.

'Margaret,' said Ah Sook, full of feeling. He bowed.

Only when he rose from the bow did he allow himself to appraise her. Like Lydia Wells, she too seemed virtually unaltered since the scene of their last encounter, at the courthouse in Sydney, when she stepped forward with the testimony—the false testimony!—that had saved his life. Her hair now showed a strip of silver down the central part, and it had turned brittle, such that the few wisps that had escaped her hairnet formed a haze about her head. Apart from this small token of her advancing age, her features seemed more or less the same: the same frightened, watery eyes; the same buck teeth; the same broken nose, broad across the bridge; the same blurred lips; the same look of fearful shock and apprehension. How well the memory is stirred by the sight of a familiar face! All in a rush Ah Sook could see her sitting down in the witness chair, folding her gloved hands neatly in her lap, blinking at the prosecutor, coughing twice into a scrap of lawn, tucking it into the cuff of her dress, folding her hands again. Telling a lie to save his life.

She was staring at him. Then she hissed, 'What on *earth*—' and gave a laugh that was almost a hiccup. 'Mr. Sook—what—what on *earth*? There is a warrant out for your arrest—did you know that? George has taken out a warrant!'

'May I come in?' said Ah Sook. He was holding the pistol against his hip, with his body half-turned to shield it: she had not seen it yet.

A gust of wind blew through the open door as he spoke, causing the interior walls of the cottage to shudder and thrum. The wind moved visibly over the stretched calico.

'Quickly,' she said. 'Quickly, now.'

She hustled him into the cottage, and shut the door.

'Why have you come?' she whispered.

'You are very kind woman, Margaret.'

Her face crumpled. 'No,' she said. 'No.'

Ah Sook nodded. 'You are very kind.'

'It's a terrible position you're putting me in,' she whispered. 'What's to say I won't send word to George? I *ought* to! There's a warrant out—and I had no idea, Mr. Sook. I had no idea you were even *here*, before this morning. Why have you come?'

Ah Sook, moving slowly, brought out the pistol from behind his back.

She brought her hand up to her mouth.

'You will hide me,' he said.

'I can't,' said Mrs. Shepard, still with her hand over her mouth. She stared at the revolver. 'You don't know what you're asking, Mr. Sook.'

'You will hide me, until dark,' Ah Sook said. 'Please.'

She worked her mouth a little, as though gnawing on her palm, and then snatched her hand away, and said, 'Where will you go when it gets dark?'

'Take Carver's life,' said Ah Sook.

'*Carver*—'

She groaned and moved on quick feet away from him, flapping her hand, as though motioning him to put the gun away, out of sight.

Ah Sook did not move. 'Please, Margaret.'

'I never dreamed I'd see you again,' she said. 'I never *dreamed*—'

She was interrupted. There came a smart rap on the door: the front door, this time, on the far side of the cottage.

Margaret Shepard's breath caught in her throat; for an instant, Ah Sook feared that she was going to vomit. Then she flew at him, pushing his chest with both hands. 'Go,' she whispered, frantic. 'Into the bedroom. Get under the bed. Get out of sight. Go. Go. *Go.*'

She pushed him into the bedroom that she shared with the gaoler. It was very tidily kept, with two chests of drawers, an iron-framed bed, and a single embroidered tract, stapled to the framing above the headboard. Ah Sook did not have time to look around him. He fell to his knees and slithered under the bed, still with the pistol in his hand. The door closed; the room darkened. Ah Sook heard steps in the passage, and then the sound of the latch being lifted. He turned to the side. Through the calico wall beside him a square of lightness widened, and a patch of blackness stepped forward into it, clouding the centre. Ah Sook felt the sudden chill of the wind.

'Good afternoon, Mrs. Shepard. I'm looking for your husband. Is he at home?'

Ah Sook stiffened. He knew that voice.

Margaret Shepard must have shaken her head, for Francis Carver said, 'Care to tell me where he might be found?'

'Up at the construction site, sir.' She spoke barely above a whisper.

'Up at Seaview, is he?'

'Yes, sir.'

Ah Sook cradled the Kerr Patent in both hands. There would be nothing easier than to slither out from beneath the bed, and stand, and press the muzzle to the wall. The cartridge would rip through the calico walls like nothing. But how could he be sure not to injure Mrs. Shepard? He looked at the patch of darkness, trying to see where Carver's shadow ended, and Mrs. Shepard's began.

'The alert's gone up,' Carver was saying. 'Shepard's just put in for a warrant. Our old friend Sook's in town. Armed and on the loose.'

The gaoler's wife said nothing. In the bedroom, Ah Sook began to ease himself out from under the bed.

'It's me he's after,' Carver said.

No answer: perhaps she only nodded.

'Well, your husband's done me a good turn, in sounding the warning,' Carver went on. 'You let him know that I appreciate it.'

'I will.'

Carver seemed to linger. 'Rumour has it that he's been in Hokitika since late last year,' he said. 'Our mutual friend. You must have seen him.'

'No,' she whispered.

'You never saw him? Or you never knew?'

'I never knew,' she said. 'Not until—not until this morning.'

In the bedroom, still with the pistol trained on the calico shadow, Ah Sook got to his knees, and then to his feet. He began to move towards the wall. If he angled the pistol sideways—if he shot obliquely, rather than head-on—

'Well, George did,' Carver was saying. 'He's known for a while now. Been keeping a watch upon the man. He didn't tell you?'

'No,' whispered Mrs. George.

Another pause.

'I suppose that figures,' Carver said.

Ah Sook had reached the timber frame of the bedroom door-way. He was perhaps six feet away from the square of lightness that was the front door; the doubled sheet of calico was all that stood between him and Francis Carver. Was Carver armed? There was no way to tell, short of opening the door and confronting him face to face—but if he did so he would lose precious seconds, and he would lose the advantage of surprise. And yet he still did not dare shoot, for fear of hurting Mrs. Shepard. He peered at the shapes on the fabric, trying to see where the woman was standing. Did the door open to the left, or to the right?

The blackness of the calico shadow seemed to thicken slightly.

'You've spent your lifetime paying for it,' Carver said. 'Haven't you?'

Silence.

'And it's never enough.'

Silence.

'He doesn't want your penance,' Carver said. 'Mark my words, Mrs. Shepard. Your penance is not what he wants. He wants something that he can take for his very own. George Shepard wants revenge.'

Mrs. Shepard spoke at last. 'George abhors the notion of revenge,' she said. 'He calls it brutish. He says revenge is an act of jealousy, not of justice.'

'He's right,' Carver said. 'But everyone's jealous of something.'

The patch of blackness in the doorway faded and dissolved, and Ah Sook heard Carver's footsteps retreating. The cottage door closed, and there came a rattling sound as Mrs. Shepard drew the bolt and chain. Then lighter footsteps, approaching, and the bedroom door opened. Mrs. Shepard looked at Ah Sook, startled, and then at the pistol in his hand.

'You fool,' she said. 'In broad daylight! And with the sergeant five paces away!'

Ah Sook said nothing. Again Mrs. George seemed to hiccup. Her voice rose to a pitch that was partly a whisper, partly a shriek. 'Are you in your right *mind*? What do you think would happen to me—to *me*—if you took that man's life on my doorstep? How could—do you think—with the duty sergeant five paces away—without a—and George—! What on *earth*!'

Ah Sook felt ashamed. 'Sorry,' he said, letting his hands fall.

'I'd be hanged,' said Margaret Shepard. 'I'd be hanged. George would see to it.'

'No harm done,' said Ah Sook.

The woman's hysteria melted into bitterness at once. 'No harm done,' she said.

'Very sorry, Margaret.'

And he did feel sorry. Perhaps he had lost his chance. Perhaps now she would turn him out into the street, or ring for her husband, or summon the sergeant . . . and he would be captured, and Carver would walk free.

She stepped forward and eased the revolver from his hand. She held it only a moment before setting it to the side, carefully, upon the whatnot, making sure the muzzle was turned away. Then she hovered a moment, not looking at him. She breathed several times, deeply. He waited. 'You'll stay here till after dark,' she said at last, and quietly. Still she did not look at him. 'You'll stay under the bed until it's dark, and it's safe to leave.'

'Margaret,' said Ah Sook.

'What?' she whispered, shrinking away, darting a quick look at the lamp fixture, then at the headboard of the bed. 'What?'

'Thank you,' said Ah Sook.

She peered at him, and then quickly dropped her gaze to his chest and stomach. 'You stand out a mile in that tunic,' she mumbled. 'You're a Chinaman through and through. Wait here.'

In ten minutes she was back with a jacket and trousers over her arm, and a soft-crowned hat in her hand. 'Try these on,' she said, 'I'll sew the trousers up for size, and you can borrow a jacket from the gaol-house. You'll leave this place looking like an Englishman, Mr. Sook, or you won't leave it at all.'

In which Mr. Staines takes his medicine, and Miss Wetherell takes a fall.

Te Rau Tauwhare reached Pritchard's Drug Hall by half past three; by the stroke of four, he and Pritchard were sitting in a rented trap, driving a pair of horses northward as fast as the trap would allow. Pritchard was half-standing, bare-headed, reckless, whipping the horses into a froth. There was a bulge in his jacket pocket: a glass jar of laudanum, sloshing thickly, so that the rusty liquid left an oily wash of colour on the inside of the glass, that thinned, and then thickened, each time the wheels of the trap went over a stone. Tauwhare was gripping the seatback with both hands, doing his best not to be sick.

'And it was me he said he wanted,' Pritchard said to himself, exhilarated. 'Not the doctor—*me!*'

Φ

Charlie Frost, queried by the lawyer Fellowes, told the truth. Yes, the fortune found on Crosbie Wells's estate had been found already retorted. The smelting was the work of the Chinese goldsmith, Quee Long, who until that morning had been the sole digger employed to work Mr. Staines's goldmine, the Aurora. Mr. Fellowes wrote this down in his pocketbook, and thanked the young banker very courteously for his help. Then he produced the charred deed of gift that Anna Wetherell had given him, and handed it word-lessly across the desk.

Frost, glancing at it, was astonished. 'It's been signed,' he said.

'Come again?' said Fellowes.

'Emery Staines has signed this document some time in the past two months,' said Frost firmly. 'Unless that signature is a fake, of course . . . but I know the man's hand: that's his mark. The last time I saw this piece of paper there was a space next to this man's name. No signature.'

'Then he's alive?' said the lawyer.

Φ

Benjamin Löwenthal, turning into Collingwood-street, was sur-prised to find that Pritchard's Drug Hall was shut and locked, with a card in the window saying the establishment was closed. He walked around to the rear of the building, where he found Pritchard's assistant, a boy named Giles, reading a paper on the back stoop.

'Where's Mr. Pritchard?' he said.

'Out,' said the boy. 'What is it that you're wanting?'

'Liver pills.'

'Repeat prescription?'

'Yes.'

'I can sort you. Come on in the back way.'

The boy put aside his paper, and Löwenthal followed him inside, through Pritchard's laboratory into the shop.

'It's not like Jo, to leave his office on a Monday afternoon,' Löwenthal said, while the boy set about making up his order.

'He went off with a native fellow.'

'Tauwhare?'

'Don't know his name,' the boy said. 'He came by all in a bother. Not two hours ago. Gave his message to Mr. Pritchard, and then Mr. Pritchard packed me off to rent a trap for the both of them, and then they tore off to the Arahura like a pair of night riders.'

'Indeed.' Löwenthal was curious. 'You didn't find out why?'

'No,' the boy said. 'But Mr. Pritchard took along a whole jar of laudanum, and a pocketful of powder, besides. The native man said, "He needs medicine"—I heard him say it. But he didn't say whom. And Mr. Pritchard kept saying something I didn't understand at all.'

'What was that?' said Löwenthal.

'"The whore's bullet",' said the boy.

Φ

'Why—Anna Wetherell!'

Clinch's tone was less astonishment than shock.

'Hello, Edgar.'

'But what are you doing here? Of course you are most welcome! But what are you doing?' He came out from behind the desk.

'I need a place to be,' she said. 'Until five o'clock. May I trespass upon your hospitality for a few hours?'

'Trespass—there's no trespassing!' Clinch cried, coming forward to take her hands in his. 'Why—yes—of course, of course! You must come into my office! Shall we take tea? With biscuits? How good it is to see you. How very lovely! Where is your mistress? And where are you going, at five o'clock?'

'I've an appointment at the Courthouse,' said Anna Wetherell, politely disengaging her hands, and stepping back from him.

Clinch's smile vanished at once. 'Have you been summoned?' he said anxiously. 'Are you to be tried?'

'It's nothing like that. I've engaged a solicitor, that's all. Of my own volition.'

'A solicitor!'

'Yes,' Anna said. 'I'm going to contest the widow's claim.'

Clinch was astonished. 'Well!' he said, smiling again, to cover his bewilderment. 'Well! You must tell me all about it, Anna—and we must take tea together. I'm so very happy you've come.'

'I'm glad to hear that,' said Anna. 'I feared you might resent me.'

'I could never resent you!' Clinch cried. 'I could never—but why?' In the next moment he understood. 'You're going to contest the widow's claim—on that fortune.'

She nodded. 'There's a document that names me as an inheritor.'

'Is there?' said Clinch, wincing. 'Signed, and everything?'

'Found in his stove. In Crosbie Wells's stove. Someone tried to burn it.'

'But is it signed?'

'Two thousand pounds,' said Anna. 'Oh—you have always been such a father to me, Edgar—I don't mind telling you. He meant it as a present! Two thousand pounds, as a present, all at once. He loves me. He's loved me all along!'

'Who?' said Edgar Clinch sourly, but he already knew.

Φ

As Löwenthal was returning to the newspaper offices on Weld-street he heard someone call his name. He turned, and saw Dick Mannering striding towards him, a paper folded beneath his arm.

'I have a juicy piece of news for you, Ben,' Mannering said. 'Though you may have heard it already. Would you like to hear a juicy piece of news?'

Löwenthal frowned, distracted. 'What is it?'

'Rumour has it that Gov. Shepard's taken out a warrant for Mr. Sook's arrest. Apparently Mr. Sook turned up in Hokitika this morning, and laid down cash money for a military weapon! How about that?'

'Does he mean to use it?'

'Why would one buy a gun,' said Mannering cheerfully, 'except to use it? I dare say that we can expect a shoot-out in the thoroughfare. A shoot-out—in the American style!'

'I have some news also,' said Löwenthal, as they turned into Revell-street, and began walking south. 'Another rumour—and no less juicy than yours.'

'About our Mr. Sook?'

'About our Mr. Staines,' said Löwenthal.

Φ

Quee Long was slicing vegetables for soup at his hut in Chinatown when he heard hoof beats approaching, and then someone shouting hello. He went to the doorway, and pulled back the hessian curtain with one hand.

'You there,' said the man on the threshold, who had just dismounted. 'You've been summoned by the law. I'm to take you to the Hokitika Courthouse.'

Quee Long put up his hands. 'Not Ah Sook,' he said. 'Ah Quee.'

'I bloody well know who you are,' the man said, 'and it's you I want. Come along: quick as you're able. There's a buggy waiting. Come.'

'Ah Quee,' said Ah Quee again.

'I know who you are. It's to do with a fortune you dug up on the Aurora.'

'The Arahura?' said Ah Quee, mishearing him.

'That's right,' the man said. 'Now get a move on. You've been summoned by a Mr. John Fellowes, on behalf of the Magistrate's Court.'

Φ

After leaving the Reserve Bank Mr. Fellowes paid a call upon Harald Nilssen, at Nilssen & Co. He found the commission merchant in his office, drawing up a balance sheet on George Shepard's behalf. The work was dreary, and Nilssen was pleased to be roused from it—pleased, that is, until the lawyer handed him the charred contract bearing the signatures of Emery Staines and Crosbie Wells. Nilssen's face drained of colour at once.

'Have you ever seen this document before?' said Fellowes.

But Nilssen was a man who learned from his mistakes.

'Before I answer you,' he said cautiously, 'I'd like to know who sent you, and what's your purpose with me.'

The lawyer nodded. 'That's fair,' he said. 'The girl Wetherell received this document this morning from an anonymous source. Slid under the front door while her mistress was out. It's a tidy sum of money, and by all appearances it's bound for her pocket, as you can see. But it stinks of a set-up. We don't know who sent it—or why.'

Nilssen had already betrayed Cowell Devlin once; he would not do so a second time. 'I see,' he said, keeping his face impassive. 'So you are working for Miss Wetherell.'

'I'm not associated with any whores,' Fellowes said sharply. 'I'm just doing a bit of research, that's all. Getting the lay of the land.'

'Of course,' Nilssen murmured. 'Forgive me.'

'You were the man who cleared Crosbie Wells's estate,' Fellowes went on. 'All I want to know is whether this piece of paper was among his possessions, when you were called in to clear the place.'

'No, it was not,' said Nilssen, truthfully. 'And we cleared that cottage top to bottom: you have my word on that.'

'All right,' Fellowes said. 'Thanks.'

He stood, and Nilssen rose also. As they did so the bells in the Wesleyan chapel rang out the hour: it was a quarter before five.

'Very fine donation you made, by the way,' said Fellowes, as he made to leave. 'Your support of the new gaol-house on Seaview. Very fine.'

'Thank you,' said Nilssen, speaking tartly.

'It's a rare thing in this day and age, to meet a truly charitable man,' said the lawyer. 'I commend you for it.'

Φ

'Mr. Staines?'

The boy's eyes fluttered open, blurred, focused, and came to rest on Joseph Pritchard, who was crouching over him.

'Why, it's Pritchard,' he said. 'The druggist.'

Pritchard reached out a gentle hand and pulled back the collar of Staines's shirt, to expose the blackened wound beneath. The boy did not protest. His eyes searched Pritchard's face as the chemist examined the wound.

'Did you manage to scrape up a piece of it?' he whispered.

Pritchard's face was sombre. 'A piece of what?'

'A piece of the resin,' the boy said. 'You said you'd stand me a piece of it.'

'I brought something to take the edge away,' Pritchard said shortly. 'You've found a thirst for the smoke, have you? That's a nasty wound you've got there.'

'A thirst,' the boy said. 'I said it was like a thorn. I never heard the shot, you know. I was in the coffin at the time.'

'How long have you been here? When was the last time you ate?'

'Three days,' the boy said. 'Was it three days? It's very good of you. Excessively kind. I suppose it was midnight. I fancied a walk.'

'He's not talking sense,' Pritchard said.

'No,' said Tauwhare. 'Will he die?'

'He doesn't look too thin,' Pritchard said, feeling Staines's cheek and forehead with the back of his hand. 'Someone's been feeding him, at least . . . or he's managed to scavenge, wherever he's been. Christ! Eight weeks. Something more than prayers is holding this one together.'

Staines's gaze drifted over Pritchard's shoulder to Tauwhare, standing behind him. 'The Maoris are the very best of guides,' he said, smiling. 'You'll do beautifully.'

'Listen,' Pritchard said to Staines, pulling his collar over the wound again. 'We've got to get you onto the trap. We're going to take you back to Hokitika, so that Dr. Gillies can take that bullet out of your shoulder. Once you're on the trap I'll give you something to take the edge away. All right?'

The boy's head had fallen forward. 'Hokitika,' he mumbled. 'Anna Magdalena.'

'Anna's in Hokitika, waiting for you,' said Pritchard. 'Come on, now. The sooner the better. We'll have you in town before dark.'

'He wrote her an aria,' said the boy. 'As a token. I never made a vow.'

Pritchard lifted Staines's good arm, draped it over his shoulder, and stood. Tauwhare grabbed the boy around the waist, and together the two men carried him out of the cottage and hauled him onto the trap. The boy was still mumbling. His skin was slick with sweat, and very hot. They arranged him on the seat of the trap in such a way that Pritchard and Tauwhare could sit on either side of him, and prevent him from falling forward, and Tauwhare tucked his woollen coat about the boy's legs. At last Pritchard produced the jar of laudanum from his pocket, and uncorked it.

'It's very bitter, I'm afraid, but it'll take the edge off,' he said, cupping the back of Staines's neck with one hand, and holding the bottle to his mouth. 'There it is,' he said. 'There it is. Goes down easy, doesn't it? One more swallow. There it is. One more. Now settle back, Mr. Staines, and close your eyes. You'll be asleep in no time.'

Φ

Alistair Lauderback, upon quitting the Hokitika Courthouse, had gone immediately to the office of the shipping agent, Thomas Balfour. He flung his copy of *Godspeed*'s bill of sale onto Balfour's desk, seated himself without invitation, and cried, 'He's still at it, Tom! Francis Carver is still at it! He'll bleed me till the bloody day I die!'

It took Balfour a very long time to make sense of this theatrical statement, to understand in full the protection and indemnity scheme under which *Godspeed* had been insured, and to venture his own opinion, finally, that perhaps Lauderback ought to admit defeat, in this round at least. Francis Carver, it seemed, had bested him. The ambiguous signature was a piece of cleverness that Lauderback could not easily contest, and as for the matter of *Godspeed*'s insurance policy, Carver *was* legally entitled to draw down those funds, and Mr. Garrity had already seen fit to approve the transaction. But the politician was loath to accept such sensible advice, and persisted in sighing, clutching his hair, and cursing Francis Carver. By five o'clock Balfour's patience was long since spent.

'I'm not the man to talk to,' he said at last. 'I don't know a scrap about the ins and outs of the law. You shouldn't be talking to me.'

'Who then?'

'Go and talk to the Commissioner.'

'He's out of town.'

'What about the Magistrate?'

'On the eve of the elections! Are you mad?'

'Shepard, then. Show this to George Shepard and see what he thinks.'

'Mr. Shepard and I are not on good terms,' Lauderback said.

'Well, all right,' Balfour said, exasperated, 'but Shepard's not on good terms with Carver, don't forget! He might be able to give you a leg-up on that account.'

'What's Shepard's beef with Carver?' Lauderback asked.

Balfour frowned at him. 'Carver did his time under Shepard,' he said. 'As a convict. Shepard was a penitentiary sergeant on Cockatoo Island at Port Jackson, and Carver did his time there.'

'Oh,' said Lauderback.

'Didn't you know that?'

'No,' said Lauderback. 'Why should I?'

'I just expected that you might,' said Balfour.

'I don't know George Shepard from a stick of chalk,' said Lauderback, stoutly.

Φ

Aubert Gascoigne had completed his business at the Reserve Bank in the mid-afternoon; when the clock struck five, he was back at the Courthouse, compiling a record of that day's petty sessions for the *West Coast Times*. He was surprised when the foyer door opened and Anna Wetherell walked in.

She gave him only a cursory greeting, however, en route to shake Mr. Fellowes' hand. They exchanged several words that Gascoigne could not hear, and then the lawyer gestured her into a private office, and closed the door.

'What's Anna doing with Fellowes?' Gascoigne said to his colleague Burke.

'Haven't the foggiest,' said Burke. 'She came by earlier, while you were at the bank. Wanted to speak to a lawyer about something private.'

'Why didn't you tell me?'

'Because it wasn't bloody news,' said Burke. 'Hello, there's Gov. Shepard.'

George Shepard was striding across the hall towards them.

'Mr. Gascoigne, Mr. Burke,' he said. 'Good afternoon.'

'Good afternoon.'

'I've come to collect a warrant for a Chinaman's arrest.'

'It's ready for you, sir.'

Burke went to fetch the warrant. Shepard waited, with restrained impatience, his hands on his hips, his fingers tapping. Gascoigne was staring at Fellowes' office door. Suddenly, from behind it, there came a muffled thump—rather like the sound of a body falling down stairs—and in the next moment Fellowes was shouting, 'Give us a hand—give us a hand in here!'

Gascoigne crossed the hall to the office and opened the door. Anna Wetherell was lying prone, her eyes closed, her mouth half-open; the lawyer Fellowes was kneeling beside her, shaking her arm.

'Out for the count,' said Fellowes. 'She just collapsed! Pitched forward, right over the table!' He turned to Gascoigne, pleading. 'I didn't do anything! I didn't touch her!'

The gaoler had come up behind them. 'What's going on?'

Gascoigne knelt and leaned close to her. 'She's breathing,' he said. 'Let's get her up.' He lifted her into a sitting position, marvelling at how thin and wasted her limbs had become. Her head lolled back; he caught it in the crook of his elbow.

'Did she hit her head?'

'Nothing like that,' said Fellowes, who was wearing a very frightened look. 'She just fell sideways. Looks like she's drunk. But she didn't seem drunk, when she walked in. I swear I didn't touch her.'

'Maybe she fainted.'

'Use your heads, both of you,' said Shepard. 'I can smell the laudanum from here.'

Gascoigne could smell it too: thick and bitter. He slipped a finger into Anna's mouth and worked her jaw open. 'There's no staining,' he said. 'If it were laudanum, her tongue would be brown, wouldn't it? Her teeth would be stained.'

'Take her to the gaol-house,' Shepard said.

Gascoigne frowned. 'Perhaps the hospital—'

'The gaol,' Shepard said. 'I've had enough of this whore and her theatrics. Take her to the Police Camp, and chain her to the rail. And sit her upright, so she can breathe.'

Fellowes was shaking his head. 'I don't know what happened,' he said. 'One moment she was stone-cold sober, the next she came over all drowsy, and the next—'

The foyer door opened again. 'A Mr. Quee for Mr. Fellowes,' came the call.

Burke had come up behind them. 'Excuse me, Mr. Shepard,' he said. 'Here's your warrant for Mr. Sook's arrest.'

'Mr. Quee?' said Gascoigne, turning. 'What's *he* doing here?'

'Take the whore away,' the gaoler said.

Φ

Sook Yongsheng, lying on the bare boards beneath George Shepard's bed, was listening to the bells in the Wesleyan chapel ring out half past five when there came another rap at the cottage door. He turned his head to the side, and listened for Margaret Shepard's footsteps. She padded down the hall, lifted the latch, and drew the bolt, and then the square of lightness on the calico wall widened again, and he felt the cool breath of the outside air. The light was bluer now, and less intense, and the shadow in the doorway was a muted grey.

'Mrs. Shepard, I presume.'

'Yes.'

'I wonder if I might have a word with your husband. Is he available?'

'No,' said Margaret Shepard, for the second time that day. 'He's gone down to the Courthouse on business.'

'What a shame. Might I wait for him?'

'You'd do better to make an appointment,' she said.

'I take it that he is not likely to return.'

'He often spends his nights at Seaview,' she said. 'And sometimes he plays billiards in town.'

'I see.'

Sook Yongsheng did not know Alistair Lauderback's voice, but he could tell from the tone and volume that the man speaking was someone of some authority.

'Forgive me for disturbing you,' Lauderback went on. 'Perhaps you might do me the favour of telling your husband that I came by.'

'Yes, of course.'

'You do know who I am, don't you?'

'You're Mr. Lauderback,' she whispered.

'Very good. Tell him that I should like to discuss a mutual acquaintance. Francis Carver is the man's name.'

'I'll tell him.'

That man will be dead before the morning, thought Sook Yongsheng. The door closed again; the bedroom darkened.

Φ

Cowell Devlin made room for Anna Wetherell in the corner of the Police Camp gaol-house, thinking, as he did so, that she made for a much more wretched picture than she had two months prior, following her attempt upon her own life. She was not feverish, as she had been then, and she did not mumble in her sleep, or lash about—but she seemed all the sorrier, for sleeping so peacefully, clad in her black mourning gown. She was so thin. Devlin manacled her with great regret, and as loosely as he was able. He asked Mrs. Shepard to bring a blanket to place beneath her head. This instruction was silently obeyed.

'What's the meaning of it?' he said to Gascoigne, as he folded the blanket over his knee. 'I saw Anna only this morning. I escorted her to the Courthouse myself! Did she go straight to Pritchard's, and buy a phial of the stuff?'

'Pritchard's is closed,' Gascoigne said. 'It's been closed all afternoon.'

Devlin slipped his palm beneath Anna's head, and slid the folded blanket beneath. 'Well then, where did she get her hands on a phial of laudanum, for heaven's sake?'

'Perhaps she'd had it all along.'

'No,' said Devlin. 'When she left the Wayfarer's Fortune this morning she wasn't carrying a reticule or wallet of any kind. She didn't even have any money on her person, as far as I'm aware. Someone must have given it to her. But why?'

Gascoigne wanted very much to know why Cowell Devlin had gone to the Wayfarer's Fortune that morning, and what had happened there; as he was thinking of a polite way to ask, however, there came the rattle and clop of a trap approaching, and then Pritchard's voice:

'Hello in there! It's Jo Pritchard, with Emery Staines!'

Devlin's face was almost comical in its astonishment. Gascoigne had already rushed outside by the time he got to his feet; the chaplain hurried after him, and saw, in the courtyard, Joseph Pritchard, climbing down from the driver's seat of a trap, and leading the horses to be tethered at the gaol-house post. On the seat of the trap Te Rau Tauwhare was sitting with both arms around a white-faced, sunken-eyed boy. Devlin stared at the boy. *This* was Emery Staines—this limp, inconsequential thing? The boy was much younger than he had envisaged. Why, he was but one-and-twenty—perhaps even younger. He was barely older than a child.

'Tauwhare found him hiding out in Crosbie's cottage,' Pritchard said shortly. 'He's very sick, as you can see. Give us a hand getting him down.'

'You're not taking him to gaol!' Devlin said.

'Of course not,' Pritchard said. 'He's going to the hospital. He needs to see Dr. Gillies at once.'

'Don't,' said Gascoigne.

'What?' said Pritchard.

'He won't last an hour if you take him there,' Gascoigne said.

'Well, we can't exactly take him back to his own rooms,' said Pritchard.

'Get him a hotel, then. Get him a room somewhere. Anywhere's better than the hospital.'

'Give us a hand,' Pritchard said again. 'And someone send for Dr. Gillies, while we're at it. He'll have the last word.'

They helped Emery Staines down from the trap.

'Mr. Staines,' said Pritchard. 'Do you know where you are?'

'Anna Magdalena,' he mumbled. 'Where's Anna?'

'Anna's right here,' said Cowell Devlin. 'She's right inside.'

His eyes opened. 'I want to see her.'

'He's not talking sense,' said Pritchard. 'He doesn't know what he's saying.'

'I want to see Anna,' said the boy, suddenly lucid. 'Where is she? I want to see her.'

'He seems coherent to me,' said Gascoigne.

'Bring him inside,' said Devlin. 'Just until the doctor gets here. Come on: it's what he wants. Bring him into the gaol.'

In which Sook Yongsheng overhears the beginning of a conversation.

Ah Sook crouched in the allotment behind the Crown Hotel, his back against the timber of the building, his knees bent, the Kerr Patent revolver cradled loosely in both his hands. He looked like an altogether different man from the one who had purchased the pistol that morning. Margaret Shepard had cut off his pigtail, shadowed his chin and throat with blacking, and thickened his eyebrows with the same; she had found a threadbare jacket for him, and a shirt of gaol-issue twill, and a red kerchief to tie about his neck. With the brim of his hat turned down, and the collar of his jacket turned up, he did not look Chinese in the slightest. Walking the three-hundred-yard distance from the Police Camp to the Crown, he had not attracted the least bit of attention from anyone at all; now, crouched in the allotment, he was all but invisible in the darkness.

Inside the hotel two people were talking: a man and a woman. Their voices came down to him quite clearly through the gap between the window shutter and the frame.

'Looks like it'll come off,' the man was saying. 'Protected an' indemnified.'

'You still sound uneasy,' said the woman.

'Yes.'

'What are you doubting? The money's in your hand, almost!'

'You know I don't trust a fellow without connexions. I couldn't dig up anything on this Gascoigne at all. He arrived in Hokitika some time before Christmas. Landed himself a job at the Courthouse without any fuss. Lives alone. No friends to speak of. *You* say he's nothing but a dandy. *I* say: how do I know that Lauderback hasn't set him up?'

'He does have one connexion. He brought a friend along to the opening of the Wayfarer's Fortune, I recall. An aristocratic type.'

'What does he go by? The friend.'

'Walter Moody was his name.'

'He can't be Adrian Moody's son?'

'That was my first thought, too. He did speak with a Scottish lilt.'

'Well, there you have it: they must be related.'

There was the clink of glasses.

'I saw him just before I left Dunedin,' the man went on. 'Adrian, I mean. Tight as all get-up.'

'And out for blood, no doubt,' said the woman.

'I don't like a man beyond his own control.'

'No,' the woman agreed, 'and Moody is of the worst variety— the kind of man who loves to be offended, so that he can vent his temper—for he knows not how to vent it, otherwise. He's a decent man when he's sober.'

'But anyway,' the man said, 'if this chap Gascoigne is in thick with one of the Moody family, he ought to do us fine. His advice ought to be fine.'

'The family resemblance is *excessively* slight. The mother's features must have been strong.'

The man laughed. 'You're never short of an opinion, Greenway. An opinion is one thing you've always got on hand.'

There was another pause, and then the woman said, 'He came over on *Godspeed*, in fact.'

'Moody?'

'Yes.'

'No. He can't have.'

'Francis! Don't contradict me. He told me himself, that evening.'

'No,' the man said. 'There was no one with the name of Moody. There were only eight of them, and I looked the paper over. I would have remembered that name.'

'Perhaps you overlooked it,' said the woman. 'You know I hate to be contradicted. Let's not disagree.'

'How would I overlook the name Moody? Why, that's like over-looking Hanover, or—or Plantagenet.'

The woman laughed. 'I would hardly compare Adrian Moody to a royal line!'

Ah Sook heard the squeak of a chair, and the shifting of weight over floorboards. 'I only mean I'd have recognised it. Would you pass over the name Carver?'

The woman made a noise in her throat. 'He most definitely said that he'd come over on *Godspeed*,' she said. 'I remember it vividly. We exchanged some words on the subject.'

'Something's not right,' the man said.

'Well, have you got the passenger list? Surely you've a copy of the *Times*—from when the ship came in. Why don't you check it?'

'Yes. You're right. Hang a bit; I'll go and look in the smoking room. They keep a stack of old broadsheets on the secretary.'

The door opened and closed.

Φ

The lamp in the next room came on, illuminating one corner of the allotment in a glow of muted yellow. Carver was in the smoking room of the Crown Hotel—and away from Lydia Wells at last. Ah Sook raised himself up slightly. He saw through the window that Carver had his back to the door, and was shuffling through the papers on the secretary. As far as he could see, there was nobody else in the room. In the bedroom, Lydia Wells began to hum a little ditty to herself.

Ah Sook got to his feet. Holding the Kerr Patent against his thigh, and moving as softly as he was able in his digger's boots, he crept around the back of the house to the tradesman's door. He turned into the alley—and froze.

'Drop your arms.'

Standing on the far side of the alley, his face in shadow, a long-handled pistol in his hand, was the gaol's governor, George Shepard. Ah Sook did not move. His eyes went to Shepard's pistol, and then back to Shepard's face.

'Drop it,' Shepard said. 'I will shoot you. Drop the piece now.'

Still Ah Sook said nothing; still he did not move.

'You will kneel down and place your revolver on the ground,' Shepard said. 'You will do that now, or you will die. Kneel.'

Ah Sook sank to his knees, but he did not release the Kerr Patent. His finger tightened on the hammer.

'I will shoot you dead before you have time to cock and aim,' Shepard said. 'Make no mistake about it. Drop your arms.'

'Margaret,' said Ah Sook.

'Yes,' Shepard said. 'She sent me a message.'

Ah Sook shook his head: he could not believe it.

'She is my wife,' Shepard said curtly. 'And she was my brother's wife before me. You remember my brother, I trust. You ought to.'

'No.' Again Ah Sook's finger tightened on the hammer.

'You do not remember him? Or you do not believe that you ought to remember?'

'No,' said Ah Sook, stubbornly.

'Let me jog your memory,' Shepard said. 'He died at the White Horse Saloon at Darling Harbour, shot through the temple at close range. Do you remember him now? Jeremy Shepard was his name.'

'I remember.'

'Good,' said Shepard. 'So do I.'

'I did not murder him.'

'Still singing the same old tune, I see.'

'Margaret,' said Sook Yongsheng again, still kneeling.

Φ

'*Francis!*'

'Hush a moment. Hush.'

'... What are you listening for?'

'Hush.'

'I can't hear anything.'

'Nor can I. That's good.'

'It was so close.'

'Poor lamb. Did it alarm you?'

'Only a bit. I thought—'

'Never mind. Most likely it was just an accident. Someone cleaning their piece.'

'I couldn't help but imagine that horrible Chinaman.'

'Nothing's going to come of him. He'll head straight to the Palace, and he'll be rounded up before the morning.'

'You've been so afraid of him, Francis.'

'Come here.'

'All right. All right. I've recovered now. Let's see what you've found.'

'Here.' There was a rustling noise. 'Look. McKitchen, Morely, Parrish. See? Eight in total—and no mention of a Walter Moody anywhere.'

There was a short period of quiet as she looked the paper over, and checked the date. Presently he said, 'Strange thing to tell a lie about. Especially when his partner shows up out of nowhere, a few weeks later, and starts yammering to me about insurance. I'm just a chap who tells another chap about loopholes, he said.'

'One of these names must be a false one. If your passengers truly numbered eight, and Walter Moody was truly among them.'

'Eight—and all accounted for. They took the lighter in to shore that afternoon—six hours, maybe seven hours, before we rolled.'

'Then he must have taken a false name.'

'Why would he do that?'

'Well, perhaps he was lying, then. About having come over on *Godspeed*.'

'Why would he do *that?*'

Evidently Lydia Wells could not produce a response to this either, for after a moment she said, 'What are you thinking, Francis?'

'I'm thinking to write my old friend Adrian a letter.'

'Yes, do,' said Mrs. Wells. 'And I shall make some inquiries of my own.'

'The insurance money *did* come through. Gascoigne was as good as his word.'

Presently she said, 'Let's to bed.'

'You've had a trying day.'

'A very trying day.'

'It'll all come out right, in the end.'

'She'll get what she deserves,' said Mrs. Wells. 'I should also like to get what I deserve, Francis.'

'It's dreary for you, waiting.'

'Frightfully.'

'Mm.'

'Are you not tired of it also?'

'Well . . . I cannot show you off in the street as I would like.'

'How would you show me off?'

Carver did not reply to this; after a short silence he said, low, 'You'll be Mrs. Carver soon.'

'I have set my sights upon it,' said Lydia Wells, and then nobody spoke for a long time.

In which the lovers sleep through much commotion.

George Shepard directed Sook Yongsheng's body to be brought into his private study at the Police Camp and laid out on the floor. The blacking on the man's chin and throat seemed all the more gruesome in death; Mrs. George, as the body was brought in, breathed very deeply, as though steadying herself internally against a wind. Cowell Devlin, arriving from the Police Camp gaol-house, looked down at the body in shock. The hatter perfectly recalled the hermit, Crosbie Wells, who had been laid out in this very way, two months prior—on the very same sheet of muslin, in fact, his lips slightly parted, one eye showing a glint of white where the lids had not been properly closed. It was a moment before Devlin realised who the dead man really was.

'The shot was mine,' said Shepard, calmly. 'He was drawing his pistol on Carver. Meaning to shoot him in the back, through the window. I caught him just in time.'

Devlin found his voice at last. 'You couldn't have—disarmed him?'

'No,' said Shepard. 'Not in the moment. It was his life or Carver's.'

Margaret Shepard let out a sob.

'But I don't understand,' Devlin said, glancing at her, and then back at Shepard. 'What was he doing, drawing a pistol on Carver?'

'Perhaps you might clear up the chaplain's confusion, Margaret,' said George Shepard, addressing his wife, who sobbed a second time. 'Reverend, I'll be wanting you to dig another grave.'

'Surely his body ought to be sent home to his people,' Devlin said, frowning.

'This one has no people,' said Shepard.

'How do you know that?' said Devlin.

'Again,' said Shepard, 'perhaps you ought to ask my wife.'

'Mrs. Shepard?' said Devlin, uncertainly.

Margaret Shepard gasped and covered her face with her hands.

Shepard turned to her. 'Compose yourself,' he said. 'Don't be a child.'

The woman took her hands from her face at once. 'Forgive me, Reverend,' she whispered, without looking at him. Her face was very white.

'That's quite all right,' said Devlin, frowning. 'You're in shock, that's all. Perhaps you ought to lie down.'

'George,' she whispered.

'I consider that you did the ethical thing today,' the gaoler said, staring at her. 'I commend you for it.'

At this Mrs. Shepard's face crumpled. She clapped her hands over her mouth, and ran from the room.

'My apologies,' said the gaoler to Devlin, when she was gone. 'My wife has a volatile temperament, as you can see.'

'I do not fault her,' Devlin said. The relations between Shepard and his wife troubled him extremely, but he knew better than to give voice to his fears. 'It is very natural to feel overcome in the presence of the dead. All the more so, if one has a personal history with the deceased.'

Shepard was staring down at Sook Yongsheng's body. 'Devlin,' he said after a moment, looking up, 'will you share a drink with me?'

Devlin was surprised: the gaoler had never made such an invitation before. 'I would be honoured,' he said, still speaking carefully. 'But perhaps we might go into the parlour ... or out onto the porch, where we will not disturb Mrs. Shepard's rest.'

'Yes.' Shepard went to his liquor cabinet. 'Do you have a taste for brandy, or for whisky? I have both.'

'Well,' Devlin said, surprised again, 'it's been an awfully long time since I had a drop of whisky. Some whisky would be very nice.'

'Kirkliston is what I have,' said Shepard, plucking out the bottle, and holding it up. 'It's tolerable stuff.' He stacked two glasses, swept them up into his great hand, and gestured for Devlin to open the door.

The Police Camp courtyard was deserted, and chilly in the dark. All the buildings opposite were shuttered, their inhabitants abed; the wind had dropped at sundown, and it was almost perfectly quiet, the silence like the surface of a pond. The only sound came from the moths bumping against the glass globe that hung in a bracket beside the cottage door. There came a fizz of light each time a moth spiralled down into the flame, and then a dusty, acrid smell, as its body burned.

Shepard set out the glasses on the banister rail, and poured them both a measure.

'Margaret was my brother's wife,' he said, handing one of the glasses to Devlin, and draining the other. 'My older brother. Jeremy. I married her after Jeremy died.'

'Thank you,' Devlin murmured, accepting the glass, and holding the liquor to his nose. The gaoler had been too modest: the whisky was more than tolerable. In Hokitika a bottle of Kirkliston cost eighteen shillings, and double that whenever spirits were scarce.

'The White Horse Saloon,' the gaoler was saying. 'That was the name of the place. A dockside tavern at Darling Harbour. He was shot through the temple.'

Devlin sipped at his whisky. The taste was smoky and slightly musty; it put him in mind of cured meats, and new books, and barnyards, and cloves.

'So I married his wife,' Shepard went on, pouring himself another measure. 'It was the moral thing to do. I am not like my brother, Reverend, neither in temperament nor in taste. He was a dissolute. I do not mean to commend myself by contrast, but the difference between us was very often remarked. It had been remarked since our childhoods. I knew virtually nothing of his marriage to Margaret. She was a barmaid. She was not a beauty, as you know. But I married her. I did the dutiful thing. I married her, and provided for her, in her loss, and together we waited for the trial.'

Devlin nodded mutely, staring at his whisky, turning the small glass around in his hand. He was thinking of Sook Yongsheng, lying cold on the floor inside—his chin and throat smeared with bootblack; his eyebrows thickened, like a clown.

'Poor, brutish Jeremy,' Shepard said. 'I never admired him, and to my knowledge, he never admired me. He was a terrible brawler. I expected that one of his brawls would turn fatal, sooner or later; they happened often enough. When I first learned that he had been murdered, I wasn't terribly surprised.'

He drained his glass again, and refilled it. Devlin waited for him to go on.

'It was a Johnny Chinaman who did it. Jeremy had kicked him about in the street, shamed him most likely. The chink came back to seek redress. Found my brother sleeping off a bottle in a rented room above the tavern. Picked up Margaret's pistol from beside his bed, put the muzzle to his temple, and that was that. Then he tried to run, of course, but he was stupid about it. He didn't get further than the edge of the quay. He was tripped up by a sergeant, and thrown in gaol that very night. The trial was scheduled for six weeks later.'

Again Shepard drained his glass. Devlin was surprised; he had never seen the gaoler drink before, except at mealtimes, or as medicine. Perhaps the death of Ah Sook had unsettled him.

'The trial ought to have been straightforward,' the gaoler went on, pouring himself a fourth measure. His face had become rather flushed. 'First, of course, the suspect was a chink. Second, he had ample provocation to wish my brother harm. Third, he had not a word of English to defend himself. There was no doubt in any-body's minds that the chink was guilty. They'd all heard the shot go off. They'd all seen him running. But then comes Margaret

Shepard into the witness box. My new wife, don't forget. We've been married less than a month. She sits down, and this is what she says. My husband wasn't murdered by that Chinaman, she says. My husband was killed by his own hand, and I know it, because I witnessed his suicide myself.'

Devlin wondered whether Margaret Shepard was listening, from inside.

'There wasn't a word of truth to it,' the gaoler said. 'Complete fabrication. She lied. Under oath. She defiled her late husband's memory—my brother's memory—by calling him a suicide ... and all to protect that worthless chink from the punishment that he deserved. He would have swung without a doubt. He should have swung. It was his crime, and it went unpunished.'

'How can you be sure that your wife wasn't telling the truth?' said Devlin.

'How can I be sure?' Shepard reached for the bottle again. 'My brother was not a suicidal type,' he said. 'That's how. You'll have another?'

'Please,' Devlin said, holding out his glass. It was rare that he tasted whisky.

'I can see that you're doubtful, Reverend,' said Shepard, as he poured, 'but there's just no other way to say it. Jeremy was not a suicidal type. No more than I am.'

'But what reason could Mrs. Shepard have had—to lie, under oath?'

'She was fond of him,' said Shepard, shortly.

'This Chinaman,' said Devlin.

'Yes,' said Shepard. 'The late Mr. Sook. They had a history together. You can be sure I didn't see *that* coming. By the time I found out, however, she was already my wife.'

Devlin sipped again at his whisky. They were silent for a long while, looking out at the shadowed forms of the buildings opposite.

Presently Devlin said, 'You haven't mentioned Francis Carver.'

'Oh—Carver,' said Shepard, swirling his glass. 'Yes.'

'What is his association with Mr. Sook?' said Devlin, to prompt him.

'They had a history,' said Shepard. 'Some bad blood. A trading dispute.'

This much Devlin knew already. 'Yes?'

'I've been keeping a watch on Sook since Darling Harbour. I got word this morning that he had bought a pistol from the outfitters on Camp-street, and I applied for a warrant for his arrest at once.'

'You would arrest a man simply for purchasing a pistol?'

'Yes, if I knew what he meant to do with it. Sook had sworn to take Carver's life. He'd sworn to it. I knew that when he finally caught up with Carver, it would be murder or nothing. As soon as I heard about the pistol I called the alarm. Staked out the Palace Hotel. Sent word ahead to Carver, letting him know. Gave the message to the bellmen, to cry along the road. I was one step behind him—until the very last.'

'And in the last?' said Devlin, after a moment.

Shepard fixed him with a cold look. 'I told you what happened.'

'It was his life or Carver's,' Devlin said.

'I acted inside the law,' Shepard said.

'I'm sure you did,' Devlin said.

'I had a warrant for his arrest.'

'I do not doubt it.'

'Revenge,' said Shepard firmly, 'is an act of jealousy, not of justice. It is a selfish perversion of the law.'

'Revenge is certainly selfish,' Devlin agreed, 'but I doubt it has very much to do with the law.'

He finished his whisky, and Shepard, after a long moment, did the same.

'I'm very sorry about your brother, Mr. Shepard,' Devlin said, placing his glass on the banister.

'Yes, well,' said Shepard, as he corked the whisky bottle, 'that was years ago. What's done is done.'

'Some things are never done,' said the chaplain. 'We do not forget those whom we have loved. We cannot forget them.'

Shepard glanced at him. 'You speak as though from experience.'

Devlin did not answer at once. After a pause he said, 'If I have learned one thing from experience, it is this: never underestimate how extraordinarily difficult it is to understand a situation from another person's point of view.'

The gaoler only grunted at this. He watched as Devlin descended the steps into the shadows of the courtyard. At the horse-post the chaplain turned and said, 'I'll be at Seaview first thing in the morning, to begin digging the grave.'

Shepard had not moved. 'Good night, Cowell.'

'Good night, Mr. Shepard.'

The gaoler watched until Devlin had rounded the side of the gaol-house, and then he pinched the empty glasses between his finger and his thumb, picked up the bottle, and went inside.

Φ

The gaol-house door stood partway open, and the duty sergeant was sitting just inside the entrance, his rifle laid across his knees. He asked with his eyebrows whether the chaplain meant to step inside.

'They're all abed, I'm afraid,' he said, his voice low.

'That's all right,' said Devlin, also speaking quietly. 'I'll only be a moment.'

The bullet had been removed from Staines's shoulder, and his wound had been stitched. His filthy clothes had been cut from his body, and the dirt washed from his face and hair; he had been dressed in moleskin trousers and a loose twill shirt, donated by Tiegreen's Hardware on promise of payment the following day. Throughout all these ministrations the boy had drifted in and out of consciousness, mumbling Anna's name; when he became aware, however, that the physician meant to install him at the Criterion Hotel opposite the Police Camp, his eyes snapped open at once. He would not leave Anna. He would not go anywhere that Anna did not go. He put up such a fuss to this effect that at length the physician agreed to placate him. A bed was made up for him at the gaol-house, next to where Anna lay, and it was decided that Staines would be manacled like the others, in the interests of preventing disharmony. The boy consented to the manacle without protest, lay down, and reached out a hand to touch Anna's cheek. After a time his eyes closed, and he slept.

Since then he had not woken. He and Anna lay facing each other, Staines lying on his left hip, and Anna, on her right, both of them with their knees drawn up to their chests, Staines with one hand tucked beneath his bandaged shoulder, Anna with one hand tucked beneath her cheek. She must have turned towards him, some time in the night: her left arm was flung outward, her fingers reaching, her palm turned down.

Devlin came closer. He felt overcome—though by what kind of sentiment, he did not exactly know. George Shepard's whisky had warmed his chest and stomach—there was a blurry tightness in his skull, a blurry heat behind his eyes—but the gaoler's story had made him feel wretched, even chilled. Perhaps he was about to weep. It would feel good to weep. What a day it had been. His heart was heavy, his limbs exhausted. He looked down at Anna and Emery, their mirrored bodies, facing in. They were breathing in tandem.

So they are lovers, he thought, looking down at them. *So they are lovers, after all.* He knew it from the way that they were sleeping.

PART FOUR

Paenga ~ wha ~ wha

27 April 1865

45° 52' 0" ♋ ∫ 170° 30' 0" E Dunedin

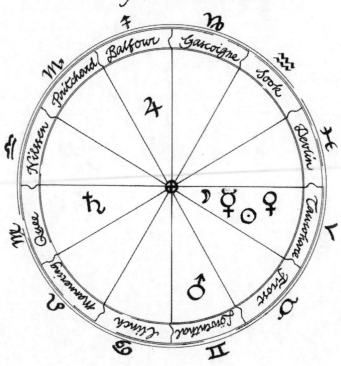

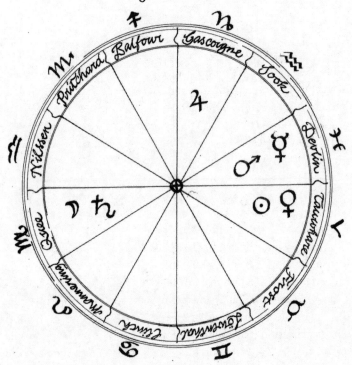

27 April 1866
42° 43' 0" S ∫ 170° 58' 0" E Hokitika

FIRST POINT OF ARIES

●

*In which a steamer arrives in Port Chalmers from Sydney,
and two passengers are roused before the rest.*

Anna Wetherell's first glimpse of New Zealand was of the rocky
heads of the Otago peninsula: mottled cliffs that dropped sharply
into the white foam of the water, and above them, a rumpled cloak
of grasses, raked by the wind. It was just past dawn. A pale fog was
rising from the ocean, obscuring the far end of the harbour, where
the hills became blue, and then purple, as the inlet narrowed, and
closed to a point. The sun was still low in the East, throwing a slick
of yellow light over the water, and lending an orange tint to the
rocks on the Western shore. The city of Dunedin was not yet visible, tucked as it was behind the elbow of the harbour, and there
were no dwellings or livestock on this stretch of coastline; Anna's
first impression was of a lonely throat of water, a clear sky, and a
rugged land untouched by human life or industry.

The first sighting had occurred in the grey hours that preceded
the dawn, and so Anna had not witnessed the smudge on the horizon growing and thickening to form the contour of the peninsula,
as the steamer came nearer and nearer to the coast. She had been
woken, some hours later, by a strange cacophony of unfamiliar
birdcalls, from which she deduced, rightly, that they must be near-
ing land at last. She eased herself from her berth, taking care not
to wake the other women, and fixed her hair and stockings in the

dark. By the time she came up the iron ladder to the deck, wrapping her shawl about her shoulders, the *Fortunate Wind* was rounding the outer heads of the harbour, and the peninsula was all around her—the relief sudden and impossible, after long weeks at sea.

'Magnificent, aren't they?'

Anna turned. A fair-haired boy in a felt cap was leaning against the portside rail. He gestured to the cliffs, and Anna saw the birds whose rancorous call had roused her from her slumber: they hung in a cloud about the cliff-face, wheeling, turning, and catching the light. She came forward to the rail. They looked to her like very large gulls, their wings black on the tops, and white beneath, their heads perfectly white, their beaks stout and pale. As she watched, one made a low pass in front of the boat, its wingtip skimming the surface of the water.

'Beautiful,' she said. 'Are they petrels—or gannets, maybe?'

'They're albatrosses!' The boy was beaming. 'They're real albatrosses! Just wait till *this* fellow comes back. He will, in a moment; he's been circling the ship for some time. Good Lord, what a feeling that must be—to *fly*! Can you imagine it?'

Anna smiled. She watched as the albatross glided away from them, turned, and began climbing on the wind.

'They're terrifically good luck, albatrosses,' the boy was saying. 'And they're the most incredible fliers. One hears stories of them following ships for months and months, and through all manner of weather—halfway around the world, sometimes. Lord only knows where these ones have been—and what they've witnessed, for that matter.'

When it turned on its side it became almost invisible. A needle of white, pale against the sky.

'So few birds are truly *mythical*,' the boy went on, still watching the albatross. 'I mean, there are ravens, I suppose, and perhaps you might say that doves have a special meaning too ... but no more than owls do, or eagles. An albatross is different. It has such a weight to it. Such symbolism. It's angelic, almost; even saying the name, one feels a kind of thrill. I'm so glad to have seen one. I feel almost touched. And how wonderful, that they guard the mouth of the harbour like they do! How's that for an omen—for a gold town! I heard them calling—that was what roused me—and I came top-side because I couldn't place the sound. I thought it was pigs at first.'

Anna looked at him sidelong. Was the boy making an overture of friendship? He was speaking as if they were close familiars, though in fact they had not exchanged more than perfunctory greetings on the journey from Sydney—Anna having kept largely to the women's quarters, and the boy, to the men's. She did not know his name. She had seen him from a distance, of course, but he had not made any particular impression upon her, good or bad. She saw now that he was something of an eccentric.

'Their calling roused me too,' she said, and then, 'I suppose I ought to go and wake the others. It's too perfect a sight to be missed.'

'Don't,' the boy said. 'Oh, don't. Would you mind? I couldn't bear to have a crowd of people jostling about. Not at this hour. Somebody's bound to say "Instead of the cross, the albatross", or "he stoppeth one of three", and then the rest of the journey would be quite lost to argument—everyone trying to piece together the poem, I mean, and quarrelling over which pieces go where, with each man trumping the next, and showing off his memory. Let's just enjoy it for ourselves. Dawn is such a private hour, don't you think? Such a solitary hour. One always hears that said of midnight, but I think of midnight as remarkably companionable—everyone together, sleeping in the dark.'

'I am afraid I am interrupting your solitude,' Anna said.

'No, no,' the boy said. 'Oh, no. Solitude is a condition best enjoyed in company.' He grinned at her, quickly, and Anna smiled back. 'Especially the company of one other soul,' he added, turning back to the sea. 'It's dreadful to feel alone and really *be* alone. But I love to enjoy the feeling when I'm not. Hark at him—the beauty! He'll circle back in a moment.'

'Birds always make me think of ships,' Anna said.

He turned to her, eyes wide. '*Do* they?' he said.

Anna blushed under his direct attention. The boy's eyes were a
deep brown. His brows were thick, and his lips very full. He was
wearing a felt cap with a flat brim; beneath it, his hair was a dark
gold, rather unruly where it curled around his temples and over his
ears. Clearly it had been cropped close some months ago, and he
had not returned to the barber since.

'It's just a fancy,' she said, becoming shy.

'But you must follow through,' said the boy. 'You must! Go on.'

'Heavy ships are so graceful in the water,' Anna said at last, looking away. 'Compared to lighter crafts, I mean. If a boat is too
light—if it bobs about on the waves—there's no grace to its
motion. I believe that it's the same with birds. Large birds are not
buffeted about by the wind. They always look so regal on the air.
This fellow. Seeing him fly is like seeing a heavy ship cut through
a wave.'

They watched as the albatross circled back to make his pass
again. Anna stole a look at the boy's shoes. They were brown
leather, tightly laced, neither too shiny nor too worn—giving her
no clues about his origin. In all likelihood he was coming to make
his fortune on the Otago goldfields, like every other man on board.

'You're quite right,' the boy cried. 'Yes, indeed! It's not at all like
watching a sparrow, is it? He's weighted—exactly like a ship,
exactly so!'

'I should like to see him in a storm,' said Anna.

'What a peculiar wish,' said the boy, delighted. 'But yes, now that
you say it, I believe I feel the same way. I should like to see him in
a storm as well.'

They lapsed into silence. Anna waited for the boy to offer his
name, but he did not speak again, and presently their solitude was
interrupted by the arrival of others on deck. The boy doffed his
hat, and Anna dropped a curtsey; in the next moment, he was
gone. Anna turned back to the ocean. The colony was behind them
now, and the grunts and squeals of the albatrosses had dwindled to
nothing—swallowed by the deep thrum of the steamer, and the
great roaring hush of the sea.

In which Cowell Devlin makes a request; Walter Moody shows his mettle; and George Shepard is unpleasantly surprised.

Since the night of the autumnal equinox both Anna Wetherell and Emery Staines had remained incarcerated in the Police Camp gaol. Anna's bail had been set at eight pounds, an outrageous sum, and one she could not possibly hope to pay without external help. This time, of course, she had no fortune sewn into her clothing to use as surety, and no employer who might consent to pay the debt on her behalf. Emery Staines might have stood her the money, had he not been remanded in custody on a charge of his own: he had been arrested, on the morning following his reappearance, on charges of fraud, embezzlement, and dereliction. His bail had been set at one pound one shilling—the standard rate—but he had opted not to pay it, preferring, instead, to remain with Anna, and to await his summons to the Magistrate's Court.

Following their reunion, Anna's health began to improve almost at once. Her wrists and forearms thickened, her face lost its pinched, starved quality, and the colour returned to her cheeks. This improvement was noted with satisfaction by the physician, Dr. Gillies, who in the weeks after the equinox had visited the Police Camp gaol-house nearly every day. He had spoken to Anna very sternly about the dangers of opium, expressing his fervent hope that her most recent collapse had cautioned her never to touch a pipe again: she had been lucky twice now, but she could not expect to be lucky a third time. 'Luck,' he said, 'has a way of running short, my dear.' He prescribed to her a decreasing dosage of laudanum, as a means of weaning her, by degrees, from her addiction.

To Emery Staines, Dr. Gillies prescribed the very same: five drams of laudanum daily, reducible by one dram a fortnight, until his shoulder had completely healed. The wound was looking much better for having been sewn and dressed, and although the joint was very stiff, and he could not yet raise his arm above his head, his health was likewise very rapidly improving. When Cowell Devlin brought the jar of laudanum into the Police Camp gaol-house each night, he watched eagerly as the chaplain poured the rust-coloured liquid into two tin cups. Staines could not account for his sudden and inconsolable thirst for the drug; Anna, however, did not seem to relish the daily dosage at all, and even wrinkled her nose at the smell. Devlin mixed the laudanum with sugar, and sometimes with sweet sherry, to allay the tincture's bitter taste—and then, under the physician's strict instruction, he stood over the two felons as they drank their twin measures down. It rarely took long for the opiate to take effect: within minutes they sighed, became drowsy, and passed into the underwater moonscape of a strange, scarlet-tinted sleep.

They slept, over the coming weeks, through a great many changes in Hokitika. On the first day of April, Alistair Lauderback was elected as the inaugural M.P. for the newly formed electoral district of Westland, achieving the majority by a triumphant margin of three hundred votes. In his speech of acceptance he praised Hokitika, calling the town 'New Zealand's nugget'; he went on to express his great sorrow at the prospect of quitting the place so soon, and assured the voting public that he would take the best interests of the common digger with him to the new capital city the following month, where he would serve his term in Parliament as a faithful Westland man. After Lauderback's speech the Magistrate shook his hand very warmly, and the Commissioner led three rounds of Huzzah.

On the 12th of April, the walls of George Shepard's gaol-house and asylum went up at last. The felons, Anna and Emery included, had been transferred from the temporary quarters at the Police Camp to the new building upon the terrace of Seaview, where Mrs. George was already installed as matron. Since Ah Sook's death she had been kept very busy hemming blankets, sewing uniforms, cooking, tabulating stores, and making up weekly rations of tobacco and salt; she was seen, if possible, even less frequently than before. She spent her evenings in the Seaview graveyard, and her nights in the residence alone.

On the 16th, Francis Carver and Lydia Wells were finally married, before a crowd that, as the society pages of the *West Coast Times* had it, 'befit, in dress, number, and demeanour, the marriage of a widowed bride'. The day after the wedding, the groom received a large cash payment from the Garrity Group, with which his creditors were paid in full, the last of the copper plating was pried from *Godspeed*'s hull, and the bones of the ship were given up, at long last, for salvage. He had ended his board at the Palace Hotel, and was now installed at the Wayfarer's Fortune with his wife.

Over this time a great many men had tramped up the switchback trail to the terrace at Seaview, in order to beg an interview with Emery Staines. Cowell Devlin, on the gaoler's strict instruction, turned each man away—assuring them that yes, Staines was alive, and that yes, he was recuperating from a very grave illness, and that yes, he would be released from custody in due course, pending the verdict of the Magistrate's Court. The only exception the chaplain made was for Te Rau Tauwhare, to whom Staines had become, over the course of the past month, extraordinarily attached. Tauwhare rarely stayed long at the gaol-house, but his visits had such an advantageous effect upon Staines's mood and health that Devlin soon began to look forward to them also.

Staines, Devlin discovered, was a sweet-natured, credulous lad, ready with a smile, and full of naïve affection for the foibles of the world around him. He spoke little of the long weeks of his absence, repeating only that he had been very unwell, and he was very glad to have returned. When Devlin asked, cautiously, whether he remembered encountering Walter Moody aboard *Godspeed*, he only frowned and shook his head. His memory of that period was very incomplete, made up, as far as Devlin could tell, of dream-like impressions, sensations, and snatches of light. He could not remember boarding a ship, and nor could he remember a ship-wreck—though he seemed to recall being washed up on the beach, coughing seawater, both arms wrapped around a cask of salt beef. He remembered approaching Crosbie Wells's cottage; he remembered passing a party of diggers, sitting around a fire; he remembered leaves and running water; he remembered the rotten hull of an abandoned canoe, and a steep-sided gorge, and the red eye of a weka; he remembered nightly dreams about the patterns of the Tarot, and gold-lined corsets, and a fortune in a flour sack, hidden beneath a bed.

'It's all a dreadful blur,' he said. 'I must have walked out into the night and got lost in the bush somehow . . . and after that I couldn't find my way back again. What a good job it was, that old Te Rau found me when he did!'

'And yet it would have been much better if he had found you sooner,' Devlin said, still speaking cautiously. 'If you had returned but three days earlier, your claims would not have been seized. You have lost all your assets, Mr. Staines.'

Staines seemed very unconcerned by this. 'There's always more gold to be had,' he said. 'Money's only money, and it does one good to be out of pocket every once in a while. In any case, I've a nest egg up in the Arahura Valley, stashed away. Thousands and thousands of pounds. As soon as I've recovered, I'll go and dig it up.'

This, naturally, took a great while to straighten out.

On the third week of April the petty sessions schedule was published in the *West Coast Times*.

The charges levelled against Mr. Emery Staines are as follows: firstly, the falsification of the January 1866 quarterly report; secondly, the theft of ore lawfully submitted by Mr. John Long Quee against the goldmine Aurora, since discovered in the possession of the late Mr. Crosbie Wells, of the Arahura Valley; thirdly, dereliction of duty to claims, mines, and other

responsibilities, the period of absence being in excess of 8 weeks. Hearing
scheduled for Thursday 27th April at the Resident Magistrate's Court,
1 P.M., before his Hon. Mr. Justice Kemp.

Devlin, reading this over his Saturday morning coffee, made for
the Crown at once.

'Yes, I saw it,' said Moody, who was breakfasting on kippers and
toast.

'You must understand the significance of the charges.'

'Of course. I shall hope for a quick hearing—as will many
others, I expect.' Moody poured his guest a cup of coffee, sat back,
and waited politely for Devlin to announce the reason for his visit.

The chaplain placed his hand upon the tabletop, palm upward.
'You have legal training, Mr. Moody,' he said, 'and from what I
know of your character you have a fair mind; that is to say, you are
not partial, one way or another. You know the facts of this case as
a lawyer ought—from all sides, I mean.'

Moody frowned. 'Yes indeed,' he said, 'which means that I know
very well that the gold in Mr. Wells's cottage never came from the
Aurora in the first place. It does not belong to Mr. Staines,
whichever way one looks at it. You can't be asking me to stand up
in court, Reverend.'

'That is precisely what I am asking,' said Devlin. 'There is a
shortage of solicitors in Hokitika, and yours is a better mind than
most.'

Moody was incredulous. 'This is a civil court,' he said. 'Do you
imagine me performing some sort of grand exposure of the whole
story—dragging every last one of you into it—not to mention
Lauderback, and Shepard, and Carver, and Lydia Wells?'

'Lydia Carver, you ought to say now.'

'Forgive me. Lydia Carver,' said Moody. 'Reverend, I do not see
how I could be of any use at all, at a court of petty sessions. Nor
do I see who would benefit, from a merciless exposure of the whole
business—the fortune in the dresses, the blackmail, Lauderback's
personal history, everything.'

He was thinking about the bastard, Crosbie Wells.

'I am not advocating for a merciless exposure,' the chaplain said. 'I am asking you to consider acting as Miss Wetherell's counsel.'

Moody was surprised. 'I thought Miss Wetherell had engaged a solicitor already.'

'I'm afraid that Mr. Fellowes has turned out to be rather less congenial than his name suggests,' Devlin said. 'He declined to take Anna on as a client, following the laudanum debacle in the Courthouse last month.'

'Citing what reason?'

'He fears being fined for corruption, apparently. She had offered to pay his retainer out of the very same fortune that she was trying to claim, which was rather unwise, all things considered.'

Moody was frowning. 'Is there not a duty solicitor at hand?'

'Yes—a Mr. Harrington—but he is very deep in the Magistrate's pocket, by all accounts. He will not do, if we are going to save Anna from a Supreme Court trial.'

'A Supreme Court trial? You must be joking,' said Moody. 'This will all be resolved at the petty sessions—and in very short time, I am sure. I do not mean to patronise your intelligence, Reverend, but there is a great deal of difference between civil and criminal law.'

Devlin gave him a strange look. 'Did you read the courthouse schedule in the paper this morning?'

'Yes indeed.'

'From start to finish?'

'I believe so.'

'Perhaps you ought to look it over once again.'

Frowning, Moody shook open his paper to the third page, flattened it, and cast his eye down the schedule a second time. And there, at the bottom of the column:

The charges levelled against Miss Anna Wetherell are as follows: firstly, forgery; secondly, public intoxication resulting in disorderly behaviour; thirdly, grievous assault. Hearing scheduled for Thursday 27th April at the Resident Magistrate's Court, 9A.M., before his Hon. Mr. Justice Kemp.

Moody was astonished. 'Grievous assault?'

'Dr. Gillies confirmed that the bullet in Staines's shoulder issued from a lady's pistol,' Devlin said. 'I'm afraid that he let this piece of information slip while in the company of the Gridiron valet, who was reminded of the shots fired in Anna's room, back in January, and fronted up with *that* story. They sent a man over to the Gridiron at once, and Mr. Clinch was obliged to hand over Anna's pistol as evidence. The match between gun and cartridge has since been confirmed.'

'But Mr. Staines cannot have been the one to bring this charge against her,' Moody said.

'No,' Devlin agreed.

'Then who's behind it?'

Devlin coughed. 'Unfortunately Mr. Fellowes is still in possession of that wretched deed of gift—the one in which Staines gives over two thousand pounds to Anna, with Crosbie Wells as witness. He has since shared it with Governor Shepard, who, as you will remember, first saw it when it was yet unsigned. Shepard asked me for the truth ... and I had to admit that Staines's signature had in fact been forged—and by Anna herself.'

'Oh dear.'

'They've got her in a corner,' Devlin said. 'If she pleads guilty to the assault, they will claim that it was an attempted murder: they can use the deed of gift to prove that she had decent provocation to wish him dead, you see.'

'And if she pleads not guilty?'

'They'll still get her on the charge of fraud; and if she denies *that*, then they'll get her on a charge of lunacy, which, as we all know, Shepard has long been keeping up his sleeve. I am afraid that he and Fellowes are very much united against her.'

'Mr. Staines will testify in her defence, of course.'

Devlin winced. 'Yes,' he said, 'but I fear that he does not really understand the gravity of the situation at hand. He has a sweet temper, but in his opinions he tends towards foolishness. When I raised the issue of Miss Wetherell's lunacy, for example, he was perfectly delighted by the idea. He said he wouldn't have her any other way.'

'What is your opinion? Is the girl of sound mind?'

'Sanity is hardly a matter of opinion,' said Devlin, archly.

'On the contrary, I'm afraid,' said Moody. 'Sanity depends for its proof upon the testimony of witnesses. Have you asked the physician to make a report?'

'I was hoping that you might be the one to do that,' Devlin said.

'Hm,' Moody said, turning back to the paper. 'If I am to provide counsel to Miss Wetherell, I'll need to speak to Mr. Staines as well.'

'That is easily arranged; they are inseparable.'

'In private—and at length.'

'You shall have everything you need.'

Moody tapped his fingers. After a moment he said, 'We shall have to ensure, first and foremost, that both sides of the story agree.'

Φ

The morning of the 27th of April dawned clear and bright in Hokitika. Walter Moody, rising with the dawn, took a very long time over his toilette. He shaved, combed and oiled his hair, and applied scent beneath his ears. The Crown maid had set his boots outside his door, freshly blackened; upon the whatnot she had laid out a burgundy vest, a grey cravat, and a standing collar with flared points. She had brushed and pressed his frock coat, and hung it up in the window so that it would not crease overnight. Moody took great care in dressing; so much so that the chapel bells were ringing out eight o'clock before he descended the stairs to breakfast, tapping the pockets of his vest to ensure his fob was correctly pinned. Half an hour later, he was striding north along Revell-street, his top hat set squarely on his brow, and his leather valise in his hand.

It seemed to Moody, as he approached the Courthouse, that all of Hokitika had turned out for the morning sessions: the queue to get into the building stretched halfway down the street, and the crowd on the portico had a breathless, eager look. He joined the shuffling queue, and in time he was shepherded into the building by a pair of grim-faced duty sergeants, who instructed him, roughly, to keep his hands to himself, not to speak unless spoken to, and to remove his hat when the justice was called. Moody shouldered his way through the gallery, holding his brief-case close to his chest, and then stepped over the rope to take his place on the barristers' bench beside the prosecution lawyers.

As defence counsel, Moody had received the list of witnesses called by the plaintiff three days before the trial. The names had been listed in the order in which they would be called: Rev. Cowell Devlin; Gov. George Shepard; Mr. Joseph Pritchard; and Mr. Aubert Gascoigne—a sequence that had furnished Moody with a fair idea of the angle that the plaintiff's laywer was likely to take, in the case against Anna. The witness list for the afternoon session was much longer: in the case of the District of Westland vs. Mr. Emery Staines, the plaintiff had called for the testimonies of Mr. Richard Mannering; Mr. John Long Quee; Mr. Benjamin Löwenthal; Mr. Edgar Clinch; Mr. Harald Nilssen; Mr. Charles Frost; Mrs. Lydia Carver; and Capt. Francis Carver. Moody, upon receiving these advance documents, had sat down at once to refine his two-part strategy—for he knew very well that the impression created in the morning would do much to shape the verdict delivered in the afternoon.

At last the clock struck nine, and those seated were requested to rise. The crowd fell silent for the arrival of the honourable Justice Kemp, who mounted the steps to the dais, seated himself heavily, waved a hand for the members of the court to be seated also, and dispatched the necessary formalities without ado. He was a florid, thick-fingered man, clean-shaven, with a thatch of wiry hair, cut oddly, so that it ballooned over his ears, and lay very flat upon the crown of his head.

'Mr. Walter Moody for the defendant,' he said, reading the names off the ledger in front of him, 'and Mr. Lawrence Broham for the plaintiff, assisted by Mr. Roger Harrington and Mr. John Fellowes of the Magistrate's Court.

'Mr. Moody, Mr. Broham'—looking up over his spectacles to fix his gaze upon the barristers' bench—'I will say two things before we begin. The first is this. I am very sensible of the fact that the crowd in this courtroom did not convene today out of love for the law; but we are here to satisfy justice, not prurience, no matter who is on that stand, and no matter what the charge. I will thank you both to restrict your interrogations of Miss Wetherell, and of all her associates, to appropriate themes. In describing Miss Wetherell's former employment, you may choose from the terms "street-walker", "lady of the night", or "member of the old profession". Do I make myself clear upon this point?'

The lawyers murmured their assent.

'Good,' said Justice Kemp. 'The second item I wish to mention is one I have already discussed with each of you in private; I repeat myself for the benefit of the public. The six charges that we will hear today—forgery, inebriation, and assault, in the case of Miss Wetherell this morning, and fraud, theft, and dereliction, in the case of Mr. Staines this afternoon—are, in a great many ways, interdependent, as I am sure every reading man in Westland is already aware. Given this interrelation, I think it prudent to delay the sentencing of Miss Wetherell until the case of Mr. Staines has been heard, so as to ensure that each trial is considered in the light, as it were, of the other. All clear? Good.' He nodded to the bailiff. 'Call the defendant.'

There was much whispering as Anna was brought forth from the cells. Moody, turning to observe her approach, was satisfied by the impression his client created. Her thinness had lost its starved, wasted quality, and now seemed merely feminine: an index of delicacy rather than of malnourishment. She was still wearing the black dress that had belonged to Aubert Gascoigne's late wife, and her hair had been fixed very plainly, gathered in a simple knot at the nape of her neck. The bailiff guided her into the makeshift witness box, and she stepped forward to place her hand upon the courthouse Bible. She gave her oath quietly and without emotion, and then turned to the justice, her expression blank, her hands loosely folded.

'Miss Anna Wetherell,' he said. 'You appear before this court to answer for three charges. Firstly, the forgery of a signature upon a deed of gift. How do you plead?'

'Not guilty, sir.'

'Secondly, public intoxication causing disorderly behaviour upon the afternoon of the twentieth of March this year. How do you plead?'

'Not guilty, sir.'

'And thirdly, the grievous assault of Mr. Emery Staines. How do you plead?'

'Not guilty, sir.'

The justice made a note of these pleas, and then said, 'You are no doubt aware, Miss Wetherell, that this court is not authorised to hear a criminal case.'

'Yes, sir.'

'The third of your indictments may be judged to warrant a trial by a higher court. If that circumstance should come to pass, you will be remanded in custody until a Supreme Court judge and jury can be convened. Do you understand?'

'Yes, sir. I understand.'

'Good. Sit.'

She sat.

'Mr. Broham,' said Justice Kemp, 'the Court will now hear your statement.'

'Thank you, sir.' Broham was a slender man with a ginger moustache and sharp, watery eyes. He rose, squaring the edges of his papers with the edge of the desk.

'Mr. Justice Kemp, fellow members of the Court, ladies and gentlemen,' he began. 'That the smoke of the poppy is a drug primitive in its temptations, devastating in its effects, and reprehensible in its associations, both social and historical, ought among all decent citizens to be a commonplace. Today we shall examine a sorry case in point: a young woman whose weakness for the drug has besmirched not only Hokitika's public countenance, but the countenance of our newly anointed District of Westland at large ...'

Broham's statement was lengthy. He reminded the members of the Court that Anna had made an attempt upon her life once before, drawing a connexion between that failed attempt and her collapse on the afternoon of the 20th of March—'both of which,' he added, with a cynical accent, 'did well to draw the attention of the public eye'. He devoted a great deal of time to her forgery of Staines's signature upon the deed of gift, casting doubt upon the validity of the document as written, and emphasising the degree to which Anna stood to gain, by falsifying it. Turning to the charge of assault, he spoke in general terms about the dangerous and unpredictable character of the opium addict, and then described Staines's gunshot wound in such frank detail that a woman in the gallery had to be escorted from the building. In closing, he invited all present to consider how much opium two thousand pounds would buy; and then he asked, rhetorically, whether the public would suffer such a quantity to be placed in the hands of such a damaged and ill-connected person as Miss Anna Wetherell, former lady of the night.

'Mr. Moody,' the justice said, when Broham sat down. 'A statement for the defence.'

Moody rose promptly. 'Thank you, sir,' he said to the justice. 'I shall be brief.' His hands were shaking: he splayed them firmly on the desktop before him, to steady himself, and then in a voice that sounded much more confident than he felt, he said,

'I will begin by reminding Mr. Broham that Miss Wetherell has in fact thrown off her dependency, an achievement for which she has earned my most sincere admiration and respect. Certainly, as Mr. Broham has taken such pleasure in describing to you all, Miss Wetherell's disposition is of the kind that leaves her prey to the myriad temptations of addiction. I myself have never touched the smoke of the poppy, as Mr. Broham has also assured you he has not, and I hazard to guess that one reason for our mutual abstinence is fear: fear of the drug's probable power over us; fear of its addictive quality; fear of what we might see, or do, were we to succumb to its effects. I make this remark to emphasise the fact that Miss Wetherell's weakness in this regard is not unique to her, and I say again that she has my commendation for having committed herself so wholeheartedly to the project of her own reform.

'But—whatever Mr. Broham might have you believe—we are not here to adjudicate Miss Wetherell's temperament, nor to deliver a verdict upon her character. We are here to adjudicate how justice might best be served with respect to three accusations: one of forgery, one of disorderly conduct, and one of assault. I do not disagree with Mr. Broham's contention that forgery is a serious crime, and nor do I find fault with his assertion that grievous assault is the close cousin of homicide; however, and as my case will shortly demonstrate, Miss Wetherell is innocent of all three crimes. She has not committed forgery; she has attempted in no way to assault Mr. Emery Staines; and her collapse on the afternoon of the twentieth of March could hardly be called disorderly, any more than the lady who was escorted from this very courtroom ten minutes ago could be accused of the same. I have not the slightest doubt that the testimony of witnesses will demonstrate my client's innocence, and that they will do so in very short order. In anticipation of this happy outcome, Mr. Justice, esteemed members of the court, ladies and gentlemen, I do not hesitate to place the matter in the good hands of the law.'

Moody sat, his heart thumping. He looked up at the justice, hoping for some token of affirmation, but Justice Kemp was bent over his ledger, taking notes. Broham was looking down the bench at Moody, a very nasty expression on his face. Fellowes, sitting next to him, leaned over to whisper something in his ear, and after a moment he smiled, and whispered something back.

'Thank you, Mr. Moody,' the justice said at last, underlining what he had written with a flourish, and putting down his pen. 'The defendant will now rise. Mr. Broham, you have the floor.'

Broham stood, and thanked the justice a second time.

'Miss Wetherell,' he said, turning to her. 'Until the night of the fourteenth of January, how did you make your living?'

'Mr. Broham!' snapped the justice at once. 'What did I just say? Miss Wetherell is a member of the old profession. Let that suffice.'

'Yes, sir,' said Broham. He began again. 'Miss Wetherell. On the night of the fourteenth of January you made a decision regarding your former employment, is that correct?'

'Yes.'

'What was it?'

'I quit.'

'What do you mean when you say that you "quit"?'

'I quit whoring.'

The justice sighed. 'Continue,' he said, with a tone of resignation.

'Did you take up alternative employment at once?' Broham said, moving on.

'Not at once,' Anna said. 'But when Mrs. Wells arrived in town she took me in at the Wayfarer's Fortune. I started learning the Tarot, and astral charts, with the idea that I might assist her in telling fortunes. I thought I might earn a living as her assistant.'

'At the time that you quit your former employment, did you have this future purpose in mind?'

'No,' said Anna. 'I didn't know that Mrs. Wells was coming before she arrived.'

'In the period before Mrs. Wells arrived in Hokitika, how then did you expect that you would support yourself?'

'I didn't have a plan,' Anna said.

'No plan at all?'

'No, sir.'

'You did not have a nest egg, perhaps? Or another form of surety?'

'No, sir.'

'In that case, you made a radical step,' said Broham, pleasantly.

'Mr. Broham!' snapped the justice.

'Yes, sir?'

'Make your point.'

'Certainly. This deed of gift'—Broham produced it—'names you, Miss Wetherell, as the lucky inheritor of *two thousand* pounds. It is dated October eleventh of last year. The donor, Mr. Emery Staines, disappeared without a trace upon the fourteenth of January—the very same day that you, as the fortunate recipient of this extraordinary sum, decided to quit walking the streets and mend your ways, a decision made *without* provocation, and *without* a plan for the future. Now—'

'I object,' said Moody, rising. 'Mr. Broham has not established

that Miss Wetherell had no provocation to change her circumstances of employment.'

The justice allowed this, and Broham, looking peeved, was
obliged to put the question to Anna: 'Did you have provocation,
Miss Wetherell, in making the decision to cease prostituting yourself?'

'Yes,' said Anna. She looked at Moody again. He nodded slightly,
encouraging her to speak. She drew a breath, and said, 'I fell in love.
With Mr. Staines. The night of the fourteenth of January was the
first night we spent together, and—well, I didn't want to keep whoring after that.'

Broham was frowning. 'That was the very same night you were
arrested for attempted suicide, was it not?'

'Yes,' Anna said. 'I thought he didn't love me—that he couldn't
love me—and I couldn't bear it—and I did a terrible thing.'

'Do you then admit you made an attempt upon your own life,
that night?'

'I meant to go under,' said Anna, 'but I never set out to do myself
real harm.'

'When you were tried for the crime of attempted suicide—in this
very courtroom—you refused to enter a plea. Why have you changed
your tune in this regard?'

This was a question that Moody and Anna had not rehearsed,
and for a moment he felt anxious that she would falter; but she
responded calmly, and with the truth. 'At that time Mr. Staines was
still missing,' she said. 'I thought he might have gone upriver, or
into the gorge, in which case he'd be reading the Hokitika papers
for news. I didn't want to say anything that he might read, and
think less of me.'

Broham coughed into the back of his knuckles, dryly. 'Please
describe what happened on the evening of the fourteenth of
January,' he said, 'in sequence, and in your own words.'

She nodded. 'I met Mr. Staines at the Dust and Nugget around
seven. We had a drink together, and then he escorted me back to
his residence on Revell-street. At about ten o'clock I went back to
the Gridiron and lit my pipe. I was feeling strange, as I've said, and

I took a little more than usual. I suppose I must have left the Gridiron while I was still under, because the next thing I remember is waking up in gaol.'

'What do you mean when you say that you were feeling strange?'

'Oh,' she said, 'just that I was melancholy—and very happy—and disconsolate, all mixed up. I can't describe it exactly.'

'At some point that same night, Mr. Staines disappeared,' Broham said. 'Do you know where he went?'

'No,' Anna said. 'Last I saw him was at his residence on Revell-street. He was asleep. He must have disappeared sometime after I left him.'

'Sometime after ten o'clock, in other words.'

'Yes,' said Anna. 'I waited for him to come back—and he didn't—and the days kept passing, with no sign of him. When Mrs. Wells offered me board at the Wayfarer, I thought it best to take it. Just for the meantime. Everyone was saying that he was surely dead.'

'Did you see Mr. Staines at any point between the fourteenth of January and the twentieth of March?'

'No, sir.'

'Did you have any correspondence with him?'

'No, sir.'

'Where do you think he went, during that period?'

Anna opened her mouth to reply, and Moody, rising quickly, said, 'I object: the defendant cannot be forced to speculate.'

Again the justice allowed the objection, and Broham was invited to continue.

'When Mr. Staines was recovered, on the afternoon of the twentieth of March, there was a bullet in his shoulder,' he said. 'At the time of your rendezvous on the fourteenth of January, was Mr. Staines injured?'

'No,' said Anna.

'Did he become injured, that evening?'

'Not that I know of,' said Anna. 'Last I saw him, he was fine. He was sleeping.'

Broham picked up a muff pistol from the barristers' desk. 'Do you recognise this firearm, Miss Wetherell?'

'Yes,' said Anna, squinting at it. 'That's mine.'

'Do you carry this weapon on your person?'

'I used to, when I was working. I kept it in the front of my dress.'

'Were you carrying it on the night of the fourteenth of January?'

'No: I left it at the Gridiron. Under my pillow.'

'But you were working on the night of the fourteenth of January, were you not?'

'I was with Mr. Staines,' Anna said.

'That was not my question,' Broham said. 'Were you working on the night of the fourteenth of January?'

'Yes,' Anna said.

'And yet—as you allege—you left your pistol at home.'

'Yes.'

'Why?'

'I didn't think I'd need it,' Anna said.

'But this was an aberration: ordinarily it would have been on your person.'

'Yes.'

'Can anyone vouch for the pistol's whereabouts that evening?'

'No,' Anna said. 'Unless someone looked under my pillow.'

'The cartridge found in Mr. Staines's shoulder issued from a pistol of this type,' Broham said. 'Did you shoot him?'

'No.'

'Do you know who did?'

'No, sir.'

Broham coughed into his knuckles again. 'Were you aware, upon the night of the fourteenth of January, of Mr. Staines's net worth as a prospector?'

'I knew he was rich,' she said. 'Everyone knows that.'

'Did you discuss the fortune discovered in the cottage of Mr. Crosbie Wells with Mr. Staines, either on that night, or on any other night?'

'No. We never spoke about money.'

'Never?' said Broham, raising an eyebrow.

'Mr. Broham,' said the justice, tiredly.

Broham inclined his head. 'When did you first learn about Mr. Staines's intentions, as described upon this deed of gift?'

'On the morning of the twentieth of March,' said Anna. She relaxed a little: this was a line she had memorised. 'The gaol-house chaplain brought that paper to the Wayfarer's Fortune to show me, and I took it straight to the Courthouse to find out what it might mean. I sat down with Mr. Fellowes, and he confirmed that the deed of gift was a legal document, and binding. He said that there might be something in it—that I might have a claim upon the fortune, I mean. Then he agreed to take the deed to the bank on my behalf.'

'What happened after that?'

'He said to meet back here at the Courthouse at five o'clock. So I came back at five, and we sat down as before. But then I fainted.'

'What induced the faint?'

'I don't know.'

'Were you under the effects of any drug or spirit at that time?'

'No,' said Anna. 'I was stone-cold sober.'

'Can anyone vouch for your sobriety that day?'

'The Reverend Devlin was with me in the morning,' Anna said, 'and I'd spent that afternoon with Mr. Clinch, at the Gridiron.'

'In his report to the Magistrate, Governor Shepard described a strong smell of laudanum in the air at the time of your faint,' Broham said.

'Maybe he made a mistake,' Anna said.

'You have a dependency upon opiates, do you not?'

'I haven't smoked a pipe since before I moved in with Mrs. Wells,' said Anna stoutly. 'I gave it up when I went into mourning: the day I was released from gaol.'

'Allow me to clarify: you attest that you have not touched opium, in any form, since your overdose upon the fourteenth of January?'

'Yes,' said Anna. 'That's right.'

'And Mrs. Carver can vouch for this?'

'Yes.'

'Can you tell the Court what happened on the afternoon of the twenth-seventh of January in the hours before Mrs. Carver's arrival at the Gridiron Hotel?'

'I was in my room, talking to Mr. Pritchard,' Anna recited. 'My pistol was in the front of my dress, like it always is. Mr. Gascoigne came into the room very suddenly, and I was startled, so I took out the pistol, and it misfired. None of us could figure out what went wrong. Mr. Gascoigne thought the piece might be broken, so he had me reload it, and then he fired it a second time into my pillow, to make sure that it was working correctly. Then he gave the piece back to me, and I put it back in my drawer, and that was the last I touched it.'

'In other words, two shots were fired that afternoon.'

'Yes.'

'The second bullet lodged in your pillow,' the lawyer said. 'What happened to the first?'

'It vanished,' Anna said.

'It vanished?' said Broham, raising his eyebrows.

'Yes,' said Anna. 'It didn't lodge anywhere.'

'Was the window open, by any chance?'

'No,' Anna said. 'It was raining. I don't know where the cartridge went. None of us could figure it out.'

'It just—vanished,' said Broham.

'That's right,' said Anna.

Broham had no further questions. He sat down, smirking slightly, and the justice invited Moody to cross-examine.

'Thank you, sir,' said Moody. 'Miss Wetherell, all three of today's charges have been brought against you by Mr. George Shepard, governor of the Hokitika Gaol. Do you have a personal acquaintance with the man?'

This was a conversation they had practised many times; Anna answered without hesitation. 'None at all.'

'And yet in addition to bringing the charges against you today, Governor Shepard has made numerous allegations about your sanity, has he not?'

'Yes: he says that I am insane.'

'Have you and Governor Shepard ever spoken at length?'

'No.'

'Have you ever transacted business of any kind together?'

'No.'

'To your knowledge, does Governor Shepard have reason to bear ill-will towards you?'

'No,' she said. 'I haven't done anything to him.'

'I understand you share a mutual acquaintance, however,' Moody said. 'Is that correct?'

'Yes,' said Anna. 'Ah Sook. A Chinaman. He ran the dragon den at Kaniere, and he was my very dear friend. He was shot dead on the twentieth of March—by Governor Shepard.'

Broham leaped up to object. 'Governor Shepard had a warrant for that man's arrest,' he said, 'and on that occasion he was acting in his capacity as a member of the police. Mr. Moody is casting aspersions.'

'I am aware of the warrant, Mr. Broham,' said Moody. 'I raise the issue because I believe the mutual acquaintance is a pertinent point of connexion between plaintiff and defendant.'

'Continue, Mr. Moody,' said the justice. He was frowning.

Broham sat down.

'What was Governor Shepard's connexion to Mr. Sook?' Moody asked Anna.

'Ah Sook was accused of murdering Governor Shepard's brother,' Anna said, speaking clearly. 'In Sydney. Fifteen years ago.'

All of a sudden the courtroom was very still.

'What was the outcome of the trial?' Moody said.

'Ah Sook was acquitted at the last minute,' said Anna. 'He walked free.'

'Did Mr. Sook ever speak of this matter to you?' said Moody.

'His English was not very good,' said Anna, 'but he often used the words "revenge", and "murder". Sometimes he talked in his sleep. I didn't understand it at the time.'

'On these occasions to which you refer,' Moody said, 'how did Mr. Sook appear to you?'

'Vexed,' Anna said. 'Perhaps frightened. I didn't think anything of it until afterwards. I didn't know about Governor Shepard's brother till after Ah Sook was killed.'

Moody turned to the justice, holding up a piece of paper. 'The defence refers the Court to the transcript of the trial, recorded in the *Sydney Herald* on the ninth of July, 1854. The original can be found at the Antipodean Archives on Wharf-street, where it is currently being held; in the meantime, I submit a witnessed copy to the Court.'

He passed the copy along the bench to be handed up to the justice, and then turned back to Anna. 'Was Governor Shepard aware of the fact that you and Mr. Sook were very dear friends?'

'It wasn't exactly a secret,' said Anna. 'I was at the den most days, and it's the only den in Kaniere. I'd say that almost everyone knew.'

'Your visits earned you a nickname, did they not?'

'Yes,' said Anna. 'Everyone called me "Chinaman's Ann".'

'Thank you, Miss Wetherell,' Moody said. 'That will be all.' He bowed to the justice, who was scanning the transcript from the *Sydney Herald*, and sat down.

Broham, to whom this insinuation had come as a very unexpected surprise, petitioned to re-examine Anna on the subject that had just been raised by the defence. Justice Kemp, however, declined his request.

'We are here this morning to consider three charges,' he said, placing the account of Ah Sook's acquittal carefully to the side, and folding his hands, 'one of forgery, one of drunk and disorderly behaviour, and one of assault. I have made note of the fact that Miss Wetherell's association with Mr. Sook was of a personal significance to the plaintiff; but I do not judge that these new developments warrant a re-examination. After all, we are not here to consider the plaintiff's motivations, but Miss Wetherell's.'

Broham looked very put out; Moody, catching Anna's eye, gave her a very small smile, which she returned in kind. This was a victory.

The first witness to be called was Joseph Pritchard, who, interrogated by Broham, echoed Anna's account of what had happened on the 27th of January in the Gridiron Hotel: the first bullet had vanished upon the event of the misfire, and the second had been fired into Anna's pillow by Aubert Gascoigne, as an experiment.

'Mr. Pritchard,' said Moody, when he was invited to cross-examine. 'What was your purpose in seeking an audience with Miss Wetherell on the afternoon of the twenty-seventh of January?'

'I figured that there was another story behind her attempted suicide,' said Pritchard. 'I thought that perhaps her store of opium might have been poisoned, or cut with something else, and I wanted to examine it.'

'Did you examine Miss Wetherell's supply, as you intended?'

'Yes.'

'What did you discover?'

'I could tell by looking at her pipe that someone had used it very recently,' Pritchard said. 'But whoever that was, it wasn't her. She was as sober as a nun that afternoon. I could see it in her eyes: she hadn't touched the drug in days. Maybe even since her overdose.'

'What about the opium itself? Did you examine her supply?'

'I couldn't find it,' Pritchard said. 'I turned over her whole drawer, looking for it—but the lump was gone.'

Moody raised his eyebrows. 'The lump was gone?'

'Yes,' said Pritchard.

'Thank you, Mr. Pritchard,' said Moody. 'That will be all.'

Harrington was bent over his ledger, writing furiously. Now he ripped out the page upon which he had been scribbling, and thrust it down the bench for the other men to read. Broham, Moody saw, was no longer smirking.

'Call the next witness,' said the justice, who was writing also.

The next witness was Aubert Gascoigne, whose testimony confirmed that the misfire had occurred, the bullet had vanished, and that the second shot had been fired, without incident, into the headboard of Anna's bed. Questioned by Broham, he admitted that he had not suspected that Emery Staines might have been present in the Gridiron Hotel on the afternoon of the twenty-seventh of January; questioned by Moody, he agreed that the notion was very possible. He returned to his place below the dais, and once he was seated again, the justice called the gaol-house chaplain, Cowell Devlin.

'Reverend Devlin,' said Broham, once the clergyman had been

sworn in. He held up the deed of gift. 'How did this document first come to be in your possession?'

'I found it in Crosbie Wells's cottage, the morning after his death,' Devlin said. 'Mr. Lauderback had brought news of Mr. Wells's death to Hokitika, and I had been charged by Governor Shepard to go to the cottage and assist in the collection of the man's remains.'

'Where exactly did you find this document?'

'I found it in the ash drawer at the bottom of the stove,' said Devlin. 'The place had an unhappy atmosphere, and the day was very wet; I decided to light a fire. I opened the drawer, and saw that document lying in the grate.'

'What did you do next?'

'I confiscated it,' said Devlin.

'Why?'

'The document concerned a great deal of money,' the chaplain said calmly, 'and I judged it prudent not to make the information public until Miss Wetherell's health had improved: she had been brought into the Police Camp late the previous night on a suspected charge of *felo de se*, and it was very plain that she was not in a fit state for surprises.'

'Was that the only reason for your confiscation?'

'No,' Devlin said. 'As I later explained to Governor Shepard, the document did not seem worth sharing with the police: it was, at that time, invalid.'

'Why was it invalid?'

'Mr. Staines had not signed his name to authorise the bequest,' said Devlin.

'And yet the document that I am holding *does* bear Mr. Staines's signature,' said Broham. 'Please explain to the Court how this document came to be signed.'

'I am afraid I can't,' Devlin said. 'I did not witness the signing first-hand.'

Broham faltered. 'When did you first become aware that the deed had been signed?'

'On the morning of the twentieth of March, when I took the

deed to Miss Wetherell at the Wayfarer's Fortune. We had been discussing other matters, and it was during our conversation that I first
noticed the document had acquired a signature.'

'Did you see Miss Wetherell sign this deed of gift?'

'No, I did not.'

Broham was plainly flummoxed by this; to regain composure, he
said, 'What were you discussing?'

'The nature of our discussion that morning was confidential to
my status as a clergyman,' Devlin said. 'I cannot be asked to repeat
it, or to testify against her.'

Broham was astonished. Devlin, however, was in the right, and
after a great deal of protestation and argument, Broham surrendered his witness to Moody, looking very upset. Moody took a
moment to arrange his papers before he began.

'Reverend Devlin,' he said. 'Did you show this deed of gift to
Governor Shepard immediately after you discovered it?'

'No, I did not,' said Devlin.

'How then did Governor Shepard become aware of its existence?'

'Quite by accident,' replied Devlin. 'I was keeping the document
in my Bible to keep it flat, and Governor Shepard chanced upon
it while browsing. This occurred perhaps a month after Mr. Wells's
death.'

Moody nodded. 'Was Mr. Shepard alone when this accidental
discovery occurred?'

'Yes.'

'What did he do?'

'He advised me to share the deed with Miss Wetherell, and I did
so.'

'Immediately?'

'No: I waited some weeks. I wanted to speak with her alone,
without Mrs. Carver's knowledge, and there were few opportunities to do so, given that the two women were living together, and
very rarely spent any length of time apart.'

'Why did you want your conversation with Miss Wetherell to
happen without Mrs. Carver's knowledge?'

'At the time I believed Mrs. Carver to be the rightful inheritor of the fortune discovered in Mr. Wells's cottage,' Devlin said. 'I did not want to drive a wedge between her and Miss Wetherell, on account of a document that, for all I knew, might have been somebody's idea of a joke. On the morning of the twentieth of March, as you may remember, Mrs. Carver was summoned to the courthouse. I read of the summons in the morning paper, and made for the Wayfarer's Fortune at once.'

Moody nodded. 'Had the deed remained in your Bible, in the meantime?'

'Yes,' said Devlin.

'Were there any subsequent occasions, following Governor Shepard's initial discovery of the deed of gift, where Governor Shepard was alone with your Bible?'

'A great many,' said Devlin. 'I take it with me to the Police Camp every morning, and I often leave it in the gaol-house office while completing other tasks.'

Moody paused a moment, to let this implication settle. Then he said, changing the subject, 'How long have you known Miss Wetherell, Reverend?'

'I had not met her personally before the afternoon of the twentieth of March, when I called on her at the Wayfarer's Fortune. Since that day, however, she has been in my custody at the Police Camp gaol-house, and I have seen her every day.'

'Have you had opportunity, over this period, to observe her and converse with her?'

'Ample opportunity.'

'Can you describe the general impression you have formed of her character?'

'My impression is favourable,' said Devlin. 'Of course she has been exploited, and of course her past is chequered, but it takes a great deal of courage to reform one's character, and I am gratified by the efforts she has made. She has thrown off her dependency, for a start; and she is determined never to sell her body again. For those things, I commend her.'

'What is your opinion of her mental state?'

'Oh, she is perfectly sane,' said Devlin, blinking. 'I have no doubt about that.'

'Thank you, Reverend,' Moody said, and then, to the justice, 'Thank you, sir.'

Next came the expert testimonies from Dr. Gillies; a Dr. Sanders, called down from Kumara to deliver a second medical opinion upon Anna's mental state; and a Mr. Walsham, police inspector from the Greymouth Police.

The plaintiff, George Shepard, was the last to be called.

As Moody had expected, Shepard dwelled long upon Anna Wetherell's poor character, citing her opium dependency, her unsavoury profession, and her former suicide attempt as proof of her ignominy. He detailed the ways in which her behaviour had wasted police resources and offended the standards of moral decency, and recommended strongly that she be committed to the newly built asylum at Seaview. But Moody had planned his defence well: following the revelation about Ah Sook, and Devlin's testimony, Shepard's admonitions came off as rancorous, even petty. Moody congratulated himself, silently, for raising the issue of Anna's lunacy before the plaintiff had a chance.

When at last Broham sat down, the justice peered down at the barristers' bench, and said, 'Your witness, Mr. Moody.'

'Thank you, sir,' said Moody. He turned to the gaoler. 'Governor Shepard. To your eye, is the signature of Emery Staines upon this deed of gift a demonstrable forgery?'

Shepard lifted his chin. 'I'd call it a near enough replica.'

'Pardon me, sir—why "near enough"?'

Shepard looked annoyed. 'It is a good replica,' he amended.

'Might one call it an *exact* replica of Mr. Staines's signature?'

'That's for the experts to say,' said Shepard, shrugging. 'I am not an expert in specialised fraud.'

'Governor Shepard,' said Moody. 'Have you been able to detect any difference whatsoever between this signature and other documents signed by Mr. Staines, of which the Reserve Bank has an extensive and verifiable supply?'

'No, I have not,' said Shepard.

'Upon what evidence do you base your claim that the signature is, in fact, a forgery?'

'I had seen the deed in question in February, and at that point, it was unsigned,' said Shepard. 'Miss Wetherell brought the same document into the courthouse on the afternoon of the twentieth of March, and it was signed. There are only two explanations. Either she forged the signature herself, which I believe to be the case, *or* she was in collusion with Mr. Staines during his period of absence—and in that case, she has perjured in a court of law.'

'In fact there is a third explanation,' Moody said. 'If indeed that signature *is* a forgery, as you so vehemently attest it is, then somebody other than Anna might have signed it. Somebody who knew that document was in the chaplain's possession, and who desired very much—for whatever reason—to see Miss Wetherell indicted.'

Shepard's expression was cold. 'I resent your implication, Mr. Moody.'

Moody reached into his wallet and produced a small slip of paper. 'I have here,' he said, 'a promissory note dated June of last year, submitted by Mr. Richard Mannering, which bears Miss Wetherell's own mark. Do you notice anything about Miss Wetherell's signature, Governor?'

Shepard examined the note. 'She signed with an X,' he said at last.

'Precisely: she signed with an X,' Moody said. 'If Miss Wetherell can't even sign her own name, Governor Shepard, what on earth makes you think that she can produce a perfect replica of someone else's?'

All eyes were on Shepard. He was still looking at the promissory note.

'Thank you, sir,' said Moody to the justice. 'I have no further questions.'

'All right, Mr. Moody,' said the justice, in a voice that might have conveyed either amusement or disapproval. 'You may step down.'

VENUS IS A MORNING STAR

In which a temptation presents itself, under a guise.

Once the *Fortunate Wind* reached her mooring at Port Chalmers, and the gangways were lowered to the docks, Anna was obliged to join the women's queue, in order to be inspected by the medical officials. From the quarantine shelter she went on to the custom-house, to have her entry papers stamped and approved. After these interviews were completed, she was directed to the depot, to see about picking up her trunk (it was a very small one, barely larger than a hatbox; she could almost hold it beneath one arm) and there she met with a further delay, her trunk having been loaded onto another lady's carriage by mistake. By the time this error was corrected, and her luggage recovered, it was well past noon. Emerging from the depot at last, Anna looked about hopefully for the golden-haired boy who had so delighted her upon the deck that morning, but she saw nobody she recognised: her fellow passengers had long since dispersed into the crush of the city. She set her trunk down on the quay, and took a moment to straighten her gloves.

'Excuse me, miss,' came a voice, approaching, and Anna turned: the speaker was a copper-haired woman, plump and smooth-complexioned; she was very finely dressed in a gown of green brocade. 'Excuse me,' she said again, 'but are you by any chance newly arrived in town?'

'Yes, ma'am,' said Anna. 'I arrived just now—this morning.'

'On which vessel, please?'

'The *Fortunate Wind*, ma'am.'

'Yes,' said the woman, 'yes: well, in that case perhaps you can help me. I'm waiting for a young woman named Elizabeth Mackay. She's around your age, plain, slim, dressed like a governess, travelling alone ...'

'I'm afraid I haven't seen her,' said Anna.

'She will be nineteen this August,' the woman went on. 'She's my cousin's cousin; I've never met her before, but by all accounts she is very well kept, and moderately pretty. Elizabeth Mackay is her name. You haven't seen her?'

'I'm very sorry, ma'am.'

'What was the name of your ship—the *Fortunate Wind*?'

'That's right.'

'Where did you board?'

'Port Jackson.'

'Yes,' said the woman. 'That was it. The *Fortunate Wind*, coming from Sydney.'

'I'm sorry to say that there were no young ladies aboard the *Fortunate Wind*, ma'am,' said Anna, squinting a little. 'There was a Mrs. Paterson, travelling with her husband, and a Mrs. Mader, and a Mrs. Yewers, and a Mrs. Cooke—but they're all on the wiser side of forty, I would say. There was no one who might have passed for nineteen.'

'Oh dear,' said the woman, biting her lip. 'Dear, dear, dear.'

'Is there a problem, ma'am?'

'Oh,' the woman said, reaching out to press Anna's hand, 'what a lamb you are, to ask. You see, I run a boarding house for girls here in Dunedin. I received a letter from Miss Mackay some weeks ago, introducing herself, paying her board in advance, and promising that she would be arriving today! Here.' The woman produced a crumpled letter. 'You can see: she makes no mistake about the date.'

Anna did not take the letter. 'I'm sorry,' she said, shaking her head. 'I'm sure there's no mistake.'

'Oh, I do apologise,' said the woman. 'You can't read.'

Anna blushed. 'Not very well.'

'Never mind, never mind,' the woman said, tucking the letter back into her sleeve. 'Oh, but I am excessively distressed about my poor Miss Mackay. I am terribly distressed! What could be the meaning of it—when she promised to be arriving on *this* day—on *this* sailing—and yet—as you attest—she never boarded at all! You're quite sure about it? You're quite sure there were no young women aboard?'

'I'm sure there's a simple explanation,' Anna said. 'Perhaps she took ill at the last minute. Or perhaps she sent a letter with apologies, and it was misdirected.'

'You are so good to comfort me,' said the woman, pressing her hand again. 'And you are right: I ought to be sensible, and not permit myself these flights of fancy. I'll only get worried, if I think of her coming to any kind of harm.'

'I'm sure that it will all come out right,' Anna said.

'Sweet child,' said the woman, patting her. 'I am so glad to make the acquaintance of such a sweet, pretty girl. Mrs. Wells is my name: Mrs. Lydia Wells.'

'Miss Anna Wetherell,' said Anna, dropping a curtsey.

'But hark at me, worrying about one girl travelling alone, when I am talking to another,' said Mrs. Wells, smiling now. 'How is it that *you* have come to be travelling without a chaperone, Miss Wetherell? You are affianced to a digger here, perhaps!'

'I'm not affianced,' said Anna.

'Perhaps you are answering a summons of some kind! Your father—or some other relative—who is here already, and has sent for you—'

Anna shook her head. 'I've just come to start over.'

'Well, you have chosen the perfect place in which to do just that,' said Mrs. Wells. 'Everyone starts anew in this country; there is simply no other way to do it! Are you quite alone?'

'Quite alone.'

'That is very brave of you, Miss Wetherell—it is excessively brave! I am cheered to know that you were not wanting for female company on your crossing, but now I should like to know at once whether you have secured lodging, here in Dunedin. There are a great many disreputable hotels in this city. Someone as pretty as you has a great need of good advice from a good quarter.'

'I thank you for your kind concern,' Anna said. 'I meant to stop in at Mrs. Penniston's; that is where I am bound this afternoon.'

The other woman looked aghast. 'Mrs. *Penniston's*!'

'The place was recommended to me,' said Anna, frowning. 'Can you not also recommend it?'

'Alas—I cannot,' said Mrs. Wells. 'If you had mentioned any lodging house in the city but Mrs. *Penniston's*! She is a very low woman, Miss Wetherell. A very low woman. You must keep your distance from the likes of her.'

'Oh,' said Anna, taken aback.

'Tell me again why you have come to Dunedin,' said Mrs. Wells, speaking warmly now.

'I came because of the rushes,' Anna said. 'Everyone says there's more gold in a camp than there is in the ground. I thought I'd be a camp follower.'

'Do you mean to find employment—as a barmaid, perhaps?'

'I can tend bar,' Anna said. 'I've done hotel work. I've a steady hand, and I'm honest.'

'Have you a reference?'

'A good one, ma'am. From the Empire Hotel in Union-street, in Sydney.'

'*Excellent*,' said Mrs. Wells. She looked Anna up and down, smiling.

'If you cannot endorse Mrs. Penniston's,' Anna began, but Mrs. Wells interrupted her.

'Oh!' she cried, 'I have the perfect solution—to solve *both* our dilemmas—yours *and* mine! It has just come to me! My Miss Mackay has paid for a week's lodging, and she is not here to occupy the room she paid for in advance. *You* must take it. *You* must come and be my Miss Mackay, until we find you some employment, and set you on your feet.'

'That is very kind, Mrs. Wells,' said Anna, stepping back, 'but I couldn't possibly accept such a handsome ... I couldn't impose upon your charity.'

'Oh, hush your protestations,' said Mrs. Wells, taking Anna's elbow. 'When we are the very best of friends, Miss Wetherell, we shall look back upon this day and call it serendipity—that we chanced upon one another in this way. I am a great believer in serendipity! And a great many other things. But what am I doing, chattering away? You must be famished—and *aching* for a hot bath. Come along. I shall take wonderful care of you, and once you are rested, I shall find you some work.'

'I don't mean to beg,' Anna said. 'I'm not going begging.'

'You haven't begged for anything at all,' said Lydia Wells. 'What a sweet child you are. Here—porter!'

A snub-nosed boy ran forward.

'Have Miss Wetherell's trunk delivered to number 35, Cumberland-street,' said Mrs. Wells.

The snub-nosed boy grinned at this; he turned to Anna, looked her up and down, and then pulled his forelock with exaggerated courtesy. Lydia Wells did not comment upon this piece of impudence, but she fixed the porter with a very severe look as she handed him a sixpence from her purse. Then she put her arm around Anna's shoulders, and, smiling, led her away.

*In which the defendant waxes philosophical; Mr. Moody
gains the upper hand; Lauderback gives a recitation; and the
Carvers are caught in a lie.*

The afternoon sessions began promptly at one o'clock.

'Mr. Staines,' said the justice, after the boy had been sworn in.
'You have been indicted for three charges: firstly, the falsification of
the January 1866 quarterly report. How do you plead?'

'Guilty, sir.'

'Secondly, the embezzlement of ore lawfully submitted by your
employee Mr. John Long Quee against the goldmine Aurora, since
discovered in the dwelling belonging to the late Mr. Crosbie Wells,
of the Arahura Valley. How do you plead?'

'Guilty, sir.'

'And lastly, dereliction of duty to claims and mines requiring
daily upkeep, the period of your absence being in excess of eight
weeks. How do you plead?'

'Guilty, sir.'

'Guilty all round,' said the justice, sitting back. 'All right. You can
be seated for the moment, Mr. Staines. We have Mr. Moody for the
defendant, again, and Mr. Broham for the plaintiff, assisted by Mr.
Fellowes and Mr. Harrington of the Magistrate's Court. Mr.
Broham: your statement please.'

As before, Broham's statement was one designed to discredit the
defendant, and as before, it was excessively long-winded. He

itemised all the trouble that had been caused by Staines's absence, casting Wells's widow, in particular, as a tragic figure whose hopes had been falsely raised by the promise of a windfall inheritance that she had mistakenly (but reasonably) supposed to be a part of her late husband's estate. He spoke of the inherent corruption of wealth, and referred to both fraud and embezzlement as 'those clear-sighted, cold-blooded crimes'. Moody's statement, when he gave it, asserted simply that Staines was very aware of the trouble he had caused by his extended absence, and very willing to pay for all damages or debts incurred as a result.

'Mr. Broham,' said Justice Kemp, when he was done. 'Your witness.'

Broham rose. 'Mr. Staines.' He held up a piece of paper in the manner of one brandishing a warrant for arrest, and said, 'I have here a document submitted by Nilssen & Co., Commission Merchants, which inventories the estate of the late Mr. Crosbie Wells. The estate, as recorded by Mr. Nilssen, includes a great deal of pure ore, since valued by the bank at four thousand and ninety-six pounds exactly. What can you tell me about this bonanza?'

Staines answered without hesitation. 'The ore was found upon the claim known as the Aurora,' he said, 'which, until recently, belonged to me. It was excavated by my employee Mr. Quee in the middle months of last year. Mr. Quee retorted the metal into squares, as was his personal custom, and then submitted these squares to me as legal earnings. When I received the bonanza, I did not bank it against the Aurora as I was legally obliged to do. Instead I bagged it up, took it to the Arahura Valley, and buried it.'

He spoke calmly, and without conceit.

'Why the Arahura, specifically?' said Broham.

'Because you can't prospect on Maori land, and most of the Arahura belongs to the Maoris,' said Staines. 'I thought it would be safest there—at least for a while; until I came back and dug it up again.'

'What did you intend to do with the bonanza?'

'I planned to cut it down the middle,' said Staines, 'and keep half of it for myself. The other half I meant to give to Miss Wetherell, as a gift.'

'Why should you wish to do such a thing?'

He looked puzzled. 'I'm afraid I don't understand the question, sir.'

'What did you mean to achieve, Mr. Staines, by presenting Miss Wetherell with this sum of money?'

'Nothing at all,' said the boy.

'You meant to achieve nothing at all?'

'Yes, exactly,' said Staines, brightening a little. 'It wouldn't be a gift otherwise, would it?'

'That fortune,' said Broham, raising his voice above the scattered laughter, 'was later discovered in the cottage belonging to the late Crosbie Wells. How did this relocation come about?'

'I don't know for sure. I expect that he dug it up and took it for himself.'

'If that was indeed the case, why do you suppose that Mr. Wells did not take it to the bank?'

'Isn't it obvious?' said Staines.

'I'm afraid it isn't,' said Broham.

'Because the ore was smelted, of course,' said Staines. 'And each one of those blocks bore the word "Aurora"—engraved into the very metal, by my Mr. Quee! He could hardly pretend he'd lifted it from the ground.'

'Why did you not bank the bonanza against the Aurora, as you were legally obliged?'

'Fifty percent shares on the Aurora belong to Mr. Francis Carver,' said Staines. 'I have a poor opinion of the man, and I did not want to see him profit.'

Broham frowned. 'You removed the bonanza from the Aurora because you did not want to pay the fifty percent dividends legally owing to Mr. Carver. However, you intended to give fifty percent of this same bonanza to Miss Anna Wetherell. Is that right?'

'Exactly right.'

'You will forgive me if I consider your intentions somewhat illogical, Mr. Staines.'

'What's illogical about it?' said the boy. 'I wanted Anna to have Carver's share.'

'For what reason?'

'Because she deserved to have it, and he deserved to lose it,' said Emery Staines.

More laughter, more widespread this time. Moody was becoming anxious: he had warned Staines against speaking too fancifully, or too pertly.

When it was quiet again the justice said, 'I do not believe that it is your prerogative, Mr. Staines, to adjudicate what a person does or does not deserve. You will kindly restrict yourself, in the future, to factual statements only.'

Staines sobered at once. 'I understand, sir,' he said.

The justice nodded. 'Continue, Mr. Broham.'

Abruptly, Broham changed the subject. 'You were absent from Hokitika for over two months,' he said. 'What caused your absence?'

'I'm ashamed to say that I've been under the effects of opium, sir,' said Staines. 'I was astonished to discover, upon my return, that over two months had passed.'

'Where have you been?'

'I believe I have spent much of the time in the opium den at Kaniere Chinatown,' said Staines, 'but I couldn't tell you for sure.'

Broham paused. 'The opium den,' he repeated.

'Yes, sir,' said Staines. 'The proprietor was a fellow named Sook. Ah Sook.'

Broham did not want to dwell on the subject of Ah Sook. 'You were discovered,' he said, 'on the twentieth of March, in the cottage that once belonged to Crosbie Wells. What were you doing there?'

'I believe I was looking for my bonanza,' said Staines. 'Only I got a little muddled—I was unwell—and I couldn't remember where I'd buried it.'

'When did you first develop a dependency upon opium, Mr. Staines?'

'I first touched the drug on the night of the fourteenth of January.'

'In other words, the very night that Crosbie Wells died.'

'So they tell me.'

'A bit of a coincidence, wouldn't you say?'

Moody objected to this. 'Mr. Wells died of natural causes,' he said. 'I cannot see how any coincidence with a natural event can be a significant one.'

'In fact,' said Broham, 'the post-mortem revealed a small quantity of laudanum in Mr. Wells's stomach.'

'A small quantity,' Moody repeated.

'Continue with your interrogation, Mr. Broham,' said the justice. 'Sit down, Mr. Moody.'

'Thank you, sir,' said Broham to the justice. He turned back to Staines. 'Can you think of a reason, Mr. Staines, why Mr. Wells might have taken *any* quantity of laudanum together with a great quantity of whisky?'

'Perhaps he was in pain.'

'Pain of what kind?'

'I am speculating,' said Staines. 'I'm afraid I can only speculate: I did not know the man's personal habits intimately, and I was not with him that evening. I mean only that laudanum is often taken as a pain relief—or as an aid to sleep.'

'Not on top of a bottle of whisky, it's not.'

'I certainly would not attempt such a combination myself. But I cannot answer for Mr. Wells.'

'Do you take laudanum, Mr. Staines?'

'Only when prescribed; not as a habit.'

'Do you have a prescription currently?'

'Currently I do,' said Staines, 'but it is a very recent prescription.'

'How recent, please?'

'It was first administered to me on the twentieth of March,' said Staines, 'as a pain relief, and as a method of weaning me from my addiction.'

'Prior to the twentieth of March, have you ever purchased or otherwise obtained a phial of laudanum from Pritchard's drug emporium on Collingwood-street?'

'No.'

'A phial of laudanum was discovered in Crosbie Wells's cottage some days after his death,' said Broham. 'Do you know how it got there?'

'No.'

'Was Mr. Wells, to your knowledge, dependent upon opiates?'

'He was a drunk,' said Staines. 'That's all I know.'

Broham studied him. 'Please tell the Court how you spent the night of the fourteenth of January, in sequence, and in your own words.'

'I met with Anna Wetherell at the Dust and Nugget around seven,' said Staines. 'We had a drink together, and after that we went back to my apartment on Revell-street. I fell asleep, and when I woke—around ten-thirty, I suppose—she had gone. I couldn't think why she might have left so suddenly, and I went out to find her. I went to the Gridiron. There was nobody at the front desk, and nobody on the landing, and the door of her room upstairs was unlocked. I entered, and saw her laid out on the floor, with her pipe and the resin and the lamp arranged around her. Well, I couldn't rouse her, and while I was waiting for her to come to, I knelt down to take a look at the apparatus. I'd never touched opium before, but I'd always longed to try it. There's such a mystique about it, you know, and the smoke is so lovely and thick. Her pipe was still warm, and the lamp was still burning, and everything seemed—serendipitous, somehow. I thought I might just taste it. She looked so marvellously happy; she was even smiling.'

'What happened next?' said Broham, when Staines did not go on.

'I went under, of course,' said Staines. 'It was heavenly.'

Broham looked annoyed. 'And after that?'

'Well, I had a pretty decent go at her pipe, and then I lay down on her bed, and slept for a bit—or dreamed; it wasn't sleep exactly. When I came up again, the lamp was cold, and the bowl of the pipe was empty, and Anna was gone. I'm ashamed to say I didn't even spare her a thought. All I wanted was another taste. It was such a thirst, you see: from the first sip, I was enchanted. I knew I couldn't rest until I tried the drug again.'

'All this from your very first taste,' said Broham, sceptically.

'Yes,' said Staines.

'What did you do?'

'I made for the den in Chinatown at once. It was early—just past dawn. I saw no one on the road at all.'

'How long did you remain in Kaniere Chinatown?'

'I think a fortnight—but it's hard to recall exactly; each day blurred into the next. Ah Sook was ever so kind to me. He took me in, fed me, made sure I never ate too much. He kept tally of my debts on a little chalkboard.'

'Did you see anyone else, over this period?'

'No,' said Staines, 'but really, I can't remember much at all.'

'What is the next thing you remember?'

'I woke up one day and Ah Sook was not there. I became very upset. He had taken his opium with him—he always did, when he left the den—and I turned the place over, looking for it, becoming more and more desperate. And then I remembered Miss Wetherell's supply.

'I set off for Hokitika at once—in a frenzy. It was raining very heavily that morning, and there were not many people about, and I made it to Hokitika without seeing anyone I knew. I entered the Gridiron by the rear door, and ascended the servants' staircase at the back. I waited until Anna went down to luncheon, and then I slipped into her room, and found the resin, and all her apparatus, in her drawer. But then I got trapped—someone struck up a conversation in the hallway, just outside the door—and I couldn't leave. And then Anna came back from lunch, and I heard her coming, and I panicked again, so I hid behind the drapes.'

'The drapes?'

'Yes,' said Staines. 'That's where I was hiding, when I took the bullet from Anna's gun.'

Broham's face was growing red. 'How long did you remain hidden behind the drapes?'

'Hours,' said Staines. 'If I were to guess, I'd say from about twelve until about three. But that is an estimation.'

'Did Miss Wetherell know that you were in her room on that day?'

'No.'

'What about Mr. Gascoigne—or Mr. Pritchard?'

'No,' said Staines again. 'I kept very quiet, and stood very still. I'm certain that none of them knew that I was there.'

Fellowes was whispering intently in Harrington's ear.

'What happened when you were shot?' said Broham.

'I kept quiet,' said Staines again.

'You kept quiet?'

'Yes.'

'Mr. Staines,' said Broham, in a voice that pretended to scold him. 'Do you mean to tell this courtroom that you were shot, quite without warning and at a very close range, and you did not cry out, or move, or make any noise at all that might have alerted any one of the *three witnesses* to your presence?'

'Yes,' said Staines.

'How on earth did you not cry out?'

'I didn't want to give up the resin,' said Staines.

Broham studied him; in the ensuing pause, Harrington passed him a piece of paper, which Broham scanned briefly, then looked up, and said, 'Do you think it possible, Mr. Staines, that Miss Wetherell might have *known* that you were present, upon the afternoon of the twenty-seventh of January, and that she might have fired her pistol *deliberately* in the direction of the drapes with the *express purpose* of causing you harm?'

'No,' said Staines. 'I do not think it possible.'

The courtroom had become very still.

'Why not?'

'Because I trust her,' said Staines.

'I am asking if you think it possible,' said Broham, 'not if you think it probable.'

'I understand the question. My answer is unchanged.'

'What induced you to place your trust in Miss Wetherell?'

'Trust cannot be *induced*,' he burst out. 'It can only be given— and given freely! How am I possibly to answer that?'

'I will simplify my question,' the lawyer said. 'Why do you trust Miss Wetherell?'

'I trust her because I love her,' said Staines.

'And how did you come to love her?'

'By trusting her, of course!'

'You make a circular defence.'

'Yes,' the boy cried, 'because I must! True feeling is always circular—either circular, or paradoxical—simply because its cause and its expression are two halves of the very same thing! Love cannot be reduced to a catalogue of reasons why, and a catalogue of reasons cannot be put together into love. Any man who disagrees with me has never been in love—not truly.'

A perfect silence followed this remark. From the far corner of the courtroom there came a low whistle, and, in response to it, smothered laughter.

Broham was plainly irritated. 'You will forgive me for remarking, Mr. Staines, that it is rather unusual to steal opiates from the person one professes to love.'

'I know it's very bad,' Staines said. 'I'm very ashamed of what I did.'

'Can anyone confirm your movements over the past two months?'

'Ah Sook can vouch for me.'

'Mr. Sook is deceased. Anyone else?'

Staines thought for a moment, and then shook his head. 'I can't think of anybody else.'

'I have no further questions,' said Broham, curtly. 'Thank you, Mr. Justice.'

'Your witness, Mr. Moody,' said the justice.

Moody thanked him also. He spent a moment putting his notes in order, and waiting for the whispering in the room to subside, before he said, 'You have testified that your opinion of Mr. Carver is a poor one, Mr. Staines. What caused this poor opinion?'

'He assaulted Anna,' said Staines. 'He beat her—in cold blood—and she was carrying a child. The child was killed.'

The courtroom was quiet at once.

'When did this assault take place?' said Moody.

'On the afternoon of the eleventh of October, last year.'

'The eleventh of October,' Moody echoed. 'Did you bear witness to this assault?'

'No, I did not.'

'How did you learn of its occurrence?'

'From Mr. Löwenthal, later that afternoon. He was the one who found her in the road—all battered and bloody. He can vouch for her condition when he found her.'

'What was your business with Mr. Löwenthal that afternoon?'

'An unrelated matter,' said Staines. 'I called on him because I wanted to put a notice in the paper.'

'Regarding—?'

'The purchase of a crate of Long Toms.'

'When you heard the news that Miss Wetherell had been assaulted,' said Moody, 'were you surprised?'

'No,' said Staines. 'I already knew Carver was a beast—and already I regretted our association ten times over. He'd offered to be my sponsor when I first arrived in Dunedin—that was how I met him, you see, when I was just off the boat, that very day. I didn't suspect anything foul. I was very green. We shook hands in good faith, and that was that, but it wasn't long before I started hearing things about him—and about Mrs. Carver too: they work as a team, of course. When I heard what they did to Mr. Wells, I was horrified. I've gone into business with a perfect swindler, I thought.'

The boy was getting ahead of himself. Moody coughed, to remind him of the narrative sequence upon which they had agreed, and said, 'Let's go back to the night of the eleventh of October. What did you do, when Mr. Löwenthal advised you that Miss Wetherell had been assaulted?'

'I made for the Arahura Valley directly, to give the news to Mr. Wells.'

'Why did you consider the information to be of importance to Mr. Wells?'

'Because he was the father of the child Miss Wetherell was carrying,' said Staines, 'and I thought he might want to know that his child had been killed.'

By now the courtroom was so quiet that Moody could hear the

distant bustle of the street. 'How did Mr. Wells respond upon receipt of the news that his unborn child was dead?'

'He was very quiet,' said Staines. 'He didn't say much at all. We had a drink together, and sat awhile. I stayed late.'

'Did you discuss any other matters with Mr. Wells that evening?'

'I told him about the fortune I had buried near his cottage. I said that if Anna survived the night—she had been very badly beaten—then I would give her Carver's share.'

'Was your intention put down in writing on that night?'

'Wells drew up a document,' said Staines, 'but I didn't sign.'

'Why not?'

'I don't exactly remember why not,' said Staines. 'I had been drinking, and by then it was very late. Perhaps the conversation turned to other themes—or perhaps I meant to, and I forgot about it. Anyway, I slept awhile, and then returned to Hokitika in the early morning to check on Miss Wetherell's progress to recovery. I never saw Mr. Wells again.'

'Did you tell Mr. Wells where the ore was buried?'

'Yes,' said Staines. 'I described the site in general terms.'

Next the Magistrate's Court heard the testimonies of Mannering, Quee, Löwenthal, Clinch, Nilssen, and Frost—all of whom described the discovery and deployment of the fortune discovered in Crosbie Wells's cottage quite as if the retorted gold had indeed been discovered upon the Aurora. Mannering testified to the conditions under which the Aurora had been sold, and Quee to the fact of the ore's retortion. Löwenthal detailed his interview with Alistair Lauderback on the night of the 14th of January, during which he learned about the death of Crosbie Wells. Clinch testified that he had purchased the estate the following morning. Nilssen described how the gold had been hidden in Crosbie Wells's cottage, and Frost confirmed its value. They made no mention whatsoever of Anna's gowns, nor of the foundered barque, *Godspeed*, nor of any of the concerns and revelations that had precipitated their secret council in the Crown Hotel three months ago. Their examinations passed without incident, and in very little time, it seemed, the justice was calling Mrs. Lydia Carver to the stand.

She was dressed in her gown of striped charcoal, and over it, a smart black riding jacket with puffed leg-o'-mutton sleeves. Her copper hair, wonderfully bright, was piled high upon her head, the chignon held in place with a black band of velvet. As she swept by the barristers' bench, Moody caught the scent of camphor, lemons, and aniseed—an emphatic scent, and one that recalled him, in a moment, to the party at the Wayfarer's Fortune, prior to the *séance*.

Mrs. Carver mounted the steps to the witness box almost briskly; but when she saw Emery Staines, seated on the stand behind the rail, she appeared momentarily to falter. Her hesitation was very brief: in the next moment she collected herself. She turned her back on Staines, smiled at the bailiff, and raised her milky hand to be sworn in.

'Mrs. Carver,' said Broham, after the bailiff had stepped back from the stand. 'Are you acquainted with the defendant, Mr. Emery Staines?'

'I'm afraid I've never had the pleasure of making the acquaintance of a Mr. Emery Staines,' said Mrs. Carver.

Moody, glancing at the boy, was surprised to see that he was blushing.

'I understand that on the night of the eighteenth of February you staged a *séance* in order to make contact with him, however,' Broham said.

'That is correct.'

'Why did you choose Mr. Staines, of all people, as the object of your *séance*?'

'The truth is rather mercenary, I'm afraid,' said Mrs. Carver, smiling slightly. 'At that time his disappearance was the talk of the town, and I thought that his name might help to draw a crowd. That was all.'

'Did you know, when you advertised this *séance*, that the fortune discovered in your late husband's cottage had originated upon the goldmine Aurora?'

'No, I did not,' said Mrs. Carver.

'Did you have any reason to connect Mr. Staines with your late husband?'

'No reason at all. He was just a name to me: all I knew about him was that he had vanished from the gorge, and that he had left a great many assets behind him.'

'Did you not know that your husband Mr. Carver owned shares in Mr. Staines's goldmine?'

'Oh,' she said, 'I don't talk investment with Francis.'

'When did you first learn of the bonanza's true origin?'

'When the Reserve Bank published the notice in the paper in late March, asserting that the gold had in fact been found smelted, and was therefore traceable.'

Broham turned to the justice. 'The Court will note that this announcement appeared in the *West Coast Times* on the twenty-third day of March this year.'

'Duly noted, Mr. Broham.'

Broham turned back to Mrs. Carver. 'You first arrived in Hokitika on Thursday the twenty-fifth of January, 1866, upon the steamer *Waikato*,' he said. 'Immediately upon landing, you made an appointment at the Courthouse to contest the sale of your late husband's cottage and land. Is that correct?'

'That is correct.'

'How had you learned of Mr. Wells's death?'

'Mr. Carver had conveyed the news to me in person,' said Mrs. Carver. 'Naturally I made for Hokitika as swiftly as I was able. I would have liked to have attended the funeral; unfortunately I was too late.'

'At the time you left Dunedin, did you know that the bulk of Mr. Wells's estate comprised a fortune of unknown origin?'

'No: it was not until I arrived in Hokitika that I read the account given in the *West Coast Times*.'

'I understand that you sold your house and business in Dunedin prior to your departure, however.'

'Yes, I did,' said Mrs. Carver, 'but it was not as radical a move as you might suppose. I am in the entertainment business, and the crowds at Dunedin are not what they once were. I had been considering a move to the West Coast for many months, and reading the *West Coast Times* with keen attention, with that future purpose in mind. When I read of Crosbie's death, it seemed the perfect opportunity. I could start anew in a place where business was sure to be good—and I could also be close to his grave, which I very much desired. As I have said, we did not have a chance to resolve our differences before his death, and our separation had cut me very keenly.'

'You and Mr. Wells were living apart at the time of his death, were you not?'

'We were.'

'How long had you been living apart?'

'Some nine months, I believe.'

'What was the reason for your estrangement?'

'Mr. Wells had violated my trust,' said Mrs. Carver.

She did not go on, so Broham, with a nervous glance at the justice, said, 'Can you elaborate on that, please?'

Mrs. Carver tossed her head. 'There was a young woman in my charge,' she said, 'whom Mr. Wells had used abominably. Crosbie and I had a dreadful row over her, and shortly after our disagreement, he quit Dunedin. I did not know where he went, and I did not hear from him. It was only when I read his obituary in the *West Coast Times* that I found out where he had gone.'

'The young woman in question . . .'

'Miss Anna Wetherell,' said Mrs. Carver, crisply. 'I had done her a charity, by taking her in, for which she was, as she asserted, very grateful. Mr. Wells tarnished that charity; Miss Wetherell abused it.'

'Did the acquaintance between Miss Wetherell and Mr. Wells continue, after their joint relocation to Hokitika?'

'I haven't the faintest idea,' said Mrs. Carver.

'Thank you, Mrs. Carver. I have no further questions.'

'Thank you, Mr. Broham,' she said, serenely.

Moody was already pushing his chair back, waiting for the invitation from the justice to rise. 'Mrs. Carver,' he said promptly, when the invitation came. 'In the month of March, 1864, your late husband Crosbie Wells made a strike in the Dunstan Valley, is that correct?'

Mrs. Carver was visibly surprised by this question, but she paused only briefly before saying, 'Yes, that is correct.'

'But Mr. Wells did not report this bonanza to the bank, is that also correct?'

'Also correct,' said Mrs. Carver.

'Instead, he employed a private escort to transport the ore from Dunstan back to Dunedin—where you, his wife, received it.'

A flicker of alarm showed in Mrs. Carver's expression. 'Yes,' she said, cautiously.

'Can you describe how the ore was packed and then transported from the field?'

She hesitated, but Moody's line of questioning had evidently caught her off guard, and she had not time enough to form an alibi.

'It was packed into an office safe,' she said at last. 'The safe was loaded into a carriage, and the carriage was escorted back to Dunedin by a team of men—armed, of course. In Dunedin I collected the safe, paid the bearers, and wrote at once to Mr. Wells to let him know that the safe had arrived safely, at which point he sent on the key.'

'Was the gold escort appointed by you, or by Mr. Wells?'

'Mr. Wells made the appointment,' said Mrs. Carver. 'They were very good. They never gave us an ounce of trouble. It was a private business. Gracewood and Sons, or something to that effect.'

'Gracewood and Spears,' Moody corrected. 'The enterprise has since relocated to Kaniere.'

'Indeed,' said Mrs. Carver.

'What did you do with the bonanza, once it was delivered safely to you?'

'The ore remained inside the safe. I installed the safe at our residence on Cumberland-street, and there it stayed.'

'Why did you not take the metal to a bank?'

'The price of gold was fluctuating daily, and the market for gold was very unpredictable,' said Mrs. Carver. 'We thought it best to wait until it was a good time to sell.'

'By your degree of caution, I would hazard to guess the value of the bonanza was considerable.'

'Yes,' she said. 'Several thousand, we thought. We never had it valued.'

'Following the strike, did Mr. Wells remain upon the field?'

'Yes, he continued to prospect for another year: until the following spring. He was buoyed by his success, and felt that he might get lucky a second time; but he did not.'

'Where is the bonanza now?' Moody asked.

She hesistated again, and then said, 'It was stolen.'

'My condolences,' said Moody. 'You must have been devastated by the loss.'

'We were,' said Mrs. Carver.

'You speak on behalf of yourself and Mr. Wells, presumably.'

'Of course.'

Moody paused again, and then said, 'I presume that the thief gained access, somehow, to the key.'

'Perhaps,' said Mrs. Carver, 'or perhaps the lock was unreliable. The safe was of a modern design; and as we all know, modern technologies are never infallible. It's also possible that a second key was cast, without our knowledge.'

'Did you have any idea who might have stolen the bonanza?'

'None at all.'

'Would you agree that it is likely to have been someone in your close acquaintance?'

'Not necessarily,' said Mrs. Carver, tossing her head. 'Any member of the gold escort might have betrayed us. *They* knew for a fact that there was a fortune in pure colour at number 35 Cumberland-street; and they knew the location of the safe, besides. It might have been anyone.'

'Did you open the safe regularly, to check upon the contents?'

'Not regularly, no.'

'When did you first discover that the fortune was missing?'

'When Crosbie returned the following year.'

'Can you describe what happened when you made this discovery?'

'Mr. Wells came back from the fields, and we sat down to take stock of our finances together. He opened the safe, and saw that it was empty. You can be sure that he was absolutely furious—as was I.'

'What month was this?'

'Oh, I don't know,' said Mrs. Carver, suddenly flustered. 'April, maybe. Or May.'

'April or May—of 1865. Last year.'

'Yes,' she said.

'Thank you, Mrs. Carver,' said Moody, and then, to the justice, 'Thank you, sir.'

He felt, as he sat down, that the atmosphere in the courtroom was quickening. Harrington and Fellowes had ceased their whispering, and the justice was no longer taking notes. Every pair of eyes in the room watched Mrs. Carver as she descended the steps from the witness box and sat down.

'The Court calls Mr. Francis Carver.'

Carver was handsome in a dark green jacket and a pinned cravat. He gave his oath with his usual terse accent, and then turned, his expression sober, to face the barristers' bench.

Broham looked up from his notes. 'Mr. Carver,' he said. 'Please describe for the Court how you first came to be acquainted with Mr. Staines.'

'I met him in Dunedin,' said Carver, 'around about this time last year. He was fresh off the boat from Sydney, and looking to set himself up as a prospector. I offered to be his sponsor, and he accepted.'

'What did this sponsorship require of each of you?'

'I'd loan him enough money to set him up on the diggings, and in return, he'd be obliged to give me half-shares in his first venture, with dividends in perpetuity.'

'What was the exact monetary value of your sponsorship?'

'I bought his swag and a store of provisions. I paid for his ticket over to the Coast. He was facing down a gambling debt in Dunedin; I paid that, too.'

'Can you guess at a total value, please?'

'I suppose I stood him eight pounds. Something in the neighbourhood of eight pounds. He got the short-term leg-up, and I got the long-term payoff. That was the idea.'

'What was Mr. Staines's first venture?'

'He bought a two-acre plot of land within a mile of Kaniere,' said Carver, 'known as the Aurora. He wrote to me from Hokitika once he'd made his purchase, and forwarded on all the papers from the bank.'

'How were the Aurora dividends paid out to you?'

'By money order, care of the Reserve Bank.'

'And in what frequency did these payments occur?'

'Every quarter.'

'What was the exact value of the dividend payment you received in October 1865?'

'Eight pounds and change.'

'And what was the exact value of the dividend payment you received in January 1866?'

'Six pounds even.'

'Over the last two quarters of last year, then, you received a total of approximately fourteen pounds in dividends.'

'That is correct.'

'In that case, Aurora's total net profit must have been recorded as approximately twenty-eight pounds, over a six-month period.'

'Yes.'

'Did Mr. Staines make any mention to you of the bonanza discovered upon the Aurora by the Chinaman John Quee?'

'No.'

'Were you aware, at the time of falsification, that Mr. Staines had falsified the Aurora's quarterly report?'

'No.'

'When did you first become aware that the bonanza discovered in the cottage of the late Mr. Wells had originated from the Aurora mine?'

'The same time everyone else did,' said Carver. 'When the bank published their records in the paper, saying that the ore had been found smelted, not pure, and that the smelting bore a signature.'

Broham nodded, then, coughing slightly, changed the subject. 'Mr. Staines has testified that he holds you in poor esteem, Mr. Carver.'

'Maybe he does,' said Carver, 'but he never spoke a word to me about it.'

'Did you, as Mr. Staines alleges, assault Miss Wetherell on the eleventh of October?'

'I slapped her face,' said Carver. 'That's all.'

From the gallery, Moody heard a low growl of disapproval.

'What provoked you to slap her face?' said Broham.

'She was insolent,' said Carver.

'Can you elaborate on that?'

'I asked her for a direction, and she had a laugh at my expense, so I slapped her. It was the first and only time I ever laid a hand on her.'

'Can you describe the encounter as you remember it, please?'

'I was in Hokitika on business,' Carver said, 'and I thought I'd ride to Kaniere to have a look at the Aurora: the quarterly report had just come in, and I could see that the claim wasn't pulling good dust, so I went to find out why. I met Miss Wetherell on the side of the road. She was up to the eyes in opium, and talking nonsense. I couldn't get anything out of her, so I remounted and rode on.'

'Mr. Staines has testified that Miss Wetherell lost her child that very same day.'

'I don't know anything about that,' said Carver. 'Last I saw her, she was still laughing, and stumbling about. Maybe she came to trouble after I left.'

'Can you remember what you asked her, that afternoon?'

'Yes. I wanted to find Wells,' said Carver.

'Why were you seeking news of Mr. Wells?'

'I had a private matter to discuss with him,' said Carver. 'I hadn't seen him since May, and I didn't know where to find him, or who to ask. As Lydia said, he up and quit Dunedin in the night. Didn't tell anyone where he was going.'

'Did Miss Wetherell divulge Mr. Wells's whereabouts to you at that time?'

'No,' said Carver. 'She only laughed. That was why I slapped her.'

'Do you believe that Miss Wetherell knew where Mr. Wells was living, and that she was concealing this information from you for a specific purpose?'

Carver thought about this, but then he shook his head. 'Don't know. Wouldn't want to say.'

'What was the nature of the business you wished to discuss with Mr. Wells?'

'Insurance,' said Carver.

'In what respect?'

He shrugged, to indicate the answer was of no consequence. 'The barque *Godspeed* was his ship,' he said, 'and I was her operating master. It wasn't pressing business; I just wanted to talk some things over.'

'Were you and Mr. Wells on good terms?'

'Fair,' said Carver. 'I'd call them fair. It's no secret that I was sweet on his wife, and quick to put my hand up when he passed, but I never came between them. I was decent to Wells, and Wells was decent to me.'

'Thank you, sir,' said Broham to the justice. 'Thank you, Mr. Carver.'

'Your witness, Mr. Moody.'

Moody stood up promptly. 'Mr. Carver,' he said. 'When did you and Mrs. Carver first become acquainted?'

'We have known each other almost twenty years,' said Carver.

'In other words, over the entire course of her marriage to the late Mr. Wells.'

'Yes.'

'I wonder if you might describe the circumstances of your engagement to Mrs. Carver.'

'I've known Lydia since I was a young man,' said Carver, 'and we'd always thought we'd marry. But then I got ten years on Cockatoo, and during that time she fell in with Wells. By the time I got my leave ticket, they were married. I couldn't fault her. Ten years is a long time to wait. I couldn't fault him either. I know what calibre of woman she is. But I said to myself, if that marriage ever comes to an end, I'll be next in line.'

'You married shortly after Mr. Wells's death, is that right?'

Carver stared at him. 'There was nothing disrespectful about it,' he said.

Moody inclined his head. 'No, I'm sure,' he said. 'I'm sorry if I implied otherwise. Allow me to backtrack a little. When was it that you were released from prison?'

'June of 'sixty-four,' said Carver. 'Nearly two years ago now.'

'What did you do, upon your release from Cockatoo Island?'

'I made for Dunedin,' said Carver. 'Found myself some work on a ship making the trans-Tasman run. That was *Godspeed*.'

'Were you captaining this craft?'

'Crew,' said Carver. 'But I made captain the following year.'

'Mr. Wells was digging the field at Dunstan at this time, is that correct?'

Carver hesitated. 'Yes,' he said.

'And Mrs. Carver—then wife of Mr. Wells—was residing in Dunedin.'

'Yes.'

'Did you see Mrs. Wells often, over this period?'

'I had a drink at her place every now and again,' said Carver. 'She kept a tavern on Cumberland-street. But I was mostly at sea.'

'In May of 1865, Crosbie Wells returned to Dunedin,' said Moody. 'I understand that he made a purchase at that time.'

Carver knew very well that he was being led into a trap, but he was powerless to stop it. 'Yes,' he said, curtly. 'He bought *Godspeed*.'

'Quite a purchase,' said Moody, nodding, 'not the least because it was made so abruptly. The fact that he chose to invest in a ship, of all things, is also curious. Had Mr. Wells any prior interest in seafaring, I wonder?'

'Couldn't tell you,' said Carver. 'But he must have done, if he made the purchase.'

Moody paused; then he said, 'I understand that the deed of sale is currently in your possession.'

'It is.'

'How did it come to be in your possession, please?'

'Mr. Wells entrusted it to me,' said Carver.

'When did he entrust this deed to you?'

'At the time of sale,' said Carver.

'Which was . . .?'

'In May,' said Carver. 'Last year.'

'Immediately before Mr. Wells quit Dunedin, in other words, and relocated to the Arahura Valley.'

Carver could not deny it. 'Yes,' he said.

'What was Mr. Wells's reason, in entrusting this deed of sale to you?' said Moody.

'So that I could act as his proxy,' said Carver.

'In case of injury, you mean,' said Moody. 'Or death.'

'Yes,' said Carver.

'Ah,' said Moody. 'Now, let me see if I have this straight, Mr. Carver. As of the beginning of last year, Mr. Wells was the rightful possessor of several thousand pounds' worth of ore, excavated from a claim in the Dunstan Valley. The ore was stashed in a safe at his residence in Dunedin, where his wife—an old and very fond acquaintance of yours—was living. In May, Mr. Wells returned home to Dunedin from the fields at Dunstan, and, without notifying his wife, cleared the safe. He immediately sank the entire bonanza into the purchase of the barque *Godspeed*, entrusted that ship and its operation to you, and promptly fled to Hokitika without informing any person of his destination or his design.

'Of course,' Moody added, 'I am making an assumption, in presuming that it was Mr. Wells, and not another party, who removed the ore from the safe ... but how else could he have purchased *Godspeed*? He possessed no shares or bonds of any kind—we are quite sure of that—and the transfer of ownership, printed in the *Otago Witness* upon the fourteenth of May that year, explicitly states that the ship was bought for gold.'

Carver was scowling. 'You're leaving out the whore,' he said. 'She was the reason he quit Dunedin. She was the reason he fell out with Lydia.'

'Perhaps she was—but I will correct you in pointing out that Miss Wetherell was not, at that point in time, a member of the old profession,' Moody said. 'The promissory note penned by Mr. Richard Mannering, which I submitted to the court this morning, explicitly states that Miss Wetherell is to be outfitted with an appropriate gown, a muff pistol, perfumes, petticoats, and all other items "in which she is currently deficient". It is dated June of last year.'

Carver said nothing.

'You will forgive me,' said Moody after a moment, 'if I remark that Mr. Wells does not seem to have benefited very greatly from the sequence of events that unfolded in Dunedin last May. You, however, seem to have benefited a very great deal.'

Justice Kemp waited until Carver had seated himself beside his wife before calling the room sharply to order. 'All right, Mr. Moody,' he said, folding his hands, 'I see that you have a clear direction here, and I will allow you to continue with your present argument, though I will make the remark that we seem to have wandered rather far from the course as set down in this morning's bulletin. Now: you have submitted the names of two witnesses for the defence.'

Moody bowed. 'Yes, sir.'

'In the case of the defence witnesses, Mr. Moody will examine, and Mr. Broham will cross-examine,' said the justice. He consulted the ledger, then looked up, over his spectacles, and said, 'Mr. Thomas Balfour.'

Thomas Balfour was duly summoned from the cells.

'Mr. Balfour,' Moody said, when he had been sworn in. 'You are in the shipping business, are you not?'

'Have been for coming up twelve years, Mr. Moody.'

'You have Mr. Lauderback's private account, I understand.'

'I do indeed,' said Balfour, happily. 'I've had Mr. Lauderback's business since the winter of 1861.'

'Can you please describe the most recent transaction between Mr. Lauderback and Balfour Shipping?'

'I most certainly can,' said Balfour. 'When Mr. Lauderback first arrived in Hokitika in January, he came over the Alps, as you might remember. His trunk and assorted effects were sent by sea. He sent down a shipping crate from Lyttelton to Port Chalmers, and once the crate reached Port Chalmers I arranged for one of my vessels—the *Virtue*—to pick it up and bring it over to the Coast. Well, she got here all right—the *Virtue*—with the crate aboard. Arrived on the twelfth of January, two days before Mr. Lauderback himself. Next day, the crate was unloaded—stacked onto the quay with all the rest of the cargo—and I signed for it to be transferred into my warehouse, where Mr. Lauderback would pick it up, after he arrived. But that never happened: the crate was swiped. Never made it into the warehouse.'

'Was the crate identified on the exterior as belonging to Mr. Lauderback?'

'Oh, yes,' said Balfour. 'You'll have seen the crates stacked along the quay—they'd be indistinguishable, you know, were it not for the bills of lading. The bill tells you who owns the goods and who's the shipper and what have you.'

'What happened when you discovered the crate was missing?'

'You can be sure I tore my hair out, looking for it: I hadn't the faintest clue where it might have gone. Well, *Godspeed* was wrecked on the bar two weeks later, and when they cleared her cargo, what should turn up but the Lauderback crate! Seems it had been loaded onto *Godspeed*, when she last weighed anchor from the Hokitika port.'

'In other words, very early on the morning of the fifteenth of January.'

'That's right.'

'What happened when the Lauderback trunk was finally recovered?'

'I did some sniffing around,' said Balfour. 'Asked some questions of the crew, and they told me how the mistake had come about. Well, here's what happened. Someone had seen the bill of lading—"Mr. Lauderback, bearer"—and remembered that their skipper—that's Carver—had been on the lookout for a crate so identified, the previous year. They saw this crate on the wharf, the night of the fourteenth, and they thought, here's a chance to earn a bit of favour with the master.

'So they open it up—just to be curious. Inside there's a trunk and a pair of carpetbags and not much else. Doesn't look terribly valuable, but they figure, you never know. They go off to find Captain Carver, but he's nowhere to be found. Not in his rooms at the hotel, not at the bars, nowhere. They decide to leave it to the morning, and off they go to bed. Then Carver himself comes flying down the quay in a terrible bother, turns them all out of their hammocks, and says *Godspeed* weighs anchor at the first light of dawn—only a few hours' hence. He won't say why. Anyway, the fellows make a decision. They pop the lid back on the crate, haul it aboard nice and quick, and when *Godspeed* weighs anchor just before first light, the crate's in the hold.'

'Was Captain Carver notified of this addition to the cargo?'

'Oh yes,' said Balfour, smiling. 'The fellows were pleased as Punch—they thought there would be a reward in it, you see. So they wait until *Godspeed* is under sail before they call him down. Carver takes one look at the bill of sale and sees they've botched the job. "Balfour Shipping?" he says. "It was *Danforth* Shipping, that was the one I lost. You've lifted the wrong bloody one—and now we've got stolen goods aboard."'

'Might we infer from this,' Moody said, 'that Captain Carver had lost a shipping crate, identified as belonging to Alistair Lauderback, with Danforth Shipping as its shipper, that contained something of great value to him?'

'Certainly looks that way,' said Balfour.

'Thank you very much for your time, Mr. Balfour.'

'My pleasure, Mr. Moody.'

Broham, who very plainly had no idea where Moody's line of questioning was going, waived his right to cross-examine the witness for the defence, and the justice, making a note of this, called the second witness.

'The Honourable Mr. Alistair Lauderback.'

Alistair Lauderback crossed the breadth of the courtroom in five strides.

'Mr. Lauderback,' said Moody, when he had given his oath. 'You are the former owner of the barque *Godspeed*, is that correct?'

'Yes,' said Lauderback. 'That is correct.'

'According to the deed of sale, you sold the ship on the twelfth of May, 1865.'

'I did.'

'Is the man to whom you sold the ship in the courtroom today?'

'He is,' said Lauderback.

'Can you identify him, please?' said Moody.

Lauderback threw out his arm and levelled his index finger squarely in Carver's face. 'That man,' he said, addressing Moody. 'That's the man, right there.'

'Can there be a mistake?' said Moody. 'I observe that the deed of sale, submitted to the court by Mr. Carver himself, was signed by a "C. Francis Wells".'

'It's an out-and-out forgery,' said Lauderback, still pointing at Carver. '*He* told me his name was Crosbie Wells, and he signed the deed as Crosbie Wells, and I sold him the ship believing all the while that I'd sold it to a man named Crosbie Wells. It wasn't until eight, nine months later that I realised I'd been played for a fool.'

Moody dared not make eye contact with Carver—who had stiffened, very slightly, at Lauderback's falsehood. Moody saw, in the corner of his eye, that Mrs. Carver had reached out a white hand to restrain him: her fingers had closed around his wrist. 'Can you describe what happened?' he said.

'He played the jilted husband,' said Lauderback. 'He knew I'd been out and about with Lydia—everyone in this room knows it too: I made my confession in the *Times*—and he saw a chance to turn a profit on it. He told me his name was Crosbie Wells and I'd been out and about with his wife. I never even dreamed he might be telling a barefaced lie. I thought, I've done this man wrong, and I've made a bad woman of his wife.'

The Carvers had not moved. Still without looking at them, Moody said, 'What did he want from you?'

'He wanted the ship,' said Lauderback. 'He wanted the ship, and he got the ship. But I was blackmailed. I sold it under duress—not willingly.'

'Can you explain the nature of the blackmail?'

'I'd been keeping Lydia in high fashion, over the course of our affair,' Lauderback said. 'Sending her old gowns over to Melbourne every month to get stitched up, and then they'd come back with the latest frills or flounces or what have you. There was a shipment that went back and forth across the Tasman in my name, and of course I used *Godspeed* as my carrier. Well, he'd intercepted it. Carver had. He'd opened up the trunk, lifted out the gowns, and packed a small fortune underneath them. The trunk was marked with my name, remember, and the arrangement with the dressmaker's in Melbourne was mine. If that bonanza shipped offshore, I'd be sunk: on paper, I'd be foul of the law on theft, evasion of duty, everything. Once I saw the trap he'd laid, I knew there was nothing to be done. I had to give him the ship. So we shook hands as men, and I apologised again—and then, in keeping with his sham, he signed the contract "Wells".'

'Did you ever hear from Mr. Carver, alias Wells, after that encounter?'

'Not a peep.'

'Did you ever see the trunk again?'

'Never.'

'Incidentally,' said Moody, 'what was the name of the shipping company you used to transport Mrs. Carver's gowns to and from the dressmaker's in Melbourne?'

'Danforth Shipping,' said Lauderback. 'Jem Danforth was the man I used.'

Moody paused, to allow the crowd in the gallery to comprehend the full implication of this, and then said, 'When did you realise Mr. Carver's true identity?'

'In December,' said Lauderback. 'Mr. Wells—the real Mr. Wells, I should say—wrote to me just before he passed. Just a voter introducing himself to a political man, that's all it was. But from his letter I knew at once that he didn't know the first thing about me and Lydia—and that's when I put it all together, and realised that I'd been had.'

'Do you have Mr. Wells's correspondence with you?'

'Yes.' Lauderback reached into his breast pocket and withdrew a folded piece of paper.

'The Court will note that the document in Mr. Lauderback's possession is postmarked the seventeenth of December, 1865,' said Moody.

'Duly noted, Mr. Moody.'

Moody turned back to Lauderback. 'Would you read out the letter, please?'

'Certainly.' Lauderback held the up the paper, coughed, and then read:

> *West Canterbury. December 1865*
>
> *Sir I observe in the 'West Coast Times' that you mean to make the passage to Hokitika overland & therefore will pass through the Arahura Valley lest you make some deliberately circuitous route. I am a voting man and as such I would be honoured to welcome a politician at my home humble though the dwelling is. I shall describe it so that you might approach or direct your course away as you see fit. The house is roofed in iron & set back thirty yards from the banks of the Arahura on that river's Southern side. There is a clearing of some thirty yards on either side of the cottage & the sawmill is some twenty yards further to the Southeast. The dwelling is a small one with a window & a chimney made of clay-fired brick. It is clad in the usual way. Perhaps even if you do not stop I shall see you riding by. I shall not expect it nor hope for it but I wish you a pleasant journey Westward & a triumphant campaign & I assure you that I remain,*
>
> *With the deepest admiration,*
> *CROSBIE WELLS*

Moody thanked him. He turned to the justice. 'The Court will note that the signature on Mr. Lauderback's private correspondence exactly resembles the signature upon the deed of gift penned by Mr. Crosbie Wells upon the eleventh of October, 1865, in which a sum of two thousand pounds is to be given over to Miss Anna Wetherell by Mr. Emery Staines, with Crosbie Wells as witness; it also exactly resembles the signature upon Mr. Wells's marriage certificate, submitted by Mrs. Lydia Carver, formerly Mrs. Wells, to the Magistrate's Court two months ago. The Court will further note that these two signatures in no way resemble the signature upon the bill of sale for the barque *Godspeed*, submitted to the Court by Mr. Francis Carver. Suffice to prove that the signature upon this bill of sale is, indeed, a forgery.'

Broham was gaping at Moody, open-mouthed.

'Just what do you mean by this, Mr. Moody?' said the justice.

'Simply that Mr. Carver obtained the barque *Godspeed* by methods of extortion, impersonation, and fraud,' Moody said, 'and used the same tactics in thieving a fortune of many thousands of pounds from Mr. Wells in May of last year—a theft he achieved, presumably, with Mrs. Carver's help, given that she is now his wife.'

Broham, who was still struggling to place the events of the past five minutes in sequence in his mind, petitioned for a recess; but his request could hardly be heard above the commotion in the gallery. Justice Kemp, raising his voice to a shout, requested the immediate presence of both Mr. Broham and Mr. Moody in the Magistrate's office; then he gave the instruction for all witnesses to be placed in custody, and adjourned the court.

THE HOUSE OF MANY WISHES

In which Lydia Wells is as good as her word; Anna Wetherell receives an unexpected visitor; and we learn the truth about Elizabeth Mackay.

The face that number 35, Cumberland-street presented to the thoroughfare was oddly blank: pale clapboard siding; a mullioned shop-window, papered over with butcher's paper; a pair of curtained sash windows on the floor above. The establishments on either side—Number 37 was a bootmaker's, and number 33, a shipping agency—had been built very close, masking any sense, from the street, of interior proportion. Walking past it, one might even have presumed the building to be unoccupied, for there were no signs or legends above the doorway, nothing on the porch, and no card in the plate above the knocker.

Mrs. Wells opened the front door with her own key. She led Anna down the silent passage to the rear of the house, where a narrow staircase led to the floor above. On the upstairs landing, which was as clean and blank as its counterpart below, she produced a second key from her reticule, unlocked a second door, and, smiling, gestured for Anna to step inside.

A more worldly soul than Anna might have formed an immediate conclusion from the scene that greeted her: the heavy lace curtains; the redundant upholstery; the heady scent of liquor and perfume; the beaded portiere, currently tied back against the door-frame to show the dimly lit bedchamber beyond. But Anna was not worldly, and if she was surprised to encounter a scene of such sweet-smelling, cushioned luxury at a boarding house for girls, she did not express it aloud. On the walk from the quay to Cumberland-street Mrs. Wells had exhibited a great range of refined tastes and particular opinions, and by the time they reached their destination Anna felt more than happy to defer to them—her own opinions seeming, all of a sudden, very pale and feeble by contrast.

'You see that I take *very* good care of my girls,' said her hostess. Anna replied that the room was exceedingly handsome, and at this encouragement Mrs. Wells proposed a turn of it, directing Anna's attention, as they walked, to several ingenuities of decoration and placement, so that her compliments might be hitherto more specifically bestowed.

Anna's chest had been delivered as promised, and was installed already at the foot of the bed—a signal that she took to mean the bed was intended to be hers. It had a handsome headboard, the wooden frame of which was all but obscured behind a great mound of white pillows, stacked in piles of three, and it was much broader and higher than the cot in which she habitually slept, at home. She wondered whether she would be required to share a bed with someone else: it seemed much too big for one person. Opposite the bed stood a high-sided copper bath, draped with towels, and beside it, a heavy bell-pull with a tasselled end. Mrs. Wells pulled this now, and from somewhere on the floor below there came a muted jingle. When the maid appeared, Mrs. Wells ordered hot water to be sent up from the kitchen, and a plate of luncheon to follow it. The maid hardly glanced at Anna, who was very grateful to be ignored, and relieved when the maid left to heat the water on the kitchen stove.

As soon as she was gone Lydia Wells turned to Anna, smiled again, and begged to take her leave.

'I have appointments uptown which I must keep; but I shall be back in time for supper, and will expect us to take it together. You may ask Lucy for whatever you desire in the world. If she can find it, it will be found. Stay in the tub as long as you like, and use anything on the washstand that strikes your fancy. I insist that you make yourself *entirely* at home.'

Anna Wetherell did just that. She washed her hair with a lavender-scented lotion, and scrubbed every inch of her body with store-bought soap, and stayed in the water for the better part of an hour. After she had dressed again—turning her stockings inside-out to show their cleaner side—she spent a long time at the looking glass, fixing her hair. There were several bottles of perfume on the washstand: she sniffed all of them, returned to the first, and dabbed a little on her wrists and beneath her ears.

The maid had left a cold luncheon on the table below the window, the plate covered with a piece of cloth. Anna lifted the cloth aside, and saw a mound of ham, shaved very nicely, a thick slice of pease pudding, evidently fried, a yellow scone spread with butter and jam, and two pickled eggs. She sat, seized the knife and fork laid out for her, and fell upon it—relishing the flavours, after so many tasteless meals at sea.

Once the plate was clean, she sat wondering for some minutes whether she ought to ring the bell for the service to be cleared away: would it be more imperious to ring, or not to ring? Eventually she decided not to. She got up from the table and went to the window, where she drew the curtains, and, feeling very contented, stood awhile to watch the traffic in the street. The clock had struck three before she heard any sound from the floor below: sudden voices in the passage, and then footsteps mounting the stairs, and then a brisk two-knuckled knock at the door.

She had barely time to rise before the door was flung open, and in strode a tall, very dirty man, dressed in yellow moleskin trousers and a faded coat. When he saw Anna, he came up short.

'Oh,' he said. 'Beg your pardon.'

'Good afternoon,' Anna said.

'You one of Lydia's girls?'

'Yes.'

'New girl?'

'I arrived today.'

'You and I both,' said the man. He had sandy hair and a slightly grizzled look. 'Good afternoon to *you*.'

'Can I help you?'

He grinned at this. 'We'll see,' he said. 'I'm looking for the mistress. Is she about?'

'She has appointments uptown.'

'What time will she be back?'

'She said by suppertime,' Anna said.

'Well: have you any appointments, before then?'

'No,' Anna said.

'Good,' the man said. 'Mind if I reserve the next dance?'

Anna did not know what to say to this. 'I'm not sure if I ought to receive company when Mrs. Wells is out.'

'*Mrs. Wells*,' said the man, and laughed. 'Sounds almost respectable, when you put it like that.' He reached back and closed the door behind him. 'Crosbie's my name. What's yours?'

'Miss Anna Wetherell,' said Anna, with increasing alarm.

He was already moving to the sideboard. 'Care for a drop of something, Miss Anna Wetherell?'

'No, thank you.'

He picked up a bottle and tilted it at her. 'No because you don't have a taste for liquor, or no because you're being polite?'

'I only just arrived.'

'You've told me so once already, my girl, and anyway, that doesn't answer the question I asked.'

'I wouldn't want to take advantage of Mrs. Wells's hospitality,' said Anna, with a slight emphasis of disapproval—as though to communicate that he ought not to, either.

Crosbie uncorked the bottle, sniffed, and recorked it. 'Oh, there's no such thing as hospitality,' he said, returning the bottle to the tray, and selecting another. 'You'll be billed for everything you touch in this room, and quick as thieves. You mark my words.'

'No,' Anna said. 'It's all been paid for. And Mrs. Wells has been wonderfully hospitable. I'm staying at her personal request.'

He was amused by this. 'Oh yes? Nearest and dearest, are you? Old friends?'

Anna frowned. 'We met at the quay this afternoon.'

'Just by accident, I suppose.'

'Yes. There was a young woman—a Miss Mackay—who didn't

make the sailing. Her cousin's cousin. When Miss Mackay didn't show, Mrs. Wells invited me in place of her. The room and board is all paid in advance.'

'Oho,' said the man, pouring out a glassful of liquor.

'Have you just returned from the fields?' said Anna, stalling for time.

'I have,' said the man. 'Up in the high country. Arrived back this morning.' He drank, expelled a breath, and then said, 'No. It's not right if I don't tell you. You've been euchred.'

'I've been what?'

'Euchred.'

'I don't know what that means, Mr. Crosbie.'

He smiled at her mistake, but did not correct her. 'There's always a Miss Mackay,' he explained. 'It's a line she spins. So you believe her, and you follow her home, and before you know it, you're beholden. Aren't you, now? She's given you a fine meal and a hot bath and nothing but the milk of kindness, and what have you given her? Oh'—he wagged his finger—'but there *will* be something, Miss Anna Wetherell. There *will* be something that you can give.' He seemed to perceive Anna's anxiety, for he added, in a gentler tone, 'Here's something you ought to know. There's no charity in a gold town. If it looks like charity, look again.'

'Oh,' said Anna.

He drained his glass and set it down. 'Are you partial to a drink or not?'

'Not today, thank you.'

He reached into his pocket, withdrew something, and then held up a closed fist. 'Can you guess what I'm holding?' he said.

'No.'

'Go on. Have a guess.'

'A coin?'

'Better than a coin. Guess again.'

'I can't think,' she said, in panic.

He opened his fist to reveal a nugget of gold around the size and shape of a chestnut, laughed again at her expression, and then tossed it to her. She caught it in the heels of her hands. 'That's enough in gold to buy every last bottle on this tray, with pounds left over,' he said. 'It's yours, if you'll keep me company until the mistress comes back. How about it? You'll have a heads-up on those debts, when they start mounting.'

'I've never touched a piece of gold,' Anna said, turning it over. It was heavier than she had imagined it would be, and more elemental. It seemed to turn dull in her hands.

'Come here,' said Crosbie. He took the brandy bottle to the little sofa, sat down, and patted the space beside him. 'Share a drink with a fellow, my girl. I've been walking for two weeks, and I'm thirsty as hell, and I want something nice to look at. Come here. I'll tell you everything you need to know about Mrs. Lydia Wells.'

CRUX

In which two verdicts are delivered, and the justice fits the sentence to the crime.

Te Rau Tauwhare had not been invited to testify at either trial. He had watched the day's proceedings from the rear of the courtroom, his expression sombre, his back against the wall. When Justice Kemp called for a final recess, giving the order for all the day's witnesses to be remanded in custody, Tauwhare left the courthouse with the rest. Outside he saw the armoured carriage, waiting to transport the felons back to the gaol, and went to greet the duty sergeant, who was standing by.

'Hello, Mr. Tauwhare,' the sergeant said.

'Hello.'

'How's your friend Staines doing, then? Kicking up his heels in there?'

'Yes,' said Tauwhare.

'I popped my head in. Couldn't hear much. Good show, is it?'

'Very good,' Tauwhare said.

'Gov. Shepard got a rap on the knuckles this morning, didn't he?'

'Yes.'

'I would have liked to have seen that,' the sergeant said.

Just then the rear door of the courthouse opened and the bailiff appeared in the doorway. 'Drake!' he called.

'Yes, sir,' said the sergeant, standing tall.

'Justice wants Francis Carver escorted to Seaview,' the bailiff said. 'Special orders. You're to take him up the hill, and then come straight back again.'

Drake ran to open the doors of the carriage. 'Only Carver?'

'Only Carver,' the bailiff said. 'Mind you're back in time for the verdict. Straight up to Seaview, and straight back again.'

'Can do.'

'Quick about it—he's coming now.'

Francis Carver was brought out into the yard, and bundled into the carriage. His hands had been cuffed behind him. Inside the carriage, Drake produced a second set of cuffs from his belt, and used these to cuff Carver's linked wrists to a clew that had been fixed to the wall behind the driver's seat.

'*That's* not going anywhere,' he said cheerfully, rattling the clew to prove his point. 'There's an inch of iron between you and the world, Mr. Carver. Hoo! What have you done, that they don't trust you with all the rest? Last I checked, you were a bloody witness; next minute, you're in irons!'

Carver said nothing.

'One hour,' the bailiff said, and returned inside.

Drake jumped out of the carriage and closed the doors. 'Hi, Mr. Tauwhare,' he said, as he set the latch. 'Care for a dash up the hill and back? You'll be down in time for the verdict.'

Tauwhare hesitated.

'What do you say?' the sergeant said. 'Beautiful day for a ride—and we'll pick up bit of speed, coming down.'

Still Tauwhare hesitated. He was staring at the latch upon the carriage door.

'How about it?'

'No,' Tauwhare said at last.

'Suit yourself,' said Drake, shrugging. He clambered up onto the driver's seat, picked up the reins, and urged the horses; the carriage rattled away.

Φ

'Mr. Emery Staines. You plead guilty to having falsified the records of the Aurora goldmine in order to avoid share payments owing to

Mr. Francis Carver, at a value of fifty percent net profit per annum, and to avoid a bonus payment owing to John Long Quee, at an undisclosed value. You plead guilty to having embezzled a great quantity of raw gold, found by John Long Quee upon the Aurora, which has since been valued at £4096. You admit that you thieved this gold from the Aurora and buried it in the Arahura Valley, with the purpose of concealment. You also plead guilty to dereliction, stating that you have been incapacitated for the past two months by excessive and prolonged consumption of opium.'

The justice laid his papers aside, and folded his hands together.

'Your counsel, Mr. Staines,' he said, 'has done a very good job of painting Mr. Carver in a poor light this afternoon. Notwithstanding his performance, however, the fact remains that provocation to break the law is not licence to break the law: your poor opinion of Mr. Carver does not give you the right to determine what he does, or does not, deserve.

'You did not witness the assault against Miss Wetherell first-hand, and nor, it seems, did anybody else; therefore you cannot know beyond a shadow of a doubt whether Mr. Carver truly *was* the author of that assault, or indeed, if an assault took place at all. Of course the loss of any child is a tragedy, and tragedy cannot be mitigated by circumstance; but in adjudicating *your* crime, Mr. Staines, we must put aside the tragic nature of the event, and consider it purely as a provocation—an *indirect* provocation, I should say—for your having committed the rather more cold-blooded crimes of embezzlement and fraud, in retaliation. Yes, you had provocation to dislike Mr. Carver, to resent Mr. Carver, even to despise him; but I feel that I state a very obvious point when I say that you might have brought your grievance to the attention of the Hokitika police, and saved us all a great deal of bother.

'Your guilty plea does you credit. I also acknowledge that you have shown courtesy and humility in your responses this morning. All this suggests contrition, and deference to the proper execution of the law. Your charges, however, show a selfish disregard for contractual obligation, a capricious and decadent temperament, and a dereliction of duty, not only to your claims, but to your fellow men. Your poor opinion of Mr. Carver, however justified that opinion might be, has led you to take the law into your own hands on more than one occasion, and in more than one respect. In light of this I consider that it will do you a great deal of good to put away your grand philosophy for a time, and learn to walk in another man's shoes.

'Mr. Carver has been a shareholder of the Aurora for nine months. He has fulfilled his contractual obligation to you, and he has been ill rewarded. Emery Staines, I hereby sentence you to nine months' servitude, with labour.'

Staines's face betrayed nothing at all. 'Yes, sir.'

The justice turned to Anna.

'Miss Anna Wetherell,' he said. 'You have pleaded not guilty to all charges brought to bear against you, and in a civilised court we hold to the principle that one is innocent until proven guilty. I am sensible of the fact that aspersions cast by Mr. Moody upon Governor Shepard are aspersions only; however they have been duly recorded by this court, and may be productive in the future, pending investigations made upon Governor Shepard and others. In the meantime, I do not see that there is sufficient evidence to prove your guilt. You are acquitted of all charges. You shall be released from gaol, effective instant. I trust that from here you will continue on the righteous path to sobriety, chastity, and other virtues of a civilised kind; needless to say that I never wish to see you in this courtroom again, on any charge, least of all a charge of public intoxication and disorderly behaviour. Do I make myself clear?'

'Yes, sir.'

'Good.' He turned to the barristers' bench. 'Now,' he said heavily, but before he got any further, there came the sound of shouting in the street, and a terrible crash, and the high whinny of panicked horses—and then a terrible thump on the courthouse door, as though someone had thrown their bodily weight against it.

'What's going on?' said the justice, frowning.

Moody had started up: he heard shouting from the porch, and a great clatter.

'Open the door, someone. See what's happening,' the justice said.

The door was thrown open.

'Sergeant Drake,' exclaimed the justice. 'What is it?'

The sergeant's eyes were wild. 'It's Carver!' he cried.

'What about him?'

'He's *dead*!'

'*What?*'

'Some point between here and Seaview—someone must have opened the doors—and I never noticed. I was driving. I opened the doors to unload him—and there he was—and he's *dead*!'

Moody whipped about, half expecting that Mrs. Carver might have fallen into a faint; but she had not. She was looking at Drake, white-faced. Quickly, Moody scanned the faces around her. All the witnesses had been remanded during the recess, including those who had testified in the morning: none of them had left the Courthouse. Shepard was there—and Lauderback—and Frost—and Löwenthal, and Clinch, and Mannering, and Quee, and Nilssen, and Pritchard, and Balfour, and Gascoigne, and Devlin. Who was missing?

'He's right outside!' cried Drake, throwing out his arm. 'His body—I came right back—I couldn't—it wasn't—'

The justice raised his voice above the commotion. 'He took his own life?'

'Hardly,' cried Drake, his voice cracking into a sob. 'Hardly!'

The crowd began crushing through the doors, past him.

'Sergeant Drake,' shouted the justice. 'How in all heaven did Francis Carver die?'

Drake was now lost in the crowd. His voice floated up: 'Somebody bashed his head in!'

The justice's face had turned purple. '*Who?*' he roared. '*Who did it?*'

'*I'm telling you I don't know!*'

There came a terrible shriek from the street, and then shouting; the courthouse emptied. Mrs. Carver, watching the last of the crowd fight its way through the doorway, brought her hands up to her mouth.

COMBUST

In which Mrs. Wells receives a false impression, and Francis Carver relays important news.

While Anna Wetherell entertained 'Mr. Crosbie' at the House of Many Wishes on Cumberland-street, Lydia Wells was doing some entertaining of her own. It was her habit, in the afternoons, to take her almanacs and star charts to the Hawthorn Hotel upon George-street, where she set up shop in a corner of the dining room, and offered to tell the fortunes of diggers and travellers newly arrived. Her sole customer, that afternoon, had been a golden-haired boy in a felt cap who, as it turned out, had also arrived on the steamer *Fortunate Wind*. He was a voluble subject, and seemed both delighted and fascinated by Mrs. Wells's affinity for the arcane; his enthusiasm was flattering, and inclined her to be generous with her prognostications. By the time his natal chart was drawn, his past and present canvassed, and his future foretold, it was coming on four o'clock.

She looked up to see Francis Carver striding across the dining room towards her.

'Edward,' she said, to the golden-haired boy, 'be a darling, would you, and ask the waiter to wrap up a pie with a hot-water crust? Tell him to put it on my account; I'll take it home for my dinner.'

The boy obliged.

'I've just had some good news,' said Carver, when the boy was gone.

'What is it?'

'Lauderback's on his way.'

'Ah,' said Lydia Wells.

'He must have seen the shipping receipt from Danforth at long last. I hear from Billy Bruce that he's bought his passage on the *Active*, sailing out of Akaroa. He arrives on the twelfth of May, and he sends an advance message that *Godspeed* is not to depart until then.'

'Three weeks away.'

'We've got him, Greenway. Like a fish in a trap, we've got him.'

'Poor Mr. Lauderback,' said Mrs. Wells, vaguely.

'You might step over to the naval club this week and make an offer to the boys. A free night of craps, or double the jackpot, or a girl with every spin of the wheel. Something to tempt Raxworthy away from the ship that night, so that I can get a chance to get at Lauderback alone.'

'I will go to the club in the morning,' said Mrs. Wells. She began to tidy her books and charts away. 'Poor Mr. Lauderback,' she said again.

'He made his own bed,' said Carver, watching her.

'Yes, he did; but you and I warmed the sheets for him.'

'Don't feel sorry for a coward,' said Carver. 'Least of all a coward with money to spare.'

'I pity him.'

'Why? Because of the bastard? I'd sooner feel sorry for the bastard. Lauderback's had nothing but good luck from start to finish. He's a made man.'

'He is; and yet he is pitiable,' said Mrs. Wells. 'He is so ashamed, Francis. Of Crosbie, of his father, of himself. I cannot help but feel pity for a man who is ashamed.'

'No chance of Wells turning up unexpectedly, is there?'

'You talk as if he and I were intimates,' snapped Mrs. Wells. 'I can't answer for him; I certainly can't control his every move.'

'How long since he was last in town?'

'Months.'

'Does he write before he comes home?'

'Good Lord,' said Mrs. Wells. 'No, he doesn't write.'

'Is there any way you can make sure he keeps away? It wouldn't do for him to come face to face with Lauderback—not at the eleventh hour.'

'A drink will always tempt him—whatever the hour.'

Carver grinned. 'Send him a mixed crate in the post? Set him up with a tally at the Diggers Arms?'

'That, in fact, is a rather good idea.' She saw the boy coming back from the kitchens with the pie wrapped in paper, and rose from the table. 'I must be getting back now. I shall call on you to-morrow.'

'I'll be waiting,' Carver said.

'Thank you, Edward,' said Mrs. Wells to the boy, taking the pie. 'And goodbye. I could wish good fortune upon you, but that would be a waste of a wish, would it not?'

The boy laughed.

Carver was smiling too. 'Did you tell his fortune, then?'

'Oh yes,' said Mrs. Wells. 'He is to become excessively rich.'

'Is he, now? Like all the rest?'

'Not like all the rest,' said Mrs. Wells. '*Exceptionally* rich. Goodbye, Francis.'

'I'll be seeing you,' said Carver.

'Goodbye, Mrs. Wells,' said the boy.

She swept from the room, and the two men gazed after her. When she was gone Carver tilted his head at the boy. 'Your name's Edward?'

'Actually—no, it isn't,' said the boy, looking a little shamefaced. 'I made the choice to travel incognito, as you might say. My father always told me, when it comes to whores and fortune tellers, never give your real name.'

Carver nodded. 'That's sense.'

'I don't know about the whores part,' the boy went on. 'It grieves me to think of my father using them—I feel a kind of repugnance about it, out of loyalty to my mother, I suppose. But I like the telling fortunes part. It was rather a thrill, to use another man's name. It made me feel invisible, somehow. Or doubled—as though I had split myself in two.'

Carver glanced at him, and then, after a moment, put out his hand. 'Francis Carver's my name.'

'Emery Staines,' said the boy.

In which a stranger arrives upon the beach at Hokitika; the bonanza is apportioned; and Walter Moody quits the Crown Hotel at last.

Even in his best suit, with his hair combed and oiled, his boots blackened, and his handkerchief scented, Mr. Adrian Moody was a great deal less handsome than his younger son. His countenance bore the symptoms of a lifetime's dependence upon hard drink—his eyes were pouched, his nose swollen, and his complexion permanently flushed—and when he moved, it was without grace or fluidity. He walked in a stiff-hipped, lumbering fashion; his gaze was restless and wary; his hands, stained yellow with tobacco smoke, were always stealing into his pockets, or picking in an anxious way at his lapels.

Upon clambering out of the skiff that had conveyed him from the steamer to the beach, Moody senior took a moment to stretch his back, shake out his aches and cramps, and pat his body down. He directed his luggage to a hotel on Camp-street, shook hands with the customs officer, who was standing by, thanked the oarsmen gruffly for their service, and finally set off down Revell-street with his hands locked behind his back. He walked the length of the street, up one side, and down the other, frowning into each window box he passed, scanning the faces in the street very closely, and smiling at no one. By now the crowd that had gathered outside the Courthouse had dispersed, and the armoured carriage containing Francis Carver's body had returned to Seaview; the double doors were shut and locked. Moody senior barely glanced at the building as he passed.

At length he mounted the steps to the Hokitika Post Office, where, inside the building, he joined the queue to the postmaster's window. As he waited, he retrieved a piece of paper from his wallet, and unfolded it, one-handed, against his breast.

'I want this to find a Mr. Walter Moody,' he said, when he reached the front of the queue.

'Certainly,' said the postmaster. 'Know where he's staying?'

As he spoke the bells in the Wesleyan chapel rang out five o'clock.

'All I know is that he's been in Hokitika these months past,' said Moody senior.

'In town? Or in the gorge?'

'In town.'

'At a hotel? Or is he tenting?'

'I'd guess a hotel, but I couldn't tell you. Walter Moody is the name.'

'Mate of yours, is he?'

'He's my son.'

'I'll have a boy look into it, and charge you collect once we find him,' said the postmaster, making a note of the name. 'You'll have to put a shilling down as surety, but if we find him to-morrow we'll likely reimburse you sixpence.'

'That's fine.'

'Would you prefer an envelope, or a seal?'

'An envelope,' said the other, 'but hang a moment: I want to read it through one more time.'

'Step aside, then, and come back when you're ready. I'm shutting the window in half an hour.'

Adrian Moody did as he was bid. He smoothed the letter flat on the countertop, and then pushed it, with his finger, closer to the light.

Hokitika. 27.Apr.66

Walter—I beg you to read this letter to its very end, and to reserve your judgment upon me until you have done so. From my postmark you will have perceived that I am in Hokitika, as you are. I am to take my lodging at the TEMPERANCE HOTEL *on Camp-street, an address which will no doubt cause you some surprise. You have long known that I have the Epicurean temperament. Now I am also of a Stoical cast. I have sworn that I will never take another drop of liquor in this life, and since this oath was made it has not been broken. It is in the spirit of repentance that I set down a brief account of those true intentions that my enslavement to the drink has occluded, even perverted, in recent years.*

I left the British Isles on account of debt, and debt alone. Frederick your brother had an acquaintance upon the field at Lawrence in Otago, and by his report the prospects there seemed very good; Frederick had determined to join him. You were in Rome, and meant to winter on the continent. I decided to make the journey in secret, in the hope that I would return as a rich man before the year was out. I confess this was a decision made with shameful provocation, for there were several men in London and also in Liverpool whom I desired very much to escape. Before I left I portioned a sum of £20 for my wife—the very last of my savings. Much later I learned that this provision never reached its destination: it was stolen, and by the very man who was to be its bearer (the blackguard PIERS HOWLAND, *may he live in shame and die in squalor). By the time I discovered this I was in Otago, half a world away; furthermore, I could not make contact without risking pursuit, even conviction, on account of crimes unpunished and debts unpaid. I did nothing. I counted my wife as abandoned, prayed that God would forgive me, and continued with Frederick on the fields.*

We made only pay dirt during our first year in Otago. I have heard it said that the men of the comfortable classes have the worst of luck upon the diggings, for they cannot bear privation as the lower orders can. This was certainly true in our case. We struggled mightily and despaired often. But we persevered, and seven months ago your brother struck upon a nugget the size of a snuffbox, caught between two boulders in the elbow of a stream. It was upon this nugget that we were able to begin to build our fortunes at long last.

You might ask why we did not send this nugget home with our apologies and blessings; that question would be a good one. Frederick your brother had long been in favour of writing to you. He had urged me to

*make contact with my abandoned wife, and even to invite her to join us
here, but I resisted. I resisted also his intimations that I should quit the
devil drink and mend my ways. We had many arguments along this theme
and finally parted on less than civil terms. I am sorry to say that I do not
know where Frederick is now.*

*You have always been the scholar of the family, Walter. I am ashamed
of a great many aspects of my life; but I have never been ashamed of you.
In taking my oath of temperance I have confronted my true soul. I have
seen myself truly as a man of weakness and of cowardice, easy prey to
vice and sin of all description. But if I am proud of one thing it is that
my sons are not like me in these degenerate respects. It is a painful joy for
a father to say of his son: 'That man is a better man than I'. I assure you
I have felt this painful joy twice over.*

*I can do no more than to beg for your forgiveness, as I must also beg for
Frederick's, and to promise that our next reunion, should you grant me one,
will be conducted 'dry'. Good fortune, Walter. Know that I have
confronted my true soul, and that I write this as a sober man. Know also
that even the briefest reply would greatly cheer the heart of*
Your father
ADRIAN MOODY

He read the letter twice over, then folded it into the envelope,
and wrote his son's name in large letters upon the front. His hand
trembled as he capped his pen.

Φ

'A Mr. Frost for Mr. Staines.'

'Send him in,' said Devlin.

Charlie Frost had a piece of paper in his hand. 'Expenses,' he
said, looking apologetic.

'Have a seat,' said Devlin.

'What's the damage, Mr. Frost?' said Staines. He was looking
very tired.

'Extensive, I'm afraid,' said Frost, drawing up a chair. 'Justice
Kemp has ruled that Francis Carver's dividend of two thousand
and forty-eight pounds must be honoured. There's a catch—the

Garrity Group is to be repaid in full for the claim taken out against *Godspeed*—but the rest will go to Mrs. Carver, as Carver's widow.'

'How is she?' Devlin said.

'Sedated,' said Frost. 'Dr. Gillies and Mr. Pritchard are waiting on her, I believe; last I saw her, she was being escorted back to the Wayfarer's Fortune.' He turned back to Staines, flattening his paper on the desk. 'May I itemise the expenses, briefly?'

'Yes.'

'As the party found guilty, you are responsible for all legal fees, including those incurred by Mr. Fellowes these months past, and including, also, Mr. Nilssen's commission, since invested in the Seaview gaol-house—as you might remember, the Magistrate ruled that because it had been charitably donated, it would not be revoked. In total all of this amounts to a little over five hundred pounds.'

'Halved, and halved again,' said Staines.

'Yes; I'm afraid you will find that a common theme with legal expenses. There's more. You have also been sued for damages by a great many diggers, in both Kaniere and the Hokitika Gorge. I don't have the exact sum for you yet; but I'm afraid it's likely to be dozens of pounds, perhaps hundreds.'

'Is that everything?'

'In terms of official expenses, yes,' said Frost. 'There are several unofficial matters to discuss, however. Do we have time?'

'Do we have time?' said Staines to Devlin.

'We have until the carriage gets here,' said Devlin.

'I will be quick,' said Frost. 'As you may be aware, the gold extracted from Anna's orange gown is still stowed beneath Mr. Gascoigne's bed. Anna owes a debt of some hundred and twenty pounds to Mr. Mannering, and she had thought to repay this amount with the pure colour extracted from the orange gown. I had the idea, however, that *you* might like to take on her debt to Mr. Mannering, and arrange for Mr. Mannering to be repaid out of your share of the bonanza, as an itemised expense. That way Anna will have something to live on, you see, during the months where you're in gaol.'

'Good,' said Staines. 'Yes—do that. Just as you say.'

Frost made a note of this. 'The second matter,' he said, 'is the bonus owing to Mr. Quee. We must keep up the sham that the fortune originated on the Aurora, you see, and every man who comes upon a bonanza deserves a reward.'

'Of course,' said Staines. 'A bonus.'

'I am given to understand,' Frost continued, 'that Mr. Quee is desirous to return to China once his Company indenture expires; furthermore, he wishes to return with exactly seven hundred and sixty-eight shillings in his pocket. According to Mr. Mannering, he has long set his mind upon this precise figure. I believe it is of some personal or spiritual significance to him.'

Ordinarily this curiosity would have tickled Emery Staines extremely, but he did not smile. It was Devlin who exclaimed, 'Seven hundred and sixty-eight shillings?'

'Yes,' said Frost.

'What a fastidious thing,' said Devlin. 'What does it augur—do you know?'

'I am afraid I do not,' said Frost. 'But if I might make a suggestion'—turning back to Staines—'perhaps your bonus payment to Mr. Quee ought to be enough to realise this ambition.'

'What does it come to, in pounds?'

'Thirty-eight pounds, eight shillings,' said Frost. 'Roughly one percent of four thousand, and one percent is a reasonable rate for a goldfields bonus, especially given that Mr. Quee is Chinese. As a gesture of good faith, you also might wish to consider buying him out of his indenture, and facilitating his passage home.'

Staines shook his head. 'I never thought of him, did I?'

'Who?' said Frost.

'Mr. Quee,' said Staines. 'I simply never thought of him.'

'Well, he did us all a very great favour this afternoon, in keeping our secret, and now we have a chance to do him one, in return. I have spoken to Mr. Mannering already. He is content to accept an early termination of Mr. Quee's contract, and has costed it at my request. If you pay Mr. Quee a bonus of sixty-four pounds, then all expenses should be adequately covered.'

Staines brought his shoulder up to his cheek, and sighed. 'Yes,' he said. 'All right.'

'Now: the third financial matter.' Frost coughed slightly. 'When we first—ah—came upon the fortune, back in January, Mr. Clinch made me a present of thirty pounds, as a gift. I'm afraid I spent it, and I have not the means to repay even a penny of it. I wonder if I might impose upon your generosity, and list those thirty pounds as bank expenses.' He said all this very fast, and then added, 'As a loan, of course: I'd repay it by the time of your release.'

'Here's the carriage,' Devlin said, rising.

'That's fine,' said Staines to Frost. 'Pay it out—just as you say. It doesn't matter.'

Frost exhaled, full of relief. 'Thank you very much, Mr. Staines.' He watched as Devlin escorted Staines from the cell. When they reached the doorway he said, raising his voice a little, 'First thing to-morrow, I'll send you up an itemised receipt.'

Φ

The chapel bells were ringing out seven o'clock as Walter Moody folded the last of his fine clothes into his trunk, closed the lid, and secured the hasp. Rising, he checked the flies of his yellow mole-skin trousers, tightened his belt, touched the red kerchief that was knotted about his neck, and finally, reached for his coat and hat— the former a plain woollen garment, cut almost to his knees, and the latter, a heavy soft-crowned thing with a wide waxed brim. He donned both, slung his swag onto his back, and left the room, removing the key from the lock as he did so.

During his absence his trunk was to be kept at Clark's Warehouse on Gibson Quay, to which place his private mail, if he received any, would also be directed. To finance this relocation, he left three silver shillings at the Crown front desk, along with his key. He slipped a fourth shilling into the hand of the Crown maid, fold-ing her small yellow hand in both his own, and thanked her very warmly for the three months' service and hospitality she had pro-vided him. Quitting the Crown, he turned down the narrow path that led to the beachfront and at once began walking north, his swag clanking on his back, his tent roll bumping the backs of his legs with each step.

He was no more than two miles out of Hokitika when he perceived that he was walking some ten paces ahead of another man, similarly clad in the digger's habitual costume; Moody glanced back, and they acknowledged one another with a nod.

'Hi there,' said the other. 'You walking north?'

'I am.'

'Heading for the beaches, are you? Charleston way?'

'So I hope. Do we share a destination?'

'Seems we do,' the other said. 'Mind if I fall into step?'

'Not at all,' said Moody. 'I shall be glad of the company. Walter Moody is my name. Walter.'

'Paddy Ryan,' said the other. 'You got a Scottish tongue on you, Walter Moody.'

'I cannot deny it,' said Moody.

'Never had any trouble with a Scot.'

'And I have never quarrelled with an Irishman.'

'That makes one of you,' said Paddy Ryan, with a grin. 'But it's the truth: I never had any trouble with a Scot.'

'I'm very glad of it.'

They walked on in silence for a time.

'I guess we're both a long way away from home,' said Paddy Ryan presently.

'I'm a long way from where I was born,' said Moody, squinting across the breakers to the open sea.

'Well,' said Paddy Ryan, 'if home can't be where you come from, then home is what you make of where you go.'

'That is a good motto,' Moody said.

Paddy Ryan nodded, seeming pleased. 'Are you fixing to stay in this country, then, Walter? After you've dug yourself a patch, and made yourself a pile?'

'I expect my luck will decide that question for me.'

'Would you call it lucky to stay, or lucky to go?'

'I'd call it lucky to choose,' said Moody—surprising himself, for that was not the answer he would have given, three months prior.

Paddy Ryan looked at him sidelong. 'How about we share our stories? Make the road a little shorter that way.'

'Our stories? Do you mean our histories?'

'Ay—or the stories you've heard, or whatever you like.'

'All right,' said Moody, a little stiffly. 'Do you want to go first, or shall I?'

'You go first,' said Paddy Ryan. 'Give us a tale, and spin it out, so we forget about our feet, and we don't notice that we're walking.'

Moody was silent for a time, wondering how to begin. 'I am trying to decide between the whole truth, and nothing but the truth,' he said presently. 'I am afraid my history is such that I can't manage both at once.'

'Hi—no need for the truth at all,' said Paddy Ryan. 'Who said anything about the truth? You're a free man in this country, Walter Moody. You tell me any old rubbish you like, and if you string it out until we reach the junction at Kumara, then I shall count it as a very fine tale.'

SUN & MOON IN CONJUNCTION (NEW MOON)

In which Mrs. Wells makes two very interesting discoveries.

When Lydia Wells returned to the House of Many Wishes a little after seven o'clock, she was informed by the maid that Anna Wetherell had received a caller in her absence: Mr. Crosbie Wells, who had returned unexpectedly after many months of absence in the Otago highlands. Mr. Wells had an appointment of some kind upon George-street that evening, the maid reported, but he had left with the assurance that he would return the next morning, in the hope of securing an interview with his wife.

Mrs. Wells received this news thoughtfully. 'How long did you say he stayed, Lucy?'

'Two hours, ma'am.'

'From when until when?'

'Three until five.'

'And Miss Wetherell . . .?'

'I haven't disturbed her,' said Lucy. 'She hasn't rung the bell since he left, and I didn't trouble them when he was here.'

'Good girl,' said Mrs. Wells. 'Now, if Crosbie does come back to-morrow, and if, for whatever reason, I am not here, you show him to Miss Wetherell's room as before.'

'Yes, ma'am.'

'And you'd better put in an order at the wine and spirit merchant first thing to-morrow. A mixed crate should do us fine.'

'Yes, ma'am.'

'Here's a pie for our supper. See that it's heated through, and then send it up. We'll eat at eight, I think.'

'Very good, ma'am.'

Lydia Wells arranged her almanacs and star charts in her arms, peered critically into the glass hanging in the hall, and then ascended the stairs to Anna's room, where she knocked briskly, and opened the door without waiting for an answer.

'Is it not better—to be fed, and dry, and clean?' she said, in lieu of a greeting.

Anna had been sitting in the window box. She leaped up when Mrs. Wells strode into the room, blushing deeply, and said, 'Very much better, ma'am. You are much too kind.'

'There is no such thing as too much kindness,' declared Mrs. Wells, depositing her books upon the table next to the settee. She glanced quickly at the sideboard, making a mental tally of the bottles, and then turned back to Anna, and smiled. 'What fun we shall have this evening! I am going to draw your chart.'

Anna nodded. Her face was still very red.

'I draw a chart each time I make a new acquaintance,' Mrs. Wells went on. 'We shall have a glorious good time, finding out what is in store for you. And I have brought home a pie for our supper: the best that can be had in all Dunedin. Isn't that fine?'

'Very fine,' said Anna, dropping her gaze to the floor.

Mrs. Wells seemed not to notice her discomfort. 'Now,' she said, sitting down at the settee, and drawing the largest book towards her. 'What is the date of your birthday, my dear?'

Anna told her.

Mrs. Wells drew back; she placed her hand over her heart. 'No!' she said.

'What?'

'How terribly odd!'

'What's odd?' said Anna, looking frightened.

'You have the same birthday as a young man I just ...' Lydia Wells trailed off, and then said, suddenly, 'How old are you, Miss Wetherell?'

'One-and-twenty.'

'One-and-twenty! And you were born in Sydney?'

'Yes, ma'am.'

'Right in town?'

'Yes.'

Lydia Wells's expression was marvellous. 'You don't happen to know the precise hour of your birth, do you?'

'I believe I was born at night,' said Anna, blushing again. 'That's the way my mother tells it. But I don't know the precise hour.'

'It is astonishing,' cried Mrs. Wells. 'I am astonished! The exact same birthday! Perhaps even beneath the very same sky!'

'I don't understand,' said Anna.

In a hushed tone of conspiracy, Lydia Wells explained. She spent her afternoons at a hotel upon George-street, where she gave astral predictions for a small fee. Her customers, for the most part, were young men about to make their fortunes on the goldfield. That afternoon—while Anna was enjoying her bath—she had given a reading to just such a man. The querent (so she described him) was *also* one-and-twenty, and had *also* been born in Sydney, upon the very same day as Anna!

Anna could not make sense of Mrs. Wells's exhilaration. 'What does it mean?' she said.

'What does it mean?' Lydia Wells's voice dropped to a whisper. 'It means that you may share a destiny, Miss Wetherell, with another soul!'

'Oh,' Anna said.

'You may have an astral soul-mate, whose path through life perfectly mirrors your own!'

Anna was not as impressed by this as Mrs. Wells might have hoped. 'Oh,' she said again.

'The phenomenon is very rare,' said Mrs. Wells.

'But I had a cousin with the same birthday as me,' Anna said, 'and we can't have shared a destiny, because he died.'

'It is not enough to share a day,' said Mrs. Wells. 'You must be born at the exact same *minute*—and at the exact same latitude and longitude: that is, under the exact same sky. Only then will your charts be identical. Even twins, you see, are born some minutes apart, and in the interim the skies have shifted a little, and the patterns have changed.'

'I don't know the exact minute I was born,' Anna said, frowning.

'Nor did he,' said Mrs. Wells, 'but I shall lay my money upon the fact that your charts are identical—for we know already that the two of you have something in common.'

'What?'

'*Me*,' said Mrs. Wells, triumphantly. 'On the twenty-seventh of April, 1865, you both arrived in Dunedin, and you both had your natal charts drawn by Mrs. Crosbie Wells!'

Anna brought her hand up to her throat. 'What?' she whispered. 'Mrs.—what?'

Lydia Wells continued with the same enthusiasm. 'And there are other correspondences! He was travelling alone, as you were, and he arrived this morning, as you did. Perhaps he made a friend by some accident of circumstances—quite as you did, when you met me!'

Anna was looking as though she might be sick.

'Edward is his name. Edward Sullivan. Oh, how I wish I had brought him back with me—how I wish I had known! Are you not *aching* to make his acquaintance?'

'Yes, ma'am,' she whispered.

'What an extraordinary thing,' said Lydia Wells, gazing at her. 'It is most extraordinary. I wonder what would happen, were you ever to meet.'

PART FIVE

Weight and Lucre

12 May 1865

45° 52' 0" S ∫ 170° 30' 0" E

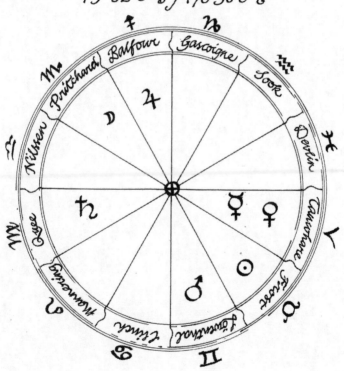

SILVER

In which Crosbie Wells makes a request; Lydia Wells is imprudent; and Anna Wetherell plays witness to a rather ugly scene.

The mortification that Anna Wetherell had suffered, upon discovering that the man whom she had entertained upon the afternoon of her arrival in Dunedin had been, in fact, the master of the house, only intensified over the weeks that followed. Crosbie Wells was now installed in the rear bedroom of number 35, Cumberland-street, and as a consequence they saw each other every day.

Anna Wetherell was painfully and perpetually conscious of the impression she created, and as a consequence of this abiding self-consciousness, her self-regard was critical to the point of fantasy. She had the inconsolable sense that there was something visible about her own character that she herself could not see, and this anxiety could not be appeased by persuasion, proof, or compliment. She was certain, when in conversation, that the unvoiced conclusions formed by those around her were both censorious and wholly apt, and because the shame she felt at this imagined censure was very real, she sought all the harder to court the good opinion of those whom she met—feeling, as she did so, that even in this project her intentions were all too visible.

Believing herself uniformly criticised, Anna would have been very surprised to learn that the impressions others formed of her were not uniform in the slightest. The artless simplicity with which she most often spoke indicated to some that she possessed an alarming store of private opinions, the frank expression of which was even more alarmingly unfeminine; to others, her speech was entirely without artifice, and refreshing for that reason. Likewise her tendency to squint upon the world was suggestive to some of fearfulness, and to others, of calculation. To Crosbie Wells, she was merely, and very simply, sweet: he found her frequent embarrassments very amusing, and had told her so more than once.

'You'd do well in a camp, my girl,' he said. 'A breath of fresh air, is what you are. Unspoiled. Nothing worse than a woman with a ready answer. Nothing worse than a woman who's forgotten how to blush.'

Lydia Wells—a woman with a great many ready answers, and who very rarely blushed—had been only infrequently seen at number 35, Cumberland-street since her husband's unexpected return. She left the house in the late morning, and often did not return until the dusk, when the gambling parlour opened for the night. Wells, in her absence, kept mostly to the first-floor boudoir, where the decanters on the sideboard were refilled daily. Drink softened him. Anna found that she liked him best in the late afternoons, when three or four glasses of whisky had turned him pensive, but not yet sad.

Wells, it transpired, had no desire to return to the fields at Dunstan. Anna learned that he had made a strike of significant value the previous year, and he now desired to put that fortune to some use: he was considering various investments, both in Dunedin and beyond, and he spent a great deal of time poring over the local papers, comparing prices for gold, and tracking the rise and fall of various stocks. 'Would you fancy me better as a flockmaster, or as a timber man, Miss Wetherell?' he said, and then laughed very freely at her rising blush.

Whether Mrs. Wells comprehended Anna's embarrassment, or the reason for it, Anna did not know. The older woman was no less warm, and her speech no less conspiratorial, than at the scene of their first meeting; but it seemed to Anna that her manner had acquired a glaze of distance—as though she were steeling herself, privately, for an impending breach in their relations. With her husband, she was similarly removed. Whenever Wells spoke she simply gazed at him, unsmiling, and then turned the conversation to an unrelated theme. Anna was devastated by these subtle tokens of displeasure, and as a consequence she strove to secure her mistress's good opinion all the more. By now she knew very well that she had been, as Crosbie Wells had phrased it, 'euchred', but any energy that she might have expended in confronting her mistress on the matter of the fictitious Elizabeth Mackay (who was never again mentioned) had been directed, instead, into a disgusted self-admonishment, and a belief, privately held, that she alone could make restitution for what she and Crosbie Wells had done.

The operations of the House of Many Wishes had been revealed to Anna gently, and in degrees. The morning after her arrival in Dunedin, Mrs. Wells had showed her the downstairs parlour, and Anna had loved it at once: the velvet booths, the green glass bottles behind the bar, the card tables, the gambling wheel, the small confessional with the saloon-style doors where Mrs. Wells occasionally told fortunes for a fee. In the daylight the room seemed somehow preserved: the motes of dust, trapped in the shafts of light that fell through the high windows, had a patient, potent feel. Anna was quite awed. At her mistress's invitation, she stepped onto the podium, and spun the gambling wheel—watching the rubber needle clack, clack, clack, towards the jackpot, only to fall, with a final clack, past it.

Mrs. Wells did not invite her to attend the evening parties immediately. From her bedroom window Anna watched the men arrive, stepping down from carriages, removing their gloves, striding up the walk to rap upon the door; soon afterwards, cigar smoke began to seep through the floorboards into her room, lending a spicy, acrid tint to the air, and turning the lamplight grey. By nine the hum of conversation had thickened to a hubbub, punctuated by snatches of laughter and applause. Anna could hear only what came up through the floor, though every time someone opened the door to the downstairs passage the noise intensified, and she could make out individual voices. Her curiosity was roused to the point of disconsolation, and after several days she inquired of Mrs. Wells, very tentatively and with much apology, whether she might be permitted to tend bar. She now did so every night, though Mrs. Wells had imposed two regulations: none of the patrons was to address her directly, and she was not permitted to dance.

'She's raising your value,' Wells explained. 'The longer they have to wait, the more you'll fetch, when it comes time to go to market.'

'Oh, Crosbie,' snapped Mrs. Wells. 'Nobody's going to market. Don't be absurd.'

'Farming,' said Wells. 'There's an enterprise. I could be a farmer—and you could be my farmer wife.' To Anna he said, 'It's quite all right. My old ma was a whore, God rest her.'

'He's only trying to frighten you,' said Mrs. Wells. 'Don't listen to him.'

'I'm not frightened,' said Anna.

'She's not frightened,' said Wells.

'There's nothing to be frightened about,' said Mrs. Wells.

In fact Anna thought the dancing girls quite marvellous. They were incurious about her, calling her either 'Sydney' or 'Port Jackson' if they addressed her at all, but she did not possess pride enough to be offended; in any case, their air of weary indifference was a sophistication to which she privately aspired. They brought up the drinks orders from the gentlemen playing cards, and waited as Anna set out the glasses and poured. 'A dash and a splash,' they said, for whisky-and-water, and 'a hard dash', for whisky poured neat. When the drinks were poured, they slid the tray onto their hip, or hoisted it high above their heads, and sashayed back through the crowd, leaving behind them the powdery-sickly scent of greasepaint and perfume.

On the 12th of May the inhabitants of number 35, Cumberland-street rose early. The House of Many Wishes was to host a party that evening in honour of naval officers and 'gentlemen with marine connexions', and there was much to be done in preparation for this grand event. Mrs. Wells had hired a fiddler, and put in an order at the store for lemons, spruce liquor, rum, and several hundred yards of rope, which she planned to cut into lengths and plait, so as to adorn each table with a knotted wreath as a centrepiece.

'I shall make the first wreath, as a template,' she said to Anna, 'and you can do the rest this afternoon: I will guide you through the steps, and show you how to tuck the ends away.'

'Waste of a good Manila line,' said Wells.

Mrs. Wells continued as if he had not spoken. 'The wreaths look quite arresting, I think; one can never over-decorate at a themed event. If there is any rope left over, we can it pin up behind the bar.'

They were eating breakfast together—an infrequent occasion, for it was rare that Wells rose before noon, and Mrs. Wells had usually quit the place by the time Anna woke. Mrs. Wells seemed nervous; perhaps she was fearful for the success of the party.

'They will look marvellous,' Anna said.

'What's next?' said Wells, who was out of humour. 'A party for diggers—with a riffle-box on each table, and a tailrace from the bar? "In honour of the common man", you could say. "A party for the unremarkable man. Gentlemen with no connexions whatsoever." There's a theme.'

'Have you had enough toast, Anna?' said Mrs. Wells.

'Yes, ma'am,' said Anna.

'One of tonight's guests is a decorated man,' Mrs. Wells went on, changing the subject. 'How about that? I think it will be the first time that I have played hostess to a naval hero. We shall have to ask him all about it—shan't we, Anna?'

'Yes,' said Anna.

'Captain Raxworthy is his name. He has a Victoria Cross; I do hope he wears it. Pass the butter, please.'

Wells passed the butter. After a moment he said, 'Have you today's *Witness*?'

'Yes, I read it already; there was nothing of consequence to report,' said Mrs. Wells. 'Friday papers are always light on the news.'

'Where is it?' said Wells. 'The paper.'

'Oh—I burned it,' said Mrs. Wells.

Wells stared at her. 'It's still morning,' he said.

'I am quite aware that it is still the morning, Crosbie!' she said, giving a little laugh. 'I used it to light the fire in my bedroom, that's all.'

'It's nine o'clock,' Wells complained. 'You don't burn today's paper at nine o'clock. Not when I haven't even seen it yet. I'll have to go out and buy another.'

'Save your sixpence,' said Mrs. Wells. 'It was nothing but gossip. Nothing to report—I've told you.' She glanced at the carriage clock—the second time she had done so in as many minutes, Anna observed.

'I like a bit of gossip,' said Wells. 'Anyway, you know that I'm looking at making an investment. How am I supposed to keep up with the stocks, without the paper?'

'Yes, well, it's done now, and it won't hurt you to wait until to-morrow. Have you had enough toast, Anna?'

Anna frowned slightly: Mrs. Wells had asked her this already. 'Yes, ma'am.'

'Good,' said Mrs. Wells. She was tapping her foot. 'What fun we shall have, tonight! I love to look forward to a party. And naval men are so high-spirited. And terribly good storytellers. Their stories are never dull.'

Wells was sulking. 'You know I spend my mornings with the paper. I do it every day.'

'You can catch up on the *Leader*,' said Mrs. Wells. 'Or last week's *Lyttelton Times*; it's on my writing desk.'

'Why didn't you burn that, then?'

'Oh, I don't know, Crosbie!' snapped Mrs. Wells. 'I'm sure it won't do you any harm to occupy yourself in some other way. Read a settler's pamphlet. I have a store of them on the bureau down-stairs.'

Wells drained his coffee and set his cup down with a clatter. 'I need the key to the safe,' he announced.

It seemed to Anna that Mrs. Wells stiffened slightly. She did not look at her husband, but concentrated on buttering her toast; after a moment, she said, 'Why is that?'

'What do you mean, why? I want to look at my dust.'

'We had agreed to wait until a more prudent time to sell,' said Mrs. Wells.

'I'm not selling anything. I just want to take stock of my affairs, that's all. Go through my papers.'

'I'd hardly call them "papers",' said Mrs. Wells, laughing slightly. 'What else?'

'Oh—you make it sound so grand, that's all.'

'My miner's right. That's a paper.'

'What need could you possibly have for your miner's right?'

He was scowling. 'What is this—a royal inquisition?'

'Of course not.'

'It's what they are,' said Wells. 'Papers. And there's a letter in there I'd like to read over.'

'Oh, come,' said Mrs. Wells. 'You must have read that thing a thousand times, Crosbie. Even I know its every phrasing by heart! *"Dear Boy—you do not know me—"*'

Wells brought his fist down on the table, causing all of the crockery to jump. 'Shut your mouth,' he said.

'Crosbie!' said Mrs. Wells, in shock.

'There's sport and then there's sporting,' said Wells. 'You just crossed over.'

For a moment, it seemed as though Mrs. Wells were about to make a retort, but she thought better of it. She dabbed her mouth with a napkin, regaining composure. 'Forgive me,' she said.

'Forgiveness doesn't cut it. I want the key.'

She tried to laugh again. 'Really, Crosbie; today is not the day. Not with the naval party this evening—and so much to organise. Let us put it off until to-morrow. We can sit down together, you and me—'

'I'm not putting it off until to-morrow,' said Wells. 'Give me the key.'

She rose from the table. 'I'm afraid you've heard my final word on the matter,' she said. 'Excuse me.'

'Excuse *me*—I'm afraid *you* haven't heard *mine*,' said Wells. He pushed his chair back from the table and rose also. 'Where is it—on your necklace?'

She edged around the table away from him. 'In actual fact, it is in a safe box at the bank,' she said. 'I don't keep a copy at home. If you wait just a—'

'Rot,' said Wells. 'It's on your necklace.'

She took another step away from him, seeming, for the first time, alarmed. 'Please, Crosbie; don't cause a scene.'

He advanced upon her. 'Give it.'

She tried to smile, but her mouth trembled. 'Crosbie,' she said again, 'be reasonable. We have—'

'Give it to me.'

'You are causing a scene.'

'I'll cause a bigger scene than this. Give it up.'

She tried to make for the door, but he was too fast: his hands shot out, and grabbed her. She twisted her body away—and for a moment they struggled—and then Wells, scrabbling with one hand at her bodice, found what he was looking for: a thin silver chain, from which a fat silver key was dangling. He wrenched it out, gathering the key in his fist, and tried to snap the chain. It tore at her neck, and would not break: she cried out. He tried again, more sharply. She was beating his chest with her fists. Grunting, he fought to restrain her, still with the chain wrapped around his fist. He tore at her neck again. 'Crosbie,' she gasped, '*Crosbie.*' At last it broke, and the key was in his hand; she gave a sob. At once he turned, panting slightly, and went to the safe. He fitted the key into the lock, rattling the handle several times before the mechanism clicked, and then the heavy door swung open.

The safe was empty.

'Where's my money?' said Crosbie Wells.

Mrs. Wells swayed, her hands cupped around her neck. Her eyes were filled with tears. 'If you calm down just a moment,' she said, 'I can explain.'

'Who needs calming?' said Wells. 'I asked a simple question, that's all. Where's my bonanza?'

'Now, Crosbie, listen,' said Mrs. Wells. 'I can get it back—the bonanza. I only put it away for a while. Somewhere safe. I can get it back for you, but not until to-morrow. All right? Tonight there are a great many distinguished gentlemen coming to the house, and I haven't the time to—to go to—to where I've hidden it. There's just too much to do.'

'Where are my papers?' said Wells. 'My miner's right. My birth certificate. The letter from my father.'

'They're with the bonanza.'

'Are they, now. And where is that?'

'I can't tell you.'

'Why not, Mrs. Wells?'

'It's complicated,' she said.

'I would imagine it is.'

'I can get them back for you.'

'Can you?'

'To-morrow. After the party.'

'Why not today? Why not this morning?'

'You can stop hectoring me,' she said, flaring up. 'I simply can't manage it today. You'll have to wait until to-morrow.'

'You're asking for time,' said Wells. 'I wonder why.'

'Crosbie, the party,' she said.

Wells looked at her for a long moment. Then he crossed the room and pulled sharply upon the bell-rope. The maid Lucy appeared within moments.

'Lucy,' said Wells, 'go on down to George-street and pick me up a copy of today's *Otago Witness*. Mrs. Wells appears to have burned our copy, by mistake.'

GOLD

The fit of whimsical good humour that had prompted Emery Staines, on the afternoon of his arrival in Dunedin, to commission a natal chart from Mrs. Lydia Wells, medium, spiritist, had been only intensified by the forecast itself, which, being uniformly providential, had put him in such high spirits that he felt inclined to celebrate. He had awoken the next morning with a terrible headache and a guilty sensation of indebtedness; upon applying to the hotelier he discovered, to his alarm, that he was in debt to the house to the tune of eight pounds, having put up a fortnight's stipend on a game of brag, only to lose every penny of it, and five pounds more. The circumstances under which he had become so grossly indebted were somewhat hazy in his memory, and he begged the hotelier for a cup of coffee on credit so that he might sit awhile and consider how best to proceed. This request was granted, and he was still sitting at the bar some three quarters of an hour later when Francis Carver appeared, sponsorship papers in hand.

Carver made his offer in plain speech and without preamble. He would provide enough capital to furnish Staines with a miner's right, a swag, and a ticket to the nearest payable goldfield; he added, casually, that he would also be happy to pay any debts that

Staines might have incurred in Dunedin since his arrival the previous day. In return, Staines would agree to sign over half-shares of
his first claim, with dividends in perpetuity, and this income would
be routed back to Carver's account in Dunedin by private mail.

Emery Staines knew at once that he had been played for a fool.
He remembered enough of the early hours of the previous evening
to know that Carver had been excessively solicitous of him, ensuring that his bets were always matched, his company was always
lively, and his glass was always filled. He also had the shadowy sense
that the gambling debt had been imposed upon him in some way,
for his weakness for cards was of a very ordinary, cheerful sort, and
he had never before thrown away such a large sum of money in a
single evening. But he was amused that he had been swindled so
soon after his adventure began, and his amusement led him to feel
a kind of affection for Carver, as one feels affection for a crafty
opponent in chess. He decided to chalk the whole business up to
experience, and accepted Carver's terms of sponsorship with characteristic good humour; but he resolved, privately, to be more
vigilant in the future. To have been bested once was diverting, but
he swore that he would not be bested a second time.

Staines was not a terribly good judge of character. He loved to
be enchanted, and so was very often drawn to persons whose
manner was suggestive of tragedy, romance, or myth. If he suspected that there was a strain of something very dastardly in
Carver, he conceived of that quality only in the most fanciful, piratical sense; had he pursued this impression, he would have found
only that it delighted him. Carver was more than twenty years
Staines's senior, and was as brawny and dark as Staines was slight
and fair. He held himself in the manner of one ready to inflict
damage at any moment, spoke gruffly, and very rarely smiled.
Staines thought him wonderful.

Once the contract had been signed, Carver's manner became
gruffer still. Otago, he said, was past its prime as a goldfield. Staines
would do much better to make for the new-built town of Hokitika
in the West, where, as rumour had it, a man could make his fortune
in a single day. The Hokitika landing was notoriously treacherous,

however, and two steamers had been wrecked already upon the bar: for this reason Carver insisted that Staines make the passage to the West Coast under sail rather than under steam. If Staines would consent to accompany him firstly to the customhouse, secondly to the outfitter's on Princes-street, and thirdly to the Reserve Bank, their arrangement could be finalised by noon. Staines did consent, and within three hours he was in possession of a miner's right, a swag, and a ticket to Hokitika upon the schooner *Blanche*, which was not due to depart Port Chalmers until the morning of the 13th of May.

Over the two weeks that followed Staines and Carver saw a great deal of one another. Carver had a month of shore leave while the barque upon which he worked was refitted and recaulked; he took his lodging, as Staines also did, at the Hawthorn Hotel on George-street. They very often breakfasted together, and occasionally Staines accompanied Carver in his chores and appointments around the city, chattering all the while. Carver did not discourage this, and although he communicated little beyond a repressed and constant anxiety, Staines flattered himself that his company was a gratifying and much-needed diversion.

Emery Staines knew very well that he created a singular impression in the minds of all those whom he met. This knowledge had become, over time, an expectation, as a consequence of which, his singularity had become even more pronounced. His manner showed a curious mixture of longing and enthusiasm, which is to say that his enthusiasms were always of a wistful sort, and his longings, always enthusiastic. He was delighted by things of an improbable or impractical nature, which he sought out with the open-hearted gladness of a child at play. When he spoke, he did so originally, and with an idealistic agony that was enough to make all but the most rigid of his critics smile; when he was silent, one had the sense, watching him, that his imagination was nevertheless usefully occupied, for he often sighed, or nodded, as though in agreement with an interlocutor whom no one else could see.

His disposition to be sunny was, it seemed, unshakeable; however this attitude had not been formed in consultation with any moral code. In general his beliefs were intuitively rather than scrupulously held, and he was not selective in choosing his society—feeling, in his intuitive way, that it was the duty of every thinking man to expose himself to a great range of characters, situations, and points of view. He had read extensively, and although he favoured the Romantics above all others, and never tired of discussing the properties of the sublime, he was by no means a strict disciple of that school, or indeed, of any school at all. A solitary, unsupervised childhood, spent for the most part in his father's library, had prepared Emery Staines for a great many possible lives without ever preferring one. He might just as soon be found in morning dress debating Cicero and Seneca as in boots and woollen trousers, ascending a mountain in search of a view, and in both cases he was bound to be enjoying himself a great deal.

On his twenty-first birthday, he was asked where he wished to go in the world, to which he immediately responded 'Otago'—knowing that the rushes in Victoria had abated, and having long been enamoured of the idea of the prospector's life, which he conceived of in terms quixotic and alchemical. He saw the metal shining, unseen, undiscovered, upon some lonely beach of some uncharted land; he saw the moon rising full and yellow over the open sea; he saw himself riding on horseback through the shallows of a creek, and sleeping on the bare earth, and running water through a wooden cradle, and twining digger's dough around a stick to bake above the embers of a fire. What a fine thing it would be, he thought, to be able to say that one's fortune was older than all the ages of men and history; to say that one had chanced upon it, had plucked it from the earth with one's own bare hands.

His request was granted: passage was duly bought upon the steamer *Fortunate Wind*, bound for Port Chalmers. On the day of his departure his father advised him to keep his wits about him, to practise kindness, and to come home once he had seen enough of the world to know his place in it. Foreign travel, he said, was the very best of educations, and it was a gentleman's duty to see and understand the world. Once they had shaken hands, he presented young Staines with an envelope of paper money, advised him not to spend it all at once, and bid him good morning, quite as if the boy were simply stepping out for a stroll, and would be back in time for dinner.

'What does he do for a living?' said Carver.

'He's a magistrate,' said Staines.

'A good one?'

The boy sighed, throwing his head back a little. 'Oh ... yes, I suppose he is good. How do I paint a picture of my father? He is a reading man, and he is well regarded in his profession, but he has a queer sense of things. For example: he tells me my inheritance comprises only his fiddle and his shaving razor—saying that if a man is to make his way in the world, all he needs is a good shave and the means to make some music. I believe he's written it into his will like that, and portioned everything else to my mother. He's a little peculiar.'

'Hm,' said Carver.

They were breakfasting together at the Hawthorn Hotel for the very last time. The next morning, the schooner *Blanche* was scheduled to depart for Hokitika, with the barque *Godspeed*, newly caulked and fitted, bound for Melbourne some hours later.

'Do you know,' Staines added, as he tapped his egg, 'that is the first time since my landing in Dunedin that somebody has asked me what my father does for a living; but I have been asked where I shall make my fortune no less than a dozen times, and I have been offered all kinds of sponsorship, and I couldn't tell you how many times I've been asked what I mean to do with my pile, once I have amassed a competence! What a curious phrase that is—a "competence". It seems to sell the notion awfully short.'

'Yes,' said Carver, his eyes on the *Otago Witness*.

'Are you expecting someone?' said Staines.

'What?' said Carver, without looking up.

'Only that you've been reading the shipping news for the past ten minutes,' said Staines, 'and you've hardly touched your breakfast.'

'I'm not waiting for anyone,' said Carver. He turned a page of the paper and began to read the goldfields correspondence.

They lapsed into silence for a time. Carver kept his eyes upon the paper; Staines finished his egg. Just as Staines was about to rise from the table and excuse himself, the front door opened, and a penny postman walked in. 'Mr. Francis Carver,' he called.

'That's me,' said Carver, raising his hand.

He tore open the envelope and scanned the paper briefly. Staines could see, through the thinness of the paper, that the letter was composed of only one line of script.

'I do hope it's not bad news,' he said.

Carver did not move for a long moment; then he crushed the paper in his hand and tossed it sideways into the fire. He reached into his pocket for a penny, and once the postman had scurried away, he turned to Staines and said, 'What would you say to a gold sovereign?'

'I don't believe I've ever addressed one before,' said Staines.

Carver stared at him.

'Do you need help?' Staines said.

'Yes. Come with me.'

Staines followed his sponsor up the stairs. He waited while Carver unlocked the door to his private quarters, and then stepped into the room after him. He had never set foot in Carver's room before. It was much larger than his own, but similarly furnished. It still held the musty, bodily smell of sleep: Carver's bedclothes were twisted in the centre of the mattress. In the centre of the room was an iron-strapped chest. Pasted to the lid was a yellow bill of lading:

BEARER ALISTAIR LAUDERBACK
SHIPPER DANFORTH SHIPPING
CARRIER GODSPEED

'I need you to watch over this,' said Carver.

'What's inside it?'

'Don't you mind what's inside it. I just need you to watch over it, until I come back. Two hours, maybe. Three hours. I've got some business up town. There'd be a sovereign in it for you.'

Staines raised his eyebrows. 'A whole sovereign—to watch a chest for three hours? Whatever for?'

'You'd be doing me a favour,' said Carver. 'I don't forget a favour.'

'It must be terribly valuable,' said Staines.

'To me it is,' said Carver. 'Do you want the job?'

'Well—all right,' said Staines, smiling. 'As a favour. I'd be glad.'

'You'd best have a pistol,' said Carver, going to the bureau.

Staines was so astonished he laughed. 'A pistol?' he said.

Carver found a single-loading revolver, snapped open the breech, and peered into it. Then he nodded, snapped it back together, and passed it to Staines.

'Should I expect to use this?' said Staines, turning it over.

'No,' said Carver. 'Just wave it about, if anyone walks in.'

'Wave it about?'

'Yes.'

'Who's going to walk in?'

'Nobody,' said Carver. 'Nobody's going to walk in.'

'What's in the trunk?' Staines said again. 'I really think I ought to know. I can keep a secret.'

Carver shook his head. 'The less you know, the better.'

'It's not a matter of knowing less; it's a matter of knowing nothing at all! Am I some kind of an accomplice? Is this some kind of a heist? Truly, Mr. Carver, I can keep a secret.'

'There's another thing,' said Carver. 'Just for today, my name isn't Carver. It's Wells. Francis Wells. If anyone comes asking, I'm Francis Wells. Never mind why.'

'Good Lord,' said the boy.

'What?'

'Only that you're being dreadfully mysterious.'

Carver rounded on him suddenly. 'If you run off, it'll be a breach of our contract. I'll have grounds to seek recompense in whatever way I see fit.'

'I won't run off,' said the boy.

'You keep your eye on that trunk until I get back, and you'll walk away with a pound coin. What's my name?'

'Mr. Wells,' said the boy.

'Mind you remember it. I'll be three hours.'

Once Carver had gone, Staines set the pistol on the bureau, the muzzle faced away, and knelt to look at the trunk. The hasp had been padlocked. He lifted the padlock to examine the profile of the keyhole—observing, to his satisfaction, that the lock was of a very simple design. Smiling suddenly, he took out his clasp knife, unfolded the blade, and fitted the point of his knife into the keyhole. He jimmied it for nearly a minute before the mechanism clicked.

COPPER

*In which Wells's suspicion deepens; Anna becomes alarmed;
and a package arrives at the House of Many Wishes,
addressed to Mrs. Wells.*

Crosbie Wells read the *Otago Witness* from top to bottom, and in
perfect silence. When he was done, he shook out the paper, folded
it crisply along the seam, and rose from his chair. Mrs. Wells was
sitting opposite him. Her expression was cold. He advanced upon
her, tossed the paper into her lap—she flinched slightly—and then
placed his hands on his hips, surveying her.

'Arrivals caught my eye,' he said.

She said nothing.

'One name in particular. *Active* is the name of the steamer.
Arriving at the top of the tide. When's that? Sundown.'

Still she said nothing.

'Seems odd you didn't tell me,' said Wells. 'I've only been waiting—what—twelve years? Twelve years, and no reply. All these
years I've been in the highlands, digging for gold. Now the man
himself arrives in town, and you knew about it, and you made no
mention. No: it's worse than keeping quiet. You set out to deceive
me. You burned the paper in the bloody stove. That's a black
deceit, Mrs. Wells. That's a cold deceit.'

She kept composure. 'You are quite right,' she said. 'I should
never have deceived you.'

'Why did you burn it?'

'I didn't want the news to spoil the party,' she said. 'If you'd discovered he was arriving tonight, you might have gone down to the quay—and he might have spurned you—and you might have become upset.'

'But that is just what has me confounded, Mrs. Wells.'

'What?' she said.

'The party.'

'It's only a party.'

'Is it?'

'Crosbie,' she said, 'don't be foolish. If you go looking for a conspiracy, you will find a conspiracy. It's a party, and that's all.'

'"Gentlemen with marine connexions",' said Wells. 'Naval types. What do you care about naval types?'

'I care that they are men of considerable rank and influence, because I care about my business, and the party will do my business good. Everybody loves a theme. It lends a flavour to an evening.'

'Does Mr. Alistair Lauderback get an invite, I wonder?'

'Of course not,' said Mrs. Wells. 'Why should I invite *him*? I've never set eyes upon the man in my life. And anyway—as I told you—it was precisely because I didn't want you to get upset that I burned this morning's paper. You're very right: I shouldn't have, and I'm very sorry to have deceived you. But the party, I assure you, is only a party.'

'What about the bonanza?' said Wells. 'And my papers? How do they fit in?'

'I'm afraid they don't,' said Mrs. Wells.

'I have half a mind to take a stroll down to Port Chalmers,' said Wells. 'Around sundown. Nice night for it. Bit chilly, perhaps.'

'By all means do so,' said Mrs. Wells.

'I'd miss the party, of course.'

'That would be a shame.'

'Would it?'

She sighed. 'Crosbie,' she said, 'you are being very silly.'

He leaned closer. 'Where's my money, Mrs. Wells?'

'It is in a vault at the Reserve.'

'Liar. Where is it?'

'It is in a vault at the Reserve.'

'Where is it?'

'It is in a vault at the Reserve.'

'*Liar.*'

'Insulting me,' said Mrs. Wells, 'will not—'

He slapped her, hard, across the face. 'You're a dirty liar,' he said, 'a rotten thief, and I'll call you worse before I'm through with you.'

A perfect silence followed. Mrs. Wells did not reach up to touch her cheek where he had slapped her. She stayed perfectly still—and Wells, suddenly vexed, turned away from her, and crossed the room to where the decanters and bottles were set out upon their silver tray. He poured himself a measure, drank it off, and then poured another. Anna kept her eyes on her rope wreath, which was becoming misshapen under her trembling fingers. She did not dare to look at Mrs. Wells.

Just then there came a swift knock at the front door, and then a voice, calling through the slot: 'Package for Mrs. Lydia Wells.'

Mrs. Wells made to rise, but Crosbie Wells shouted, '*No.*' He had become very flushed. 'You'll stay right there.' He pointed to Anna with the hand that held his glass. 'You,' he said. 'Go and see.'

She did. It was a bottle, pint-sized, wrapped in brown paper, and stamped with the matrix of the chemist on George-street.

'What is it?' called Wells, from the floor above.

'It's a package from the chemist's,' Anna called back.

There was a pause, and then Mrs. Wells said, speaking clearly, 'Oh: I know what it is. It's hair tonic. I placed the order last week.'

Anna returned upstairs, the package in her hand.

'Hair tonic,' said Wells.

'Really, Crosbie,' said Mrs. Wells, 'you are becoming paranoiac.' To Anna she said, 'You can put it in my room. On the nightstand, please.'

Wells was still glaring at his wife. 'You're not going anywhere,' he said. 'Not until you tell me the truth. You're staying right here—where I can keep an eye on you.'

'In that case I look forward to a very dull afternoon,' said Mrs. Wells.

Crosbie Wells responded angrily to this, and they continued bickering. Anna, glad to have a reason to exit, took the paper-wrapped bottle across the hallway and into the hushed darkness of Mrs. Wells's bedroom. She went to set the bottle down upon the nightstand when something caught her eye: a bottle of hair tonic, half the size of the bottle she was holding in her hand, and not at all alike in its dimensions. Frowning, she looked at the package in her hand—and then, on a sudden impulse, slid her finger underneath the wrapping, and sloughed the paper away. The bottle was unmarked; it had been corked, and the cork had been sealed with candle wax. She held it up to the light. It contained a thick, treacly liquid, the colour of rust.

'Laudanum,' she whispered.

WU XING

In which Emery Staines does Carver's bidding, and Ah Sook is effectively deceived.

Staines held the gown up to the light, wondering. There were five in total—one of orange silk, and the rest of muslin—but apart from them the chest was quite empty. What was the meaning of it? Perhaps they held some sentimental value for Carver ... but if so, then why had he outfitted Staines with a pistol, in watching over them? Perhaps they were stolen goods, though they did not look at all valuable ... or perhaps, Staines thought, Carver was going mad. This thought cheered him; he chuckled aloud, and then, shaking his head, returned the gowns to the chest.

There came a sharp knock upon the door.

'Who is it?' said Staines.

There was no answer; but after a moment the caller knocked again.

'Who's there?' said Staines again.

The caller knocked a third time, more urgently. Staines felt his heartbeat quicken. He went to the bureau and picked up the pistol. Holding it flat against his thigh, he walked to the door, unlatched it, and opened it a crack.

'Yes?' he said.

In the hallway stood a Chinese man of perhaps thirty years, dressed in a tunic and a woollen cape.

'Francis Carver,' he said.

Staines remembered Carver's instruction. 'I'm afraid there's nobody of that name here,' he said. 'You don't mean Mr. Wells— Francis Wells?'

The Chinese man shook his head. 'Carver,' he said. He produced a piece of paper from his breast, and held it out. Curious, Staines took it. It was a letter from the Cockatoo Island Penitentiary, thanking Mr. Yongsheng for his inquiry, and informing him that upon his release from gaol Mr. Francis Carver had sailed for Dunedin, New Zealand, upon the steamer *Sparta*. At the bottom of the letter—and in a much darker shade of ink—somebody else had written *Hawthorn Hotel*. Staines stared at the note for a long time. He had not known that Carver was a former convict; the news was striking to him, but he found, upon further reflection, that it was not wholly unexpected. At last, and with great reluctance, he shook his head. 'I'm sorry,' he said, passing the piece of paper back to the Chinese man, and smiling apologetically. 'There's nobody named Francis Carver here.'

IRON

In which Crosbie Wells puts two and two together.

An interminable afternoon passed at number 35, Cumberland-street. Together Anna and Mrs. Wells had constructed fifteen plaited wreaths, which they installed in the parlour downstairs, watched over by Wells, who drank steadily and did not speak. Behind the rostrum they had fashioned a 'mainsail' made from an oar and a white bedsheet, which they reefed with lengths of twine; behind the bar they had hung a string of admiralty flags. Once the wreaths had been arranged, they set out lemons and spruce liquor, trimmed candles, polished glasses, refilled the spirit lamps, and dusted—stretching each task out as long as possible, and taking every excuse to make small trips upstairs and to the kitchen, so as to avoid the dreadful silence of embittered company.

They were interrupted, a little after four, by a brisk knock at the front door.

'Who can that be?' said Mrs. Wells, frowning. 'The girls aren't due until seven. I never receive callers at this time of day.'

'I'll answer it,' said Wells.

On the threshold was a Chinese man in a tunic and a woollen cape.

'What have we got here?' said Wells. '*You're* not a naval man.'

'Good afternoon,' said the other. 'I look for Francis Carver.'

'What?' said Crosbie Wells.

'I look for Francis Carver.'

'Carver, you said?'

'Yes.'

'Never heard of him.'

'He live here,' said the Chinese man.

'Afraid he doesn't, mate. This place belongs to a Mrs. Lydia Wells. I'm her lucky husband. Crosbie's my name.'

'Not Carver?'

'I don't know anyone by the name of Carver,' said Wells.

'Francis Carver,' the man supplied.

'Can't help you, I'm afraid.'

The Chinese man frowned. He reached into his pocket and withdrew the same letter that he had presented to Emery Staines, some two hours prior. He handed it to Wells. The words *Hawthorn Hotel* had been scratched out; beneath them, in a different hand, someone had written *House of Many Wishes, Cumb'd-st.*

'Someone gave you this address?' said Wells.

'Yes,' said the Chinese man.

'Who?' said Wells.

'Harbourmaster,' said the Chinese man.

'I'm afraid the Harbourmaster's put you wrong, mate,' said Wells, passing the letter back to him. 'There's no one of that name at this address. What's it you're wanting him for?'

'To bring to justice,' said the Chinese man.

'Justice,' said Wells, grinning. 'All right. Well, I hope he deserves it. Good luck.'

He closed the door—and then suddenly stopped, his hand upon the frame. Suddenly he turned, and, taking the steps two at a time, returned upstairs to the boudoir, where the *Otago Witness* was folded upon the bureau. He snatched it up. After scanning the columns for several minutes he saw, listed among the projected departures for the following day:

Jetty Four: Godspeed, *dest. Port Phillip. Crew comprising J. RAX-WORTHY (captain), P. LOGAN (mate), H. PETERSEN (second mate), J. DRAFFIN (steward), M. DEWEY (cook), W. COLLINS (boatswain), E. COLE, M. JERISON, C. SOLBERG, F. CARVER (seamen).*

'Who was that at the door?'

Anna had come up behind him. She was holding a brass candleholder in each hand. 'Was it Lucy, back from the store? Mrs. Wells is wanting her.'

'It was a Chinaman,' said Wells.

'What did he want?'

'He was looking for someone.'

'Who?'

Wells studied her. 'Do you know anyone who ever did time at Cockatoo Island?'

'No.'

'Nor do I.'

'That's hard labour,' said Anna. 'Cockatoo is hard labour.'

'Not for the faint-hearted, I should think.'

'Who was he looking for?'

Wells hesitated, but then he said, 'Ever heard of a Francis Carver?'

'No.'

'Ever seen an ex-con?'

'How would I know one?'

'I suppose you wouldn't,' said Wells.

There was a pause; presently she said, 'Should I tell Mrs. Wells?'

'No,' said Wells. 'Stop a moment.'

'I was only supposed to come up for these,' said Anna, holding up the candleholders. 'I really ought to be getting back.'

Wells rolled the *Otago Witness* into a tube. 'She's a heartless woman, Anna. Not a bone of true feeling in Mrs. Lydia Wells: it's profit or bust. She's taken my money, and she'll take yours, and we'll be ruined—both of us. We'll be ruined.'

'Yes,' Anna said, miserably. 'I know.'

He brandished the rolled paper. 'Do you know what this says? Man named Carver listed as a crewman on a private charter. Leaving on to-morrow's tide. A gentleman with a marine connexion, in other words.'

'I suppose that means he'll be at the party,' Anna said.

'And another thing: the master of the craft. Raxworthy.'

'Mrs. Wells mentioned him at breakfast,' Anna said.

'Indeed she did,' said Wells, striking the paper upon his leg. 'Everything's beginning to add up. Only I can't quite see it yet. The picture.'

'What's adding up?'

'All day,' he explained, 'I've been wondering one thing: what could *she* possibly want with my papers? My miner's right. My birth certificate. I've no doubt she lifted them, as she lifted the bonanza too; but she wouldn't bother with anything unless it could be put to some use, and what use for an old man's papers could she possibly have? None at all, I thought. In that case, she must have dispatched them somehow. Passed them on. But to whom? What kind of a man might have need for another man's papers? That's when it struck me. A man running from his past, I thought. A man with a tarnished name, who wants to start over with a better one. A man looking to put some chapter of his life behind him.'

Anna waited, frowning.

'Here's a d—n certainty,' said Wells, holding up the rolled paper like a sceptre. 'I don't know how, and I don't know why or what for, but I'll tell you here and now, little Anna, that tonight I'll be making the acquaintance of a Mr. Francis Carver.'

TIN

In which Carver takes an alias, and Lauderback signs his name.

'Wells,' said Lauderback, coming up short.

'Good evening,' said Francis Carver. He was sitting in a chair facing the gangway. There was a pistol in his hand.

'What is this?' said Lauderback.

'Do come in.'

'What is this?' he said again.

'A conversation,' said Carver.

'But what's it about?'

'I recommend that you step into the cabin, Mr. Lauderback.'

'Why?'

Carver said nothing, but the muzzle of the pistol twitched a little.

'I haven't laid my eyes on her since last we spoke,' Lauderback said. 'Upon my honour. When you told me to step away, Mr. Wells, I stepped away. I've been in Akaroa these nine months past. I only just arrived back in town tonight—just now, in fact; this very moment. I've kept away—just as you asked of me.'

'Says you,' said Carver.

'Yes, says me! Do you doubt my word?'

'No.'

'Then what do you mean—says me?'

'Only that on paper it says different.'

Lauderback faltered. 'I have not the slightest idea what paper you're talking about,' he said after a moment, 'I shall hazard to guess, however, that you are alluding in some way to the Danforth receipt.'

'I am,' said Carver.

With a swift look over his shoulder, Lauderback stepped into the cabin and pulled the hatch closed behind him. 'All right,' he said, when he was inside. 'Something's cooking. Or cooked.'

'Yes,' said Carver.

'Is this about Crosbie?' said Lauderback. 'Is this something to do with Crosbie?'

'You know,' said Carver, 'I worry about old Crosbie.'

He did not go on. After a moment Lauderback said, in a fearful voice, 'Do you?'

'Yes, I do,' said Carver. 'One of these days, that poor man is going to drink himself to death.'

Lauderback had begun to sweat. 'Where's Raxworthy?' he said.

'Getting drunk on Cumberland-street, I believe.'

'What about Danforth?'

'The same,' said Carver.

'They're in your pocket, are they?'

'No,' said Carver. 'You are.'

TAR

In which Carver comes to finish the deed; Crosbie Wells
makes a counter-attack; and the laudanum takes effect.

When Francis Carver rapped upon the door of number 35 Cumberland-street some two hours later, the naval party was in full swing: he could hear rhythmic clapping and the stamp of feet, and raucous laughter. He knocked again, more sharply. The maid Lucy appeared after his fourth knock; once she saw that it was Carver, she invited him inside, and flew down the passage to summon Mrs. Wells.

'Oh, Francis,' she said, when she saw him. 'Thank heavens.'

'It came off,' said Carver. He patted his breast, where the deed of sale lay folded in his inside pocket. 'Everything signed, effective instant. I've got a boy keeping an eye on him—Lauderback—until the morning. But I doubt he'll do any talking.'

'You didn't hurt him, did you?'

'No: he's feeling very sorry for himself, that's all. What's been happening here?'

She dropped her voice to a whisper. 'Well,' she said, 'after that awful brawl this morning—and a wretched day—we've had the most incredible luck. Crosbie's taken up with my new girl. Perhaps he thought to spite me, by taking her to bed ... but I couldn't have thought of anything I wanted more, than to have the two of them out of the way for the evening. The moment they were alone, I sent up Lucy with a fresh decanter.'

'Laced?'

'Of course.'

'How strong?'

'I used half the bottle.'

'Anything come of it?'

'I haven't heard a peep,' she said. 'Not a sound.'

'All right,' he said. 'I'll go up. I'll need fifteen minutes.'

'He's very angry. He knows about the gold—as I told you—and he found out about Lauderback arriving. You must be careful.'

'I won't need to be careful if he's sauced.'

'You won't shoot him—will you, Francis?'

'Don't worry your head about it.'

'I want to know.'

'I'll tap him on the head,' said Carver, 'that's all.'

'Not here!'

'No—not here. I'll take him someplace else.'

'The girl's still up there, you know. She might have gone down with him. I don't know.'

'I'll deal with her. I'll tell her to leave before anything happens. Don't you worry.'

'What should I do?'

'Get on back to the party. Pour Raxworthy another drink.'

Φ

Carver put his ear to the door; hearing nothing, he eased the door handle, very quietly. It opened without a sound. The room was dark, but in the chamber beyond, a small lamp was burning. There was someone in the bed: the bedclothes were mounded, and he could see a splash of dark hair on the pillow. Keeping his hand on his hip, he moved slowly forward, into the room.

He heard the whistle of something heavy slicing through air, and almost turned—but before he could do so, he was clubbed on the back of the head, and he stumbled to his knees. He whirled about, his hand closing around the grip of his pistol—but Crosbie Wells swung the poker again, cracking him across the knuckles, and again, across the jaw. Carver recoiled in pain. He brought his hands up, instinctively, to protect his face. A fourth strike made contact with his elbow, and a fifth cracked him just above his temple. He collapsed sideways, suddenly weak, upon the floor.

Wells darted forward and tried to yank the pistol from the man's belt with his free hand. Carver grabbed his arm, and they tussled a moment, until Wells cracked him another time across the side of the head with the poker. He lost his grip, and fell back. At last Wells gained purchase on the pistol, and wrenched it free; once it was in his hand he cocked it, levelled it in Carver's face, and stood a moment, panting. Carver grunted, bringing his arms up to his face. He was dazed: the lights in the room had begun to pulse.

'Who are you?'

Carver peered at him. There was blood in his mouth.

Wells was holding the pistol in his left hand, and the poker in his right. He raised the poker a little, threatening to strike again. 'Are you Francis Carver? You speak or I'll shoot you dead. Is your name Carver?'

'Used to be,' said Carver.

'What is it now?'

Carver grinned at him, showing bloody teeth. 'Crosbie Wells,' he said.

Wells came closer. 'I'll kill you,' he said.

'Go ahead,' said Carver, and closed his eyes.

Wells raised the poker again. 'Where's my bonanza?'

'Gone.'

'Where is it, I said?'

'Shipped offshore.'

'Who shipped it? You?'

Carver opened his eyes. 'No,' he said. 'You did.'

Wells brought the poker down. It glanced off the other man's temple—and Carver fainted away. Wells waited a moment, to see if he was shamming, but the faint was plainly real: he was showing the whites of his eyes, and one of his hands was twitching.

Wells laid the poker down, out of Carver's reach. He transferred the pistol to his right hand. Tentatively, he pushed the muzzle of the pistol into Carver's cheek, and nudged him. The man's head rolled back.

'Is he dead?' said Anna, from the doorway. Her face was white.

'No. He's breathing.'

With his left hand Wells took his bowie knife from his boot, and unsheathed the blade.

'Will you kill him?' Anna whispered.

'No.'

'What will you do?'

Wells did not answer. Using his pistol to keep Carver's head steady, he inserted the point of his knife just below the outer corner of Carver's left eye. Blood welled up instantly, running thickly down his cheek. With a sudden flick of his wrist, Wells twisted the blade, slicing from his eye down to his jaw. He leaped back—but Carver did not wake; he only gurgled. His cheek was now awash with blood; it was running off the line of his jaw and soaking into his collar.

'C for Carver,' said Wells quietly, staring at him. 'You're a man to remember now, Francis Carver. You're the man with the scar.'

He looked up and caught Anna's eye. Her hands were over her mouth; she looked horrified. He jerked his chin at the decanter on the sideboard. 'Have a drink,' he said. 'You'll be asleep in a minute. Only you'd better do it fast.'

Anna glanced at the decanter. The laudanum had darkened the whisky very slightly, giving the liquid a coppery glow. 'How much?' she said.

'As much as you can stomach,' said Wells. 'And then lie down on your side—not your back. You'll drown on your own self, otherwise.'

'How long will it take?'

'No time at all,' said Crosbie Wells. He wiped his knife on the carpet, sheathed it, and then stood, ready to leave.

'Wait.' Anna ran into the bedroom. A moment later she returned with the gold nugget that he had first given her, the afternoon of their first encounter. 'Here,' she said, pressing it into his hands. 'Take it. You can use it to get away.'

MAKEWEIGHTS

In which Crosbie Wells asks for help; a customs agent becomes angry; and a bill of lading is recalled.

'Psst—Bill!'

The official looked up from his newspaper. 'Who's that?'

'It's Wells. Crosbie Wells.'

'Come out where I can see you.'

'Here.' He emerged into the light, palms up.

'What are you doing—creeping about in the dark?'

Wells took another step forward. Still with his palms up, he said, 'I need a favour.'

'Oh?'

'I need to get on a ship first light.'

The official's eyes narrowed. 'Where you bound?'

'It doesn't matter,' said Wells. 'Anywhere. I just need to go quiet.'

'What's in it for me?'

Wells opened his left fist: there, against his palm, was the nugget that Anna had returned to him. The official looked at it, making a mental estimation of its worth, and then said, 'What about the law?'

'I'm on side with the law,' said Wells.

'Who's on your heels, then?'

'Man named Carver,' said Wells.

'What's he got on you?'

'My papers,' said Wells. 'And a fortune. He lifted a fortune from my safe.'

'When did you ever make a fortune?'

'At Dunstan,' said Wells. 'Maybe a year ago. Fifteen months.'

'You kept bloody quiet about it.'

'Course I did. I never told a soul but Lydia.'

The man laughed. 'That was your first mistake, then.'

'No,' said Wells, 'my last.'

They looked at each other. Presently Bill said, 'Might not be worth it. For me.'

'I go aboard tonight, hide away, sail first thing. You keep this nugget, and I keep my life. That's all. You don't need to get me on board—just tell me which ship is leaving, and turn a blind eye as I walk past.'

The official wavered. He put aside his paper and leaned forward to check the schedule pinned above his desk. 'There's a schooner bound for Hokitika leaving at first light,' he said after a moment. 'The *Blanche*.'

'You tell me where she's anchored,' said Wells. 'Give me a window. That's all I'm asking, Bill.'

The official pursed his lips, considering it. He turned back to the schedule, as though the best course of action might somehow present itself to him in writing. Then his gaze sharpened, and he said, 'Hang on—Wells!'

'What?'

'This inventory says it was authorised by you.'

Frowning, Wells stepped forward. 'Let me see.'

But Bill pulled the log towards him, away from Wells's reach. 'There's a crate going to Melbourne,' he said, scanning the entry. 'It's been loaded on *Godspeed*—and you signed for it.' He looked up, suddenly angry. 'What's all this about?'

'I don't know,' said Wells. 'Can I see it?'

'You're spinning me a line,' said Bill.

'I'm not,' said Wells. 'I never signed that bloody thing.'

'Your money's in that crate,' said Bill. 'You're sending your colour offshore, while you hop over to Hokitika to cover your tracks, and when it's all safe and sound, you'll sally across the Tasman and make yourself over, tax-free.'

'No,' said Wells. 'That wasn't me.'

The official flapped his hand, disgustedly. 'Go on. Keep your bloody nugget. I don't want a part in any scheme.'

Wells said nothing for a moment. He stared at the dark shapes of the ships at anchor, the broken needles of light upon the water, the hanging lanterns, squeaking in the wind. Then he said, speaking carefully, 'That wasn't me who signed.'

Bill scowled. 'No,' he said. 'Don't start. You won't take me for a fool.'

'My certificates,' said Wells. 'My miner's right—my papers—everything. It was all in the safe at Cumberland-street. I swear to you. This man Carver. He's an ex-convict. Served time at Cockatoo. He took it all. I have nothing but the shirt on my back, Bill. Francis Carver is using my name.'

Bill shook his head. 'No,' he said. 'That crate's not going offshore. I'm pulling the inventory, first thing in the morning.'

'Pull it now,' said Wells. 'I'll take the crate with me—to Hokitika. Nothing's going offshore that way, is it? Everything's legal that way.'

The official looked down at the inventory, and then back at Wells. 'I don't want a part in any racket.'

'You'll have done nothing wrong,' said Wells. 'Nothing at all. It's only evasion of duty if you send it offshore. I'll even sign for it. I'll sign anything you like.'

Bill did not say anything for a long moment, and Wells knew that he was considering it. 'I can't get it on the *Blanche*,' he said at last. 'She's sailing first light, and Parrish has signed off on the cargo already. There isn't time.'

'Send it on after, then. I'll sign a transfer right now. I'm begging you.'

'No need to beg,' said Bill, frowning.

Wells came forward and placed the nugget on the desk. For a moment the thing seemed to shiver, like the needle of a compass.

Bill looked at the nugget for a long moment. Then he looked up, and said, 'No. You keep your nugget, Crosbie Wells. I don't want a part in any scheme.'

PART SIX

The Widow and the Weeds

18 June 1865

42° 43' 0" S ∫ 170° 58' 0" E

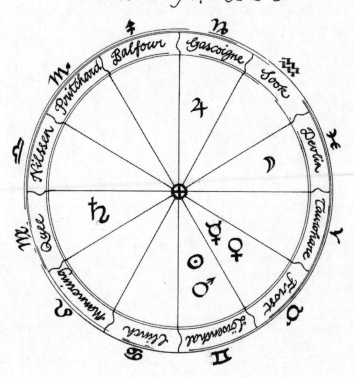

FIXED EARTH

In which Emery Staines takes his metal to the bank; Crosbie Wells proposes a deceit; and Staines begins to doubt his first impression, much too late.

Emery Staines was yet to make a strike in Hokitika. He had not yet found a patch of ground he liked well enough to stake, or indeed, a company he liked well enough to join. He had amassed a small 'competence' in dust, but the pile had been collected variously, from beaches both north and south of the river, and from small gullies on the far side of the Hokitika Gorge: it was an inconstant yield, of which the greater portion by far had already disappeared. Staines tended towards profligacy whenever the time and money spent were his very own: he far preferred to sleep and dine in the society of others than to do so alone in his tent beneath the stars, the romance of which did not endure, he discovered, past the first experience. He had not been prepared for the bitterness of the West Canterbury winter, and was very frequently driven indoors by the rain; with poor weather as his excuse, he drank wine and ate salt beef and played at cards every evening, venturing out the next morning to fill his handkerchief anew. Had it not been for his agreement with Francis Carver, he might have continued in this haphazard way indefinitely, which is to say, following a two-part pattern of excess and recovery; but he had not forgotten the conditions of his sponsorship, under which he would shortly be obliged to 'throw down an anchor', as the diggers termed it, and invest.

On the morning of the 18th of June Staines woke early. He had spent the night at a flophouse in Kaniere, a long, low clapboard shanty with a lean-to kitchen and hammocks strung in tiers. There was a damp chill in the air; as he dressed, his breath showed white. Outside, he paid a halfpenny for a plate of porridge, ladled from a steaming vat, and ate standing, gazing eastward to where the ridge of the high Alps formed a crisp silhouette against the winter sky. When the plate was clean he returned it to the hatch, tipped his hat to his fellows, and set off for Hokitika, where he intended to make an appointment with a gold buyer preparatory to purchasing a claim.

As he came around the river to the spit he perceived a ship make its stately approach into the neck of the harbour; it glided into the roadstead and seemed to hover, broadside to the river, in the deep water on the far side of the bar. Staines admired the craft as he walked around the long curve of the quay. It was a handsome three-masted affair, none too large, with a figurehead carved in the shape of an eagle, its beak wide and screaming, its wings outspread. There was a woman at the portside rail: from this distance Staines could not make out her face, much less her expression, but he supposed that she was lost in a reverie, for she stood very still, both hands gripping the rail, her skirts whipping about her legs, the strings of her bonnet slapping at her breast. He wondered what preoccupied her—whether she was absorbed in a memory, a scene recalled, or in a forecast, something that she wished for, something that she feared.

At the Reserve Bank he produced his kid pouch of dust, and, at the banker's request, surrendered its contents to be examined and weighed. The valuation took some time, but the eventual price offered was a good one, and Staines left the building with a paper note made out for twenty pounds folded in his vest pocket, against his heart.

'Stop you there, lad.'

Staines turned. On the steps of the bank, just rising, was a sandy-haired man, perhaps fifty in age. His skin was very weathered, and his nose very red. He sported a patchy week-old beard, the stubble of which was quite white.

'Can I help you?' said Staines.

'You can answer me a couple of questions,' said the man. 'Here's the first. Are you a Company man?'

'I'm not a Company man.'

'All right. Here's the second. Honesty or loyalty?'

'Excuse me?'

'Honesty or loyalty,' said the man. 'Which do you value higher?'

'Is this a trick?'

'A genuine inquiry. If you wouldn't mind.'

'Well,' said Staines, frowning slightly, 'that's very difficult to say—which to value higher. Honesty or loyalty. From a certain point of view one might say that honesty is a kind of loyalty—a loyalty to the truth ... though one would hardly call loyalty a kind of honesty! I suppose that when it came down to it—if I had to choose between being dishonest but loyal, or being disloyal but honest—I'd rather stand by my men, or by my country, or by my family, than by the truth. So I suppose I'd say loyalty ... in myself. But in others ... in the case of others, I feel quite differently. I'd much prefer an honest friend to a friend who was merely loyal to me; and I'd much rather *be* loyal to an honest friend than to a sycophant. Let's say that my answer is conditional: in myself, I value loyalty; in others, honesty.'

'That's good,' said the man. 'That's very good.'

'Is it?' said Staines, smiling now. 'Have I passed some kind of a test?'

'Almost,' said the man. 'I'm after a favour. In good faith—and on your terms. Look here—'

He reached into his pocket and withdrew a nugget, around the size of a short cigar. He held it up, so that it caught the light. 'Nice, isn't it?'

'Very nice,' said Staines, but he was no longer smiling.

The man continued. 'Picked this up in the Clutha Valley. Otago way. Been carrying it about for a month—two months—but I'm wanting to turn it into land, you see—got my eye on a patch of land—and the land agent won't touch anything but paper money. Here's the problem. I've been robbed. Got no proof of my own identity. My papers, my miner's right. Everything's gone. So I can't bank this nugget on my own accord.'

'Ah,' said Staines.

'What I'm after is a favour. You take this nugget into the bank. Say it's your own—that you found it, on Crown land. Change it into paper money for me. It wouldn't take you half an hour, all up. You can name your price.'

'I see,' said Staines, uncertainly. He hovered a moment. 'Surely,' he said, 'you might simply explain your situation to the fellows inside. You might tell them that you've been robbed—as you've just told me.'

'I can't do that,' said the man.

'There are always records,' said Staines. 'Even if you don't have your papers, they'll have other ways of tracking who you are. The shipping news and so forth.'

The man shook his head. 'I was on an Otago certificate,' he said, 'and I never came through the customhouse when I arrived. There's no record of me here.'

'Oh,' said Staines—who was beginning to feel very uncomfortable.

The man stepped forward. 'I'm telling you a straight story, lad. The nugget's mine. Picked it up in the Clutha Valley. I'll sketch the place for you. I'll draw you a bloody map. My story's straight.'

Staines looked again at the nugget. 'Can anyone vouch for you?' he said.

'I haven't gone waving this about,' the man snapped, shaking his fist. 'Where would be the sense in that? I've been robbed already; I won't be robbed again. There's only one soul on earth who's touched this piece besides me. Young woman by the name of Anna Wetherell. *She'd* vouch for the truth of what I'm telling you; but she's in Dunedin, isn't she, and I can't stand about waiting for the post.'

The name Anna Wetherell meant nothing to Staines, and he registered it only dimly as he considered the best way to withdraw. The man's story was not at all convincing (it seemed obvious to Staines that the nugget had been stolen, and that the thief, fearing capture, was now attempting to cover his tracks by employing an innocent third man to turn the evidence to untraceable cash) and his countenance did not reassure. He had the weary, bloodshot look of a man long since ruined by drink; even at a distance of several paces, Staines could smell yesterday's liquor on his clothes and on his breath. Stalling for time, he said, 'Land agent, did you say?'

The man nodded. 'There's an acreage I'm keen on. Arahura way. Timber, that's the business. I'm through with chasing gold. I had a fortune, and now it's gone, and that's the end of the game as far as I'm concerned. Timber—that's honest work.'

'What's your name?'

'Crosbie Wells,' said the man.

Staines paused. 'Wells?' he said.

'That's right,' said the man. Suddenly he scowled. 'What's it to you?'

Staines was remembering the strange injunction that Francis Carver had given him at the Hawthorn Hotel in George-street, one month prior: 'Just for today,' he had said, 'my name's Wells. Francis Wells.'

'*Crosbie* Wells,' Staines repeated now.

'That's it,' said Wells, still scowling. 'No middle name, no nick-name, no alias, nothing but plain old Crosbie Wells, ever since the day I was born. Can't prove it, of course. Can't prove a d—ned thing, without my papers.'

Staines hesitated again. After a moment he put out his hand and said, 'Emery Staines.'

Wells transferred the nugget to his other hand, and they shook. 'Care to name your price, Mr. Staines? I'd be very much obliged to you.'

'Listen,' said Staines suddenly. 'You don't happen to know—I mean, forgive me, but—you don't happen to know a man named Francis Carver?'

For he still did not know the full story of what had happened on the day before he left Dunedin—where Carver had gone that after-noon; why he had chosen to assume an alias; why he had afforded such importance to a small chest containing nothing but five unre-markable gowns.

Wells had stiffened. He said, in a voice that was newly hard, 'Why?'

'I'm very sorry,' said Staines. 'Perhaps it's of no consequence. I only ask because—well, about a month ago, a man named Carver took on your surname—just for an afternoon—and never told me why or what for.'

Wells's hands had balled into fists. 'What's Carver to you?'

'I don't know him well,' said Staines, taking a step back. 'He stood me some money, that's all.'

'What kind of money? How much?'

'Eight pounds,' said Staines.

'What?'

'Eight,' said Staines, and then, again, 'Eight pounds.'

Wells advanced on him. 'Friend, is he?'

'Not in the least,' said Staines, stepping back again. 'I found out later that he was a con—that he'd served ten years, with labour—but it was too late by then; I'd signed.'

'Signed what?'

'A sponsorship agreement,' said Staines.

'And he signed in *my* name.'

'No,' said Staines, putting up his hands, 'he only used it—your name, I mean—but I don't know what for. Look, I'm ever so sorry to distress you—'

'He was the one,' said Crosbie Wells. 'He was the one who took my papers. Cheated me out of a pile in pure. Turned my own wife against me. He took my name, and my money, and he tried to take my life—only the job didn't come off, did it? I got out. I'm still here. Working for a pittance, and living hand to mouth, and keeping my head down, and looking over my shoulder every moment till I'm fairly driven mad. *This*'—he brandished the nugget—'is all I've got left.'

'Why do you not bring the law against him?' said Staines. 'All that sounds like evidence enough.'

Wells did not reply at once. Then he said, 'Where is he?'

'I believe he's in Dunedin still.'

'Are you sure about that?'

'As much as I can be,' said Staines. 'I've his address; I'm to write to him as soon as I make my first venture.'

'You're his *partner*.' Wells spat out the word.

'No: I'm obliged to him, that's all. He stood me eight pounds, and I'm to make him an investment, in return.'

'You're his partner. You're his man.'

'Look,' said Staines, alarmed again, 'whatever Mr. Carver's done to you, Mr. Wells—and whatever his reasons—I don't know anything about it. Truly. Why—if I'd known anything, I'd never have mentioned his name to you just now, would I? I'd have kept my mouth shut.'

Wells said nothing. They stared at one another, each searching the other's expression. Then Staines said, 'I'll do it. I'll take your nugget to the bank.'

MARS IN CANCER

In which Carver begins his search for Crosbie Wells; Edgar Clinch offers his services; and Anna Wetherell hardens her resolve.

Godspeed crossed the Hokitika bar at the highest point of the tide. It took Captain Carver the better part of an hour to negotiate the traffic in the river mouth, for several crafts were departing, and he was obliged to wait for a signal from Gibson Quay before he could approach the wharf; Anna Wetherell, standing alone on deck, had ample time to take a measure of the view. Hokitika was smaller than she had envisaged, and much more exposed. Compared with the city of Dunedin, which was tucked away down the long arm of the Otago Harbour, and enclosed on all sides by hills, Hokitika's proximity to the ocean seemed almost fearsome. To Anna the buildings had a grim, forsaken look, made somehow wretched by the strings of red and yellow bunting that crossed back and forth between the rooflines and the awnings of the waterfront hotels.

A sudden clanging directed her attention to the quay, where a ginger-haired man with a moustache was standing on the wharf, swinging a brass hand-bell, and shouting into the wind. He was plainly advertising something, but his litany of recommendations was quite inaudible beneath the peal of the bell, the mouth of which was big enough to admit a round of bread, and the clapper, as thick and heavy as a bar of bullion. It produced a dolorous, inexorable sound, muffled by the distance, and by the wind.

The journey from Dunedin had marked *Godspeed*'s inaugural voyage under the command of Francis Carver, who had been so incapacitated by the multiple injuries that he had incurred on the night of the 12th of May that he had failed to make *Godspeed*'s scheduled departure for Melbourne the following afternoon; he had missed, as a consequence, any opportunity to inform Captain Raxworthy that the ship's ownership had changed. Raxworthy was punctual by nature, and would not suffer the barque's departure to be delayed on account of a tardy crewman: he had sailed on schedule, his own severe headache notwithstanding, and after *Godspeed* left her anchor at Port Chalmers Carver could do nothing but wait for her return. He passed the next four weeks in convalescence, watched over by an anxious Mrs. Wells, who could not look upon his facial disfigurement without despair. The wound had been stitched, and the stitches since removed: it now formed an ugly pinkish weal, as thick as a length of sisal, and puckered at both ends. He touched the scar very often with his fingertips, and had taken to covering it with his hand when he spoke.

When *Godspeed* returned from Port Phillip on the 14th of June, Carver met with James Raxworthy to inform him that his tenure as captain had come to an end. The barque had been sold from under him, and by order of the ship's new owner, a Mr. Wells, Carver himself had been promoted to the captaincy, an honour that gave him the licence to disband Raxworthy's crew, and assemble his own. The meeting between Carver and his former captain was long, and not at all cordial; relations became further strained when Carver discovered that a certain item had been struck from *Godspeed*'s inventory one month ago. He appealed to Raxworthy, who only shrugged: as far as he could see, there had been no breach of regulation or protocol in the trunk's having been recalled. Carver's fury turned to anguish. He applied to the customhouse, and to all the shipping firms along the quay, and to all the doss-houses in the sailors' district. His inquiries turned up nothing. Poring over the shipping news of the *Otago Witness* later that evening, he discovered that, besides *Godspeed*, there had been only one departure from Port Chalmers on the 13th of May: the schooner *Blanche*, bound for Hokitika.

'It's hardly even a clue,' he said to Mrs. Wells, 'but I can't stand to do nothing. If I do nothing I'll go mad. I've still got his birth certificate, after all—and the miner's right. I'll say my name is Crosbie Wells, and I'll say I've lost a shipping crate. I'll offer a reward for its return.'

'But what about Crosbie himself?' said Mrs. Wells. 'There's a chance—'

'If I see him,' said Carver, 'I'll kill him.'

'Francis—'

'I'll kill him.'

'He will be expecting you to pursue him. He won't be caught off guard—not a second time.'

'Neither will I.'

The day before *Godspeed*'s departure, Anna Wetherell was summoned to the downstairs parlour, where she found Mrs. Wells waiting for her.

'Now that Mr. Carver has recovered his health,' said Mrs. Wells, 'I can turn my mind to less pressing matters, such as the matter of your future. You cannot remain in my household even a moment longer, Miss Wetherell, and you know the reason why.'

'Yes, ma'am,' Anna whispered.

'I might have turned a blind eye to your betrayal,' Mrs. Wells went on, 'and suffered in silence, as is a woman's lot; the violence brought upon Mr. Carver, however, I cannot ignore. Your alliance with my husband has passed beyond the realm of wickedness, and into the realm of evil. Mr. Carver has been permanently disfigured. Indeed he was lucky to have kept his life, given the severity of the injuries he sustained. He will bear that scar forever.'

'I was asleep,' said Anna. 'I didn't see any of it.'

'Where is Mr. Wells?'

'I don't know.'

'Are you telling me the truth, Miss Wetherell?'

'Yes,' she said. 'I swear.'

Mrs. Wells drew herself up. 'Mr. Carver sails to the West Coast tomorrow, as you know,' she said, changing the subject, 'and as it happens I have an acquaintance in a Hokitika man. Dick Mannering is his name. He will set you up in Hokitika as he sees fit: you will become a camp follower, as was your original ambition, and you and I will not cross paths again. I have taken the liberty of costing all of your expenses over the last two months, and passing the debt to him. I can see you are surprised. Perhaps you believe that liquor grows on trees. Do you believe that liquor grows on trees?'

'No, ma'am,' she whispered.

'Then it will not come as a surprise to you that your habit of drinking alone has cost me more than pennies, this month past.'

'No, ma'am.'

'Evidently you are not as stupid as you are wicked,' said Mrs. Wells, 'though given the scope and degree of your wickedness, this hardly signifies as an intellectual achievement. Mr. Mannering, I ought to inform you, is unmarried, so you are in no danger of bringing shame upon his household as you have done upon mine.'

Anna choked; she could not speak. When Mrs. Wells dismissed her she flew to the boudoir, went to her bureau, pulled the stopper from the decanter of laudanum-laced whisky and drank straight from the neck, in two desperate, wretched slugs. Then she threw herself upon her bed, and sobbed until the opiate took effect.

Anna knew very well what awaited her in Hokitika, but her guilt and self-reproach were such that she had steeled herself against all impending fates, as a body against a wind. She might have protested any or all of Mrs. Wells's arrangements; she might have fled in the night; she might have formed a plan of her own. But she was no longer in any doubt about the fact of her condition, and she knew that it would not be long before she began to show. She needed to quit Mrs. Wells's household as soon as possible, before the other woman guessed her secret, and she would do so by whatever method available to her.

A gull made a long, low pass down Gibson Quay; once it reached the spit it turned and began climbing on the updraft, circling back to make the pass again. Anna pulled her shawl tighter around her shoulders. By now *Godspeed* had received clearance to drop anchor. A line had been thrown ashore, and the sails were being furled and reefed at Carver's instruction; slowly, the barque rolled towards the wharf. A small crowd of stevedores had gathered to assist, and Anna, blinking suddenly, saw that several of them were pointing at her and talking behind their hands. When they saw that she was looking, they doffed their hats, and bowed, and laughed, hoisting up their trousers by the buckles of their belts. Anna flushed. Suddenly wretched, she crossed the deck to the starboard rail, gripped it with both hands, and, breathing deeply, looked out over the high shelf of the spit, to where the breakers threw up a fine mist of white, blurring the line of the horizon. She remained there until Carver, calling her name with a curt accent, bid her to descend to the quay; a Mr. Edgar Clinch, acting proprietor of the Gridiron Hotel, had made her an offer of lodging, which Carver had accepted on her behalf.

In which Crosbie Wells makes for the Arahura Valley, and the steamer Titania *is wrecked upon the bar.*

Wells's nugget, banked by Staines, fetched over a hundred pounds in cash money. While the buyer completed his evaluation, and the banker made his notes, Staines was interrogated from a great many quarters about the nugget's origin. He gave vague replies to these inquiries, waving his hand in an easterly direction, and mentioning general landmarks such as 'a gully' and 'a hill', but his attempts to downplay the yield were unsuccessful. When the nugget's value was chalked onto the board above the buyer's desk, the banker led a round of applause, and the diggers chanted his name.

'If you like, we could have it copied, before it's smelted down,' said the banker, Frost, as Staines made to depart. 'You could paint the copy gold, and keep it—or you could send it home to a sweet-heart, as a token. It's a handsome piece.'

'I don't need a replica,' said Staines. 'Thanks anyway.'

'You might want to remember it,' said Frost. 'Your luckiest day.'

'I hope my luckiest day is yet to come,' said Staines—prompting another round of applause, and more admiration, and propositions to 'go mates' from at least half a dozen men. By the time he had extracted himself from the crowd and returned outside, he felt more than a little annoyed.

'I have been declared the luckiest man in Hokitika,' he said, as he handed Crosbie Wells his envelope. 'I have been advised to keep hold of my luck, and to share my luck around, and to confess the secret of my luck, and I don't know what else. I fancy that the story you told me was not at all true, Mr. Wells; you simply knew what would happen to a man foolish enough to walk into the Reserve Bank with a nugget of that size at this hour of the day.'

Wells was grinning. 'The luckiest man in Hokitika,' he said. 'Quite an expectation. I trust you'll bear up.'

'I will do my best,' said the boy.

'Well, I'm very much obliged to you,' said Wells, thumbing through the paper notes quickly, and then tucking the envelope into his vest. 'The Arahura Valley is where I mean to buy. Some ten miles to the north. The river crosses the beach—you can't miss it. You're welcome any time, and for any reason.'

'I'll remember,' said Staines.

Wells paused. 'You still don't quite believe my story, do you, Mr. Staines?'

'I'm afraid I don't, Mr. Wells.'

'Maybe you'll spill the beans to your man Carver.'

'Carver's not my man.'

'But maybe you'll drop my name. Casual mention. Just to see.'

'I won't.'

'It would be as good as murder, Mr. Staines. He's got a score to settle. He wants me dead.'

'I can keep a secret,' said Staines. 'I won't tell anyone.'

'I believe it,' said Wells. He put out his hand. 'Good luck.'

'Yes—good luck.'

'Perhaps I'll be seeing you.'

'Perhaps you will.'

Staines remained on the steps of the Reserve Bank for a long time after Crosbie Wells stepped down into the street. He watched the other man thread through the crowd towards the land agent's office, where he mounted the steps, removed his hat, and stepped inside without a backwards glance. Fifteen minutes passed. Staines rested his elbows on the rail, and kept watching.

'Shipwreck—shipwreck—shipwreck on the bar!'

Staines watched the bellman approach. 'What's the name of the craft?' he called.

'The *Titania*,' said the bellman. 'A steamer. Run aground.'

Staines had never heard of the *Titania*. 'Where was she coming from?'

'Dunedin, by way of Auckland,' the bellman replied. When Staines nodded, dismissing him, he continued on: 'Shipwreck—shipwreck—shipwreck on the bar!'

At long last, the door of the land agency office opened, and two men walked out: Crosbie Wells, and a second man, presumably a land agent, who was putting his arms into his coat. They stood talking on the porch for several minutes; presently a small two-horse cab came clopping around the side of the building, and stopped to let Wells and the land agent climb aboard. Once they were seated, and the doors closed, the driver spoke to the horses, and the small vehicle clattered off to the north.

ACCIDENTAL DIGNITY

*In which two chance acquaintances are reunited, and Edgar
Clinch is less than pleased.*

Mr. Edgar Clinch proved a guide both solicitous and thorough.
During the short walk from Gibson Quay he maintained a constant
and richly detailed commentary upon everything they passed:
every shopfront, every warehouse, every vendor, every horse, every
trap, every pasted bill. Anna's responses were few, and barely
uttered; as they approached the Reserve Bank, however, she interrupted his chatter with a sudden exclamation of surprise.

'What is it?' said Clinch, alarmed.

Leaning against the porch railing was the golden-haired boy
from the *Fortunate Wind*—who was gazing at her with an expression
likewise incredulous.

'It's you!' he cried.

'Yes,' said Anna. 'Yes.'

'The albatrosses!'

'I remember.'

They regarded one another shyly.

'How good to see you again,' Anna said after a moment.

'It is perfectly serendipitous,' said the boy, descending the steps to
the street. 'Fancy that—us meeting a second time! Of course I have
wished for it, very much—but they were vain wishes; the kind one
makes in twilight states, you know, idly. I remember just what you

said, as we rounded the heads of the harbour—in the dawn light. "I should like to see him in a storm", you said. I have thought of it many times, since; it was the most delightfully original of speeches.'

Anna blushed at this: not only had she never heard herself described as an original before, she had certainly never supposed that her utterances qualified as 'speeches'. 'It was only a fancy,' she said.

Clinch was waiting to be introduced; he cleared his throat.

'Have you been in Hokitika long?' said the boy.

'I arrived this morning. Just now, in fact—we dropped anchor not an hour ago.'

'So recently!' The boy seemed even more astonished, as though her recent arrival meant that their chance reunion was even more remarkable to him.

'And you?' Anna said. 'Have you been here long?'

'I've been here over a month,' said the boy. He beamed suddenly. 'How good it is to see you—how very wonderful. It has been a great age since I have seen a familiar face.'

'Are you a—a member of the camp?' said Anna, blushing again.

'Yes; here to make my fortune, or at least, to chance upon it: I confess I do not quite understand the difference. Oh!' He snatched off his hat. 'How outrageously rude of me. I haven't introduced myself. Staines is my name. Emery Staines.'

Clinch used this opportunity to interject. 'And how do you like Hokitika, Mr. Staines?'

'I like it very well indeed,' replied the boy. 'It's a perfect hive of contradictions! There is a newspaper, and no coffee house in which to read it; there is a druggist for prescriptions, but one can never find a doctor, and the hospital barely deserves its name. The store is always running out of either boots or socks, but never both at once, and all the hotels along Revell-street only serve breakfast, though they do so at all hours of the day!'

Anna was smiling. She opened her mouth to reply, but Clinch cut across her.

'Gridiron does a hot dinner,' he said. 'We've a threepenny plate and a sixpenny plate—and the sixpenny comes with beer.'

'Which one is the Gridiron?' said Staines.

'Revell-street,' said Clinch, as if this destination were address enough.

Staines turned back to Anna. 'What has brought you to the Coast?' he said. 'Have you come at somebody's request? Are you to make your living here? Will you stay?'

Anna did not want to use Mannering's name. 'I mean to stay,' she said cautiously. 'I am to take my lodging at the Gridiron Hotel—at the kind request of Mr. Clinch.'

'That's me,' said Clinch, putting out his hand. 'Clinch. Edgar is my Christian name.'

'I am delighted to meet you,' said Staines, shaking his hand briefly; then, turning back to Anna, he said, 'I still don't know your name ... but perhaps I won't ask for it, just yet. Shall you keep it a secret—so that I have to make inquiries, and find you out?'

'Her name is Anna Wetherell,' said Clinch.

'Oh,' said the boy. His expression had suddenly given way to astonishment; he was looking at Anna very curiously, as though her name bore a significance that he could not, for some reason, articulate aloud.

'We'd best be getting on,' said Clinch.

He leaped aside. 'Oh—yes, of course. You'd best be getting on. A very good morning to you both.'

'It was very nice to see you again,' said Anna.

'May I call upon you?' said Staines. 'Once you're settled?'

Anna was surprised, and thanked him; she might have said more, but Clinch was already leading her away, seizing her hand where it was tucked beneath his elbow and drawing it, firmly, closer to his chest.

ARIES, RULED BY MARS

In which Francis Carver asks Te Rau Tauwhare for information; but Tauwhare, having not yet made the acquaintance of a Mr. Crosbie Wells, cannot help him.

The Maori man carried a greenstone club upon his hip, thrust through his belt in the way that one might wear a crop or a pistol. The club had been carved into the shape of a paddle, and polished to a shine: the stone was a rippled olive green, shot through with bursts of yellow, as if tiny garlands of kowhai had been melted and then pressed into glass.

Carver, having delivered his message, was about to bid the other man goodbye when the stone caught the light, and seemed suddenly to brighten; curious, he pointed at it, saying, 'What's that—a paddle?'

'*Patu pounamu,*' said Tauwhare.

'Let me see,' said Carver, holding out his hand. 'Let me hold it.'

Tauwhare took the club off his belt, but he did not hand it to the other man. He stood very still, staring at Carver, the club loose in his hand, and then suddenly, he leaped forward, and mimed jabbing Carver in the throat, and then in the chest; finally he raised the club up high above his shoulder, and brought it down, very slowly, stopping just before the weapon made contact with Carver's temple. 'Harder than steel,' he said.

'Is it?' said Carver. He had not flinched. 'Harder than steel?'

Tauwhare shrugged. He stepped back and thrust the club back into his belt; he appraised Carver for a long moment, his chin lifted, his jaw set, and then he smiled coldly, and turned away.

In which Benjamin Löwenthal perceives an error, and Staines acts upon a whim.

'Bother,' said Löwenthal. He was scowling at his forme—reading the text both right-to-left and backwards, for the type was both mirrored and reversed. 'I've got a widow.'

'A what?' said Staines, who had just entered the shop.

'It's called a widow. A typographical term. I have one too many words to fit into the column; when there's a word hanging over, that's a widow. Bother, bother, bother. I was in such a rush, this morning—I let a man pay for a two-inch advertisement without tallying his letters, and his notice won't fit into a two-inch square. Ah! I must put it aside, and come back with fresh eyes later: that is the only thing to do, when one is in a muddle. What can I do for you, Mr. Staines?' Löwenthal pushed the forme aside and, smiling, reached for a rag to wipe the ink from his fingers.

Staines explained that he had banked his competence that morning in exchange for cash. 'I was meaning to invest in a claim,' he explained, 'but I don't want to do that—not just yet. I'm still— well, I'm still of two minds about a number of things. I would like to know what's on offer in the camp instead. Hotels, dining halls, warehouses, shops . . . anything that's for sale.'

'Certainly,' said Löwenthal. He moved to the cabinet, opened the topmost drawer, and began to thumb through the files;

presently he extracted a piece of paper, and handed it to Staines. 'Here.'

Staines scanned the document. When he reached the bottom of the list, his expression slackened very slightly; in surprise, he looked up.

'The Gridiron,' he said.

Löwenthal spread his hands. 'It is as good a venture as any,' he said, 'Mr. Maxwell is the current owner; Mr. Clinch, the acting proprietor. Both are good men.'

'I'll take it,' said Staines.

'Oh?' said Löwenthal. 'Should I inform Mr. Maxwell that you would like to look it over?'

'I don't want to look it over,' said Staines. 'I want to buy it outright—and at once.'

SCORPIO, RULED BY MARS

In which Francis Carver makes an acquaintance at the Imperial Hotel.

Carver held little hope that the notice he had placed in the *West Coast Times* that morning would bear fruit. He doubted that anyone would be so foolish as to surrender a wanted trunk unopened, still less when a fifty-pound reward was offered for that trunk's return. The very best that he could hope for was that the trunk would be opened, the contents rifled, and the dresses presumed to be of sentimental value only, in which case the finder—if he or she had read the *Times*, and was aware of the reward offered—might surrender them; but that contingency, itself unlikely, depended upon the still more unlikely contingency that the trunk had been sent to West Canterbury, of all possible destinations in the world! No: the fact that it had been removed from *Godspeed*'s hold on the night of the 12th of May could mean only one thing: someone must have been aware of the colossal fortune the trunk contained. It would hardly have been recalled at the last minute, only to be shipped at hazard, elsewhere. If it had been Crosbie Wells who had recalled the trunk at the last moment— by far the most likely guess—then he would surely have quit the country as soon as he was able, using the gold to bribe the custom-house officials, or perhaps, paying another man for his papers or his name. The fortune was gone for good. Carver cursed aloud, and, to accent his frustration, slammed the base of his glass against the bar.

'Amen,' said the man nearest him.

Carver turned to glare at him, but the man was beckoning the bartender.

'Pour that man another drink,' he said. 'We'll both have another. On my tab.'

The bartender uncorked the brandy bottle and refilled Carver's glass.

'Pritchard's my name,' said the man, watching as the bartender poured.

Carver glanced at him. 'Carver,' he said.

'Took you for a sailor,' Pritchard said. 'Salt on your jacket.'

'Captain,' said Carver.

'Captain,' said Pritchard. 'Well, good on you. I never had a stomach for the sea. I might have gone back home, otherwise; only I'm put off by the thought of the journey. I'd rather die here than suffer that again. Arse end of the world, isn't it?'

Carver grunted, and they both drank.

'Captain, though,' said Pritchard presently. 'That's good.'

'And you?' said Carver.

'Chemist.'

Carver was surprised. 'Chemist?'

'Only one in town,' said Pritchard. 'A true original, that's what I am.'

They sat in silence for a time. When their glasses were empty Pritchard signalled again to the bartender, who refilled them both as before. Suddenly Carver rounded on him, and said, 'What have you got in the way of opium? Have you a ready supply?'

'Afraid I can't help,' Pritchard said, shaking his head. 'Nothing but tincture, that's all I've got, and it's poor. Weaker than whisky, twice the headache. You won't find anything south of the Grey. Not if you've a real thirst for it. Go north.'

'I'm not buying,' Carver said.

PART SEVEN

Domicile

28 July 1865

42°43'0"S ∫ 170°58'0"E

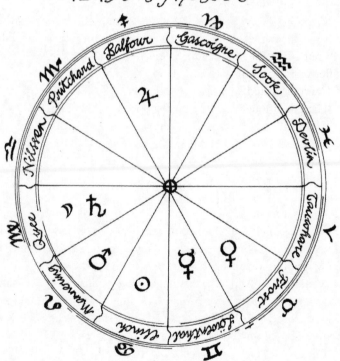

CANCER & THE MOON

*In which Edgar Clinch attempts to exercise his authority,
having deduced that Anna's recent decline in health owes
much to a new dependency both facilitated and encouraged by
her employer, Mannering; and Anna Wetherell, whose
obstinacy of feeling is more than a match for Clinch's own,
does not indulge him.*

'I don't have anything against the Chinese,' said Clinch. 'I just don't
like the look of it, that's all.'

'What does it matter what it looks like?'

'I don't like the feel of it. That's what I meant. The situation.'

Anna smoothed down the skirt of her dress—muslin, with a
cream skirt and a crocheted bust, one of five that she had purchased from the salvage vendors following the wreck of the *Titania*
some weeks ago. Two of the gowns had been speckled with black
mould, the kind that any amount of washing would not remove.
They were all very heavy, and the corsets, very fortified, tokens by
which she presumed them to be relics of an older, more rigid age.
The salvage man, as he wrapped the purchases in paper, had
informed her that, very strangely, the *Titania* had been conveying
no female passengers at all on the day she came to ground; stranger
still, nobody had come forward to claim this particular trunk after
the cargo had been recovered from the wreck. None of the shipping firms seemed to know the first thing about it. The bill of
lading had been rendered illegible by salt water, and the log did not

list the item by name. It was certainly a mystery, the salvage man concluded. He hoped that she would not come to any embarrassment or difficulty, in wearing them.

Clinch pressed on. 'How are you to keep your wits about you, when you're under? How are you to defend yourself, if—if—well, if you encounter something—untoward?'

Anna sighed. 'It isn't your concern.'

'It's my concern when I can see plain as day that he's got your advantage, and he's using you for ill.'

'He will always have my advantage, Mr. Clinch.'

Clinch was becoming upset. 'Where did it come from—your thirst? Answer me that! You just picked up a pipe, did you, and that was all it took? Why did you do it, if you weren't compelled by Mr. Mannering himself? He knows the way he wants you: without any room to move, that's how. Do you think I haven't seen it before, this method? The other girls won't touch the stuff. He knows that. But he tried it on you. He set you up. He took you there.'

'Edgar—'

'What?' said Clinch. 'What?'

'Please leave me be,' said Anna. 'I can't bear it.'

> *In which Emery Staines enjoys a long luncheon with the magnate Mannering, who, over the past month, has made a concerted effort to court his friendship, behaving mayorally, as he prefers to do, as though all goldfields triumphs are his to adjudicate, and his to commend.*

'You're a man who wears his success, Mr. Staines,' said Mannering. 'That's a uniform I like.'

'I'm afraid,' said Staines, 'my luck has been rather awfully exaggerated.'

'That's modesty talking. It was a hell of a find, you know, that nugget. I saw the banker's report. What did it fetch—a hundred pounds?'

'More or less,' said Staines, uncomfortably.

'And you picked it up in the gorge, you said!'

'Near the gorge,' Staines corrected. 'I can't remember exactly where.'

'Well, it was a piece of good luck, wherever it came from,' said Mannering. 'Will you finish up these mussels, or shall we move on to cheese?'

'Let's move on.'

'A hundred pounds!' said Mannering, as he signalled to the waiter to come and take their plates away. 'That's a d—n sight more than the price of the Gridiron Hotel, whatever you paid for the freehold. What did you pay?'

Staines winced. 'For the Gridiron?'

'Twenty pounds, was it?'

He could hardly dissemble. 'Twenty-five,' he said.

Mannering slapped the table. 'There you have it. You're sitting on a pile of ready money, and you haven't spent a single penny in four weeks. Why? What's your story?'

Staines did not answer immediately. 'I have always considered,' he said at last, 'that there is a great deal of difference between keeping one's own secret, and keeping a secret for another soul; so much so that I wish we had two words, that is, a word for a secret of one's own making, and a word for a secret that one did not make, and perhaps did not wish for, but has chosen to keep, all the same. I feel the same about love; that there is a world of difference between the love that one gives—or wants to give—and the love that one desires, or receives.'

They sat in silence for a moment. Then Mannering said, gruffly, 'What you're telling me is that this isn't the whole picture.'

'Luck is never the whole picture,' said Staines.

AQUARIUS & SATURN

In which Sook Yongsheng, having recently taken up residence in Kaniere Chinatown, journeys into Hokitika to outfit himself with various items of hardware, where he is observed by the gaoler George Shepard, known to him as the brother of the man he had been accused of having murdered, and also, as the husband of that man's true murderer, Margaret.

Margaret Shepard stood in the doorway of the hardware store, waiting for her husband to complete his purchases and pay; Sook Yongsheng, though not eight feet distant from her, was shielded from her view by the dry goods cabinet. Shepard, coming around the side of the cabinet, saw him first. He stopped at once, and his expression hardened; in a voice that was quite ordinary, however, he said,

'Margaret.'

'Yes, sir,' she whispered.

'Go back to the camp,' said Shepard, without taking his eyes from Sook Yongsheng. 'At once.'

She did not ask why; mutely she turned and fled. When the door had slammed shut behind her, Shepard's right hand moved, very slowly, to rest upon his holster. In his left hand he was holding a paper sack containing a roll of paper, two hinges, a ball of twine, and a box of bugle-headed nails. Sook Yongsheng was kneeling by the paraffin cans, making some kind of calculation on his fingers; he had placed his parcels beside him on the floor.

Shepard was aware, dimly, that the atmosphere in the store had become very still. From somewhere behind him someone said, 'Is there a problem, sir?'

Shepard did not answer at once. Then he said, 'I will take these.' He held up the paper sack, and waited; after a moment he heard whispering, and then tentative footsteps approaching, and then the sack was lifted from his hand. Nearly a minute passed. Sook Yongsheng continued counting; he did not look up. Then the same voice said, almost in a whisper, 'That will be a shilling sixpence, sir.'

'Charge it to the gaol-house,' Shepard said.

In which Alistair Lauderback, believing his half-brother Crosbie Wells to be the half-brother, on his mother's side, of the blackguard Francis Carver, and believing, consequently, that Crosbie Wells had been in some way complicit in the blackmail under which he, Lauderback, surrendered his beloved barque Godspeed, *is perplexed to receive a letter with a Hokitika postmark, the contents of which make clear that his apprehension has been quite false, a revelation that prompts him, after a great deal of solemn contemplation, to write a letter of his own.*

It would be an exaggeration to say that the renewed correspondence of Mr. Crosbie Wells comprised the sole reason for Alistair Lauderback's decision to run for the Westland seat in Parliament; the letter did serve, however, to tip the scales in the district's favour. Lauderback read the letter through six times, then, sighing, tossed it onto his desk, and lit his pipe.

West Canterbury. June 1865

Sir you will notice from my postmark that I am no longer a resident of the province of Otago but have 'upped my sticks' as the saying goes. You most likely have had little cause to venture west of the mountains so I shall tell you that West Canterbury is a world apart from the grasses of the South. The sunrise over the coastline is a scarlet marvel & the snowy peaks hold the colour of the sky. The bush is wet & tangled & the water very white. It is a lonely place though not quiet for the birdsong is constant & very pleasant for its constancy. As you may have guessed already I have put my former life behind me. I am estranged from my wife. I ought to tell you that I concealed much in my correspondence with you fearing that if you knew the bitter truth you might think less of me. I shall not trouble you with the details of my escape to this place for it is a sorry tale & one that saddens me to recall. I am twice bitten three times shy which is a less admirable ratio than other men can boast but suffice to say that I have learned my lesson. Enough upon that subject instead I shall speak about the present & the future. I mean to dig for gold no longer though West Canterbury is flush with colour & men are making fortunes every day. No I will not prospect & have my fortune stolen once again. Instead I shall try my hand at the timber trade. I have made a fine acquaintance of a Maori man Terou Tow-Faray. This name in his native tongue means 'The Hundred House of Years'. What poor names we British fellows have compared to these! I fancy it might be a line from a poem. Tow-Faray is a noble savage of the first degree & we are fast becoming friends. I confess it lifts my spirits to be in the companionship of men again.

    Yours &c,

    CROSBIE WELLS

In which Emery Staines pays a call upon Anna Wetherell at the Gridiron Hotel, where he begs her, after some preamble, to narrate her version of Crosbie Wells's escape; and Anna, made curious by the urgency and frankness of his appeal, sees no reason not to recount the tale in full.

Emery Staines did not recognise the dress that Anna was wearing as one of the five that he had been charged to safeguard, pistol in hand, at the Hawthorn Hotel on the afternoon of the 12th of May. It did strike him, when he first appraised her, that the garment fit her rather oddly—it had clearly been tailored for a woman much more buxom than she—but he put the thought aside just as quickly. They greeted one another warmly, but with mutual uncertainty, and after an awkward pause Anna invited him into the parlour, where they sat down on the straight-backed chairs that faced the hearth.

'Miss Wetherell,' said Staines at once, 'there's something I would like to ask you—something terribly impertinent—and you must knock me back at once if—if you don't want to give an answer—if you do not want to indulge me, I should say—for whatever reason at all.'

'Oh,' said Anna—and then she drew a breath, as if to steel herself, and turned her face away.

'What is it?' said Staines, drawing back.

Abruptly she rose from her chair and crossed the room; she stood a moment, breathing deeply, her face turned towards the wall. 'It's stupid,' she said thickly. 'It's stupid. Don't mind me. I'll be all right in a moment.'

Staines had risen also, in astonishment. 'Have I offended you?' he said. 'I'm terribly sorry if I have—but what is the matter? Whatever can be the matter?'

Anna wiped her face with her hand. 'It's nothing,' she said, still without turning. 'It came as a surprise, that's all—but I was stupid to think otherwise. It's not your fault.'

'What has come as a surprise?' said Staines. 'What's otherwise?'

'Only that you—'

'Yes? Please tell me—so that I can put it right. Please.'

She composed herself at last and turned. 'You may ask your question,' she said, managing a smile.

'Are you quite sure you're all right?'

'Quite sure,' Anna said. 'Please ask.'

'Well, all right,' said Staines. 'Here. It's about a man named Crosbie Wells.'

Anna's expression of misery dissolved into one of shock. '*Crosbie Wells?*'

'He is a mutual friend of ours, I think. At least—that is to say— he has my loyalty; I am under the impression that he also has yours.'

She did not reply; after squinting at him a moment she said, 'How do you know him?'

'I can't tell you that exactly,' said Staines. 'He charged me to keep it a secret—his whereabouts, I mean; and the circumstances of our having met. But he mentioned your name in connexion with a gold nugget, and a man named Francis Carver, and a robbery of some kind; and if you don't think me too impertinent—which I am; I know I am—then I should very much like to hear the whole story. I can't say that it's a matter of life or death, because it isn't, and I can't say that very much depends on my knowing, because really, nothing at all depends on it; except that I've gone into a kind of partnership with Mr. Carver—I was a fool to do it; I know that now—and I've got the sense, the awful sense, that I was wrong about him; that he's a villain after all.'

'Is he here?' she said. 'Crosbie. Is he in Hokitika?'

'I'm afraid I can't tell you that,' said Staines.

Her hands had moved to her belly. 'You don't need to tell me where he is,' she said. 'But I need you to take him a message. An important message—from me.'

THE ASCENDANT

In which Te Rau Tauwhare declines to mention Francis Carver's name to Crosbie Wells, much less to describe the circumstances of their brief interaction one month prior, an omission that owes in equal parts to a deeply private nature and to a certain cunning when it comes to financial profit; the next time he sees Francis Carver, Tauwhare thinks, he will make an easy shilling, perhaps more.

Crosbie Wells had bought four panes of glass for a quartered window, but he had yet to cut the hole, and set the sill; for the moment, the panes were propped against the wall, reflecting, faintly, the flickering lamplight, and the square grating of the stove.

'I knew a man who lost an arm in the floods at Dunstan,' Wells was saying. He was lying on his bolster, a bottle of spirits on his chest; Tauwhare sat opposite, nursing a bottle of his own. 'Got caught in a rapid, you see, and his arm got trapped, and they couldn't save it. He had a plain name. Smith or Stone or something like that. Anyway—the point is—he talked of it afterwards, the incident, and his real sorrow, he said, was that the arm he'd lost had been tattooed. A full-rigged ship was the picture—a present to himself, after coming round the Horn—and it bothered him extremely that he'd lost it. For some reason it stayed with me—that story. Losing a tattoo. I asked him if he mightn't just tattoo the other arm, but he was strange about it. I'll never do that, he said. I'll never do it.'

'It is painful,' said Tauwhare. '*Ta moko.*'

Wells looked over at him. 'Is it sometimes a shock,' he said, 'to see yourself? After you haven't been near a looking glass in a while, I mean. Do you forget?'

'No,' Tauwhare said. 'Never.' His face was shadowed; the lamp-light accented the lines around his mouth, giving his expression a hawkish, solemn look.

'I think I would.'

'We have a saying,' Tauwhare said. '*Taia a moko hei hoa matenga mou.*'

'I cut a man's face with a knife,' Wells said, still staring at him. 'Gave him a scar. Right here. Eye to mouth. It bled like anything. Did yours bleed like anything?'

'Yes.'

'Have you ever killed a man, Tauwhare?'

'No.'

'No,' said Wells, turning back to his bottle. 'Nor have I.'

PART EIGHT

The Truth About Aurora

22 August 1865

42° 43' 0" S / 170° 58' 0" E

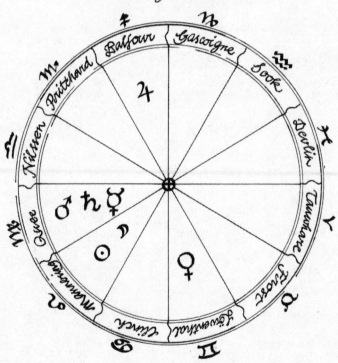

SATURN IN VIRGO

In which Quee Long brings a complaint before the law, and George Shepard, whose personal hatred of Sook Yongsheng has grown, over time, to include all Chinese men, declines to honour it, an injustice for which he does not, either then, or afterwards, feel any compunction.

'I do not understand what you are saying.'

Ah Quee sighed. He pointed a third time to his certificate of indenture, which lay between them on Shepard's desk. In the box marked 'present site of employment' was written the word *Aurora*.

'Duffer,' he explained. 'Aurora is duffer claim.'

'The Aurora is a duffer claim, and you work the Aurora, yes. That much I understand.'

'Mannering,' said Ah Quee. 'Mannering make duffer *not* duffer.'

'Mannering make duffer not duffer,' Shepard repeated.

'Very good,' said Ah Quee, nodding. 'Very bad man.'

'Which is he—very good or very bad?'

Ah Quee frowned; then he said, 'Very bad man.'

'How does he make the duffer not a duffer? How? *How?*'

Ah Quee took his purse and held it up. Moving very deliberately, so that the action would not be lost on Shepard, he extracted a silver penny, which he then transferred to his left pocket. He waited a moment, and then he took the penny from his pocket, and returned it to his purse, as before.

Shepard sighed. 'Mr. Quee,' he said. 'I see that the term of your indenture will not expire for some years; the term of my patience, however, reached its expiration some minutes ago. I have neither the resources nor the inclination to launch an investigation into Mr. Mannering's finances on the strength of a half-articulated tip. I suggest you return to the Aurora, and count yourself lucky that you have any kind of work at all.'

JUPITER IN SAGITTARIUS

In which Alistair Lauderback, having now officially announced his intention to run for the Westland seat in the Fourth New Zealand Parliament, an ambition that, in addition to furthering his already illustrious political career, will take him over the Alps to Westland proper in the coming months, thus granting the interview his bastard brother has so long desired, now turns his mind to practical matters, or, more accurately, entreats an old associate to turn his mind to practical matters on his, Lauderback's, behalf.

Akaroa. 22 Aug.

My dear Tom—

I expect you know already of my ambition to run for the Westland seat; but if this news comes as a surprise to you, I have enclosed an article from the Lyttelton Times *that explains the announcement, and my reasons for it, in more detail than I have time for here. You can be sure that I am eager to see the fine sights of West Canterbury with my own eyes. I plan to arrive in Hokitika by 15 January, an estimate dependent upon weather, as I will make the journey overland, rather than by sea, in order to follow and inspect the future Christchurch-road. I prefer to travel light, as you know; I have arranged for a trunk of personal effects to be transferred from Lyttelton in the last days of December. Might the* Virtue *collect the trunk in Dunedin prior to her departure on the 10th of January, and convey it to the Coast? As a West Canterbury foreigner I shall defer to your expertise on questions of Hokitika lodging, dining, coach hire, club membership &c. I trust fully in your good taste and capability, and remain,*

Yours, &c.,

A. LAUDERBACK

In which Mannering, driving Anna Wetherell to Kaniere, perceives in her a new quality, a hardness, a kind of distance; an observation that moves him, internally, to pity, though when he speaks, some three miles after this observation is first made, it is not to console her, the intervening miles having wrought in him a hardness of his own.

'Misery won't do. Misery is bad for business, whatever the business. A man won't bet on it, and a man won't bet against it—and it has to be one or the other, you see, in our line of work. Do you see?'

'Yes,' Anna said. 'I see.'

He was driving her to Chinatown, where Ah Sook was waiting with his resin and his pipe.

'I've never had a girl murdered, and I've never had a girl beat,' he said.

'I know,' she said.

'So you can trust me,' he said.

*In which Staines confides in Mannering to the extent that he
admits regret in having entered into a sponsorship agreement
with Mr. Francis Carver, explaining that the initial opinion
that he, Staines, formed of Carver's character and history was
and is grievously in error, his opinion now being that Carver
is a villain of the first degree, and one not at all deserving of
good fortune; to which Mannering, chuckling slightly, proposes
a somewhat thrilling, because dastardly, solution.*

'There's only one true crime upon a goldfield,' said Mannering to
Staines as they stamped through the undergrowth towards the
southern edge of the Aurora claim. 'Don't you bother your head
about murder, or theft, or treason. No: it's fraud that's the crime of
crimes. Making sport of a digger's hopes, you see, and a digger's
hopes are all he has. Digger fraud has two varieties. Salting a claim
is the first. Crying a duffer is the second.'

'Which is considered to be the more grievous?'

'Depends on what you call grievous,' said Mannering, swiping
away a vine. 'Salt a claim and get caught, you might get murdered
in your bed; cry a duffer and get caught, you're liable to get
lynched. Cold-blooded, hot-blooded. That's your choice.'

Staines smiled. 'Am I to do business with a cold-blooded man?'

'You can decide for yourself,' said Mannering, throwing out his
arm. 'Here it is: the Aurora.'

'Ah,' said Staines, stopping also. They were both panting slightly
from the walk. 'Well—very good.'

They surveyed the land together. Staines perceived a Chinese man, squatting some thirty yards distant, his panning dish loose in his hands.

'What's the opposite of a homeward-bounder?' said Mannering presently. 'A never-going-homer? A stick-it-to-Mr.-Carver?'

'Who's that?' said Staines.

'That's Quee,' said Mannering. 'He'll stay on.'

Staines dropped his voice. 'Does he know?'

Mannering laughed. '"Does he know?" What have I just told you? I'm not keen on getting murdered in my bed, thank you.'

'He must think this a terribly poor enterprise.'

'I haven't the first idea what that man thinks,' said Mannering, scornfully.

ANOTHER KIND OF DAWN

In which Ah Quee, placing his hands upon the armoured curve of Anna's bodice, makes a curious discovery, the full significance of which he will not appreciate until eight days later, when the complete rotation of Anna's four muslin gowns has given him a mental estimation of the extent of the riches they contain, excluding, of course, the dust contained within the gown of orange silk, which Anna never wears to Kaniere.

Anna lay perfectly still, her eyes closed, as Ah Quee ran his hands over her gown. He tapped every part of her corset with his fingers; he traced each flounce; he picked up the weighted hem and poured the fabric through his hands. His methodical touch seemed to anchor her in time and space; she felt that it was imperative that he touched every part of the garment before he touched her, and this certainty filled her with a lucid, powerful calm. When he slid his arm beneath her shoulders to roll her over, she complied without a sound, bringing her limp hands up to her mouth, like a baby, and turning her face towards his chest.

PART NINE

Mutable Earth

20 September 1865

42° 43' 0" S ∫ 170° 58' 0" E

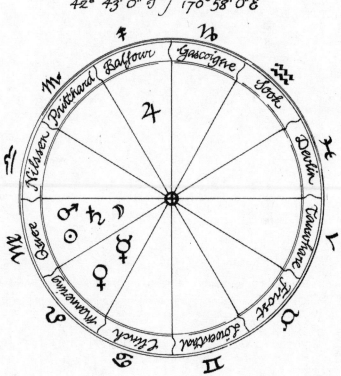

MOON IN VIRGO, CRESCENT

In which Ah Quee fills his firebox with charcoal, meaning to smelt the last of the dust excavated from Anna's gown, and to inscribe the smelted bars with the name of the goldmine to which he is indentured, the Aurora; and Anna, as she sleeps, mutters syllables of distress, and moves her hand to her cheek, as if intending to staunch a wound.

When Anna woke, it was morning. Ah Quee had moved her to the corner of his hut. He had placed a folded blanket beneath her cheek, and had covered her with a woollen cape, his own. She knew upon waking that she had been talking in her sleep, for she felt flushed and disturbed, and much too hot; her hair was damp. Ah Quee had not yet noticed that she had woken. She lay still and watched him as he fussed over his breakfast, and examined his fingernails, and nodded, and hummed, and bent to rake the coals.

SUN IN VIRGO

In which Emery Staines, to whom Crosbie Wells has since narrated the full story of his betrayal at the hands of Francis Carver, each having won the other's trust and loyalty, decides in a moment to falsify the quarterly report, removing all evidence of the bonanza from the goldfield records, and quite forgetting as he does so the determined worker Quee, who, according to protocol, and notwithstanding the circumstances of his indenture, is nevertheless deserving of a bonus.

Emery Staines, arriving at the camp station, was surprised to see that the Aurora's box was flagged, meaning that a yield had been submitted. He requested the gold escort to unlock the box. Inside there was a neat lattice of smelted gold bars. Staines took one of the bars in his hand. 'If I asked you to turn your back a moment,' he said presently, 'while I transferred the contents of this box elsewhere, what would be your price?'

The escort thought a moment, running his fingers up and down the barrel of his rifle. 'I'd do it for twenty pounds,' he said. 'Sterling. Not pure.'

'I'll give you fifty,' said Staines.

A PARTIAL ECLIPSE OF THE SUN

In which Emery Staines journeys to the Arahura Valley, sack in hand, with the intention of burying the bonanza, for a period of safekeeping, upon a portion of land set aside for Maori use, having not considered the possibility that Francis Carver might soon return to Hokitika to investigate why the Aurora goldmine, such a promising investment, has become a veritable duffer.

In the flax at Staines's shoulder a tui dipped its head and gave its rattling cry—sounding, to his ear, like a stick being dragged across pickets, while a reedy whistle played a tune. How wonderfully strange the sound! He stretched out his palm and touched the waxy blades of the flax, noting the vivid colours with pleasure: purple at the blade's edges, melting to a whitish green in the very centre of the leaf.

The tui beat away, and it was quiet. Staines reached down and took up the smelted bars. He laid them carefully at the bottom of the hole that he had dug. After they were buried, he arranged above them several flat-topped stones in a sequence that he was sure to recognise, and then kicked away his footprints.

In which, some half mile downriver from the site of the newly buried gold, Crosbie Wells and Tauwhare are sitting down to a hangi, a meal cooked in a fire pit that was covered in earth, later to be excavated, and the leaves around the meat unwrapped to yield a feast that is moist and richly flavoured with smoke and tannin and the rich, loamy flavours of the soil.

'What I'm saying is that there's nothing in it. You with your greenstone, us with our gold. It might just as well be the other way about. The greenstone rushes, we might call them. A greenrush, we might say.'

Tauwhare thought about this, still chewing. After a moment he swallowed and shook his head. 'No,' he said.

'There's no difference,' Wells insisted, reaching for another piece of meat. 'You might not like it—but you have to admit—there's no difference. It's just one mineral or another. One rock or another.'

'No,' Tauwhare said. He looked angry. 'It is not the same.'

PART TEN
Matters of Succession
11 October 1865
42° 43' 0" S ∫ 170° 58' 0" E

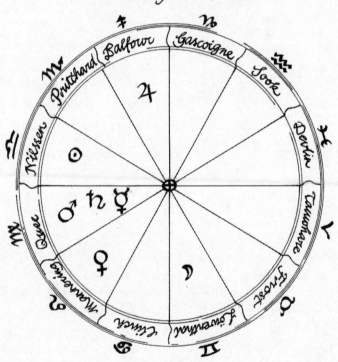

DETRIMENT

In which Anna Wetherell, who remembers the assault that occurred in the boudoir of the House of Many Wishes in Dunedin upon the night of the 12th of May with a stricken, nauseated clarity, and who is made wretched, daily, by the memory of that assault, a wretchedness not assuaged by the knowledge that her collusion, however tacit, helped an innocent man to escape unharmed, is surprised by the appearance of the disfigured man himself, and, in a moment of weakness, forgets herself.

Francis Carver was riding inland on the Kaniere-road when he spotted a familiar figure on the roadside. He reined in, dismounted his horse, and approached her, perceiving that her walk was unsteady and her face, very flushed. She was smiling.

'He got away,' she mumbled. 'I helped him.'

Carver came closer. He put his finger beneath her chin, and tilted her face. 'Who?'

'Crosbie.'

Carver stiffened at once. 'Wells,' he said. 'Where is he?'

She hiccupped; suddenly she looked frightened.

'Where?' He pulled back and slapped her, hard, across the face. 'Answer me. Is he here?'

'No!'

'In Otago? Canterbury? Where?'

In desperation, she turned to run. Carver caught her by the

shoulder, jerked her back—but just then there came the clap of gunshot, nearby—

'Whoa,' Carver shouted, spinning away—

And the horse shied up—

FALL

In which Anna Wetherell tells a falsehood to protect Crosbie Wells, attempting, in this belated act of loyalty, to atone for an earlier betrayal, the partial memory of which shifts and recedes, uncertainly, for her mind has been thrice fogged, once by smoke, a second time by violence, and lastly by the opiate administered by the physician Dr. Gillies, preparatory to a most unhappy procedure, during which Anna sobbed, and groaned, and clawed herself, becoming so distressed that Dr. Gillies was obliged to ask for help in restraining her, and Löwenthal, ordinarily a man of some fortitude in times of injury or upheaval, wept freely as he pried her hands away.

When Anna opened her eyes Löwenthal was standing over her, a white cloth in one hand, a jar of laudanum in the other; beside him stood Edgar Clinch, white-faced.

'She's awake,' said Clinch.

'Anna,' Löwenthal said. 'Anna. Dear heart.'

'Mnh,' she said.

'Tell us what happened. Tell us who it was.'

'Carver,' she said thickly.

'Yes?' said Löwenthal, leaning in.

She must not betray Crosbie Wells. She had sworn not to betray him. She must not mention his name.

'Carver . . .' she said again, her mind focusing, unfocusing.

'Yes?'

'. . . Was the father,' Anna said.

THE DESCENDANT

In which Emery Staines, learning of Anna's assault from Benjamin Löwenthal, saddles up at once and rides for the Arahura Valley, his jaw set, his eyes pricking tears, these being the external tokens of an emotional disturbance for which he does not, over the course of the journey north, admit true cause, much less attempt to articulate, inasmuch as any powerful emotion can be immediately articulated or understood by the sufferer, who, in this case, had been so distressed by Löwenthal's frank account of the injuries sustained, and by the blood that soaked his printer's apron from chest to hip, that he forgot both his wallet and his hat at the stables, and as he rode out, almost charged down Harald Nilssen as the latter exited Tiegreen's Hardware with a paper sack beneath his arm.

Wells opened his door. There upon the threshold, doubled over, was Emery Staines.

'The baby's gone,' he sobbed. 'Your baby's gone.'

Wells helped him inside, and listened to the story. Then he fetched a bottle of brandy, poured them each a glassful, downed it, poured them each another, downed it, poured them a third.

When the bottle was empty Staines said, 'I'll give her half. I'll share it with her. I've a fortune—secret—buried in the ground. I'll dig it up.'

Wells stared at him. After a time he said, 'How much is half?'

'Why,' mumbled Staines, 'I'd guess perhaps two thousand.' He put his head down upon the table, and closed his eyes.

Wells fetched down a tin box from his shelf, opened it, and withdrew a clean sheet of paper and a reservoir pen. He wrote:

On this 11th day of October 1865 a sum of two thousand pounds is to be given to MISS ANNA WETHERELL, formerly of New South Wales, by MR. EMERY STAINES, formerly of New South Wales, as witnessed by MR. CROSBIE WELLS, presiding.

'There,' said Wells. He signed his name, and pushed the sheet to Staines. 'Sign.'

But the boy was asleep.

PART ELEVEN

Orion Sets when Scorpio Rises

3 December 1865

42° 43' 0" S / 170° 58' 0" E

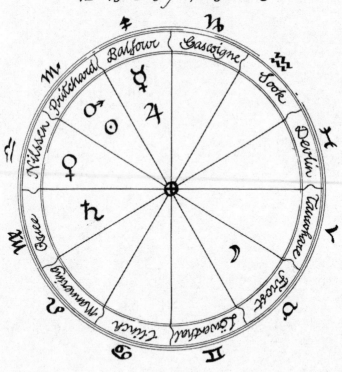

MOON IN TAURUS (ORION'S REACH)

In which Anna Wetherell, lost to meditation, tallies her obligations, a project that gives rise to such disconsolation that her mind averts its eye, so to speak, and casts about for another, lighter subject, alighting, inevitably, upon the smiling, bright-eyed form of Emery Staines, whose good opinion she has come to desire above all the others of her acquaintance, a desire quashed just as often as it is expressed, knowing his situation to be a world above her own, his prospects as bright and numerous as hers are dark and few, and presuming his regard for her to be likewise contrary, that is, the very opposite of hers for him, a belief held in spite of the fact that he has called upon her thrice since her recovery, and recently made her a present of a bottle of Andalusian brandy, the last bottle of its kind in all of Hokitika, though as she took it from his hands he became suddenly stricken, and begged to recover it and return with another, more suitable gift, to which she replied, honestly, that she was very flattered to be given a gift that did not attempt in any way to be suitable, and anyway, it was the last bottle of its kind in all of Hokitika, and for that, much rarer and more singular than any favour or trinket she had ever received.

Anna's debt to Mannering had doubled in the past month. A hundred pounds! It would take her a decade to repay that amount, perhaps even longer, if one considered the rates of usury, and the cost of opium, and the fact that her own value, inevitably, would come to fall. Her breath had fogged the corner of the window: she reached out to touch it. There was a snatch of something in her head, a maxim. *A woman fallen has no future; a man risen has no past.* Had she heard it spoken somewhere? Or had she composed it of her own accord?

In which Emery Staines, lost to meditation, doubts his own intentions, his natural frankness having accepted very readily the fact of his desire, and the fact of his delight, and the ease with which his pleasure might be got, expressions that cause him no shame, but that nevertheless give him pause, for he feels, whatever the difference in their respective stations, a certain bond with Anna Wetherell, a connexion, by virtue of which he feels less, rather than more, complete, in the sense that her nature, being both oppositional to and in accord with his own, seems to illumine those internal aspects of his character that his external manner does not or cannot betray, leaving him feeling both halved and doubled, or in other words, doubled when in her presence, and halved when out of it, and as a consequence he becomes suddenly doubtful of those qualities of frankness and good-natured curiosity upon which he might ordinarily have acted, without doubt and without delay; these meditations being interrupted, frequently, by a remark of Joseph Pritchard's—'if it weren't for her debt, her dependency, she'd have had a dozen propositions from a dozen men'—that keeps returning, uncomfortably and without variation, to his mind.

Perhaps he could buy her for the night. In the morning, he could take her to the Arahura, where he would show her the fortune he had buried there. He could explain that he meant to give exactly half of it to her. Would it defeat the purpose of the gift, if he had already paid for the pleasure of her company? Perhaps. But could he endure it, that other men knew her in a way that he, Staines, did not? He did not know. He crushed a leaf against his palm, and then lifted his palm to his nose, to smell the juices.

THE LUMINARIES

In which Anna Wetherell is purchased for the night; Alistair Lauderback rides to meet his bastard brother; Francis Carver makes for the Arahura Valley on a tip; Walter Moody disembarks upon New Zealand soil; Lydia Wells spins her wheel of fortune; George Shepard sits in the gaol-house, his rifle laid across his knees; a shipping crate on Gibson Quay is opened; the lovers lie down together; Carver uncorks a phial of laudanum; Moody turns his face to unfamiliar skies; the lovers fall asleep; Lauderback rehearses his apology; Carver comes upon the excavated fortune; Lydia spins her wheel again; Emery Staines wakes to an empty bed; Anna Wetherell, in need of solace, lights her pipe; Staines falls and strikes his head; Anna is concussed; in drugged confusion Staines sets out into the night; in concussed confusion Anna sets out into the night; Lauderback spies his brother's cottage from the ridge; Crosbie Wells drinks half the phial; Moody checks into an hotel; Staines makes a misstep on Gibson Quay, and collapses; Anna makes a misstep on the Christchurch-road, and collapses; the lid of the shipping crate is nailed in place; Carver commits a piece of paper to the stove; Lydia Wells laughs long and gaily; Shepard blows his lantern out; and the hermit's spirit detaches itself, ever so gently, and begins its lonely passage upwards, to find its final resting place among the stars.

'Tonight shall be the very beginning.'
  'Was it?'
  'It shall be. For me.'
  'My beginning was the albatrosses.'

'That is a good beginning; I am glad it is yours. Tonight shall be mine.'

'Ought we to have different ones?'

'Different beginnings? I think we must.'

'Will there be more of them?'

'A great many more. Are your eyes closed?'

'Yes. Are yours?'

'Yes. Though it's so dark it hardly makes a difference.'

'I feel—more than myself.'

'I feel—as though a new chamber of my heart has opened.'

'Listen.'

'What is it?'

'The rain.'

ACKNOWLEDGEMENTS

I am very grateful for the support and encouragement of the New Zealand Arts Foundation, the estate of Louis Johnson, Creative New Zealand, the New Zealand Society of Authors, the Taylor-Chehak family, the Schultz family, the Iowa Arts Foundation, the University of Canterbury English Department, the Michael King Writers' Centre, the University of Auckland English Department, the Manukau Institute of Technology Faculty of Creative Arts, and my colleagues and teachers at the Iowa Writers' Workshop. I feel very fortunate in having found a home at Granta in the UK, at Little, Brown in the USA, and at Victoria University Press in New Zealand.

This book is not a factual account by any means; however I owe a debt of inspiration to Colin Townsend's account of the Seaview prison, *Misery Hill*, and Stevan Eldred-Grigg's history of the New Zealand gold rushes, *Diggers, Hatters and Whores*. I am also indebted to the National Library of New Zealand newspaper archives (paperspast.natlib.govt.nz); the extensive and sometimes hilarious astrological resources at www.astro.com; and the work of astrologers Stella Starsky and Quinn Cox. In charting stellar and planetary positions I used the interactive sky chart provided at www.starandtelescope.com and also the Mac application *Stellarium*.

My love and thanks to Max Porter, Sara Holloway, and Fergus Barrowman; to Philip Gwyn Jones and Reagan Arthur; to Caroline Dawnay, Olivia Hunt, Jessica Craig, Linda Shaughnessy, Sarah Thickett, Zoe Ross, and Sophie Scard; and of course to Emma

Borges-Scott, Justin Torres, Evan James, Katie Parry, and Thomas Fox Parry, whose friendship and conversation inspired this book in countless ways. Sincere thanks also to XuChong Judy Guan, who translated sections of this book into phonetic Cantonese; to Christine Lo, Sarah Bance, Ilona Jasiewicz, and Anne Meadows, who helped to edit the manuscript; to Barbara Hilliam, who drew the charts so beautifully; to Philip Catton, who explained the stars, the planets, and the golden ratio; and to Joan Oakley, who sent me the shipping news, across the sea.

Lastly and above all: to Steven Toussaint, who was there for every conjunction, every opposition, and every dawn; who was Outermost and Innermost; who had faith in relation, and shared that faith with me. I cannot place a measure on your influence. Thank you—I to Thou.